HELEN

MARIA EDGEWORTH (1768-1849) was born in Oxfordshire, the eldest daughter of Richard Lovell Edgeworth, a reforming educationalist, scientist and inventor. At the age of fourteen the family moved to his estate at Edgeworthstown in County Longford, Ireland, where Maria became his amenuensis and the teacher of her growing number of half-siblings (twenty-two by four marriages).

Her first stories were written for and about children, some in collaboration with her father. They were considered a significant breakthrough in our understanding of the world of childhood. In 1800 she published her first novel, *Castle Rackrent*, anonymously and to instant acclaim. It was the first of four pioneering *Irish Tales*. King George III declared on reading it, 'I know something now of my Irish subjects.'

Yet it was her sparkling comedies of high-life English manners – *Belinda* (1801) *Patronage* (1814) and *Helen* (1834) – that were to secure Maria Edgeworth's status as the pre-eminent author of her day. Her books were a major influence on Jane Austen (a self-proclaimed admirer), Sir Walter Scott and the young Turgenev. John Ruskin described her novels 'the most re-readable books in existence.'

Maria Edgeworth never married. A brief courtship at age thirty-four failed as she felt unable to leave home and live abroad. During the potato famine of 1845 to 1847 she worked tirelessly for the relief of the Irish peasants. She died two years later at Edgeworthstown.

THANKS

Thanks to Dr Katherine MacDonald and Miranda Davies for expert help in translating and compiling the footnotes; to Nikky Twyman for proofreading; Gabriella Jaffe for inputting; Peter Dyer for design; and John Mullan for his introduction and encouragement.

First published 1834

This edition first published in 2010 by
Sort Of Books, PO Box 18678, London NW3 2FL.

2

Introduction © John Mullan, 2010

Typeset in Bembo and Gill Sans to a design by Susan Lamble
Printed in England by Clays Ltd, St Ives plc

528pp.
A catalogue record for this book is available from the British Library

978-0-95600-389-8

—⚜— HELEN ⚜—

MARIA EDGEWORTH

Introduced by John Mullan

Sort Of
BOOKS

—⊰ CONTENTS ⊱—

Introduction

by John Mullan

This is a book about lying. Maria Edgeworth, its author, was a supremely worldly and intelligent novelist, who was interested not in lies that are told in malice (though there are these too in the novel), but in the lies a woman tells to those whom she loves. Though it begins as if it were a novel of courtship, destined to end with the happy betrothal of its heroine, Helen, it soon becomes something more audacious: the story of Helen's friend Lady Cecilia Clarendon, and the crumbling of her marriage. Readers of Edgeworth's near-contemporary Jane Austen will recognize some things: the drawing-room jousts, the female rivalries, the comedy of manners. Yet Helen looks forward to later nineteenth-century novels of marital discontent or disaster. It was Edgeworth's last completed novel, at the end of a successful career, and has both the polish of achievement and the energy of something experimental.

It seems extraordinary that such a sophisticated novel should long have been available only in secondhand shops or university libraries. Early nineteenth-century readers thought of Maria Edgeworth as the leading woman novelist of the day. Jane Austen acknowledges one of her novels, along with two of Fanny Burney's, in a famous vindication of modern fiction in Chapter V of *Northanger Abbey*. She names Edgeworth's *Belinda* (1801) as one of those works that have proved the intellectual power, the insight and the wit to be found in the best novels. When Austen herself began publishing with *Sense and Sensibility* in 1811, Edgeworth was the most widely admired and best remunerated living novelist. Her work was respectfully reviewed; it also sold very well. We know just how much she earned from her books because she kept a list, rightly believing that copyright prices were the best measure of an author's standing. She received over £1000 for *Tales of Fashionable Life* (2nd series) and over £2000 for *Patronage*. These were very large sums: £500 might be a good income for a professional gentleman with a family to support. Edgeworth's fame had faded somewhat by the time of *Helen*, which was completed when she was in her sixties. Yet her publisher Richard Bentley still paid her £1100 for the three volumes (a sum adroitly negotiated by her friend J.G. Lockhart, Walter Scott's son-in-law).

Maria Edgeworth was an extraordinary woman. Her father was the Irish landowner, politician and self-styled intellectual Richard Lovell Edgeworth. Maria became his protégée, and from him she inherited an interest in education and a cosmopolitan bookishness. She tutored some of her many siblings and published works on education, notably her *Letters for Literary Ladies* (1795), advocating women's education. Her novels, beginning with the hilarious *Castle Rackrent* in 1800, increased her renown and, despite living mostly on the family estate in rural Ireland, she came to know leading writers of the day such as Jeremy Bentham, Sir Humphrey Davy and Sir Walter Scott. (In *Helen*, Lady Davenant gives a sketch of Scott's person and manners that is really Edgeworth's own). She was herself a literary celebrity: well read, well traveled, and thoroughly intellectual. You can hear Edgeworth's sophistication in her narrative voice, for she is certainly present in her novel, coolly judging the characters whom she has set in motion. Describing how the bitchy Lady Katrine foolishly supposes herself likely to snare Horace Churchill in marriage, she typically asks us to notice how often 'hope increases as all probability of success decreases'.

But she cannot stop there. 'This aberration of the intellect is usually to be observed to be greatest in very clever women', she adds. She has seen all this before. Edgeworth offered – and still offers – her readers the pleasure of being in worldly and enlightened company. It is also highly literary company. Her characters like to lob quotes at each other, and are sometimes enjoyably absurd for doing so, but the novelist herself loves her allusions. Literature-lovers will enjoy spotting the quotations. In particular, anyone with a liking for the sharp glitter of Alexander Pope's satirical verse will find plenty of his lines gleaming from the narrative.

In some ways, however, *Helen* is less high-minded than Edgeworth's earlier novels. She felt it worth pointing out that this was a novel 'depending more on the development of various characters and on the *interest* excited by Helen herself than on any particular point or moral'. Didactic design was implicit in many of the titles of early nineteenth-century novels by women, where abstract nouns abounded. Edgeworth published *Ennui* and *Patronage*; Mary Brunton produced *Self-Control* and *Discipline*; Susan Ferrier, *Marriage* and *Destiny*. Austen, of course, wrote three novels whose titles apparently proclaim their designs, *Sense and Sensibility*, *Pride and Prejudice* and *Persuasion* (even if her admirers find that the novels themselves undermine moralistic intent). Edgeworth was clearly serious in attempting to escape lesson-teaching. In *Helen* the protagonist has a moral guide, the formidable Lady Davenant, who is gifted with many of the author's own insights. But she is as much an interrogator as an adviser. For Lady Davenant, moral scruple is the female province. It is for women to worry about the ethics of everyday life. When her husband Lord Davenant arrives from London, to interrupt one of her sagacious conversations with the heroine, she exclaims amusedly, 'Now for politics – farewell morality, a long farewell.'

Helen is a novel of two halves: the first a study of manners and narrative of conversations, the second an accelerating drama of marital distrust. Part of the pleasure of the second half is in recognizing how this drama has been prepared in apparently incidental episodes early in the novel. It would spoil things for the reader to point these out in an introduction, except to say that Cecilia's fibs are introduced with beguiling harmlessness. Much of the time it seems that amused, clever dialogue is an end in itself for the novelist. The social milieu she depicts is unabashedly patrician. Helen, who was preparing herself for a quietly genteel life with the local vicar and his wife, finds herself thrust into grand company at Clarendon Park, Lord and Lady Davenant's country house. At one stage there is even a weekend's hawking party. This was the period of 'silver fork' fiction, novels of fashionable, upper-class society that were hugely popular with readers who did not themselves belong to this class. Some of them were written by actual aristocrats; all purported to give an insider's account of a gilded, usually scandalous, world. Edgeworth is sensitive to this fashion. She herself moved in high society in the 1820s and 1830s. Certainly there is a kind of respect for social standing shown by this novelist of liberal sympathies that one would never expect from the supposedly conservative Jane Austen.

Indeed, politeness is so elegantly exercised that the reader is likely to warm to those vulgar or tactless enough to break its surface. The jumped-up Lady Bearcroft is one such. Her apparently blundering conversation often contains gems of satire. Professing her respect for the superbly grand Lady Davenant, she observes, 'even her pride I like – it well became her – birth and all, for I hear she is straight from Charlemagne'. In the pressing silence of a formidably refined tea, to which various political potentates have been invited, it is she who wonderfully acknowledges the overwhelming awkwardness of the occasion. 'Amazing entertaining we are! So many clever people got together too, for what?' It is a good question. A few moments later she finds herself laughing so much at the pained gravity of the other ladies' countenances that she has to run from the room. She uses deliciously incorrect words ('coggledy', 'boggle-de-botch') with a happy sense of their incongruity: 'when people are warm, they cannot stand picking terms'.

Nothing very bad seems likely to happen at Clarendon Park. When the novel moves with its heroine to London, however, the mood shifts decisively. To the reader's (and perhaps the novelist's) private delight, London high society is evidently nasty and scandal-addicted. The first metropolitan occasion is Lady Castlefort's party, where Helen and Beauclerc arrive as expectant guests to encounter a world of stage whispers and knowing glances. It is quite a baptism. Most of the women at this do seem to cluster to exchange choice slanders. In an inner room Lady Katrine Hawksby stirs the cauldron of her malice with her scandalmongering confidantes. At a fashion-able London picture sale, a story about the amorous provenance of a certain locket is told 'for the amusement of the whole room' by 'a party of fashionables'. Though names are knowingly avoided, it is Cecilia who is being cheerfully defamed. This is a social world where calumny seems a sport, yet where proprieties are rigidly maintained. An intriguing sub-plot involves the efforts of the cunning Madame de St Cymon, a woman ostracized for some unspecified sexual misdemeanour, to win her way back into high society. Separated from her husband because of a 'terrible discovery', she has become a kind of untouchable. She challenges disgrace by using her knowl-edge of Cecilia's past into blackmailing her into communication. It is like a glimpse into a Henry James novel.

Just talking to someone can be dangerous. There is a good deal of conversation in the novel, but then we have to judge people from how they talk. As Lady Davenant puts it, 'if women would avail themselves of their daily, hourly, opportunities of judging people by their words, they would get at the natural char-acters'. Sometimes you seem to hear the tone of worldly reflec-tiveness that Edgeworth must have taken from her own evenings in drawing rooms and salons. Commenting on the 'fireworks' of

Horace Churchill's satirical conversation, Lady Davenant says, 'it's all *feu d'artifice* after all' – which dismisses the artificiality of his wit with a witty play upon the meanings of a French phrase. French plays a big part in the novel, a trace of its author's sophistication. Edgeworth visited Paris in 1802 with her father and was much influenced by French intellectual urbanity. After her return, French literature played almost as important a role in her private reading as books written in English. In 1820 she spent almost a year in France and Switzerland with her stepsisters Fanny and Harriet, including several months in Paris, renting elegant apartments and moving in high society. Edgeworth wrote at length to her stepmother and sisters back in Ireland, detailing her conversations with aristocrats and intellectuals. Her command of French as much as her status as an author was her passport into the best salons.

So a sense of the nuances of French is one of the author's resources. Describing Horace Churchill's ill humour one morning, the narrator uses the word that the character himself chooses, *journalier*; Edgeworth cannot resist adding in parentheses, 'a French word settles everything'. This is a joke, naturally, about how cultivated people show their subtlety by using French words to indicate that nothing in English precisely quite catches their meaning. Horace Churchill is always flourishing his French, as if he were finding nice words for the cruel things that he always wants to say. When a cash-strapped member of the upperclasses marries someone rich but vulgar, it is, he says, '*mettre du fumier sur nos terres*' ('to put dung on our fields'). The overall effect seems irresistibly camp. Coming upon some ladies swapping scandal over tea and punch at a London party, he comments, 'Tea and *ponch*' (he naturally prefers the French word), 'you know, in London, is now quite *à la Française*'. But Edgeworth is mocking only a little. She did not have to use so much French and distribute it so widely amongst her characters. When we hear that Cecilia's lady's maid Felicie has 'a certain *petite metaphysique de toilette*', the elaborate phrase is suited to the character (French herself, naturally) but also seems an authorial flourish. When Edgeworth wants to explain Lady Castlefort's behaviour towards Beauclerc, whom she had once fancied as a partner, she tells us that 'she was not of the violent vindictive sort, with her there was no long-lasting *dépit amoreux*', a phrase that translates as 'the resentment of spurned love'; but why choose French for this? Because it is the language of *les amours*, and naturally adopted by a sophisticated narrator. The fact that Edgeworth had little amorous experience on which to base her observations — she never married and seems hardly to have had a single romantic attachment — makes the linguistic artfulness all the more necessary.

Yet it is characteristic of Edgeworth's fictional skill that this linguistic resourcefulness should be used to arouse our suspicions. Even the francophile Horace regrets the sacrifices of candour he has made 'for this *reputation de salon*'. It is fun to be able to use French, but perhaps an evasion of honesty. Cecilia loves using French. The truthful Helen understands it very well, but does not use it. General Clarendon's blunt, good-hearted sister Esther, the one person who sees through Cecilia's lies, amazes the French by declaring that a just-told anecdote is entirely untrue. Such impolite truthfulness is '*bien Anglaise*'. Parisians are appalled. French phrasing returns us to the ways in which a clever person might avoid truthfulness.

This story about untruthfulness turns on one question: can a woman love more than once? Before marrying, General Clarendon has asked Cecilia, his wife-to-be, 'if she had ever loved any other man'. Cecilia has taken it that only a firm 'no' will win his hand, and has duly given the desired answer. We might remember Marianne in Austen's *Sense and Sensibility*, with her conviction that a person can only love once (even though she is the daughter of her father's second wife). Cecilia's assurance is an untruth, since she was once admired by the disreputable Colonel D'Aubigny and appeared (in letters, dangerously enough) to return his endearments. The error is small, we might think. In the verse tale by George Crabbe that gave Edgeworth her idea, 'The Confidant', Anna – the equivalent of Cecilia – has had a love affair and an illegitimate child. Cecilia's secret is a smaller thing. Yet her husband's very rectitude invests it with huge significance.

We watch Helen being recruited to her friend's deception, with Edgeworth exploiting her heroine's unselfishness and making it look like pliability. Yet Cecilia is the one in danger, and in its second half *Helen* becomes the gripping story of how her lies take her marriage to the brink of destruction. Increasingly fearful of her husband, her every effort to extricate herself involves another untruth. Deception becomes a kind of illness. In a nice twist, there is a moment when Clarendon begins to worry about his wife's health, and the modern reader assumes that her anxiety about her lies is making her ill. A contemporary reader would have inferred the truth: she is pregnant, and potentially has a new claim on his affections.

While the moralist in Edgeworth seeks to teach a lesson, the novelist in her is simply interested in the ramifying consequences of deceit, as one lie leads to another. Through the third and last volume of the novel, the entanglements become ever more complicated and painful. The clever thing is to begin with an untruth for which the reader finds it easy to forgive Cecilia. Her utterly principled, and therefore utterly daunting, husband-to-be, with his countenance 'rigid as iron', has terrified his wife into deception. The code by which he lives, and her own respect for it, may be foreign to us, but the dilemmas it produces are entirely credible. What disgrace might you suffer to save a dear friend from a worse disgrace? What lies would you not tell your husband to protect your marriage? Can you love a man you can so completely deceive? These are the questions that push the reader on to the novel's dénouement. Can it all possibly end happily? You will have to find out.

VOLUME ONE

CHAPTER 1

'THERE IS HELEN in the lime-walk,' said Mrs Collingwood to her husband, as she looked out of the window. The slight figure of a young person in deep mourning appeared between the trees. 'How slowly she walks! She looks very unhappy!'

'Yes,' said Mr Collingwood with a sigh, 'she is young to know sorrow, and to struggle with difficulties to which she is quite unsuited both by nature and by education, difficulties which no one could ever have foreseen. How changed are all her prospects!'

'Changed indeed!' said Mrs Collingwood, 'pretty young creature! Do you recollect how gay she was when first we came to Cecilhurst? and even last year, when she had hopes of her uncle's recovery, and when he talked of taking her to London, how she enjoyed the thoughts of going there! The world was bright before her then. How cruel of that uncle, with all his fondness for her, never to think what was to become of her the moment he was dead: to breed her up as an heiress, and leave her a beggar!'

'But what is to be done, my dear?' said her husband.

'I am sure I do not know; I can only feel for her, you must think for her.'

'Then I must tell her directly of the state in which her uncle's affairs are left, and that there is no provision for her.'

'Not yet, my dear,' said Mrs Collingwood: 'I don't mean about there being no provision for herself, that would not strike her, but her uncle's debts, – there is the point: she would feel dreadfully the disgrace to his memory – she loved him so tenderly!'

'Yet it must be told,' said Mr Collingwood resolutely; 'and perhaps it will be better now: she will feel it less, while her mind is absorbed by grief for him.'

Helen was the only daughter of Colonel and Lady Anne Stanley; her parents had both died when she was too young to know her loss, nor had she felt till now that she was an orphan, for she had been adopted and brought up with the greatest tenderness by her uncle, Dean Stanley, a man of genius, learning, and sincere piety, with the most affectionate heart, and a highly-cultivated understanding. But on one subject he really had not common sense: in money matters he was inconceivably imprudent and extravagant – extravagant from charity, from taste, from habit. He possessed rich benefices in the church and an ample private fortune, and it was expected that his niece would be a great heiress – he had often said so himself, and his fondness for her confirmed every one in this belief. But the Dean's taste warred against his affection: his too hospitable, magnificent establishment had exceeded his income; he had too much indulged his passion for all the fine arts, of which he was a liberal patron: he had collected a magnificent library, and had lavished immense sums of money on architectural embellishments. Cursed with too fine a taste, and with too soft a heart – a heart too well knowing how to yield – never could he deny himself, much less any other human being, any gratification which money could command; and soon the necessary consequence was, that he had no money to command, his affairs fell into embarrassment – his estate was sold; but, as he continued to live with his accustomed hospitality and splendour, the world believed him to be as rich as ever.

Some rise superior from the pressure of pecuniary difficulties, but that was not the case with Dean Stanley; not from want of elasticity of mind, but perhaps because his ingenuity continually suggested resources, and his sanguine character led him to plunge into speculations: they failed, and in the anxiety and agitation which his embarrassments occasioned him, he fell into bad health, his physicians ordered him to Italy. Helen, his devoted nurse, the object upon which all his affections centred, accompanied him to Florence. There his health and spirits seemed at first, by the change of climate, to be renovated; but in Italy he found fresh temptations to extravagance, his learning and his fancy combined to lead him on from day to day to new expense, and he satisfied his conscience by saying to himself that all the purchases which he now made were only so much capital, which would, when sold in England, bring more than their original price, and would, he flattered himself, increase the fortune he intended for his niece. But one day, while he was actually bargaining for an antique, he was seized with a fit of apoplexy. From this fit he recovered, and was able to return to England with his niece. Here he found his debts and difficulties had been increasing; he was harassed with doubts as to the monied value of his last-chosen chef-d'œuvre; his mind preyed upon his weakened frame, he was seized with another fit, lost his speech, and after struggles the most melancholy for Helen to see, conscious as she was that she could do nothing for him, he expired – his eyes fixed on her face, and his powerless hand held between both hers.

All was desolation and dismay at the deanery; Helen was removed to the vicarage by the kindness of the good vicar and his wife, Mr and Mrs Collingwood.

It was found that the Dean, instead of leaving a large fortune, had nothing to leave. All he had laid out at the deanery was sunk and gone; his real property all sold; his imaginary wealth, his pictures, statues – his whole collection, even his books, his immense library, shrunk so much in value when estimated after his death, that the demands of the creditors could not nearly be answered: as to any provision for Miss Stanley, that was out of the question.

These were the circumstances which Mrs Collingwood feared to reveal, and which Mr Collingwood thought should be told immediately to Helen; but hitherto she had been so much absorbed in sorrow for the uncle she had loved, that no one had ventured on the task.

Though Mr and Mrs Collingwood had not known her long (for they had but lately come to the neighbourhood), they had the greatest sympathy for her orphan state; and they had seen enough of her during her uncle's illness to make them warmly attached to her. Everybody loved her that knew her, rich or poor, for in her young prosperity, from her earliest childhood, she had always been sweet-tempered and kind-hearted; for though she had been bred up in the greatest luxury, educated as an heiress to a large fortune, taught every accomplishment, used to every fashionable refinement, she was not spoiled – she was not in the least selfish. Indeed, her uncle's indulgence, excessive though it was, had been always joined with so much affection that it had early touched her heart, and filled her whole soul with ardent gratitude.

It is said that the ill men do lives after them – the good is oft interred with their bones. It was not so with Dean Stanley: the good he had intended for Helen, his large fortune, was lost and gone; but the real good he had done for his niece remained in full force, and to the honour of his memory: the excellent education he had given her – it was excellent not merely in the worldly meaning of the word, as regards accomplishments and elegance of manners, but excellent in having given her a firm sense of duty, as the great principle of action, and as the guide of her naturally warm, generous affections.

And now, when Helen returned from her walk, Mr Collingwood, in the gentlest and kindest manner he was able, informed her of the confusion in her uncle's affairs, the debts, the impossibility of paying the creditors, the total loss of all fortune for herself.

Mrs Collingwood had well foreseen the effect this intelligence would have on Helen. At first, with fixed incredulous eyes, she could not believe that her uncle could have been in any way to blame. Twice she asked – 'Are you sure – are you certain – is there no mistake?' And when the conviction was forced upon her, still her mind did not take in any pan of the facts, as they regarded herself. Astonished and shocked, she could feel nothing but the disgrace that would fall upon the memory of her beloved uncle.

Then she exclaimed, 'One part of it is not true, I am certain'; and hastily leaving the room, she returned immediately with a letter in her hand, which, without speaking, she laid before Mr Collingwood, who wiped his spectacles quickly and read.

It was addressed to the poor Dean, and was from an old friend of his, Colonel Munro, stating that he had been suddenly ordered to India, and was obliged to return a sum of money which the Dean had many years before placed in his hands, to secure a provision for his niece Miss Stanley.

This letter had arrived when the Dean was extremely ill. Helen had been afraid to give it to him, and yet thought it right to do so. The moment her uncle had read the letter, which he was still able to do, and to comprehend, though he was unable to speak, he wrote on the back with difficulty, in a sadly trembling hand, yet quite distinctly, these words: − 'That money is yours, Helen Stanley: no one has any claim upon it. When I am gone consult Mr Collingwood; consider him as your guardian.'

Mr Collingwood perceived that this provision had been made by the Dean for his niece before he had contracted his present debts − many years before, when he had sold his paternal estate − and that, knowing his own disposition to extravagance, he had put this sum out of his own power.

'Right − all right, my dear Miss Stanley,' said the vicar; 'I am very glad − it is all justly yours.'

'No,' said Helen, 'I shall never touch it: take it, my dear Mr Collingwood, take it, and pay all the debts before any one can complain.'

Mr Collingwood pressed her to him without speaking; but after a moment's recollection he replied − 'No, no, my dear child, I cannot let you do this: as your guardian, I cannot allow such a young creature as you are, in a moment of feeling, thus to give away your whole earthly fortune − it must not be.'

'It must, indeed it must, my dear sir. Oh, pay everybody at once − directly.'

'No, not directly, at all events,' said Mr Collingwood − 'certainly not directly: the law allows a year.'

'But if the money is ready,' said Helen, 'I cannot understand why the debt should not be paid at once. Is there any law against paying people immediately?'

Mr Collingwood half smiled, and on the strength of that half smile Helen concluded that he wholly yielded. 'Yes, do,' cried she, 'send this money this instant to Mr James, the solicitor: he knows all about it, you say, and he will see everybody paid.'

'Stay, my dear Miss Stanley,' said the vicar; 'I cannot consent to this, and you should be thankful that I am steady. If I were at this minute to consent, and to do what you desire – pay away your whole fortune, you would repent, and reproach me with my folly before the end of the year – before six months were over.'

'Never, never,' said Helen.

Mrs Collingwood strongly took her husband's side of the question. Helen could have no idea, she said, how necessary money would be to her. It was quite absurd to think of living upon air; could Miss Stanley think she was to go on in this world without money?

Helen said she was not so absurd; she reminded Mrs Collingwood that she should still have what had been her mother's fortune. Before Helen had well got out the words, Mrs Collingwood replied –

'That will never do, you will never be able to live on that; the interest of Lady Anne Stanley's fortune, I know what it was, would just do for pocket-money for you in the style of life for which you have been educated. Some of your uncle's great friends will, of course, invite you presently, and then you will find what is requisite with that set of people.'

'Some of my uncle's friends perhaps will,' said Helen; 'but I am not obliged to go to great or fine people, and if I cannot afford it I will not, for I can live independently on what I have, be it ever so little.'

Mrs Collingwood allowed that if Helen were to live always in the country in retirement, she might *do* upon her mother's fortune.

'Wherever I live – whatever becomes of me, the debts must be paid – I will do it myself'; and she took up a pen as she spoke – 'I will write to Mr James by this day's post.'

Surprised at her decision of manner and the firmness of one in general so gentle, yielding, and retired, and feeling that he had no legal power to resist, Mr Collingwood at last gave way, so far as to agree that he would in due time use this money in satisfying her uncle's creditors; *provided she lived for the next six months within her income.*

Helen smiled, as if that were a needless provision.

'I warn you,' continued Mr Collingwood, 'that you will most probably find before six months are over that you will want some of this money to pay debts of your own.'

'No, no, no,' cried she; 'of that there is not the slightest chance.'

'And now, my dear child,' said Mrs Collingwood, 'now that Mr Collingwood has promised to do what you wish, will you do what we wish? Will you promise to remain with us? to live here with us, for the present at least; we will resign you whenever better friends may claim you, but for the present will you try us?'

'Try!' in a transport of gratitude and affection she could only repeat the words. 'Try! oh, my dear friends, how happy I am, an orphan, without a relation, to have such a home.'

But though Mr and Mrs Collingwood, childless as they were, felt real happiness in having such a companion, such an adopted daughter, yet they were sure that some of Dean Stanley's great friends and acquaintance in high life would ask his niece to spend the spring in town, or the summer in the country, with them; and post after post came letters of condolence to Miss Stanley from all these personages of high degree, professing the greatest regard for their dear, amiable friend's memory, and for Miss Stanley, his and their dear Helen; and these polite and kind expressions were probably sincere at the moment, but none of these dear friends seemed to think of taking any trouble on her account, or to be in the least disturbed by the idea of never seeing their dear Helen again in the course of their lives.

Helen, quite touched by what was said of her uncle, thought only of him; but when she showed the letters to Mr and Mrs Collingwood, they marked the oversight, and looked significantly as they read, folded the letters up and returned them to Helen in silence. Afterwards, between themselves, they indulged in certain comments.

'Lady C— does not invite her, for she has too many daughters, and they are too ugly, and Helen is too beautiful,' said Mrs Collingwood.

'Lady L— has too many sons,' said Mr Collingwood, 'and they are too poor, and Helen is not an heiress now.'

'But old Lady Margaret Dawe, who has neither sons nor daughters, what stands in the way there? Oh! her delicate health – delicate health is a blessing to some people – excuses them always from doing anything for anybody.'

Then came many who hoped, in general, to see Miss Stanley as soon as possible; and some who were 'very anxious indeed' to have their dear Helen with them; but when or where never specified – and a general invitation, as everybody knows, means nothing but 'Good morning to you.'

'Mrs Coldstream ends with, "I forbear to say more at present," without giving any reason.'

'And here is the Dean's dear duchess, always in the greatest haste, with "You know my heart," in a parenthesis, "ever and ever most sincerely and affec' – yours." '

'And the Davenants,' continued Mrs Collingwood, 'who were such near neighbours, and who were so kind to the Dean at Florence; they have not even written!'

'But they are at Florence still,' said Mr Collingwood; 'they can hardly have heard of the poor Dean's death.'

The Davenants were the great people of this part of the country; their place, Cecilhurst, was close to the deanery and to the vicarage, but they were not known to the Collingwoods, who had come to Cecilhurst during the Dean's absence abroad.

'And here is Mrs Wilmot too,' continued Mrs Collingwood, 'wondering, as usual, at everybody else: wondering that Lady Barker has not invited Miss Stanley to Castleport; and it never enters into Mrs Wilmot's head that she might invite her to Wilmot's Fort. And this is friendship, as the world goes!'

'And as it has been ever since the beginning of the world, and will he to the end,' replied Mr Collingwood. 'Only I thought in Dean Stanley's case – however, I am glad his niece does not see it as we do.'

No – with all Helen's natural quickness of sensibility, she suspected nothing, saw nothing in each excuse but what was perfectly reasonable and kind; she was sure that her uncle's friends could not mean to neglect her. In short, she had an undoubting belief in those she loved, and she loved all those who she thought had loved her uncle, or who had ever shown her kindness. Helen had never yet experienced neglect or detected insincerity, and nothing in her own true and warm heart could suggest the possibility of double-dealing, or even of coldness in friendship. She had yet to learn that

> No after-friendship e'er can raze
> Th' endearments of our early days,
> And ne'er the heart such fondness prove,
> As when it first began to love;
> Ere lovely nature is expelled,
> And friendship is romantic held.
> But prudence comes with hundred eyes,
> The veil is rent, the vision flies,
> The dear illusions will not last,
> The era of enchantment's past:
> The wild romance of life is done,
> The real history begun!

CHAPTER 2

SOME TIME AFTER THIS, Mr Collingwood, rising from the breakfast table, threw down the day's paper, saying there was nothing in it; Mrs Collingwood glancing her eye over it exclaimed –

'Do you call this nothing? Helen, hear this!

' "Marriage in high life. – At the Ambassador's chapel, Paris, on the 16th instant, General Clarendon to Lady Cecilia Davenant, only daughter of Earl and Countess Davenant." '

'Married! absolutely married!' exclaimed Helen: 'I knew it was to be, but so soon I did not expect. Ambassador's chapel – where did you say? – Paris? No, that must be a mistake, they are all at – Florence settled there, I thought their letters said.'

Mrs Collingwood pointed to the paragraph, and Helen saw it was certainly Paris – there could be no mistake. Here was a full account of the marriage, a list of all 'the fashionables who attended the fair bride to the hymeneal altar. Her father gave her away.'

'Then it is certainly so,' said Helen; and she came to the joyful conclusion that they must all be on their way home: – 'Dear Lady Davenant coming to Cecilhurst again!'

Lady Cecilia, 'the fair bride,' had been Helen's most intimate friend; they had been when children much together, for the deanery was so close to Cecilhurst that the shrubbery opened into the park.

'But is it not rather extraordinary, my dear Helen,' said Mrs Collingwood, 'that you should see this account of your dear Lady

Cecilia's marriage in the public papers only, without having heard of it from any of your friends themselves – not one letter, not one line from any of them?'

A cloud came over Helen's face, but it passed quickly, and she was sure they had written – something had delayed their letters. She was certain Lady Davenant or Lady Cecilia had written; or, if they had not, it was because they could not possibly, in such a hurry, such agitation as they must have been in. At all events, whether they had written or not, she was certain they could not mean anything unkind; she could not change her opinion of her friend for a letter more or less.

'Indeed!' said Mrs Collingwood; 'how long is it since you have seen them?'

'About two years; just two years it is since I parted from them at Florence.'

'And you have corresponded with Lady Cecilia constantly ever since?' asked Mrs Collingwood.

'Not constantly.'

'Not constantly – oh!' said Mrs Collingwood, in a prolonged and somewhat sarcastic tone.

'Not constantly – so much the better,' said her husband: 'a constant correspondence is always a great burthen, and moreover, sometimes a great evil, between young ladies especially – I hate the sight of ladies' long cross-barred letters.'

Helen said that Lady Cecilia's letters were never cross-barred, always short and far between.

'You seem wonderfully fond of Lady Cecilia,' said Mrs Collingwood.

'Not wonderfully,' said Helen, 'but very fond, and no wonder, we were bred up together. And,' continued she, after a little pause – 'and if Lady Cecilia had not been so generous as she is, she might have been – she must have been, jealous of the partiality, the fondness, which her mother always showed me.'

'But was not Lady Davenant's heart large enough to hold two?' asked Mrs Collingwood. 'Was she not fond of her own daughter?'

'Yes, as far as she knew her, but she did not know Lady Cecilia.'

'Not know her own daughter!' Mr and Mrs Collingwood both at once exclaimed. 'How could that possibly be?'

'Very easily,' Helen said, 'because she saw so little of her.'

'Was not Lady Cecilia educated at home?'

'Yes, but still Lady Cecilia, when a child, was all day long with her governess, and at Cecilhurst the governess's apartments were quite out of the way, in one of the wings at the end of a long corridor, with a separate staircase; she might as well have been in another house.'

'Bad arrangement,' said Mr Collingwood, speaking to himself as he stood on the hearth. 'Bad arrangement which separates mother and daughter.'

'At that time,' continued Helen, 'there was always a great deal of company at Cecilhurst. Lord Davenant was one of the ministers then. I believe – I know he saw a great many political people, and Lady Davenant was forced to be always with them talking.'

'Talking! yes, yes,' said Mr Collingwood, 'I understand it all. Lady Davenant is a great politician, and female politicians, with their heads full of the affairs of Europe, cannot have time to think of the affairs of their families.'

'What is the matter, my dear Helen?' said Mrs Collingwood, taking her hand. Helen had tears in her eyes and looked unhappy.

'I have done very wrong,' said she: 'I have said something that has given you a bad, a false opinion of one for whom I have the greatest admiration and love – of Lady Davenant. I am excessively sorry; I have done very wrong.'

'Not the least, my dear child; you told us nothing but what everybody knows – that she is a great politician; you told us no more.'

'But I should have told you more, and what nobody knows better than I do,' cried Helen, 'that Lady Davenant is a great deal more, and a great deal better, than a politician. I was too young to judge, you may think, but, young as I was, I could see and feel, and children can and do often see a great deal into character, and I assure you Lady Davenant's is a sort of deep, high character that you would admire.'

Mrs Collingwood observed with surprise that Helen spoke of her with even more enthusiasm than of her dear Lady Cecilia.

'Yes, because she is a person more likely to excite enthusiasm.'

'You did not feel afraid of her, then?'

'I do not say that,' replied Helen; 'yet it was not fear exactly, it was more a sort of awe, but still I liked it. It is so delightful to have something to look up to. I love Lady Davenant all the better, even for that awe I felt of her.'

'And I like you all the better for everything you feel, think and say about your friends,' cried Mrs Collingwood; 'but let us see what they will do; when I see whether they can write, and what they write to you, I will tell you more of my mind – if any letters come.'

'If – !' Helen repeated, but would say no more – and there it rested, or at least stopped. By common consent the subject was not recurred to for several days. Every morning at post-time Helen's colour rose with expectation, and then faded with disappointment; still, with the same confiding look, she said, 'I am sure it is not their fault.'

'Time will show,' said Mrs Collingwood.

At length, one morning when she came down to breakfast, 'Triumph, my dear Helen!' cried Mrs Collingwood, holding up two large letters, all scribbled over with 'Try this place and try that, missent to Cross-keys – Over moor, and Heaven knows where – and – no matter.'

Helen seized the packets and tore them open; one was from Paris, written immediately after the news of Dean Stanley's death; it contained two letters, one from Lady Davenant, the other from Lady Cecilia – 'written, only think!' cried she, 'how kind! – the very day before her marriage; signed "Cecilia Davenant, for the last time," and Lady Davenant, too – to think of me in all their happiness.'

She opened the other letters, written since their arrival in England, she read eagerly on, – then stopped, and her looks changed.

'Lady Davenant is not coming to Cecilhurst. Lord Davenant is to be sent ambassador to Petersburg, and Lady Davenant will

go along with him! Oh! there is an end of everything, I shall
never see her again! Stay – she is to be first with Lady Cecilia at
Clarendon Park, wherever that is, for some time – she does not
know how long – she hopes to see me there – oh! how kind,
how delightful!'

Helen put Lady Davenant's letter proudly into Mrs Collingwood's hand, and eagerly opened Lady Cecilia's.

'So like herself! so like Cecilia,' cried she. Mrs Collingwood
read, and acknowledged that nothing could be kinder, for here
was an invitation, not vague or general, but particular, and pressing as heart could wish or heart could make it. 'We shall be at
Clarendon Park on Thursday, and shall expect you, dearest Helen,
on Monday – just time, the General says, for an answer; so write
and say where horses shall meet you,' etc. etc.

'Upon my word, this is being in earnest, when it comes to
horses meeting,' cried Mrs Collingwood. 'Of course you will go
directly?'

Helen was in great agitation.

'Write – write – my dear, directly,' said Mrs Collingwood, 'for
the post-boy waits.'

Helen wrote she scarcely knew what, but in short an acceptance, signed, sealed, delivered, and then she took breath. Off cantered the boy with the letters bagged, and scarcely was he out of
sight, when Helen saw under the table the cover of the packet, in
which were some lines that had not yet been read. They were in
Lady Cecilia's handwriting – a postscript.

'I forgot, dear Helen, the thing that is most essential (you
remember our friend Dumont's definition of *une bêtise: c'est
d'oublier la chose essentielle*)[1] – I forgot to tell you that the General
declares he will not hear of a mere visit from you. He bids me tell
you that it must be "till death or marriage." So, my dear friend,
you must make up your mind in short to live with us till you find
a General Clarendon of your own. To this postscript no reply –
silence gives consent.'

---

[1] an act of stupidity: to forget something truly essential

'If I had seen this!' said Helen, as she laid it before Mr and Mrs Collingwood; 'I ought to have answered, but, indeed, I never saw it'; she sprang forward instantly to ring the bell, exclaiming, 'It is time yet – stop the boy – "silence gives consent." I must write. I cannot leave you, my dear friends, in this way. I did not see that postscript, believe me! I did not.'

They believed her, they thanked her, but they would not let her ring the bell; they said she had better not bind herself in any way either to themselves or to Lady Cecilia. Accept of the present invitation she must – she must go to see her friend on her marriage; she must take leave of her dear Lady Davenant before her departure.

'They are older friends than we are,' said Mr Collingwood, 'they have the first claim upon you; but let us think of it as only a visit now. As to a residence for life, that you can best judge of for yourself after you have been some time at Clarendon Park; if you do not like to remain there, you know how gladly we shall welcome you here again, my child; or, if you decide to live with those you have known so long, and loved so much, we cannot be offended at your choice.'

This generous kindness, this freedom from jealous susceptibility, touched Helen's heart and increased her agitation. She could not bear the thoughts of either the reality or appearance of neglecting these kind people the moment she had other prospects, and frequently, in all the hurry of her preparations, she repeated, 'It will only be a visit at Clarendon Park. I will return to you; I shall write to you, my dear Mrs Collingwood, at all events, constantly.'

When Mr Collingwood gave her his parting blessing he reminded her of his warning about her fortune. Mrs Collingwood reminded her of her promise to write. The carriage drove from the door. Helen's heart was full of the friends she was leaving, but by degrees the agitation of the parting subsided, her tears ceased, her heart grew lighter, and the hopes of seeing her friends at Clarendon Park arose bright in her mind, and her thoughts all turned upon Cecilia and Lady Davenant.

CHAPTER 3

HELEN LOOKED EAGERLY out of the carriage window for the first view of Clarendon Park. It satisfied – it surpassed her expectations. It was a fine, aristocratic place: ancestral trees, and a vast expanse of park; herds of deer, yellow and dark, or spotted, their heads appearing in a distance just above the fern, or grazing near, startled as the carriage passed. Through the long approach she caught various views of the house, partly gothic, partly of modern architecture; it seemed of great extent and magnificence.

All delightful so far; but now for her own reception. Her breath grew quick and quicker as she came near and nearer to the house. Some one was standing on the steps. Was it General Clarendon? No; only a servant. The carriage stopped, more servants appeared, and as Helen got out, a very sublime-looking personage informed her that 'Lady Cecilia and the General were out riding – only in the park – would be in immediately.'

And as she crossed the grand hall, the same sublime person informed her that there would be still an hour before dinner-time, and inquired whether she would be pleased to be shown to her own apartment, or to the library. Helen felt chilled and disappointed, because this was not exactly the way she had expected things would be upon her arrival. She had pictured to herself Cecilia running to meet her in the hall.

Without answering the groom of the chambers, she asked, 'Is Lady Davenant out too?'

'No; her ladyship is in the library.'

'To the library then.'

And through the antechamber she passed rapidly, impatient of a momentary stop of her conductor to open the folding-doors, while a man, with a letter-box in hand, equally impatient, begged that Lady Davenant might be told 'the General's express was waiting.'

Lady Davenant was sealing letters in great haste for this express, but when the door opened, and she saw Helen, she threw wax and letter from her, and pushing aside the sofa-table, came forward to receive her with open arms.

All was in an instant happy in Helen's heart; but there was the man of the letter-box: he must be attended to. 'Beg your pardon, Helen, my dear – one moment. Letters of consequence – must not be delayed.'

By the time the letters were finished, before they were gone, Lady Cecilia came in. The same as ever, with affectionate delight in her eyes – her beautiful eyes. The same, yes, the same Cecilia as ever; yet different: less of a girl, less lively, but more happy. The moment she had embraced her, Lady Cecilia turned quick to present General Clarendon, thinking he had followed, but he had stopped in the hall.

'Send off the letters,' were the first words of his which Helen heard. The tone commanding, the voice remarkably gentleman-like. An instant afterwards he came in. A fine figure, a handsome man; in the prime of life; with a high-born, high-bred military air. English decidedly – proudly English. Something of the old school – composed self-possession, with voluntary deference to others – rather distant. Helen felt that his manner of welcoming her to Clarendon Park was perfectly polite, yet she would have liked it better had it been less polite – more cordial. Lady Cecilia, whose eyes were anxiously upon her, drew her arm within hers, and hurried her out of the room. She stopped at the foot of the stairs, gathered up the folds of her riding-dress, and turning suddenly to Helen, said –

'Helen, my dear, you must not think *that* – '

'Think what?' said Helen.

'Think *that* – for which you are now blushing. Oh, you know what I mean! Helen, your thoughts are just as legible in your face

as they always were to me. His manner is reserved – cold, maybe
– but not his heart. Understand this, pray – once for all. Do you?
Will you, dearest Helen?'

'I do, I will,' cried Helen; and every minute she felt that she
better understood and was more perfectly pleased with her friend.
Lady Cecilia showed her through the apartment destined for her,
which she had taken the greatest pleasure in arranging: everything there was not only most comfortable, but particularly to
her taste; and some little delicate proofs of affection, recollections
of childhood, were there – keepsakes, early drawings, nonsensical
things, not worth preserving, but still preserved.

'Look how near we are together,' said Cecilia, opening a door
into her own dressing-room.'You may shut this up whenever you
please, but I hope you will never please to do so.You see how I
leave you your own free will, as friends usually do, with a proviso,
a hope at least, that you are never to use it on any account – like
the child's half-guinea pocket-money, never to be changed.'

Her playful tone relieved, as she intended it should, Helen's
too keen emotion; and this too was felt with the quickness with
which every touch of kindness ever was felt by her. Helen pressed
her friend's hand, but smiled without speaking.

They were to be some time alone before the commencement
of bridal visits, and an expected succession of troops of friends.
This was a time of peculiar enjoyment to Helen: she had leisure
to grow happy in the feeling of reviving hopes from old associations.

She did not forget her promise to write to Mrs Collingwood;
nor afterwards (to her credit be it here marked) – even when
the house was full of company, and when, by amusement or by
feeling, she was most pressed for time – did she ever omit to write
to those excellent friends. Those who best know the difficulty
will best appreciate this proof of the reality of her gratitude.

As Lady Cecilia was a great deal with her husband riding or
walking, Helen had opportunities of being much alone with Lady
Davenant, who now gave her a privilege that she had enjoyed in
former times at Cecilhurst, that of entering her apartment in

the morning at all hours without fear of being considered an intruder.

The first morning, however, on seeing her ladyship immersed in papers with a brow of care, deeply intent, Helen paused on the threshold, 'I am afraid I interrupt – I am afraid I disturb you.'

'Come in, Helen, come in,' cried Lady Davenant, looking up, and the face of care was cleared, and there was a radiance of pleasure. 'Interrupt – yes; disturb – no. Often in your little life, Helen, you have interrupted – never disturbed me. From the time you were a child till this moment, never did I see you come into my room without pleasure.'

Then sweeping away heaps of papers, she made room for Helen on the sofa beside her.

'Now tell me how things are with you – somewhat I have heard reported of my friend the Dean's affairs – tell me all.'

Helen told all as briefly as possible; she hurried on through her uncle's affairs with a tremulous voice, and before she could come to a conclusion, Lady Davenant exclaimed –

'I foresaw it long since: with all my friend's virtues, all his talents – but we will not go back upon the painful past. You, my dear Helen, have done just what I should have expected from you, – right; – right, too, the condition Mr Collingwood has made – very right. And now to the next point: – where are you to live, Helen? or rather with whom?'

Helen was not quite sure yet; she said she had not quite determined.

'Am I to understand that your doubt lies between the Collingwoods and my daughter?'

'Yes; Cecilia most kindly invited me, but I do not know General Clarendon yet, and he does not know me yet. Cecilia might wish most sincerely that I should live with her, and I am convinced she does; but her husband must be considered.'

'True,' said Lady Davenant – 'true; a husband is certainly a thing *to be cared for* – in Scottish phrase, and General Clarendon is no doubt a person to be considered, – but it seems that I am not a person to be considered in your arrangements.'

Even the altered, dry, and almost acrid tone in which Lady Davenant spoke, and the expression of disappointment in her countenance, were, as marks of strong affection, deeply gratifying to Helen. Lady Davenant went on –

'Was not Cecilhurst always a home to you, Helen Stanley?'

'Yes, yes, – always a most happy home!'

'Then why is not Cecilhurst to be your home?'

'My dear Lady Davenant! how kind! – how very, very kind of you to wish it – but I never thought of – '

'And why did you not think of it, Helen?'

'I mean – I thought you were going to Russia.'

'And have you settled, my dear Helen,' said Lady Davenant, smiling –'have you settled that I am never to come back from Russia? Do you not know that you are – that you ever were – you ever will be to me a daughter?' and drawing Helen fondly towards her, she added, 'as my own very dear – I must not say dear*est* child, – must not, because as I well remember once – little creature as you were then – you whispered to me, "Never call me dear*est*," – generous-hearted child!' And tears came into her eyes as she spoke; but at that moment came a knock at the door. 'A packet from Lord Davenant, by Mr Mapletofft, my lady.'

Helen rose to leave the room, but Lady Davenant laid a detaining hand upon her, saying, 'You will not be in my way in the least;' and she opened her packet, adding that while she read Helen might amuse herself 'with arranging the books on that table, or in looking over the letters in that portfolio.'

Helen had hitherto seen Lady Davenant only with the eyes of early youth; but now, after an absence of two years – a great space in her existence – it seemed as if she looked upon her with new eyes, and every hour made fresh discoveries in her character. Contrary to what too often happens when we again see and judge of those whom we have early known, Lady Davenant's character and abilities, instead of sinking and diminishing, appeared to rise and enlarge, to expand and be ennobled to Helen's view. Strong lights and shades there were, but these only excited and fixed her attention. Even her defects – those inequalities of temper of which she had already had some example, were interesting as evidences of the power and warmth of her affections.

The books on the table were those which Lady Davenant had had in her travelling carriage. They gave Helen an idea of the range and variety of the reader's mind. Some of them were presentation copies, as they are called, from several of the first authors of our own and foreign countries; some with dedications to Lady Davenant; others with inscriptions expressing respect or propitiating favour, or anxious for judgment.

The portfolio contained letters whose very signatures would have driven the first of modern autograph-collectors distracted with joy – whose meanest scrap would make a scrap-book the envy of the world.

But among the letters in this portfolio there were none of those nauseous notes of compliment, none of those epistles adulatory, degrading to those who write, and equally degrading to those to whom they are written: letters which are, however cleverly turned, inexpressibly wearisome to all but the parties concerned.

After opening and looking at the signature of several of these letters, Helen sat in a delightful *embarras de richesse*. To read them all – at once, was impossible; with which to begin she could not determine. One after another was laid aside as too good to be read first, and after glancing at the contents of each, she began to deal them round alphabetically till she was struck by a passage in one of them – she looked to the signature, it was unknown to fame – she read the whole, it was striking and interesting. There were several letters in the same hand, and Helen was surprised to find them arranged according to their dates, in Lady Davenant's own writing – preserved with those of persons of illustrious reputation! These she read on without further hesitation. There was no sort of affectation in them – quite easy and natural, 'real feeling, and genius,' certainly genius, she thought! – and there seemed something romantic and uncommon in the character of the writer. They were signed 'Granville Beauclerc!'

Who could he be, this Granville Beauclerc? She read on till
Lady Davenant, having finished her packet, rang a silver handbell,
as was her custom, to summon her page. At the first tinkle of the
bell Helen started, and Lady Davenant asked, "Whose letter, my
dear, has so completely abstracted you?'

Carlos, the page, came in at this instant, and after a quick
glance at the handwriting of the letters, Lady Davenant gave her
orders in Portuguese to Carlos, and then returning to Helen,
took no further notice of the letters, but went on just where she
had left off. 'Helen, I remember when you were about nine years
old, timid as you usually were, your coming forward, bold as a
little lion, to attack me in Cecilia's defence; I forget the particulars, but I recollect that you said I was unjust, and that I did not
know Cecilia, and there you were right; so, to reward you, you
shall see that now I do her perfect justice, and that I am as fond
of her as your heart can wish. I really never did know Cecilia till
I saw her heartily in love: I had imagined her incapable of real
love; I thought the desire of pleasing universally had been her
ruling passion – the ruling passion that of a little mind and a cold
heart; but I did her wrong. In another more material point, too,
I was mistaken.'

Lady Davenant paused and looked earnestly at Helen, whose
eyes said, 'I am glad,' and yet she was not quite certain she knew
to what she alluded.

'Cecilia righted herself, and won my good opinion, by the
openness with which she treated me from the very commencement of her attachment to General Clarendon.'

Lady Davenant again paused to reflect, and played for some
moments with the tablets in her hand.

'Some one says that we are apt to flatter ourselves that we
leave our faults when our faults leave us, from change of situation,
age, and so forth; and perhaps it does not signify much which it
is, if the faults are fairly gone, and if there be no danger of their
returning: all our former misunderstandings arose on Cecilia's
part from cowardice of character; on mine from – no matter what
– no matter which of us was most wrong.'

'True, true,' cried Helen eagerly; and, anxious to prevent recurrence to painful recollections, she went on to ask rapidly several questions about Cecilia's marriage.

Lady Davenant smiled, and promised that she should have the whole history of the marriage in true gossip detail.

'When I wrote to you, I gave you some general ideas on the subject, but there are little things which could not well be written, even to so safe a young friend as you are, for what is written remains, and often for those by whom it was never intended to be seen: the *dessous des cartes*[1] can seldom be either safely or satisfactorily shown on paper; so give me my embroidery-frame, I never can tell well without having something to do with my hands.'

And as Helen set the embroidery-frame, Lady Davenant searched for some skeins of silk and silk winders.

'Take these, my dear, and wind this silk for me, for I must have my hearer comfortably established, not like the agonised listener in the *World* leaning against a table, with the corner running into him all the time.'

[1] the face of the cards

'I MUST GO BACK,' continued Lady Davenant, 'quite to the dark ages, the time when I knew nothing of my daughter's character but by the accidental lights which you afforded me. I will take up my story before the reformation, in the middle ages, when you and your dear uncle left us at Florence; about two years ago, when Cecilia was in the height of her conquests, about the time when a certain Colonel D'Aubigny flourished, – you remember him?'

Helen answered 'Yes,' in rather a constrained voice, which caused Lady Davenant to look up, and on seeing that look of inquiry, Helen coloured, though she would have given the world not to be so foolish. The affair was Cecilia's, and Helen only wished not to have it recurred to, and yet she had now, by colouring, done the very thing to fix Lady Davenant's attention, and as the look was prolonged, she coloured more and more.

'I see I was wrong,' said Lady Davenant: 'I had thought Colonel D'Aubigny's ecstasy about that miniature of you was only a feint; but I see he really was an admirer of yours, Helen?'

'Of mine! oh no, never!' Still from her fear of saying something that should implicate Cecilia, her tone, though she spoke exactly the truth, was not to Lady Davenant's discriminative ear quite natural. Helen, seeing doubt, added –

'Impossible, my dear Lady Davenant! you know I was then so young, quite a child!'

'No, no, not quite; two from eighteen and sixteen remain, I think, and in our days sixteen is not absolutely a child.'

Helen made no answer; her thoughts had gone back to the time when Colonel D'Aubigny was first introduced to her, which was just before her uncle's illness, and when her mind had been so engrossed by him, that she had but a confused recollection of all the rest.

'Now you are right, my dear,' said Lady Davenant; 'right to be absolutely silent. In difficult cases say nothing; but still you are wrong in sitting so uneasily under it, for that seems as if there was something.'

'Nothing upon earth!' cried Helen, 'if you would not look at me so, Lady Davenant.'

'Then, my dear Helen, do not break my embroidery silk; that jerk was imprudent, and trust me, my dear, the screw of that silk winder is not so much to blame as you would have me think; take patience with yourself and with me. There is no great harm done, no unbearable imputation, you are not accused of loving or liking, only of having been admired.'

'Never!' cried Helen.

'Well, well! it does not signify in the least now; the man is either dying or dead.'

'I am glad of it,' cried Helen.

'How barbarous!' said Lady Davenant; 'but let it pass, I am neither glad nor sorry: contempt is more dignified and safer than hatred, my dear.'

'Now to return to Cecilia; soon after, I will not say the D'Aubigny era, but soon after you left us, I fell sick, – Cecilia was excessively kind to me. In kindness her affectionate heart never failed, and I felt this the more, from a consciousness that I had been a little harsh to her. I recovered but slowly; I could not bear to have her confined so long in a sick-room, and yet I did not much like either of the chaperons with whom she went out, though they were both of rank, and of unimpeachable character – the one English, one of the best women in the world, but the most stupid; the other a foreigner, one of the most agreeable women in the world, but the most false. I prevailed upon Cecilia to break off that – I do not know what to call it, friendship it was not – and my daughter and I drew nearer together. Better times began to dawn; but still there was little sympathy between us: my mind was intent on Lord Davenant's interests, hers on amusement and admiration. Her conquests were numerous, and she gloried in their number, for, between you and me, Cecilia was, before the reformation, not a little of a coquette. You will not allow it, you did not see it, you did not go out with her, and being three or four years younger, you could not be a very good critic of Cecilia's conduct; and depend upon it I am right, she was not a little of a coquettte. She did not know, and I am sure I did not know, that she had a heart, till she became acquainted with General Clarendon.

'The first time we met him,' – observing a quickening of attention in Helen's eyes, Lady Davenant smiled, and said, 'Young ladies always like to hear of "the first time we saw him." – The first time we saw General Clarendon was – forgive me the day of the month – in the gallery at Florence. I forget how it happened that he had not been presented to me – to Lord Davenant he must have been. But so it was, and it was new to Cecilia to see a man of his appearance who had not on his first arrival shown himself ambitious to be made known to her. He was admiring a beautiful Magdalene, and he was standing with his back towards us. I recollect that his appearance when I saw him as a stranger – the time when one can best judge of appearance – struck me as that of a distinguished person; but little did I think that there stood Cecilia's husband! so little did my maternal instinct guide me.

'As we approached, he turned and gave one look at Cecilia; she gave one look at him. He passed on; she stopped me to examine the picture he had been admiring.

'Every English mother at Florence, except myself, had their eyes fixed upon General Clarendon from the moment of his arrival. But whatever I may have been, or may have been sup-posed to be, on the great squares of politics, I believe I have never been accused or even suspected of being a manoeuvrer on the small domestic scale.

'My reputation for imbecility in these matters was perhaps advantageous. He did not shun me as he did the tribe of knowing ones; a hundred reports flew about concerning him, settling in one, that he was resolved never to marry. Yet he was a passionate admirer of beauty and grace, and it was said that he had never been unsuccessful where he had wished to please. The secret of his resolution against marriage was accounted for by the gossiping public in many ways variously absurd. The fact was, that in his own family, and in that of a particular friend, there had been about this time two or three scandalous intrigues, followed by "the public brand of shameful life." One of these "sad affairs," as they are styled, was marked with premeditated treachery and turpitude. The lady had been, or had seemed to be, for years a pattern wife, the mother of several children; yet she had long betrayed, and at last abandoned, a most amiable and confiding husband, and went off with a man who did not love her, who cared for nought but himself, a disgusting monster of selfishness, vanity, and vice! This woman was said to have been once good, but to have been corrupted and depraved by residence abroad – by the contagion of foreign profligacy. In the other instance, the seduced wife had been originally most amiable, pure-minded, uncommonly beautiful, loved to idolatry by her husband, Clarendon's particular friend, a man in high public estimation. The husband shot himself. The seducer was, it is said, the lady's first love. That these circumstances should have made a deep impression on Clarendon is natural; the more feeling – the stronger the mind, the more deep and lasting it was likely to be. Besides his resolution against marriage in general, we heard that he had specially resolved against marrying any travelled lady, and most especially against any woman with whom there was danger of a first love. How this danger was to be avoided or ascertained mothers and daughters looked at one another, and did not ask, or at least did not answer.

'Cecilia, apparently unconcerned, heard and laughed at these high resolves, after her gay fashion, with her young companions, and marvelled how long the resolution would be kept. General

Clarendon, of course, could not but be introduced to us, could
not but attend our assemblies, nor could he avoid meeting us in
all the good English and foreign society at Florence; but whenever he met us, he always kept at a safe distance: this caution
marked his sense of danger. To avoid its being so construed,
perhaps, he made approaches to me, politely cold; we talked very
wisely on the state of the Continent and the affairs of Europe;
I did not, however, confine myself or him to politics, I gave
him many unconscious opportunities of showing in conversation, not his abilities, for they are nothing extraordinary; but his
character, which is first-rate. Gleams came out of a character
born to subjugate, to captivate, to attach for life. It worked first
on Cecilia's curiosity; she thought she was only curious, and
she listened at first, humming an opera air between times, with
the least concerned look conceivable. But her imagination was
caught, and thenceforward through everything that everybody
else might be saying, and through all she said herself, she heard
every word that fell from our General, and even all that was
repeated of his saying at second or third hand. So she learned in
due season that he had seen women as handsome, handsomer
than Lady Cecilia Davenant; but that there was something in
her manner peculiarly suited to his taste – his fastidious taste!
so free from coquetry, he said she was. And true, perfectly true,
from the time he became acquainted with her: no hypocrisy
on her part, no mistake on his; at the first touch of a real love,
there was an end of vanity and coquetry. Then her deference
– her affection for her mother, was so charming, he thought;
such perfect confidence – such quick intelligence between us.
No deceit here either, only a little self-deception on Cecilia's
part. She had really grown suddenly fonder of me; what had
become of her fear she did not know. But I knew full well my
new charm and my real merit: I was a good and safe conductor
of the electric shock.

'It chanced one day, when I was listening only as one listens to
a man who is talking at another through oneself, I did not immediately catch the meaning, or I believe hear what the General

said. Cecilia, unawares, answered for me, and showed that she perfectly understood: – he bowed – she blushed.

'Man is usually quick-sighted to woman's blushes. But our General was not vain, only proud; the blush he did not set down to his own account, but very much to hers. It was a proof, he thought, of so much simplicity of heart, so unspoiled by the world, so unlike – in short, so like the very woman he had painted in his fancy, before he knew too much – Lady Cecilia was now a perfect angel. Not one word of all this did he say, but it was understood quite as well as if it had been spoken: his lips were firm compressed, and the whole outer man composed – frigidly cold; – yet through all this Cecilia saw – such is woman's penetration in certain cases – Cecilia saw what must sooner or later happen. He, still proud of his prudence, refrained from word, look, or sigh, resolved to be impassive till his judgment should be perfectly satisfied. At last this judgment was perfectly satisfied; that is, he was passionately in love – fairly "caught," my dear, "in the strong toils of grace," and he threw himself at Cecilia's feet. She was not quite so much surprised as he expected, but more pleased than he had ventured to hope. There was, that, however, in his proud humility, which told Cecilia that there must be no trifling.

> He either fears his fate too much,
>   Or his deserts are small,
> Who dare not put it to the touch,
>   To win or lose it all.

He put it to the test, and won it all. General Clarendon, indeed, is a man likely to win and keep the love of woman, for this, among other good reasons, that love and honour being with him inseparable, the idol he adores must keep herself at the height to which he has raised her, or cease to receive his adoration. She must be no common vulgar idol for every passing worshipper.'

As Lady Davenant paused, Helen looked up, hesitated, and said, 'I hope that General Clarendon is not disposed to jealousy.'

'No; he's too proud to be jealous,' replied Lady Davenant.

Are proud men never jealous? thought Helen.

'I mean,' continued Lady Davenant, 'that General Clarendon is too proud to be jealous of his wife. For aught I know, he might have felt jealousy of Cecilia before she was his, for then she was but a woman, like another; but once HIS – once having set his judgment on the cast, both the virtues and the defects of his character join in security for his perfect confidence in the wife "his choice and passion both approve." From temper and principle he is unchangeable. I acknowledge that I think the General is a little inclined perhaps to obstinacy; but, as Burke says, though obstinacy is certainly a vice, it happens that the whole line of the great and masculine virtues, constancy, fidelity, fortitude, magnanimity, are closely allied to this disagreeable quality, of which we have so just an abhorrence.

'It is most peculiarly happy for Cecilia that she has a husband of this firm character, one on whom she can rely – one to whom she may, she must, look up, if not always, yet upon all important occasions where decision is necessary, or integrity required. It is between her and her General as it should be in marriage, each has the compensating qualities to those which the other possesses: General Clarendon is inferior to Cecilia in wit, but superior in judgment; inferior in literature, superior in knowledge of the world; inferior to my daughter altogether in abilities, in what is called genius, but far superior in that rifling power, *strength of mind*. Strength of mind is an attaching as well as a ruling power: all human creatures, women especially, become attached to those who have power over their minds. Yes, Helen, I am satisfied with their marriage, and with your congratulations: yours are the sort I like. Vulgar people – by vulgar people I mean all who think vulgarly – very great vulgar people have congratulated me upon this establishment of my daughter's fortune and future rank (a dukedom in view), all that could be wished in worldly estimation. But I rejoice in it as the security for my daughter's character and happiness. Thank you again, my dear young friend, for your sympathy; you can understand me, you can feel with me.'

Sympathy, intelligent, quick, warm, unwearied, unweariable, such as Helen's, is really a charming accomplishment in a friend;

the only obligation a proud person is never too proud to receive; and it was most gratifying to Helen to be allowed to sympathise with Lady Davenant – one who, in general, never spoke of herself, or unveiled her private feelings, even to those who lived with her on terms of intimacy. Helen felt responsible for the confidence granted to her thus upon credit, and a strong ambition was excited in her mind to justify the high opinion her superior friend had formed of her. She determined to become all that she was believed to be; as the flame of a taper suddenly rises towards what is held over it, her spirit mounted to the point to which her friend pointed.

CHAPTER 5

HELEN'S PERFECT HAPPINESS at Clarendon Park was not of long duration. People who have not been by nature blessed or cursed with nice feelings, or who have well rubbed off their delicacy in roughing through the world, can be quite happy, or at least happy enough, without ascertaining whether they are really esteemed or liked by those with whom they live. Many, and some of high degree, when well sheltered and fed, and provided with all the necessaries, and surrounded by all the luxuries of life, and with appearances tolerably well kept up by outward manner, care little or nought about the inside sentiments.

But Helen was neither of the case-hardened philosophic nor the naturally obtuse-feeling class; she belonged to the over-anxious. Surrounded at Clarendon Park with all the splendour of life, and with the immediate expectation of seeing and being seen by the first society in England; with the certainty also of being tenderly loved and highly esteemed by two of the persons she was living with, yet a doubt about the third began to make her miserable. Whether General Clarendon really liked her or not, was a question that hung upon her mind sometimes as a dead weight; then vibrating backwards and forwards, she often called to mind, and endeavoured to believe, what Cecilia the first day told her, that this reserved manner was natural to him with strangers, and would wear off. But to her the icy coldness did not thaw. So she felt, or so she fancied, and which it was she could not decide. She had never before lived with any one about whose liking for her she could doubt, therefore, as she said to herself, 'I know I am a bad judge.' She feared to open her mind to Cecilia. Lady Davenant would be the safest person to consult; yet Helen, with all her young delicacy fresh about her, scrupled, and could not screw her courage to the sticking-place. Every morning, going to Lady Davenant's room, she half resolved, and yet came away without speaking. At last, one morning, she began -

'You said something the other day, my dear Lady Davenant, about a visit from Miss Clarendon. Perhaps − I am afraid − in short I think, − I fear, the General does not like my being here; and I thought, perhaps, he was displeased at his sister's not being here, − that he thought Cecilia's having asked me prevented his sister's coming; but then you told me he was not of a jealous temper, did not you?'

Distinguez,[1] said Lady Davenant; '*distinguons*,[2] as the old French metaphysicians used to say, *distinguons*, there be various kinds of jealousy, as of love. The old romancers make a distinction between *amour*[3] and *amour par amours*.[4] Whatever that means, I beg leave to take a distinction full as intelligible, I trust, between *jalousie par amour*[5] and *jalousie par amitié*.[6] Now, to apply; when I told you that our General was not subject to jealousy, I should have distinguished, and said, *jalousie par amour* − jealousy in love, but I will not ensure him against *jalousie par amitié* − jealousy in friendship − of friends and relations, I mean. Methinks I have seen symptoms of this in the General; he does not like my influence over Cecilia, nor yours, my dear.'

'I understand it all,' exclaimed Helen, 'and I was right from the very first; I saw he disliked me, and he ever will and must dislike and detest me − I see it in every look, hear it in every word, in every tone.'

'Now, my dear Helen, if you are riding off on your imagination, I wish you a pleasant ride, and till you come back again I will write my letter,' said Lady Davenant, taking up a pen.

Helen begged pardon, and protested she was not going to ride off upon any imagination, − she had no imagination now − she entreated Lady Davenant to go on, for she was very anxious to know the whole truth, whatever it might be. Lady Davenant laid

[1] You distinguish; [2] Let us distinguish; [3] love; [4] love in love; [5] jealousy in love;
[6] jealousy in friendship

down her pen, and told her all she knew. In the first place, that
Cecilia did not like Miss Clarendon, who, though a very estimable person, had a sort of uncompromising sincerity, joined with
a *brusquerie* of manner which Cecilia could not endure. How her
daughter had managed matters to refuse the sister without offending the brother, Lady Davenant said she did not know; that was
Cecilia's secret, and probably it lay in her own charming manner
of doing things, aided by the whole affair having occurred a few
days before marriage, when nothing could be taken ill of the
bride-elect. 'The General, as Cecilia told me, desired that she
would write to invite you, Helen; she did so, and I am very glad
of it. This is all I know of this mighty matter.'

But Helen could not endure the idea of being there, contrary
to the General's wishes, in the place of the sister he loved. Oh,
how very, very unfortunate she was to have all her hopes blighted,
destroyed – and Cecilia's kindness all in vain. Dear, dear Cecilia!
– but for the whole world Helen would not be so selfish – she
would not run the hazard of making mischief. She would never
use her influence over Cecilia in opposition to the General. Oh,
how little he knew of her character, if he thought it possible.

Helen had now come to tears. Then the keen sense of injustice turned to indignation; and the tears wiped away, and pride
prevailing, colouring she exclaimed, 'That she knew what she
ought to do, she knew what she should do – she would not stay
where the master of the house did not wish for her. Orphan
though she was, she could not accept of protection or obligation
from any human being who neither liked nor esteemed her. She
would shorten her visit at Clarendon Park – make it as short
as his heart could desire – she would never be the cause of any
disagreement – poor, dear, kind Cecilia! She would write directly
to Mrs Collingwood.'

At the close of these last incoherent sentences, Helen was
awestruck by the absolute composed immovability and silence of
Lady Davenant. Helen stood rebuked before her.

'Instead of writing to Mrs Collingwood, had you not better
go at once?' said her ladyship, speaking in a voice so calm, and in

a tone so slightly ironical, that it might have passed for earnest on any but an acutely-feeling ear – 'Shall I ring, and order your carriage?' putting her hand on the bell as she spoke, and resting it there, she continued – 'It would be so spirited to be off instantly; so wise, so polite, so considerate towards dear Cecilia – so digni-fied towards the General, and so kind towards me, who am going to a far country, Helen, and may perhaps not see you ever again.'

'Forgive me!' cried Helen; 'I never could go while you were here.'

'I did not know what you might think proper when you seemed to have lost your senses.'

'I have recovered them,' said Helen; 'I will do whatever you please – whatever you think best.'

'It must not be what I please, my dear child, nor what I think best, but what you judge for yourself to be best; else what will become of you when I am in Russia? It must be some higher and more stable principle of action that must govern you. It must not be the mere wish to please this or that friend; – the defect of your character, Helen, remember I tell you, is this – ordinate desire to be loved, this impatience of not being loved – that which but a moment ago made you ready to abandon two of the best friends you have upon earth, because you imagine, or you suspect, or you fear, that a third person, almost a stranger, does not like before he has had time to know you.'

'I was very foolish,' said Helen; 'but now I will be wise, I will do whatever is – right. Surely you would not have me live here if I were convinced that the master of the house did not wish it?'

'Certainly not – certainly not,' repeated Lady Davenant; 'but let us see our way before us; never gallop, my dear, much less leap; never move, till you see your way; – once it is ascertained that General Clarendon does not wish you to be here, nor approve of you for the chosen companion of his wife. I, as your best friend, would say, begone, and speed you on your way; then as much pride, as much spirit, as you will; but those who are conscious of possessing real spirit should never be – seldom are – in a hurry to show it; that kind of ostentatious haste is undignified in man, and ungraceful in woman.'

Helen promised that she would be patience itself. 'But tell me exactly,' said she, 'what you would have me do.'

'Nothing,' said Lady Davenant.

'Nothing! that is easy at least,' said Helen, smiling.

'No, not so easy as you imagine; it requires sometimes no small share of strength of mind.'

'Strength of mind!' said Helen, 'I am afraid I have not any.'

'Acquire it then, my dear,' said her friend.

'But can I?'

'Certainly; strength of mind, like strength of body, is improved by exercise.'

'If I had any to begin with – ' said Helen.

'You have some, Helen, a great deal in one particular, else why should I have any more regard for you, or more hope of you, than of any other well-dressed, well-taught beauty, any of the tribe of young ladies who pass before me without ever fixing my mind's eye for one moment?'

'But in what particular, my dear Lady Davenant, do you mean?' said Helen, anxiously; 'I am afraid you are mistaken; in what do you think I ever showed strength of mind? Tell me, and I will tell you the truth.'

'That you will, and there is the point that I mean. Ever since I have known you, you have always, as at this moment, coward as you are, been brave enough to tell the truth; and truth I believe to be the only real lasting foundation for friendship; in all but truth there is a principle of decay and dissolution. Now good-bye, my dear; – stay, one word more – there is a line in some classic poet, which says "the suspicion of ill-will never fails to produce it." – Remember this in your intercourse with General Clarendon; show no suspicion of his bearing you ill-will, and to show none, you must feel none. Put absolutely out of your head all that you may have heard or imagined about Miss Clarendon, or her brother's prejudices on her account.'

'I will – I will indeed,' said Helen, and so they parted.

A few words have sometimes a material influence on events in human life. Perhaps even among those who hold in general that advice never does good, there is no individual who cannot recollect some few words – some conversation which has altered the future colour of their lives.

Helen's over-anxiety concerning General Clarendon's opinion of her being now balanced by the higher interest Lady Davenant had excited, she met him with new-born courage; and Lady Cecilia, not that she suspected it was necessary, but merely by way of prevention, threw in little douceurs of flattery, on the General's part, repeated sundry pretty compliments, and really kind things which he had said to her of Helen. These always pleased Helen at the moment, but she could never make what she was told he said of her quite agree with what he said to her; indeed, he said so very little, that no absolute discrepancy could be detected between the words spoken and the words reported to have been said; but still the looks did not agree with the opinions or the cordiality implied.

One morning Lady Cecilia told her that the General wished that she would ride out with them; 'and you must come, indeed, you must, and try his pretty Zelica; he wishes it of all things, he told me so last night.'

The General chancing to come in as she spoke, Lady Cecilia appealed to him with a look that almost called upon him to enforce her request; but he only said that if Miss Stanley would do him the honour, he should certainly be happy, if Zelica would not be too much for her; but he could not take it upon him to advise. Then looking for some paper of which he came in search, and passing her with the most polite and deferential manner possible, he left the room.

Half vexed, half smiling, Helen looked at Cecilia, and asked whether all she had told her was not just a little more attractive than the truth.

Lady Cecilia, blushing slightly, poured out rapid protestations that all she had ever repeated to Helen of the General's sayings was perfect truth – 'I will not swear to the words – because in the first place it is not pretty to swear, and next, because I can never recollect anybody's words, or my own, five minutes after they have been said.'

Partly by playfulness, and partly by protestations, Lady Cecilia half convinced Helen; but from this time she refrained from repeating compliments which, true or false, did no good; and things went on better; observing this, she left them to their natural course, upon all such occasions the best way.

And now visitors began to appear, and some officers of the General's staff arrived. Clarendon Park happened to be in the district which General Clarendon commanded, so that he was able usually to reside there. It was in what is called a good neighbourhood, and there was much visiting, and many entertainments.

One day at dinner, Helen was seated between the General and a fine young gentleman, who, as far as his deep sense of his own merit and his fashionable indifference to young ladies would permit, had made some demonstrations of a desire to attract her notice. He was piqued when, in the midst of something he had wonderfully exerted himself to say, he observed that her attention was distracted by a gentleman opposite, who had just returned from the Continent, and who, among other pieces of news, marriages and deaths of English abroad, mentioned that 'poor D'Aubigny' was at last dead.

Helen looked first at Cecilia, who, as she saw, heard what was said with perfect composure; and then at Lady Davenant, who had meantime glanced imperceptibly at her daughter, and then upon Helen, whose eyes she met – and Helen coloured merely from association, because she had coloured before – provoking! yet impossible to help it. All passed in less time than it can be told, and Helen had left the guardsman in the midst of his sentence, discomfited, and his eyes were now upon her; and in confusion she turned from him, and there were the General's eyes; but he was only inviting her to taste some particular wine, which he thought she would like, and which she willingly accepted, and praised, though she assuredly did not know in the least what manner of taste it had. The General now exerted himself to occupy the guardsman in a conversation about promotion, and drew all observation from Helen.

Yet not the slightest indication of having seen, heard, or understood appeared in his countenance, not the least curiosity or interest about Colonel D'Aubigny. Of one point Helen was, however, intuitively certain, that he had noticed that confusion which he had so ably, so coolly covered. One ingenuous look from her thanked him, and his look in return was most gratifying; she could not tell how it was, but it appeared more as if he understood her and liked her than any look she had ever seen from him before. They were both more at their ease. Next day, he certainly justified Cecilia's former assurances, by the urgency with which he desired to have her of the riding-party. He put her on horseback himself, bade the aide-de-camp ride on with Lady Cecilia – three several times set the bridle right in Miss Stanley's hands, assuring her that she need not be afraid, that Zelica was the gentlest creature possible, and he kept his fiery horse, Fleetfoot, to a pace that suited her during the whole time they were out. Helen took courage, and her ride did her a vast deal of good.

The rides were repeated, the General evidently became more and more interested about Miss Stanley; he appealed continually to her taste, and marked that he considered her as part of his family; but, as Helen told Lady Davenant, it was difficult, with a person of his high-bred manners and reserved temper, to ascertain what was to be attributed to general deference to her sex, what to particular regard for the individual, how much to hospitality to his guest, or attention to his wife's friend, and what might be considered as proof of his own desire to share that friendship, and of a real wish that she should continue to live with them.

While she was in this uncertainty, Lord Davenant arrived from London; he had always been fond of Helen, and now the first sight of her youthful figure in deep mourning, the recollection of the great changes that had taken place since they had last met, touched him to the heart – he folded her in his arms, and was unable to speak. He! a great bulky man, with a face of constitutional joy – but so it was; he had a tender heart, deep feelings of all kinds under an appearance of *insouciance* which deceived the world. He was distinguished as a political leader – but, as he said of himself, he had been three times inoculated with ambition – once by his mother, once by his brother, and once by his wife; but it had never taken well; the last the best, however, – it had shown at least sufficiently to satisfy his friends, and he was happy to be no more tormented. With talents of the first order, and integrity unblenching, his character was not of that stem stuff – no, not of that corrupt stuff – of which modern ambition should be made.

He had now something to tell Helen, which he would say even before he opened his London budget of news. He told her, with a congratulatory smile that he had an opportunity of showing his sense of Mr Collingwood's merits; and as he spoke he put a letter into her hand.

The letter was from her good friend Mr Collingwood, accepting a bishopric in the West Indies, which had been offered to him by Lord Davenant. It enclosed a letter for Helen, desiring in the most kind manner that she would let him know immediately and decidedly where and with whom she intended to live; and there was a postscript from Mrs Collingwood full of affection, and doubts, and hopes, and fears.

The moment Helen had finished this letter, without seeming to regard the inquiring looks of all present, and without once looking towards any one else, she walked deliberately up to General Clarendon, and begged to speak to him alone. Never was the General more surprised, but of course he was too much of a general to let that appear. Without a word, he offered his arm, and led her to his study; he drew a chair towards her –

'No misfortune, I hope, Miss Stanley? If I can in any way be of service – '

'The only service, General Clarendon,' said Helen, her manner becoming composed, and her voice steadying as she went on – 'the only service you can do me now is to tell me the plain truth, and this will prevent what would certainly be a misfortune to me – perhaps to all of us. Will you read this letter?'

He received it with an air of great interest, and again moved the chair to her. Before she sat down, she added –

'I am unused to the world, you see, General Clarendon. I have been accustomed to live with one who always told me his mind sincerely, so that I could judge always what I ought to do. Will you do so now? It is the greatest service, as well as favour, you can do me.'

'Depend upon it, I will,' answered General Clarendon.

'I should not ask you to tell me in words – that might be painful to your politeness; only let me see it,' said Helen, and she sat down.

The General read on without speaking, till he came to the mention of Helen's original promise of living with the Collingwoods. He did not comprehend that passage, he said, showing it to her. He had always, on the contrary, understood that it had been a long *settled* thing, a promise between Miss Stanley and Lady Cecilia, that Helen should live with Lady Cecilia when she married.

'No such thing!' Helen said. 'No such agreement had ever been made.'

So the General now perceived; but this was a mistake of his which he hoped would make no difference in her arrangements, he said: 'Why should it? – unless Miss Stanley felt unhappy at Clarendon Park?'

He paused, and Helen was silent; then, taking some desperate resolution, she answered –

'I should be perfectly happy here, if I were sure of your wishes, your feelings about me – about it.'

'Is it possible that there has been anything in my manner,' said he, 'that could give Miss Stanley pain? What could have put a doubt into her mind?'

'There might be some other person nearer, and naturally dearer to you,' said Helen, looking up in his face ingenuously – 'one whom you might have desired to have in my place: – your sister, Miss Clarendon, in short.'

'Did Cecilia tell you of this?'

'No, Lady Davenant; and since I heard it I never could be happy – I never can be happy till I know your feeling.'

His manner instantly changed.

'You shall know my feelings, then,' said he. 'Till I knew you, Helen, my wish was that my sister should live with my wife; now I know you, my wish is that you should live with us. You

will suit Cecilia better than my sister could – will suit us both
better, having the same truth of character, and more gentleness of
manner. I have answered you with frankness equal to your own.
And now,' said he, taking her hand, 'you know Cecilia has always
considered you as her sister – allow me to do the same: consider
me as a brother – such shall you find me. Thank you. This is
settled for life,' added he, drawing her arm through his, and taking
up her letters, he led her back towards the library.

But her emotion, the stronger for being suppressed, was too
great for reappearing in company: she withdrew her arm from
his when they were passing through the hall, and turning her
face away, she had just voice enough to beg he would show her
letters to –

He understood. She ran upstairs to her own room, glad to be
alone; a flood of joy came over her.

'A brother in Cecilia's husband! – a brother!'

The word had a magical charm, and she could not help repeating it aloud – she wept like a child. Lady Cecilia soon came flying
in, all delight and affection, reproaches and wonder alternately,
in the quickest conceivable succession. 'Delighted it is settled for
ever and ever! my dear, dear Helen! But how could you ever
think of leaving us, you wicked Helen! Well! now you see what
Clarendon really is! But, my dear, I was so terrified when I heard
it all. You are, and ever were, the oddest mixture of cowardice and
courage. I – do you know I, brave *I* – never should have advised
– never should have ventured as you have? But he is delighted at
it all, and so I am now it has all ended so charmingly, now I have
you safe. I will write to the Collingwoods; you shall not have a
moment's pain; I will settle it all, and invite them here before they
leave England; Clarendon desired I would – oh, he is! – now you
will believe me! The Collingwoods, too, will be glad to be asked
here to take leave of you, and all will be right; I love, as you do,
dear Helen, that everybody should be pleased when I am happy.'

When Lady Davenant heard all that had passed, she did not
express that prompt unmixed delight which Helen expected:
a cloud come over her brow, something painful regarding her

daughter seemed to strike her, for her eyes fixed on Cecilia, and her emotion was visible in her countenance; but pleasure unmixed appeared as she turned to Helen, and to her she gave, what was unusual, unqualified approbation.

'My dear Helen, I admire your plain straightforward truth; I am satisfied with this first essay of your strength of mind and courage.'

'Courage!' said Helen, smiling.

'Not such as is required to take a lion by the beard, or a bull by the horns,' replied Lady Davenant; 'but there are many persons in this world who, brave though they be, would rather beard a lion, sooner seize a bull by the horns, than, when they get into a dilemma, dare to ask a direct question and tell plainly what passes in their own minds. Moral courage is, believe me, uncommon in both sexes, and yet in going through the world it is equally necessary to the virtue of both men and women.'

'But do you really think,' said Helen, 'that strength of mind, or what you call moral courage, is as necessary to women as it is to men?'

'Certainly, show me a virtue, male or female – if virtues admit of grammatical distinctions, if virtues acknowledge the more worthy gender and the less worthy of the grammar, show me a virtue male or female that *can* long exist without truth. Even that emphatically termed the virtue of our sex, on which social happiness rests, society depends, on what is it based? is it not on that single-hearted virtue truth? – and truth on what? on courage of the mind. They who dare to speak the truth will not ever dare to go irretrievably wrong. Then what is falsehood but cowardice? – and a false woman! – does not that say all in one word?

'But whence arose all this? you wonder, perhaps,' said Lady Davenant; 'and I have not inclination to explain. Here comes Lord Davenant. Now for politics – farewell morality, a long farewell. Now for the London budget, and "what news from Constantinople? Grand Vizier certainly strangled, or not?" '

CHAPTER 6

THE LONDON BUDGET of news was now opened, and gone through by Lord Davenant, including quarrels in the Cabinet and all that with fear of change perplexes politicians. But the fears and hopes of different ages are attached to such different subjects, that Helen heard all this as though she heard it not, and went on with her drawing, touching and retouching it, without ever looking up, till her attention was wakened by the name of Granville Beauclerc; this was the name of the person who had written those interesting letters which she had met with in Lady Davenant's portfolio.

'What is he doing in town?' asked the General.

'Amusing himself, I suppose,' replied Lord Davenant.

'I believe he forgets that I am his guardian,' said the General.

'I am sure he cannot forget that you are his friend,' said Lady Cecilia; 'for he has the best heart in the world.'

'And the worst head for anything useful,' said the General.

'He is a man of genius,' said Lady Davenant.

'Did you speak to him, my lord,' pursued the General, 'about standing for the county?'

'Yes.'

'And he said what?'

'That he would have nothing to do with it.'

'Why?'

'Something about not being tied to party, and somewhat he said about patriotism,' replied Lord Davenant.

'Nonsense!' said the General, 'he is a fool.'

'Only young,' said Lady Davenant.

'Men are not so very young in these days at two-and-twenty,' said the General.

'In some,' said Lady Davenant, 'the classical touch, the romance of political virtue, lasts for months, if not years, after they leave college; even those who, like Granville, go into high life in London, do not sometimes, for a season or two, lose their first enthusiasm for patriotism.'

The General's lips became compressed. Lord Davenant, throwing himself back in his easy-chair, repeated 'Patriotism! yes, every young man of talent is apt to begin with a fit of that sort.'

'My dear lord,' cried Lady Davenant, 'you, of all men, to speak of patriotism as a disease!'

'And a disease that can be had but once in life, I am afraid,' replied her lord, laughing; 'and yet,' as if believing in that at which he laughed, 'it evaporates in most men in words, written or spoken, lasts till the first pamphlet is published, or until the maiden-speech in Parliament is fairly made, and fairly paid for – in all honour – all honourable men.'

Lady Davenant passed over these satirical observations, and somewhat abruptly asked Lord Davenant if he recollected the late Mr Windham.

'Certainly, he was not a man to be easily forgotten; but what in particular?'

'The scales of his mind were too fine,' said Lady Davenant, 'too nicely adjusted for common purposes: diamond scales will not do for weighing wool. Very refined, very ingenious, very philosophical minds, such as Windham, Burke, Bacon, were all too scrupulous weighers; their scales turned with the millionth of a grain, and all from the same cause, subject to the same defect, indecision. They saw too well how much can be said on both sides of the question. There is a sort of philosophical doubt, arising from enlargement of understanding, quite different from that irresolution of character which is caused by infirmity of will; and I have observed,' continued Lady Davenant, 'in some of these over-scrupulous weighers, that when once they come to a balance, that instant they become most wilful; so it will be, you will see, with Beauclerc. After excessive indecision, you will see him start perhaps at once to rash action.'

'Rash of wrong, resolute of right,' said Lord Davenant.

'He is constitutionally wilful, and metaphysically vacillating,' said Lady Davenant.

The General waited till the metaphysics were over, and then said to Lord Davenant that he suspected there was something more than mere want of ambition in Beauclerc's refusal to go into Parliament. Some words were here inaudible to Helen, and the General began to walk up and down the room with so strong a tread, that at every step the china shook on the table near which Helen sat, so that she lost most part of what followed, and yet it seemed interesting, about some Lord Beltravers, and a Comtesse de Saint- something, or a Lady Blanche- somebody.

Lady Davenant looked anxious, the General's steps became more deliberately, more ominously firm; till Lady Cecilia came up to him, and playfully linking her arm in his, the steps were moderated, and when a soothing hand came upon his shoulder, the compressed lips were relaxed – she spoke in a low voice – he answered aloud.

'By all means! write to him yourself, my love; get him down here and he will be safe; he cannot refuse you.'

'Tuesday, then?' she would name the earliest day if the General approved.

He approved of everything she said: 'Tuesday let it be.' Following him to the door, Lady Cecilia added something which seemed to fill the measure of his contentment.

'Always good and kind,' said he; 'so let it be.'

'Then shall I write to your sister, or will you?'

'You,' said the General; 'let the kindness come from you, as it always does.'

Lady Cecilia, in a moment at the writing-table, ran off, as far as pen could go, two notes, which she put into her mother's hand, who gave an approving nod; and, leaving them with her to seal and have franked, Cecilia darted out on the terrace, carrying Helen along with her, to see some Italian garden she was projecting.

And as she went, and as she stood directing the workmen, at every close of her directions she spoke to Helen. She said she was very glad that she had settled that Beauclerc was to come to them immediately. He was a great favourite of hers.

'Not for any of those grandiose qualities which my mother sees in him, and which I am not quite clear exist; but just because he is the most agreeable person in nature, and really natural; though he is a man of the world, yet not the least affected. Quite fashionable, of course, but with true feeling. Oh! he is delightful, just-' then she interrupted herself to give directions to the workmen about her Italian garden –

'Oleander in the middle of that bed; vases nearer to the balustrade –

'Beauclerc has a very good taste, and a beautiful place he has, Thorndale. He will be very rich. Few very rich young men are agreeable now, women spoil them so. – ["Border that bed with something pretty."] – Still he is, and I long to know what you will think of him; I know what I think he will think, but, however, I will say no more; people are always sure to get into scrapes in this world when they say what they think. – ["That fountain looks beautiful."] I forgot to tell you he is very handsome. The General is very fond of him, and he of the General, except when he considers him his guardian, for Granville Beauclerc does not particularly like to be controlled – who does? It is a curious story. – ["Unpack those vases, and by the time that is done I will be back."] – Take a turn with me, Helen, this way. It is a curious story: Granville Beauclerc's father but I don't know it perfectly, I only know that he was a very odd man, and left the General, though he was so much younger than himself, guardian to Granville, and settled that he was not to be of age, I mean not to come into possession of his large estates, till he is five-and-twenty: shockingly hard on poor Granville, and enough to make him hate Clarendon, but he does not, and that is charming, that is one reason I like him! So amazingly respectful to his guardian always, considering how impetuous he is – amazingly respectful, though I cannot say I think he is what the gardening books call *patient of the knife* – I don't think he likes his fancies to be lopped; but then he is so clever. Much more what you would call a reading man than the General, distinguished at college, and all that which usually makes a young man conceited; but Beauclerc is only a little headstrong – all the more agreeable, it keeps one in agitation; one never knows how it will end, but I am sure it will all go on well now. It is curious, too, that mamma knew him also when he was at Eton, I believe – I don't know how, but long before we ever heard of Clarendon, and she corresponded with him, but I never knew him till he came to Florence, just after it was all settled with me and the General; and he was with us there and at Paris, and travelled home with us, and I like him. Now you know all, except what I do not choose to tell you, so come back to the workmen. – "That vase will not do there, move it in front of these evergreens; that will do." '

Then returning to Helen – 'After all, I did so right, and I am so glad I thought in time of inviting Esther, now Mr Beauclerc is coming – the General's sister – half-sister. Oh, so unlike him! you would never guess that Miss Clarendon was his sister, except from her pride. But she is so different from other people; she knows nothing, and wishes to know nothing, of the world. She lives always at an old castle in Wales, Llan – something, which she inherited from her mother, and she has always been her own mistress, living with her aunt in melancholy grandeur, till her brother brought her to Florence, where – oh, how she was out of her element! Come this way and I will tell you more. The fact is, I do not much like Miss Clarendon, and I will tell you why – I will describe her to you.'

'No, no, do not,' said Helen; 'do not, my dear Cecilia, and I will tell you why.'

'Why – why?' cried Cecilia.

'Do you recollect the story my uncle told us about the young bride and her old friend, and the bit of advice?'

No, Cecilia did not recollect anything of it. She should be very glad to hear the anecdote, but as to the advice, she hated advice.

'Still, if you knew who gave it – it was given by a very great man.'

'A very great man! now you make me curious. Well, what is it?' said Lady Cecilia.

'That for one year after her marriage she would not tell to her friends the opinion she had formed, if unfavourable, of any of her husband's relations, as it was probable she might change that opinion on knowing them better, and would afterwards be sorry for having told her first hasty judgment. Long afterwards the lady told her friend that she owed to this advice a great part of the happiness of her life, for she really had, in the course of the year, completely changed her first notions of some of her husband's family, and would have had sorely to repent if she had told her first thoughts.'

Cecilia listened, and said it was all 'vastly well! excellent. But I had nothing in the world to say of Miss Clarendon, but that she was too good – too sincere for the world we live in. For instance, at Paris, one day a charming Frenchwoman was telling some anecdote of the day in the most amusing manner. Esther Clarendon all the while stood by, grave and black as night, and at last turning upon our charmer at the end of the story, pronounced, "There is not one word of truth in all you have been saying!" Conceive it, in full salon! The French were in such amazement. "Inconceivable!" as they might well say to me, as she walked off with her tragedy-queen air; "*Inconcevable – mais, vraiment inconcevable*"; and "*Bien Anglaise,*" they would have added, no doubt, if I had not been by.'

'But there must surely have been some particular reason,' said Helen.

'None in the world, only the story was not true, I believe. And then another time, when she was with her cousin, the Duchess of Lisle, at Lisle-Royal, and was to have gone out the next season in London with the Duchess, she came down one morning, just before they were to set off for town, and declared that she had heard such a quantity of scandal since she had been there, and such shocking things of London society, that she had resolved not to go out with the Duchess, and not to go to town at all! So absurd – so prudish!'

Helen felt some sympathy in this, and was going to have said so, but Cecilia went on with –

'And then to expect that Granville Beauclerc – should – '

Here Cecilia paused, and Helen felt curious, and ashamed of her curiosity; she turned away, to raise the branches of some shrub, which were drooping from the weight of their flowers.

'I know something *has* been thought of,' said Cecilia. 'A match has been in contemplation – do you comprehend me, Helen?'

'You mean that Mr Beauclerc is to marry Miss Clarendon,' said Helen, compelled to speak.

'I only say it has been thought of,' replied Lady Cecilia; 'that is, as everything in this way is thought of about every couple not within the prohibited degrees, one's grandmother inclusive. And the plainer the woman, the more sure she is to contemplate such things for herself, lest no one else should think of them for her. But, my dear Helen, if you mean to ask – '

'Oh, I don't mean to ask anything,' cried Helen.

'But, whether you ask or not, I must tell you that the General is too proud to own, even to himself, that he could ever think of any man for his sister who had not first proposed for her.'

There was a pause for some minutes.

'But,' resumed Lady Cecilia, 'I could not do less than ask her here for Clarendon's sake, when I know it pleases him; and she is very – estimable, and so I wish to make her love me if I could! But I do not think she will be nearer her point with Mr Beau-clerc, if it is her point, by coming here just now. Granville has eyes as well as ears, and contrasts will strike. I know who I wish should strike him, as she strikes me – and I think – I hope – '

Helen looked distressed.

'I am as innocent as a dove,' pursued Lady Cecilia; 'but I suppose even doves may have their own private little thoughts and wishes.'

Helen was sure Cecilia had meant all this most kindly, but she was sorry that some things had been said. She was conscious of having been interested by those letters of Mr Beauclerc's; but a particular thought had now been put into her mind, and she could never more say, never more feel, that such a thought had not come into her head. She was very sorry; it seemed as if somewhat of the freshness, the innocence, of her mind was gone from her. She was sorry, too, that she had heard all that Cecilia had said about Miss Clarendon; it appeared as if she was actually doomed to get into some difficulty with the General about his sister; she felt as if thrown back into a sea of doubts, and she was not clear that she could, even by opposing, end them.

On the appointed Tuesday, late, Miss Clarendon arrived; a fine figure, but ungraceful, as Helen observed, from the first moment when she turned sharply away from Lady Cecilia's embrace to a great dog of her brother's – 'Ah, old Neptune! I'm glad you're still here.'

And when Lady Cecilia would have put down his paws – 'Let him alone, let him alone, dear, honest, old fellow.'

'But the dear, honest, old fellow's paws are wet, and will ruin your pretty new pelisse.'

'It may be new, but you know it is not pretty,' said Miss Clarendon, continuing to pat Neptune's head as he jumped up with his paws on her shoulder.

'Oh, my dear Esther, how can you bear him? he is so rough in his love.'

'I like rough better than smooth.' The rough paw caught in her lace frill, and it was torn to pieces before 'down! down!' and the unified efforts of Lady Cecilia and Helen could extricate it. 'Don't distress yourself about it, pray; it does not signify in the least. Poor Neptune, how really sorry he looks – there, there, wag your tail again – no one shall come between us two old friends.'

Her brother came in, and, starting up, her arms were thrown round his neck, and her bonnet falling back, Helen, who had thought her quite plain before, was surprised to see that, now her colour was raised, and there was life in her eyes, she was really handsome.

Gone again that expression when Cecilia spoke to her; whatever she said, Miss Clarendon differed from; if it was a matter of taste, she was always of the contrary opinion; if narrative or assertion, she questioned, doubted, seemed as if she could not believe. Her conversation, if conversation it could be called, was a perpetual rebating and regrating, especially with her sister-in-law; if Lady Cecilia did but say there were three instead of four, it was taken up as 'quite a mistake,' and marked not only as a mistake, but as 'not true.' Every, the slightest error, became a crime against majesty, and the first day ended with Helen's thinking her really the most disagreeable, intolerable person she had ever seen.

And the second day went on a little worse. Helen thought Cecilia took too much pains to please, and said it would be better to leave her quite alone. Helen did so completely, but Miss Clarendon did not let Helen alone; but watched her with penetrating eyes continually, listened to every word she said, and seeming to weigh every syllable, – 'Oh, my words are not worth your weighing,' said Helen, laughing.

'Yes, they are, to settle my mind.'

The first thing that seemed at all to settle it was Helen's not agreeing with Cecilia about the colour of two ribands which Helen said she could not flatter her were good matches. The next was about a drawing of Miss Clarendon's, of Llansillan, her place in Wales; a beautiful drawing indeed, which she had brought for her brother, but one of the towers certainly out of the perpendicular. Helen was appealed to, and could not say it was upright; Miss Clarendon instantly took up a knife, cut the paper at the back of the frame, and, taking out the drawing, set the tower to rights.

'There's the use of telling the truth.'

'Of listening to it,' said Helen.

'We shall get on, I see, Miss Stanley, if you can get over the first bitter outside of me – a hard outside, difficult to crack – stains delicate fingers, may be,' continued she, as she replaced her drawing in its frame – 'stains delicate fingers, may be, in the opening, but a good walnut you will find it, taken with a grain of salt.'

Many a grain seemed necessary, and very strong nutcrackers in very strong hands. Lady Cecilia's evidently were not strong enough, though she strained hard. Helen did not feel inclined to try.

Cecilia invited Miss Clarendon to walk out and see the alterations her brother had made. As they passed the new Italian garden,
Miss Clarendon asked, 'What's all this? – I don't like this – how I
regret the Old English garden, and the high beech hedges. Everything is to be changed here, I suppose, – pray do not ask my
opinion about any of the alterations.'

'I do not wonder,' said Cecilia, 'that you should prefer the old
garden, with all your early associations; warm-hearted, amiable
people must always be so fond of what they have loved in childhood.'

'I never was here when I was a child, and I am not one of
your amiable people.'

'Very true, indeed,' thought Helen.

'Miss Stanley looks at me as if I had seven heads,' said Miss
Clarendon, laughing; and, a minute after, overtaking Helen as she
walked on, she looked full in her face, and added, 'Do acknowledge that you think me a savage.' Helen did not deny it, and from
that moment Miss Clarendon looked less savagely upon her. She
laughed and said, 'I am not quite such a bear as I seem, you'll find;
at least I never hug people to death. My growl is worse than my
bite, unless someone should flatter my classical, bearish passion,
and offer to feed me with honey, and when I find it all comb and
no honey, who would not growl then?'

Lady Cecilia now came up, and pointed out views to which
the General had opened. 'Yes, it's well, he has done very well, but
pray don't stand on ceremony with me. I can walk alone, you may
leave me to my own cogitations, as I like best.'

Surely, as you like best,' said Lady Cecilia; 'pray consider yourself, as you know you are, at home here.'

'No, I shall never be at home here,' said Esther.

'Oh! don't say that, let me hope – let me hope –' and she
withdrew. Helen just stayed to unlock a gate for Miss Clarendon's
'rambles further,' and, as she unlocked it, she heard Miss Clarendon sigh as she repeated the word, 'Hope, I do not like to hope,
hope has so often deceived me.'

'You will never be deceived in Cecilia,' said Helen.

'Take care – stay till you try.'

'I have tried,' said Helen, 'I know her.'

'How long?'

'From childhood!'

'You're scarcely out of childhood yet.'

'I am not so very young. I have had trials of my friends – of Cecilia in particular, much more than you could ever have had.'

'Well, this is best thing I ever heard of her, and from good authority too; her friends abroad were all false,' said Miss Clarendon.

'It is very extraordinary,' said Helen, 'to hear such a young person as you talk so – '

'So – how?'

'Of false friends – you must have been very unfortunate.'

'Pardon me – very fortunate – to find them out in time.' She looked at the prospect, and liked all that her brother was doing, and disliked all that she even guessed Lady Cecilia had done. Helen showed her that she guessed wrong here and there, and smiled at her prejudices; and Miss Clarendon smiled again, and admitted that she was prejudiced, 'but everybody is; only some show and tell, and others smile and fib. I wish that word fib was banished from the English language, and white lie drummed out after it. Things by their right names and we should all do much better. Truth must be told, whether agreeable or not.'

'But whoever makes truth disagreeable commits high treason against virtue,' said Helen.

'Is that yours?' cried Miss Clarendon, stopping short.

'No,' said Helen.

'It is excellent, whoever said it.'

'It was from my uncle Stanley I heard it,' said Helen.

'Superior man that uncle must have been.'

'I will leave you now,' said Helen.

'Do; I see we shall like one another in time, Miss Stanley; in time – I hate sudden friendships.'

That evening Miss Clarendon questioned Helen more closely about her friendship with Cecilia, and how it was she came to live with her. Helen plainly told her.

'Then it was not an original promise with you?'

'Not at all,' said Helen.

'Lady Cecilia told me it was. Just like her, – I knew all the time it was a lie.'

Shocked and started at the word, and at the idea, Helen exclaimed, 'Oh, Miss Clarendon, how can you say so? anybody may be mistaken. Cecilia mistook – '

Lady Cecilia joined them at this moment. Miss Clarendon's face was flushed. 'This room is unsufferably hot. What can be the use of a fire at this time of year?'

Cecilia said it was for her mother, who was apt to be chilly in the evenings; and as she spoke, she put a screen between the flushed cheek and the fire. Miss Clarendon pushed it away, saying, 'I can't talk, I can't hear, I can't understand with a screen before me. What did you say, Lady Cecilia, to Lady Davenant, as we came out from dinner, about Mr Beauclerc?'

'That we expect him to-morrow.'

'You did not tell me so when you wrote.'

'No, my dear.'

'Why, pray?'

'I don't know.'

'You don't know, Lady Cecilia? why should people say they do not know, when they do know perfectly well?'

'If I had thought it was of any consequence to you, Esther,' said Cecilia, with an arch look.

'Now you expect me to answer that it was not of the least consequence to me – that is the answer you would make; but my answer is, that it was of consequence to me, and you knew it was.'

'And if I did?'

'If you did, why say "If I had thought it of any consequence to you?" – why say so? answer me truly!'

'Answer me truly!' repeated Lady Cecilia, laughing. 'Oh, my dear Esther, we are not in a court of justice.'

'Nor in a court of honour.'

'Well, well! let it be a court of love at least,' said Lady Cecilia. 'What a pretty proverb that was, Helen, that we met with the other day in that book of old English proverbs – "Love rules his kingdom without a sword."'

'Very likely; but to the point,' said Miss Clarendon, 'when do you expect Mr Beauclerc?'

'To-morrow.'

'Then I shall go to-morrow.'

'My dear Esther, why?'

'You know why; you know what reports have been spread; it suits neither my character nor my brother's to give any foundation for such reports. Let me ring the bell, and I will give my own orders.'

'My dear Esther, but your brother will be so vexed – so surprised.'

'My brother is the best judge of his own conduct, he will do what he pleases, or what you please. I am the judge of mine, and certainly shall do what I think right.'

She ran accordingly, and ordered that her carriage should be at the door at six o'clock in the morning.

'Nay, my dear Esther,' persisted Cecilia, 'I wish you would not decide so suddenly; we were so glad to have you come to us – '

'Glad! why, you know – '

'I know,' interrupted Lady Cecilia, colouring, and she began as fast as possible to urge every argument she could think of to persuade Miss Clarendon: but no arguments, no entreaties of hers or the General's, public or private, were of any avail, – go she would, and go she did, at six o'clock.

'I suppose,' said Helen to Lady Davenant, 'that Miss Clarendon is very estimable, and she seems to be very clever; but I wonder with all her abilities she does not learn to make her manners more agreeable.'

'My dear,' said Lady Davenant, 'we must take people as they are; you may graft a rose upon an oak, but those who have tried the experiment tell us the graft will last but a short time, and the operation ends in the destruction of both; where the stocks have no common nature, there is ever a want of conformity which sooner or later proves fatal to both.'

But Beauclerc, what was become of him? – that day passed, and no Beauclerc; another and another came, and on the third day, only a letter from him, which ought to have come on Tuesday. – But '*too late*,' the shameful brand of procrastination was upon it – and it contained only a few lines blotted in the folding, to say that he could not possibly be at Clarendon Park on Tuesday, but would on Wednesday or Thursday if possible.

Good-natured Lord Davenant observed, 'When a young man in London, writing to his friends in the country, names two days for leaving town, and adds an "*if possible*," his friends should never expect him till the last of the two named.'

The last of the two days arrived – Thursday. The aide-de-camp asked if Mr Beauclerc was expected to-day.

'Yes, I expect to see him to-day,' the General answered.

'I hope, but do not expect,' said Lady Davenant, 'for, as learned authority tells me, "to expect is to hope with some degree of certainty" – '

The General left the room repeating, 'I expect him to-day, Cecilia.'

The day passed, however, and he came not – the night came. The General ordered that the gate should be kept open, and that a servant should sit up. The servant sat up all night, cursing Mr Beauclerc. And in the morning he replied with malicious alacrity to the first question his master asked, 'No, sir, Mr Beauclerc is not come.'

At breakfast, the General, after buttering his bread in silence for some minutes, confessed that he loved punctuality. It might be a military prejudice, – it might be too professional, martinet perhaps, – but still he owned he did love punctuality. He considered it as a part of politeness, a proper attention to the convenience and feelings of others; indispensable between strangers it is usually felt to be, and he did not know why intimate friends should deem themselves privileged to dispense with it.

His eyes met Helen's as he finished these words, and smiling, he complimented her upon her constant punctuality. It was a voluntary grace in a lady, but an imperative duty in a man – and a very young man.

'You are fond of this young man, I see, General,' said Lord Davenant.

'But not of his fault.'

Lady Cecilia said something about forgiving a first fault.

'Never!' said Lady Davenant. 'Lord Collingwood's rule was – never forgive a first fault, and you will not have a second. You love Beauclerc, I see, as Lord Davenant says.'

'Love him!' resumed the General; 'with all his faults and follies, I love him as if he were my brother.'

At which words Lady Cecilia, with a scarcely perceptible smile, cast a furtive glance at Helen.

The General called for his horses, and, followed by his aide-de-camp, departed, saying that he should be back at luncheon-time, when he hoped to find Beauclerc. In the same hope, Lady Davenant ordered her pony-phaeton earlier than usual; Lady Cecilia further hoped most earnestly that Beauclerc would come this day, for the next the house would be full of company, and she really wished to have him one day at least to themselves, and she gave a most significant glance at Helen.

'The first move often secures the game against the best players,' said she.

Helen blushed, because she could not help understanding; she was ashamed, vexed with Cecilia, yet pleased by her kindness, and half amused by her arch look and tone.

They were neither of them aware that Lady Davenant had heard the words that passed, or seen the looks; but immediately afterwards, when they were leaving the breakfast-room, Lady Davenant came between the two friends, laid her hand upon her daughter's arm, and said,

'Before you make any move in a dangerous game, listen to the voice of old experience.'

Lady Cecilia, startled, looked up, but as if she did not comprehend.

'Cupid's bow, my dear,' continued her mother, 'is, as the Asiatics tell us, strung with bees, which are apt to sting – sometimes fatally – those who meddle with it.'

Lady Cecilia still looked with an innocent air, and still as if she could not comprehend.

'To speak more plainly, then, Cecilia,' said her mother, 'build no matrimonial castles in the air; standing or falling they do mischief – either to the builder, or to those for whom they may be built.'

'Certainly if they fall they disappoint one,' said Lady Cecilia, 'but if they stand?'

Seeing that she made no impression on her daughter, Lady Davenant turned to Helen, and gravely said,

'My dear Helen, do not let my daughter inspire you with false, and perhaps vain imaginations, certainly premature, therefore unbecoming.'

Helen shrank back, yet instantly looked up, and her look was ingenuously grateful.

'But, mamma,' said Lady Cecilia, 'I declare I do not understand what all this is about.'

'About Mr Granville Beauclerc,' said her mother.

'How can you, dear mamma, pronounce his name so *tout au long*'[1]

'Pardon my indelicacy, my dear; delicacy is a good thing, but truth a better. I have seen the happiness of many young women sacrificed by such false delicacy, and by the fear of giving a moment's pain, which it is sometimes the duty of a true friend to give.'

'Certainly, certainly, mamma, only not necessary now; and I am so sorry you have said all this to poor dear Helen.'

'If you have said nothing to her, Cecilia, I acknowledge I have said too much.'

'I said – I did nothing,' cried Lady Cecilia; 'I built no castles – never built a regular castle in my life; never had a regular plan in my existence; never mentioned his name, except about another person – '

An appealing look to Helen was however protested.

[1] in full

'To the best of my recollection, at least,' Lady Cecilia immediately added.

'Helen seems to be blushing for your want of recollection,
Cecilia.'

'I am sure I do not know why you blush, Helen. I am certain
I never did say a word distinctly.'

'Not *distinctly* certainly,' said Helen in a low voice. 'It was my
fault if I understood – '

'Always true, you are,' said Lady Davenant.

'I protest I said nothing but the truth,' cried Lady Cecilia
hastily.

'But not the whole truth, Cecilia,' said her mother.

'I did, upon my word, mamma,' persisted Lady Cecilia, repeating, 'upon my word.'

'Upon your word, Cecilia! that is either a vulgar expletive or
a most serious asseveration.'

She spoke with a grave tone, and with her severe look, and
Helen dared not raise her eyes; Lady Cecilia now coloured deeply.

'Shame! Nature's hasty conscience,' said Lady Davenant.
'Heaven preserve it!'

'Oh, mother!' cried Lady Cecilia, laying her hand on her
mother's, 'surely you do not think seriously – surely you are not
angry – I cannot bear to see you displeased,' said she, looking
up imploringly in her mother's face, and softly, urgently pressing
her hand. No pressure was returned; that hand was slowly and
with austere composure withdrawn, and her mother walked away
down the corridor to her own room.

Lady Cecilia stood still, and the tears came into her eyes.

'My dear friend, I am exceedingly sorry,' said Helen. She
could not believe that Cecilia meant to say what was not true,
yet she felt that she had been to blame in not telling all, and her
mother in saying too much.

Lady Cecilia, her tears dispersed, stood looking at the impression which her mother's signet-ring had left in the palm of her
hand. It was at that moment a disagreeable recollection that the
motto of that ring was 'Truth.' Rubbing the impress from her

hand, she said, half speaking to herself, and half to Helen, – 'I am sure I did not mean anything wrong; and I am sure nothing can be more true than that I never formed a regular plan in my life. After all, I am sure that so much has been said about nothing, that I do not understand anything: I never do, when mamma goes on in that way, making mountains out of molehills, which she always does with me, and did ever since I was a child; but she really forgets that I am not a child. Now, it is well the General was not by; he would never have borne to see his wife so treated. But I would not, for the world, be the cause of any disagreement. O Helen, my mother does not know how I love her, let her be ever so severe to me! But she never loved me; she cannot help it. I believe she does her best to love me – my poor, dear mother!'

Helen seized this opportunity to repeat the warm expressions she had heard so lately from Lady Davenant, and melting they sank into Cecilia's heart. She kissed Helen again and again, for a dear, good peacemaker, as she always was – and 'I'm resolved' – but in the midst of her good resolve, she caught a glimpse, through the glass door opening on the park, of the General, and a fine horse they were ringing, and she hurried out; all light of heart she went, as though

> Her treading would not bend a blade of grass,
> Or shake the downy *blowball* from her stalk.

CHAPTER 7

SINCE LORD DAVENANT'S arrival, Lady Davenant's time was so much taken up with him, that Helen could not have many opportunities of conversing with her, and she was the more anxious to seize every one that occurred. She always watched for the time when Lady Davenant went out in her pony phaeton, for then she had her delightfully to herself, the carriage holding only two.

It was at the door, and Lady Davenant was crossing the hall followed by Helen, when Cecilia came in with a look, unusual in her, of being much discomfited.

'Another put-off from Mr Beauclerc! He will not be here to-day. I give him up.'

Lady Davenant stopped short, and asked whether Cecilia had told him that probably she should soon be gone?

'To be sure I did, mamma.'

'And what reason does he give for his delay?'

'None, mamma, none – not the least apology. He says, very cavalierly indeed, that he is the worst man in the world at making excuses – shall attempt none.'

'There he is right,' said Lady Davenant. 'Those who are good at excuses, as Franklin justly observed, are apt to be good for nothing else.'

The General came up the steps at this moment, rolling a note between his fingers, and looking displeased. Lady Davenant inquired if he could tell her the cause of Beauclerc's delay. He could not.

Lady Cecilia exclaimed – 'Very extraordinary! Provoking! Insufferable! Intolerable!'

'It is Mr Beauclerc's own affair,' said Lady Davenant, wrapping her shawl round her; and, taking the General's arm, she walked on to her carriage. Seating herself, and gathering up the reins, she repeated – 'Mr Beauclerc's own affair, completely.'

The lash of her whip was caught somewhere, and, while the groom was disentangling it, she reiterated 'That will do; let the horses go'; and with half-suppressed impatience thanked Helen, who was endeavouring to arrange some ill-disposed cloak – 'Thank you, thank you, my dear; it's all very well; sit down, Helen.'

She drove off rapidly, through the beautiful park scenery. But the ancient oaks, standing alone, casting vast shadows, the distant massive woods of magnificent extent and of soft and varied foliage, the secluded glades, all were lost upon her. Looking straight between her horses' ears, she drove on in absolute silence.

Helen's idea of Mr Beauclerc's importance increased wonderfully. What must he be whose coming or not coming could so move all the world, or those who were all the world to her? And, left to her own cogitations, she was picturing to herself what manner of man he might be, when suddenly Lady Davenant turned, and asked what she was thinking of? 'I beg your pardon for startling you so, my dear; I am aware that it is a dreadfully imprudent, impertinent question – one which, indeed, I seldom ask. Few interest me sufficiently to make me care of what they think: from fewer still could I expect to hear the truth. Nay – nothing upon compulsion, Helen. Only say plainly, if you would rather not tell me. That answer I should prefer to the ingenious formula of evasion, the solecism in metaphysics, which Cecilia used the other day, when unwittingly I asked her of what she was thinking – "Of a great many different things, mamma." '

Helen, still more alarmed by Lady Davenant's speech than by her question, and aware of the conclusions which might be drawn from her answer, nevertheless bravely replied that she had been thinking of Mr Beauclerc, of what he might be whose coming or not coming was of such consequence. As she spoke, the expression of Lady Davenant's countenance changed.

'Thank you, my dear child, you are truth itself, and truly do I love you therefore. It's well that you did not ask me of what I was thinking, for I am not sure that I could have answered so directly.'

'But I could never have presumed to ask such a question of you,' said Helen, 'there is such a difference.'

'Yes,' replied Lady Davenant; 'there is such a difference as age and authority require to be made, but nevertheless, such as is not quite consistent with the equal rights of friendship. You have told me the subject of your day-dream, my love, and if you please, I will tell you the subject of mine. I was rapt into times long past: I was living over again some early scenes – some which are connected, and which connect me, in a curious manner, with this young man, Mr Granville Beauclerc.'

She seemed to speak with some difficulty, and yet to be resolved to go on.

'Helen, I have a mind,' continued she, 'to tell you what, in the language of affected biographers, I might call "some passages of my life." '

Helen's eyes brightened, as she eagerly thanked her: but hearing a half-suppressed sigh, she added – 'Not if it is painful to you though, my dear Lady Davenant.'

'Painful it must be,' she replied, 'but it may be useful to you; and a weak friend is that who can do only what is pleasurable. You have often trusted me with those little inmost feelings of the heart, which, however innocent, we shrink from exposing to any but the friends we most love; it is unjust and absurd of those advancing in years to expect of the young that confidence should come all and only on their side: the human heart, at whatever age, opens only to the heart that opens in return.'

Lady Davenant paused again, and then said, 'It is a general opinion that nobody is the better for advice.'

'I am sure I do not think so,' said Helen.

'I am glad you do not; nor do I. Much depends upon the way in which it is offered. General maxims, drawn from experience are, to the young at least, but as remarks – moral sentences – mere dead letter, and take no hold of the mind. "I have felt" must come before "I think", especially in speaking to a young friend; and, though I am accused of being so fond of generalising that I never come to particulars, I can and will: therefore, my dear, I will tell you some particulars of my life, in which, take notice, there are no adventures. Mine has been a life of passion – of feeling, at least, – not of incidents: nothing, my dear, to excite or to gratify curiosity.'

'But, independent of all curiosity about events,' said Helen, 'there is such an interest in knowing what has been really felt and thought in their former lives by those we know and love.'

'I shall sink in your esteem,' said Lady Davenant – 'so be it.

'I need not begin, as most people do, with "I was born" –' but, interrupting herself, she said, 'this heat is too much for me.'

They turned into a long shady drive through the woods. Lady Davenant drew up the reins, and her ponies walked slowly on the grassy road; then, turning to Helen, she said, –

'It would have been well for me if any friend had, when I was of your age, put me on my guard against my own heart: but my too indulgent, too sanguine mother led me into the very danger against which she should have warned me – she misled me, though without being aware of it. Our minds, our very natures, differed strangely.

'She was a castle-builder – yes, now you know, my dear, why I spoke so strongly and, as you thought, so severely, this morning. My mother was a castle-builder of the ordinary sort: a worldly plan of a castle was hers, and little care had she about the knight within; yet she had sufficient tact to know that it must be the idea of the *preux chevalier* [1] that would lure her daughter into the castle. Prudent for herself, imprudent for me, and yet she loved me – all she did was for love of me. She managed with so much address, that I had no suspicion of my being the subject of any speculation – otherwise, probably, my imagination might have

[1] valiant knight

revolted, my self-will have struggled, my pride have interfered, or my delicacy might have been alarmed, but nothing of all that happened; I was only too ready, too glad, to believe all that I was told, all that appeared in that spring-time of hope and love. I was very romantic, not in the modern fashionable young-lady sense of the word, with the mixed ideas of a shepherdess's hat and the paraphernalia of a peeress – love in a cottage, and a fashionable house in town. No; mine was honest, pure, real romantic love – absurd if you will; it was love nursed by imagination more than by hope. I had early, in my secret soul, as perhaps you have at this instant in yours, a pattern of perfection – something chivalrous, noble, something that is no longer to be seen nowadays – the more delightful to imagine, the moral sublime and beautiful; more than human, yet with the extreme of human tenderness. Mine was to be a demigod whom I could worship, a husband to whom I could always look up, with whom I could always sympathise, and to whom I could devote myself with all a woman's self-devotion. I had then a vast idea – as I think you have now, Helen – of self-devotion; you would devote yourself to your friends, but I could not shape any of my friends into a fit object. So after my own imagination I made one, dwelt upon it, doated upon it, and at last threw this bright image of my own fancy full upon the being to whom I thought I was most happily destined – destined by duty, chosen by affection. The words "I love you" once pronounced, I gave my whole heart in return, gave it, sanctified, as I felt, by religion. I had high religious sentiments; a vow once past the lips, a look, a single look of appeal to Heaven, was as much for me as if pronounced at the altar, and before thousands of witnesses. Some time was to elapse before the celebration of our marriage. Protracted engagements are unwise, yet I should not say so; this gave me time to open my eyes – my bewitched eyes: still, some months I passed in a trance of beatification, with visions of duties all performed – benevolence universal, and gratitude, and high success, and crowns of laurel, for my hero, for he was military; it all joined well in my fancy. All the pictured tales of vast heroic deeds were to be his. Living, I was to live in the radiance of his honour; or dying, to die with him, and then to be most blessed.

'It is all to me now as a dream, long past, and never told; no, never, except to him who had a right to know it – my husband, and now to you, Helen. From my dream I was awakened by a rude shock – I saw, I thank Heaven I first, and I alone, saw that his heart was gone from me – that his heart had never been mine – that it was unworthy of me. No, I will not say that; I will not think so. Still I trust he had deceived himself, though not so much as he deceived me. I am willing to believe he did not know that what he professed for me was not love till he was seized by that passion for another, a younger, fairer – Oh! how much fairer. Beauty is a great gift of Heaven – not for the purposes of female vanity; but a great gift for one who loves, and wishes to be loved. But beauty I had not.'

'Had not!' interrupted Helen, 'I always heard – '

'*He* did not think so, my dear; no matter what others thought, at least so I felt at that time. My identity is so much changed that I can look back upon this now, and tell it all to you calmly.

'It was at a rehearsal of ancient music; I went there accidentally one morning without my mother, with a certain old duchess and her daughters; the dowager full of some Indian screen which she was going to buy; the daughters intent, one of them, on a quarrel between two of the singers; the other upon loves and hates of her own. I was the only one of the party who had any real taste for music. I was then particularly fond of it.

'Well my dear, I must come to the point,' her voice changing as she spoke. – 'After such a lapse of time, during which my mind, my whole self, has so much changed, I could not have believed before I began to speak on this subject that these reminiscences could have so moved me; but it is merely this sudden wakening of ideas long dormant, for years not called up, never put into words.

'I was sitting, rapt in a silent ecstasy of pleasure, leaning back behind the whispering party, when I saw him come in, and, thinking only of his sharing my delight, I made an effort to catch his attention, but he did not see me – his eye was fixed on another; I followed that eye, and saw that most beautiful creature on which it was fixed; I saw him seat himself beside her – one look was enough – it was conviction. A pang went through me; I grew cold, but made no sound or motion; I gasped for breath, I believe, but I did not faint. None cared for me; I was unnoticed – saved from the abasement of pity. I struggled to retain my self-command, and was enabled to complete the purpose on which I then, even *then*, resolved. That resolve gave me force.

'In any great emotion we can speak better to those who do not care for us than to those who feel for us. More calmly than I now speak to you, I turned to the person who then sat beside me, to the dowager whose heart was in the Indian screen, and begged that I might not longer detain her, as I wished that she would carry me home – she readily complied; I had presence of mind enough to move when we could do so without attracting attention. It was well that woman talked as she did all the way home: she never saw, never suspected, the agony of her to whom she spoke. I ran up to my own room, bolted the door, and threw myself into a chair; that is the last thing I remember, till I found myself lying on the floor, wakening from a state of insensibility. I know not what time had elapsed: so as soon as I could I rang for my maid; she had knocked at my door, and supposing I slept, had not disturbed me – my mother, I found, had not yet returned.

'I dressed for dinner; HE was to dine with us. It was my custom to see him for a few minutes before the rest of the company arrived. No time ever appeared to me so dreadfully long as the interval between my being dressed that day and his arrival.

'I heard him coming upstairs; my heart beat so violently that I feared I should not be able to speak with dignity and composure, but the motive was sufficient.

'What I said I know not; I am certain only that it was without one word of reproach. What I had at one glance foreboded was true – he acknowledged it. I released him from all engagement to me. I saw he was evidently relieved by the determined tone of my refusal – at what expense to my heart he was set free, he saw not – never knew – never suspected. But after that first involuntary expression of the pleasure of relief, I saw in his countenance surprise, a sort of mortified astonishment at my self-possession. I own my woman's pride enjoyed this; it was something better than pride – the sense of the preservation of my dignity. I felt that in this shipwreck of my happiness I made no cowardly exposure of my feelings, but he did not understand me. Our minds, as I now found, moved in different orbits. We could not comprehend each other. Instead of feeling, as the instinct of generosity would have taught him to feel, that I was sacrificing my happiness to his, he told me that he now believed I had never loved him. My eyes were opened – I saw him at once as he really was. The ungenerous look upon self-devotion as madness, folly, or art: he could not think me a fool, he did not think me mad, artful I believe he did suspect me to be; he concluded that I made the discovery of his inconstancy an excuse for my own; he thought me, perhaps, worse than capricious, interested – for, our engagement being unknown, a lover of higher rank had, in the interval, presented himself. My perception of this base suspicion was useful to me at the moment, as it roused my spirit, and I went through the better, and without relapse of tenderness, with that which I had undertaken. One condition only I made; I insisted that this explanation should rest between us two; that, in fact, and in manner, the breaking off the match should be left entirely to me. And to this part of the business I now look back with satisfaction, and I have honest pride in telling you, who will feel the same for me, that I practised in the whole conduct of the affair no deceit of any kind, not one falsehood was told. The world knew nothing; there my mother had been prudent. She was the only person to whom I was bound to explain – to speak, I mean, for I did not feel myself bound to explain. Perfect confidence only can command perfect confidence in whatever relation of life. I told her all that she had a right to know. I announced to her that the intended marriage could never be – that I objected to it; that both our minds were changed; that we were both satisfied in having released each other from our mutual engagement. I had, as I foresaw, to endure my mother's anger, her entreaties, her endless surprise, her bitter disappointment; but she exhausted all these, and her mind turned sooner than I had expected to that hope of higher establishment which amused her during the rest of the season in London. Two months of it were still to be passed – to me the two most painful months of my existence. The daily, nightly, effort of appearing in public, while I was thus wretched, in the full gala of life in the midst of the young, the gay, the happy – broken-hearted as I was – it was an effort beyond my strength. That summer was, I remember, intolerably hot. Whenever my mother observed that I looked pale, and that my spirits were not so good as formerly, I exerted myself more and more; accepted every invitation because I dared not refuse; I danced at this ball, and the next, and the next; urged on, I finished to the dregs the dissipation of the season.

'My mother certainly made me do dreadfully too much. But I blame others, as we usually do when we are ourselves the most to blame – I had attempted that which could not be done. By suppressing all outward sign of suffering, allowing no vent for sorrow in words or tears – by actual force of compression – I thought at once to extinguish my feelings. Little did I know of the human heart when I thought this! The weak are wise in yielding to the first shock. They cannot be struck to the earth who sink prostrate; sorrow has little power where there is no resistance. – "The flesh will follow where the pincers tear." Mine was a presumptuous – it had nearly been a fatal struggle. That London season at last over, we got into the country; I expected rest, but found none. The pressing necessity for exertion over, the stimulus ceasing, I sank – sank into a fit of apathy.

'Time enough had elapsed between the breaking off of my marriage and the appearance of this illness to prevent any ideas on my mother's part of cause and effect, ideas indeed which were never much looked for, or well joined in her mind. The world knew nothing of the matter. My illness went under the convenient head "nervous." I heard all the opinions pronounced on my case, and knew they were all mistaken, but I swallowed whatever they pleased. No physician, I repeated to myself, can "minister to a mind diseased."

'I tried to call religion to my aid; but my religious sentiments were at that time tinctured with the enthusiasm of my early character. Had I been a Catholic, I should have escaped from my friends and thrown myself into a cloister; as it was, I had formed a strong wish to retire from that world which was no longer anything to me: the spring of passion, which I then thought the spring of life, being broken, I meditated my resolution secretly and perpetually as I lay on my bed. They used to read to me, and, among other things some papers of *The Rambler*, which I liked not at all; its tripod sentences tired my ear, but I let them go on – as well one sound as another.

'It chanced one night, as I was going to sleep, an eastern story in *The Rambler* was read to me, about some man, aweary of the world, who took to the peaceful hermitage. There was a regular moral tagged to the end of it, a thing I hate; the words were, "No life pleasing to God that is not useful to man." When I wakened in the middle of that night, this sentence was before my eyes, and the words seemed to repeat themselves over and over again to my ears when I was sinking to sleep. The impression remained in my mind, and though I never voluntarily recurred to it, came out long afterwards, perfectly fresh, and became a motive of action.

'Strange, mysterious connection between mind and body; in mere animal nature we see the same. The bird wakened from his sleep to be taught a tune sung to him in the dark, and left to sleep again, – the impression rests buried within him, and weeks afterwards he comes out with the tune perfect. But these are only phenomena of memory – mine was more extraordinary. I am not sure that I can explain it to you. In my weak state, my understanding enfeebled as much as my body – my reason weaker than my memory, I could not help allowing myself to think that the constant repetition of that sentence was a warning sent to me from above. As I grew stronger, the superstition died away, but the sense of the thing still remained with me. It led me to examine and reflect. It did more than all my mother's entreaties could effect. I had refused to see any human creature, but now I consented to admit a few. The charm was broken. I gave up my longing for solitude, my plan of retreat from the world; suffered myself to be carried where they pleased – to Brighton it was – to my mother's satisfaction. I was ready to appear in the ranks of fashion at the opening of the next London campaign. Automatically I "ran my female exercises o'er" with as good grace as ever. I had followers and proposals; but my mother was again thrown into despair by what she called the short work I made with my admirers, scarcely allowing decent time for their turning into lovers, before I warned them not to think of me. I have heard that women who have suffered from man's inconstancy are disposed afterwards to revenge themselves by inflicting pain such as they have themselves endured, and delight in all the cruelty of coquetry. It was not so with me. Mine was too deep a wound – skinned over – not callous, and all danger of its opening again I dreaded. I had lovers the more, perhaps, because I cared not for them; till amongst them there came one who, as I saw, appreciated my character, and, as I perceived, was becoming seriously attached. To prevent danger to his happiness, as he would take no other warning, I revealed to him the state of my mind. However humiliating the confession, I thought it due to him. I told him that I had no heart to give – that I had received none in return for that with which I had parted, and that love was over with me.

' "As a passion, it may be so, not as an affection," was his reply.

'The words opened to me a view of his character. I saw, too, by his love increasing with his esteem, the solidity of his understanding and the nobleness of his nature. He went deeper and deeper into my mind, till he came to a spring of gratitude, which rose and overflowed, vivifying and fertilising the seemingly barren waste. I believe it to be true that, after the first great misfortune, persons never return to be the same that they were before, but this I know – and this it is important you should be convinced of, my dear Helen – that the mind, though sorely smitten, can recover its powers. A mind, I mean, sustained by good principles, and by them made capable of persevering efforts for its own recovery. It may be sure of regaining, in time – observe, I say in time – its healthful tone.

'Time was given to me by that kind, that noble being, who devoted himself to me with a passion which I could not return – but, with such affection as I could give, and which he assured me would make his happiness, I determined to devote to him the whole of my future existence. Happiness for me, I thought, was gone, except in so far as I could make him happy.

'I married Lord Davenant – much against my mother's wish, for he was then the younger of three brothers, and with a younger brother's very small portion. Had it been a more splendid match, I do not think I could have been prevailed on to give my consent. I could not have been sure of my own motives, or rather my pride would not have been clear as to the opinion which others might form. This was a weakness, for in acting we ought to depend upon ourselves, and not to look for the praise or blame of others; but I let you see me as I am, or as I was: I do not insist, like Queen Elizabeth, in having my portrait without shade.

CHAPTER 8

'I'M PROUD TO TELL YOU that at the time I married we were so poor that I was obliged to give up many of those luxuries to which I was entitled, and to which I had been so accustomed that the doing without them had till then hardly come within my idea of possibility. Our whole establishment was on the most humble scale.

'I look back to this period of my life with the greatest satisfaction. I had exquisite pleasure, like all young people of sanguine temperament and generous disposition, in the consciousness of the capability of making sacrifices. This notion was my idol, the idol of the inmost sanctuary of my mind, and I worshipped it with all the energies of body and soul.

'In the course of a few years, my husband's two elder brothers died. If you have any curiosity to know how, I will tell you, though indeed it is as little to the purpose as half the things people tell in their histories. The eldest, a home-bred lordling, who, from the moment he slipped his mother's apron-strings, had fallen into folly, and then, to show himself manly, run into vice, lost his life in a duel about some lady's crooked thumb, or more crooked mind.

'The second brother distinguished himself in the navy; he died the death of honour; he fell gloriously, and was by his country honoured – by his country mourned.

'After the death of this young man, the inheritance came to my husband. Fortune soon after poured in upon us a tide of wealth, swelled by collateral streams.

'You will wish to know what effect this change of circumstances produced upon my mind, and you shall, as far as I know
it myself. I fancied that it would have made none, because I had
been before accustomed to all the trappings of wealth; yet it did
make a greater change in my feelings than you could have imagined, or I could have conceived. The possibility of producing a
great effect in society, of playing a distinguished part, and attain-
ing an eminence which pleased my fancy, had never till now been
within my reach. The incense of fame had been wafted near me,
but not to me – near my husband I mean, yet not to him; I had
heard his brother's name from the trumpet of fame, I longed to
hear his own. I knew, what to the world was then unknown, his
great talents for civil business, which, if urged into action, might
make him distinguished as a statesman even beyond his hero
brother, but I knew that in him ambition, if it ever awoke, must
be awakened by love. Conscious of my influence, I determined
to use it to the utmost.

'Lord Davenant had not at that time taken any part in politics,
but from his connections he could ask and obtain; and there was
one in the world for whom I desired to obtain a favour of importance. It chanced that he, whom I have mentioned to you as my
inconstant lover, now married to my lovely rival, was at this time
in some difficulty about a command abroad. His connections,
though of very high rank, were not now in power. He had failed
in some military exploit which had formerly been entrusted
to him. He was anxious to retrieve his character; his credit, his
whole fate in life, depended on his obtaining this appointment,
which, at my request, was secured to him by Lord Davenant. The
day it was obtained was, I think, the proudest of my life. I was
proud of returning good for evil; that was a Christian pride, if
pride can be Christian. I was proud of showing that in me there
was none of the fury of a woman scorned – no sense of the injury
of charms despised.

'But it was not yet the fullness of success; it had pained me
in the midst of my internal triumph, that my husband had been
obliged to use intermediate powers to obtain that which I should

have desired should have been obtained by his own. Why should he not be in that first place of rule? He could hold the balance with a hand as firm, an eye as just. That he should be in the House of Peers was little satisfaction to me, unless distinguished among his peers. It was this distinction that I burned to see obtained by Lord Davenant; I urged him forward then by all the motives which make ambition virtue. He was averse from public life, partly from indolence of temper, partly from sound philosophy: power was low in the scale in his estimate of human happiness; he saw how little can be effected of real good in public by any individual; he felt it scarcely worth his while to stir from his easy chair of domestic happiness. However, love urged him on, and inspired him, if not with ambition, at least with what looked like it in public. He entered the lists, and in the political tourna-ment tilted successfully. Many were astonished, for, till they came against him in the joust, they had no notion of his weight, or of his skill in arms; and many seriously inclined to believe that Lord Davenant was only Lady Davenant in disguise, and all he said, wrote, and did, was attributed to me. Envy gratifies herself continually by this shifting the merit from one person to another; in hopes that the actual quantity may be diminished, she tries to make out that it is never the real person, but somebody else, who does that which is good. This silly, base propensity might have cost me dear, would have cost me my husband's affections, had he not been a man, as there are few, above all jealousy of female influence or female talent; in short, he knew his own superior-ity, and needed not to measure himself to prove his height. He is quite content, rather glad, that everybody should set him down as a commonplace character. Far from being jealous of his wife's ruling him, he was amused by the notion: it flattered his pride, and it was convenient to his indolence; it fell in, too, with his peculiar humour. The more I retired, the more I was put forward, he, laughing behind me, prompted and forbade me to look back.

'Now, Helen, I am coming to a point where ambition ceased to be virtue. But why should I tell you all this? no one is ever the better for the experiences of another.'

'Oh! I cannot believe that,' cried Helen; 'pray, pray go on.'

'Ambition first rose in my mind from the ashes of another passion. Fresh materials, of heterogeneous kinds, altered the colour and changed the nature of the flame: I should have told you, but narrative is not my forte – I never can remember to tell things in their right order. I forgot to tell you that when Madame de Staël's book, *Sur la Revolution Française,* came out, it made an extraordinary impression on me. I turned, in the first place, as everybody did, eagerly to the chapter on England, but, though my national feelings were gratified, my female pride was dreadfully mortified by what she says of the ladies of England; in fact, she could not judge of them. They were afraid of her. They would not come out of their shells. What she called timidity, and what I am sure she longed to call stupidity, was the silence of overawed admiration, or mixed curiosity and discretion. Those who did venture had not full possession of their powers, or in a hurry showed them in a wrong direction. She saw none of them in their natural state. She asserts that though there may be women distinguished as writers in England, there are no ladies who have any great conversational and political influence in society, of that kind which, during the old regime, was obtained in France by what they would call their *femmes marquantes*[2], such as Madame de Tencin, Madame de Deffand, Mademoiselle de l'Espinasse. This remark stung me to the quick, for my country and for myself, and raised in me a foolish, vainglorious emulation, an ambition false in its objects, and unsuited to the manners, domestic habits, and public virtue of our country. I ought to have been gratified by her observing that a lady is never to be met with in England, as formerly in France, at the Bureau du Ministre; and that in England there has never been any example of a woman's having known in public affairs, or at least told, what ought to have been kept secret. Between ourselves, I suspect she was a little mistaken in some of these assertions; but, be that as it may, I determined to prove that she was mistaken; I was conscious that I had more

---

[1] outstanding women

within me than I had yet brought out; I did not doubt that I had eloquence, if I had but courage to produce it. It is really astonishing what a mischievous effect those few passages produced on my mind. In London, one book drives out another, one impression, however deep, is effaced by the next shaking of the sand; but I was then in the country, for, unluckily for me, Lord Davenant had been sent away on some special embassy. Left alone with my nonsense, I set about, as soon as I was able, to assemble an audience round me, to exhibit myself in the character of a female politician, and I believe I had a notion, at the same time of being the English Corinne. Rochefoucault, the dextrous anatomist of self-love, says that we confess our small faults, to persuade the world that we have no large ones. But, for my part, I feel that there are some small faults more difficult to me to confess than any large ones. Affectation, for instance; it is something so little, so paltry, it is more than a crime, it is a ridicule: I believe I did make myself completely ridiculous: I am glad Lord Davenant was not by, it lasted but a short time. Our dear good friend Dumont (you knew Dumont at Florence?) could not bear to see it; his regard for Lord Davenant urged him the more to disenchant me, and bring me back, before his return, to my natural form. The disenchantment was rather rude.

'One evening, after I had been snuffing up incense till I was quite intoxicated, when my votaries had departed, and we were alone together, I said to him, "Allow that this is what would be called at Paris *un grand succès*." [1]

'Dumont made no reply, but stood opposite to me playing in his peculiar manner with his great snuff-box, slowly swaying the snuff from side to side. Knowing this to be a sign that he was in some great dilemma, I asked of what he was thinking. "Of you," said he. "And what of me?" In his French accent he repeated those two provoking lines –

"New wit, like wine, intoxicates the brain,
Too strong for feeble women to sustain."

[1] a great success

' "To my face?" said I, smiling, for I tried to command my temper.

' "Better than behind your back, as others do," said he.

' "Behind my back!" said I; "impossible."

' "Perfectly possible," said he, "as I could prove if you were strong enough to bear it."

' "Quite strong enough," I said, and bade him speak on.

' "Suppose you were offered," said he, "the fairy-ring that rendered the possessor invisible, and enabled him to hear everything that was said, and all that was thought of him, would you throw it away, or put it on your finger?"

' "Put it on my finger," I replied; "and this instant, for a true friend is better than a magic ring, I put it on."

' "You are very brave," said he, "then you shall hear the lines I heard in a rival salon, repeated by him who last wafted the censer to you tonight." He repeated a kind of doggrel pasquinade, beginning with

> "Tell me, gentles, have you seen
> The prating she, the mock Corinne?"

'Dumont, who had the courage for my good to inflict the blow, could not stay to see its effect, and this time I was left alone, not with my nonsense, but with my reason. It was quite sufficient. I was cured. My only consolation in my disgrace was that I honourably kept Dumont's counsel. The friend who composed the lampoon, from that day to this, never knew that I had heard it; though I must own I often longed to tell him, when he was offering his incense again, that I wished he would reverse his practice, and let us have the satire in my presence, and keep the flattery for my absence. The graft of affectation, which was but a poor weak thing, fell off at once, but the root of the evil had not yet been reached. My friend Dumont had not cut deep enough, or perhaps feared to cut away too much that was sound and essential to life: my political ambition remained, and on Lord Davenant's return sprang up in hill vigour.

'Now it is all over I can analyse and understand my own motives: when I first began my political course, I really and truly had no love for power; full of other feelings, I was averse from it; it was absolutely disagreeable to me; but as people acquire a taste for drams after making faces at first swallowing, so I, from experience of the excitation, acquired the habit, the love, of this mental dram-drinking; besides, I had such delightful excuses for myself: I didn't love power for its own sake, it was never used for myself, always for others; ever with my old principle of sacrifice in full play: this flattering unction I laid to my soul, and it long hid from me its weakness, its gradual corruption.

'The first instance in which I used my influence, and by my husband's intervention obtained a favour of some importance, the thing done, though actually obtained by private favour, was in a public point of view well done and fit to be done; but when in time Lord Davenant had reached that eminence which had been the summit of my ambition, and when once it was known that I had influence (and in making it known between jest and earnest Lord Davenant was certainly to blame), numbers of course were eager to avail themselves of the discovery, swarms born in the noontide ray, or such as salute the rising morn, buzzed round me. I was good-natured and glad to do the service, and proud to show that I could do it. I thought I had some right to share with Lord Davenant, at least, the honours and pleasures of patronage, and so he willingly allowed it to be, as long as my objects were well chosen, though he said to me once with a serious smile, "The patronage of Europe would not satisfy you; you would want India, and if you had India, you would sigh for the New World." I only laughed, and said, "The same thought as Lord Chesterfield's, only more neatly put." "If all Ireland were given to such a one for his patrimony, he'd ask for the Isle of Man for his cabbage-garden." Lord Davenant did not smile. I felt a little alarmed, and a feeling of estrangement began between us.

'I recollect one day his seeing a note on my table from one of my *protégés*, thanking me outrageously, and extolling my very obliging disposition. He read, and threw it down, and with one of his dry-humour smiles, repeated, half to himself,

– "By flatterers besieged,
And so obliging that she ne'er obliged."

'I thought these lines were in the Characters of Women, and I hunted all through them in vain; at last I found them in the character of a man, which could not suit me, and I was pacified, and, what is extraordinary, my conscience quite put at ease.

'The week afterwards I went to make some request for a friend: my little boy – for I had a dear little boy then – had come in along with mamma. Lord Davenant complied with my request, but unwillingly I saw, and as if he felt it a weakness; and, putting his hand upon the curly-pated little fellow's head, he said, "This boy rules Greece, I see." The child was sent for the Grecian history, his father took him on his knee, while he read the anecdote, and as he ended he whispered in the child's ear, "Tell mamma this must not be; papa should be ruled only by justice." He really had public virtue, I only talked of it.

'After this you will wonder that I could go on, but I did.

'I had at that time a friend, who talked always most romantically, and acted most selfishly, and for some time I never noticed the inconsistency between her words and actions. In fact she had two currents in her mind, two selves, one romantic from books, the other selfish from worldly education and love of fashion, and of the goods of this world. She had charming manners, which I thought went for nothing with me, but which I found stood for everything. In short, she was as caressing, as graceful, in her little ways, and as selfish as a cat. She had claws too, but at first I only felt the velvet.

'It was for this woman that I hazarded my highest happiness – my husband's esteem – and for the most paltry object imaginable. She wanted some petty place for some man who was to marry her favourite maid. When I first mentioned it to him, Lord Davenant coldly said, "It can't be done," and his pen went on very quickly with the letter he was writing. Vexed and ashamed, and the more vexed because ashamed, I persisted. "Cannot be done for *me*?" said I. "Not for anybody," said he – "by me, at least." – I thought – Helen, I am ashamed to tell you what I thought; but I will tell it you, because it will show you how a mind may be debased by the love of power, or rather by the consequence which its possession bestows. I thought he meant to point out to me that, although he would not do it, I might *get it done*. And, speaking as if to myself, I said, "Then I'll go to such a person; then I'll use such and such ways and means."

'Looking up from his writing at me, with a look such as I had never seen from him before, he replied, in the words of a celebrated minister, "*C'est facile de se servir de pareils moyens, c'est difficile de s'y résoudre.*" [1]

'I admired him, despised myself, left the room, and went and told my friend decidedly it could not be done. That instant she became my enemy, and I felt her claws. I was proud of the wounds, and showed them to my husband. Now, Helen, you think I am cured for ever, and safe. Alas! no, my dear, it is not so easy to cure habit. I have, however, some excuse – let me put it forward; the person for whom I again transgressed was my mother, and for her I was proud of doing the utmost because she had, as I could not forget, been ready to sacrifice my happiness to her speculations. She had left off building castles in the air, but she had outbuilt herself on earth. She had often recourse to me in her difficulties, and I supplied funds, as well I might, for I had a most liberal allowance from my most liberal lord; but schemes of my own, very patriotic, but not overwise, had in process of time drained my purse. I had a school at Cecilhurst, and a lace-manufactory; and to teach my little girls I must needs bring over lace-makers from Flanders, and Lisle thread, at an enormous expense: I shut my lace-makers up in a room (for secrecy was necessary), where, like spiders, they quarrelled with each other and fought, and the whole failed.

'Another scheme, very patriotic too, cost me an immensity; trying to make Indian cachemires in England, very beautiful they were, but they left not the tenth part of a penny in my private purse, and then my mother wanted some thousands for a new dairy; dairies were then the fashion, and hers was to be floored with the finest Dutch tiles, furnished with Sevres china, with

---

[1] It's easy to make use of such means, but difficult to decide to do so

plate glass windows, and a porch hung with French mirrors; so she set me to represent to Lord Davenant her very distressed situation, and to present a petition from her for a pension. The first time I urged my mother's request, Lord Davenant said, "I am sure, Anne, that you do not know what you are asking." I desisted. I did not indeed well understand the business, nor at all comprehend that I was assisting a fraudulent attempt to obtain public money for a private purpose, but I wished to have the triumph of success, I wished to feel my own influence.

'Had it been foretold to me that I could so forget myself in the intoxication of political power, how I should have disdained the prophecy – "Lord, is thy servant a dog that he should do this thing?" There is a fine sermon of Blair's on this subject; it had early made a great impression on me; but what are good impressions, good feelings, good impulses, good intentions, any good thing, without principle?

'My mother wondered how I could so easily take a refusal; she piqued my pride by observing that she was sorry my influence had declined; her pity, so near contempt, wounded me, and I unadvisedly exclaimed that my influence had in no way declined. Scarcely had I uttered the words, when I saw the inference to which they laid me open, that I had not used my influence to the utmost for her. My mother had quite sense and just feeling enough to refrain from marking this in words. She noted it only by an observing look, followed by a sigh. She confessed that I had always been so kind, so much kinder than she could have expected, that she would say no more. This was more to the purpose with me than if she had talked for hours. I heard fresh sighs, and saw tears begin to flow – a mother's sighs and tears it is difficult, and I felt it was shameful, to bear. I was partly melted, much confused, and hurried, too, by visitors coming in, and I hastily promised that I would try once more what I could do. The moment I had time for reflection I repented of what I had promised. But the words were past recall. It was so disagreeable to me to speak about the affair to my husband, that I wanted to get it off my mind as soon as possible, but the day passed without my being able to find a moment when I could speak to Lord Davenant in private. Company stayed till late, my mother the latest. At parting, as she kissed me, calling me her dearest Anne, she said she was convinced I could do whatever I pleased with Lord Davenant, and as she was going downstairs, added she was sure the first words she should hear from me in the morning would be "Victory, victory!"

'I hated myself for admitting the thought, and yet there it was; I let it in, and could not get it out. From what an indescribable mixture of weak motives or impulses, and often without one reasonable principle, do we act in the most important moments of life. Even as I opened the door of his room I hesitated, my heart beat forebodingly, but I thought I could not retreat, and I went in.

'He was standing on the hearth looking weary, but a reviving smile came on seeing me, and he held out his hand – "My comfort always," said he.

'I took his hand, and, hesitating, was again my better self but I would not go back, nor could I begin with any preface. – Thank Heaven that was impossible. – I began: –

' "Davenant, I am come to ask you a favour, and you must do it for me."

' "I hope it is in my power, my dear," said he; "I am sure you would not ask – " and there he stopped.

'I told him it was in his power, and that I would not ask it for any creature living, but – He put his hand upon my lips, told me he knew what I was going to say, and begged me not to say it; but I, hoping to carry it off playfully, kissed his hand, and putting it aside said, "I must ask, and you must grant this to my mother." He replied, "It cannot be, Anne, consistently with public justice, and with my public duty. I – "

"Nonsense, nonsense," I said, "such words are only to mask a refusal." *Mask*, I remember, was the word that hurt him. Of all I could have used, it was the worst: I knew it the instant I had said it. Lord Davenant stepped back, and with such a look! You, Helen, who have seen only his benign countenance, his smiling eyes, cannot conceive it. I am sure he must have seen how much it alarmed me, for suddenly it changed, and I saw all the melting softness of love.

'O fool! vain wicked fool that I was! I thought of "victory," and pursued it. My utmost power of persuasion – words – smiles – and tears I tried – and tried in vain; and then. I could not bear to feel that I had in vain made this trial of power and love. Shame and pride and anger seized me by turns, and raised such a storm within me – such confusion – that I knew not what I did or said. And he was so calm! looked so at least, though I am sure he was not. His self-possession piqued and provoked me past all bearing. I cannot tell you exactly how it was – it was so dreadfully interesting to me that I am unable to recall the exact words; but I remember at last hearing him say, in a voice I had never before heard, "Lady Davenant!" – He had never called me so before; he had always called me "Anne": it seemed as if he had dismissed me from his heart.

"Call me Anne! Oh, call me Anne!"

'And he yielded instantly, he called me Anne, and caressing me, "his Anne."

'O Helen! never do as I did. I whispered, "Then, my love, you will do this for me – for me, your own Anne?"

'He put me gently away, and leaned against the chimney-piece in silence. Then turning to me, in a low suppressed voice, he said,

' "I have loved you – love you as much as man can love woman, there is nothing I would not sacrifice for you except -

' "No exceptions!" cried I, in an affected tone of gaiety.

' "Except honour," he repeated firmly. – Helen, my dear, you are of a generous nature, so am I, but the demon of pride was within me, it made me long to try the extent of my power. Disappointed, I sank to meanness; never, never, however tempted, however provoked, never do as I did, never reproach a friend with any sacrifices you have made for them; this is a meanness which your friend may forgive, but which you can never forgive yourself.

'I reproached him with the sacrifice of my feelings, which I had made in marrying him! His answer was, "I feel that what you say is true: I am now convinced you are incapable of loving me; and since I cannot make you happy, we had better – part."

'These were the last words I heard. The blow was wholly unexpected.

'Whether I sank down, or threw myself at his feet, I know not; but when I came to myself he was standing beside me. There were other faces, but my eyes saw only his: I felt his hand holding mine; I pressed it, and said, "Forget." He stooped down and whispered, "It is forgotten."

'I believe there is nothing can touch a generous mind so much as the being treated with perfect generosity – nothing makes us so deeply feel our own fault.'

Lady Davenant was here so much moved that she could say no more. By an involuntary motion, she checked the reins, and the horses stopped, and she continued quite silent for a few minutes: at length two or three deeply-drawn sighs seemed to relieve her; she looked up, and her attention seemed to be caught by a bird that was singing sweetly on a branch over their heads. She asked what bird it was. Helen showed it to her where it sat: she looked up and smiled, touched the horses with her whip, and went on where she had left off –

'The next thing was the meeting my mother in the morning; I prepared myself for it, and thought I was now armed so strong in honesty that I could go through with it well: my morality, however, was a little nervous, was fluttered by the knock at the door, and when I heard her voice as she came towards my room, asking eagerly if I was alone, I felt a sickness at the certainty that I must at once crush her hopes. But I stood resolved; my eyes fixed on the door through which she was to enter. She came in, to my astonishment, with a face radiant with joy, and hastening to me she embraced me with the warmest expression of fondness and gratitude. – I stood petrified as I heard her talk of my kindness – my generosity. I asked what she could mean, said there must be some mistake. But holding before my eyes a note, "Can there be any mistake in this?" said she. That note, for I can never forget it, I will repeat to you.

' "What you wish can be done in a better manner than you proposed. The public must have no concern with it; Lady Davenant must have the pleasure of doing it her own way; an annuity to the amount required shall be punctually paid to your banker. The first instalment will be in his hands by the time you receive this – DAVENANT."

'When I had been formerly disenchanted from my trance of love, the rudeness of the shock had benumbed all my faculties, and left me scarcely power to think; but now, when thus recovered from the delirium of power, I was immediately in perfect possession of my understanding, and when I was made to comprehend the despicable use I would have made of my influence, or the influence my husband possessed, I was so shocked that I have ever since, I am conscious, in speaking of any political corruption, rather exaggerated my natural abhorrence of it. Not from the mean and weak idea of convincing the world how foreign all such wrong was to my soul, but because it really is foreign to it, because I know how it can debase the most honourable characters; I feel as much shocked at the criminal as at the crime, because I saw it once in all its hideousness so near myself.

'A change in the ministry took place this year, Lord Davenant's resignation was sent in and accepted, and in retirement I had not only leisure to be good, but also leisure to cultivate my mind. Of course I had read all such reading as ladies read, but this was very different from the kind of study that would enable me to keep pace with Lord Davenant and his highly-informed friends. Many of these, more men of thought than of show, visited us from time to time in the country. Though I had passed very well in London society, blue, red, and green, literary, fashionable, and political, and had been extolled as both witty and wise, especially when my husband was in place; yet when I came into close contact with minds of a higher order, I felt my own deficiencies. Lord Davenant's superiority I particularly perceived in the solidity of the ground he uniformly took and held in reasoning. And when I, too confident, used to venture rashly, and often found myself surrounded, and in imminent danger in argument, he used to bring me off and ably cover my retreat, and looked so pleased, so proud, when I made a happy hit, or jumped to a right conclusion.

'But what I most liked, most admired, in him, was that he never triumphed or took unfair advantages on the strength of his learning, of his acquirements, or of what I may call his logical training.

'I mention these seeming trifles because it is not always in the great occasions of life that a generous disposition shows itself in the way which we most feel. Little instances of generosity shown in this way, unperceived by others, have gone most deeply into my mind; and have most raised my opinion of his character. The sense that I was over rather than under valued made me the more ready to acknowledge and feel my own deficiencies. I felt the truth of an aphorism of Lord Verulam's, which is now come down to the copy books; that "knowledge is power." Having made this notable discovery, I set about with all my might to acquire knowledge. You may smile, and think that this was only in a new form the passion for power; no, it was something better. Not to do myself injustice, I now felt the pure desire of knowledge, and enjoyed the pure pleasure of obtaining it; assisted, supported, and delighted, by the sympathy of a superior mind.

'As to intellectual happiness, this was the happiest time of my life. As if my eyes had been rubbed by your favourite dervise in the Arabian tales with his charmed ointment, which opened at once to view all the treasures of the earth, I saw and craved the boundless treasures opened to my view. I now wanted to read all that Lord Davenant was reading, that I might be up to his ideas, but this was not to be done in an instant. There was a Frenchwoman who complained that she never could learn anything, because she could not find anybody to teach her all she wanted to know in two words. I was not quite so demanding as this lady; but, after having skated easily and rapidly, far on the superficies of knowledge, it was difficult and rather mortifying to have to go back and begin at the beginning. Yet, when I wanted to go a little deeper, and really to understand what I was about, this was absolutely necessary. I could not have got through without the assistance of one who showed me what I might safely leave unlearned, and who pointed out what fruit was worth climbing for, what would only turn to ashes.

'This happy time of my life too quickly passed away. It was interrupted, however, not by any fault or folly of my own, but by an infliction from the hand of Providence, to which I trust I submitted with resignation – we lost our dear little boy; my second boy was born dead, and my confinement was followed by long and severe illness. I was ordered to try the air of Devonshire.

'One night – now, my dear, I have kept for the last the only romantic incident in my life – one night, a vessel was wrecked upon our coast; one of the passengers, a lady, an invalid, was brought to our house; I hastened to her assistance – it was my beautiful rival!

'She was in a deep decline, and had been at Lisbon for some time, but she was now sent home by the physicians, as they send people from one country to another, to die. The captain of the ship in which she was mistook the lights upon the coast, and ran the ship ashore near to our house.

'Of course we did for her all we could, but she was dying: she knew nothing of my history, and I trust I soothed her last moments – she died in my arms.

'She had one child, a son, then at Eton: we sent for him; he arrived too late; the feeling he showed interested us deeply; we kept him with us some time; he was grateful; and afterwards as he grew up he often wrote to me. His letters you have read.'

'Mr Beauclerc!' said Helen.

'Mr Beauclerc. – I had not seen him for some time, when General Clarendon presented him to me as his ward at Florence, where I had opportunities of essentially serving him.

'You may now understand, my dear, why I had expected that Mr Granville Beauclerc might have preferred coming to Clarendon Park this last month of my stay in England to the pleasures of London. I was angry, I own, but after five minutes' grace I cooled, saw that I must be mistaken, and came to the just conclusion of the old poet, that no one sinks at once to the depth of ill, and ingratitude I consider as the depth of ill. I opine, therefore, that some stronger feeling than friendship now operates to detain Granville Beauclerc. In that case I forgive him, but, for his own sake, and with such a young man I should say for the sake of society – of the public good – for he will end in public life, I hope the present object is worthy of him, whoever she may be.

'Have I anything more to tell you? Yes, I should say that, when by changes in the political world Lord Davenant was again in power, I had learned, if not to be less ambitious, at least to show it less. D——, who knew always how to put sense into my mind, so that I found it there, and thought it completely my own, had once said that "every public man who has a cultivated and high-minded wife has in fact two selves, each holding watch and ward for the other." The notion pleased me – pleased both my fancy and my reason; I acted on it, and Lord Davenant assures me that I have been this second self to him, and I am willing to believe it, first because he is a man of strict truth, and secondly, because every woman is willing to believe what she wishes.'

Lady Davenant paused, and after some minutes of reflection said, 'I confess, however, that I have not reason to be quite satisfied with myself as a mother; I did not attend sufficiently to Cecilia's early education: engrossed with politics, I left her too much to governesses, at one period to a very bad one. I have done what I can to remedy this, and you have done more perhaps; but I much fear that the early neglect can never be completely repaired; she is, however, married to a man of sense, and when I go to Russia I shall think with satisfaction that I leave you with her.'

After expressing how deeply she had been interested in all that she had heard, and how grateful she felt for the confidence reposed in her, Helen said she could not help wishing that Cecilia knew all that had been just told her of Lady Davenant's history. If Cecilia could but know all the tenderness of her mother's heart, how much less would she fear, how much more would she love her!

'It would answer no purpose,' replied Lady Davenant; 'there are persons with intrinsic differences of character, who, explain as you will, can never understand one another beyond a certain point. Nature and art forbid – no spectacles you can furnish will remedy certain defects of vision. Cecilia sees as much as she can ever see of my character, and I see, in the best light, the whole of hers. So Helen, my dear, take the advice of a Scotch proverb – proverbs are vulgar because they usually contain common sense – "Let well alone."

'You are a very good little friend,' added she, 'but keep my present narrative for your own use.'

CHAPTER 9

IT WAS LATE BEFORE they reached home, and Helen dressed as fast as possible, for the General's punctual habits required that all should assemble in the drawing-room five minutes at least before dinner. She was coming down the private turret stair-case, which led from the family apartments to the great hall, when, just at the turn, and in the most awkward way possible, she met a gentleman, a stranger, where never stranger had been seen by her before, running up full speed, so that they had but barely space and time to clear out of each other's way. Pardons were begged of course. The manner and voice of the stranger were particularly gentlemanlike. A servant followed with his portmanteau, inquiring into which room Mr Beauclerc was to go.

'Mr Beauclerc!' – When Helen got to the drawing-room, and found that not even the General was there, she thought she could have time to run up the great staircase to Lady Davenant's room, and tell her that Mr Beauclerc was come.

'My dear Lady Davenant, Mr Beauclerc' – He was there! and she made her retreat as quickly as possible. The quantity that had been said about him, and the awkward way in which they had thus accidentally met, made her feel much embarrassed when they were regularly introduced.

At the beginning of dinner Helen fancied that there was unusual silence and constraint; perhaps this might be so, or perhaps people were really hungry, or perhaps Mr Beauclerc had not yet satisfied the General and Lady Davenant: however, towards the end of dinner, and at the dessert, he was certainly entertaining; and Lady Cecilia appeared particularly amused by an account which he was giving of a little French piece he had seen just before he left London, called 'Les Premières Amours,' and Helen might have been amused too, but that Lady Cecilia called upon her to listen, and, Mr Beauclerc turning his eyes upon her, she saw, or fancied, that he was put out in his story, and though he went on with perfect good breeding, yet it was evidently with diminished spirit. As soon as politeness permitted, at the close of the story, she, to relieve him and herself, turned to the aide-de-camp on her other side, and devoted, or seemed to devote, to him her exclusive attention. He was always tiresome to her, but now more than ever; he went on, when once set a-going, about his horses and his dogs, while she had the mortification of hearing, almost immediately after her seceding, that Mr Beauclerc recovered the life and spirit of his tone, and was in full and delightful enjoyment of conversation with Lady Cecilia. Something very entertaining caught her ear every now and then; but, with her eyes fixed in the necessary direction, it was impossible to make it out, through the aide-de-camp's never-ending tediousness. She thought the sitting after dinner never would terminate, though it was in fact rather shorter than usual.

As soon as they reached the drawing-room, Lady Cecilia asked her mother what was the cause of Granville's delay in town, and why he had come to-day, after he had written it was impossible.

Lady Davenant replied that he had 'trampled,' as Lord Chatham did, 'on impossibilities.' 'It was not a physical impossibility, it seems.'

'I'm sure – I hope,' continued Cecilia, 'that none of the Beltravers set had anything to do with his delay, yet from a word or two the General let fall, I'm almost sure that they have – Lady Blanche, I'm afraid – 'There she stopped. 'If it were only a money difficulty with Lord Beltravers,' resumed she, 'that might be easily settled, for Beauclerc is rich enough.'

'Yes,' said Lady Davenant, 'but rashly generous; an uncommon fault in these days, when young men are in general selfishly prudent or selfishly extravagant.'

'I hope,' said Cecilia, – 'I hope Lady Blanche Forrester will not –' there she paused, and consulted her mother's countenance; her mother answered that Beauclerc had not spoken to her of Lady Blanche. After putting her hopes and fears, questions and conjectures, into every possible form and direction, Lady Cecilia was satisfied that her mother knew no more than herself, and this was a great comfort.

When Mr Beauclerc reappeared, Helen was glad that she was settled at her embroidery frame, at the farthest end of the room, as there, apart from the world, she felt safe from all cause for embarrassment, and there she continued happy till some one came to raise the light of the lamp over her head. It was Mr Beauclerc, and, as she looked up, she gave a foolish little start of surprise, and then all her confusion returning, with thanks scarcely audible, her eyes were instantly fixed on the vine-leaf she was embroidering. He asked how she could by lamplight distinguish blue from green? a simple and not very alarming question, but she did not hear the words rightly, and thinking he had asked whether she wished for a screen, she answered, 'No, thank you.'

Lady Cecilia laughed, and covering Helen's want of hearing by Beauclerc's want of sight, explained – 'Do not you see, Granville, the silk-cards are written upon, "blue" and "green"? there can be no mistake.'

Mr Beauclerc made a few more laudable attempts at conversation with Miss Stanley, but she, still imagining that this was forced, could not in return say anything but what seemed forced and unnatural, and as unlike her usual self as possible. Lady Cecilia tried to relieve her; she would have done better to have let it alone, for Beauclerc was not of the French wit's opinion that *La modestie n'est bonne qu'à quinze ans* [1], and to him it appeared only a graceful timidity. Helen retired earlier than anyone else, and, when she thought over her foolish awkwardness, felt as much ashamed as if Mr Beauclerc had actually heard all that Lady Cecilia had said about him – had seen all her thoughts,

---

[1] Modesty is only good for a fifteen-year-old

and understood the reason of her confusion. At last, when Lady Cecilia came into her room before she went to bed, she began with – 'I am sure you are going to scold me, and I deserve it, I am so provoked with myself, and the worst of it is, that I do not think I shall ever get over it – I am afraid I shall be just as foolish again tomorrow.'

'I could find it in my heart to scold you to death,' said Lady Cecilia, 'but that I am vexed myself.'

Then, hesitating, and studying Helen's countenance, she seemed doubtful how to proceed. Either she was playing with Helen's curiosity, or she was really herself perplexed. She made two or three beginnings, each a little inconsistent with the other.

'Mamma is always right; with her – "coming events" really and truly "cast their shadows before." I do believe she has the fatal gift, the coming ill to know!'

'Ill!' said Helen; 'what ill is coming?'

'After all, however, it may not be an ill,' said Lady Cecilia, 'it may be all for the best, yet I am shockingly disappointed, though I declare I never formed any – '

'Oh, my dear Cecilia, do tell me at once what it is you mean.'

'I mean that Granville Beauclerc, like all men of genius, has acted like the greatest fool.'

'What has he done?'

'He is absolutely – you must look upon him in future – as a married nun.'

Helen was delighted. Cecilia could form no further schemes on her account, and she felt relieved from all her awkwardness.

'Dearest Helen, this is well at all events,' cried Cecilia, seeing her cleared countenance. 'This comforts me; you are at ease; and, if I have caused you one uncomfortable evening, I am sure you are consoled for it by the reflection that my mother was right, and I, as usual, wrong. But, Helen,' continued she earnestly, 'remember that this is not to be known; remember you must not breathe the least hint of what I have told you to mamma or the General.'

Something more than astonishment appeared in Helen's countenance. 'And is it possible that Mr Beauclerc does not tell

them – does not trust his guardian and such a friend as your
mother?' said Helen.

'He will tell them, he will tell them – but not yet; perhaps
not till – he is not to see his *fiancée* – they have for some reason
agreed to be separated for some time – I do not know exactly, but
surely everybody may choose their own opportunity for telling
their own secrets. In fact, Helen, the lady, I understand, made it a
point with him that nothing should be said of it yet – to any one.'

'But he told it to you?'

'No, indeed, he did not tell it: I found it out, and he could
not deny it; but he charged me to keep it secret, and I would not
have told it to anybody living but yourself; and to you, after all
I said about him, I felt it was necessary – I thought I was bound
– in short, I thought it would set things to rights, and put you at
your ease at once.'

And then, with more earnestness, she again pressed upon
Helen a promise of secrecy, especially towards Lady Davenant.
Helen submitted. Cecilia embraced her affectionately, and left
the room. Quite tired and happy, Helen was in bed and asleep in
a few minutes.

Not the slightest suspicion crossed her mind that all her
friend had been telling her was not perfectly true. To a more
practised, a less confiding, person, the perplexity of Lady Cecilia's
prefaces, and some contradictions or inconsistencies might have
suggested doubts; but Helen's general confidence in her friend's
truth had never yet been seriously shaken. Lady Davenant she
had always thought prejudiced on this point, and too severe. If
there had been in early childhood a bad habit of inaccuracy in
Cecilia, Helen thought it long since cured; and so perhaps it was,
till she formed a friendship abroad with one who had no respect
for truth.

But of this Helen knew nothing; and, in fact, till now Lady
Cecilia's aberrations had been always trifling, almost impercep-
tible, errors, such as only her mother's strictness or Miss Clarendon's scrupulosity could detect. Nor would Cecilia have ventured
upon a decided, an important, false assertion, except for a kind

purpose. Never in her life had she told a falsehood to injure any human creature, or one that she could foresee might, by any possibility, do harm to any living being. But here was a friend, a very dear friend, in an awkward embarrassment, and brought into it by her means; and by a little innocent stretching of the truth she could at once, she fancied, set all to rights. The moment the idea came into her head, upon the spur of the occasion, she resolved to execute it directly. It was settled between the drawing-room door and her dressing-room. And when thus executed successfully, with happy sophistry she justified it to herself. 'After all,' said she to herself, though it was not absolutely true, it was as near the truth, perhaps, as possible. Beauclerc's friends really feared that he was falling in love with the lady in question. It was very likely, and too likely, it might end in his marrying this Lady Blanche Forrester. And, on every account, and every way, it was far the best that Helen should consider him as a married man. This would restore Helen by one magical stroke to herself, and release her from that wretched state in which she could neither please nor be pleased.' And as far as this good effect upon Helen was concerned, Lady Cecilia's plan was judicious; it succeeded admirably.

Wonderful! how a few words spoken, a single idea taken out of or put into the mind, can make such a difference, not only in the mental feelings, but in the whole bodily appearance, and in the actual powers of perception and use of our senses.

When Helen entered the breakfast-room the next morning, she looked, and moved, and felt, quite a different creature from what she had been the preceding day. She had recovered the use of her understanding, and she could hear and see quite distinctly; and the first thing she saw was, that nobody was thinking particularly about her; and now she for the first time actually saw Mr Beauclerc. She had before looked at him without seeing him, and really did not know what sort of looking person he was, except that he was like a gentleman; of that she had a sort of intuitive perception; – as Cuvier could tell from the first sight of a bone what the animal was, what were its habits, and to what class it belonged, so any person early used to good company can, by the first gesture, the first general manner of being, passive or active, tell whether a stranger, even scarcely seen, is or is not a gentleman.

At the beginning of breakfast Mr Beauclerc had all the perfect English quiet of looks and manners, with somewhat of a high-bred air of indifference to all sublunary things, yet saying and doing whatever was proper for the present ceremony; yet it was done and said like one in a dream, performed like a somnambulist, correctly from habit, but all unconsciously. He awakened from his reverie the moment General Clarendon came in, and he asked eagerly,

'General, how far is it to Old Forest?' These were the first words which he pronounced like one wide awake. 'I must ride there this morning; it's absolutely necessary.'

The General replied that he did not see the necessity.

'But when I do, sir,' cried Beauclerc; the natural vivacity of the young man breaking through the conventional manner. Next moment, with a humble look, he hoped that the General would accompany him, and the look of proud humility vanished from his countenance the next instant, because the General demurred, and Beauclerc added, 'Will you not oblige me so far? Then I must go by myself.'

The General, seeming to want to go on with his own thoughts, and not to be moved by his ward's impatience, talked of a review that was to be put off, and at length found that he could accompany him. Beauclerc then, delighted, thanked him warmly.

'What is the object of this essential visit to Old Forest, may I ask?' said Lady Davenant.

'To see a dilapidated house,' said the General.

'To save a whole family from ruin,' cried Beauclerc; 'to restore a man of first-rate talents to his place in society.'

'Pshaw!' said the General.

'Why that contemptuous exclamation, my dear General?' said Beauclerc.

'I have told you, and again I tell you, the thing is impossible!' said the General.

'So I hear you say, sir,' replied his ward; 'but till I am convinced, I hold to my project.'

'And what is your project, Granville?' said Lady Davenant.

'I will explain it to you when we are alone,' said Beauclerc.

'I beg your pardon, I was not aware that there was any mystery,' said Lady Davenant.

'No mystery,' said Beauclerc, 'only about lending some money to a friend.'

'To which I will not consent,' said the General.

'Why not, sir?' said Beauclerc, throwing back his head with an air of defiance in his countenance; there was as he looked at his guardian a quick, mutable succession of feelings, in striking contrast with the fixity of the General's appearance.

'I have given you my reasons, Beauclerc,' said the General. 'It is unnecessary to repeat what I have said, you will do no good.'

'No good, General? When I tell you that if I lend Beltravers the money, to put his place in repair, to put it in such a state that his sisters could live in it, he would no longer be a banished man, a useless absentee, a wanderer abroad, but he would come and settle at Old Forest, re-establish the fortune and respectability of his family, and above all, save his own character and happiness. Oh, my dear General!'

General Clarendon, evidently moved by his ward's benevolent enthusiasm, paused and said that there were many recollections which made it rather painful to him to revisit Old Forest. Still he would do it for Beauclerc, since nothing but seeing the place would convince him of the impractibility of his schemes. 'I have not been at Old Forest,' continued the General, 'since I was a boy – since it was deserted by the owners, and sadly changed I shall find it.

'In former times these Forresters were a respectable, good old English family, till the second wife, pretty and silly, took a fancy for figuring in London, where of course she was nobody. Then, to make herself somebody, she forced her husband to stand for the county. A contested election – bribery – a petition – another election – ruinous expense. Then that Beltravers title coming to them: and they were to live up to it, – and beyond their income. The old story – over head and shoulders in debt. Then the new story, – that they must go abroad for economy!'

'Economy! The cant of all those who have not courage to retrench at home,' said Lady Davenant.

' "They must," they said, "live abroad, it is so cheap," ' continued the General. 'So cheap to leave their house to go to ruin! Cheap education too! and so good – and what does it come to?'

'A cheap provision it is for a family in many cases,' said Lord Davenant. 'Wife, son, and daughter, Satan, are thy own.'

'Not in this case,' cried Beauclerc; 'you cannot mean, I hope.'

'I can answer for one, the daughter at least,' said Lady Davenant; 'that Madame de St Cymon, whom we saw abroad, at Florence, you know, Cecilia, with whom I would not let you form an acquaintance.'

'Your ladyship was quite right,' said the General.

Beauclerc could not say, 'Quite wrong,' – and he looked – suffering.

'I know nothing of the son,' pursued Lady Davenant.

'I do,' said Beauclerc, 'he is my friend.'

'I thought he had been a very distressed young man, that young Beltravers,' said the aide-de-camp.

'And if he were, that would not prevent my being his friend, sir,' said Beauclerc.

'Of course,' said the aide-de-camp, 'I only asked.'

'He is a man of genius and feeling,' continued Beauclerc, turning to Lady Davenant.

'But I never heard you mention Lord Beltravers before. How long has he been your friend?' said Lady Davenant.

Beauclerc hesitated. The General without hesitation answered, 'Three weeks and one day.'

'I do not count my friendship by days or weeks,' said Beauclerc.

'No, my dear Beauclerc,' said the General: 'well would it be for you if you would condescend to any such common-sense measure.' He rose from the breakfast-table as he spoke, and rang the bell to order the horses.

'You are prejudiced against Beltravers, General; but you will think better of him, I am sure, when you know him.'

'You will think worse of him when you know him, I suspect,' replied the General.

'Suspect! But since you only *suspect*,' said Beauclerc, 'we English do not condemn on suspicion, unheard, unseen.'

'Not unheard,' said the General; 'I have heard enough of him.'

'From the reports of his enemies,' said Beauclerc.

'I do not usually form my judgment,' replied the General, 'from reports either of friends or enemies; I have not the honour of knowing any of Lord Beltravers' enemies.'

'Enemies of Lord Beltravers!' exclaimed Lady Davenant. 'What right has he to enemies as if he were a great man? – a person of whom nobody ever heard, setting up to have enemies! But nowadays, these candidates for fame, these would-be celebrated, set up their enemies as they would their equipages, on credit – then, by an easy process of logic, make out the syllogism thus: – Every great man has enemies, therefore, every man who has enemies must be great – hey, Beauclerc?'

Beauclerc vouchsafed only a faint, absent smile, and, turning to his guardian, asked – 'Since Lord Beltravers was not to be allowed the honour of enemies, or the benefit of pleading prejudice, on what *did* the General form his judgment?'

'From his own words.'

'Stay judgment, my dear General,' cried Beauclerc; 'words repeated! by whom?'

'Repeated by no one – heard from himself, by myself.'

'Yourself! I was not aware you had ever met; – when? where?' Beauclerc started forward on his chair, and listened eagerly for the answer.

'Pity,' said Lady Davenant, speaking to herself, – 'pity that "with such quick affections kindling into flame," they should burn to waste.'

'When, where?' repeated Beauclerc, with his eyes fixed on his guardian, and his soul in his eyes.

Soberly and slowly his guardian answered, and categorically, 'When did I meet Lord Beltravers? A short time before his father's death. Where? At Lady Grace Bland's.'

'At Lady Grace Bland's! – where he could not possibly appear to advantage! Well, go on, sir.'

'One moment – pardon me, Beauclerc; I have curiosity as well as yourself. May I ask why Lord Beltravers could not possibly have appeared to advantage at Lady Grace Bland's?'

'Because I know he cannot endure her; I have heard him, speaking of her, quote what Johnson or somebody says of Clariss – "a prating, preaching, frail creature." '

'Good!' said the General, 'he said this of his own aunt!'

'Aunt! You cannot mean that Lady Grace is his aunt?'

'She is his mother's sister,' replied the General, 'and therefore is, I conceive, his aunt.'

'Be it so,' cried Beauclerc; 'people must tell the truth sometimes, even of their own relations they must know it best, and therefore I conclude that what Beltravers said of Lady Grace is true.'

'Bravo! well jumped to a conclusion, Granville, as usual,' said Lady Davenant. 'But go on, General, tell us what you have heard from this precious lord; can you have better than what Beauclerc, his own witness, gives in evidence?'

'Better, I think, and in the same line,' said the General; 'his lordship has the merit of consistency. At table, servants of course present, and myself a stranger, I heard Lord Beltravers begin by cursing England and all that inhabit it. "But your country!" remonstrated his aunt. He abjured England; he had no country, he said, no liberal man ever has; he had no relations – what nature gave him without his consent he had a right to disclaim, I think he argued. But I can swear to these words, with which he con-cluded – "My father is an idiot, my mother a brute, and my sister may go to the devil her own way!" '

'Such bad taste!' said the aide-de-camp.

Lady Davenant smiled at the unspeakable astonishment in Helen's face. 'When you have lived one season in the world, my dear child, this power of surprise will be worn out.'

'But even to those who have seen the world,' said the aide-de-camp, who had seen the world, 'as it strikes me, really it is such extraordinary bad taste!'

'Such ordinary bad taste! as it strikes me,' said Lady Davenant 'base imitation, and imitation is always a confession of poverty, a want of original genius. But then there are degrees among the race of imitators. Some choose their originals well, some come near them tolerably; but here, all seems equally bad, clumsy, Birmingham counterfeit; don't you think so, Beauclerc? a counterfeit that falls and makes no noise. There is the worst of it for your *protégé*, whose great ambition I am sure it is to make a noise in the world. However, I may spare my remonstrances, for I am quite aware that you would never let drop a friend.'

'Never, never!' cried Beauclerc.

'Then, my dear, Granville, do not take up with this man, this Lord Beltravers, for, depend upon it, he will never do. If he had made a bold stroke for a reputation, like a great original, and sported some deed without a name, to work upon the wonder-loving imagination of the credulous English public, one might have thought something of him. But this cowardly, negative sin, *not* honouring his father and mother! so common-place, too, neutral tint – no effect. Quite a failure, one cannot even stare, and you know, Granville, the object of all these strange speeches is merely to make fools stare. To be the wonder of the London world for a single day is the great ambition of these ephemeral fame-hunters, "insects that shine, buzz, and fly-blow in the setting sun." '

Beauclerc pushed away his tea-cup half across the table, exclaiming, 'How unjust! to class him among a tribe he detests and despises as much as you can, Lady Davenant. And all for that one unfortunate speech. – Not quite fair, General, not quite philosophical, Lady Davenant, to decide on a man's character from the specimen of a single speech: this is like judging of a house from the sample of a single brick. All this time I know how Beltravers came to make that speech – I know how it was, as well as if I had been present – better!'

'Better!' cried Lady Cecilia.

'Ladies and gentleman may laugh,' resumed Beauclerc, 'but I seriously maintain – better!'

'How better than the General, who was present, and heard and saw the whole?' said Lady Cecilia.

'Yes, better, for he saw only effects, and I know causes; and I appeal to Lady Davenent, – from Lady Davenant sarcastic to Lady Davenant philosophic I appeal – may not the man who discovers causes say he knows more than he who merely sees effects?'

'He may say he knows more, at all events,' replied Lady Davenant; 'but now for the discovery of causes, metaphysical sir.'

'I have done,' cried the General, turning to leave the breakfast-room, 'when Beauclerc goes to metaphysics I give it up.'

'No, no, do not give it up, my dear General,' cried Lady Cecilia; 'do not stir till we have heard what will come next, for I am sure it will be something delightfully absurd.'

Beauclerc bowed, and feared he should not justify her ladyship's good opinion, for he had nothing delightfully absurd to say, adding that the cause of his friend's appearing like a brute was, that he feared to be a hypocrite among hypocrites.

'Lord Beltravers was in company with a set who were striving, with all their might of dissimulation, to appear better than they are, and he, as he always does, strove to make himself appear worse than he really is.'

'Unnecessary, I should think,' said Lady Davenant.

'Impossible, I should think,' said the General.

'Impossible I know it is to change your opinion, General, of any one,' said Beauclerc.

'For my own part, I am glad of that,' said Lady Cecilia, rising; 'and I advise you, Granville, to rest content with the General's opinion of yourself, and say no more.'

'But,' said Beauclerc; 'one cannot be content to think only of oneself always.'

'Say no more, say no more,' repeated Lady Cecilia, smiling as she looked back from the door, where she had stopped the General. 'For my sake say no more, I entreat; I do dislike to hear so much said about anything, or anybody. What sort of a road is it to Old Forest?' continued she; 'why should not we ladies go with you, my dear Clarendon, to enliven the way?'

Clarendon's countenance brightened at this proposal. The road was certainly beautiful, he said, by the banks of the Thames. Lady Cecilia and the General left the room, but Beauclerc remained sitting at the breakfast-table, apparently intently occupied in forming a tripod of three tea-spoons; Lady Davenant opposite to him, looking at him earnestly. 'Granville!' said she. He started. 'Granville! set my mind at ease by one word, tell me the *mot d'énigme* [1] of this sudden friendship.'

'Not what you suppose,' said he steadily, yet colouring deeply. 'The fact is, that Beltravers and I were school-fellows; a generous little fellow he was as ever was born; he got me out of a sad scrape once at his own expense, and I can never forget it. We had never met since we left Eton, till about three weeks ago in town, when I found him in great difficulties, persecuted too, by a party – I could not turn my back on him – I would rather be shot!'

'No immediate necessity for being shot, my dear Granville, I hope,' said Lady Davenant. 'But if this be indeed *all*, I will never say another word against your Lord Beltravers; I will leave it to you to find out his character, or to time to show it. I shall be quite satisfied that you throw away your money, if it be only money that is in the question; be this Lord Beltravers what he may. Let hint say, "or let them do, it is all one to me," provided that he does not marry you to his sister.'

'He has not a thought of it,' cried Beauclerc; 'and if he had, do you conceive, Lady Davenant, that any man on earth could dispose of me in marriage, at his pleasure?'

'I hope not,' said Lady Davenant.

'Be assured not; my own will, my own heart alone, must decide that matter.'

'The horses are at the door!' cried Cecilia, as she entered; 'but where's Helen?'

[1] key to the mystery

Helen had made her escape out of the room when Lady Davenant had pronounced the words, 'Set my mind at rest, Granville,' as she felt it must then be embarrassing to him to speak, and to herself to hear. Her retreat had not, however, been effected without considerable loss, she had been compelled to leave a large piece of the crape-trimming of her gown under the foot of Lady Davenant's inexorable chair.

'Here is something that belongs to Miss Stanley, if I mistake not,' said the General, who first spied the fragment. The aide-de-camp stooped for it – Lady Cecilia pitied it – Lady Davenant pronounced it to be Helen's own fault – Beauclerc understood how it happened, and said nothing. 'But, Helen,' cried Lady Cecilia, as she reappeared, – 'but, Helen, are you not coming with us?'

Helen had intended to have gone in the pony-carriage with Lady Davenant but her ladyship now declared that she had business to do at home; it was settled therefore that Helen was to be of the riding party, and that party consisted of Lady Cecilia and the General, Beauclerc and herself.

CHAPTER 10

IT WAS A DELIGHTFUL DAY, sun shining, not too hot, air balmy, birds singing, all nature gay; and the happy influence was quickly felt by the riding party. Unpleasant thoughts of the past or future, if any such had been, were now lost in present enjoyment. The General, twice a man on horseback, as he always felt himself, managed his own and Helen's horse to admiration, and Cecilia, riding on with Beauclerc, was well pleased to hear his first observation, that he had been quite wrong last night, in not acknowledging that Miss Stanley was beautiful. 'People look so different by daylight and by candlelight,' said he; 'and so different when one does not know then at all, and when one begins to know something of them.'

'But what can you know yet of Helen?'

'One forms some idea of character from trifles light as air. How delightful this day is!'

'And now you really allow she may be called beautiful?'

'Yes, that is, with some expression of mind, heart, soul, which is what I look for in general,' said Beauclerc.

'In general, what can you mean by in general?'

'Not in particular; in particular cases I might think – I might feel – otherwise.'

'In particular, then, do you like fools that have no mind, heart, or soul, Granville? Answer me.'

'Take care,' said he, 'that horse is too spirited for a lady.'

'Not for me,' said Lady Cecilia; 'but do not think you shall get off so; what did you mean?'

'My meaning lies too deep for the present occasion.'

'For the present company – eh?'

Beauclerc half smiled and answered – 'You know you used to tell me that you hated long discussions on words and nice distinctions.'

'Well, well, but let me have the nice distinction now.'

'Between love and friendship, then, there is a vast difference in what one wishes for in a woman's face; there are "faces which pale passion loves."'

'To the right, turn,' the General's voice far behind was heard to say.

To the right they turned, into a glade of the park, which opened to a favourite view of the General's, to which Cecilia knew that all attention must be paid. He came up, and they proceeded through a wood which had been planted by his father, and which seemed destined to stand for ever secure from sacrilegious axe. The road led them next into a village, one of the prettiest of that sort of scattered English villages, where each habitation seems to have been suited to the fancy as well as to the convenience of each proprietor; giving an idea at once of comfort and liberty, such as can be seen only in England. Happy England, how blest, would she but know her bliss!

This village was inhabited by the General's tenants. His countenance brightened and expanded, as did theirs, whenever he came amongst them; he saw them happy, and they knew that they owed their happiness in just proportion to their landlord and themselves; therefore there was a comfortable mixture in their feelings of gratitude and self-respect. Some old people who were sitting on the stone benches, sunning themselves at their doors, rose as he passed, cap in hand, with cordial greeting. The oldest man, the father of the village, forgot his crutch as he came forward to see his landlord's bride, and to give him joy. At every house where they stopped, out came husband, wife, and children, even 'wee toddling things'; one of these, while the General was speaking to its mother, made its way frightfully close to his horse's heels: Helen saw it, and called to the mother. The General, turning and leaning back on his horse, said to the bold little urchin as the mother snatched him up, 'My boy, as long as you live never again go behind a horse's heels.'

'And remember, it was General Clarendon gave you this advice,' added Beauclerc, and turning to Lady Cecilia – ' "*Et souvenez vous que c'est Marechal Turenne qui vous l'a dit.*" '[1]

While the General searched for that English momento, six-pence, Lady Cecilia repeated, 'Marshall Turenne! I do not understand.'

'Yes, if you recollect,' said Helen, 'you do.'

'I daresay I know, but I don't remember,' said Cecilia.

'It was only,' said Helen, 'that the same thing had happened to Marshal Turenne, that he gave the same advice to a little child.'

Lady Cecilia said she owed Beauclerc an acknowledgement down to her saddle-bow, for the compliment to her General, and a bow at least as low to Helen, for making her comprehend it; and, having paid both these debts with graceful promptitude, she observed, in an aside to Beauclerc, that she quite agreed with him, that 'In friendship it was good not to have to do with fools.'

He smiled.

'It is always permitted,' continued Cecilia, 'for woman to use her intellects so far as to comprehend what man says; her knowledge, of whatever sort, never comes amiss when it serves only to illustrate what is said by one of the lords of creation. Let us note this, my dear Helen, as a general maxim, for future use, and pray, since you have so good a memory, remember to tell mamma, who says I never generalise, that this morning I have actually made and established a philosophical maxim, one that may be of some use too, which cannot be said of all reflections, general or particular.'

They rode on through a lane bright and fragrant with primroses and violets; gradually winding, this lane opened at last upon the beautiful banks of the Thames, whose 'silver bosom' appeared at once before them in the bright sunshine, silent, flowing on, seeming, as Beauclerc said, as if it would for ever flow

[1] "And remember, it was Marechal Turenne who told you". (Turenne was Marshal of France and an outstanding commander in Louis XIV's early campaigns.)

on unaltered in full, broad, placid dignity. 'Here,' he exclaimed, as
they passed to contemplate the view, 'the throng of commerce,
the ponderous barge, the black steamboat, the hum and din
of business, never have violated the mighty current. No lofty
bridge insultingly overarches it, no stone-built wharf confines
it; nothing but its own banks, coeval with itself, and, like itself,
uncontaminated by the petty uses of mankind! They spread into
large parks, or are hung with thick woods, as nature wills. No
citizen's box, no chimera villa destroys the idea of repose; but
nature, uninterrupted, carries on her own operations in field, and
flood, and tree.'

The General, less poetically inclined, would name to Helen
all the fine places within view – 'Residences,' as he practically
remarked, 'such as cannot be seen in any country in the world
but England; and not only fine places such as these, but from the
cottage to the palace – "the homes of Old England" are the best
homes upon earth.'

'The most candid and sensible of all modern French travel-
lers,' said Beauclerc, 'was particularly struck with the superiority
of our English country residences, and the comfort of our homes.'

'You mean M de Staël?' said the General; 'true English sense in
that book, I allow.'

When the General and Beauclerc did agree in opinion about a
book, which was not a circumstance of frequent occurrence, they
were mutually delighted; one always feeling the value of the other's
practical sense, and the other then acknowledging that literature
is good for something. Beauclerc in the fulness of his heart and
abundance of his words, began to expatiate on M de Staël's merits,
in having better than any foreigner understood the actual workings
and balances of the English constitution, that constitution so much
talked of abroad, and so little understood.

'So little understood anywhere,' said the General.

Reasonably as Beauclerc now spoke, Helen formed a new idea
of his capacity, and began to think more respectfully of his common
sense, than when she had heard him in the Beltravers cause. He
spoke of the causes of England's prosperity, the means by which

she maintains her superiority among nations – her equal laws and their just administration. He observed that the hope which every man born in England, even in the lowest station, may have of rising by his own merits to the highest eminence, forms the great spring of industry and talent. He agreed with the intelligent foreigner's observation, that the aristocracy of talent is superior in England to the aristocracy of birth.

The General seemed to demur at the word superior, drew himself up, but said nothing in contradiction.

'Industry, and wealth, and education, and fashion, all emulous act in England beneficially on each other,' said Beauclerc.

The General sat at ease again.

'And above all,' pursued Beauclerc, – 'above all, education and the diffusion of knowledge – '

'Knowledge – yes, but take care of what kind,' said his guardian.

'All kinds are good,' said Beauclerc.

'No, only such as are safe,' said the General. The march of intellect was not a favourite march with him, unless the step were perfectly kept, and all in good time.

But now, on passing a projecting bend in the wood, they came within sight of a place in melancholy contrast to all they had just admired. A park of considerable extent, absolutely bereft of trees, except a few ragged firs on each side of a large dilapidated mansion on the summit of a bleak hill: it seemed as if a great wood had once been there.

'Old Forest!' exclaimed the General; 'Old Forest, now no more! Many a happy hour, when I was a boy, have I spent shooting in those woods,' and he pointed to where innumerable stumps of trees, as far as the eye could reach, marked where the forest had once stood: some of the white circles on the ground showed the magnificent size of those newly felled. Beauclerc was quite silent.

The General led the way on to the great gate of entrance: the porter's lodge was in ruins.

A huge rusty padlock hung upon one of the gates, which had been dragged half open, but, the hinge having sunk, there it stuck – the gate could not be opened further. The other could not be stirred without imminent hazard of bringing down the pier on which it hung, and which was so crazy, the groom said, 'he was afraid, if he shook it never so little, all would come down together.'

'Let it alone,' said the General, in the tone of one resolved to be patient; 'there is room enough for us to get in one by one – Miss Stanley, do not be in a hurry, if you please; follow me quietly.'

In they filed. The avenue, overgrown with grass, would have been difficult to find, but for deep old cart-ruts which still marked the way. But soon, fallen trees, and lopped branches, dragged many a rood and then left there, made it difficult to pass. And there lay exposed the white bodies of many a noble tree, some wholly, some half, stripped of their bark, some green in decay, left to the weather – and every here and there little smoking pyramids of burning charcoal.

As they approached the house – 'How changed,' said the General, 'from that once cheerful hospitable mansion!' It was a melancholy example of a deserted home: the plaster dropping off, the cut stone green, the windows broken, the shutters half shut, the way to the hall-door steps blocked up. They were forced to go round through the yards. Coach-houses and stables, grand ranges, now all dilapidated. Only one yelping cur in the great kennel. The back-door being ajar, the General pushed it open, and they went in, and on to the great kitchen, where they found in the midst of wood smoke one little old woman, whom they nearly scared out of her remaining senses. She stood and stared. Beauclerc stepped towards her to explain; but she was deaf; he raised his voice – in vain. She was made to comprehend by the General, whose voice, known in former times, reached her heart – 'that they only came to see the place.'

'See the place! ah! a sad sight to see.' Her eyes reverted to Beauclerc, and, conceiving that he was the young lord himself, she waxed pale, and her head shook fearfully; but, when relieved from this mistake, she went forward to show them over the house.

As they approached the great staircase, she confided to her friend, the General, that she was glad it was not the young lord, for she was told he was a fiery man, and she dreaded his coming unawares.

Lady Cecilia asked if she did not know him.

No, she had never seen him since he was a little fellow; 'he has been always roaming about, like the rest, in foreign places, and has never set foot in the place since he came to man's estate.'

As the General passed a window on the landing-place, he looked out. 'You are missing the great elm, sir. Ah! I remember you here, a boy; you was always good. It was the young lord ordered specially the cutting of that, which I could not stomach; the last of the real old trees! Well, well! I'm old and foolish – I'm old and foolish, and I should not talk.'

But still she talked on, and as this seemed her only comfort, they would not check her garrulity. In the hope that they were come to take the house, she now bustled as well as she could, to show all to the best advantage, but bad was the best now, as she sorrowfully said. She was very unwilling that the gentleman should go up to inspect the roof. They went, however; and the General saw and estimated, and Beauclerc saw and hoped.

The General, recollecting the geography of the house, observed that she had not shown them what used to be the picture-gallery, which looked out on the terrace; he desired to see it. She reluctantly obeyed; and, after trying sundry impossible keys, repeating all the while that her heart was broke, that she wished it had pleased God never to give her a heart, unlock the door she could not in her trepidation. Beauclerc gently took the keys from her, and looked so compassionately upon her, that she God-blessed him, and thought it a pity her young lord was not like him; and while he dealt with the lock, Lady Cecilia, saying they would trouble her no further, slipped into her hand what she thought would be some comfort. The poor old creature thanked her ladyship, but said gold could be of no use to her now in life; she should soon let the parish bury her, and be no cost to the young lord. She could forgive many things, she said, but she could never forgive him for parting with the old pictures. She turned away as the gallery-door opened.

Only one old daub of a grandmother was there; all the rest had been sold, and their vacant places remained discoloured on the walls. There were two or three dismembered old chairs, the richly-dight windows broken, the floor rat-eaten. The General stood and looked, and did not sigh, but absolutely groaned. They went to the shattered glass door, which looked out upon the terrace – that terrace which had cost thousands of pounds to raise, and he called Cecilia to show her the place where the youngsters used to play, and to point out some of his favourite haunts.

'It is melancholy to see a family-place so gone to ruin,' said Beauclerc; 'if it strikes us so much, what must it be to the son of this family, to come back to the house of his ancestors, and find it thus desolate! Poor Beltravers!'

The expression of the General's eye changed.

'I am sure you must pity him, my dear General,' continued Beauclerc.

'I might, had he done anything to prevent, or had he done less to hasten, this ruin.'

'How? he should not have cut down the trees, do you mean? – but it was to pay his father's debts – '

'And his own,' said the General.

'He told me his father's, sir.'

'And I tell you his own.'

'Even so,' said Beauclerc, 'debts are not crimes, for which we ought to shut the gates of mercy on our fellow-creatures – and so young a man as Beltravers, left to himself, without a home, his family abroad, no parent, no friend – no guardian friend.'

'But what is it you would do, Beauclerc?' said the General.

'What you must wish to be done,' said Beauclerc. 'Repair this ruin, restore this once hospitable mansion, and put it in the power of the son to be what his ancestors have been.'

'But how – my dear Beauclerc? Tell me plainly – how?'

'Plainly, I would lend him money enough to make this house fit to live in.'

'And he would never repay you, and would never live in it.'

'He would, sir – he promised me he would.'

'Promised you!'

'And I promised him that I would lend him the money.'

'Promised! Beauclerc? Without your guardian's knowledge? Pray, how much – ?'

'Confound me if I remember the words. The sense was, what would do the business, what would make the house fit for him and his sisters to live in.'

'Ten thousand! – fifteen thousand would not do.'

'Well, sir. You know what will be necessary better than I do. A few thousands more or less, what signifies, provided a friend be well served? The superfluous money accumulated during my long minority cannot be better employed.'

'All that I have been saving for you with such care from the time your father died.'

'My dear guardian, my dear friend, do not think me ungrateful; but the fact is, – in short, my happiness does not depend, never can depend, upon money; as my friend, therefore, I beseech you to consider my moneyed interest less, and my happiness more.'

'Beauclerc, you do not know what your happiness is. One hour you tell me it is one thing, the next another. What is become of the plan for the new house you wanted to build for yourself? I must have common sense for you, Beauclerc, as you have none for yourself. I shall not give you this money for Lord Beltravers.'

'You forget, sir, that I told you I had promised.'

'You forget, Beauclerc, that I told you that such a promise, vague and absurd in itself, made without your guardian's concurrence or consent, is absolutely null and void.'

'Null and void in law, perhaps it may be,' cried Beauclerc; 'but for that very reason, in honour, the stronger, the more binding, and I am speaking to a man of honour.'

'To one who can take care of his own honour,' said the General.

'And of mine, I trust.'

'You do well to trust it, as your father did, to me: it shall not be implicated – '

'When once I am of age,' interrupted Beauclerc.

'You will do as you please,' said the General. 'In the meantime I shall do my duty.'

'But, sir, I only ask you to let me *lend* this money.'

'Lend – nonsense! lend to a man who cannot give any security.'

'Security!' said Beauclerc, with a look of unutterable contempt. 'When a friend is in distress, to talk to him like an attorney, of security! Do, pray, sir, spare me that. I would rather give the money at once.'

'I make no doubt of it; then at once I say No, sir.'

'No, sir! and why do you say no?'

'Because I think it my duty, and nothing I have heard has at all shaken my opinion.'

'Opinion! and so I am to be put down by opinion, without any reason!' cried Beauclerc. Then trying to command his temper, 'But tell me, my dear General, why I cannot have this cursed money?'

'Because, my dear Beauclerc, I am your guardian, and can say *no*, and can adhere to a refusal as firmly as any man living, when it is necessary.'

'Yes, and when it is unnecessary. General Clarendon, according to your own estimate, fifteen thousand pounds is the utmost sum requisite to put this house in a habitable state – by that sum I abide!'

'Abide!'

'Yes, I require it, to keep my promise to Beltravers, and have it I MUST.'

'Not from me.'

'From some one else then, for have it I WILL.'

'Dearest Clarendon,' whispered Lady Cecilia, 'let him have it, since he has promised – '

Without seeming to hear her whisper, without a muscle of his countenance altering, General Clarendon repeated, 'Not from me.'

'From some one else then – I can.'

'Not while I have power to prevent.'

'Power! power! power! Yes, that is what you love, above all things and all persons, and I tell you plainly, General Clarendon,' pursued Beauclerc, too angry to heed or see Lady Cecilia's remonstrating looks, 'at once I tell you that you have not the power. You had it. It is past and gone. The power of affection you had, if not of reason; but force, General Clarendon, despotism, can never govern me. I submit to no man's mere will, much less to any man's sheer obstinacy.'

At the word obstinacy, the General's face, which was before rigid, grew hard as iron. Beauclerc walked up and down the room with great strides, and as he strode he went on talking to himself.

'To be kept from the use of my own money, treated like a child – an idiot – at my time of life! Not considered at years of discretion, when other men of the meanest capacity, by the law of the land, can do what they please with their own property! By heavens! – that will of my father's – '

'Should be respected, my dear Granville, since it was your father's will,' said Lady Cecilia, joining him as he walked. 'And respect – ' He stopped short.

'My dear Lady Cecilia, for your sake – ' he tried to restrain himself.

'Till this moment never did I say one disrespectful word to General Clarendon. I always considered him as the representative of my father and when most galled I have borne the chains in which it was my father's pleasure to leave me. Few men of my years would have so submitted to a guardian not many years older than himself.'

'Yes, and indeed that should be considered,' said Lady Cecilia, turning to the General.

'I have always considered General Clarendon more as my friend than my guardian.'

'And have found him so, I had hoped,' said the General, relaxing in tone but not in looks.

'I have never treated you, sir, as some wards treat their guardians. I have dealt openly, as man of honour to man of honour, gentleman to gentleman, friend to friend.'

'Acknowledged, and felt by me, Beauclerc.'

'Then now, my dear Clarendon, grant the only request of any consequence I ever made you – say yes.' Beauclerc trembled with impatience.

'No,' said the General, 'I have said it – No.'

The gallery rang with the sound.

'No!' repeated Beauclerc.

Each walked separately up and down the room, speaking without listening to what the other said. Helen heard an offer from Beauclerc, to which she extremely wished that the General had listened. But he was deaf with determination not to yield to anything Beauclerc could say further; the noise of passion in their ears was too great for either of them to hear the other.

Suddenly turning, Beauclerc exclaimed, –

'Borne with me, do you say? 'Tis I that have to bear – and by heavens!' cried he, 'more than I can – than I will – bear. Before to-morrow's sun goes down I will have the money.'

'From whom?'

'From any money-lending Jew – usurer – extortioner – cheat – rascal – whatever he be. You drive me to it – you – you my friend – you, with whom I have dealt so openly; and to the last it shall be open. To no vile indirections will I stoop. I tell you, my guardian, that if you deny me my own, I will have what I want from the Jews.'

'Easily,' said his guardian. 'But first, recollect that a clause in your father's will, in such case, sends his estates to your cousin Venables.'

'To my cousin Venables let them go – all – all; if such be your pleasure, sir, be it so. The lowest man on earth that has feeling keeps his promise. The slave has a right to his word! Ruin me if you will, and as soon as you please; disgrace me you cannot; bend my spirit you cannot; ruin in any shape I will meet, rather than submit to such a guardian, such a – '

Tyrant he was on the point of saying, but Lady Cecilia stopped that word by suddenly seizing upon his arm: forcibly she carried him off, saying, 'Come out with me on the terrace, Granville, and recover your senses.'

'My senses! I have never lost them; never was cooler in my life,' said he, kicking open the glass door upon its first resistance, and shattering its remaining panes to fragments. Unnoticing, not hearing the crash, the General stood leaning his elbow on the mantelpiece, and covering his eyes with his hand. Helen remained near him, scarce breathing loud enough to be heard; he did not know she was there, and he repeated aloud, in an accent of deep feeling, 'Tyrant! from Beauclerc!'

A sigh from Helen made him aware of her presence, and as he removed his hand from his eyes, she saw his look was more in sorrow than in anger: she said softly, 'Mr Beauclerc was wrong, very wrong, but he was in a passion, he did not know what he meant.'

There was silence for a few moments. 'You are right, I believe,' said the General, 'it was heat of anger – '

'To which the best are subject,' said Helen, 'and the best and kindest most easily forgive.'

'But Beauclerc said some things which were – '

'Unpardonable – only forget them; let all be forgotten.'

'Yes,' said the General, 'all but my determination; that, observe, is fixed. My mind, Miss Stanley, is made up, and, once made up, it is not to be changed.'

'I am certain of that,' said Helen, 'but I am not clear that your mind is made up.'

The General looked at her with astonishment.

'Your refusal is not irrevocable.'

'You do not know me, Miss Stanley.'

'I think I do.'

'Better than I know myself?'

'Yes, better, if you do yourself the injustice to think that you would not yield, if it were right to do so. At this very instant,' pursued Helen, disregarding his increasing astonishment, 'you would yield if you could reasonably, honourably – would not you? If you could without injury to your ward's fortune or character, would you not? Surely it is for his good only that you are so resolute?'

'Certainly!' He waited with eyes fixed, bending forward, but with intensity of purpose in his calmness of attention.

'There was something which I heard Mr Beauclerc say, which, I think, escaped your attention,' said Helen. 'When you spoke of the new house he intended to build for himself, which was to cost so much, he offered to give that up.'

'I never heard that offer.'

'I heard him,' said Helen, 'I assure you; it was when you were both walking up and down the room.'

'This may be so, I was angry *then*,' said the General.

'But you are not angry now,' said Helen.

He smiled, and in truth he desired nothing more than an honourable loophole – a safe way of coming off without injury to his ward – without hurting his own pride, or derogating from the dignity of guardian. Helen saw this, and, thanking him for his condescension, his kindness, in listening to her, she hastened as quickly as possible, lest the relenting moment might not be seized; and running out on the terrace, she saw Beauclerc, his head down upon his arms, leaning upon an old broken stone lion, and Lady Cecilia standing beside him, commiserating; and as she approached, she heard her persuading him to go to the General, and speak to him again, and say *so* – only say so.

Whatever it was, Helen did not stay to inquire, but told Cecilia, in as few words as she could, all that she had to say; and ended with, 'Was I right?'

'Quite right, was not she, Granville?'

Beauclerc looked up – a gleam of hope and joy came across his face, and with one grateful look to Helen, he darted forward. They followed, but could not keep pace with him; and when they reached the gallery, they found him appealing, as to a father, for pardon.

'Can you forgive, and will you?'

'Forgive my not hearing you, not listening to you, as your father would? My dear Beauclerc, you were too hot, and I was too cold; and there is an end of it.'

This reconciliation was as quick, as warm, as the quarrel had been. And then explanations were made, as satisfactorily as they are when the parties are of good understanding, and depend on each other's truth, past, present, and future.

Beauclerc, whose promise all relied on, and for reasons good, none more implicitly than the General, promised that he would ask for no more than just what would do to put this Old Forest house in habitable trim; he said he would give up the new house for himself, till as many thousands as he now lent, spent, or wasted – take which word you will – should be again accumulated from his income. It was merely a sacrifice of his own vanity, and perhaps a little of his own comfort, he said, to save a friend, a human being, from destruction.

'Well, well, let it rest so.'

It was all settled, witness present – 'two angels to witness,' as Beauclerc quoted from some play.

And now in high good-humour, up again to nonsense pitch, they all felt that delightful relief of spirits, of which friends, after perilous quarrel, are sensible in perfect reconciliation. They left this melancholy mansion now, with Beauclerc the happiest of the happy, in the generous hope that he should be the restorer of its ancient glories and comfort. The poor old woman was not forgotten as they passed, she curtsying, hoping, and fearing; Lady Cecilia whispered, and the deaf ear heard,

'The roof will not fall – all will be well: and there is the man that will do it all.'

'Well, well, my heart inclined to him from the first – at least from the minute I knew him not to be my young lord.'

They were to go home by water. The boat was in readiness, and, as Beauclerc carefully handed Helen into it, the General said – 'Yes, you are right to take care of Miss Stanley, Beauclerc; she is a good friend in need, at least, as I have found this morning;' added he, as he seated himself beside her.

Lady Cecilia was charming, and everything was delightful, especially the cold chicken.

CHAPTER 11

NO TWO PEOPLE COULD BE more unlike in their habits of mind than this guardian and ward. General Clarendon referred in all cases to old experience, and dreaded innovation; Beauclerc took for his motto, 'My mind leadeth me to new things.' General Clarendon was what is commonly called a practical man; Granville Beauclerc was the flower of theorists. The General, fit for action, prompt and decided in all his judgments, was usually right and just in his conclusions – but if wrong, there was no setting him right; for he not only would not, but could not, go back over the ground – he could not give in words any explanation of his process of reasoning – it was enough for him that it was right, and that it was *his*; while Beauclerc, who cared not for any man's opinion, was always so ingeniously wrong, could show all the steps of his reasoning so plausibly, that it was a pity he should be quite out of the right road at last. The General hated metaphysics, because he considered them as taking a flight beyond the reach of discipline, as well as of common sense: he continually asked, of what use are they? While Lady Davenant answered, –

'To invigorate and embellish the understanding. "This turning the soul inward on itself concentrates its forces, and fits it for the strongest and boldest flights; and in such pursuits, whether we take or whether we lose the game, the chase is certainly of service." '

Possibly, the General said; he would not dispute the point with Lady Davenant, but a losing chase, however invigorating, was one in which he never wished to engage: as to the rest, he altogether hated discussions, doubts, and questionings. He had 'made up his fagot of opinions,' and would not let one be drawn out for examination, lest he should loosen the bundle.

Beauclerc, on the contrary, had his dragged out and scattered about every day, and each particular stick was tried, and bent, and twisted, this way and that, and peeled, and cut, and hacked; and unless they proved sound to the very core, not a twig of them should ever go back into his bundle, which was to be the bundle of bundles, the best that ever was seen, when once tied so that it would hold together – of which there seemed little likelihood, as every knot slipped, and all fell to pieces at each pull.

While he was engaged in this analysis, he was, as his guardian thought, in great moral peril, for not a principle had he left to bless himself with; and, in any emergency, if any temptation should occur, what was to become of him? The General, who was very fond of him, but also strongly attached to his own undeviating rule of right, was upon one occasion about peremptorily to interpose, not only with remonstrances as a friend, but with authority as a guardian.

This occurred when Beauclerc was with them at Florence, and when the General's love for Lady Cecilia, and intimacy with her mother, commenced. Lady Davenant, being much interested for young Beauclerc, begged that the patient might be left to her, and that his guardian would refrain from interfering. This was agreed to the more readily by the General, as his thoughts and feelings were then more agreeably engrossed, and Beauclerc found in Lady Davenant the very friend he wanted and wished for most ardently – one whose mind would not blench at any moral danger, would never shrink from truth in any shape, but, calm and self-possessed, would examine whether it were indeed truth, or only a phantom assuming her form. Besides, there was in Lady Davenant towards Beauclerc a sort of maternal solicitude and kindness, of which the effect was heightened by her dignified manner and pride of character.

She, in the first place, listened to him patiently; she, who could talk, would listen; this was, as she said, her first merit in his estimation. To her he poured forth all those doubts, of which she was wise enough not to make crimes: she was sure of his honourable intentions, certain that there was no underhand motive, no bad passion, no concealed vice, or disposition to vice, beneath his boasted freedom from prejudice, to be justified or to be indulged by getting rid of the restraints of principle. Had there been any danger of this sort, which with young men who profess themselves *ultra-liberal* is usually the case, she would have joined in his guardian's apprehensions; but in fact Beauclerc, instead of being '*le philosophe sans le savoir*,'[1] was '*le bon enfant sans le savoir*';[2] for, while he questioned the rule of right in all his principles, and while they were held in abeyance, his good habits and good natural disposition held fast and stood him in stead; while Lady Davenant, by slow degrees, brought him to define his terms, and presently to see that he had been merely saying old things in new words, and that the systems which had dazzled him as novelties were old to older eyes; in short, that he was merely a resurrectionist of obsolete heresies, which had been gone over and over again at various long-past periods, and over and over again abandoned by the common sense of mankind; so that, after puzzling and wandering a weary way in the dark labyrinth he had most ingeniously made for himself, he saw light, followed it, and at length, making his way out, was surprised, and sorry perhaps, to perceive that it was the common light of day.

It is of great consequence to young enthusiastic tyros, like Beauclerc, to have safe friends to whom they can talk of their opinions privately, otherwise they will talk their ingenious non-sense publicly, and so they bind themselves, or are bound, to the stake, and live or die martyrs to their own follies.

From these and all such dangers Lady Davenant protected him, and she took care that nobody hurt him in his defenceless state,

---

[1] A philosopher without knowing it;   [2] A good child without knowing it

before his shell was well formed and hardened. She was further of peculiar service in keeping all safe and smooth between the ward and guardian. All Beauclerc's romance the General would have called by the German word '*Schwärmerey*,' – not fudge – not humbug – literally 'sky-rocketing' – visionary enthusiasm; and when it came to arguments, they might have turned to quarrels, but for Lady Davenant's superior influence, while Lady Cecilia's gentleness and gaiety usually succeeded in putting all serious dangerous thoughts to flight.

Nature never having intended Lady Cecilia for a manoeuvrer, she was now perpetually on the point of betraying herself; and one day, when she was alone with Helen, she exclaimed, 'Never was anything better managed than I managed this, my dear Helen! I am so glad I told you – ' Recollecting herself just in time, she ended with, 'so glad I told you the truth.'

'Oh yes! thank you,' said Helen. 'My uncle used to say no one could be a good friend who does not tell the whole truth.'

'That I deny,' thought Cecilia. The twinge of conscience was felt but very slightly; not visible in any change of countenance, except by a quick twinkling motion of the eyelashes, not noticed by unsuspicious Helen.

Everything now went on as happily as Cecilia could have desired; every morning they rode or boated to Old Forest to see what was doing. The roof was rather hastily taken off; Lady Cecilia hurried forward that measure, aware that it would prevent the possibility of any of the ladies of the family coming there for some time. Delay was all she wanted, and she would now, as she promised herself, leave the rest to time. She would never interfere further in word or look, especially when her mother might be by. One half of this promise she kept faithfully, the other she broke continually.

There were plans to be made of all the alterations and improvements at Old Forest. Beauclerc applied to Lady Cecilia for her advice and assistance. Her advice she gave, but her assistance she ingeniously contrived to leave to Helen; for whenever Beauclerc brought to her a sketch or a plan of what was to be done, Lady

Cecilia immediately gave it to Helen, repeating, 'Never drew a regular plan in my life, you know, my dear, you must do this'; so that Helen's pencil and her patience were in constant requisition. Then came apologies from Beauclerc, and regrets at taking up her time, all which led to an intimacy that Lady Cecilia took care to keep up by frequent visits to Old Forest, so that Helen was necessarily joined in all his present pursuits.

During one of these visits they were looking over some old furniture which Lord Beltravers had commissioned Beauclerc to have disposed of at some neighbouring auction. There was one curiously-carved oak arm-chair, belonging to 'the old old gentlemen of all' which the old woman particularly regretted should go. She had sewn it up in a carpet, and when it came out, Helen was struck with its likeness to a favourite chair of her uncle's; many painful recollections occurred to her, and tears came into her eyes. Ashamed of what appeared so like affectation, she turned away, that her tears might not be seen, and when Cecilia, following her, insisted on knowing what was the matter, she left Helen immediately to the old woman, and took the opportunity of telling Beauclerc all about Dean Stanley, and how Helen was an heiress and no heiress, and her having determined to give up all her fortune to pay her uncle's debts. There was a guardian, too, in the case, who would not consent; and, in short, a parallelism of circumstances, a similarity of generous temper, and all this she thought must interest Beauclerc – and so it did. But yet its being told to him would have gone against his nice notions of delicacy, and Helen would have been ruined in his opinion had he conceived that it had been revealed to him with her consent and connivance. She came back before Lady Cecilia had quite finished, and a few words which she heard made her aware of the whole. The blush of astonishment – the glance of indignation – which she gave at Lady Cecilia, settled Beauclerc's opinion; and Cecilia was satisfied that she had done her friend good service against her will; and as to the means thought she – what signifies going back to consider when they succeed?

The Collingwoods gladly availed themselves of Lady Cecilia Clarendon's kind invitation, as they were both anxious to take leave of Helen Stanley before their departure. They were to sail very soon, so that their visit was but short; a few days of painful pleasure to Helen – a happy meeting, but enjoyed with the mournful sense that they were so soon to separate, and for long a time; perhaps for ever.

Mr Collingwood told Helen that if she still agreed to his conditions, he would arrange with Mr James, the solicitor, that all the money left to her by her uncle, should be appropriated to the payment of his debts. 'But,' continued he, 'pause and consider well, whether you can do without this money, which is still yours; you are, you know, not bound by any promise, and it is not yet too late to say you have altered your decision.'

Helen smiled and said, 'You cannot be serious in saying this, I am sure.'

Mr Collingwood assured her that he was. Helen simply said that her determination was unalterable. He looked pleased, yet his last words in taking leave of her were, 'Remember, my dear, that when you have given away your fortune, you cannot live as if you had it.'

The Collingwoods departed; and, after a decent time had elapsed, or what she deemed a decent time had elapsed, Lady Cecilia was anxious to ascertain what progress had been made; how, relatively to each other, Lady Blanche Forrester and Helen stood in Beauclerc's opinion, or rather in his imagination. But this was not quite so easy a matter to determine as she had conceived it would be, judging from the frankness of Beauclerc's temper, and from the terms of familiarity on which they had lived while abroad. His confidence was not to be won, surprised, or forced. He was not only jealous of his free will, as most human beings are in love affairs, but, like all men of true feeling, he desired in these matters perfect mental privacy.

When Psyche is awakened, it should be by Cupid alone. Beauclerc did not yet wish that she should be awakened. He admired, he enjoyed that repose: he was charmed by the perfect confiding simplicity of Helen's mind, so unlike what he had seen in others – so real. The hope of that pure friendship which dawned upon him he wished to prolong, and dreaded lest, by any doubt raised, all might be clouded and changed. Lady Cecilia was, however, convinced that, without knowing it, he was falling comfortably in love through friendship; a very easy convenient way.

And Helen, had she too set out upon that easy convenient road of friendship? She did not think about the road, but she felt that it was very agreeable, and thought it was quite safe, as she went on so smoothly and easily. She could not consider Mr Beauclerc as a new acquaintance, because she had heard so much about him. He was completely one of the family, so that she, as part of that family, could not treat him as a stranger. Her happiness, she was sensible, had much increased since his arrival; but so had everybody's. He gave a new spring, a new interest, to everything; added so much to the life of life; his sense and his nonsense were each of them good in their kind; and they were of various kinds, from the high sublime of metaphysics to the droll realities of life. But everybody blaming, praising, scolding, laughing *at*, or *with* him, he was necessary to all, and with all, for some reason or other, a favourite.

But the General was always as impatient as Lady Cecilia herself both of his hypercriticism and of his never-ending fancies, each of which Beauclerc pursued with an eagerness and abandoned with a facility which sorely tried the General's equanimity.

One day, after having ridden to Old Forest, General Clarendon returned chafed. He entered the library, talking to Cecilia, as Helen thought, about his horse.

'No managing him! Curb him ever so little, and he is on his hind-legs directly. Give him his head, put the bridle on his neck, and he stands still; does not know which way he would go, or what he would do. The strangest fellow for a rational creature.'

Now it was clear it was of Beauclerc that he spoke. 'So rash and yet so resolute,' continued the General.

'How is that?' said Lady Davenant.

'I do not know, but so it is,' said the General. 'As you know,' appealing to Helen and to Lady Cecilia, 'he was ready to run me through till he had his own way about that confounded old house; and now there are all the workmen at a stand, because Mr Beauclerc cannot decide what he will have done or undone.'

'Oh, it is my fault!' cried Helen, with the guilty recollection of the last alteration not having been made yesterday in drawing the working plan, and she hastened to look for it directly; but when she found it, she saw to her dismay that Beauclerc had scribbled it all over with literary notes; it was in no state to meet the General's eye; she set about copying it as fast as possible.

'Yes,' pursued the General; 'forty alterations – shuffling about continually. Cannot a man be decided?'

'Always with poor Beauclerc,' said Lady Cecilia, '*le mieux est l'ennemi du bien.*' [1]

'No, my dear Cecilia, it is all his indolence; there he sat with a book in his hand all yesterday! with all his impetuosity, too indolent to stir in his own business,' said the General.

'His mind is too active sometimes to allow his body to stir,' said Lady Davenant; 'and because he cannot move the universe, he will not stir his little finger.'

'He is very fond of paradoxes, and your ladyship is very fond of him,' said the General; 'but indolent he is; and as to activity of mind, it is only in pursuit of his own fancies.'

'And your fancies and his differ,' said Lady Davenant.

'Because he never fancies anything useful,' said the General.

'*C'est selon! c'est selon!*' [2] cried Lady Cecilia gaily; 'he thinks his fancies useful, and especially all he. is doing at Old Forest; but I confess he tends most to the agreeable. Certainly he is a most agreeable creature.'

'Agreeable! satisfied to be called an agreeable man!' cried the General indignantly; 'yes, he has no ambition.'

'There I differ from you, General,' said Lady Davenant; 'he has too much: have patience with him; he is long-sighted in his visions of glory.'

---

[1] The better is the enemy of the good [2] It all depends! It all depends!

'Visions indeed!' said the General.

'Those who are really ambitious,' continued Lady Davenant, 'must think before they act. "What shall I do to be for ever known?" is a question which deserves at least a little more thought than those which most young men ask themselves, which commonly are, "What shall I do to be known to-morrow – on the Turf or at Brook's – or in Doctors' Commons – or at some exclusive party at charming Lady Nobody's?"'

'What will you do for the plan for these workmen in the meantime, my dear Clarendon?' said Cecilia, afraid that some long discussion would ensue.

'Here it is!' said Helen, who had managed to get it ready while they were talking. She gave it to the General, who thanked her, and was off directly. Cecilia then came to divert herself with looking at Beauclerc's scribbled plan, and she read the notes aloud for her mother's amusement. It was a sketch of a dramatical, metaphysical, entertainment, of which half a dozen proposed tides had been scratched out, and there was finally left 'Tarquin the Optimist, or the Temple of Destiny.' It was from an old story begun by Laurentius Valla, and continued by Leibnitz; – she read,

' "*Act i. Scene* I. *Sextus Tarquin goes to consult the Oracle, who foretells the crime he is to commit.*"

'And then,' cried Lady Cecilia, 'come measures of old and new front of Old Forest, wings included. Now he goes on with his play.

' "*Tarquin's complaint to Jupiter of the Oracle – Modern Predestination compared to Ancient Destiny.*"

'And here,' continued Cecilia, 'come prices of Norway deal and a great blot, and then we have "*Jupiter's answer that Sextus may avoid his doom if he pleases, by staying away from Rome; but he does not please to do so, because he must then renounce the crown. Good speech here on vanity, and inconsistency of human wishes.*"

' "Kitchen 23 ft. by 21. Query with hobs?"

'I cannot conceive, my dear Helen,' continued Lady Cecilia, 'how you could make the drawing out through all this,' and she continued to read,

' "*Scene 3rd.*

' "*High Priest of Delhi asks Jupiter why he did not give Sextus a better* WILL – *why not* MAKE *him choose to give up the crown, rather than commit the crime? Jupiter refuses to answer, and sends the High Priest to consult Minerva at Athens.*"

' "NB. Old woman at Old Forest, promised her an oven," – "*Leibnitz gives –* "

'Oh! if he goes to Leibnitz,' said Lady Cecilia, 'he will be too grand for me, but it will do for you, mamma.

' "*Leibnitz gives in his Temple of the Destinies a representation of every possible universe from the worst to the best – This could not be done on the stage.*"

'Very true indeed,' said Lady Cecilia, 'but, Helen, listen, Granville has really found an ingenious resource.

' "*By Ombres Chinoises, suppose; or a gauze curtain, as in Zemire et Azore, the audience might be made to understand the main point, that* GOOD *resulted from Tarquin's* BAD *choice. Brutus, Liberty, Rome's grandeur, and the Optimist right at last.* QED."

'Well, well,' continued Lady Cecilia; 'I don't understand it; but I understand this, – "Bricks wanting." '

Lady Davenant smiled at this curious specimen of Beauclerc's versatility, but said, 'I fear he will fritter away his powers on a hundred different petty objects, and do nothing at last worthy of his abilities. He will scatter and divide the light of his genius, and show us every change of the prismatic colours – curious and beautiful to behold, but dispersing, wasting the light he should concentrate on some one, some noble object.'

'But if he has light enough for little objects and great too?' said Lady Cecilia, 'I allow, *qu'il faudrait plus d'un cœur pour aimer tant de choses à la fois;*[1] but as I really think Granville has more heart than necessary, he can well afford to waste some of it, even on the old woman at Old Forest.'

---

[1] One would need more than one heart to love so many things at once

CHAPTER 12

ONE EVENING, Helen was looking over a beautiful scrap-book of Lady Cecilia's. Beauclerc, who had stood by for some time, eyeing it in rather scornful silence, at length asked whether Miss Stanley was a lover of albums and autographs.

Helen had no album of her own, she said, but she was curious always to see the autographs of celebrated people.

'Why?' said Beauclerc.

'I don't know. It seems to bring one nearer to them. It gives more reality to our imagination of them perhaps,' said Helen.

'The imagination is probably in most cases better than the reality,' replied he.

Lady Davenant stooped over Helen's shoulder to look at the handwriting of the Earl of Essex – the writing of the gallant Earl of Essex, at sight of which, as she observed, the hearts of queens have beat high. 'What a crowd of associated ideas rise at the sight of that autograph! who can look at it without some emotion?'

Helen could not. Beauclerc in a tone of raillery said he was sure, from the eager interest Miss Stanley took in these autographs that she would in time become a collector herself; and he did not doubt that he should see her with a valuable museum, in which should be preserved the old pens of great men, that of Cardinal Chigi, for instance, who boasted that he wrote with the same pen for fifty years.

'And by that boast you know,' said Lady Davenant, 'convinced the Cardinal de Retz that he was not a great, but a very little man. We will not have that pen in Helen's museum.'

'Why not?' Beauclerc asked; 'it was full as worth having as many of the relics to be found in most young ladies' and even old gentlemen's museums. It was quite sufficient whether a man had been great or little that he had been talked of, – that he had been something of a *lion* – to make anything belonging to him valuable to collectors, who preserve and worship even "the parings of lions' claws."'

That class of indiscriminate collectors Helen gave up to his ridicule; still he was not satisfied. He went on to the whole class of 'lion-hunters,' as he called them, condemning indiscriminately all those who were anxious to see celebrated people; he hoped Miss Stanley was not one of that class.

'No, not a lion-hunter,' said Helen; she hoped she never should be one of that set, but she confessed she had a great desire to see and to know distinguished persons, and she hoped that this sort of curiosity, or, as she would rather call it, enthusiasm, was not ridiculous, and did not deserve to be confounded with the mere trifling vulgar taste for sight-seeing and lion-hunting.

Beauclerc half smiled, but, now answering immediately, Lady Davenant said that for her part she did not consider such enthusiasm as ridiculous; on the contrary, she liked it, especially in young people. 'I consider the warm admiration of talent and virtue in youth as a promise of future excellence in maturer age.'

'And yet,' said Beauclerc, 'the maxim "not to admire" is, I believe, the most approved in philosophy, and in practice is the great secret of happiness in this world.'

'In the *fine* world, it is a fine air, I know,' said Lady Davenant. 'Among a set of fashionable young somnambulists, it is doubtless the only art they know to make men happy or to keep them so; but this has nothing to do with philosophy, Beauclerc, though it has to do with conceit or affectation.'

Mr Beauclerc, now piqued, with a look and voice of repressed feeling, said that he hoped her ladyship did not include him amongst that set of fashionable somnambulists.

'I hope you will not include yourself in it,' answered Lady Davenant; 'it is contrary to your nature, and if you join the *nil admirari* coxcombs, it can only be for fashion's sake – mere affectation.'

Beauclerc made no reply, and Lady Davenant, turning to Helen, told her that several celebrated people were soon to come to Clarendon Park, and congratulated her upon the pleasure she would have in seeing them. 'Besides being a great pleasure, it is a real advantage,' continued she, 'to see and be acquainted early in life with superior people. It enables one to form a standard of excellence, and raises that standard high and bright. In men, the enthusiasm becomes glorious ambition to excel in arts or arms; in women, it refines and elevates the taste, and is so far a preventive against frivolous, vulgar company, and all their train of follies and vices. I can speak from my own recollection, of the great happiness it was to me, when I early in life became acquainted with some of the illustrious of my day.'

'And may I ask,' said Beauclerc, 'if any of them equalled the expectations you formed of them?'

'Some far exceeded them,' said Lady Davenant.

'You were fortunate. Everybody cannot expect to be happy,' said Beauclerc. 'I believe, in general it is found that few great men of any times stand the test of near acquaintance. No man – '

'Spare me!' cried Lady Davenant, interrupting him, for she imagined she knew what he was going to say; 'oh! spare me that old sentence, "No man is a hero to his valet de chambre." I cannot endure to hear that for the thousandth time; I heartily wish it had never been said at all.'

'So do I,' replied Beauclerc; but Lady Davenant had turned away, and he now spoke in so low a voice that only Helen heard him. 'So do I detest that quotation, not only for being hackneyed, but for having been these hundred years the comfort both of lean-jawed envy and fat mediocrity.'

He took up one of Helen's pencils and began to cut it – he looked vexed, and low to her observed, 'Lady Davenant did not do me the honour to let me finish my sentence.'

'Then,' said Helen, 'if Lady Davenant misunderstood you, why do you not explain?'

'No, no, it is not worth while, if she could so mistake me.'

'But anybody may be mistaken; do explain.'

'No, no,' said he, very diligently cutting the pencil to pieces; 'she is engaged, you see, with somebody – somebody else.'

'But now she has done listening.'

'No, no, not now; there are too many people, and it's of no consequence.'

By this time the company were all eagerly talking of every remarkable person they had seen or that they regretted not having seen. Lady Cecilia now called upon each to name the man among the celebrated of modern days whom they should most like to have seen. By acclamation they all named Sir Walter Scott, 'The Ariosto of the North!'

All but Beauclerc; he did not join the general voice; he said low to Helen with an air of disgust – 'How tired I am of hearing him called "The Ariosto of the North!" '

'But by whatever name,' said Helen, 'surely you join in that general wish to have seen him?'

'Yes, yes, I am sure of your vote,' cried Lady Cecilia, coming up to them. 'You, Granville, would rather have seen Sir Walter Scott than any author since Shakespeare – would not you?'

'Pardon me, on the contrary, I am glad that I have never seen him.'

'Glad not to have seen him! – *not?*'

The word *not* was repeated with astonished incredulous emphasis by all voices. 'Glad not to have seen Sir Walter Scott! How extraordinary! What can Mr Beauclerc mean?'

'To make us all stare,' said Lady Davenant, 'so do not gratify him. Do not wonder at him; we cannot believe what is impossible, you know, only because it is impossible. But,' continued she, laughing, 'I know how it is. The spirit of contradiction – the spirit of singularity – two of your familiars, Granville, have got possession of you again, and we must have patience while the fit is on.'

'But I have not, and will not have, patience,' said Lord Davenant, whose good-nature seldom failed, but who was now quite indignant.

'I wonder you are surprised, my dear lord,' said Lady Davenant, 'for Mr Beauclerc likes so much better to go wrong by
himself than to go right with all the world, that you could not
expect that he would join the loud voice of universal praise.'

'I hear the loud voice of universal execration,' said Beauclerc;
'you have all abused me, but whom have I abused? What have I
said?'

'Nothing,' replied Lady Cecilia; 'that is what we complain
of. I could have better borne any abuse than indifference to Sir
Walter Scott.'

'Indifference!' exclaimed Beauclerc – 'what did I say, Lady
Cecilia, from which you could infer that I felt indifference? Indifferent to him whose name I cannot pronounce without emotion?
I alone, of all the world, indifferent to that genius, pre-eminent
and unrivalled, who has so long commanded the attention of the
whole reading public, arrested at will the instant order of the day
by tales of other times, and in this commonplace, this everyday
existence of ours, created a holiday world, where, undisturbed by
vulgar cares, we may revel in a fancy region of felicity, peopled
with men of other times – shades of the historic dead, more illustrious and brighter than in life!'

'Yes, the great Enchanter,' cried Cecilia.

'Great and good Enchanter,' continued Beauclerc, 'for in his
magic there is no dealing with unlawful means. To work his
ends, there is never aid from any one of the bad passions of our
nature. In his writings there is no private scandal – no personal
satire – no bribe to human frailty – no libel upon human nature.
And among the lonely, the sad, and the suffering, how has he
medicined to repose the disturbed mind, or elevated the dejected
spirit! – perhaps fanned to a flame the unquenched spark in souls
not wholly lost to virtue. His morality is not in purple patches,
ostentatiously obtrusive, but woven in through the very texture
of the stuff. He paints man as he is, with all his faults, but with his
redeeming virtues – the world as it goes, with all its compensating good and evil, yet making each man better contented with
his lot. Without our well knowing how, the whole tone of our

minds is raised – for, thinking nobly of our kind, he makes us think more nobly of ourselves!'

Helen, who had sympathised with Beauclerc in every word he had said, felt how trite it is that

– Next to genius, is the power
Of feeling where true genius lies.

'Yet after all this, Granville,' said Lady Cecilia, 'you would make us believe you never wished to have seen this great man?'

Beauclerc made no answer.

'Oh, how I wish I had seen him!' said Helen to Lady Davenant, the only person present who had had that happiness.

'If you have seen Raeburn's admirable pictures, or Chantrey's speaking bust,' replied Lady Davenant, 'you have as complete an idea of Sir Walter Scott as painting or sculpture can give. The first impression of his appearance and manner was surprising to me, I recollect, from its quiet, unpretending good nature; but scarcely had that impression been made before I was struck with something of the chivalrous courtesy of other times. In his conversation you would have found all that is most delightful in his works – the combined talent and knowledge of the historian, novelist, antiquary, and poet. He recited poetry admirably, his whole face and figure kindling as he spoke: but whether talking, reading, or reciting, he never tired me, even with admiring; and it is curious that, in conversing with him, I frequently found myself forgetting that I was speaking to Sir Walter Scott; and what is even more extraordinary, forgetting that Sir Walter Scott was speaking to me, till I was awakened to the conviction by his saying something which no one else could have said. Altogether he was certainly the most perfectly agreeable and perfectly amiable great man I ever knew.'

'And now, mamma,' said Lady Cecilia, 'do make Granville confess honestly he would give the world to have seen him.'

'Do, Lady Davenant,' said Helen, who saw, or thought she saw, a singular emotion in Beauclerc's countenance and fancied he was upon the point of yielding; but Lady Davenant, without looking at him, replied – 'No, my dear, I will not ask him – I will not encourage him in *affectation*.'

At that word dark grew the brow of Beauclerc, and he drew back, as it were, into his shell, and out of it came no more that night, nor the next morning at breakfast. But, as far as could be guessed, he suffered internally, and no effort made to relieve him did any good, so every one seemed to agree that it was much better to leave him alone, or let him be moody in peace, hoping that in time the mood would change; but it changed not till the middle of that day, when, as Helen was sitting working in Lady Davenant's room, while she was writing, two quick knocks were heard at the door.

'Come in!' said Lady Davenant.

Mr Beauclerc stood pausing on the threshold.

'Do not go, Miss Stanley,' said he, looking very miserable and ashamed, and proud, and then ashamed again.

'What is the matter, Granville?' said Lady Davenant.

'I am come to have a thorn taken out of my mind,' said he – 'two thorns which have sunk deep, kept me awake half the night. Perhaps, I ought to be ashamed to own I have felt pain from such little things. But so it is; though, after all, I am afraid they will be invisible to you, Lady Davenant.'

'I will try with a magnifying-glass,' said she; 'lend me that of your imagination, Granville – a high power, and do not look so very miserable, or Miss Stanley will laugh at you.'

'Miss Stanley is too good to laugh.'

'That is being too good indeed,' said Lady Davenant. 'Well, now to the point.'

'You were very unjust to me, Lady Davenant, yesterday, and unkind.'

'Unkind is a woman's word; but go on.'

'Surely man may mark "unkindness' altered eye" as well as woman,' said Beauclerc; 'and from a woman and a friend he may and must feel it, or he is more or less than man.'

'Now what can you have to say, Granville, that will not be anticlimax to this exordium?'

'I will say no more if you talk of exordiums and anticlimaxes,' cried he. 'You accused me yesterday of affectation – twice, when I was no more affected than you are.'

'Oh! is that my crime? Is that what has hurt you so dreadfully? Here is the thorn that has gone in so deep! I am afraid that, as is usual, the accusation hurt the more because it was – '

'Do not say "true," ' interrupted Beauclerc, 'for you really cannot believe it, Lady Davenant. You know me, and all my faults, and I have plenty; but you need not accuse me of one that I have not, and which from the bottom of my soul I despise. Whatever are my faults, they are at least real, and my own.'

'You may allow him that,' said Helen.

'Well, I will – I do,' said Lady Davenant; 'to appease you, poor injured innocence; though any one in the world might think you affected at this moment. Yet I, who know you, know that it is pure real folly. Yes, yes, I acquit you of affectation.'

Beauclerc's face instantly cleared up.

'But you said two thorns had gone into your mind – one is out, now for the other.'

'I do not feel that other now,' said Beauclerc, 'it was only a mistake. When I began with "No man," I was not going to say, "No man is a hero to his valet de chambre." If I had been allowed to finish my sentence, it would have saved a great deal of trouble. I was going to say that no man admires excellence more fervently than I do, and that my very reason for wishing not to see celebrated people is, lest the illusion should be dispelled.

'No description ever gives us an exact idea of any person, so that when any one has been much described and talked of, before we see them we form in our mind's eye some image, some notion of our own, which always proves to be unlike the reality; and when we do afterwards see it, even if it be fairer or better than our imagination, still at first there is a sort of disappointment, from the non-agreement with our previously formed conception. Everybody is disappointed the first time they see Hamlet, or Falstaff, as I think Dugald Steward observes.'

'True; and I remember,' said Lady Davenant, 'Madame de la Rochejaquelin once said to me, "I hate that people should come to see me. I know it destroys the illusion."'

'Yes,' cried Beauclerc; 'how much I dread to destroy any of those blessed illusions, which make the real happiness of life. Let me preserve the objects of my idolatry; I would not approach too near the shrine; I fear too much light. I would not know that they were false!'

'Would you then be deceived?' said Lady Davenant.

'Yes,' cried he; 'sooner would I believe in all the fables of the Talmud than be without the ecstasy of veneration. It is the curse of age to be thus miserably disenchanted; to outlive all our illusions, all our hopes. That may be my doom in age, but, in youth, the high spring-time of existence, I will not be cursed with such a premature ossification of the heart. Oh! rather, ten thousand times rather, would I die this instant!'

'Well! but there is not the least occasion for your dying,' said Lady Davenant, 'and I am seriously surprised that you should suffer so much from such slight causes; how will you ever get through the world if you stop thus to weigh every light word?'

'The words of most people,' replied he, 'pass by me like the idle wind; but I do weigh every word from the very few whom I esteem, admire, and love; with my friends, perhaps, I am too susceptible, I love them so deeply.'

This is an excuse for susceptibility of temper which flatters friends too much to be easily rejected. Even Lady Davenant admitted it, and Helen thought it was all natural.

CHAPTER 13

LADY CECILIA WAS NOW impatient to have the house filled with company. She gave Helen a *catalogue raisonné*[1] of all who were expected at Clarendon Park, some for a fashionable three days' visit; some for a week; some for a fortnight or three weeks, be the same more or less. 'I have but one fixed principle,' said she, 'but I *have* one — never to have tiresome people when it can possibly be avoided. Impossible, you know, it is sometimes. One's own and one's husband's relations one must have; but, as for the rest, it's one's own fault if one fails in the first and last maxim of hospitality — to welcome the coming and speed the parting guest.'

The first party who arrived were of Lady Davenant's particular friends, to whom Cecilia had kindly given the precedence, if not the preference, that her mother might have the pleasure of seeing them, and that they might have the honour of taking leave of her, before her departure from England.

They were political, fashionable, and literary; some of ascendency in society, some of parliamentary promise, and some of ministerial eminence — the aristocracy of birth and talents well mixed.

The aristocracy of birth and the aristocracy of talents are words now used more as a commonplace antithesis, than as denoting a real difference or contrast. In many instances, among those now living, both are united in a manner happy for themselves and glorious for their country. England may boast of having among her young nobility *'The first in birth, the first in fame'* — men

---

[1] descriptive catalogue

distinguished in literature and science, in senatorial eloquence and statesmanlike abilities.

But in this party at Clarendon Park there were more of the literary and celebrated than without the presence of Lady Davenant could perhaps have been assembled, or perhaps would have been desired by the General and Lady Cecilia. Cecilia's beauty and grace were of all societies, and the General was glad for Lady Davenant's sake and proud for his own part to receive these distinguished persons at his house.

Helen had seen some of them before at Cecilhurst and at the Deanery. By her uncle's friends she was kindly recognised, by others of course politely noticed; but miserably would she have been disappointed and mortified, if she had expected to fix general attention, or excite general admiration. Past and gone for ever are the days, if ever they were, when a young lady, on her entrance into life, captivated by a glance, overthrew by the first word, and led in triumph her train of admirers. These things are not to be done nowadays.

Yet even when unnoticed Helen was perfectly happy. Her expectations were more than gratified in seeing and in hearing these distinguished people, and she sat listening to their conversation in delightful enjoyment, without even wanting to have it seen how well she understood.

There is a precious moment for young people, if taken at the prime, when first introduced into society, yet not expected, not called upon to take a part in it, they, as standers-by, may see not only all the play, but the characters of the players, and may learn more of life and of human nature in a few months than afterwards in years, when they are themselves actors upon the stage of life, and become engrossed by their own parts. There is a time, before the passions are awakened, when the understanding, with all the life of nature, fresh from all that education can do to develop and cultivate, is at once eager to observe and able to judge, for a brief space blessed with the double advantages of youth and age. This time once gone is lost irreparably; and how often it is lost – in premature vanity, or premature dissipation!

Helen had been chiefly educated by a man, and a very sensible man, as Dean Stanley certainly was in all but money matters. Under his masculine care, while her mind had been brought forward on some points, it had been kept back on others, and while her understanding had been cultivated, it had been done without the aid of emulation or competition; not by touching the springs of pride, but by opening sources of pure pleasure; and this pure pleasure she now enjoyed, grateful to that dear uncle.

For the single inimitable grace of simplicity which she possessed, how many mothers, governesses, and young ladies themselves, willingly, when they see how much it charms, would too late exchange half the accomplishments, all the acquirements, so laboriously achieved!

Beauclerc, who had seen something of the London female world, was, both from his natural taste and from contrast, pleased with Helen's fresh and genuine character, and he sympathised with all her silent delight. He never interrupted her in her enthusiastic contemplation of the great stars, but he would now and then seize an interval of rest to compare her observations with his own; anxious to know whether she estimated their relative magnitude and distances as he did. These snatched moments of comparison and proof of agreement in their observations, or the pleasure of examining the causes of their difference of opinion, enhanced the enjoyment of this brilliant fortnight; and not a cloud obscured the deep serene.

Notwithstanding all the ultra-refined nonsense Beauclerc had talked about his wish not to see remarkable persons, no one could enjoy it more, as Helen now perceived; and she saw also that he was considered as a man of promise among all these men of performance. But there were some, perhaps very slight things, which raised him still more in her mind, because they showed superiority of character. She observed his manner towards the General in this company, where he had himself the 'vantage ground – so different now from what it had been in the Old Forest battle, when only man to man, ward to guardian. Before these distinguished persons there was a look – a tone of deference at once most affectionate and polite.

'It is so generous,' said Lady Cecilia to Helen; 'is not it?' and Helen agreed.

This brilliant fortnight ended too soon, as Helen thought, but Lady Cecilia had had quite enough of it. 'They are all to go to-morrow morning, and I am not sorry for it,' said she at night, as she threw herself into an arm-chair in Helen's room; and, after having indulged in a refreshing yawn, she exclaimed, 'Very delightful, very delightful! as you say, Helen, it has all been; but I am not sure that I should not be very much tired if I had much more of it. Oh yes, I admired them all amazingly, but then admiring all day long is excessively wearisome. The very attitude of looking up fatigues both body and mind. Mamma is never tired, because she never has to look up; she can always look down, and that's so grand and so easy. She has no idea how the neck of my poor mind aches this minute; and my poor eyes! blasted with excess of light. How yours have stood it so well, Helen, I cannot imagine! how much stronger they must be than mine. I must confess, that, without the relief of music now and then, and ecarté, and that quadrille, bad as it was, I should never have got through it tonight alive or awake. But,' cried she, starting up in her chair, 'do you know Horace Churchill stays to-morrow? Such a compliment from him to stay a day longer than he intended! And do you know what he says of your eyes, Helen? – that they are the best listeners he ever spoke to. I should warn you though, my dear, that he is something, and not a little, I believe, of a male coquette. Though he is not very young, but he well understands all the advantages of a careful toilette. He has, like that George Herbert in Queen Elizabeth's time, "a genteel humour for dress." He is handsome still, and his fine figure, and his fine feelings, and his fine fortune, have broken two or three hearts; nevertheless I am delighted that he stays, especially that he stays on your account.'

'Upon my account!' exclaimed Helen. 'Did not you see that, from the first day when Mr Churchill had the misfortune to be placed beside me at dinner, he utterly despised me? he began to talk to me, indeed, but left his sentence unfinished, his good story untold, the instant he caught the eye of a grander auditor.'

Lady Cecilia had seen this, and marvelled at a well-bred man so far forgetting himself in vanity; but this, she observed, was only the first day; he had afterwards changed his manner towards Helen completely.

'Yes, when he saw Lady Davenant thought me worth speaking to. But, after all, it was quite natural that he should not know well what to say to me. I am only a young lady. I acquit him of all peculiar rudeness to me, for I am sure Mr Churchill really could not talk for only one insignificant hearer, could not bring out his good things, unless he felt secure of possessing the attention of the whole dinner-table, so I quite forgive him.'

'After this curse of forgiveness, my dear Helen, I will wish you a good-night,' said Lady Cecilia, laughing; and she retired with a fear that there would not be jealousy enough between the gentlemen, or that Helen would not know how to play them one against another.

There is a pleasure in seeing a large party disperse; in staying behind when others go: – there is advantage as well as pleasure, which is felt by the timid, because they do not leave their characters behind them; and rejoiced in by the satirical, because the characters of the departed and departing are left behind, fair game for them. Of this advantage no one could be more sensible, no one availed himself of it with more promptitude and skill, than Mr Churchill; for well he knew that though wit may fail, humour may not take – though even flattery may pall upon the sense, scandal, satire, and sarcasm are resources never failing for the lowest capacities, and sometimes for the highest.

This morning, in the library at Clarendon Park, he looked out of the window at the departing guests, and, as each drove off, he gave to each his *coup de patte*.[1] To Helen, to whom it was new, it

[1] cutting remark

was wonderful to see how each, even of those next in turn to go, enjoyed the demolition of those who were just gone; how, blind to fate, they laughed, applauded, and licked the hand just raised to strike themselves. Of the first who went – 'Most respectable people,' said Lady Cecilia;'a *bonne mère de famille.*' [2]

'Most respectable people!' repeated Horace – 'most respectable people, old coach and all.' And then, as another party drove off – 'No fear of anything truly respectable here.'

'Now, Horace, how can you say so? – she is so amiable and so clever.'

'So clever? only, perhaps, a thought too fond of English liberty and French dress. *Poissarde bien coiffée.*' [3]

'*Poissarde*! of one of the best-born, best-bred women in England!' cried Lady Cecilia;'*bien coiffée* [3] I allow.'

'Lady Cecilia is *si coiffée de sa belle amie* [4] that I see I must not say a word against her, till – the fashion changes. But, hark! I hear a voice I never wish to hear.'

'Yet nobody is better worth hearing – '

'Oh yes, the queen of the Blues – the Blue Devils!'

'Hush!' cried the aide-de-camp,'she is coming in to take leave.'

Then, as the queen of the Blue Devils entered, Mr Churchill, in the most humbly respectful manner, begged – 'My respects – I trust your Grace will do me the favour – the justice to remember me to all your party who – do me the honour to bear me in mind' – then, as she left the room, he turned about and laughed.

'Oh! you sad, false man!' cried the lady next in turn to go. 'I declare, Mr Churchill, though I laugh, I am quite afraid to go off before you.'

'Afraid! what could malice or envy itself find to say of your ladyship, *intacte* as you are? *Intacte!*' repeated he, as she drove off, '*intacte!* – a well-chosen epithet, I flatter myself.'

'Yes, *intacte* – untouched – above the breath of slander,' cried Lady Cecilia.

---

[1] a good family woman   [2] well-groomed fishwife   [3] well-groomed;
[4] as well turned out as her beautiful friend

'I know it: so I say,' replied Churchill: 'fidelity that has stood all temptations – to which it has ever been exposed; and her husband is – '

'A near relation of mine,' said Lady Cecilia. 'I am not prudish as to scandal in general,' continued she, laughing; ' "a chicken, too, might do me good," but then the fox must not prey at home. No one ought to stand by and hear their own relations abused.'

'A thousand pardons! I depended too much on the general maxim – that the nearer the bone the sweeter the slander.'

'Nonsense!' said Lady Cecilia.

'I meant to say, the nearer the heart the dearer the blame. A cut against a first cousin may go wrong – but a bosom friend – oh! how I have succeeded against best friends; scolded all the while, of course, and called a monster. But there is Sir Stephen bowing to you.' Then, as Lady Cecilia kissed her hand to him from the window, Churchill went on: 'By the bye, without any scandal, seriously I heard something – I was quite concerned – that he had been of late less in his study and more in the boudoir of – . Surely it cannot be true!'

'Positively false,' said Lady Cecilia.

'At every breath a reputation dies,' said Beauclerc.

''Pon my soul, that's true!' said the aide-de-camp. 'Positively, hit or miss, Horace has been going on, firing away with his wit, pop, pop, pop! till he has bagged – how many brace?'

Horace turned away from him contemptuously, and looked to see whereabouts Lady Davenant might be all this time.

CHAPTER 14

LADY DAVENANT WAS at the far end of the room engrossed, Churchill feared, by the newspaper; as he approached she laid it down, and said, –

'How scandalous some of these papers have become, but it is the fault of the taste of the age. "Those who live to please, must please to live." '

Horace was not sure whether he was cut or not, but he had the presence of mind not to look hurt. He drew nearer to Lady Davenant, seated himself, and taking up a book as if he was tired of folly, to which he had merely condescended, he sat and read, and then sat and thought, the book hanging from his hand.

The result of these profound thoughts he gave to the public, not to the aide-de-camp; no more of the little popgun pellets of wits – but now were brought out reason and philosophy. In a higher tone he now reviewed the literary, philosophical, and political world, with touches of La Bruyère and Rochefoucauld in the characters he drew and in the reflections he made; with an air, too, of sentimental contrition for his own penetration and fine moral sense, which compelled him to see and to be annoyed by the faults of such superior men.

The analysis he made of every mind was really perfect – in one respect, not a grain of bad but was separated from the good, and held up clean and clear to public view. And as an anatomist he showed such knowledge both of the brain and the heart, such an admirable acquaintance with all their diseases, and handled the probe and scalpel so well, with such a practised hand!

'Well, really this is comfortable,' said Lord Davenant, throwing himself back in his arm-chair – 'true English comfort, to sit at ease and see all one's friends so well dissected! Happy to feel that it is our duty to our neighbour to see him well cut up – ably anatomised for the good of society; and when I depart – when my time comes – as come it must, nobody is to touch me but Professor Churchill. It will be a satisfaction to know that I shall be carved as a dish fit for gods, not hewed as a carcase for hounds. So now remember, Cecilia, I call on you to witness – I hereby, being of sound mind and body, leave and bequeath my character, with all my defects and deficiencies whatever, and all and any singular curious diseases of the mind, of which I may die possessed, wishing the same many for his sake, – to my good friend Doctor Horace Churchill, professor of moral, philosophic, and scandalous anatomy, to be by him dissected at his good pleasure for the benefit of society.'

'Many thanks, my good lord; and I accept your legacy for the honour – not the value of the gift, which everybody must be sensible is nothing,' said Churchill, with a polite bow – 'absolutely nothing. I shall never be able to make anything of it.'

'Try – try, my dear friend,' answered Lord Davenant. 'Try, don't be modest.'

'That would be difficult when so distinguished,' said Beauclerc, with an admirable look of proud humility.

'Distinguished Mr Horace Churchill assuredly is,' said Lady Davenant, looking at him from behind her newspaper. 'Distinguished above all his many competitors in this age of scandal; he has really raised the art to the dignity of a science. Satire, scandal, and gossip, now hand-in-hand – the three new graces: all on the same elevated rank – three, formerly considered as so different, and the last left to our inferior sex, but now, surely, to be a male gossip is no reproach.'

'Oh, Lady Davenant! – male gossip – what an expression!'

'What a reality!'

'Male gossip! – "*Tombe sur moi le ciel!*" '[1] cried Churchill.

---

[1] Heaven forbid

' *"Pourvu que je me venge"*[1] always understood,' pursued Lady Davenant; 'but why be so afraid of the imputation of gossiping, Mr Churchill? It is quite fashionable, and if so, quite respectable, you know, and in your style quite grand.

'And *gossiping* wonders at being so fine!

Malice, to be hated, needs but to be seen, but now when it is elegantly dressed we look upon it without shame or consciousness of evil; we grow to dote upon it – so entertaining, so graceful, so refined. When vice loses half its grossness, it loses all its deformity. Humanity used to be talked of when our friends were torn to pieces, but now there is such a philosophical perfume thrown over the whole operation, that we are irresistibly attracted. How much we owe to men such as Mr Churchill, who makes us feel detraction virtue!'

He bowed low and Lady Davenant, summoned by her lord, left the room, and there he stood as one condemned but not penitent.

'If I have not been well sentenced,' said he, as the door closed, 'and made "to feel detraction virtue!" But since Lady Cecilia cannot help smiling at that, I am acquitted, and encouraged to sin again at the first opportunity. But Lady Davenant shall not be by, nor Lord Davenant either.'

Lady Cecilia sat down to write a note, and Mr Churchill walked round the room in a course of critical observation on the pictures, of which, as of everything else, he was a supreme judge. At last he put his eye and his glass down to something which singularly attracted his attention on one of the marble tables.

'Pretty!' said Lady Cecilia, 'pretty are not they? – though one's so tired of them everywhere now – those doves.'

'Doves!' said Churchill, 'what I am admiring are gloves, are not they, Miss Stanley?' said he, pointing to an old pair of gloves, which, much wrinkled and squeezed together, lay on the beautiful marble in rather an unsightly lump.

[1] So long as I get my revenge

'Poor Doctor V—,' cried Helen to Cecilia; 'that poor Doctor V— is as absent as ever! he is gone, and has forgotten his gloves!'

'Absent! oh, as ever!' said Lady Cecilia, going on with her note, 'the most absent man alive.'

'Too much of that sort of thing I think there is in Doctor V—,' pursued Churchill: 'a touch of absence of mind, giving the idea of high abstraction, becomes a learned man well enough; but then it should only be slight, as a *soupçon* of rouge, which may become a pretty woman: all depends on the measure, the taste, with which these things are managed – put on.'

'There is nothing managed, nothing *put on*, in Doctor V—,' cried Helen eagerly, her colour rising; 'it is all perfectly sincere, true in him, whatever it be.'

Beauclerc put down his book.

'All perfectly true! You really think so, Miss Stanley?' said Churchill, smiling, and looking superior down.

'I do, indeed,' cried Helen.

'Charming – so young! How I do love that freshness of mind!'

'Impertinent fellow! I could knock him down,' felt Beauclerc.

'And you think all Doctor V—'s humility true?' said Churchill.

'Yes, perfectly!' said Helen; 'but I do not wonder you are surprised at it, Mr Churchill.'

She meant no *malice*, though for a moment he thought she did; and he winced under Beauclerc's smile.

'I do not wonder that any one who does not know Doctor V— should be surprised by his great humility,' added Helen.

'You are sure that it is not pride that apes humility?' asked Churchill.

'Yes, quite sure!'

'Yet – ' said Churchill (putting his malicious finger through a great hole in the thumb of the doctor's glove), 'I should have fancied that I saw vanity through the holes in these gloves, as through the philosopher's cloak of old.'

'Horace is a famous fellow for picking holes and making much of them, Miss Stanley, you see,' said the aide-de-camp.

'Vanity! Doctor V— has no vanity!' said Helen, 'if you knew him.'

'No vanity! Whom does Miss Stanley mean?' cried the aide-de-camp. 'No vanity? that's good. Who? Horace?'

'*Mauvais plaisant!*' [1] Horace put him by, and, happily, not easily put out of countenance, he continued to Helen, –

'You give the good doctor credit, too, for all his *naïveté?*'

'He does not want credit for it,' said Helen, 'he has it.'

'I wish I could see things as you do, Miss Stanley.'

'Show him that, Helen,' cried Lady Cecilia, looking at a table beside them, on which lay one of those dioramic prints which appear all a confusion of lines till you look at them in their right point of view. 'Show him that – it all depends, and so does seeing characters, on getting the right point of view.'

'Ingenious!' said Churchill, trying to catch the right position; 'but I can't, I own – ' then abruptly resuming, '*Naïveté* charms me at fifteen,' and his eye glanced at Helen, then was retracted, then returning to his point of view, 'at eighteen perhaps may do,' and his eyes again turned to Helen, 'at eighteen – it captivates me quite,' and his eye dwelt. 'But *naïveté* at past fifty, verging to sixty, is quite another thing, really rather too much for me. I like all things in season, and above all, simplicity will not bear long keeping. I have the greatest respect possible for our learned and excellent friend, but I wish this could be any way suggested to him, and that he would lay aside this out-of-season simplicity.'

'He cannot lay aside his nature,' said Helen, 'and I am glad of it, it is such a good nature.'

'Kind-hearted creature he is, I never heard him say a severe word of anyone,' said Lady Cecilia.

'What a sweet man he must be!' said Horace, making a face at which none present, not even Helen, could forbear to smile. 'His heart, I am sure, is in the right place always. I only wish one could say the same of his wig. And would it be amiss if he sometimes (I would not be too hard upon him, Miss Stanley),

---

[1] one who makes jokes at another's expense

once a fortnight, suppose – brushed, or caused to be brushed, that coat of his?'

'You have dusted his jacket for him famously, Horace, I think,' said the aide-de-camp.

At this instant the door opened, and in came the doctor himself.

Lady Cecilia's hand was outstretched with her note, thinking, as the door opened, that she should see the servant come in, for whom she had rung.

'What surprises you all so, my good friends?' said the doctor, stopping and looking round in all his native simplicity.

'My dear doctor,' said Lady Cecilia, 'only we thought you were gone – that's all.'

'And I am not gone, that's all. I stayed to write a letter, and am come here to look for – but I cannot find – my – '

'Your gloves, perhaps, doctor, you are looking for,' said Churchill, going forward, and with an air of the greatest respect and consideration, both for the gloves and for their owner, he presented them; then shook the doctor by the hand, with a cordiality which the good soul thought truly English, and, bowing him out, added, 'How proud he had been to make his acquaintance, – *au revoir*, he hoped, in Park Lane.'

'Oh you treacherous – ' cried Lady Cecilia, turning to Horace, as soon as the unsuspecting philosopher was fairly gone. 'Too bad really! If he were not the most simple-minded creature extant, he must have seen, suspected, something from your look; and what would have become of you if the doctor had come in one moment sooner, and had heard you – ? I was really frightened.'

'Frightened! so was I, almost out of my wits,' said Churchill. '*Les revenans*[1] always frighten one; and they never hear any good of themselves, for which reason I make it a principle, when once I have left a room, full of friends especially, never – never to go back. My gloves, my hat, my coat, I'd leave, sooner than lose my friends. Once I heard it said, by one who knew the world and human

---

[1] Those who come back from the dead

nature better than any of us – once I heard it said in jest, but in sober earnest I say, that I would not for more than I am worth be places, without his knowing it, within earshot of my best friend.'

'What sort of a best friend can yours be?' cried Beauclerc.

'Much like other people's, I suppose,' replied Horace, speaking with perfect nonchalance – 'much like other people's best friends. Whosoever expects to find better, I guess, will find worse, if he live in the world we live in.'

'May I go out of the world before I believe or suspect any such thing!' cried Beauclerc. 'Rather than have the Roman curse light upon me, "May you survive all your friends and relations!" may I die a thousand times!'

'Who talks of dying, in a voice so sweet – a voice so loud?' said provoking Horace, in his calm, well-bred tone; 'for my part, I who have the honour of speaking to you, can boast, that never since I was of years of discretion (counting new style, beginning at thirteen, of course) – never have I lost a friend, a sincere friend – never, for this irrefragable reason – since that nonage, never was I such a neophyte as to fancy I had found that freak of nature, a friend perfectly sincere.'

'How I pity you!' cried Beauclerc; 'if you are in earnest, but in earnest you can't be.'

'Pardon me, I can, and I am. And in earnest you will oblige me, Mr Beauclerc, if you will spare me your pity; for, all things in this world considered,' said Horace Churchill, drawing himself up, 'I do not conceive that I am much an object of pity.' Then, turning upon his heel, he walked away, conscious, however, half an instant afterwards, that he had drawn himself up too high, and that for a moment his temper had spoiled his tune, and betrayed him into a look and manner too boastful, bordering on the ridiculous. He was in haste to repair the error.

Not Garrick, in the height of his celebrity and of his susceptibility, was ever more anxious than Horace Churchill to avert the stroke of ridicule – to guard against the dreaded smile. As he walked away, he felt behind his back that those he left were smiling in silence.

Lady Cecilia had thrown herself on a sofa, resting after the labour of *l'éloquence de billet*.[1] He stopped, and leaning over the back of the sofa on which she reclined, repeated an Italian line in which was the word '*pavoneggiarsi.*'

'My dear Lady Cecilia, you, who understand and feel Italian so well, how expressive are some of their words! *Pavoneggiarsi!* – untranslatable. One cannot say well in English to peacock oneself. To make oneself like unto a peacock is flat; but *pavoneggiarsi* – action, passion, picture, all in one! To plume oneself comes nearest to it but the word cannot be given, even by equivalents, in English; nor can it be naturalised, because, in fact, we have not the feeling. An Englishman is too proud to boast – too bashful to strut; if ever he *peacocks himself* it is in a moment of anger, not in display. The language of every country,' continued he, raising his voice, in order to reach Lady Davenant, who just then returned to the room, as he did not wish to waste a philosophical observation on Lady Cecilia, – 'the language of every country is, to a certain degree, evidence, record, history of his character and manners.' Then, lowering his voice almost to a whisper, but very distinct, turning while he spoke so as to make sure that Miss Stanley heard – 'Your young friend this morning quite captivated me by her nature – nature, the thing that now is most uncommon, a real natural woman; and when in a beauty, how charming! How delicious when one meets with *effusion de cœur* a young lady, too, who speaks pure English, not a leash of language at once; and cultivated, too, your friend is, for one does like ignorance, if one could have knowledge without pretension – so hard to find the golden mean! – and if one could find it, one might not be nearer to – '

Lady Cecilia listened for the finishing word, but none came. It all ended in a sigh, to be interpreted as she pleased. A look towards the ottoman, where Beauclerc had now taken his seat beside Miss Stanley, seemed to point the meaning out: but Lady Cecilia knew her man too well to understand him.

[1] epistolary eloquence

Beauclerc, seated on the ottoman, was showing to Helen some passages in the book he was reading; she read with attention, and from time to time looked up with a smile of intelligence and approbation. What either said Horace could not hear, and he was the more curious, and when the book was put down, after carelessly opening others he took it up. Very much surprised was he to find it neither novel nor poem: many passages were marked with pencil notes of approbation, he took it for granted these were Beauclerc's; there he was mistaken, they were Lady Davenant's. She was at her work-table. Horace, book in hand, approached; the book was not in his line, it was more scientific than literary – it was for posterity more than for the day; he had only turned it over as literary men turn over scientific books, to seize what may serve for a new simile or a good allusion; besides, among his philosophical friends, the book being talked of, it was well to know enough of it to have something to say, and he had said well, very *judiciously* he had praised it among the elect; but now it was his fancy to depreciate it with all his might; not that he disliked the author or the work now more than he had done before, but he was in the humour to take the opposite side from Beauclerc, so he threw the book from him contemptuously.

'Rather a slight hasty thing, in my opinion,' said he.

Beauclerc's eyes took fire as he exclaimed, 'Slight! hasty! this most noble, most solid work!'

'Solid in your opinion,' said Churchill, with a smile deferential, slightly sneering.

'Our own opinion is all that either of us can give,' said Beauclerc; 'in my opinion it is the finest work of the progress of natural philosophy, the most enlarged, the most just in its judgments of the past, and in its prescience of the future; in the richness of experimental knowledge, in its theoretical invention, the greatest work by any one individual since the time of Bacon.'

'And Bacon is under your protection, too?'

'Protection! my protection?' said Beauclerc.

'Pardon me, I simply meant to ask if you are one of those who swear by Lord Verulam.'

'I swear by no man, I do not swear at all, not on philosophical subjects especially; swearing adds nothing to faith,' said Beauclerc.

'I stand corrected,' said Churchill, 'and I would go further, and add that in argument enthusiasm adds nothing to reason – much as I admire, as we all admire,' glancing at Miss Stanley, 'that enthusiasm with which this favoured work has been advocated.'

'I could not help speaking warmly,' said Beauclerc; 'it is a book to inspire enthusiasm; there is such a noble spirit all through it, so pure from petty passions, from all vulgar jealousies, all low concerns! Judge of a book, somebody says, by the impression it leaves on your mind when you lay it down; this book stands that test, at least with me; I lay it down with such a wish to follow – with steps ever so unequal still to follow – where it points the way.'

'Bravo! bravissimo! hear him, hear him! print him, print him! hot-press from the author to the author, hot-press!' cried Churchill, and he laughed.

Like one suddenly awakened from the trance of enthusiasm by the cold touch of ridicule, stood Beauclerc, brought down from heaven to earth, and by that horrid little laugh, not the heart's laugh.

'But my being ridiculous does not make my cause so, and that is a comfort.'

'And another comfort you may have, my dear Granville,' said Lady Davenant, 'that ridicule is not the test of truth; truth should be the test of ridicule.'

'But where is the book?' continued Beauclerc.

Helen gave it to him.

'Now, Mr Churchill,' said Beauclerc; 'I am really anxious, I know you are such a good critic, will you show me these faults? blame as well as praise must always be valuable from those who themselves excel.'

'You are too good,' said Churchill.

'Will you then be good enough to point out the errors for me?'

'Oh, by no means,' cried Churchill, 'don't note me, do not quote me, I am nobody, and I cannot give up my authorities.'

'But the truth is all I want to get at,' said Beauclerc.

'Let her rest, my dear sir, at the bottom of her well; there she is, and there she will be for ever and ever, and depend upon it none of our windlassing will ever bring her up.'

'Such an author as this,' continued Beauclerc, 'would have been so glad to have corrected any error.'

'So every author tells you, but I never saw one of them who did not look blank at a list of errata – if you knew how little one is thanked for them!'

'But you would be thanked now,' said Beauclerc: – 'the faults in style, at least.'

'Nay, I am no critic,' said Churchill, confident in his habits of literary detection; 'but if you ask me,' said he, as he disdainfully flirted the leaves back and forward with a 'There now!' and a 'Here now!' 'We should not call that good writing – you could not think this correct? I may be wrong, but I should not use this phrase. Hardly English that – colloquial, I think; and this awkward ablative absolute – never admitted now.'

'Thank you,' said Beauclerc, 'these faults are easily mended.'

'Easily mended, say you? I say, better make a new one.'

'WHO COULD?' said Beauclerc.

'How many faults you see,' said Helen, 'which I should never have perceived unless you had pointed them out, and I am sorry to know them now.'

Smiling at Helen's look of sincere mortification, in contrast at this moment with Mr Churchill's air of satisfied critical pride, Lady Davenant said, –

'Why sorry, my dear Helen? No human work can be perfect; Mr Churchill may be proud of that strength of eye which in such a powerful light can count the spots. But whether it be the best use to make of his eyes, or the best use that can be made of the light, remains to be considered.'

BEYOND MEASURE was Churchill provoked to find Lady Davenant against him and on the same side as Granville Beauclerc – all unused to contradiction in his own society, where he had long been supreme, he felt a difference of opinion so sturdily maintained as a personal insult.

For so young a man as Beauclerc, yet unknown to fame, not only to challenge the combat but to obtain the victory, was intolerable; and the more so, because his young opponent appeared no ways elated or surprised, but seemed satisfied to attribute his success to the goodness of his cause.

Churchill had hitherto always managed wisely his great stakes and pretensions in both the fashionable and literary world. He had never actually published anything except a clever article or two in a review, or an epigram, attributed to him but not acknowledged. Having avoided giving his measure, it was believed he was above all who had been publicly tried – it was always said – 'If Horace Churchill would but publish, he would surpass every other author of our times.'

Churchill accordingly dreaded and hated all who might possibly approach the throne of fashion, or interfere with his dictatorship in a certain literary set in London, and from this moment he began cordially to detest Beauclerc – he viewed him with scornful, yet with jealous eyes; but his was the jealousy of vanity, not of love; it regarded Lady Davenant and his fashionable reputation in the first place – Helen only in the second.

Lady Davenant observed all this, and was anxious to know how much or how little Helen had seen, and what degree of interest it excited in her mind. One morning, when they were alone together, looking over a cabinet of cameos, Lady Davenant pointed to one which she thought like Mr Beauclerc. Helen did not see the likeness. 'People see likenesses very differently,' said Lady Davenant. 'But you and I, Helen, usually see characters, if not faces, with the same eyes. I have been thinking of these two gentleman, Mr Churchill and Mr Beauclerc – which do you think the most agreeable?'

'Mr Churchill is amusing certainly,' said Helen, 'but I think Mr Beauclerc's conversation much more, interesting – though Mr Churchill is agreeable, sometimes – when – '

'When he flatters you,' said Lady Davenant.

'When he is not satirical – I was going to say,' said Helen.

'There is a continual petty brilliancy, a petty effort too,' continued Lady Davenant, 'in Mr Churchill, that tires me'– sparks struck perpetually, but then you hear the striking of the flints, the clink of the tinder-box.'

Helen, though she admitted the tinder-box, thought it too low a comparison. She thought Churchill's were not mere sparks.

'Well, fireworks, if you will,' said Lady Davenant, 'that rise, blaze, burst, fall, and leave you in darkness, and with a disagreeable smell too; and it's all *feu d'artifice*[1] after all. Now in Beauclerc there is too little art and too ardent nature. Some French friends of mine, who knew both, said of Mr Churchill, "*De l'esprit on ne peut pas plus même à Paris*,"[2] the highest compliment a Parisian can pay, but they allowed that Beauclerc had "*beaucoup plus d'ame*."'[3]

'Yes,' said Helen; 'how far superior!'

'It has been said,' continued Lady. Davenant, 'that it is safer to judge of men by their actions than by their words, but there are few actions and many words in life; and if women would

---

[1] fireworks [2] One cannot even find such wit in Paris; [3] much more soul

avail themselves of their daily, hourly, opportunities of judging people by their words, they would get at the natural characters, or, what is of just as much consequence, they would penetrate through the acquired habits; and here, Helen, you have two good studies before you.'

Preoccupied as Helen was with the certainty of Beauclerc being an engaged, almost a married man, and looking, as she did, on Churchill as one who must consider her as utterly beneath his notice, she listened to Lady Davenant's remarks as she would have done to observations about two characters in a novel or on the stage.

As Churchill could not immediately manifest his hatred of Mr Beauclerc, it worked inwardly the more. He did not sleep well this night, and when he got up in the morning, there was something the matter with him. Nervous, bilious – cross it could not be; – *journalier* [1](a French word settles everything) – *journalier* he allowed he was; he rather gloried in it, because his being permitted to be so proved his power, – his prerogative of fortune and talent combined.

In the vast competition of the London world, it is not permitted to every man to be in his humour or out of his humour at pleasure; but, by an uncommon combination of circumstances, Churchill had established his privilege of caprice. He was allowed to have his bad and his good days, and the highest people and the finest smiled and submitted to his stamp of approval or disapproval, and when he was sulky, rude, or snappish, called it only Horace Churchill's way. They even prided themselves on his preferences and his aversions. 'Horace is always charming when he is with us.' 'With me you have no idea how delightful he is. Indeed I must do him the justice to say that I never found him otherwise. While the less favoured permitted him to be as rude as he pleased, and only petted him, and told of his odd ways to those who sighed in vain to have him at their parties. But Lady Davenant was not a person to pet

[1] day labourer

or spoil a child of any age, and to the General Mr Churchill was not particularly agreeable – not his sort; while to Lady Cecilia, secure in grace, beauty, and fashion, his humours were only matter of amusement, and she bore with him pleasantly and laughingly.

'Such weather!' cried he in a querulous tone; 'how can a man have any sense in such weather? Some foreigner says that the odious climate of England is an over-balance for her good constitution. The sun of the south is in truth well worth the liberty of the north. It is a sad thing,' said he, with a very sentimental air, 'that a free-born Briton should be senile to these skyey influences'; and grumbling on, he looked out of the window as cross as he pleased, and nobody minded him. The aide-de-camp civilly agreed with him that it was horrid weather, and likely to rain, and it did rain; and everyone knows how men, like children, are in certain circumstances, affected miserably by a rainy day. There was no going out; horses at the door, and obliged to be dismissed. Well, since there could be no riding, the next best thing the aide-de-camp thought was to talk of horses, and the officers all grew eager, and Churchill had a mind to exert himself so far as to show them that he knew more of the matter than they did; that he was no mere book-man; but on this unlucky day all went wrong. It happened that Horace fell into some grievous error concerning the genealogy of a famous race-horse, and, disconcerted more than he would have been at being convicted of any degree of moral turpitude, vexed and ashamed, he talked no more of Newmarket or of Doncaster, left the race-ground to those who prided themselves on the excellences of their four-footed betters, and lounged into the billiard-room.

He found Lady Cecilia playing with Beauclerc; Miss Stanley was looking on. Churchill was a famous billiard-player, and took his turn to show how much better than Beauclerc he performed, but this day his hand was out, his eye not good; he committed blunders of which a novice might have been ashamed. And there was Miss Stanley and there was Beauclerc by to see! and Beauclerc pitied him!

O line extreme of human misery!

He retreated to the book-room, but there the intellectual Horace, with all the sages, poets, and novelists of every age within his reach, reached them not; but, with his hands in his pockets, like any squire or schoolboy under the load of ignorance or penalties of idleness, stood before the chimney-piece, eyeing the pendule, and verily believing that this morning the hands went backward. Dressing-time came at last, and dinner-time, bringing relief how often to man and child ill-tempered; but this day to Churchill dinner brought only discomfiture worse discomfited.

Some of the neighbouring families were to dine at Clarendon Park. Mr Churchill abhorred country neighbours and country gentlemen. Among these, however, were some not unworthy to be perceived by him; and besides these, there were some foreign officers; one in particular, from Spain, of high rank and birth, of the *sangre azul*, the *blue blood*, who have the privilege of the silken cord if they should come to be hanged. This Spaniard was a man of distinguished talent, and for him Horace might have been expected to shine out; it was his pleasure, however, this day to disappoint expectations, and to do 'the dishonours of his country.' He would talk only of eating, of which he was privileged not only to speak but to judge, and pronounce upon in the last resort, though this was only an air, for he was not really a gourmand; but after ogling through his glass the distant dishes, when they with a wish came nigh, he, after a cursory glance or a close inspection, made them with a nod retire.

At last he thought an opportunity offered for bringing in a well-prepared anecdote which he had about Cambacérès, and a hot blackbird and white feet, but unluckily a country gentleman would tell some history of a battle between poachers and gamekeepers, which fixed the attention of the company till the moment for the anecdote was past.

Horace left his tale untold, and spoke word never more
till a subject was started on which he thought he could come
out unrivalled. General Clarendon had some remarkably good
wines. Churchill was referred to as a judge, and he allowed
them to be all good, but he prided himself on possessing a
certain Spanish wine, esteemed above all price, because not to
be had for money – *amontillado* is its name. Horace appealed to
the Spanish officer, who confirmed all he said of this vinous
phenomenon. 'No cultivator can be certain of producing it. It
has puzzled, almost to death, all the growers of Xeres: – it is a
variety of sherry, almost as difficult to judge of as to procure.'

But Mr Churchill boasted he had some, undoubtedly
genuine; he added, 'that Spanish judges had assured him his
taste was so accurate he might venture to pronounce upon the
difficult question of amontillado or not!'

While he yet spoke, General Clarendon, unawares, placed
before him some of this very fine wine, which, as he finished
speaking, Churchill swallowed without knowing it from some
other sherry which he had been drinking. He would have questioned that it was genuine, but the Spaniard, as far as he could
pretend to judge, thought it unquestionable.

Churchill's countenance fell in a manner that quite surprised
Helen, and exceedingly amused Lady Cecilia. He was more
mortified and vexed by this failure than by all the rest, for the
whole table smiled.

The evening of this day of misfortune was not brighter than
the morning, everything was wrong – even at night – at night
when at last the dinner company, the country visitors, relieved
him from their presence, and when some comfort might be had,
he thought, stretched in a good easy-chair – Lord Davenant
had set him the example. But something had happened to all
the chairs, – there was a variety of fashionable kinds; he tried
them by turns, but none of them this night would suit him. Yet
Lady Cecilia maintained (for the General had chosen them)
that they were each and all of them in their way comfortable,
in the full English spirit of the word, and according to the

French explanation of *confortable*,[1] given to us by the Duchess d'Abrantes, *convenablement bon*[2]; but in compassion to Mr Churchill's fastidious restlessness, she would now show him a perfection of a chair which she had just had made for her own boudoir. She ordered that it should be brought, and in it rolled, and it was looked at in every direction and sat in, and no fault could be found with it, even by the great fault-finder; but what was it called? It was neither a lounger, nor a dormeuse, nor a Cooper, nor a Nelson, nor a kangaroo: a chair without a name would never do; in all things fashionable the name is more than half. Such a happy name as kangaroo Lady Cecilia despaired of finding for her new favourite, but she begged some one would give it a good one; whoever gave her the best name should be invited to the honours and pleasures of the sitting in this chair for the rest of the night.

Here eyes, and all eyes, turned upon Mr Churchill; but whether the occasion was too great, or that his desire to satisfy the raised expectation of the public was too high strained, or that the time was out of joint, or that he was out of sorts, the fact was he could find no name.

Beauclerc, who had not yet tried the chair, sank into its luxurious depth, and leaning back, asked if it might not be appropriately called the 'Sleepy-hollow.'

'Sleepy-hollow!' repeated Lady Cecilia, 'excellent!' and by acclamation 'Sleepy-hollow' was approved; but when Beauclerc was invited to the honours of the sitting, he declined, declaring that the name was not his invention, only his recollection; it had been given by a friend of his to some such chair.

This magnanimity was too much for Horace; he looked at his watch, found it was bed-time, pushed the chair out of his way, and departed; Beauclerc, the first and last idea in this his day of mortifications.

Seeing a man subject to these petty irritations lowers him in the eyes of woman. For that susceptibility of temper arising

[1] comfortable   [2] reasonably good

from the jealousy of love, even when excited by trifles, woman
makes all reasonable, all natural allowance; but for the jealousy
of self–love she has no pity. Unsuited to the manly character! –
so Helen thought, and so every woman thinks.

CHAPTER 16

IT WAS EXPECTED by all who had witnessed his discomfiture and his parting push to the chair, that Mr Churchill would be off early in the morning – such was his wont when he was disturbed in vanity: but he reappeared at breakfast.

This day was a good day with Horace; he determined it should be so, and though it was again a wet day, he now showed that he could rule the weather of his own humour, when intensity of will was awakened by rivalry. He made himself most agreeable, and the man of yesterday was forgotten or remembered only as a foil to the man of to-day. The words he so much loved to hear, and to which he had so often surreptitiously listened, were now repeated, 'No one can be so agreeable as Horace Churchill is on his good days!'

Bright he shone out, all gaiety and graciousness; the stamp of favour was for all, but its finest impression was for Helen. He tried flattery, and wit, each playing on the other with reflected and reflecting lustre, for a woman naturally says to herself, 'When this man has so much wit, his flattery even must be worth something.'

And another day came, and another, and another party of friends filled the house, and still Mr Churchill remained, and was now the delight of all. As far as concerned his successes in society, no one was more ready to join in applause than Beauclerc; but when Helen was in question he was different, though he had reasoned himself into the belief that he could not yet love Miss Stanley, therefore he could not be jealous. But he had been glad to observe that she had from the first seemed to see what sort of person Mr Churchill was. She was now only amused, as every-body must be, but she would never be interested by such a man as Horace Churchill, a wit without a soul. If she were — why he could never feel any further interest about her — that was all!

So it went on; and now Lady Cecilia was as much amused as she expected by these daily jealousies, conflicts, and compari-sons, the feelings perpetually tricking themselves out, and strut-ting about, calling themselves judgments, like the servants in *Gil Blas*[1] in their masters' clothes, going about as counts, dukes, and grandees.

'Well, really,' said Lady Cecilia to Helen one day, as she was standing near her tambour frame, 'you are an industrious creature, and the only very industrious person I ever could bear. I have myself a natural aversion to a needle, but that tambour needle I can better endure than a common one, because, in the first place, it makes a little noise in the world; one not only sees but hears it getting on; one finds that without dragging it draws at every link a lengthened chain.'

'It is called chainstitch, is it not?' said the aide-de-camp; 'and Miss Stanley is working on so famously fast at it she will have us all in her chains by and by.'

'Bow, Miss Stanley,' said Lady Cecilia; 'that pretty compliment deserves at least a bow, if not a look-up.'

'I should prefer a look-down, if I were to choose,' said Churchill.

'Beggars must not be choosers,' said the aide-de-camp.

'But the very reason I can bear to look at you working, Helen,' continued Lady Cecilia, 'is because you do look up so often — so refreshingly. The professed *Notables* I detest — those who never raise their eyes from their everlasting work; whatever is said, read, thought, or felt, is with them of secondary importance to that bit of muslin in which they are making holes, or that bit of canvas on which they are perpetrating such figures or flowers as nature scorns to look upon. I did not mean anything against you,

---

[1] Series of picaresque novels by Lesage, published from 1715 to 1735

mamma, I assure you,' continued Cecilia, turning to her mother, who was also at her embroidering frame, 'because, though you do work, or have work before you, to do you justice, you never attend to it in the least.'

'Thank you, my dear Cecilia,' said Lady Davenant, smiling; 'I am, indeed, a sad bungler, but still I shall always maintain a great respect for work and workers, and I have good reasons for it.'

'And so have I,' said Lord Davenant. 'I only wish that men who do not know what to do with their hands were not ashamed to sew. If custom had but allowed us this resource, how many valuable lives might have been saved, how many rich *ennuyés* would not have hung themselves, even in November! What years of war, what overthrow of empires, might have been avoided, if princes and sultans, instead of throwing handkerchiefs, had but hemmed them!'

'No, no,' said Lady Davenant; 'recollect that the race of Spanish kings has somewhat deteriorated since they exchanged the sword for the tambour frame. We had better have things as they are; leave us the privilege of the needle, and what a valuable resource it is; sovereign against the root of all evil – an antidote both to love in idleness and hate in idleness – which is most to be dreaded, let those who have felt both decide. I think we ladies must be allowed to keep the privilege of the needle to ourselves, humble though it be, for we must allow it is a good one.'

'Good at need,' said Churchill. 'There is an excellent print, by Bouck, I believe, of an old woman beating the devil with a distaff; distaffs have been out of fashion with spinsters ever since, I fancy.'

'But as she was old, Churchill,' said Lord Davenant, 'might not your lady have defied his black majesty without her distaff?'

'His *black* majesty!' I admire your distinction, my lord,' said Churchill, 'but give it more emphasis; for all kings are not black in the eyes of the fair, it is said, you know.' And here he began an anecdote of regal scandal in which Lady Cecilia stopped him –

'Now, Horace, I protest against your beginning with scandal so early in the morning. None of your *on dits*, for decency's sake, before luncheon; wait till evening.'

Churchill coughed, and shrugged, and sighed, and declared he would be temperate; he would not touch a character, upon his honour; he would only indulge in a few little personalities; it could not hurt any lady's feelings that he should criticise or praise absent beauties. So he just made a review of all he could recollect, in answer to a question one of the officers, Captain Warmsley, had asked him, and which, in an absent fit, he had had the ill-manners yesterday, as now he recollected, not to answer – Whom he considered as altogether the handsomest woman of his acquaintance? Beauclerc was now in the room, and Horace was proud to display, before him in particular, his infinite knowledge of all the fair and fashionable, and all that might be admitted fashionable without being fair – all that have the *je ne sais quoi* which is than beauty dearer. As one conscious of his power to consecrate or desecrate, by one look of disdain or one word of praise, he stood; and beginning at the lowest conceivable point, his uttermost notion of want of beauty – his ideal of ugliness, naming one whose image, no doubt, every charitable imagination will here supply, Horace next fixed upon another for his mediocrity point – what he should call 'just well enough' – *assez bien, assez* – just up to the Bellasis motto, '*Bonne et belle assez.*'[1] Then, in the ascending scale, he rose to those who, in common parlance, may be called charming, fascinating; and still for each he had his fastidious look and depreciating word. Just keeping within the verge, Horace, without exposing himself to the ridicule of coxcombry, ended by sighing for that being 'made of every creature's best' – perfect, yet free from the curse of perfection. Then, suddenly turning to Beauclerc, and tapping him on the shoulder – 'Do give us your notions – to what sort of body or mind, now, would you willingly bend the knee?'

Beauclerc could not or would not tell – 'I only know that whenever I bend the knee,' said he, 'it will be because I cannot help it!'

Beauclerc could not be drawn either by Churchill's persiflage or flattery, and he tried both, to talk of his tastes or opinions of

[1] good and fine enough

women. He felt too much perhaps about love to talk much about it. This all agreed well in Helen's imagination with what Lady Cecilia had told her of his secret engagement. She was sure he was thinking of Lady Blanche, and that he could not venture to describe her, lest he should betray himself and his secret. Then, leaving Churchill and the talkers, he walked up and down the room alone, at the farther side, seeming as if he were recollecting some lines which he repeated to himself, and then stopping before Lady Cecilia, repeated to her, in a very low voice the following –

> 'I saw her upon nearer view;
> A spirit, yet a woman too!
> Her household motions light and free,
> And steps of virgin liberty;
> A countenance in which did meet
> Sweet records, promises as sweet;
> A creature not too bright or good
> For human nature's daily food;
> For transient sorrows, simple wiles,
> Praise, blame, love, kisses, tears, and smiles.'

Helen thought Lady Blanche must be a charming creature if she was like this picture; but somehow, as she afterwards told Lady Cecilia, she had formed a different idea of Lady Blanche Forrester. Cecilia smiled and asked, 'How? different how?'

Helen did not exactly know, but altogether she had imagined that she must be more of a heroine, or perhaps more of a woman of rank and fashion. She had not formed any exact idea – but different altogether from this description. Lady Cecilia again smiled, and said, 'Very natural; and after all not very certain that the Lady Blanche is like this picture, which was not drawn for her or from her assuredly – a resemblance found only in the imagination, to which we are, all of us, more or less, dupes; and so much the better say I – 'too bad,' says mamma – and all mothers.'

'There is one thing I like better in Mr Beauclerc's manners than in Mr Churchill,' said Helen.

'There are a hundred I like better,' said Lady Cecilia, 'but what is your one thing?'

'That he always speaks of women in general with respect – as if he had more confidence in them, and more dependence upon them for his happiness. Now Mr Churchill, with all the adoration he professes, seems to look upon them as idols that he can set up or pull down, bend the knee to or break to pieces, at pleasure – I could not like a man for a friend who had a bad, or even a contemptuous, opinion of women – could you, Cecilia?'

'Certainly not,' Lady Cecilia said; 'the General had always, naturally, the greatest respect for women. Whatever prejudices he had taken up had been only caught from others, and lasted only till he had got rid of the impression of certain "untoward circumstances." Even a grave, serious dislike, both Lady Cecilia and Helen agreed that they could bear better than that persiflage which seemed to mock even while it most professed to admire.

Horace presently discovered the mistakes he had made in his attempts, and repaired them as fast as he could by his versatility. The changes shaded off with a skill which made then run easily into each other. He perceived that Mr Beauclerc's respectful air and tone were preferred, and he now laid himself out in the respectful line, adding, as he flattered himself, something of a finer point, more polish in whatever he said, and with more weight of authority.

But he was mortified to find that it did not produce the expected effect, and, after having done the respectful one morning, as he fancied, in the happiest manner, he was vexed to perceive that he not only could not raise Helen's eyes from her work, but that even Lady Davenant did not attend to him: and that, as he was rounding one of his best periods, her looks were directed to the other side of the room, where Beauclerc sat apart; and presently she called to him, and begged to know what it was he was reading. She said she quite envied him the power he possessed of being rapt into future times or past, completely at his author's bidding, to be transported how and where he pleased.

Beauclerc brought the book to her, and put it into her hand. As she took it she said, 'As we advance in life, it becomes more and more difficult to find in any book the sort of enchanting, entrancing interest which we enjoyed when life, and books, and we ourselves, were new. It were vain to try and settle whether the fault is most in modern books, or in our ancient selves; probably not in either: the fact is, that not only does the imagination cool and weaken as we grow older, but we become, as we live on in this world, too much engrossed by the real business and cares of life, to have feeling or time for factitious, imaginary interests. But why do I say factitious? while they last, the imaginative interests are as real as any others.'

'Thank you,' said Beauclerc, 'for doing justice to poor imagination, whose pleasures are surely, after all, the highest, the most real, that we have, unwarrantably as they have been decried both by metaphysicians and physicians.'

The book which had so fixed Beauclerc's attention was Segur's *History of Napoleon's Russian Campaign*. He was at the page where the burning of Moscow is described – the picture of Buonaparte's despair, when he met resolution greater than his own, when he felt himself vanquished by the human mind, by patriotism, by virtue – in which he could not believe, the existence of which, with all his imagination, he could not conceive: the power which his indomitable will could not conquer.

Beauclerc pointed to the account of that famous description on the iron gate of a church which the French found still standing, the words written by Rostopchin after the burning of his 'delightful home.'

'*Frenchmen, I have been eight years in embellishing this residence; I have lived in it happily in the bosom of my family. The inhabitants of this estate (amounting to seventeen hundred and twenty) have quitted it at your approach; and I have, with my own hands, set fire to my own house, to prevent it from being polluted by your presence.*'

'See what one, even one, magnanimous individual can do for his country,' exclaimed Beauclerc. 'How little did this sacrifice cost him! Sacrifice do I say? It was a pride – a pleasure.'

Churchill did not at all like the expression of Helen's countenance, for he perceived she sympathised with Beauclerc's enthusiasm. He saw that romantic enthusiasm had more charm for her than wit or fashion; and now he meditated another change of style. He would try a noble style. He resolved that the first convenient opportunity he would be a little romantic, and perhaps, even take a touch at chivalry, a burst like Beauclerc's, but in a way of his own, at the degeneracy of modern times. He tried it – but it was quite a failure; Lady Cecilia, as he overheard, whispered to Helen what was once so happily said –

'*Ah! le pauvre homme! comme il se batte les flancs d'un enthousiasme de commande.*'[1]

Horace was too clever a man to persist in a wrong line, or one in which his test of right, *success*, did not crown his endeavours. If this did not do, something else would – should. It was impossible that with all his spirit of resource he should ultimately fail. To please, and to make an impression on Helen, a greater impression than Beauclerc – to annoy Beauclerc, in short, was still, independently of all serious thoughts, the utmost object of Churchill's endeavours.

---

[1] Oh! The poor man! How he struggles to control himself.

VOLUME TWO

ABOUT THIS TIME a circumstance occurred, which seemed to have nothing to do with Churchill, or Beauclerc, but which eventually brought both their characters into action and passion.

Lord Davenant had purchased, at the sale of Dean Stanley's pictures, several of those which had been the Dean's favourites, and which, independently of their positive merit, were peculiarly dear to Helen. He had ordered that they should be sent down to Clarendon Park; at first, he only begged house-room for them from the General while he and Lady Davenant were in Russia; then he said that in case he should never return he wished the pictures should be divided between his two dear children, Cecilia and Helen; and that, to prevent disputes, he would make the distribution of them himself now, and in the kindest and most playful manner he allotted them to each, always finding some excellent reason for giving to Helen those which he knew she liked best; and then there was to be a *hanging committee*, for hanging the pictures, which occasioned a great deal of talking, Beauclerc always thinking most of Helen, or of what was really best for the paintings; Horace most of himself and his amateurship.

Among these pictures were some fine Wouvermans, and other hunting and hawking pieces, and one in particular of the duchess and her ladies, from Don Quixote. Beauclerc, who had gone round examining and admiring, stood fixed when he came to this picture, in which he fancied he discovered in one of the figures some likeness to Helen; the lady had a hawk upon her wrist. Churchill came up eagerly to the examination, with glass at eye. He could not discern the slightest resemblance to Miss Stanley; but he was in haste to bring out an excellent observation of his own, which he had made his own from a *Quarterly Review,* illustrating the advantage it would be to painters to possess knowledge, even of kinds most distant from the line of their profession.

'For instance now, *a priori,* one should not insist upon a great painter's being a good ornithologist, and yet, for want of being something of a bird-fancier, look here what he has done – quite absurd, a sort of hawk introduced, such as never was or could be at any hawking affair in nature: would not sit upon lady's wrist or answer to her call – would never fly at a bird. Now you see this is a ridiculous blunder.'

While Churchill plumed himself on this critical remark, Captain Warmsley told of who still kept hawks in England, and of the hawking parties he had seen and heard of – 'even this year, that famous hawking in Wiltshire, and that other in Norfolk.'

Churchill asked Warmsley if he had been at Lord Berner's when Landseer was there studying the subject of his famous hawking scene. 'Have you seen it, Lady Cecilia?' continued he; 'it is beautiful; the birds seem to be absolutely coming out of the picture'; and he was going on with some of his connoisseurship, and telling of his mortification in having missed the purchase of that picture; but Warmsley got back to the hawking he had seen, and he became absolutely eloquent in describing the sport.

Churchill, though eager to speak, listened with tolerably polite patience till Warmsley came to what he had forgot to mention, – to the label with the date of place and year that is put upon the heron's leg; to the heron brought from Denmark, where it had been caught, with the label of having been let fly from Lord Berner's; 'for,' continued he, 'the heron is always to be saved if possible, so, when it is down, and the hawk over it, the falconer has some raw beef ready minced, and lays it on the heron's back, or a pigeon, just killed, is sometimes used; the hawk devours it, and the heron, quite safe, as soon as it recovers from its fright, mounts slowly upward and returns to its heronry.'

Helen listened eagerly, and so did Lady Cecilia, who said, 'You know, Helen, our favourite Washington Irving quotes that in days of yore "a lady of rank did not think herself completely equipped in riding forth, unless she had her tassel – gentel held by jesses on her delicate hand." '

Before her words were well finished, Beauclerc had decided what he would do, and the business was half done that is well begun. He was at the library table, writing as fast as pen could go, to give *carte blanche* to a friend to secure for him immediately a whole hawking establishment which Warmsley had mentioned, and which was now upon public sale, or privately to be parted with by the present possessor.

At the very moment when Beauclerc was signing and sealing at one end of the room, at the other Horace Churchill, to whom something of the same plan had occurred, was charming Lady Cecilia Clarendon by hinting to her his scheme – anticipating the honour of seeing one of his hawks borne upon her delicate wrist.

Beauclerc, after despatching his letter, came up just in time to catch the sound and the sense, and took Horace aside to tell him what he had done. Horace looked vexed, and haughtily observed that he conceived his place at Erlesmede was better calculated for a hawking party than most places in England; and he had already announced his intentions to the ladies. The way was open to him – but Beauclerc did not see why he should recede; the same post might carry both their letters – both their orders.

'How far did your order go, may I ask?' said Churchill.

'*Carte blanche*.'

Churchill owned, with a sarcastic smile, that he was not prepared to go quite so far. He was not quite so young as Granville; he, unfortunately, had arrived at years of discretion – he said unfortunately; without ironical reservation, he protested from the bottom of his heart he considered it as a misfortune to have become that slow circumspect sort of creature which looks before it leaps. Even though this might save him from the fate of the man who was in Sicily, still he considered it as unfortunate to have lost so much of his natural enthusiasm.

'Natural enthusiasm!' Beauclerc could not help repeating to himself, and he went on his way. It must be confessed, as even Beauclerc's best friends allowed, that never was man of sense more subject to that kind of temporary derangement of the reasoning powers which results from being what is called bit by a fancy; he would then run on straight forward, without looking to the right or the left, in pursuit of his object, great or small. That hawking establishment now in view completely shut out, for the moment, all other objects; 'of tercels and of lures he talks'; and before his imagination were hawking scenes, and Helen with a hawk on her wrist, looking most graceful – a hawk of his own training it should be.

Then, how to train a hawk became the question. While he was waiting for the answer to his *carte blanche*, nothing better, or so good, could be done, as to make himself master of the whole business, and for this purpose he found it essential to consult every book on falconry that could be found in the library, and a great plague he became to everybody in the course of this book-hunt.

'What a bore!' Warmsley might be excused for muttering deep and low between the teeth. General Clarendon sighed and groaned. Lady Davenant bore and forbore philosophically – it was for Beauclerc; and to her great philosophy she gave all the credit of her indulgent partiality. Lady Cecilia, half-annoyed yet ever good-natured, carried her complaisance so far as to consult the catalogue and book-shelves sundry times in one hour; but she was not famous for patience, and she soon resigned him to a better friend – Helen, the most indefatigable of book-hunters. She had been well trained to it by her uncle; had been used to it all her life; and really took pleasure in the tiresome business. She assured Beauclerc it was not the least trouble, and he thought she looked beautiful when she said so. Whosoever of the male kind, young, and of ardent, not to say impatient, spirit, has ever been aided and abetted in a sudden whim, assisted, forwarded, above all, sympathised with, through all the changes and chances of a reigning fancy, may possibly conceive how charming, and more charming every hour, perhaps minutes, Helen became in Beauclerc's eyes. But, all in the way of friendship observe. Perfectly so – on her part, for she could not have another idea, and it was for this reason she was so much at her ease. He so understood it, and, thoroughly a gentleman, free from coxcombry, as he was, and interpreting the language and manners of women with instinctive delicacy, they went on delightfully. Churchill was on the watch, but he was not alarmed; all was so undisguised and frank, that now he began to feel assured that love on her side not only was, but ever would be, quite out of the question.

Beauclerc was, indeed, in the present instance, really and truly intent upon what he was about; and he pursued the History of Falconry, with all its episodes, from the olden time of the Boke of St Alban's down to the last number of the *Sporting Magazine*, including Colonel Thornton's latest flight, with the adventures of his red falcons, Miss M'Ghee and Lord Townsend; and his red tercels, Messrs Croc Franc and Craignon; – not forgetting that never-to-be-forgotten hawking of the Emperor Arambombamboberus with Trebizonian eagles, on the authority of a manuscript in the Grand Signior's library.

Beauclerc had such extraordinary dependence upon the sympathy of his friends, that, when he was reading anything that interested him, no matter what they might be doing, he must have their admiration for what charmed him. He brought his book to Lord Davenant, who was writing a letter. 'Listen, oh listen! to this pathetic lament of the falconer. – "Hawks, heretofore the pride of royalty, the insignia of nobility, the ambassador's present, the priest's indulgence, companion of the knight, and nursling of the gentle mistress, are now uncalled for and neglected."

'Ha! very well that,' said good-natured Lord Davenant, stopping his pen, dipping again, dotting, and going on.

Then Beauclerc passaged to Lady Davenant, and, interrupting her in Scoff's *Lives of the Novelists*, on which she was deeply intent, 'Allow me, my dear Lady Davenant, though you say you are no great topographer, to show you this, it is so curious; this royal falconer's proclamation – Henry the Eighth's – to preserve

his partridges, pheasants, and herons, from his palace at Westminster to St Giles's in the Fields, and from thence to Islington,
Hampstead, and Highgate, under penalty for every bird killed of
imprisonment, or whatever other punishment to his highness
may seem meet.'

Lady Davenant vouchsafed some suitable remark, consonant
to expectation, on the changes of times and places, and men
and manners, and then motioned the quarto away, with which
motion the quarto reluctantly complied; and then following Lady
Cecilia from window to window, as she *tended* her flowers, he
would insist upon her hearing the table of precedence for hawks.
She, who never cared for any table of precedence in her life, even
where the higher animals were concerned, would only undertake
to remember that the merlin was a lady's hawk, and this only
upon condition that she should have one to sit upon her wrist
like the fair ladies in Wouvermans' pictures. But further, as to
Peregrine, Gerfalcon, or Gerkin, she would hear nought of them,
nor could she listen, though Granville earnestly exhorted, to the
several good reasons which make a falcon dislike her master –

1st, If he speak rudely to her.

2nd, If he feed her carelessly.

Before he could get thirdly out, Lady Cecilia stopped him,
declaring that in all her life she never could listen to anything that
began with *first* and *secondly* – reasons especially.

Horace, meanwhile, looked superior down, and thought
with ineffable contempt of Beauclerc's little skill in the arts of
conversation, thus upon unwilling ears to squander anecdotes
which would have done him credit at some London dinner.
'What I could have made of them! and may make of them yet,'
thought he; 'but some there are, who never can contrive, as some
others cleverly do, to ride their hobby-horses to good purpose
and good effect; – now Beauclerc's hobbies, I plainly see, will
always run away with him headlong, cost him dear certainly, and
may be, leave him in the mire at last.'

What this fancy was to cost him, Beauclerc did not yet
know. Two or three passages in the *Sporting Magazine* had given

some hints of the expense of this 'most delectable of all country contentments,' which he had not thought it necessary to read aloud. And he knew that the late Lord Orford, an ardent pursuer of this 'royal and noble' sport, had expended one hundred a-year on every hawk he kept, each requiring a separate attendant, and being moreover indulged in an excursion to the Continent every season during moulting-time: but Beauclerc said to himself he had no notion of humouring his hawks to that degree; they should, aristocratic birds though they be, content themselves in England, and not pretend to 'damn the climate like a lord.' And he flattered himself that he should be able to pursue his fancy more cheaply than any of his predecessors; but as he had promised his guardian that, after the indulgence granted him in the Beltravers cause, he could not call upon him for any more extraordinary supplies, he resolved, in case the expense exceeded his ways and means, to sell his hunters, and so indulge in a new love at the expense of an old one.

The expected pleasure of the first day's hawking was now bright in his imagination; the day was named, the weather promised well, and the German cadgers and trainers who had been engaged, and who, along with the whole establishment, were handed over to Beauclerc, were to come down to Clarendon Park, and Beauclerc was very happy teaching the merlins to sit on Lady Cecilia's and on Miss Stanley's wrist. Helen's voice was found to be peculiarly agreeable to the hawk, who, as Beauclerc observed, loved, like Lear, that excellent thing in woman, a voice ever soft, gentle, and low.

The ladies were to wear some pretty dresses for the occasion, and all was gaiety and expectation; and Churchill was mortified, when he saw how well the thing was likely to take, that he was not to be the giver of the *fête*, especially as he observed that Helen was particularly pleased – when, to his inexpressible surprise, Granville Beauclerc came to him, a few days before that appointed for the hawking-party, and said that he had changed his mind, that he wished to get rid of the whole concern – that he should be really obliged to Churchill if he would take his engagement off his hands. The only reason that he gave was, that the establishment would altogether be more than he could afford, he found he had other calls for money, which were incompatible with his fancy, and therefore he would give it up.

Churchill obliged him most willingly by taking the whole upon himself, and he managed to do so in a very ingenious way, without incurring any preposterous expense. He was acquainted with a set of rich, fashionable young men, who had taken a sport-ing lodge in a neighbouring county, who desired no better than to accede to the terms proposed, and to distinguish themselves by giving a fête out of the common line, while Churchill, who understood, like a true man of the world, the worldly art of bar-gaining, contrived, with off-hand gentlemanlike jockeying, to have every point settled to his own convenience, and he was to be the giver of the entertainment to the ladies at Clarendon Park.

When this change in affairs was announced, Lady Cecilia, the General, Lady Davenant, and Helen, were all, in various degrees, surprised, and each tried to guess what could have been the cause of Beauclerc's sudden relinquishment of his purpose. He was – very extraordinary for him – impenetrable: he adhered to the words 'I found I could not afford it.' His guardian could not believe in this wonderful prudence, and was almost certain 'there must be some imprudence at the bottom of it all.'

Granville neither admitted nor repelled that accusation. Lady Cecilia worked away with perpetual little strokes, hoping to strike out the truth, but, as she said, you might as well have worked at an old flint. Nothing was elicited from him, even by Lady Davenant; nor did the collision of all their opinions throw any light upon the matter.

Meanwhile the day for the hawking-party arrived. Churchill gave the *fête*, and Beauclerc, as one of the guests, attended and enjoyed it without the least appearance even of disappointment; and, so far from envying Churchill, he assisted in remedying any little defects, and did all he could to make the whole go off well.

The party assembled on a rising round; a flag was displayed to give notice of the intended sport; the falconers appeared,

picturesque figures in their green jackets and their long gloves,
and their caps plumed with herons' feathers – some with the
birds on their wrists – one with the frame over his shoulder
upon which to set the hawk. *Set*, did we say? – no: '*cast* your hawk
on the perch' is, Beauclerc observed, the correct term; for, as
Horace sarcastically remarked, Mr Beauclerc might be detected as
a novice in the art by his over-exactness; his too correct, too attic,
pronunciation of the hawking language. But Granville readily
and gaily bore all this ridicule and raillery, sure that it would
neither stick nor stain, enjoying with all his heart the amusement
of the scene – the assembled ladies, the attendant cavaliers; the
hood-winked hawks, the ringing of their brass bells; the falconers
anxiously watching the clouds for the first appearance of the
bird; their skill in loosening the hoods, as, having but one hand
at liberty, they used their teeth to untie the string. And now the
hoods are off, and the hawks let fly.

They were to fly many casts of hawks this day: the first was
after a curlew; and the riding was so hard, so dangerous, from
the broken nature of the ground, that the ladies gave it up, and
were contented to view the sport from the eminence where they
remained.

And now there was a question to be decided among the
sportsmen as to the comparative rate of riding at a fox-chase, and
in 'the short, but terrifically hard gallop, with the eyes raised to
the clouds, which is necessary for the full enjoyment of hawking';
and then the gentlemen, returning, gathered round the ladies,
and the settling the point, watches in hand, and bets depending,
added to the interest of flight the first, and Churchill, master of
the revels, was in the highest spirits.

But presently the sky was overcast, the morning lowered, the
wind rose, and changed was Churchill's brow; there is no such
thing as hawking against the wind – that capricious wind!

'Curse the wind!' cried Churchill; 'and confusion seize the
fellow who says there is to be no more hawking today!'

The chief falconer, however, was a phlegmatic German,
and proper-behaved, as good falconers should be, who, as 'Old

Tristram's booke' has it, even if a bird should be lost, should never swear, and only say, '*Dieu soit loué*,'[1] and 'remember that the mother of hawks is not dead.'

But Horace, in the face of reason and in defiance of his German counsellors, insisted upon letting the hawks fly in this high wind; and it so fell out that, in the first place, all the terms he used in his haste and spleen were wrong; and in the next, that the quarry taking down the wind, the horsemen could not keep up with the hawks; the falconers in great alarm called to them by the names they gave them – 'Miss Didlington,' 'Lord Berners.' 'Ha! Miss Didlington's off; – off, with Blucher, and Lady Kirby, and Lord Berners, and all of 'em after her.' Miss Didlington flew fast and far, and farther still, till she and all the rest were fairly out of sight – lost, lost, lost!

'And as fine a cast of hawks they were as ever came from Germany!' – the falconers were in despair, and Churchill saw that the fault was his; and it looked so like cockney sportsmanship! If Horace had been in a towering rage, it would have been well enough; but he only grew pettish, snappish, waspish: now none of those words ending in *ish* become a gentleman; ladies always think so, and Lady Cecilia now thought so, and Helen thought so too, and Churchill saw it, and he grew pale instead of red, and that looks ugly in an angry man.

But Beauclerc excused him when he was out of hearing, and when others said he had been cross, and crosser than became the giver of a gala, Beauclerc pleaded well for him, that falconry has ever been known to be 'an extreme stirrer-up of the passions, being subject to mischances infinite.'

However, a cold and hot collation under the trees for some, and under a tent for others, set all to rights for the present. Champagne sparkled, and Horace pledged and was pledged, and all were gay; even the Germans at their own table, after their own fashion, with their Rhenish and their foaming ale, contrived to drown the recollection of the sad adventure of the truant hawks.

---

[1] God be praised

And when all were refreshed and renewed in mind and body, to the hawking they went again. For now that

The wind was laid, and all their fears asleep,

there was to be a baffle between heron and hawk, one of the finest sights that can be in all falconry.

'Look! look! Miss Stanley,' cried Granville; 'look! follow that high-flown hawk — that black speck in the clouds. Now! now! right over the heron; and now she will *canceleer* — turn on her wing, Miss Stanley, as she comes down, whirl round, and balance herself — *chanceler*. Now! now look! canceleering gloriously!'

But Helen at this instant recollected what Captain Warmsley had said of the fresh-killed pigeon, which the falconer in the nick of time is to lay upon the heron's back; and now, even as the canceleering was going on — three times most beautifully, Helen saw only the dove, the white dove, which that black-hearted German held, his great hand round the throat, just raised to wring it. 'Oh, Beauclerc, save it, save it!' cried Lady Cecilia and Helen at once.

Beauclerc sprang forward, and, had it been a tiger instead of a dove, would have done the same no doubt at that moment; the dove was saved, and the heron killed. If Helen was pleased, so was not the chief falconer, nor any of the falconers, the whole German council in combustion! and Horace Churchill deeming it 'rather extraordinary that any gentleman should so interfere with other gentlemen's hawks.'

Lady Cecilia stepped between them, and never stepped in vain. She drew a ring from her finger — a seal; it was the seal of peace — no great value — but a well-cut bird — a bird for the chief falconer — a guinea-hen, with its appropriate cry, its polite mono, 'Come back, come back'; and she gave it as a pledge that the ladies would come back another day, and see another hawking; and the gentlemen were pleased, and the aggrieved attendant falconers pacified by a promise of another heron from the heronry at Clarendon Park; and the clouded faces brightened, and 'she smoothed the raven down of darkness till it smiled,' whatever that may mean; but, as Milton said it, it must be sense as well as sound.

At all events, in plain prose, be it understood that everybody was satisfied, even Mr Churchill; for Beauclerc had repaired for him, just in time, an error which would have been a blot on his gallantry of the day. He had forgotten to have some of the pretty gray hairs plucked from the heron, to give to the ladies to ornament their bonnets, but Beauclerc had secured them for him, and also two or three of those much-valued, smooth, black feathers, from the head of the bird, which are so much prized that a plume of them is often set with pearls and diamonds. Horace presented these most gracefully to Lady Cecilia and Helen, and was charmed with Lady Cecilia's parting compliments, which finished with the words, 'Quite chivalrous.'

And so, after all the changes and chances of weather, wind, and humour, all ended well, and no one rued the hawking of this day.

CHAPTER 18

'BUT ALL THIS TIME,' said Lady Davenant, 'you have not told me whether you have, any of you, found out what changed Granville's mind about this falconry scheme – why he so suddenly gave up the whole to Mr Churchill. Such a point-blank weathercock turn of fancy in most young men would no more surprise me than the changes of those clouds in the sky, now shaped and now unshaped by the driving wind; but in Granville Beauclerc there is always some reason for apparent caprice, and the reason is so often ingeniously wrong that it amuses me to hear it; and even as a study in human nature, I am curious to know the simple fact.'

But no one could tell the simple fact, no one could guess his reason, and from him it never would have been known – never could have been found out, but from a mistake – from a letter of thanks coming to a wrong person.

One morning, when Helen was sitting in Lady Davenant's room with her, Lord Davenant came in, reading a letter, like one walking in his sleep.

'What is all this, my dear? Can you explain it to me? Some good action of yours, I suppose, for which I am to be thanked.'

Lady Davenant looked at the letter. She had nothing to do with the matter, she said; but, on second thoughts, exclaimed, 'This is Granville Beauclerc's doing, I am clear!'

The letter was from Count Polianski, one of the poor banished Poles; now poor, but who had been formerly master of a property estimated at about one hundred and sixty-five thousand *available individuals*. In attempting to increase the happiness and secure the liberty of these available individuals, the count had lost everything, and had been banished from his country – a man of high feeling as well as talents, and who had done all he could for that unhappy country, torn to pieces by demagogues from within and tyrants from without.

Lady Davenant now recollected that Beauclerc had learned from her all this, and had heard her regretting that the circumstances in which Lord Davenant was placed at this moment prevented the possibility of his affording this poor count assistance for numbers of his suffering fellow-countrymen who had been banished along with him, and who were now in London in the utmost distress. Lady Davenant remembered that she had been speaking to Granville on this subject the very day that he had abandoned his falconry project. 'Now I understand it all,' said she; 'and it is like all I know and all I have hoped of him. These hundreds a-year which he has settled on these wretched exiles are rather better disposed of in a noble national cause, than in pampering one set of birds that they may fly at another set.'

'And yet this is done,' said Lord Davenant, 'by one of the much-reviled high-bred English gentlemen – among whom, let the much-reviling low-bred English democrats say what they will, we find every day instances of subscription for public purposes from private benevolence, in a spirit of princely charity to be found only in our own dear England – " England with all her faults." '

'But this was a less ordinary sort of generosity of Granville's,' said Lady Davenant, – 'the giving up a new pleasure, a new whim with all its gloss fresh upon it, full and bright in his eye.'

'True,' said Lord Davenant; 'I never saw a strong-pulling fancy better thrown upon its haunches.'

The white dove, whose life Helen had saved, was brought home by Beauclerc, and was offered to her and accepted. Whether she had done a good or a bad action, by thus saving the life of a pigeon at the expense of a heron, may be doubted, and will be decided according to the several tastes of ladies and gentlemen for herons or doves. As Lady Davenant remarked, Helen's humanity (or dove-anity, as Churchill called it) was of that equivocal sort which is ready to destroy one creature to save another which may happen to be a greater favourite.

Be this as it may, the favourite had a friend upon the present occasion, and no less a friend than General Clarendon, who presented it with a marble basin, such as doves should drink out of, by right of long prescription.

The General feared, he said, 'that this vase might be a little too deep – dangerously perhaps – '

But Helen thought nothing could be altogether more perfect in taste and kindness – approving Beauclerc's kindness too – a remembrance of a day most agreeably spent.

Churchill, to whom she looked as she said the last words, with all becoming politeness bowed and accepted the compliment, but with a reserve of jealousy on the brow; and as he looked again at the dove, caressing and caressed, and then at the classic vase, he stood vexed, and to himself he said, –

'So this is the end of all my pains – hawking and all, "quite chivalrous"! Beauclerc carries off the honours and pleasures of the day, and his present and his dove are to be all in all. Yet still,' continued he to himself in more consolatory thought – 'she is so open in her very love for the bird, that it is plain she has not yet any love for the man. She would be somewhat more afraid to show it, delicate as she is. It is only friendship – honest friend-ship, on her side; and if her affections be not engaged somewhere else – she may be mine: if I please – if – I can bring myself fairly to propose – we shall see – shall think of it.'

And now he began to think of it seriously. Miss Stanley's indifference to him, and the unusual difficulty which he found in making any impression, stimulated him in an extraordinary degree. Helen now appeared to him even more beautiful than he had at first thought her – 'Those eyes that fix so softly,' thought he, 'those dark eyelashes – that blush coming and going so beauti-fully – and there is a timid grace in all her motions, with that fine figure too – and that high-bred turn of the neck! – altogether she is charming! and she will be thought so! – she must be mine!'

She would do credit to his taste; he thought she would, when she had a little more *usage du monde*, do the honours of his house well; and it would be delightful to train her! If he could but engage her affections, before she had seen more of the world, she might really love him for his own sake – and Churchill wished to be really loved, if possible, for his own sake; but of the reality of modern love he justly doubted, especially for a man of his fortune and his age; yet, with Helen's youth and innocence he began to think he had some chance of disinterested attachment, and he determined to bring out for her the higher powers of his mind – the better parts of his character.

One day Lady Davenant had been speaking of London conversation. 'So brilliant,' said she, 'so short-lived, as my friend Lady Emmeline K— once said, "London wit is like gas, which lights at a touch, and at a touch can be extinguished";' and Lady Davenant concluded with a compliment to him who was known to have this '*touch and go*' of good conversation to perfection.

Mr Churchill bowed to the compliment, but afterwards sighed, and it seemed an honest sigh from the bottom of his heart. Only Lady Davenant and Helen were in the room, and turning to Lady Davenant he said,

'If I have it, I have paid dearly for it, more than it is worth, much too dearly, by the sacrifice of higher powers; I might have been a very different person from what I am.'

Helen's attention was instantly fixed; but Lady Davenant suspected he was now only talking for effect. He saw what she thought – it was partly true, but not quite. He felt what he said at the moment; and besides, there is always a sincere pleasure in speaking of oneself when one can do it without exposing oneself to ridicule, and with a chance of obtaining real sympathy.

'It was my misfortune,' he said, 'to be spoiled, even in childhood, by my mother.'

As he pronounced the word 'mother,' either his own heart or Helen's eyes made him pause with a look of respectful tenderness. It was cruel of a son to blame the fond indulgence of a mother; but the fact was, she brought him too forward early as a child, fed him too much with that sweet dangerous fostering dew of praise. The child – the man – must suffer for it afterwards.

'True, very true,' said Lady Davenant; 'I quite agree with you.'

'I could do nothing without flattery,' continued he, pursuing the line of confession which he saw had fixed Lady Davenant's attention favourably. 'Unluckily, I came too early into possession of a large fortune, and into the London world, and I lapped the stream of prosperity as I ran, and it was sweet with flattery, intoxicating, and knew it, and yet could not forbear it. Then in a London life everything is too stimulating – over-exciting. If there are great advantages to men of science and literature in museums and public libraries, the more than *Avicenna* advantages of having books come at will, and ministering spirits in waiting on all your pursuits – there is too much of everything except time, and too little of that. The treasures are within our reach, but we cannot clutch; we have, but we cannot hold. We have neither leisure to be good nor to be great; who can think of living for posterity, when he can scarcely live for the day? and sufficient for the day are never the hours thereof. From want of time, and from the immense quantity that nevertheless must be known, comes the necessity, the unavoidable necessity, of being superficial.'

'Why should it be unavoidable necessity?' asked Lady Davenant.

'Because *should* waits upon *must*, in London always, if not elsewhere,' said Churchill.

'A conversation answer,' replied Lady Davenant.

'Yes, I allow it; it is even so, just so, and to such tricks, such playing upon words, do the bad habits of London conversation lead'; and Lady Davenant wondered at the courage of his candour, as he went on to speak of the petty jealousies, the paltry envy, the miserable selfish susceptibility generated by the daily competition of London society. Such dissensions, such squabbles – an ignoble but appropriate word – such deplorable, such scandalous squabbles among literary, and even among scientific men. 'And who,' continued he, 'who can hope to escape in such a tainted atmosphere – an atmosphere overloaded with life, peopled with myriads of little buzzing stinging vanities? It really requires the strength of Hercules, mind and body, to go through our labours, fashionable, political, *bel esprit*, altogether too much for mortal. In Parliament, in politics, in the tug of war, you see how the strongest minds fail, come to untimely – '

'Do not touch upon that subject,' cried Lady Davenant, suddenly agitated. Then, commanding herself, she calmly added – 'As you are not now, I think, in Parliament, it cannot affect you. What were you saying? – your health of mind and body, I think you said, you were sensible had been hurt by – '

'These straining, incessant competitions have hurt me. My health suffered first, then my temper. It was originally good, now, as you have seen, I am afraid' – glancing at Helen, who quickly looked down, 'I am afraid I am irritable.'

There was an awkward silence. Helen thought it was for Lady Davenant to speak; but Lady Davenant did not contradict Mr Churchill. Now, the not contradicting a person who is abusing himself is one of the most heinous offences to self-love that can be committed; and it often provokes false candour to pull off the mask and throw it in your face; but either Mr Horace Churchill's candour was true, or it was so well guarded at the moment that no such catastrophe occurred.

'Worse than this bad effect on my temper,' continued he, 'I feel that my whole mind has been deteriorated – my ambition dwindled to the shortest span – my thoughts contracted to the narrow view of mere effect; what would please at the dinner-table or at the clubs – what will be thought of me by this literary coterie, or in that fashionable boudoir. And for this *reputation de salon* I have sacrificed all hope of other reputation, all power of obtaining it, all hope of – ' (here he added a few words, murmured down to Lady Davenant's embroidery frame, yet still in such a tone that Helen could not help thinking he meant she should hear) – 'If I had a heart such as – ' he paused, and, as if struck with some agonising thought, he sighed deeply, and then added – 'but I have not a heart worth such acceptance, or I would make the offer.'

Helen was not sure what these words meant, but she now pitied him, and she admired his candour, which she thought was so far above the petty sort of character he had at first done himself the injustice to seem, and she seized the first opportunity to tell Beauclerc all Mr Churchill had said to Lady Davenant and to her, and of the impression it had made upon them both. Beauclerc had often discussed Mr Churchill's character with her, but she was disappointed when she saw that what she told made no agreeable impression on Beauclerc: at first he stood quite silent, and when she asked what he thought, he said – 'It's all very fine, very clever.'

'But it is all true,' said Helen. 'And I admire Mr Churchill's knowing the truth so well and telling it so candidly.'

'Everything Mr Churchill has said may be true – and yet I think the truth is not in him.'

'You are not usually so suspicious,' said Helen. 'If you had heard Mr Churchill's voice and emphasis, and seen his look and manner at the time, I think you could not have doubted him.'

The more eager she grew, the colder Mr Beauclerc became. 'Look and manner, and voice and emphasis,' said he, 'make a great impression, I know, on ladies.'

'But what is your reason, Mr Beauclerc, for disbelief? I have as yet only heard that you believe everything that Mr Churchill said was true, and yet that you do not believe in his truth,' said Helen, in a tone of raillery.

And many a time before had Beauclerc been the first to laugh when one of his own paradoxes stared him in the face; but now he was more out of countenance than amused, and he looked seriously about for reasons to reconcile his seeming self-contradiction.

'In the first place, all those allusions and those metaphorical expressions, which you have so wonderfully well remembered, and which no doubt were worth remembering, all those do not give the idea of a man who is really feeling in earnest, and speaking the plain truth about faults, for which, if he felt at all, he must be too much ashamed to talk in such a grand style; and to talk of them at all, except to most intimate friends, seems so unnatural, and quite out of character in a man who had expressed such horror of egotists, and who is so excessively circumspect in general.'

'Yes, but Mr Churchill's forgetting all his little habits of circumspection, and all fear of ridicule, is the best proof of his being quite in earnest – that all he said was from his heart.'

'I doubt whether he has any heart,' said Beauclerc.

'Poor man, he said – ', Helen began, and then recollecting the words, 'or I would make the offer,' she stopped short, afraid of the construction they might bear, and then, ashamed of her fear, she coloured deeply.

'Poor man, he said – ' repeated Beauclerc, fixing his eyes upon her; 'what did he say, may I ask?'

'No, – ' said Helen; 'I am not so sure that I distinctly heard or understood Mr Churchill.'

'Oh, if there was any mystery!' Beauclerc begged pardon.

And he went away very quickly. He did not touch upon the subject again, but Helen saw that he never forgot it and, by few words which she heard him say to Lady Davenant about his dislike to half-confidences, she knew he was displeased, and she thought he was wrong. She began to fear that his mistrust of Churchill arose from envy at his superior success in society; and, though she was anxious to preserve her newly-acquired good opinion of Churchill's candour, she did not like to lose her esteem for Beauclerc's generosity. Was it possible that he could be seriously hurt at the readiness with which Mr Churchill availed himself of any idea which Beauclerc threw out, and which he dressed up, and passed as his own? Perhaps this might be what he meant by 'the truth is not in him.' She remembered one day when she sat between him and Beauclerc, and when he did not seem to pay the least attention to what Mr Beauclerc was saying to her, yet, fully occupied as he had apparently been in talking for the company in general, he had through all heard Granville telling the Chinese fable of the 'Man in the Moon, whose business it is to knit together with an invisible silken cord those who are predestined for each other.' Presently, before the dessert was over, Helen found the 'Chinese Man in the Moon,' whom she thought she had all to herself, figuring at the other end of the table, and received with great applause. And was it possible that Beauclerc, with his abundant springs of genius, could grudge a drop thus stolen from him? but without any envy in the case, he was right in considering such theft, however petty, as a theft, and right in despising the meanness of the thief. Such meanness was strangely incompatible with Mr Churchill's frank confession of his own faults. Could that confession be only for effect?

Her admiration had been sometimes excited by a particular happiness of thought, beauty of expression, or melody of language, in Mr Churchill's conversation. Once Beauclerc had been speaking with enthusiasm of modern Greece, and his hopes that she might recover her ancient character; and Mr Churchill, as if admiring the enthusiasm, yet tempering it with better judgment, smiled, paused, and answered,

'But Greece is a dangerous field for a political speculator; the imagination produces an illusion resembling the beautiful appearances which are sometimes exhibited in the Sicilian straits; the reflected images of ancient Grecian glory pass in a rapid succession before the mental eye; and, delighted with the captivating forms of greatness and splendour, we forget for a moment that the scene is in reality a naked waste.'

Some people say they can distinguish between a written and a spoken style, but this depends a good deal on the art of the speaker. Churchill could give a colloquial tone to a ready-written sentence, and could speak it with an off-hand grace, a carelessness which defied all suspicions of preparation; and the look, the pause, and precipitation – each and all came in aid of the actor's power of perfecting the illusion. If you had heard and seen him, you would have believed that, in speaking this passage, the thought of the *Fata Morgana* rose in his mind at the instant, and that, seeing it pleased you, and pleased with it himself, encouraged by your look of intelligence, and borne along by your sympathy, the eloquent man followed his own idea with a happiness more than care, admirable in conversation. A few days afterwards, Helen was very much surprised to find her admired sentence word for word in a book, from which Churchill's card fell as she opened it.

Persons without a name Horace treated as barbarians who did not know the value of their gold; and he seemed to think that, if they chanced to possess rings and jewels, they might be plucked from them without remorse, and converted to better use by some lucky civilised adventurer. Yet in his most successful piracies he was always haunted by the fear of discovery, and he especially dreaded the acute perception of Lady Davenant; he thought she suspected his arts of appropriation, and he took the first convenient opportunity of sounding her opinion on this point.

'How I enjoy,' said he to Lady Cecilia, 'telling a good story to you, for you never ask if it is a fact. Now, in a good story, no one sticks to absolute fact; there must be some little embellishment. No one would send his own or his friend's story into the world without "putting a hat on its head, and a stick into his hand," ' Churchill triumphantly quoted; this time he did not steal.

'But,' said Lady Davenant, 'I find that even the pleasure I have in mere characteristic or humorous narration is heightened by my dependence on the truth – the character for truth – of the narrator.'

Not only Horace Churchill, but almost everybody present, except Helen, confessed that they could not agree with her. The character for truth of the story-teller had nothing to do with his story, unless it was *historique*, or that he was to swear to it.

'And even if it were *historique*,' cried Horace, buoyed up at the moment by the tide in his favour, and floating out farther than was prudent – 'and even if it were *historique*, how much pleasanter is graceful fiction than grim, rigid truth; and how much more amusing in my humble opinion!'

'Now,' said Lady Davenant, 'for instance, this book I am reading' – (it was Dumont's *Mémoires de Mirabeau*) – 'this book which I am reading gives me infinitely increased pleasure, from my certain knowledge, my perfect conviction, of the truth of the author. The self-evident nature of some of the facts would support themselves, you may say, in some instances; but my perceiving the scrupulous care he takes to say no more than what he knows to be true, my perfect reliance on the relater's private character for integrity, gives a zest to every anecdote he tells – a specific weight to every word of conversation which he repeats – appropriate value to every trait of wit or humour characteristic of the person he describes. Without such belief, the characters would not have to me, as they now have, all the power, and charm, and life, of nature and reality. They are all now valuable as records of individual varieties that have positively so existed. While the most brilliant writer could, by fiction, have produced an effect, valuable only as representing the general average of human nature, but adding nothing to our positive knowledge, to the data from which we can reason in future.'

Churchill understood Lady Davenant too well to stand quite unembarrassed as he listened; and when she went on to say how differently she should have felt in reading these memoirs if they had been written by Mirabeau himself; with all his brilliancy, all his talents, how inferior would have been her enjoyment as well as instruction; his shrinking conscience told him how this might all be applied to himself; yet, strange to say, though somewhat abashed, he was nevertheless flattered by the idea of a parallel between himself and Mirabeau. To *Mirabeauder* was no easy task; it was a certain road to notoriety, if not to honest fame.

But even in the better parts of his character, his liberality in money matters, his good-natured patronage of rising genius, the meanness of his mind broke out. There was a certain young poetess whom he had encouraged; she happened to be sister to Mr Mapletofft, Lord Davenant's secretary, and she had spoken with enthusiastic gratitude of Mr Churchill's kindness. She was going to publish a volume of Sonnets under Mr Churchill's patronage, and, as she happened to be now at some country town in the neighbourhood, he requested Lady Cecilia to allow him to introduce this young authoress to her. She was invited for a few days to Clarendon Park, and Mr Churchill was zealous to secure subscriptions for her and eager to lend the aid of his fashion and his literary reputation to bring forward the merits of her book. 'Indeed,' he whispered, 'he had given her some little help in the composition,' and all went well till, in an evil hour, Helen praised one of the sonnets rather too much – more, he thought, than she had praised another, which was his own. His jealousy awakened – he began to criticise his *protégée*'s poetry. Helen defended her admiration, and reminded him that he had himself recommended these lines to her attention.

'Well! – yes, I did say the best I could for the whole thing, and for her it is surprising – that is, I am anxious the publication should take. But if we come to compare – you know this cannot stand certain comparisons that might be made. Miss Stanley's own taste and judgment must perceive – when we talk of genius – that is quite out of the question, you know.'

Horace was so perplexed between his philanthropy and his jealousy, his desire to show the one and his incapability of concealing the other, that he became unintelligible; and Helen laughed, and told him that she could not now understand what his opinion really was. She was quite ready to agree with him, she said, if he would but agree with himself; this made him disagree still more with himself and unluckily with his better self, his benevolence quite gave way before his jealousy and ill-humour, and he vented it upon the book; and, instead of prophecies of its success, he now groaned over 'sad careless lines,' – 'passages that lead to nothing,' – 'similes that will not hold when you come to examine them.'

Helen pointed out the dedication, a pretty, happy thought.

Horace smiled, and confessed that was his own.

What! in the dedication to himself? – and in the blindness of his vanity he did not immediately see the absurdity.

The more he felt himself in the wrong, of course the more angry he grew, and it finished by his renouncing the dedication altogether, declaring he would have none of it. The book and the lady might find a better patron.

There are things which no man of real generosity could say or do, or think, put him in ever so great a passion. He would not be harsh to an inferior – a woman – a *protégée* on whom he had conferred obligations; but Mr Churchill was harsh – he showed neither generosity nor feeling; and Helen's good opinion of him sank to rise no more.

Of this, however, he had not enough of the sympathy or penetration of feeling to be aware.

CHAPTER 19

THE PARTY NOW at Clarendon Park consisted chiefly of young
people. Among them were two cousins of Lady Cecilia's, whom
Helen had known at Cecilhurst before they went abroad, while
she was still almost a child. Lady Katrine Hawksby, the elder,
was several years older than Cecilia. When Helen last saw her,
she was tolerably well-looking, very fashionable, and remarkable for high spirits, with a love for *quizzing*, and for all that is
vulgarly called *fun*, and a talent for ridicule, which she indulged
at everybody's expense. She had always amused Cecilia, who
thought her more diverting than really ill-natured; but Helen
thought her more ill-natured than diverting, never liked her,
and had her own private reasons for thinking that she was
no good friend to Cecilia: but now, in consequence either of
the wear and tear of London life, or of a disappointment in
love or matrimony, she had lost the fresh plumpness of youth;
and gone too was that spirit of mirth, if not of good humour,
which used to enliven her countenance. Thin and sallow, the
sharp features remained, and the sarcastic without the arch
expression; still she had a very fashionable air. Her pretensions
to youth, as her dress showed, were not gone; and her hope of
matrimony, though declining, not set. Her many-years-younger
sister, Louisa, now Lady Castlefort, was beautiful. As a girl she
had been the most sentimental, refined, delicate creature conceivable; always talking poetry – and so romantic – with such
a soft, sweet, die-away voice – lips apart – and such fine eyes,
that could so ecstatically turn up to heaven, or be so cast down,

charmingly fixed in contemplation: – and now she is married, just the same. There she is, established in the library at Clarendon Park, with the most sentimental fashionable novel of the day, beautifully bound, on the little rosewood table beside her, and a manuscript poem, a great secret, 'Love's Last Sigh,' in her bag with her smelling-bottle and embroidered handkerchief and on that beautiful arm she leaned so gracefully, with her soft languishing expression; so perfectly dressed too – handsomer than ever.

Helen was curious to know what sort of man Lady Louisa had married, for she recollected that no hero of any novel that ever was read, or talked of, came up to her idea of what a hero ought to be, of what a man must be, whom she could ever think of loving. Cecilia told Helen that she had seen Lord Castlefort, but that he was not Lord Castlefort, or likely to be Lord Castlefort, at that time; and she bade her guess, among all she could recollect having ever seen at Cecilhurst, who the man of Louisa's choice could be. Lady Katrine, with infinite forbearance, smiled, and gave no hint, while Helen guessed and guessed in vain. She was astonished when she saw him come into the room. He was a little deformed man, for whom Lady Louisa had always expressed to her companions a peculiar abhorrence. He had that look of conceit which unfortunately sometimes accompanies personal deformity, and which disgusts even Pity's self. Lord Castlefort was said to have declared himself made for love and fighting! Helen remembered that kind-hearted Cecilia had often remonstrated for humanity's sake, and stopped the quizzing which used to go on in their private coteries, when the satirical elder sister would have it that *le petit bossu*[1] was in love with Louisa.

But what *could* make her marry him? Was there anything within to make amends for the exterior? Nothing – nothing that could 'rid him of the lump behind.' But superior to the metamorphoses of love, or of fairy tale, are the metamorphoses of fortune. Fortune had suddenly advanced him to uncounted

[1] the little hunchback

thousands and a title, and no longer *le petit bossu*, Lord Castle-fort obtained the fair hand, the very fair hand, of Lady Louisa Hawksby, more lovely than a fairy!

Still Helen could not believe that Louisa had married him voluntarily; but Lady Cecilia assured her that it was voluntarily, quite voluntarily. 'You could not have so doubted had you seen the *trousseau* and the wedding gifts, for you know, " The **present** makes one forget the future."

Helen could scarcely smile.

'But Louisa had feeling – really some,' continued Lady Cecilia; 'but she could not afford to follow it. She had got into such debt, I really do not know what she would have done if Lord Castlefort had not proposed; but she has some little heart, and I could tell you a secret; but no, I will leave you the pleasure of finding it out.'

'It will be no pleasure to me,' said Helen.

'I never saw anybody so out of spirits,' said Lady Cecilia, laughing, 'at another's unfortunate marriage, which all the time she thinks very fortunate. She is quite happy, and even Katrine does not laugh at him any longer, it is to be supposed; it is no laughing matter now.'

'No indeed,' said Helen.

'Nor a crying matter either,' said Cecilia. 'Do not look shocked at me, my dear, I did not do it; but so many do, and I have seen it so often, that I cannot wonder with such a foolish face of blame – I do believe, my dear Helen, that you are envious because Louisa is married before you! for shame, my love! Envy is a naughty passion, you know our Madame Bonne used to say; but here's mamma, now talk to her about Louisa Castlefort, pray.'

Lady Davenant took the matter with great coolness, was neither shocked nor surprised at this match, she had known so many worse; Lord Castlefort, as well as she recollected, was easy enough to live with. 'And after all,' said she, 'it is better than what we see every day, the fairest of the fair knowingly, willingly, giving themselves to the most profligate of the profligate. In short, the market is so overstocked with accomplished young ladies on the one hand, and on the other men find wives and establishments

so expensive, clubs so cheap and so much more luxurious than
any home, liberty not only so sweet but so fashionable, that their
policy, their maxim, is, "Marry not at all, or if marriage be ultimately necessary to pay debts and leave heirs to good names,
marry as late as possible"; and thus the two parties with their
opposite interests stand at bay, or try to outwit or outbargain
each other. And if you wish for the moral of the whole affair,
here it is: from the vulgar nursery-maids, with their broad sense
and bad English, and the good or bad French of the governess,
to the elegant innuendo of the drawing-room, all is working to
the same effect; dancing-masters, music-masters, and all the tribe,
what is it all for, but to prepare young ladies for the grand event;
and to raise in them, besides the natural, a factitious, an abstract
idea of good in being married? Every girl in these days is early
impressed with the idea that she must be married, that she cannot
be happy unmarried. Here is an example of what I meant the
other day by strength of mind; it requires some strength of mind
to be superior to such a foolish, vain, and vulgar belief.'

'It will require no great strength of mind in me,' said Helen,
'for I really never have formed such notions. They never were
early put into my head; my uncle always said a woman might be
very happy unmarried. I do not think I shall ever be seized with
a terror of dying an old maid.'

'You are not come to the time yet, my dear,' said Lady Davenant, smiling. 'Look at Lady Katrine; strength of mind on this
one subject would have saved her from being a prey to envy, and
jealousy, and all the vulture passions of the mind.

'In the old French *régime*,' continued Lady Davenant, 'the
young women were at least married safely out of their convents;
but our young ladies, with their heads full of high-flown poetry
and sentimental novels, are taken out into the world before marriage, expected to see and not to choose, shown the most agreeable, and expected, doomed, to many the most odious. But in
all these marriages for establishments the wives who have least
feelings are not only likely to be the happiest, but also most likely
to conduct themselves well. In the first place, they do not begin

with falsehood. If they have no hearts, they cannot pretend to give any to the husband, and that is better than having given them to somebody else. Husband and wife, in this case, clearly understand the terms of agreement, expect, imagine no more than they have, and jog-trot they go on together to the end of life very comfortably.'

'Comfortably!' exclaimed Helen, 'it must be most miserable.'

'Not most miserable, Helen,' said Lady Davenant; 'keep your pity for others; keep your sighs for those who need them – for the heart which no longer dares to utter a sigh for itself, the faint heart that dares to love, but dares not abide by its choice. Such infatuated creatures, with the roots of feeling left aching within them, must take what opiates they can find; and in after-life, through all their married existence, their prayer must be for indifference, and thankful may they be if that prayer is granted.'

These words recurred to Helen that evening, when Lady Castlefort sang some tender and passionate airs; played on the harp with a true Saint Cecilia air and attitude; and at last, with charming voice and touching expression, sang her favourite – 'Too late for redress.'

Both Mr Churchill and Beauclerc were among the group of gentlemen; neither was a stranger to her. Mr Churchill admired and applauded as a connoisseur. Beauclerc listened in silence. Mr Churchill entreated for more – more – and named several of his favourite Italian airs. Her ladyship really could not. But the slightest indication of a wish from Beauclerc was, without turning towards him, heard and attended to, as her sister failed not to remark and to make others remark.

Seizing a convenient pause while Mr Churchill was searching for some masterpiece, Lady Katrine congratulated her sister on having recovered her voice, and declared that she had never heard her play or sing since she was married till tonight.

'You may consider it as a very particular compliment, I assure you,' continued she, addressing herself so particularly to Mr Beauclerc that he could not help being a little out of countenance, – 'I have so begged and prayed, but she was never in voice or humour, or heart, or something. Yesterday, even Castlefort was almost on his knees for a song, – were not you, Lord Castlefort?'

Lord Castlefort pinched his pointed chin, and casting up an angry look, replied in a dissonant voice, – 'I do not remember!'

'*Tout voir, tout entendre, tout oublier,*'[1] whispered Lady Katrine to Mr Churchill, as she stooped to assist him in the search for a music-book – '*Tout voir, tout entendre, tout oublier*, should be the motto adopted by all married people.'

Lady Castlefort seemed distressed, and turned over the leaves in such a flutter that she could not find anything, and she rose, in spite of all entreaties, leaving the place to her sister, who was, she said, 'so much better a musician and not so foolishly nervous.' Lady Castlefort said her 'voice always went away when she was at all – '

There it ended as far as words went; but she sighed, and retired so gracefully that all the gentlemen pitied her.

There is one moment in which ill-nature sincerely repents – the moment when it sees pity felt for its victim.

Horace followed Lady Castlefort to the ottoman, on which she sank. Beauclerc remained leaning on the back of Lady Katrine's chair, but without seeming to hear what she said or sang. After some time Mr Churchill, not finding his attentions well received, or weary of paying them, quitted Lady Castlefort, but sat down by Helen; and in a voice to be heard by her, but by no one else, he said –

'What a relief! – I thought I should never get away!' then, favoured by a loud bravura of Lady Katrine's, he went on – 'That beauty, between you and me, is something of a bore – she – I don't mean the lady who is now screaming – she should always sing. Heaven blessed her with song, not sense – but here one is made so fastidious!'

He sighed, and for some minutes seemed to be given up to the duet which Lady Katrine and an officer were performing; and then exclaimed, but so that Helen only could hear, – 'Merciful Heaven! how often one wishes one had no ears: that Captain Jones

[1] see all, hear all, forget all

must be the son of Stentor, and that lady! – if angels sometimes saw themselves in a looking-glass when singing – there would be peace upon earth.'

Helen, not liking to be the secret receiver of his contraband good things, was rising to change her place, when, softly detaining her, he said, 'Do not be afraid, no danger – trust me, for I have studied under Talma.'

'What can you mean?'

'I mean,' continued he, 'that Talma taught me the secret of his dying scenes – how every syllable of his dying words might be heard to the farthest part of the audience; and I – give me credit for my ingenuity – know how, by reversing the art, to be perfectly inaudible at ten paces' distance, and yet, I trust, perfectly intelligible, always, to you.'

Helen now rose decidedly, and retreated to a table at the other side of the room, and turned over some books that lay there – she took up a volume of the novel Lady Castlefort had been reading – *Love unquestionable*. She was surprised to find it instantly, gently, but decidedly drawn from her hand: she looked up – it was Beauclerc.

'I beg your pardon, Miss Stanley, but – '

'Thank you! thank you!' said Helen; 'you need not beg my pardon!'

This was the first time Beauclerc had spoken in his friendly, cordial, natural manner, to her, since their incomprehensible misunderstanding. She was heartily glad it was over, and that he was come to himself again. And now they conversed very happily together for some time; thought what they said might not be particularly worth recording. Lady Katrine was at Helen's elbow before she perceived her 'looking for her sac'; and Lady Castlefort came for her third volume, and gliding off, wished to all, '*Felice, felicissima notte.*'

Neither of these sisters had ever liked Helen; she was too true for the one, and too good-natured for the other. Lady Katrine had always, even when she was quite a child, been jealous of Lady Cecilia's affection for Helen; and now her indignation and disappointment were great at finding her established at Clarendon Park – to live with the Clarendons, to *go out* with Lady Cecilia. Now, it had been the plan of both sisters that Lady Katrine's present visit should be eternal. How they would ever have managed to fasten her ladyship upon the General, even if Helen had been out of the question, need not now be considered. Their disappointment and dislike to Helen were as great as if she had been the only obstacle to the fulfilment of their scheme.

These two sisters had never agreed –

– Doom'd by Fate
To live in all the elegance of hate;

and since Lady Castlefort's marriage, the younger, the beautiful, being now the successful lady of the ascendant, the elder writhed in all the combined miseries of jealousy and dependence, and an everyday lessening chance of bettering her condition. Lord Castlefort, too, for good reasons of his own, well remembered, detested Lady Katrine, and longed to shake her off. In this wish, at least, husband and wife united; but Lady Castlefort had no decent excuse for her ardent impatience to get rid of her sister. She had magnificent houses in town and country, ample room everywhere – but in her heart. She had the smallest heart conceivable, and the coldest; but had it been ever so large, or ever so warm, Lady Katrine was surely not the person to get into it, or into any heart, male or female: there was the despair. 'If Katrine was but married – Mr Churchill, suppose?'

Faint was the *suppose* in Lady Castlefort's imagination. Not so the hope which rose in Lady Katrine's mind the moment she saw him here. 'How fortunate!' Her ladyship had now come to that no particular age, when a remarkable metaphysical phenomenon occurs; on one particular subject hope increases as all probability of success decreases. This aberration of intellect is usually observed to be greatest in very clever women; while Mr Churchill, the flattered object of her present hope, knew how to manage with great innocence and modesty, and draw her on to overt acts of what is called flirtation.

Rousseau says that a man is always awkward and miserable when placed between two women to whom he is making love. But Rousseau had never seen Mr Churchill, and had but an imperfect idea of the dexterity, the ambiguity, that in our days can be successfully practised by an accomplished male coquette. Absolutely to blind female jealousy may be beyond his utmost skill; but it is easy, as every day's practice shows, to keep female vanity pleasantly perplexed by ocular deception – to make her believe that what she really sees she does not see, and that what is unreal is reality; to make her, to the amusement of the spectators, continually stretch out her hand to snatch the visionary good that for ever eludes her grasp, or changes, on near approach, to grinning mockery.

This delightful game was now commenced with Lady Katrine, and if Helen could be brought to take a snatch, it would infinitely increase the interest and amusement of the on-lookers. Of this, however, there seemed little chance; but the evil eye of envy was set upon her, and the demon of jealousy was longing to work her woe.

Lady Castlefort saw with scornful astonishment that Mr Beauclerc's eyes, sometimes when she was speaking, or when she was singing, would stray to that part of the room where Miss Stanley might be; and when she was speaking to him, he was wonderfully absent. Her ladyship rallied him, while Lady Katrine, looking on, cleared her throat in her horrid way, and longed for an opportunity to discomfit Helen, which supreme pleasure her ladyship promised herself upon the first convenient occasion, – convenient meaning when Lady Davenant was out of the room; for Lady Katrine, though urged by prompting jealousy, dared not attack her when under cover of that protection. For long habit, even her sarcastic nature stood in awe of a certain power of moral indignation, which had at times flashed upon her, and of which she had a sort of superstitious dread, as of an incomprehensible, incalculable power.

But temper will get the better of all prudence. Piqued by some little preference which Lady Cecilia had shown to Helen's taste in the choice of the colour of a dress, an occasion offered of signalising her revenge, which could not be resisted. It was a question to be publicly decided, whether blue, green, or white should be adopted for the ladies' uniforms at an approaching *fête*. She was deputed to collect the votes. All the company were assembled; Lady Davenant, out of the circle, as it was a matter that concerned her not, was talking to the gentlemen apart.

Lady Katrine went round canvassing. 'Blue, green, or white? say blue, *pray*.' But when she came to Helen, she made a full stop, asked no question – preferred no prayer, but after fixing attention by her pause, said, 'I need not ask Miss Stanley's vote or opinion, as I know my cousin's, and with Miss Stanley it is always, "I say ditto to Lady Cecilia"; therefore, to save trouble, I always count two for Cecilia – one for herself and one for her *double*.'

'Right, Lady Katrine Hawksby,' cried a voice from afar, which made her start; 'you are quite right to consider Helen Stanley as my daughter's double, for my daughter loves and esteems her as her second self – her better self. In this sense Helen is Lady Cecilia's double, but if you mean – '

'Bless me! I don't know what I meant, I declare. I could not have conceived that Lady Davenant – Miss Stanley, I beg a thousand million of pardons.'

Helen, with anxious good-nature, pardoned before she was asked, and hastened to pass on to the business of the day, but Lady Davenant would not so let it pass; her eye still fixed, she pursued the quailing enemy – 'One word more. In justice to my daughter, I must say her love has not been won by flattery, as none knows better than the Lady Katrine Hawksby.'

The unkindest cut of all, and on the tenderest part. Lady Katrine could not stand it. Conscious and trembling, she broke through the circle, fled into the conservatory, and closing the doors behind her, would not be followed by Helen, Cecilia, or anybody.

Lady Castlefort sighed, and first breaking the silence that ensued, said, ' 'Tis such a pity that Katrine will always so let her wit run away with her – it brings her so continually into – For my part, in all humility, I must confess, I can't help thinking that, what, with its being unfeminine, and altogether so incompatible with what in general is thought amiable – I cannot but consider wit in a woman as a real misfortune. What say the gentlemen? they must decide, gentlemen being always the best judges.'

With an appealing tone of interrogation she gracefully looked up to the gentlemen; and after a glance towards Granville Beauclerc, unluckily unnoticed or unanswered, her eyes expected reply from Horace Churchill. He, well feeling the predicament in which he stood, between a fool and a *femme d'esprit*,[1] answered, with his ambiguous smile, 'that no doubt it was a great misfortune to have "*plus d'esprit qu'on ne sait mêner.*" '[2]

'This is a misfortune,' said Lady Davenant, 'that may be deplored for a great genius once in an age, but is really rather of uncommon occurrence. People complain of wit where, nine times in ten, poor wit is quite innocent; but such is the consequence of having kept bad company. Wit and ill-nature having been too often found together, when we see one we expect the other; and such an inseparable false association has been formed, that half the world would take it for granted that there is wit if they do but see ill-nature.'

At this moment Mr Mapletofft, the secretary, entered with his face full of care, and his hands full of papers. Lady Katrine needed not to feign or feel any further apprehensions of Lady Davenant; for, an hour afterwards, it was announced that Lord and Lady Davenant were obliged to set off for town immediately. In the midst of her hurried preparations Lady Davenant had found a moment to comfort Helen with the assurance that, whatever happened, she would see her again. It might end in Lord Davenant's embassy being given up. At all events she would see her again – she hoped in a few weeks, perhaps in a few days. 'So no leave-takings, my dear child, and no tears – it is best as it is. On my return let me find – '

'Lord Davenant's waiting, my lady,' and she hurried away.

---

[1] woman of wit [2] more wit than she knows what to do with

CHAPTER 20

ABSENT OR PRESENT, the guardian influence of a superior friend is one of the greatest blessings on earth, and after Lady Davenant's departure Helen was so full of all she had said to her, and of all that she would approve or disapprove, that every action, almost every thought, was under the influence of her friend's mind. Continually she questioned her motives as well as examined her actions, and she could not but condemn some of her conduct, or if not her conduct, her manner, towards Horace Churchill; she had been flattered by his admiration, and had permitted his attentions more than she ought, when her own mind was perfectly made up as to his character. Ever since the affair of the poetess, she had been convinced that she could never make the happiness or redeem the character of one so mean.

According to the ladies' code, a woman is never to understand that a gentleman's attentions mean anything more than common civility; she is supposed never to see his mind, however he may make it visible, till he declares it in words. But, as Helen could not help understanding his manner, she thought it was but fair to make him understand her by her manner. She was certain that if he were once completely convinced, not only that he had not made any impression, but that he never could make any impressions, on her heart, his pursuit would cease. His vanity, mortified, might revenge itself upon her, perhaps; but this was a danger which she thought she ought to brave; and now she resolved to be quite sincere, as she said to herself, at whatever hazard (probably meaning at the hazard of displeasing Cecilia) she would make her own sentiments clear, and put an end to Mr Churchill's ambiguous conduct: and this should be done on the very first opportunity.

An opportunity soon occurred – Horace had a beautiful little topaz ring with which Lady Katrine Hawksby fell into raptures; such a charming device! – Cupid and Momus making the world their plaything.

It was evident that Lady Katrine expected that the seal should be presented to her. Besides being extravagantly fond of baubles, she desired to have this homage from Horace. To her surprise and mortification, however, he was only quite flattered by her approving of his taste: – it was his favourite seal, and so 'he kept the topaz, and the rogue was bit.'

Lady Katrine was the more mortified by this failure, because it was witnessed by many of the company, among whom, when she looked round, she detected smiles of provoking intelligence. Soon afterwards the dressing-bell rang and she quitted the room; one after another every one dropped off, except Helen, who was finishing a letter, and Horace, who stood on the hearth playing with his seal. When she came to sealing-time, he approached and besought her to honour him by the acceptance of this little seal. 'If he could obliterate Momus – if he could leave only Cupid, it would be more appropriate. But it was a device invented for him by a French friend, and he hoped she would pardon his folly, and think only of his love!'

This was said so that it might pass either for mere jest or for earnest; his look expressed very sentimental love, and Helen seized the moment to explain herself decidedly.

It was a surprise – a great surprise – to Mr Churchill, a severe disappointment, not only to his vanity, but to his heart, for he had one. It was some comfort, however, that he had not quite committed himself, and he recovered – even in the moment of disappointment he recovered himself time enough dexterously to turn the tables upon Helen.

He thanked her for her candour – for her great care of his happiness, in anticipating a danger which might have been so fatal to him; but he really was not aware that he had said anything which required so serious an answer.

Afterwards he amused himself with Lady Katrine at Miss Stanley's expense, representing himself as in the most pitiable case of Rejected Addresses – rejected before he had offered. He had only been guilty of Folly, and he was brought in guilty of Love.

Poor Helen had to endure not only this persiflage, which was soon made to reach her ear, but also the reproaches of Lady Cecilia, who said, 'I should have warned you, Helen, not to irritate that man's relentless vanity; now you see the consequences.'

'But, after all, what harm can he do me?' thought Helen. 'It is very disagreeable to be laughed at, but still my conscience is satisfied, and that is a happiness that will last; all the rest will soon be over. I am sure I did the thing awkwardly, but I am glad it is done.'

Mr Churchill soon afterwards received an invitation – a command to join a royal party now at some watering-place; an illustrious person could not live another day without Horace *le désiré*. He showed the note, and acted despair at being compelled to go, and then he departed. To the splendid party he went, and drowned all recollections of whatever love he had felt in the fresh intoxication of vanity – a diurnal stimulus which, however degrading, and he did feel it degrading, was now become necessary to his existence.

His departure from Clarendon Park was openly regretted by Lady Cecilia, while Lady Katrine secretly mourned over the downfall of her projects, and Beauclerc attempted not to disguise his satisfaction.

He was all life and love, and would then certainly have declared his passion, but for an extraordinary change which now appeared in Helen's manner towards him. It seemed unaccountable; it could not be absolute caprice, she did not even treat him as a friend, and she evidently avoided explanation. He thought, and thought, and came as near the truth without touching it as possible. He concluded that she had understood his joy at Churchill's departure; that she now clearly perceived his attachment; and was determined against him. Not having the slightest idea that she considered him as a married man, he could not even guess the nature of her feelings.

And all the time Helen did not well understand herself; she began to be extremely alarmed at her own feelings – to dread that there was something not quite right. This dread, which had come and gone by fits, – this doubt as to her own sentiments, – was first excited by the death of her dove – Beauclerc's gift. The poor dove was found one morning drowned in the marble vase in which it went to drink. Helen was very sorry – that was surely natural; but she was wonderfully concerned. Lady Katrine scoffingly said, and before everybody, before Beauclerc, worse than all, her ladyship represented to the best of her ability the attitude in which she had found Helen mourning over her misfortune, the dove in her hand pressed close to her bosom – 'And in tears – absolutely.' She would swear to the tears.

Helen blushed, tried to laugh, and acknowledged it was very foolish. Well, that passed off as only foolish, and she did not at first feel that it was a thing much to be ashamed of in any other way. But she was sorry that Beauclerc was by when Lady Katrine mimicked her; most sorry that he should think her foolish. But then did he? His looks expressed tenderness. He was very tender-hearted. Really manly men always are so; and so she observed to Lady Cecilia. Lady Katrine heard the observation, and smiled – her odious smile – implying more than words could say. Helen was not quite clear, however, what it meant to say.

Some days afterwards Lady Katrine took up a book, in which Helen's name was written in Beauclerc's hand. '*Gage d'amitié?*'[1] said her ladyship; and she walked up and down the room, humming the air of an old French song; interrupting herself now and then to ask her sister if she could recollect the words. 'The *refrain*, if I remember right, is something like this –

"Sous le nom d'amitié – sous le nom d'amitié,
   La moitié du monde trompe l'autre moitié,
   Sous le nom, sous le nom, sous le nom d'amitié.[2]

[1] token of friendship   [2] Under the name of friendship – under the name of friendship, Half the world deceives the other half, under the name etc

And it ends with

> "Sous le nom d'amitié, Damon, je vous adore, [1]
>   Sous le nom d'amitié – sous le nom d'amitié."

Miss Stanley, do you know that song?' concluded her malicious ladyship.

No – Miss Stanley had never heard it before; but the marked emphasis with which Lady Katrine sang and looked made Helen clear that she meant to apply the words tauntingly to herself and Beauclerc, – but which of them her ladyship suspected was cheating, or cheated, '*sous le nom d'amitié*,' she did not know. All was confusion in her mind. After a moment's cooler reflecting, however, she was certain it could not be Beauclerc who was to blame – it must be herself, and she now very much wished that everybody, and Lady Katrine in particular, should know that Mr Beauclerc was engaged – almost married; if this were but known, it would put an end to all such imputations.

The first time she could speak to Cecilia on the subject, she begged to know how soon Mr Beauclerc's engagement would be declared. Lady Cecilia slightly answered she could not tell – and when Helen pressed the question she asked, –

'Why are you so anxious, Helen?'

Helen honestly told her, and Lady Cecilia only laughed at her for minding what Lady Katrine said, – 'When you know yourself, Helen, how it is, what can it signify what mistakes others may make?'

But Helen grew more and more uneasy, for she was not clear that she did know how it was, with herself at least. Her conscience faltered, and she was not sure whether she was alarmed with or without reason. She began to compare feelings that she had read of, and feelings that she had seen in others, and feelings that were new to herself, and in this maze and mist nothing was distinct – much was magnified – all alarming.

One day Beauclerc was within view of the windows on horseback, on a very spirited horse, which he managed admirably;

---

[1] Under the name of friendship, Damon, I adore you

but a shot fired suddenly in an adjoining preserve so startled the horse that it – oh! what it did Helen did not see, she was so terrified: and why was she so much terrified? She excused herself by saying it was natural to be frightened for any human creature. But, on the other hand, Tom Isdall was a human creature, and she had seen him last week actually thrown from his horse, and had not felt much concern. But then he was not a friend; and he fell into a soft ditch: and there was something ridiculous in it which prevented people from caring about it.

With such nice casuistry she went on pretty well; and besides, she was so innocent, so ignorant, that it was easy for her to be deceived. She went on, telling herself that she loved Beauclerc as a brother – as she loved the General. But when she came to comparisons, she could not but perceive a distinction. Her heart never bounded on the General's appearance, let him appear ever so suddenly, as it did one day when Beauclerc returned unexpectedly from Old Forest. Her whole existence seemed so altered by his approach, his presence, or his absence. Why was this? Was there anything wrong in it? She had nobody whose judgment she could consult – nobody to whom she could venture to describe her feelings, or lay open her doubts and scruples. Lady Cecilia would only laugh; and she could not quite trust either her judgment or her sincerity, though she knew her affection. Besides, after what Cecilia had said of her being safe; after all she had told her of Beauclerc's engagement, how astonished and shocked Cecilia would be!

Then Helen resolved that she would keep a strict watch over herself, and repress all emotion, and be severe with her own mind to the utmost; and it was upon this resolution that she had changed her manner, without knowing how much, towards Beauclerc; she was certain he meant nothing but friendship. It was her fault if she felt too much pleasure in his company; the same things were, as she wisely argued, right or wrong according to the intention with which they were said, done, looked, or felt. Rigidly she inflicted on herself the penance of avoiding his delightful society, and to make sure that she did not try to attract, she repelled him with all her power – though she never could make herself cold, and stiff, and disagreeable enough to satisfy her conscience.

Then she grew frightened at Beauclerc's looks of astonishment – feared he would ask explanation – avoided him more and more. Then, on the other hand, she feared he might guess and interpret *wrong*, or rather *right*, this change; and back she changed, tried in vain to keep the just medium – she had lost the power of measuring – altogether she was very unhappy, and so was Beauclerc; he found her incomprehensible, and thought her capricious. His own mind was fluttered with love, so that he could not see or judge distinctly, else he might have seen the truth; and sometimes, though free from conceit, he did hope it might be all love. But why then so determined to discourage him? he had advanced sufficiently to mark his intentions, she could not doubt his sincerity. He would see farther before he ventured farther. He thought a man was a fool who proposed before he had tolerable reason to believe he should not be refused.

Lord Beltravers and his sisters were now expected at Old Forest immediately, and Beauclerc went thither early every morning, to press forward the preparations for the arrival of the family, and he seldom returned till dinner-time; and every evening Lady Castlefort contrived to take possession of him. It appeared to be indeed as much against his will as it could be between a well-bred man and a high-bred belle; but to do her bidding seemed, if not a moral, at least a polite necessity. She had been spoiled, she owned, by foreign attentions, not French, for that is all gone now at Paris, but Italian manners, which she so much preferred. She did not know how she could live out of Italy, and she must convince Lord Castlefort that the climate was necessary for her health. Meanwhile she adopted, she acted, what she conceived to be foreign manners, and with an exaggeration common with those who have very little sense and a vast desire to be fashionable with a certain set. Those who knew her best (all but her sister Katrine, who shook her head) were convinced that there was really no harm in Lady Castlefort, 'only vanity and folly.' How frequently folly leads farther than fools ever, or wise people often, foresee, we need not here stop to record. On the present occasion, all at Clarendon Park, even those most inclined to scandal. – persons who, by the bye, may always be known by their invariable preface of 'I hate all scandal,' – agreed that no one *so far* could behave better than Granville Beauclerc – 'so far,' – 'as yet.' But all the elderly who had any experience of this world, all the young who had any intuitive prescience in these matters, could not but fear that things could not long go on as they were now going. It was sadly to be feared that so young a man, and so very handsome a man, and such an admirer of beauty, and grace, and music, and of such an enthusiastic temper, must be in danger of being drawn on farther than he was aware, and before he knew what he was about.

The General heard all and saw all that went on without seeming to take heed, only once he asked Cecilia how long she thought her cousins would stay. She did not know, but she said 'she saw he wished them to be what they were not – cousins once removed – and quite agreed with him.' He smiled, for a man is always pleased to find his wife agree with him in disliking her cousins.

One night – one fine moonlight night – Lady Castlefort, standing at the conservatory door with Beauclerc, after talking an inconceivable quantity of nonsense about her passion for the moon, and her notions about the stars, and congenial souls born under the same planet, proposed to him a moonlight walk.

The General was at the time playing at chess with Helen, and had the best of the game, but at that moment, he made a false move, was checkmated, rose hastily, threw the men together on the board, and forgot to regret his shameful defeat, or to compliment Helen upon her victory. Lady Castlefort, having just discovered that the fatality nonsense about the stars would not quite do for Beauclerc, had been the next instant seized with a sudden passion for astronomy; she must see those charming rings of Saturn, which she had heard so much of, which the General was showing Miss Stanley the other night; she must beg him to lend his telescope; she came up with her sweetest smile to trouble the General for his glass. Lord Castlefort, following, objected strenuously to her going out at night; she had been complaining of a bad cold when he wanted her to walk in the daytime, she would only make it worse by going out in the night air. If she wanted to see Saturn and his rings, the General, he was sure, would fix a telescope at the window for her.

But that would not do, she must have a moonlight walk; she threw open the conservatory door, beckoned to Mr Beauclerc, and how it ended Helen did not stay to see. She thought that she ought not even to think on the subject, and she went away as fast as she could. It was late, and she went to bed wishing to be up early, to go on with a drawing she was to finish for Mrs Colling-wood – a view by the riverside, that view which had struck her fancy as so beautiful the day she went first to Old Forest. Early the next morning – and a delightful morning it was – she was up and out, and reached the spot from which her sketch was taken. She was surprised to find her little camp-stool, which she had looked for in vain in the hall, in its usual place, set here ready for her, and on it a pencil nicely cut.

Beauclerc must have done this. But he was not in general an early riser. However, she concluded that he had gone over thus early to Old Forest, to see his friend Lord Beltravers, who was to have arrived the day before, with his sisters. She saw a boat rowing down the river, and she had no doubt he was gone. But just as she had settled to her drawing, she heard the joyful bark of Beauclerc's dog, Nelson, who came bounding towards her, and the next moment his master appeared, coming down the path from the wood. With quick steps he came till he was nearly close to her, then slackened his pace.

'Good morning!' said Helen; she tried to speak with compo-sure, but her heart beat – she could not help feeling surprise at seeing him – but it was only surprise.

'I thought you were gone to Old Forest?' said she.

'Not yet,' said he.

His voice sounded different from usual, and she saw in him some suppressed agitation. She endeavoured to keep her own manner unembarrassed – she thanked him for the nicely-cut pencil, and the exactly well-placed seat. He advanced a step or two nearer, stooped, and looked close at her drawing, but he did not seem to see or know what he was looking at.

At this moment Nelson, who had been too long unnoticed, put up one paw on Miss Stanley's arm, unseen by his master, and encouraged by such gentle reproof as Helen gave, his audacious paw was on the top of her drawing-book the next moment, and the next was upon the drawing – and the paw was wet with dew. 'Nelson!' exclaimed his master in an angry tone.

'Oh do not scold him!' cried Helen, 'do not punish him; the drawing is not spoiled – only wet, and it will be as well as ever when it is dry.'

Beauclerc ejaculated something about the temper of an angel while she patted Nelson's penitent head.

'As the drawing must be left to dry,' said Beauclerc, 'perhaps Miss Stanley would do me the favour to walk as far as the landing-place, where the boat is to meet me – to take me – if – if I MUST go to Old Forest!' and he sighed.

She took his offered arm and walked on – surprised – confused; – wondering what he meant by that sigh and that look – and that strong emphasis on *must*. 'If I *must* go to Old Forest.' Was it not a pleasure? – was it not his own choice? – what could he mean? What could be the matter?

A vague agitating idea rose in her mind, but she put it from her, and they walked on for some minutes, both silent. They entered the wood, and feeling the silence awkward, and afraid that he should perceive her embarrassment, and that he should suspect her suspicion, she exerted herself to speak – to say something, no matter what.

'It is a charming morning!'

After a pause of absence of mind, he answered,

'Charming! – very!'

Then stopping short, he fixed his eyes upon Helen with an expression that she was afraid to understand. It could hardly bear any interpretation but one – and yet that was impossible – ought to be impossible – from a man in Beauclerc's circumstances – engaged

– almost a married man, as she had been told to consider him. She did not know at this moment what to think – still she thought she must mistake him, and she should be excessively ashamed of such a mistake, and now more strongly felt the dread that he should see and misinterpret or interpret too rightly her emotion; she walked on quicker, and her breath grew short, and her colour heightened. He saw her agitation – a delightful hope rose in his mind. It was plain she was not indifferent – he looked at her, but dared not look long enough – feared that he was mistaken. But the embarrassment seemed to change its character even as he looked, and now it was more like displeasure – decidedly, she appeared displeased. And so she was; for she thought now that he must either be trifling with her, or, if serious, must be acting most dishonourably; – her good opinion of him must be destroyed for ever, if, as now it seemed, he wished to make an impression upon her heart – yet still she tried not to think, not to see it. She was sorry, she was very wrong to let such an idea into her mind – and still her agitation increased.

Quick as she turned from him these thoughts passed in her mind, alternately angry and ashamed, and at last, forcing herself to be composed, telling herself she ought to see farther and at least to be certain before she condemned him – condemned so kind, so honourable a friend, while the fault might be all her own; she now, in a softened tone, as if begging pardon for the pain she had given, and the injustice she had done him, said some words, insignificant in themselves, but from the voice of kindness charming to Beauclerc's ear and soul.

'Are we not walking very fast?' said she, breathless. He slackened his pace instantly, and with a delighted look, while she, in a hurried voice, added, 'But do not let me delay you. There is the boat. You must be in haste – impatient!'

'In haste! impatient! to leave you, Helen!' She blushed deeper than he had ever seen her blush before. Beauclerc in general knew

Which blush was anger's, which was love's!

But now he was so much moved he could not decide at the first glance: at the second, there was no doubt; it was anger – not love.

Her arm was withdrawn from his. He was afraid he had gone too far. He had called her Helen!

He begged pardon, half humbly, half proudly. 'I beg pardon; Miss Stanley, I should have said. I see I have offended. I fear I have been presumptuous, but Lady Davenant taught me to trust to Miss Stanley's sincerity, and I was encouraged by her expressions of confidence and friendship.'

'Friendship! Oh yes! Mr Beauclerc,' said Helen, in a hurried voice, eagerly seizing on and repeating the word friendship; 'yes, I have always considered you as a friend. I am sure I shall always find you a sincere, good friend.'

'Friend!' he repeated in a dissatisfied tone – all his hopes sank. She took his arm again, and he was displeased even with that. She was not the being of real sensibility he had fancied – she was not capable of real love. So vacillated his heart and his imagination, and so quarrelled he alternately every instant with her and with himself. He could not understand her, or decide what he should next do or say himself; and there was the boat nearing the land, and they were going on, on, towards it in silence. He sighed.

It was a sigh that could not but be heard and noticed; it was not meant to be noticed, and yet it was. What could she think of it? She could not believe that Beauclerc meant to act treacherously. This time she was determined not to take anything for granted, not to be so foolish as she had been with Mr Churchill.

'Is that not your boat that I see, rowing close?'

'Yes, I believe – certainly. Yes,' said he.

But now the vacillation of Beauclerc's mind suddenly ceased. Desperate, he stopped her, as she would have turned down that path to the landing-place where the boat was mooring. He stood full across the path. 'Miss Stanley, by one word – by one word, one look, decide. You must decide for me whether I stay – or go – forever!'

'I! – Mr Beauclerc!'

The look of astonishment – more than astonishment, almost of indignation – silenced him completely, and he stood dismayed. She pressed onwards, and he no longer stopped her path. For an instant he submitted in despair. 'Then I must not think of it. I must go – must I, Miss Stanley? Will you not listen to me, Helen? Advise me; let me open my heart to you as a friend.'

She stopped under the shady tree beneath which they were passing, and leaning against it, she repeated, 'As a friend – but no, no, Mr Beauclerc – no; I am not the friend you should consult – the General, your guardian.'

'I have consulted him, and he approves.'

'You have! That is well, that is well at all events,' cried she; 'if he approves, then all is right.'

There was a ray of satisfaction on her countenance. He looked as if considering what she exactly meant. He hoped again, and was again resolved to hazard the decisive words. 'If you knew all!' and he pressed her arm closer to him – 'if I might tell you all – '

Helen withdrew her arm decidedly. 'I know all,' said she; 'all I ought to know, Mr Beauclerc.'

'You know all!' cried he, astonished at her manner. 'You know the circumstances in which I am placed?'

He alluded to the position in which he stood with Lady Castlefort; she thought he meant with respect to Lady Blanche, and she answered – 'Yes: I know all!' and her eye turned towards the boat.

'I understand you,' said he; 'you think I ought to go?'

'Certainly,' said she. It never entered into her mind to doubt the truth of what Lady Cecilia had told her, and she had at first been so much embarrassed by the fear of betraying what she felt she ought not to feel, and she was now so shocked by what she thought his dishonourable conduct, that she repeated almost in a tone of severity – 'Certainly, Mr Beauclerc, you ought to go.'

The words, 'since you are engaged,' – 'you know you are engaged,' she was on the point of adding, but Lady Cecilia's injunctions not to tell him that she had betrayed his secret stopped her.

He looked at her for an instant, and then abruptly, and in great agitation, said: 'May I ask, Miss Stanley, if your affections are engaged?'

'Is that a question, Mr Beauclerc, which you have a right to ask me?'

'I have no right – no right, I acknowledge – I am answered.'

He turned away from her, and ran down the bank towards the boat, but returned instantly, and exclaimed, 'If you say to me, Go! I am gone forever!'

'Go!' Helen firmly pronounced. 'You never can be more than a friend to me. Oh, never be less! – go!'

'I am gone,' said he, 'you shall never see me more.'

He went, and a few seconds afterwards she heard the splashing of his oars. He was gone! Oh! how she wished that they had parted sooner – a few minutes sooner, even before he had so looked – so spoken!

'Oh that we had parted while I might have still perfectly esteemed him; but now – !'

WHEN HELEN ATTEMPTED to walk, she trembled so much that she could not move, and leaning against the tree under which she was standing, she remained fixed for some time almost without thought. Then she began to recollect what had been before all this, and as soon as she could walk she went back for her drawing-book, threw from her the pencil which Beauclerc had cut, and made her way home as fast as she could, and up to her own room, without meeting anybody; and as soon as she was there she bolted the door and threw herself upon her bed. She had by this time a dreadful headache, and she wanted to try and get rid of it in time for breakfast – that was her first object; but her thoughts were so confused that they could not fix upon anything rightly. She tried to compose herself, and to think the whole affair over again; but she could not. There was something so strange in what had passed! The sudden – the total change in her opinion – her total loss of confidence! She tried to put all thoughts and feelings out of her mind, and just to lie stupefied if she could, that she might get rid of the pain in her head. She had no idea whether it was late or early, and was going to get up to look at her watch, when she heard the first bell, half an hour before breakfast, and this was the time when Cecilia usually opened the door between their rooms. She dreaded the sound, but when she had expected it some minutes, she became impatient even for that which she feared; she wanted to have it over, and she raised herself on her elbow, and listened with acute impatience; at last the door was thrown wide open, and, bright and gay as ever, in came Cecilia, but at the first sight of Helen on her bed, wan and miserable, she stopped short.

'My dearest Helen! what can be the matter?'

'Mr Beauclerc – '

'Well, what of him?' cried Cecilia, and she smiled.

'Oh, Cecilia! do not smile; you cannot imagine – '

'Oh yes, but I can,' cried Cecilia; 'I see how it is; I understand it all; and, miserable and amazed as you look at this moment, I will set all right for you in one word. He is not going to be married – not engaged.'

Helen started up. 'Not engaged?'

'No more than you are, my dear! Oh, I am glad to see your colour come again!'

'Thank Heaven!' cried Helen; 'then he is not – '

'A villain! not at all. He is all that's right; all that is charming, my dear. So thank Heaven, and be as happy as you please.'

'But I cannot understand it,' said Helen, sinking back; 'I really cannot understand how it is, Cecilia.'

Cecilia gave her a glass of water in great haste, and was very sorry, and very glad, and begged forgiveness, and all in a breath: but as yet Helen did not know what she had to forgive, till it was explained to her in direct words that Cecilia had told her not only what was not true, but what she at the time of telling knew to be false.

'For what purpose, O my dear Cecilia! All to save me from a little foolish embarrassment at first, you have made us miserable at last.'

'Miserable! my dear Helen; at worst miserable only for half an hour. Nonsense! lie down again, and rest your poor head. I will go this minute to Granville. Where is he?'

'Gone! Gone for ever! Those were his last words.'

'Impossible! absurd! Only what a man says in a passion. But where is he gone? Only to Old Forest! Gone for ever – gone till dinner-time! Probably coming back at this moment all in haste, like a true lover, to beg your pardon for your having used him abominably ill. Now, smile; do not shake your head, and look so wretched; but tell me exactly, word for word and look for look, all that passed between you, and then I shall know what is best to be done.'

Word for word Helen could not answer, for she had been so much confused, but she told to the best of her recollection; and Cecilia still thought no great harm was done. She only looked a little serious from the apprehension, now the real, true apprehension, of what might happen about Lady Blanche, who, as she believed, was at Old Forest. 'Men are so foolish; men in love so rash. Beauclerc, in a fit of anger and despair on being so refused by the woman he loved, might go and throw himself at the feet of another for whom he did not care in the least, in a strange sort of revenge. But I know how to settle it all, and I will do it this moment.'

But Helen caught hold of her hand, and firmly detaining it, absolutely objected to her doing anything without telling her exactly and truly what she was going to do.

Lady Cecilia assured her that she was only going to inquire from the General whether Lady Blanche was with her sister at Old Forest, or not. 'Listen to me, my dear Helen; what I am going to say can do no mischief. If Lady Blanche is there, then the best thing to be done is, for me to go immediately, this very morning, to pay the ladies a visit on their coming to the country, and I will bring back Granville. A word will bring him back. I will only tell him there was a little mistake, or if you think it best, I will tell him the whole truth. Let me go – only let me go and consult the General before the breakfast-bell rings, for I shall have no time afterwards.'

Helen let her go, for as Beauclerc had told her that he had opened his mind to the General, she thought it was best that he should hear all that had happened.

The moment the General saw Lady Cecilia come in, he smiled and said, 'Well! my dear Cecilia, you have seen Helen this morning, and she has seen Beauclerc – what is the result? Does he stay, or go?'

'He is gone!' said Cecilia. The General looked surprised and sorry. 'He did not propose for her,' continued Cecilia, 'he did not declare himself – he only began to sound her opinion of him, and she – she contrived to misunderstand, to offend him, and he is gone, but only to Old Forest, and we can have him back again directly.'

'That is not likely,' said the General, 'because I know that Beauclerc had determined that if he went he would not return for some time. Your friend Helen was to decide. If she gave him any hope, that is, permitted him to appear as her declared admirer, he could, with propriety, happiness, and honour, remain here; if not, my dear Cecilia, you must be sensible that he is right to go.'

'Gone for some time!' repeated Cecilia, 'you mean as long as Lady Castlefort is here.'

'Yes,' said the General.

'I wish she was gone, I am sure, with all my heart,' said Cecilia; 'but in the meantime, tell me, my dear Clarendon, do you know whether Lord Beltravers's sisters are at Old Forest?'

The General did not think that Lady Blanche had arrived; he was not certain, but he knew that the Comtesse de St Cymon had arrived yesterday.

'Then,' said Cecilia, 'it would be but civil to go to see the Comtesse. I will go this morning.'

General Clarendon answered instantly, and with decision, that she must not think of such a thing – that it could not be done. 'Madame de St Cymon is a woman of doubtful reputation, not a person with whom Lady Cecilia Clarendon ought to form any acquaintance.'

'No, not form an acquaintance – I'm quite aware of that'; and eagerly she pleaded that she had no intention of doing anything; 'but just one morning visit paid and returned, you know, leads to nothing. Probably we shall neither of us be at home, and never meet; and really it would be such a marked thing not to pay this visit to the Beltravers family on their return to the country. Formerly there was such a good understanding between the Forresters and your father; and really hospitality requires it. Altogether this one visit must be paid, it cannot be helped, so I will order the carriage.'

'It must not be done!' the General said; 'it is a question of right, not of expediency.'

'Right, but there is nothing really wrong, surely; I believe all that has been said of her is scandal. Nobody is safe against reports – the public papers are so scandalous! While a woman lives with her husband, it is but charitable to suppose all is right. That's the rule. Besides, we should not throw the first stone.' Then Lady Cecilia pleaded, lady this and lady that, and the whole county, without the least scruple, would visit Madame de St Cymon.

'Lady this and lady that may do as they please, or as their husbands think proper or improper, that is no rule for Lady Cecilia Clarendon; and as to the whole county, or the whole world, what is that to me, when I have formed my own determination?'

The fact was, that at this time Madame de St Cymon was about to be separated from her husband. A terrible discovery had just been made. Lord Beltravers had brought his sister to Old Forest to hide her from London disgrace; there he intended to leave her to rusticate, while he should follow her husband to Paris immediately, to settle the terms of separation or divorce.

'Beauclerc, no doubt, will go to Paris with him,' said the General.

'To Paris! when will he set out?'

'To-day – directly, if Helen has decidedly rejected him; but you say he did not declare himself. Pray tell me all at once.'

And if she had done so, all might have been well; but she was afraid. Her husband was as exact about *some things* as her mother; he would certainly be displeased at the deception she had practised on Helen; she could not tell him that, not at this moment, for she had just fooled him to the top of his bent about this visit; she would find a better time; she so dreaded the instant change of his smile – the look of disapprobation; she was so cowardly; in short, the present pain of displeasing – the consequences even of her own folly, she never could endure, and to avoid it she had always recourse to some new evasion; and now, when Helen – her dear Helen's happiness was at stake, she faltered – she would not for the world do her any wrong; but still she thought she could manage without telling the whole – she would tell nothing *but* the truth. So, after a moment's hesitation, while all these thoughts went through her mind, when the General repeated his question, and begged to know at once what was passing in her little head, she smiled in return for that smile which played on her husband's face while he fondly looked upon her, and she answered, 'I am thinking of poor Helen. She has made a sad mistake – and has a horrid headache at this moment – in short she has offended Beauclerc past endurance – past his endurance – and he went off in a passion before she found out her mistake. In short, we must have him back again; could you go, my dear love – or write directly?'

'First let me understand,' said the General. 'Miss Stanley has made a mistake – what mistake?'

'She thought Beauclerc was engaged to Lady Blanche.'

'How could she think so? What reason had she?'

'She had been told so by somebody.'

'Somebody! – that eternal scandal-monger Lady Katrine, I suppose.'

'No – not Lady Katrine,' said Cecilia; 'but I am not at liberty to tell you whom.'

'No matter; but Miss Stanley is not a fool; she could not believe somebody or anybody, contrary to common sense.'

'No, but Beauclerc did not come quite to proposing – and you know she had been blamed for refusing Mr Churchill before she was asked – and in short – in love, people do not always know what they are about.'

'I do not understand one word of it,' said the General; 'nor I am sure do you, my dear Cecilia.'

'Yes, I really do, but – '

'My dear Cecilia, I assure you it is always best to let people settle their love affairs their own way.'

'Yes, certainly – I would not interfere in the least – only to get Granville back again – and then let them settle it in their own way. Cannot you call at Old Forest?'

'No.'

'Could you not write?'

'No – not unless I know the whole. I will do nothing in the dark. Always tell your confessor, your lawyer, your physician, your friend, your whole case, or they are fools or rogues if they act for you: go back and repeat this to Helen Stanley from me.'

'But, my dear, she will think it so unkind.'

'Let her show me how I can serve her, and I will do it.'

'Only write a line to Beauclerc – say, "Beauclerc, come back – here has been a mistake." ' She would have put a pen into his hand, and held paper to him.

'Let me know the whole, and then, and not till then, can I judge whether I should be doing right for her or not.' The difficulty of telling the whole had increased to Lady Cecilia, even from the hesitation and prevarication she had now made. 'Let me see Helen – let me speak to her myself, and learn what this strange nonsensical mystery is.' He was getting impatient. 'Cannot I see Miss Stanley?'

'Why no, my dear, not just now, she has such a headache! She is lying down. There is the breakfast-bell – after breakfast, if you please. But I am clear she would rather not speak to you herself on the subject.'

'Then come down to breakfast, my dear, and let her settle it her own way – that is much the best plan. Interference in love matters always does mischief. Come to breakfast, my dear – I have no time to lose – I must be off to a court-martial.'

He looked at his watch, and Cecilia went half down stairs with him, and then ran back to keep Helen quiet by the assurance that all would be settled – all would be right, and that she would send her up some breakfast – she must not think of coming down; and Cecilia lamented half breakfast-time how subject to headaches poor Helen was; and through this and through all other conversation she settled what she would do for her. As the last resource, she would tell the whole truth – not to her husband, she loved him too well to face his displeasure for one moment – but to Beauclerc: and writing would be so much easier than speaking – without being put to the blush she could explain it all to Beauclerc, and turn it playfully; and he would be so happy that he would be only too glad to forgive her, and to do anything she asked. She concocted and wrote a very pretty letter, in which she took all the blame fully on herself – did perfect justice to Helen; said she wrote without her knowledge, and depended entirely upon his discretion, so he must come back of his own accord, and keep her counsel. This letter, however, she could not despatch so soon as she had expected; she could not send a servant with it till the General should be off to his court-martial. Now had Cecilia gone the straightforward way to work, her husband could in that interval, and would, have set all to rights; but this to Cecilia was impossible; she could only wait in an agony of impatience till the General and his officers were all out of the way, and then she despatched a groom with her letter to Old Forest, and desired him to return as fast as possible, while she went to Helen's room, to while away the time of anxious suspense as well as she could; and she soon succeeded in talking herself into excellent spirits again. 'Now, my dear Helen, if that unlucky mistake had not been made, – if you had not fancied that Granville was married already, – and if he had actually proposed for you, – what would you have said? – in short – would you have accepted him?'

'O Cecilia, I do hope he will understand how it all was; I hope he will believe that I esteem him as I always did; as to love – '

Helen paused, and Lady Cecilia went on: 'As to love, nobody knows anything about it till it comes – and here it is coming, I do believe!' continued she, looking out of the window. No! not Mr Beauclerc, but the man she had sent with her letter, galloping towards the house. Disappointed not to see Beauclerc himself, she could only conclude that as he had not his horse with him, he was returning in the boat. The answer to her letter was brought in. At the first glance on the direction, her countenance changed. 'Not Granville's hand! – what can have happened?' She tore open the note, 'He is gone! – gone with Lord Beltravers! – set off – gone to Paris!' Helen said not one word, and Cecilia, in despair, repeated, 'Gone! – gone! – absolutely gone! Nothing more can be done. Oh that I had done nothing about it! All has failed!

Heaven knows what may happen now! Oh if I could but have let it all alone! I never, never can forgive myself! My dear Helen, pray be angry with me – reproach me: pray – pray reproach me as I deserve!' But Helen could not blame one who so blamed herself – one who, however foolish and wrong she had been, had done it all from the kindest motives. In the agony of her penitence, she now told Helen all that had passed between her and the General; that, to avoid the same of confessing to him her first deception, she had gone on another and another step in these foolish evasions, contrivances, and mysteries; how, thinking she could manage it, she had written without his knowledge; and now, to complete her punishment, not only had everything which she had attempted failed, but a consequence which she could never have foreseen had happened. 'Here I am, with a note actually in my hand from this horrid Madame de St Cymon, whom Clarendon absolutely would not hear of my even calling upon! Look what she writes to me. She just took advantage of this opportunity to begin a correspondence before an acquaint- ance: but I will never answer her. Here is what she says: –

' "The Comtesse de St Cymon exceedingly regrets that Lady Cecilia Clarendon's servant did not arrive in time to deliver her ladyship's letter into Mr Beauclerc's own hand. Mr B left Old Forest with Lord Beltravers early to-day for Paris. The Comtesse de St Cymon, understanding that Lady Cecilia Clarendon is anxious that there should be as little delay as possible in forward- ing her letter, and calculating that if returned by her ladyship's servant it must be too late for this day's post from Clarendon Park, has forwarded it immediately with her own letters to Paris, which cannot fail to meet Mr Beauclerc directly on his arrival there."

'Oh!' cried Lady Cecilia, 'how angry the General would be if he knew of this!' She tore the note to the smallest bits as she spoke, and threw them away; and next she begged that Helen would never say a word about it. There was no use in telling the General what would only vex him, and what could not be helped; and what could lead to nothing, for she should never answer this note, nor have any further communication of any kind with Madame de St Cymon.

Helen, nevertheless, thought it would be much better to tell the General of it, and she wondered how Cecilia could think of doing otherwise, and just when she had so strongly reproached herself, and repented of these foolish mysteries; and this was going on another step. 'Indeed, Cecilia,' said Helen, 'I wish – on my own account I wish you would not conceal anything. It is hard to let the General suspect me of extreme folly and absurdity, or of some sort of double dealing in this business, in which I have done my utmost to do right and to go straight forward.' Poor Helen, with her nervous headache beating worse and worse, remonstrated and entreated, and came to tears; and Lady Cecilia promised that it should all be done as she desired; but again she charged and besought Helen to say nothing herself about the matter to the General: and this acceded to, Lady Cecilia's feelings being as transient as they were vehement, all her self-reproaches, penitence, and fears passed away, and, taking her bright view of the whole affair, she ended with the certainty that Beauclerc would return the moment he received her letter; that he would have it in a very few days, and all would end well, as quite as well as if she had not been a fool.

——✦ CHAPTER 22 ✦——

THE FIRST TIDINGS of Beauclerc came in a letter from him to the General, written immediately after his arrival at Paris. But it was plain that it must have been written before Lady Cecilia's letter, forwarded by Madame de St Cymon, could have reached him. It was evident that matters were as yet unexplained, from his manner of writing about 'the death-blow to all his hopes,' and now he was setting off with Lord Beltravers for Naples, to follow M de St Cymon, and settle the business of the sister's divorce. Lady Cecilia could only hope that her letter would follow him thither, enclosed in this Madame de St Cymon's despatches to her brother; and now they could know nothing more till they could hear from Naples.

Meanwhile, Helen perceived that, though the General continued to be as attentive and kind to her as usual, yet that there was something more careful and reserved in his manner than formerly, less of spontaneous regard, and cordial confidence. It was not that he was displeased by her having discouraged the addresses of his ward, fond as he was of Beauclerc, and well as he would have been pleased by the match. This he distinctly expressed the only time he touched upon the subject. He said that Miss Stanley was the best and the only judge of what would make her happy; but he could not comprehend the nature of the mistake she had made; Cecilia's explanations, whatever they were, had not made the matter clear. There was either some caprice, or some mystery, which he determined not to inquire into, upon his own principle of leaving people to settle their love affairs in their own way. Helen's spirits were lowered: naturally of great sensibility, she depended more for her happiness on her inward feelings than upon any external circumstances. A great deal of gaiety was now going on constantly among the young people at Clarendon Park, and this made her want of spirits more disagreeable to herself, more obvious, and more observed by others. Lady Katrine rallied her unmercifully. Not suspecting the truth, her ladyship presumed that Miss Stanley repented of having, before she was asked, said No instead of Yes to Mr Churchill. Ever since his departure she had evidently worn the willow.

Lady Cecilia was excessively vexed by this ill-natured raillery: conscious that she had been the cause of all this annoyance to Helen, and of much more serious evil to her, the zeal and tenderness of her affection now increased, and was shown upon every little occasion involuntarily, in a manner that continually irritated her cousin Katrine's jealousy. Helen had been used to live only with those by whom she was beloved, and she was not at all prepared for the sort of welfare which Lady Katrine carried on; her perpetual sneers, innuendoes, and bitter sarcasms, Helen did not resent, but she felt them. The arrows, ill-aimed and weak, could not penetrate far; it was not with their point they wounded, but by their venom – wherever that touched it worked inward mischief.

Often to escape from one false imputation she exposed herself to another more grievous. One night, when the young people wished to dance, and the usual music was not to be had, Helen played quadrilles, and waltzes, for hours with indefatigable good-nature, and when some of the party returned their cordial thanks, Lady Katrine whispered, 'Our musician has been well paid by Lord Estridge's admiration of her white hands.' His lordship had not danced, and had been standing all the evening beside Helen, much to the discomfiture of Lady Katrine, who intended to have had him for her own partner. The next night Helen did not play, but joined the dance, and with a boy partner, whom nobody could envy her. The General, who saw wonderfully quickly the by-play of society, marked all this, and now

his eye followed Helen through the quadrille, and he said to
some one standing by that Miss Stanley danced charmingly, to
his taste, and in such a ladylike manner. He was glad to see her in
good spirits again; her colour was raised; and he observed that she
looked remarkably well. 'Yes,' Lady Katrine answered, 'remarkably well; and black is so becoming to that sort of complexion,
no doubt this is the reason Miss Stanley wears it so much longer
than is customary for an uncle. Short or long mournings are, to
be sure, just according to fashion, or feeling, as some say. For my
part, I hate long mournings — so like ostentation of sentiment;
whatever I did, at any rate I would be consistent. I never would
dance in black. Pope, you know, has such a good cut at that sort
of thing. Do you recollect the lines?

> "And bear about the mockery of woe
> To midnight dances and the public show." '

Lady Castlefort took Miss Stanley aside, after the dance was over,
to whisper to her good-naturedly, how shockingly severe Katrine
had been; faithfully repeating every word that her sister had said.
'And so cruel, to talk of your bearing about the *mockery* of woe!
But, my sweet little lamb, do not let me distress you so.' Helen,
withdrawing from the false caresses of Lady Castlefort, assured
her that she should not be hurt by anything Lady Katrine could
say, as she so little understood her real feelings; and at the moment
her spirit rose against the injustice, and felt as much superior to
such petty malice as even Lady Davenant could have desired.

She had resolved to continue in mourning for the longest
period in which it is worn for a parent, because, in truth, her
uncle had been a parent to her; but the morning after Lady
Katrine's cruel remarks, Cecilia begged that Helen would oblige
her by laying aside black. 'Let it be on my birthday.' Lady Cecilia's
birthday was to be celebrated the ensuing week. 'Well, for that
day certainly I will,' Helen said; 'but only for that day.' This would
not satisfy Cecilia. Helen saw that Lady Katrine's observations
had made a serious impression, and, dreading to become the
subject of daily observation, perhaps altercation, she yielded. The

mourning was thrown aside. Then everything she wore must be new. Lady Cecilia and Mademoiselle Felicie, her waiting-maid, insisted upon taking the matter into their own hands. Helen really intended only to let one dress for her friend's birthday be bespoken for her; but from one thing she was led on to another. Lady Cecilia's taste in dress was exquisite. Her first general principle was admirable – 'Whatever you buy, let it be the best of its kind, which is always the cheapest in the end.' Her second maxim was – 'Never have anything but from such and such people, or from such and such places,' naming those who were at the moment accredited by fashion. 'These, of course, make you pay high for the name of the thing; but that must be. The name is all,' said Lady Cecilia. 'Does your hat, your bonnet, whatever it be, come from the reigning fashionable authority? then it is right, and you are quite right. You can put down all objections and objectors with the magic of a name. You need think no more about your dress; you have no trouble; while the poor creatures who go toiling and rummaging in cheap shops – what comes of it but total exhaustion and disgrace? Yesterday, now, my dear Helen, recollect. When Lady Katrine, after dinner, asked little Miss Isdall where she bought that pretty hat, the poor girl was quite out of countenance. "Really, she did not know; she only knew it was very cheap." You saw that nobody could endure the hat afterwards; so that, cheap as it might be, it was money to all intents and purposes absolutely thrown away, for it did not answer its purpose.'

Helen, laughing, observed that if its purpose had been to look well, and to make the wearer look well, it had fully succeeded.

'Sophistry, my dear Helen. The purpose was not to look well, but to have a distinguished air. Dress, and what we call fashion and taste altogether, you know, are mere matters of opinion, association of ideas, and so forth. When will you learn to reason, as mamma says? Do not make me despair of you.'

Thus, half in jest, half in earnest, with truth and falsehood, sense and nonsense, prettily blended together, Lady Cecilia prevailed in overpowering Helen's better judgment, and obtained a hasty submission. In economy, as in morals, false principles are far more dangerous than any one single error. One false principle as to laying out money is worse than any bad bargain that can be made, because it leads to bad bargains innumerable. It was settled that all Helen wanted should be purchased, not only from those who sold the best goods but from certain very expensive houses of fashionable high name in London. And the next point Lady Cecilia insisted upon was, that Helen's dress should always be the same as her own. 'You know it used to be so, my dear Helen, when we were children; let it be so now.'

'But there is such a difference *now*,' said Helen; 'and I cannot afford – '

'Difference! Oh! don't talk of differences – let there be none ever between us. Not afford! – nonsense, my dear – the expense will be nothing. In these days you get the materials of dress absolutely for nothing – the fashion – the making-up is all, as Felicie and I, and everybody who knows anything of the matter, can tell you. Now all that sort of thing we can save you – here is my wedding paraphernalia all at your service – patterns ready cut – and here is Felicie, whose whole French soul is in the toilette – and there is your own little maid, who has hands, and head, and heart, all devoted to you – so leave it to us – leave it to us, my dear – take no thought but what you shall put on – and you will put it on all the better.' Felicie was summoned. 'Felicie, remember Miss Stanley's dress is always to be the same as my own. It must be so, my dear. It will be the greatest pleasure to me,' and with her most persuasive caressing manner, she added, 'My own dear Helen, if you love me, let it be so.'

This was an appeal which Helen could not resist. She thought she could not refuse without vexing Cecilia; and, from a sort of sentimental belief that she was doing Cecilia 'a real kindness,' – that it was what Cecilia called 'a sisterly act,' she yielded to what she knew was unsuited to her circumstances – to what was quite contrary to her better judgment. It often so happens that our friends doubly guard one obvious point of weakness, while another exists undiscovered by them, and unknown to ourselves. Lady Davenant had warned Helen against the dangers of indecision and coquetry with her lovers, but this danger of extravagance in dress she had not foreseen – and into how much expense this one weak compliance would lead her, Helen could not calculate. She had fancied that, at least, till she went to town, she should not want anything expensive – this was a great mistake. Formerly in England, as still in every other country but England, a marked difference was made in the style of dress in the country and in town. Formerly, overdressing in the country was rebrobated as quite vulgar; but now, even persons of birth and fashion are guilty of this want of taste and sense. They display almost as much expensive dress in the country as in town.

It happened that among the succession of company at Clarendon Park this summer, there came, self-invited, from the royal party in the neighbourhood, a certain wealthy lady, by some called 'Golconda,' by others 'the Duchess of Baubleshire.' She was passionately fond of dress, and she eclipsed all rivals in magnificence and variety of ornaments. At imminent peril of being robbed, she brought to the country, and carried about everywhere with her, an amazing number of jewels, wearing two or three different sets at different times of the day – displaying them on the most absurdly improper occasions – at a *fête champêtre*, [1] or a boat-race.

Once, after a riding-party, at a picnic under the trees, when it had been resolved unanimously that nobody should change their dress at dinner-time, Golconda appeared in a splendid necklace, displayed over her riding-dress, and when she was reproached with having broken through the general agreement not to dress she replied that 'really she had put the thing on in the greatest hurry, without knowing well what it was, just to oblige her little page who had brought three sets of jewels for her choice – she had chosen the *most undressed* of the three, merely because she could not disappoint the poor little fellow.'

Every one saw the affectation and folly, and above all, the vulgarity of this display, and those who were most envious were most eager to comfort themselves by ridicule. Never was the

[1] rural feast or open-air entertainment

'Golconda' out of hearing, but Lady Katrine was ready with some instance of her 'absurd vanity.' 'If fortune had but blessed her with such jewels,' Lady Katrine said, 'she trusted she should have worn them with better grace'; but it did not appear that the taste for baubles was diminished by the ridicule thrown upon them – quite the contrary, it was plain that the laughers were only envious, and envious because they could not be envied.

Lady Cecilia, who had no envy in her nature – who was really generous – entered not into this vain competition; on the contrary, she refrained from wearing any of her jewels, because Helen had none; besides, simplicity was really the best taste, the General said so – this was well thought and well done for some time, but there was a little lurking love of ornaments in Cecilia's mind, nor was Helen entirely without sympathy in that taste. Her uncle had early excited it in her mind by frequent fond presents of the prettiest trinkets imaginable; the taste had been matured along with her love for one for whom she had such strong affection, and it had seemed to die with its origin. Before she left Cecilhurst, Helen had given away every ornament she possessed; she thought she could never want them again, and she left them as remembrances with those who had loved her and her uncle.

Cecilia on her birthday brought her a set of forget-me-nots, to match those which she intended to wear herself, and which had been long ago given to Lady Cecilia by the dear good Dean himself. This was irresistible to Helen, and they were accepted. But this was only the prelude to presents of more value, which Helen scrupled to receive; yet –

Oft to refuse and never once offend

was not so easily done as said, especially with Lady Cecilia; she was so urgent, so caressing, and had so many plausible reasons, suitable to all occasions. On the General's birthday, Lady Cecilia naturally wished to wear his first gift to her – a pair of beautiful pearl bracelets, but then Helen must have the same. Helen thought that Roman pearl would do quite as well for her. She had seen some such excellent imitations that no eye could detect the difference.

'No eye! very likely; but still your own conscience, my dear!' replied Lady Cecilia. 'And if people ask whether they are real, what would you say? You know there are everywhere impertinent people; malicious Lady Katrines, who will ask questions. Oh! positively I cannot bear to think of your being detected in passing off counterfeits. In all ornaments, it should be genuine or none – none or genuine.'

'None, then, let it be for me this time, dear Cecilia.'

Cecilia seemed to submit, and Helen thought she had well settled it. But on the day of the General's *fête*, the pearl bracelets were on her dressing-table. They were from the General, and could not be refused. Cecilia declared she had nothing to do with the matter.

'Oh, Cecilia!'

'Upon my word!' cried Lady Cecilia; 'and if you doubt me, the General shall have the honour of presenting, and you the agony of refusing or accepting, them in full salon.'

Helen sighed, hesitated, and submitted. The General, on her appearing with the bracelets, bowed, smiled, and thanked her with his kindest look; and she was glad to see him look kindly upon her again.

Having gained her point so pleasantly this time, Lady Cecilia did not stop there; and Helen found there was no resource but to bespeak beforehand for herself whatever she apprehended would be pressed upon her acceptance.

Fresh occasions for display, and new necessities for expense, continually occurred. Reviews, and races, and race balls, and archery meetings, and archery balls, had been, and a regatta was to be. At some of these the ladies had appeared in certain uniforms, new, of course, for the day; and now preparations for the regatta had commenced, and were going on. It was to last several days; and after the boat-races in the morning, there were to be balls at night. The first of these was to be at Clarendon Park, and Mademoiselle Felicie considered her lady's dress upon this occasion as one of the objects of first importance in the universe. She had often sighed over the long unopened jewel-box. Her lady might as well be nobody.

Mademoiselle Felicie could no ways understand a lady well born not wearing that which distinguished her above the common; and if she was ever to wear jewels, the ball-room was surely the proper place. And the sapphire necklace would look *à ravir* [1] with her lady's dress, which, indeed, without it, would have no effect; would be quite *mésquine* and *manquée*. [2]

Now Lady Cecilia had a great inclination to wear that sapphire necklace, which probably Felicie saw when she commenced her remonstrances, for it is part of the business of a well-trained waiting-woman to give utterance to those thoughts which her lady wishes should be divined and pressed into accomplishment. Cecilia considered whether it would not be possible to divide the double rows of her sapphires, to make out a set for Helen as well as for herself; she hesitated only because they had been given to her by her mother, and she did not like to run the hazard of spoiling the set; but still she could manage it, and she would do it. Mademoiselle Felicie protested the attempt would be something very like sacrilege; to prevent which, she gave a hint to Helen of what was in contemplation.

Helen knew that with Cecilia, when once she had set her heart upon a generous feat of this kind, remonstrance would be in vain; she dreaded that she would, if prevented from the meditated division of the sapphires, purchase for her a new set: she had not the least idea what the expense was, but, at the moment, she thought anything would be better than letting Cecilia spoil her mother's present, or put her under fresh obligations of this sort. She knew that the sapphires had been got from the jewellers with whom her uncle had dealt, and who were no strangers to her name; she wrote, and bespoke a similar set to Lady Cecilia's.

'*Charmante!* the very thing,' Mademoiselle Felicie foresaw, 'a young lady so well born would determine on doing. And if she

[1] delightful [2] stingy and lacking

might add a little word, it would be good at the same opportunity to order a ruby brooch, the same as her lady's, as that would be the next object in question for the second day's regalia ball, when it would be indispensable for that night's appearance; *positivement*, she knew her lady would do it for Miss Stanley if Miss Stanley did not do it of her own head.'

Helen did not think that a brooch could be very expensive; there was not time to consider about it – the post was going – she was afraid that Lady Cecilia would come in and find her writing, and prevent her sending the letter. She hastily added an order for the brooch, finished the letter, and despatched it. And when it was gone she told Cecilia what she had done. Cecilia looked startled; she was well aware that Helen did not know the high price of what she had bespoken. But, determining that she would settle it her own way, she took care not to give any alarm, and shaking her head, she only reproached Helen playfully with having stolen a march upon her.

'You think you have out-generaled me, but we shall see. Remember, I am the wife of a general, and not without resources.'

OF THE REGATTA, of the fineness of the weather, the beauty of the spectacle, and the dresses of the ladies, a full account appeared in the papers of the day, of which it would be useless here to give a repetition, and shameful to steal or seem to steal a description. We shall record only what concerns Helen.

With the freshness of youth and of her naturally happy temper, she was delighted with the whole, to her a perfectly new spectacle, and everybody was pleased except Lady Katrine, who, in the midst of every enjoyment, always found something that annoyed her, something that 'should not have been so.' She was upon this occasion more cross than usual, was most particularly so to Miss Stanley, as all the gentlemen observed.

Just in time before the ladies went to dress for the ball at night, the precious box arrived, containing the set of sapphires. Cecilia opened it eagerly, to see that all was right. Helen was not in the room. Lady Katrine stood by, and when she found that these were for Helen, her jealous indignation broke forth. 'The poor daughters of peers cannot indulge in such things,' cried she; 'they are fit only for rich heiresses! I understood,' continued she, 'that Miss Stanley had given away her fortune to pay her uncle's debts, but I presume she has thought better of that, as I always prophesied she would. Generosity is charming, but, after all, sapphires are so becoming!'

Helen came into the room just as this speech was ended. Lady Katrine had one of the bracelets in her hand. She looked miserably cross, for she had been disappointed about some ornaments she had expected by the same conveyance that brought Miss Stanley's. She protested that she had nothing fit to wear tonight. Helen looked at Cecilia; and though Cecilia's look gave her no encouragement, she begged that Lady Katrine would do her the honour to wear these sapphires this night, since she had not received what her ladyship had ordered. Lady Katrine suffered herself to be prevailed upon, but accepted with as ill a grace as possible. The ball went on, and Helen at least was happier than if she had worn the bracelets. She had no pleasure in being the object of envy, and now, when she found that Cecilia could be and was satisfied, though their ornaments were not exactly alike, it came full upon her mind that she had done foolishly in bespeaking these sapphires: it was at that moment only a transient self-reproach for extravagance, but before she went to rest this night it became more serious.

Lady Davenant had been expected all day, but she did not arrive till late in the midst of the ball, and she just looked in at the dancers for a few minutes before she retired to her own apartment. Helen would have followed her, but that was not allowed. After the dancing was over, however, as she was going to her room, she heard Lady Davenant's voice calling to her as she passed by; and, opening the door softly, she found her still awake, and desiring to see her for a few minutes, if she was not too much tired.

'Oh no, not in the least tired; quite the contrary,' said Helen.

After affectionately embracing her, Lady Davenant held her at arm's length, and looked at her as the light of the lamp shone full upon her face and figure. Pleased with her whole appearance, Lady Davenant smiled, and said, as she looked at her – 'You seem, Helen, to have shared the grateful old fairy's gift to Lady Georgiana B of the never-fading rose in the cheek. But what particularly pleases me, Helen, is the perfect simplicity of your dress. In the few minutes that I was in the ball-room tonight, I was struck with that over-dressed duchess: her figure has been before my eyes ever since, hung round with jewellery, and with that halo a foot and a half high on her head: like the Russian bride's

head-gear, which Heber so well called "the most costly deformity he ever beheld." Really, this passion for baubles,' continued
Lady Davenant, 'is the universal passion of our sex. I will give
you an instance to what extravagance it goes. I know a lady of
high rank, who hires a certain pair of emerald earrings at fifteen
hundred pounds per annum. She rents them in this way from
some German countess in whose family they are an heirloom,
and cannot be sold.' Helen expressed her astonishment. 'This is
only one instance, my dear; I could give you hundreds. Over the
whole world, women of all ages, all ranks, all conditions, have
been seized with this bauble insanity – from the counter to the
throne. Think of Marie Antoinette and the story of her necklace;
and Josephine and her Cisalpine pearls, and all the falsehoods
she told about them to the emperor she reverenced, the husband
she loved – and all for what? – a string of beads! But I forget,'
cried Lady Davenant, interrupting herself, 'I must not forget how
late it is: and I am keeping you up, and you have been dancing:
forgive me! When once my mind is moved I forget all hours.
Good-night – or good-morning, my dear child; go and rest.' But
just as Helen was withdrawing her hand, Lady Davenant's eye
fixed on her pearl bracelets – 'Roman pearls, or real? Real, I see,
and very valuable! – given to you, I suppose, by your poor dear
extravagant uncle?'

Helen cleared her uncle's memory from this imputation, and
explained that the bracelets were a present from General Clarendon. She did not know they were so 'very valuable,' but she hoped
she had not done wrong to accept of them in the circumstances;
and she told how she had been induced to take them.

Lady Davenant said she had done quite right. The General
was no present-maker, and this exception in his favour could not
lead to any future inconvenience. 'But Cecilia,' continued she, 'is
too much addicted to trinket-giving, which ends often disagree-
ably even between friends, or at all events fosters a foolish taste,
and moreover associates it with feelings of affection in a way particularly deceitful and dangerous to such a little, tender-hearted
person as I am speaking to, whose common sense would too

easily give way to the pleasure of pleasing or fear of offending a friend. Kiss me, and don't contradict me, for your conscience tells you that what I say is true.'

The sapphires, the ruby brooch, and all her unsettled accounts, came across Helen's mind; and if the light had shone upon her face at that moment, her embarrassment must have been seen; but Lady Davenant, as she finished the last words, laid her head upon the pillow, and she turned and settled herself comfortably to go to sleep. Helen retired with a disordered conscience; and the first thing she did in the morning was to look in the red case in which the sapphires came, to see if there was any note of their price; she recollected having seen some little bit of card – it was found on the dressing-table. When she beheld the price, fear took away her breath – it was nearly half her whole year's income; still she *could* pay it. But the ruby brooch that had not yet arrived – what would that cost? She hurried to her accounts; she had let them run on for months unlooked at, but she thought she must know the principal articles of expense in dress by her actual possessions. There, was a heap of little crumpled bills which, with Felicie's griffonage, Helen had thrown into her table-drawer. In vain did she attempt to decipher the figures, like apothecaries' marks, linked to quarters and three-quarters, and yards, of gauzes, silks, and muslins, altogether inextricably puzzling. They might have been at any other moment laughable, but now they were quite terrible to Helen; the only thing she could make clearly out was the total; she was astonished when she saw to how much little nothings can amount, an astonishment felt often by the most experienced – how much more by Helen, all unused to the arithmetic of economy! At this instant her maid came in smiling with a packet, as if sure of being the bearer of the very thing her young lady most wished for; it was the brooch – the very last thing in the world she desired to see. With a trembling hand she opened the parcel, looked at the note of the price, and sank upon her chair half stupefied, with her eyes fixed upon the sum. She sat she knew not how long, till, roused by the opening of Cecilia's door, she hastened to put away the papers.

'Let me see them, my dear, don't put away those papers,' cried Cecilia; 'Felicie tells me that you have been at these horrid accounts these two hours, and – you look – my dear Helen, you must let me see how much it is!' She drew the total from beneath Helen's hand. It was astounding even to Cecilia, as appeared by her first unguarded look of surprise. But, recovering herself immediately, she in a playfully-scolding tone told Helen that all this evil came upon her in consequence of her secret machinations. 'You set about to counteract me, wrote for things that I might not get them for you, you see what has come of it! As to these bills, they are all from tradespeople who cannot be in a hurry to be paid; and as to the things Felicie has got for you, she can wait, is not she a waiting-woman by profession? Now, where is the ruby brooch? Have you never looked at it? – I hope it is pretty – I am sure it is handsome,' cried she, as she opened the case. 'Yes, I like it prodigiously, I will take it off your hands, my dear; will that do?'

'No, Cecilia, I cannot let you do that, for you have one the same, I know, and you cannot want another – no, no.'

'You speak like an angel, my dear, but you do not look like one,' said Cecilia. 'So woebegone, so pale a creature, never did I see! do look at yourself in the glass; but you are too wretched to plague. Seriously, I want this brooch, and mine it must be – it is mine: I have a use for it, I assure you.'

'Well, if you have a use for it, really,' said Helen, 'I should indeed be very glad – '

'Be glad, then, it is mine,' said Cecilia; 'and now it is yours, my dear Helen, now, not a word, pray, if you love me!'

Helen could not accept of it; she thanked Cecilia with all her heart, she felt her kindness – her generosity, but even the hitherto irresistible words, 'If you love me,' were urged in vain. If she had not been in actual need of money, she might have been over-persuaded, but now her spirit of independence strengthened her resolution, and she persisted in her refusal. Lady Davenant's bell rang, and Helen, slowly rising, took up the miserable accounts, and said, 'Now I must go – '

'Where!' said Cecilia; 'you look as if you had heard a knell that summoned you – what are you going to do?'

'To tell all my follies to Lady Davenant.'

'Tell your follies to nobody but me,' cried Lady Cecilia. 'I have enough of my own to sympathise with you, but do not go and tell them to my mother, of all people; she, who has none of her own, how can you expect any mercy?'

'I do not; I am content to bear all the blame I so richly deserve, but I know that after she has heard me, she will tell me what I ought to do, she will find out some way of settling it all rightly, and if that can but be, I do not care how much I suffer. So the sooner I go to her the better,' said Helen.

'But you need not be in such a hurry; do not be like the man who said, "*Je veux être l'enfant prodigue, je veux être l'enfant perdu.*" [1] *L'enfant prodigue*, well and good, but why *l'enfant perdu*?'

'My dear Cecilia, do not play with me – do not stop me,' said Helen anxiously. 'It is serious with me now, and it is as much as I can do – '

Cecilia let her go, but trembled for her, as she looked after her, and saw her stop at her mother's door.

Helen's first knock was too low, it was unheard, she was obliged to wait; another, louder, was answered by 'Come in.' And in the presence she stood, and in the middle of things she rushed at once; the accounts, the total, lay before Lady Davenant. There it was: and the culprit, having made her confession, stood waiting for the sentence.

The first astonished change of look was certainly difficult to sustain. 'I ought to have foreseen this,' said Lady Davenant; 'my affection has deceived my judgment. Helen, I am sorry for your sake, and for my own.'

'Oh do not speak in that dreadful calm voice, as if – do not give me up at once,' cried Helen.

'What can I do for you? what can be done for one who has no strength of mind?' I have some, thought Helen, or I should not

---

[1] 'I want to be the prodigal child, I want to be the lost child'.

be here at this moment. 'Of what avail, Helen, is your good heart
– your good intentions, without the power to abide by them?
When you can be drawn aside from the right by the first paltry
temptation – by that most contemptible of passions – the passion
for baubles! You tell me it was not that, what then? a few words of
persuasion from any one who can smile, and fondle, and tell you
that they love you; – the fear of offending Cecilia? how absurd!
Is this what you both call friendship? But weaker still, Helen, I
perceive that you have been led blindfold in extravagance by a
prating French waiting-maid – to the very brink of ruin, the very
verge of dishonesty.'

'Dishonesty! how?'

'Ask yourself, Helen: is a person honest, who orders and takes
from the owner that for which he cannot pay? Answer me, honest
or dishonest?'

'Dishonest! If I had intended not to pay. But I did intend to
pay, and I will.'

'You will. The weak have no will – never dare to say I will. Tell
me how you will pay that which you owe. You have no means –
no choice, except to take from the fund you have already *willed*
to another purpose. See what good intentions come to, Helen,
when you cannot abide by them!'

'But I can,' cried Helen; 'whatever else I do, I will not touch
that fund, destined for my dear uncle – I have not touched it. I
could pay it in two years, and I will – I will give up my whole
allowance.'

'And what will you live upon in the meantime?'

'I should not have said my whole allowance, but I can do with
very little, I will buy nothing new.'

'Buy nothing – live upon nothing!' repeated Lady Davenant;
'how often have I heard these words said by the most improvi-
dent, in the moment of repentance, even then as blind and uncal-
culating as ever! And you, Helen, talk to me of your powers of
forbearance, – you, who, with the strongest motive your heart
could feel, have not been able for a few short months to resist the
most foolish – the most useless fancies.'

Helen burst into tears. But Lady Davenant, unmoved, at least to all outward appearance, coldly said, 'It is not feeling that you want, or that I require from you; I am not to be satisfied by words or tears.'

'I deserve it all,' said Helen; 'and I know you are not cruel. In the midst of this, I know you are my best friend.'

Lady Davenant was now obliged to be silent, lest her voice should betray more tenderness than her countenance chose to show.

'Only tell me what I can do now,' continued Helen; 'what can I do?'

'What you CAN do, I will tell you, Helen. Who was the man you were dancing with last night?'

'I danced with several; which do you mean?'

'Your partner in the quadrille you were dancing when I came in.'

'Lord Estridge: but you know him – he has often been here.'

'Is he rich?' said Lady Davenant.

'Oh yes, very rich, and very self-sufficient: he is the man Cecilia used to call "*Le prince de mon mérite*." [1]

'Did she? I do not remember. He made no impression on me, nor on you, I daresay.'

'Not the least, indeed.'

'No matter, he will do as well as another, since he is rich. You can marry him, and pay your present debts, and contract new, for thousands instead of hundreds: – this is what you CAN do, Helen.'

'Do you think I can?' said Helen.

'You can, I suppose, as well as others. You know that young ladies often marry to pay their debts.'

'So I once heard,' said Helen, 'but is it possible?'

'Quite. You might have been told more – that they enter into regular partnerships, joint-stock companies with dress-makers and jewellers, who make their ventures and bargains on the more or less reputation of the young ladies for beauty or for

[1] The prince I deserve

fashion, supply them with finery, speculate on their probabilities of matrimonial success, and trust to being repaid after marriage. Why not pursue this plan next season in town? You must come to it like others, whose example you follow – why not begin it immediately?'

There is nothing so reassuring to the conscience to hear, in the midst of blame that we do deserve, suppositions of faults, imputations which we know to be unmerited – impossible. Instead of being hurt or alarmed by what Lady Davenant had said, the whole idea appeared to Helen so utterly beneath her notice, that the words made scarcely any impression on her mind, and her thoughts went earnestly back to the pressing main question – 'What can I do, honestly to pay this money that I owe?' She abruptly asked Lady Davenant if she thought the jeweller could be prevailed upon to take back the sapphires and the brooch.

'Certainly not, without a considerable loss to you,' replied Lady Davenant; but with an obvious change for the better in her countenance, she added, 'Still the determination to give up the bauble is good; the means, at whatever loss, we will contrive for you, if you are determined.'

'Determined! – oh yes.' She ran for the bracelets and brooch, and eagerly put them into Lady Davenant's hand. And now another bright idea came into her mind: she had a carriage of her own – a very handsome carriage, almost new; she could part with it – yes, she would, though it was a present from her dear uncle – his last gift; and he had taken such pleasure in having it made perfect for her. She was very, very fond of it, but she would part with it; she saw no other means of abiding by her promise, and paying his debts and her own. This passed rapidly through her mind; and when she had expressed her determination, Lady Davenant's manner instantly returned to all its usual kindness, and she exclaimed as she embraced her, drew her to her, and kissed her again and again – 'You are my own Helen! These are deeds, Helen, not words: I am satisfied – I may be satisfied with you now.

'And about that carriage, my dear, it shall not go to a stranger, it shall be mine. I want a travelling chaise – I will purchase it from you; I shall value it for my poor friend's sake, and for yours, Helen. So now it is settled, and you are clear in the world again. I will never spoil you, but I will always serve you, and a greater pleasure I cannot have in this world.'

After this happy termination of the dreaded confession, how much did Helen rejoice that she had had the courage to tell all to her friend. The pain was transient – the confidence permanent.

As Helen was going into her own room, she saw Cecilia flying upstairs towards her, with an open letter in her hand, her face radiant with joy. 'I always knew it would all end well! Churchill might well say that all the sand in my hour-glass was diamond sand. There, my dear Helen – there,' cried Cecilia, embracing her as she put the letter into her hand. It was from Beauclerc, his answer to Lady Cecilia's letter, which had followed him to Naples. It was written the very instant he had read her explanation, and, warm from his heart, he poured out all the joy he felt on hearing the truth, and, in his transport of delight, he declared that he quite forgave Lady Cecilia, and would forget, as she desired, all the misery she had made him feel. Some confounded quarantine he feared might detain him, but he would certainly be at Clarendon Park in as short a time as possible. Helen's first smile, he said, would console him for all he had suffered, and make him forget everything.

Helen's first smile he did not see, nor the blush which spread and rose as she read. Cecilia was delighted. 'Generous, affectionate Cecilia!' thought Helen; 'if she has faults, and she really has but one, who could help loving her?' Not Helen, or she would have been the most ungrateful of human beings. Besides her sympathy in Helen's happiness, Cecilia was especially rejoiced at this letter, coming, as it did, the very day after her mother's return; for though she had written to Lady Davenant on Beauclerc's departure, and told her that he was gone only on Lord Beltravers's account, yet she dreaded that, when it came to speaking, her mother's penetration would discover that something extraordinary had happened. Now all was easy. Beauclerc was coming back: he had finished his friend's business, and, before he returned to Clarendon Park he wished to know if he might appear that as the acknowledged admirer of Miss Stanley – if he might with any chance of success pay his addresses to her. Secure that her mother would never ask to see the letter, considering it either as a private communication to his guardian, or as a love-letter to Helen, Cecilia gave this version of it to Lady Davenant; and how she settled it with the General Helen never knew; but it seemed all smooth and right.

And now, the regatta being at an end, the archery meetings over, and no hope of further gaiety for this season at Clarendon Park, the Castleforts and Lady Katrine departed. Lady Katrine's last satisfaction was the hard haughty look with which she took leave of Miss Stanley – a look expressing, as well as the bitter smile and cold form of good breeding could express it, unconquered, unconquerable hate.

CHAPTER 24

THERE IS NO BETTER TEST of the strength of affection than the ready turning of the mind to the little concerns of a friend, when preoccupied with important interests of our own. This was a proof of friendship which Lady Davenant had lately given to Helen, for, at the time when she had entered with so much readiness and zeal into Helen's little difficulties and debts, great political affairs and important interests of Lord Davenant's were in suspense, and pressed heavily upon her mind. What might be the nature of these political embarrassments had not been explained. Lady Davenant had only hinted at them. She said, 'she knew from the terror exhibited by the inferior creatures in office that some change of administration was expected, as beasts are said to howl and tremble before storm, or earthquake, or any great convulsion of nature takes place.'

Since Lady Davenant's return from town, where Lord Davenant still remained, nothing had been said of the embassy to Russia but that it was delayed. Lady Cecilia, who was quick, and where she was not herself concerned, usually right, in interpreting the signs of her mother's discomfiture, guessed that Lord Davenant had been circumvented by some diplomatist of inferior talents, and she said to Helen, 'When an ass kicks you never tell it, is a maxim which mamma heard from some friend, and she always acts upon it; but a kick, whether given by ass or not, leaves a bruise, which sometimes tells in spite of ourselves, and my mother should remember another maxim of that friend's, that the faults and follies of the great are the delight and comfort of the little. Now, my mother, though she is so well suited, from her superior abilities and strength of mind, and all that, to be the wife of a great political leader, yet in some respects she is the most unfit person upon earth for *the situation*; for, though she feels the necessity of conciliating, she cannot unbend with her inferiors, that is, with half the world. As Catalani said of singing, it is much more difficult to descend than to ascend well. Shockingly mamma shows in her manner sometimes how tired she is of the stupid, and how she despises the mean; and all the underlings think she can undo them with papa, for it has gone abroad that she *governs*, while, in fact, though papa asks her advice, to be sure, because she is so wise, she never does interfere in the least; but, now it has once got into the world's obstinate head that she does, it cannot be put out again, and mamma is the last person upon earth to take her own part, or condescend to explain and set things right. She is always thinking of papa's glory and the good of the public, but the public will never thank him and much less her; so there she is, a martyr without her crown; now, if I were to make a martyr of myself, which Heaven forbid! I would at least take right good care to secure my crown, and to have my full glory round my head, and set on becomingly. But seriously, my dear Helen,' continued Lady Cecilia, 'I am unhappy about papa and mamma, I assure you. I have seen little clouds of discontent long gathering, lowering, and blackening, and I know they will burst over their heads in some tremendous storm at last.'

Helen hoped not, but looked frightened.

'Oh, you may hope not, my dear, but I know it will be – we may not hear the thunder, but we shall see the lightning all the more dangerous. We shall be struck down, unless – ' she paused.

'Unless what?' said Helen.

'Unless the storm be dispersed in time.'

'And how?'

'The lightning drawn off by some good conductor – such as myself; I am quite serious, and though you were angry with me for laughing just now, as if I was not the best of daughters, even though I laugh, I can tell you I am meditating an act of self-devotion for my mother's sake – a grand *coup d'état*.'

'*Coup d'état*? You, Cecilia! my dear – '

'I, Helen, little as you think of me.'

'Of your political talents you don't expect me to think much, do you?'

'My political talents! you shall see what they are. I am capable of a grand *coup d'état*. I will have next week a three-days' congress, anti-political, at Clarendon Park, where not a word of politics shall be heard, nor anything but nonsense if I can help it, and the result shall be, as you shall see, goodwill between all men and all women? Yes, there's the grand point. Mamma has so affronted two ladies, very influential as they call it, each – Lady Masham, a favourite at court, and Lady Bearcroft, risen from the ranks, on her husband's shoulders; he, "a man of law," Sir Benjamin Bearcroft, and very clever she is I hear, but loud and coarse; absolutely inadmissible she was thought till lately, and now, only tolerated for her husband's sake, but still have her here I must.'

'I think you had better not,' remonstrated Helen; 'if she is so very vulgar, Lady Davenant and the General will never endure her.'

'Oh, he will; the General will bear a great deal for mamma's sake, and more for papa's. I must have her, my dear, for her husband is of consequence and, though he is ashamed of her, for that very reason he cannot bear that anybody should neglect her, and terribly mamma has neglected her! Now, my dear Helen, do not say a word more against it.' Very few words had Helen said. 'I must ponder well,' continued Cecilia, 'and make out my list of worthies, my concordatum party.'

Helen much advised the consulting Lady Davenant first; but Lady Cecilia feared her mother might be too proud to consent to any advance on her own part. Helen still feared that the bringing together such discordant people would never succeed, but Lady Cecilia, always happy in paying herself with words answerable to her wishes, replied 'that discords well managed often produced the finest harmony.' The only point she feared was, that

she should not gain the first step, that she should not be able to
prevail upon the General to let her give the invitations. In truth,
it required all her persuasive words and more persuasive looks
to accomplish this preliminary, and to bring General Clarendon
to invite, or permit to be invited, to Clarendon Park, persons
whom he knew but little, and liked not at all. But as Lady Cecilia
pleaded and urged that it would soon be over, 'the whole will
be over in three days – only a three-days' visit; and for mamma!
– I am sure, Clarendon – you will do anything for her, and for
papa, and your own Cecilia?' – the General smiled, and the notes
were written, and the invitations were accepted, and when once
General Clarendon had consented, he was resolutely polite in his
reception of these to him unwelcome guests. His manner was
not false; it was only properly polite, not tending to deceive any
one who understood the tokens of conventional good breeding.
It however required considerable power over himself to keep
the line of demarcation correctly, with one person in particular to whom he had a strong political aversion: Mr Harley. His
very name was abhorrent to General Clarendon, who usually
designated him as 'that Genius, Cecilia – that favourite of your
mother's!' – while to Lady Davenant Mr Harley was the only
person from whose presence she anticipated any pleasure, or who
could make the rest of the party to her endurable.

Helen, though apprehensive of what might be the ultimate
result of this congress, yet could not help rejoicing that she should
now have an opportunity of seeing some of those who are usually
considered 'high as human veneration can look.' It is easy, after
one knows who is who, to determine that we should have found
out the characteristic qualities and talents in each countenance.
Lady Cecilia, however, would not tell Helen the names of the
celebrated unknown who were assembled when they went into
the drawing-room before dinner, and she endeavoured to guess
from their conversation the different characters of the speak-
ers; but only a few sentences were uttered, signifying nothing;
snuff-boxes were presented, pinches taken and inclinations made
with becoming reciprocity, but the physiognomy of a snuff-box

Helen could not interpret, though Lavater asserts that everything in nature, even a cup of tea, has a physiognomy.

Dinner was announced, and the company paired off, seemingly not standing on the order of their going; yet all, especially as some were strangers, secretly mindful of their honours, and they moved on in precedence just, and found themselves in places due at the dinner-table.

But Helen did not seem likely to obtain more insight into the characters of these great personages in the dining-room than she had done in the drawing-room. For it often happens that, when the most celebrated, and even the most intellectual persons are brought together expressly for the purpose of conversation, then it does not flow, but sinks to silence, and ends at last in the stagnation of utter stupidity. Each seems oppressed with the weight of his own reputation, and, in the pride of high celebrity, and the shyness, real or affected, of high rank, each fears to commit himself by a single word. People of opposite parties, when thrown together, cannot at once change the whole habit of their minds, nor without some effort refrain from that abuse of their opposites in which they are accustomed to indulge when they have it all to themselves. Now every subject seemed laboured – for in the pedantry of party spirit no partisan will speak but in the slang or cant of his own craft. Knowledge is not only at one entrance, but at every entrance, quite shut out, and even literature itself grows perilous, so that to be safe they must all be dumb.

Lady Cecilia Clarendon was little aware of what she undertook when she called together this heterogeneous assembly of uncongenials and dissimilars round her dinner-table. After she had in vain made what efforts she could, and, well skilled in throwing the ball of conversation, had thrown it again and again without rebound from either side, she felt that all was flat, and that the silence and the stupidity were absolutely invincible. Helen could scarcely believe, when she tried afterwards to recollect, that she had literally this day, during the whole of the first course, heard only the following sentences, which came out at long intervals between each couple of questions and answers – or observations and acquiescences: – 'We had a shower.' – 'Yes, I think so.' 'But very fine weather we have had.' – 'Only too hot.' – 'Quite.' 'The new buildings at Marblemore – are they getting on, my lord?' – 'Do not know; did not come that way.' 'Whom have they now at Dunstanbury?' was the next question. Then in reply came slowly a list of fashionable names. 'Sir John died worth a million, they say.' – 'Yes, a martyr to the gout.' 'Has Lady Rachel done anything for her eyes?' – 'Gone to Brighton, I believe.' 'Has anything been heard of the North Pole expedition?' – 'Not a word.' 'Crockly has got a capital cook, and English too.' – 'English! eh?' – 'English – yes.' Lord Davenant hoped this English cook would, with the assistance of several of his brother *artistes* of the present day, redeem our country from one-half of the Abbé Gregoire's reproach. The abbé has said that England would be the finest country in the world, but that it wants two essentials, *sunshine* and *cooks*. 'Good! Good! Very!' voices from different sides of the table pronounced; and there was silence again.

At the dessert, however, after the servants had withdrawn, most people began to talk a little to their next neighbours; but by this Helen profited not, for each pair spoke low, and those who were beside her on either hand were not disposed to talk; she was seated between Sir Benjamin Bearcroft and Mr Harley – Sir Benjamin the man of law, and Mr Harley the man of genius, each eminent in his kind; but he of law seemed to have nothing in him but law, of which he was very full. In Sir Benjamin's economy of human life it was a wholesome rule, which he practised invariably, to let his understanding sleep in company, that it might waken in the courts, and for his repose he needed not what some great men have professed so much to like – 'the pillow of a woman's mind.' Helen did not much regret the silence of this great legal authority, but she was very sorry that the man of genius did not talk; she did not expect him to speak to her, but she wished to hear him converse with others. But something was the matter with him; from the moment he sat down to dinner Helen saw he seemed discomfited. He first put his hand across his eyes, then pressed his forehead; she feared he had a bad headache.

The hand went next to his ear, with a shrinking, excruciating gesture; it must be the earache, thought Helen. Presently his jaws were pinched together; toothache perhaps. At last she detected the disturbing cause. Opposite to Mr Harley, and beside Lady Davenant, sat a person whom he could not endure; one, in the first place, of an opposite party, but that was nothing; a man who was, in Mr Harley's opinion, a disgrace to any party, and what could bring him here? They had had several battles in public, but had never before met in private society, and the aversion of Mr Harley seemed to increase inversely as the squares of the distance. Helen could not see in the object adequate cause for this antipathy: the gentleman looked civil, smiling, rather mean, and quite insignificant, and he really was as insignificant as he appeared – not of consequence in any point of view. He was not high in office, nor ambassador, nor *chargé-d'affaires*; not certain that he was an *attaché* even, but he was said to have the ear of *somebody*, and was reputed to be secretly employed in diplomatic transactions of equivocal character; disclaimed, but used, by his superiors, and courted by his timid inferiors, whom he had persuaded of his great influence *somewhere*. Lady Cecilia had been assured, from good authority, that he was one who ought to be propitiated on her father's account, but now, when she perceived what sort of creature he was, sorely did she repent that he had been invited, and her mother, by whom he sat, seemed quite oppressed and nauseated.

So ended the dinner. And, as Lady Cecilia passed the General in going out of the room, she looked her contrition, her acknowledgment that he was perfectly right in his prophecy that it would never do.

⟨⟨⟨ CHAPTER 25 ⟩⟩⟩

IT WAS RATHER WORSE when the ladies were by themselves. Some of the party were personally strangers to Lady Davenant; all had heard of her sufficiently; most had formed a formidable and false opinion of her. Helen was quite astonished at the awe her ladyship inspired in strangers. Lady Davenant's appearance and manner at this moment were not, indeed, calculated to dispel this dread. She was unusually distant and haughty, from a mistaken sort of moral pride. Aware that some of the persons now before her had, in various ways, by their own or their husbands' means, power to serve or to injure Lord Davenant, she disdained to propitiate them by the slightest condescension.

But how any persons in England – in London – could be strangers to Lady Davenant, was to a foreign lady who was present matter of inexpressible surprise. She could not understand how the wives of persons high in political life, some of opposite, but some of the same parties, should often be personally strangers to each other. Foreigners are, on first coming to England, apt to imagine that all who act together in public life must be of the same private society; while, on the contrary, it often happens that the ladies especially of the same party are in different grades of fashion – moving in different orbits. The number of different circles and orbits in London is, indeed, astonishing to strangers, and the manner in which, though touching at tangents, these keep each their own path, attracted and repelled, or mutually influential, is to those who have not seen and studied the planisphere absolutely incomprehensible. And, as she pondered on this difficulty, the ambassadress, all foreigner as she was, and all unused to silence, spoke not, and no one spoke; and nought was heard but the cup on the saucer, or the spoon in the cup, or the buzzing of a fly in the window.

In the midst of this awful calm it was that Lady Bearcroft blurted out with loud voice – 'Amazing entertaining we are! so many clever people got together, too, for what?' It was worth while to have seen Lady Masham's face at that moment! Lady Bearcroft saw it, and, fearing no mortal, struck with the comic of that look of Lady Masham's, burst into laughter uncontrolled, and the contrast of dignity and gravity in Lady Davenant only made her laugh the more, till out of the room at last she ran. Lady Masham all the while, of course, never betrayed the slightest idea that she could by any possibility have been the object of Lady Bearcroft's mirth. But Lady Davenant – how did she take it? To her daughter's infinite relief, quite quietly; she looked rather amused than displeased. She bore with Lady Bearcroft, altogether, better than could have been expected; because she considered her only as a person unfortunately out of her place in society, and, without any fault of her own, dragged up from below to a height of situation for which nature had never intended, and neither art nor education had ever prepared her; whose faults and deficiencies were thus brought into the flash of the day at once, before the malice of party and the fastidiousness of fashion, which knows not how to distinguish between lack of wit and lack of learning.

Not so Lady Davenant: she made liberal and philosophic allowance for even those faults of manner which were most glaring, and she further suspected that Lady Bearcroft purposely exaggerated her own vulgarity, partly for diversion, partly to make people stare, and partly to prevent their seeing what was habitual, and what involuntary, by hiding the bounds of reality. Of this Lady Masham had not the most distant conception; on the contrary, she was now prepared to tell a variety of odd anecdotes of Lady Bearcroft. She had seen, she said, this extraordinary person before, but had never met her in society, and delighted she was unexpectedly to find her here – 'quite a treat.' Such characters are indeed seldom met with at a certain height in the atmosphere of society, and such were peculiarly and justly Lady Masham's delight, for they relieved and at the same time fed a sense of superiority insufficient to itself. Such a person is fair, privileged, safe game, and Lady Masham began, as does a reviewer determined to be especially severe, with a bit of praise.

'Really very handsome Lady Bearcroft must have been! Yes, as you say, Lady Cecilia, she is not out of blow yet, certainly, only too full-blown rather for some tastes — fortunately not for Sir Benjamin; he married her, you know, long ago, for her beauty; she is a very correct person — always was; but they do repeat the strangest things she says — so very odd! and they tell such curious stories, too, of the things she does.' Lady Masham then detailed a variety of anecdotes, which related chiefly to Lady Bearcroft's household cares, which never could she with haste despatch; then came stories of her cheap magnificence and extraordinary toilette expedients. 'I own,' continued Lady Masham, 'that I always thought the descriptions I heard must be exaggerated; but one is compelled to acknowledge that there is here in reality a terrible want of tact. Poor Sir Benjamin! I quite pity him, he must so see it! Though not of the first water himself, yet still he must feel, when he sees Lady Bearcroft with other people! He has feelings, though nobody would guess it from his look, and he shows it too, I am told: sadly annoyed he is sometimes by her *mal-apropoisms*. One day, she at one end of the table and he at the other, her ladyship in her loud voice called out to him, "Sir Benjamin, Sir Benjamin! this is our wedding-day!" He, poor man, did not hear; she called out again louder, "Sir Benjamin, my dear, this day fifteen years ago you and I were married!" "Well, my dear," he answered, "well, my dear, how can I possibly help that now?" '

Pleased with the success of this anecdote, which raised a general smile, Lady Masham vouched for its perfect correctness; 'she had it from one, who heard it from a person who was actually present at the time it happened.' Lady Davenant had not the least doubt of the correctness of the story, but she believed the names of the parties were different; she had heard it years ago of another person. It often happens, as she observed, to those who make themselves notoriously ridiculous, as to those who become famous for wit, that all good things in their kinds are attributed to them; though the one may have no claim to half the witticisms, and the other may not be responsible for half the absurdities, for which they have the reputation. It required all Lady Masham's politeness to look pleased, and all her candour to be quite happy to be set right as to that last anecdote. But many she had heard of Lady Bearcroft were really incredible. 'Yet one would almost believe anything of her.' While she was yet speaking, Lady Bearcroft returned, and her malicious enemy, leaning back in her chair as if in expectation of the piece beginning, waited for her puppet to play or be played off.

All this time Lady Cecilia was not at ease; she, well aware what her mother would feel, and had felt, while Lady Masham was going on with this gossip-talk, had stood between her ladyship and Lady Davenant, and, as Lady Masham did not speak much above her breath, Cecilia had for some time flattered herself that her laudable endeavours to intercept the sound, or to prevent the sense from reaching her mother's ear, had succeeded, especially as she had made as many exclamations as she could of 'Really!' 'Indeed!' 'How extraordinary!' 'You do not say so?' which, as she pronounced them, might have excited the curiosity of common-place people, but which she knew would in her mother's mind deaden all desire to listen. However, Lady Masham had raised her voice, and from time to time had stretched her neck of snow beyond Lady Cecilia's intercepting drapery, so as actually to claim Lady Davenant's attention. The consequences her daughter heard and felt. She heard the tap, tap, tap of the ivory folding-knife upon the table; and well interpreting, she knew, even before she saw her mother's countenance, that Lady Masham had undone herself, and, what was of much more consequence, had destroyed all chance of accomplishing that reconciliation with 'mamma,' that projected coalition which was to have been of such ultimate advantage to 'papa.'

Notwithstanding Lady Bearcroft's want of knowledge of the great world, she had considerable knowledge of human nature, which stood her wonderfully in stead. She had no notion of being made sport of for the *élégantes*, and, with all Lady Masham's plausibility of persiflage, she never obtained her end, and never elicited anything really absurd by all attempts to draw her out – out she would not be drawn. After an unconquerable silence and all the semblance of dead stupidity, Lady Bearcroft suddenly showed signs of life, however, and she, all at once, began to talk – to Helen of all people! And why? – because she had taken, in her own phrase, a monstrous fancy to Miss Stanley; she was not sure of her name, but she knew she liked her nature, and it would be a pity that her reason should not be known, and in the words in which she told it to Lady Cecilia, 'Now I will just tell you why I have taken such a monstrous fancy to your friend here, Miss Hanley – '

'Miss Stanley – give me leave to mention,' said Lady Cecilia. 'Let me introduce you regularly.'

'Oh! by no means; don't trouble yourself now, Lady Cecilia, for I hate regular introductions. But, as I was going to tell you how, before dinner to-day, as I came down the great staircase, I had an uncommon large, big, and, for aught I know, yellow corking-pin, which that most careless of all careless maids of mine – a good girl, too – had left sticking point foremost out of some part of me. Miss Hanley – Stanley (beg pardon) was behind, and luckily saw and stopped. Out she pulled it, begging my pardon; so kindly too, I only felt the twitch on my sleeve, and turned, and loved the first sight I had of that pretty face, which need never blush, I am sure, though it's very becoming the blush too. So good-natured, you know, Lady Cecilia, it was, when nobody was looking, and before anybody was the wiser. Not like some young ladies, or old even, that would have *showed one up*, rather than help one out in any pin's point of a difficulty.'

Lady Cecilia herself was included in Lady Bearcroft's good graces, for she liked that winning way, and saw there was a real good-nature there too. She opened to both friends cordially, *à propos* to some love of a lace trimming. Of lace she was a famous judge, and she went into details of her own good bargains, with histories of her expeditions into the extremity of the City in search of cheap goods and unheard-of wonders at prime cost, in regions unknown. She told how it was her clever way to leave her carriage and her *people*, and go herself down narrow streets and alleys, where only wheel-barrows and herself could go; she boasted of her feats in diving into dark dens in search of run goods, charming things – French warranted – that could be had for next to nothing, and, in exemplification, showed the fineness of her embroidered cambric handkerchiefs, and told their price to a farthing!

Lady Masham's 'Wonderful!' was worthy of any Jesuit, male or female, that ever existed.

From her amazing bargains, the lady of the law-knight went on to smuggling; and, as she got into spirits, talking loudly, she told of some amber satin, a whole piece capitally got over in an old gentleman's 'Last Will and Testament,' tied up with red tape so nicely, and sealed and superscribed and all, got through untouched! 'But a better thing I did myself,' continued she; 'the last trip I made to Paris – coming back, I set at defiance all the searchers and *stabbers*, and custom-house officers of both nations. I had hundreds of pounds worth of Valenciennes and Brussels lace hid – you would never guess where. I never told a servant – not a mortal maid even; that's the only way; had only a confidant of a coachmaker. But when it came to packing-up time, my own maid smelt out the lace was missing; and gave notice, I am confident, to the custom-house people to search me. So much the more glory to me. I got off clear; and, when they had stabbed the cushions, and torn the inside of my carriage all to pieces, I very coolly made them repair the mischief at their own cost. Oh, I do love to do things bravely! and away I drove triumphant with the lace, well stuffed, packed, and covered within the pole leather of the carriage they had been searching all the time.'

At this period of her narrative the gentlemen came into the drawing-room. 'But here comes Sir Benjamin! mum, mum! not a word more for my life! You understand, Lady Cecilia, husbands must be minded. And let me whisper a favour – a whist-party I must beg; nothing keeps Sir Ben in good humour so certainly as whist – when he wins, I mean.'

The whist-party was made, and Lady Cecilia took care that Sir Benjamin should win, while she lost with the best grace possible. By her conciliating manners and good management in dividing to govern, all parties were arranged to general satisfaction. Mr Harley's antipathy, the *attaché*, she settled at *écarté* with Lady Masham, who found him 'quite a well-mannered, pleasant person.' Lady Cecilia explained to Mr Harley that it was her fault – her mistake entirely – that this person had been invited. Mr Harley was now himself again, and happy in conversation with Lady Davenant, beside whom he found his place on the sofa.

After Helen had done her duty at harp and pianoforte, Cecilia relieved her, and whispered that she might now go to her mother's sofa, and rest and be happy. 'Mamma's work is in some puzzle; you must go and set it to rights, my dear.' Lady Davenant welcomed her with a smile, made room for her on the sofa, and made over to her the tambour-frame; and now that Helen saw and heard Mr Harley in his natural state, she could scarcely believe that he was the same person who had sat beside her at dinner. Animated and delightful he was now, and, what she particularly liked in him, there was no display – nothing in the Churchill style. Whenever any one came near, and seemed to wish to hear or speak, Mr Harley not only gave them fair play, but helped them in their play. Helen observed that he possessed the art which she had often remarked in Lord Davenant, peculiar to good-natured genius – the art of drawing something good out of everybody; sometimes more than they knew they had in them, till it was brought out. Even from Lord Masham, insipid and soulless though he was, as any courtier-lord in waiting could be, something was extracted; Lord Masham, universally believed to have nothing in him, was this evening surprisingly entertaining. He gave Lady Davenant a description of what he had been so fortunate to see – the first public dinner of the King of France on his restoration, served according to all the former ceremonials, and in the etiquette of Louis the Fourteenth's time. Lord Masham represented in a lively manner the Marquis de Dreux, in all his antiquarian glory, going through the whole form described: first knocking with his cane at the door; then followed by three guards with shouldered carbines, marching to buttery and hall, each and every officer of the household making reverential obeisance as they passed to the *Nef* – the *Nef* being, as Lord Masham explained to Miss Stanley, a piece of gilt plate in the shape of the hull of a ship, in which the napkins for the king's table are kept. 'But why should the hull of a ship be appropriated to the royal napkins?' was asked. Lord Masham confessed that this was beyond him, but he looked amazingly considerate – delicately rubbed his polished forehead with the second finger of the right hand, then regarded his ring, and turned it thrice slowly round, but the talismanic action produced nothing, and he received timely relief by a new turn given to the conversation, in which he was not, he thought, called upon to take any share – the question indeed appeared to him irrelevant, and retiring to the card-table, he 'left the discussion to abler heads.'

The question was, why bow to the Nef at all? – This led to a discussion upon the advantages of ceremonials in preserving respect for order and reverence for authority, and then came an inquiry into the abuses of this real good. It was observed that the signs of the times should always be consulted, and should guide us in these things. How far? was next to be considered. All agreed on the principle that 'order is Heaven's first law,' yet there were in the application strong shades of difference between those who took part in the conversation. On one side, it was thought that overturning the *tabouret* at the court of France had been the signal for the overthrow of the throne; while, on the other hand, it was suggested that a rigid adherence to forms unsuited to the temper of the times only exasperates, and that, wherever reliance on forms is implicit, it is apt to lead princes and their counsellors to depend too much on the strength of that fence which, existing only in the imagination, is powerless when the fashion changes.

In a court quite surrounded and enveloped by old forms, the light of day cannot penetrate to the interior of the palace, the eyes long kept in obscurity are weakened, so that light cannot be borne: when suddenly it breaks in, the royal captive is bewildered, and if obliged to act, he gropes, blunders, injures himself, and becomes incapable of decision in extremity of danger, reduced to the helplessness which marks the condition of the Eastern despot, or puppet monarchs of any time or country.

As Helen sat by, listening to this conversation, what struck and interested her most was the manner in which it went on and went off without leading to any unpleasant consequences, notwithstanding the various shades of opinion between the parties. This she saw depended much on the good sense and talents, but far more on the good breeding and temper of those who spoke and those who listened. Time in the first place was allowed and taken for each to be understood, and no one was urged by exclamation, or misconception, or contradiction, to say more than just the thing he thought.

Lady Cecilia, who had now joined the party, was a little in pain when she heard Louis the Fourteenth's love for punctuality alluded to. She dreaded, when the General quoted 'Punctuality is the virtue of princes,' that Mr Harley, with the usual impatience of genius, would have ridiculed so antiquated a notion; but, to Lady Cecilia's surprise, he even took the part of punctuality; in a very edifying manner he distinguished it from mere ceremonial etiquette – the ceremonial of the German courts, where 'they lose time at breakfast, at dinner, at supper; at court, in the antechamber, on the stairs, everywhere'; – punctuality was, he thought, a habit worthy to be ranked with the virtues, by its effects upon the mind, the power it demands and gives of self-control, raising in us a daily, hourly sense of duty, of something that ought, that must be done, one of the best habits human creatures can have, either for their own sake or the sake of those with whom they live. And to kings and courtiers particularly, because it gives the idea of stability – of duration; and to the aged, because it gives a sort of belief that life will last for ever. The General had often thought this, but said he had never heard it so well expressed; he afterwards acknowledged to Cecilia that he found Mr Harley was quite a different person from what he had expected – 'He has good sense, as well as genius and good breeding. I am glad, my dear Cecilia, that you asked him here.' This was a great triumph.

Towards the close of the evening, when mortals are beginning to think of bed-chamber candles, Lady Cecilia looked at the *écarté* table, and said to her mother, 'How happy they are, and how comfortable we are! A card-table is really a necessary of life – not even music is more universally useful.' Mr Harley said, 'I doubt,' and then arose between Lady Davenant and him an argument upon the comparative power in modern society of music and cards. Mr Harley took the side of music, but Lady Davenant inclined to think that cards, in their day, and their day is not over yet, have had a wider range of influence. 'Nothing like that happy board of green cloth; it brings all intellects to one level,' she said. Mr Harley pleaded the cause of music, which, he said, hushes all passions, calms even despair. Lady Davenant urged the silent superiority of cards, which rests the weary talker, and relieves the perplexed courtier, and, in support of her own opinion, she mentioned an old ingenious essay on cards and tea, by Pinto, she thought; and she begged that Helen would some time look for it in the library. Helen went that instant. She searched, but could not find; where it ought to have been, there it of course was not. While she was still on the book-ladder, the door opened, and enter Lady Bearcroft.

'Miss Hanley!' cried she, 'I have a word to say to you, for, though you are a stranger to me, I see you are a dear good creature, and I think I may take the liberty of asking your advice in a little matter.'

Helen, who had by this time descended from the steps, stood and looked a little surprised, but said all that was properly civil, 'gratified by Lady Bearcroft's good opinion – happy to be of any service,' – etc.

'Well, then – sit ye down one instant, Miss Hanley.' Helen suggested that her name was Stanley.

'Stanley! – eh? – Yes, I remember. But I want to consult you, since you are so kind to allow me, on a little matter – but do sit down, I can never talk of business standing. Now I just want you, my dear Miss Hanley, to do a little job for me with Lady Davenant, who, with half an eye I can see, is a great friend of yours. – 'Arn't I right?'

Helen said Lady Davenant was indeed a very kind friend of hers, but still what it could be in which Lady Bearcroft expected her assistance she could not imagine.

'You need not be frightened at the word job; if that is what alarms you,' continued Lady Bearcroft; 'put your heart at ease, there is nothing of that sort here. It is only a compliment that I want to make, and nothing in the world expected in return for it – as it is a return in itself. But in the first place look at this cover.' She produced the envelope of a letter. 'Is this Lady Davenant's handwriting, think you?' She pointed to the word '*Mis-sent*,' written on the corner of the cover. Helen said that it was Lady Davenant's writing. 'You are certain? – Well, that is odd! – Mis-sent! when it was directed to herself, and nobody else on earth, as you see as plain as possible – Countess Davenant, surely that is right enough?' Then opening a red morocco case she showed a magnificent diamond Sévigné. 'Observe now,' she continued, 'these diamonds are so big, my dear Miss Hanley – Stanley – they would have been quite out of my reach, only for that late French invention which maybe you may not have heard of, nor should I, but for the hint of a friend at Paris, who is in the jewellery line. The French, you must know, have got the art of sticking small di'monds together so as to make little worthless ones into large, so that, as you see, you would never tell the difference; and as it was a new discovery, and something ingenious and scientific, and Lady Davenant being reported to be a scientific lady, as well as political and influential, and all that, I thought it a good opportunity, and a fine excuse for paying her a compliment, which I had long wished to pay, for she was once on a time very kind to Sir Ben, and got him appointed to his present station; and though Lord Davenant was the ostensible person, I considered her as the prime mover behind the curtain. Accordingly, I sat me down, and wrote as pretty a note as I could pen, and Sir Ben approved of the whole thing; but I don't say that I'm positive he was as off-handed and as clean-hearted in the matter as I was, for between you and I his gratitude, as they say of some people's, is apt to squint with one eye to the future as well as one to the past – you comprehend?'

Helen was not clear that she comprehended all that had been said; still less had she any idea what she could have to do in this matter; she waited for further explanation.

'Now all I want from you then, Miss Hanley – Stanley I would say, I beg pardon, I'm the worst at proper names that lives – but all I want of you, Miss Hanley, is – first, your opinion as to the validity of the handwriting, – well, you are positive, then, that this *mis-sent* is her hand. Now then, I want to know, do you think Lady Davenant knew what she was about when she wrote it?'

Helen's eyes opened to their utmost power of distension, at the idea of anybody's questioning that Lady Davenant knew what she was about.

'La! my dear,' said Lady Bearcroft; 'spare the whites of your eyes, I didn't mean she didn't know what she was about in *that* sense.'

'What sense?' said Helen.

'Not in any particular sense,' replied Lady Bearcroft. 'But let me go on, or we shall never come to an understanding; I only meant that her ladyship might have just sat down to answer my note, as I often do myself, without having read the whole through, or before I have taken it in quite.'

Helen thought this very unlikely to have happened with Lady Davenant.

'But still it might have happened,' continued Lady Bearcroft, 'that her ladyship did not notice the delicacy of the way in which the thing was *put* – for it really was put so that nobody could take hold of it against any of us – you understand; and after all, such a curiosity of a Sévigné as this, and such fine "di'monds," was too pretty and too good a thing to be refused hand-over-head, in that way. Besides, my note was so respectable, and respectful, it surely required and demanded something more of an answer, methinks, from a person of birth or education than the single bald word "mis-sent," like the postman! Surely, Miss Hanley, now, putting your friendship apart, candidly you must think as I do? And, whether or no, at least you will be so obliging to do me the favour to find out from Lady Davenant if she really made the reply with her eyes open or not, and really meant what she said.'

Helen being quite clear that Lady Davenant always meant what she said, and had written with her eyes open, declined, as perfectly useless, making the proposed inquiry. It was plain that Lady Davenant had not thought proper to accept of this present, and to avoid any unpleasant explanations had presumed it was not intended for her, but had been sent by mistake. Helen advised her to let the matter rest.

'Well, well!' said Lady Bearcroft, 'thank you, Miss Hanley, at all events for your good advice. But, neck or nothing, I am apt to go through with whatever I once take into my head, and, since you cannot aid and abet, I will trouble you no further, only not to say a word of what I have mentioned. But all the time I thank you, my dear young lady, as much as if I took your dictum. So, my dear Miss Hanley – Stanley – do not let me interrupt you longer in your book-hunt. Take care of that step-ladder, though; it is *coggledy*, as I observed when you came down – Good-night, good-night.'

'MY DEAR HELEN, there is an end of everything!' cried Lady Cecilia, the next day, bursting into Helen's room, and standing before her with an air of consternation. 'What has brought things to this sad pass, I know not,' continued she, 'for, but an hour before, I left everybody in good-humour with themselves – all in good train. But now – '

'What?' said Helen, 'for you have not given me the least idea of what has happened.'

'Because I have not the least idea myself, my dear. All I know is, that something has gone wrong, dreadfully, between my mother and Lady Bearcroft. Mamma would not tell me what it is; but her indignation is at such a height she declares she will not see that *woman* again: – positively she will not come forth from her chamber as long as Lady Bearcroft remains in the house. So there is a total break-up – and I wish I had never meddled with anything. Oh that I had never brought together these unsuitabiities, these incompatibilities! O Helen! what shall I do?'

Quite pale, Lady Cecilia stood, really in despair; and Helen did not know what to advise.

'Do you know anything about it, Helen, for you look as if you did?'

An abrupt knock at the door interrupted them, and, without waiting for permission, in came Lady Bearcroft, as if blown by a high wind, looking very red: half angry, half frightened, and then laughing, she exclaimed – 'A fine *boggle-de-botch* I have made of it!' But seeing Lady Cecilia she stopped short – 'Beg pardon – thought you were by yourself, Miss Hanley.'

Lady Cecilia instantly offered to retire, yet intimated, as she moved towards the door, a wish to stay, if it were not too much, to ask what was meant by –

'By *boggle-de-botch*, do you mean?' said Lady Bearcroft. 'I am aware it is not a canonical word – classical, I mean; nor in nor out of any dictionary, perhaps – but when people are warm, they cannot stand picking terms.'

'Certainly not,' said Lady Cecilia; 'but what is the matter? I am sorry anything unpleasant has occurred.'

'Unpleasant indeed!' cried Lady Bearcroft; 'I have been treated actually like a dog, while paying a compliment too, and a very handsome compliment, beyond contradiction. Judge for yourself, Lady Cecilia, if this Sévigné is to be *sneezed at*.'

She opened the case; Lady Cecilia said the diamonds were certainly very handsome, but –

'But!' repeated Lady Bearcroft, 'I grant you there may be a but to everything in life; still it might be said civilly, as you say it, Lady Cecilia, or looked civilly, as you look it, Miss Hanley: and if that had been done, instead of being affronted, I might after all have been well enough pleased to pocket my diamonds; but nobody can without compunction pocket an affront.'

Lady Cecilia was sure her mother could not mean any affront.

'Oh, I do not know what she could or could not mean; but I will tell you what she did – all but threw the diamonds in my face.'

'Impossible!' cried Helen.

'Possible – and I will show you how, Miss Hanley. This way: just shut down the case – snap! –and across the table she threw it, just as you would deal a card in a passion, only with a Mrs Siddons air to boot. I beg your pardons, both ladies, for mimicking your friend and your parent, but flesh and blood could not stand that sort of style, you know, and a little wholesome mimicry breaks no bones, and is not very offensive, I hope?' The mimicry could not indeed be very offensive, for the imitation

was so utterly unlike the reality, that Lady Cecilia and Helen with
difficulty repressed their smiles. 'Ladies may smile, but they would
smile on the wrong sides of their pretty little mouths if they had
been treated as I have been – so ignominiously. I am sure I wish
I had taken your advice, Miss Hanley; but the fact was, last night
I did not quite believe you: I thought you were only saying the
best you could to set off a friend; for, since I have been among
the great, and indeed even when I lived with the little, I have
met with so many fair copies of false countenances, that I could
not help suspecting there might be something of that sort with
your Lady Davenant, but I am entirely convinced all you told me
is true, for I peeped quite close at her, lifted up the hood, and
found there were not two faces under it – only one very angry
one for my pains. But I declare I would rather see that than a
double one, like my Lady Masham's, with her spermaceti smile.
And after all, do you know,' continued Lady Bearcroft, in a right
vulgarly-cordial tone – 'do you know now, really, the first anger
over, I like Lady Davenant – I protest and vow, even her pride I
like – it well became her – birth and all, for I hear she is straight
from Charlemagne! But I was going to mention, now my recollection is coming to me, that when I began talking to her ladyship of Sir Ben's gratitude about that place she got for him, she
cut me short with her queer look, and said she was sure that Lord
Davenant (and if he had been the king himself, instead of only
her husband, and your father, Lady Cecilia, she could not have
pronounced his name with more distinction) – she was sure, she
said, that Lord Davenant would not have been instrumental in
obtaining that place for Sir Benjamin Bearcroft if he had known
any man more worthy of it, which indeed I did not think at the
time over and above civil – for where, then, was the particular
compliment to Sir Ben?'

But when Lady Bearcroft saw Lady Cecilia's anxiety and real
distress at her mother's indignant resolution, she, with surprising
good-humour, said, – 'I wish I could settle it for you, my dear. I
cannot go away directly, which would be the best move, because
Sir Benjamin has business here to-day with Lord Davenant –

some job of his own, which must take place of any movements of mine, he being the more worthy gender. But I will tell you what I can do, and will, and welcome. I will keep my room instead of your mother keeping hers; so you may run and tell Lady Davenant that she is a prisoner at large, with the range of the whole house, without any danger of meeting me, for I shall not stir till the carriage is at the door to-morrow morning, when she will not be up, for we will have it at six. I will tell Sir Benjamin, he is in a hurry back to town, and he always is. So all is right on my part. And go you to your mother, my dear Lady Cecilia, and settle her. I am glad to see you smile again; it is a pity you should ever do anything else.'

It was not long before Cecilia returned, proclaiming, 'Peace, Peace!' She had made such an amusing report to her mother of all that Lady Bearcroft had said and done, and purposed to do, that Lady Davenant could not help seeing the whole in a ludicrous light, felt at once that it was beneath her serious notice, and that it would be unbecoming to waste indignation upon such a person. The result was, that she commissioned Helen to release Lady Bearcroft as soon as convenient, and to inform her that an act of oblivion was passed over the whole transaction.

There had been a shower, and it had cleared up. Lady Cecilia thought the sky looked bluer, and birds sang sweeter, and the air felt pleasanter, than before the storm. 'Nothing like a storm,' said she, 'for clearing the air; nothing like a little honest hurricane. But with Lady Masham there never is anything like a little honest hurricane. It is all still and close with an indescribable volcano-like feeling; one is not sure of what one is standing upon. Do you know, Helen,' continued she, 'I am quite afraid of some explosion between mamma and Lady Masham. If we came to any difficulty with her, we could not get out of it quite so well as with Lady Bearcroft, for there is no resource of heart or frankness of feeling with her. Before we all meet at dinner, I must sound mamma, and see if all is tolerably safe.' And when she went this day at dressing-time with a bouquet, as was her custom, for her mother, she took Helen with her.

At the first hint of Lady Cecilia's fears that Lady Masham could do her any mischief, Lady Davenant smiled in scorn. 'The will she may have, my dear, but she has not the power.'

'She is very foolish, to be sure,' said Lady Cecilia; 'still she might do mischief, and there is something monstrously treacherous in that smile of hers.'

'Monstrously!' repeated Lady Davenant. 'No, no, my dear Cecilia; nothing monstrous. Leave to Lady Bearcroft the vulgar belief in court-bred monsters; we know there are no such things. Men and women there, as everywhere else, are what nature, education, and circumstances have made them. Once an age, once in half-a-dozen ages, nature may make a Brinvilliers, or art allow of a Zeluco; but, in general, monsters are mere fabulous creatures – mistakes often, from bad drawings, like the unicorn.'

'Yes, mamma, yes; now I feel much more comfortable. The unicorn has convinced me,' said Lady Cecilia, laughing and singing

' 'Tis all a mere fable; there's nothing to fear.

'And I shall think of her henceforth as nothing but what she appears to be, a well-dressed, well-bred, fine lady. Ay – every inch a fine lady; every word, look, motion, thought, suited to that *métier.*'

'That vocation,' said Lady Davenant; 'it is above a trade; with her it really is a sacred duty, not merely a pleasure, to be fine. She is a fine lady of the first order; nothing too professional in her manner – no obvious affectation, for affectation in her was so early wrought into a habit as to have become second nature, scarcely distinguished from real – all easy.'

'Just so, mamma; one gets on so easy with her.'

'A curious illusion,' continued Lady Davenant, 'occurs with every one making acquaintance with such persons as Lady Masham, I have observed; perhaps it is that some sensation of the tread-mill life she leads communicates itself to those she is talking to; which makes you fancy you are always getting on, but you never do get beyond a certain point.'

'That is exactly what I feel,' said Helen, 'while Lady Masham speaks, or while she listens, I almost wonder how she ever existed without me.'

'Yes, and though one knows it is all an illusion,' said Lady Cecilia, 'still one is pleased, knowing all the time that she cannot possibly care for one in the least; but then one does not expect everybody to care for one really; at least I know I cannot like all my acquaintances as much as my friends, much less can I love all my neighbours as myself – '

'Come, come, Cecilia!' said her mother.

'By "come, come!" mamma means, don't go any further, Cecilia,' said she, turning to Helen. 'But now, mamma, I am not clear whether you really think her your friend or your enemy, inclined to do you mischief or not. Just as it may be for her interest or not, I suppose.'

'And just as it may be the fashion or not,' said Lady Davenant. 'I remember hearing old Lady M—, one of the cleverest women of the last century, and one who had seen much of the world, say, "If it was the fashion to burn me, and I at the stake, I hardly know ten persons of my acquaintance who would refuse to throw on a faggot." '

'O mamma – O Lady Davenant!' exclaimed Helen and Cecilia.

'It was a strong way of putting the matter,' said Lady Davenant, laughing: – 'but fashion has, I assure you, more influence over weak minds, such as Lady Masham's, than either party or interest. And since you do not like my illustration by fire, take one by water – She is just a person to go out with, on a party of pleasure, on the smooth surface of a summer sea, and if a slight shower comes on would pity your bonnet sincerely, but if a serious squall arose and all should be in danger – '

'Then, of course, everybody would take care of themselves,' interrupted Lady Cecilia, 'excepting such a simpleton as Helen, who would take care of you first, mamma, of me next, and of herself last.'

'I believe it – I do believe it,' cried Lady Davenant, and, her eyes and thoughts fixing upon Helen, she quite forgot what further she was going to say of Lady Masham.

The perfectly unimpassioned tone in which her mother had discussed this lady's character, even the candour, convinced Lady Cecilia as well as Helen that nothing further could be done as to drawing them together. No condescension of manner, no conciliation, could be expected from Lady Davenant towards Lady Masham, but at the same time there was no fear of any rupture. And to this humble consolation was Lady Cecilia brought. She told Helen that she gave up all hope of doing any good, she would now be quite content if she avoided doing harm, and if this visit ended without coming to any further outrage on the part of Lady Bearcroft, and without her mother's being *guilty of contempt* to Lady Masham. She had done some little service, however, with respect to the ambassadress, and her mother knew it. It was well known that the ambassadress governed the ambassador, and Lady Cecilia had quite won her heart, 'so that he will be assuredly a friend to papa. Indeed, this has been almost promised. Madam l'Ambassadrice assured me that her husband looks upon Lord Davenant as one of the first sages of England, that is to say, of Europe; and she says he is well acquainted with all Lord Davenant's works – and it is my belief,' concluded Lady Cecilia, 'that all Sir William Davenant's works go with her to papa's credit, for as she spoke she gave a polite glance towards the bookcase where she saw their gilded backs, and I found the ambassador himself, afterwards, with "Davenant on Trade" in his hand! Be it so: it is not, after all, you know, robbing the dead, only inheriting by mistake from a namesake, which with foreigners is allowable, because impossible to avoid, from the time of "*Monsieur Robinson parent apparemment de Monsieur Crusoe?*" [1] to the present day.'

By dint of keeping well asunder those who would not thaw well together, Lady Cecilia did contrive to get through the remaining morning of this operose visit; some she sent out to drive with gallant military outriders to see places in the neighbourhood famed for this or that; others walked, or boated, or went through the customary course of conservatories, pheasantry,

[1] Mr Robinson, apparently a relative of Mr Crusoe

flower-garden, pleasure-grounds, and best views of Clarendon Park – and billiards always.

The political conferences were held in Lord Davenant's apartment: to what these conferences tended we never knew and never shall; we consider them as matters of history, and leave them with due deference to the historian; we have to do only with biography. Far be it from us to meddle with politics – we have quite enough to do with manners and morality.

CHAPTER 27

THE NEXT DAY, as Helen was going across the hall, she saw the members of the last political conclave coming out of Lord Davenant's room, each looking as if the pope had not been chosen according to his wish – dark and disappointed; even Mr Harley's radiant countenance was dimmed, and the dry symptomatic cough which he gave after taking leave of Lady Davenant convinced Helen that all was not well within. He departed, and there seemed to be among those who remained a greater constraint than ever. There appeared to be in each an awakened sense that there were points on which they could never agree; all seemed to feel how different it would have been if Mr Harley had remained. True, the absence or presence of a person of genius makes as much difference in the whole appearance of things as sunshine or no sunshine on the landscape.

Dinner, however, was got through, for time and the hour, two hours, or three, will get through the roughest dinner or the smoothest. 'Never saw a difficult dinner-party better bothered!' was Lady Bearcroft's compliment, whispered to Cecilia as they went into the drawing-room; and Helen, notwithstanding Lady Bearcroft's vulgarity, could not help beginning absolutely to like her for her good-nature and amazingly prompt sympathy; but, after all, good nature without good manners is but a blundering ally, dangerous to its best friend.

This evening, Lady Cecilia felt that every one was uncomfortable, and, flitting about the room, she touched here and there to see how things were going on. They were not

going on well, and she could not make them better; even
her efforts at conciliation were ineffectual: she had stepped
in between her mother, some of the gentlemen, and the
General, in an argument in which she heard indications of
strife, and she set about to explain away contradictions, and
to convince everybody that they were really all of the same
opinion. With her sweet voice and pretty persuasive look, this
might have done for the General, as a relaxing smile seemed to
promise; but it would not do at all with Lady Davenant, who,
from feelings foreign to the present matter, was irritated, and
spoke, as Helen thought, too harshly: – 'Cecilia, you would act
Harmony in the comedy to perfection; but, unfortunately, I am
not one of those persons who can be persuaded that when I
say one thing I mean quite another – probably because it is
not my practice to do so. That old epigram, Sir Benjamin, do
you know it,' continued she, 'which begins with a bankrupt's
roguish "*Whereas*"?

> 'Whereas the religion and fate of three nations
> Depend on th'importance of our conversations:
> Whereas some objections are thrown in our way,
> And words have been construed to mean what they say, –
> Be it known from henceforth to each friend and each brother,
> Whene'er we say one thing we mean quite another.'

Sir Benjamin gravely remarked that it was good law practice.
The courts themselves would be shut up if some such doctrine
were not understood in the practice there, *subaudito*, if not publicly proclaimed with an absolute 'Whereas be it known from
henceforth.'

Whether this was dry humour of Sir Benjamin's, or plain
matter of fact and serious opinion, the gravity with which it was
delivered indicated not; but it produced the good effect of a smile,
a laugh, at him or with him. Lady Cecilia did not care which,
the laugh was good at all events; her invincible good-nature and
sweetness of temper had not been soured or conquered even by
her mother's severity; and Lady Davenant, observing this, forgave
and wished to he forgiven.

'My dearest Cecilia,' said she, 'clasp this bracelet for me, would you? It would really be a national blessing if, in the present times, all women were as amiable as you,

'Fond to spread friendships, but to cover heats.'

Then, turning to a French gentleman, she spoke of the change she had observed, when she was last at Paris, from the over-whelming violence of party spirit on all sides.

'Dreadfully true,' the French gentleman replied – 'party spirit, taking every Proteus form, calling itself by a hundred names and with a thousand devices and watchwords, which would be too ridiculous if they were not too terrible – domestic happiness destroyed, all society disordered, disorganised – literature not able to support herself, scarcely appearing in company – all precluded, superseded by the politics of the day.'

Lady Davenant joined with him in his regrets, and added that she feared society in England would soon be brought to the same condition.

'No,' said the French gentleman; 'English ladies will never be so vehement as my countrywomen; they will never become, I hope, like some of our lady politicians, "*qui heurlent comme des demons.*" [1]

Lady Cecilia said that, from what she had seen at Paris, she was persuaded that if the ladies did bawl too loud it was because the gentlemen did not listen to them; that above half the party-violence which appeared in Parisian belles was merely dramatic, to produce a sensation, and draw the gentlemen, from the black *pelotons* [2] in which they gathered, back to their proper positions round the armchairs of the fair ladies.

The foreigner, speaking to what he saw passing in Lady Davenant's mind, went on; – 'Ladies can do much, however, in this as in all other dilemmas where their power is, and ought to be, omnipotent.'

'Female *influence* is and ought to be *potent*,' said the General, with an emphasis on influence, contradistinguishing it from

[1] who screech like demons   [2] small groups

power, and reducing the exaggeration of omnipotent by the short
process of lopping off two syllables.

'So long as ladies keep in their own proper character,' said Lady
Davenant, 'all is well; but, if they once cease to act as women, that
instant they lose their privilege – their charm: they forfeit their
exorcising power; they can no longer command the demon of
party nor themselves, and he transforms them directly, as you say,'
said she to the French gentleman, 'into actual furies.'

'And, when so transformed, sometimes unconscious of their
state,' said the General, drily, his eye glancing towards the other
end of the room, and lighting upon Lady Bearcroft, who was at
the instant very red and very loud; and Lady Cecilia was standing, as if watchful for a moment's pause, in which to interpose
her word of peace. She waited for some time in vain, for when
she hastened from the other end of the room to this, the scene
of action, things had come to such a pass between the ladies
Masham and Bearcroft, that mischief, serious mischief, must have
ensued, had not Lady Cecilia, at utmost need, summoned to her
aid the happy genius of Nonsense – the genius of Nonsense, in
whose elfin power even Love delights; on whom Reason herself
condescends often to smile, even when Logic frowns, and chops
him on his block: but, cut in twain, the ethereal spirit soon unites
again, and lives, and laughs.

But mark him well – this little happy genius of Nonsense; see
that he be the true thing – the genuine spirit. You will know him
by his well-bred air and tone, which none can counterfeit; and
by his smile; for while most he makes others laugh, the arch little
rogue seldom goes beyond a smile himself! Graceful in the midst
of all his pranks, he never goes too far – though far enough he has
been known to go: he has crept into the armour of the great hero,
convulsed the senate in the wig of a chancellor, and becomingly,
decorously, put on now and then the mitre of an archbishop. 'If
good people,' said Archbishop Usher, 'would but make goodness
agreeable, and smile, instead of frowning in their virtue, how
many they would win to the good cause!' Lady Cecilia in this was
good at need, and at her utmost need, obedient to her call, came

this happy little genius, and brought with him song and dance, riddle and charade, and comic prints; and on a half-opened parcel of books Cecilia darted, and produced a *Comic Annual*, illustrated by him whom no risible muscles can resist.

All smiled who understood, and mirth admitted of her crew all who smiled, and party-spirit fled. But there were foreigners present. Foreigners cannot well understand our local allusions; our Cruikshank is to them unintelligible, and Hood's *Sorrows of Number One* quite lost upon them. Then Lady Bearcroft thought she would do as much as Lady Cecilia, and more – that she would produce what these poor foreigners could comprehend. But not at her call came the genius of lively nonsense, he heard her not. In his stead came that counterfeit, who thinks it witty to be rude:

> And placing raillery in railing,
> Will tell aloud your greatest failing –

that vulgar imp Fun – known by his broad grin, by his loud tone, and by his rude banter. Head foremost forcing himself in, came he, and brought with him a heap of coarse caricatures, and they were party caricatures.

'Capital!' Lady Bearcroft, however, pronounced them, as she spread all upon the table for applause – but no applause ensued.

Not such, these, as real good English humour produces and enjoys, independently of party – these were all too broad, too coarse. Lady Davenant despised, the General detested, Helen turned away, and Lady Cecilia threw them under the table, that they might not be seen by the foreigners. 'For the honour of England do not let them be spread abroad, pray, Lady Bearcroft.'

'The world is grown mighty nice!' said Lady Bearcroft; 'for my part, give me a good laugh when it is to be had.'

'Perhaps we shall find one here,' said Lady Cecilia, opening a portfolio of caricatures in a different style, but they were old, and Lady Bearcroft would have thrown them aside; but Lord Davenant observed that, if they have lasted so long, they must be good, because their humour can only ensure their permanence;

the personality dies with the person: for instance, in the famous old print of the minister rat-catcher, in the Westminster election, the likeness to each rat of the day is lost upon us, but the ridicule on placeman ratters remains. The whole, however is perfectly incomprehensible to foreigners.

'Rats! rats!' repeated one of the foreigners, as he looked at and studied the print. It was amusing to see the gravity with which this foreign diplomatist, quite new to England, listened to Lady Bearcroft's explanation of what is meant in English by a *rat political*. She was at first rather good on this topic, professing a supernatural acuteness of the senses, arising from an unconquerable antipathy, born with her, to the whole race of *rats*. She declared that she could see a rat a mile off in any man – could, from the moment a man opened his mouth in Parliament, or on the hustings, prophesy whether he would turn into a rat at last, or not. She, moreover, understood the language of rats of every degree, and knew even when they said 'No,' that they meant 'Yes,' – two monosyllables, the test of rats, which betray them all sooner or later, and transform the biped into the quadruped, who then turns tail, and runs always to the other side, from whatever side he may be of.

The *chargé-d'affaires* stood in half-bow, lending deferential ear and serious attention the whole time of this lecture upon rats, without being able from beginning to end to compass its meaning, and at the close, with a disconsolate shrug, he exclaimed, '*Ah! Je renonce à ça –* ' [1]

Lady Bearcroft went on – 'Since I cannot make your excellency understand what I mean by an English rat-political, I must give you an example or two, dead and living – living best, and I have more than one noted and branded rat in my eye.'

But Lady Cecilia, anxious to interrupt this perilous business, hastily rang for wine and water; and as the gentlemen went to help themselves she gave them a general toast, as, sitting down to

[1] I give up

the pianoforte, to the tune of 'Here's to the maiden of blushing fifteen', she sang –

> 'Here's to rats and rat-catchers of every degree,
> The rat that is trapped, and the rat that is free,
> The rat that is shy, sir, the rat that is bold, sir,
> The rat upon sale, sir, the rat that is sold, sir.
> Let the rats rat! Success to them all,
> And well off to the old ones before the house fall!'

CHAPTER 28

SIR BENJAMIN AND LADY BEARCROFT departed at six o'clock the next morning, and all the rest of the political and diplomatic corps *left* immediately after breakfast.

Lady Davenant looked relieved, the General satisfied, and Lady Cecilia consoled herself with the hope that, if she had done no good, she had not done any harm. This was a bad slide, perhaps, in the magic lantern, but would leave no trace behind. She began now to be very impatient for Beauclerc's appearance; always sanguine, and as rapid in her conclusions as she was precipitate in her actions, she felt no doubt, no anxiety, as to the future; for, though she refrained from questioning Helen as to her sentiments for Beauclerc, she was pretty well satisfied on that subject. Helen was particularly grateful to Lady Cecilia for this forbearance, being almost ashamed to own, even to herself, how exceedingly happy she felt; and now that it was no longer wrong in her to love, or dishonourable in him to wish to be loved, she was surprised to find how completely the idea of Beauclerc was connected with and interwoven through all her thoughts, pursuits, and sentiments. He had certainly been constantly in her company for several months, a whole summer, but she could scarcely believe that during this time he could have become so necessary to her happiness. While, with still-increasing agitation, she looked forward to his arrival, she felt as if Lady Davenant's presence was a sort of protection, a something to rely on, in the new circumstances in which she was to be placed. Lord Davenant had returned to town, but Lady Davenant remained. The Russian embassy seemed still in abeyance.

One morning as Helen was sitting in Lady Davenant's room alone with her, she said suddenly: 'At your age, Helen, I had as little taste for what are called politics as you have, yet you see what I am come to, and by the same road you may, you will, arrive at the same point.'

'I! oh, I hope not!' cried Helen, almost before she felt the whole inference that might be drawn from this exclamation.

'You hope not?' repeated her ladyship calmly. 'Let us consider this matter rationally, and put our hopes, and our fears, and our prejudices out of the question, if possible. Let me observe to you that the position of women in society is somewhat different from what it was a hundred years ago, or as it was sixty, or I will say thirty years since. Women are now so highly cultivated, and political subjects are at present of so much importance, of such high interest, to all human creatures who live together in society, you can hardly expect, Helen, that you, as a rational being, can go through the world as it is now, without forming any opinion on points of public importance. You cannot, I conceive, satisfy yourself with the common namby-pamby little missy phrase, "ladies have nothing to do with politics." '

Helen blushed, for she was conscious that, wrong or right, namby-pamby, little missy, or not, she had hitherto satisfied herself very comfortably with some such thought.

'Depend upon it, Helen,' resumed Lady Davenant, 'that when you are married, your love for a man of superior abilities, and of superior character, must elevate your mind to sympathy with all his pursuits, with all the subjects which claim his attention.'

Helen felt that she must become strongly interested in every subject in which the man she loved was interested; but still she observed that she had not abilities or information, like Lady Davenant's, that could justify her in attempting to follow her example. Besides, Helen was sure that, even if she had, it would not suit her taste; and besides, in truth, she did not think it well suited to a woman – she stopped when she came to that last thought. But what kindness and respect suppressed was clearly understood by her penetrating friend. Fixing her eyes upon Helen, she said with a smile, the candour and nobleness of her character rising above all little irritation of temper,

'I agree with you, my dear Helen, in all you do not say, and were I to begin life over again, my conduct should in some respects be different. Of the public dangers and private personal inconveniences that may result from women becoming politicians, or, as you better express our meaning, interfering with public affairs, no one can be more aware than I am. *Interfering*, observe I say, for I would mark and keep the line between influence and interference. Female influence must, will, and ought to exist on political subjects as on all others; but this influence should always be domestic, not public – the customs of society have so ruled it. Of the thorns in the path of ambitious men all moralists talk, but there are little, scarcely visible, thorns of a peculiar sort that beset the path of an ambitious woman, the venomous prickles of the *domestic bramble*, a plant not perhaps mentioned in Withering's Botany, or the *Hortus Kewensis*, but it is too well known to many, and to me it has been sorely known.'

At this instant General Clarendon came in with some letters, which had been forwarded to him express. One, for Lady Davenant, he had been desired to put into her hands himself: he retired, and Lady Davenant opened the letter. By the first glance at her countenance, Helen saw that there was something in it which had surprised and given her great concern. Helen withdrew her eyes, and waited till she should speak. But Lady Davenant was quite silent, and Helen, looking at her again, saw her put her hand to her heart, as if from some sudden sense of violent bodily pain, and she sank on the sofa, fell back, and became as pale as death and motionless. Excessively frightened, Helen threw open the window, rang the bell for Lady Davenant's own woman, and sent the page for Lady Cecilia. In a few moments Lady Cecilia and Elliott came. Neither was as much alarmed as Helen had expected they would be. They had seen Lady Davenant under similar attacks – they knew what remedies to apply. Elliott was a remarkably composed, steady person. She now went on doing all that was necessary without speaking a word. The paroxysm lasted longer than usual, as Lady Cecilia observed; and, though she continued her assurances to Helen that 'it was all nervous – only nerves,' she began evidently to be herself alarmed. At length symptoms of returning animation appeared, and then Cecilia retired, beckoning to Helen to follow her into the next room. 'We had better leave mamma to Elliott, she will be happier if she thinks we know nothing of the matter.' Then, recollecting that Helen had been in the room when this attack came on, she added – 'But no, you must go back, for mamma will remember that you were present – take as little notice, however, as possible of what has happened.'

Cecilia said that her mother, when they were abroad, had been subject to such seizures at intervals, 'and in former times, before I was born, I believe,' said Lady Cecilia; 'she had some kind of extraordinary disease in the heart; but she had a particular aversion to being thought nervous. Every physician who has ever pronounced her nervous has always displeased her, and has been dismissed. She was once quite vexed with me for barely suggest-ing the idea. There,' cried Cecilia, 'I hear her voice, go to her.'

Helen followed Lady Cecilia's suggestion, and took as little notice as possible of what had happened. Elliott disappeared as she entered – the page was waiting at the door, but to Helen's satisfaction Lady Davenant did not admit him. 'Not yet: tell him I will ring when I want him,' said she. The door closed: and Lady Davenant, turning to Helen, said, 'Whether I live or die is a point of some consequence to the friends who love me; but there is another question, Helen, of far more importance to me, and, I trust, to them. That question is, whether I continue to live as I have lived, honoured, and respected, or live and die dishonoured and despised,' – her eye glanced towards the letter she had been reading. 'My poor child,' continued Lady Davenant, looking at Helen's agitated countenance, – 'my poor child, I will not keep you in suspense.' She then told Helen that she was suspected of having revealed a secret of state that had been confided to her husband, and which it was supposed, and truly supposed, that Lord Davenant had told her. Beyond its political importance, the disclosure involved a charge of baseness, in her having betrayed confidence, having suffered a copy of a letter from an illustrious personage to be handed about and read by several people. 'Lord Davenant as yet knows nothing of this, the effect upon him is what I most dread. I cannot show you this,' continued she, opening again the letter she had just received, 'because it concerns others as well as myself. I am, at all events, under obligations that can never be forgotten to the person who gave me this timely notice, which could no otherwise have reached me, and the person to whom I am thus obliged is one, Helen, whom neither you nor I like, and whom Cecilia particularly dislikes – Miss Clarendon! Her manner of doing me this service is characteristic: she begins –

' "Miss Clarendon is aware that Lady Davenant has no liking for her, but that shall not prevent Miss Clarendon from doing what she thinks an act of justice towards a noble character falsely attacked." ' – Lady Davenant read no more.

'Had not you better wait till you are stronger, my dear Lady Davenant?' said Helen, seeing her prepare to write.

'It was once said, gloriously well,' replied Lady Davenant, 'that the duties of life are more than life itself – so I think.'

While she wrote, Helen thought of what she had just heard, and she ventured to interrupt Lady Davenant to ask if she had formed any idea of the means by which the secret could have been betrayed – or the copy of the letter obtained.

'Yes, she had a suspicion of one person, the diplomatist to whom Mr Harley had shown such a mortal antipathy. She recollected that the last morning the *Congress* had sat in Lord Davenant's cabinet, she had left her writing-desk there, and this letter was in it; she thought that she had locked the desk when she had left the room, it certainly was fast when she returned, but it had a spring Bramah lock, and its being shut down would have fastened it. She had no proof one way or other, her suspicion rested where was her instinctive dislike. It was remarkable, however, that she at once did justice to another person whom she did not like, Mr Mapletofft, Lord Davenant's secretary. 'His manners do not please me,' she said, 'but I have perfect confidence in his integrity.'

Helen felt and admired this generous candour, but her suspicions were not of the diplomatist alone: she thought of one who might perhaps have been employed by him – Carlos the page. And many circumstances, which she recollected and put together, now strengthened this suspicion. She wondered it had not occurred to Lady Davenant; she thought it must, but that she did not choose to mention it. Helen had often heard Lady Davenant's particular friends complain that it was extremely disagreeable to them to have this boy constantly in the room, whatever might be the conversation. There was the page, either before or behind a screen, always within hearing.

Lady Davenant said that, as Carlos was a Portuguese, and had never been in England till she had brought him over, a few months before, he could not understand English well enough to comprehend what was going on. This was doubted, especially by Helen, who had watched his countenance, and had represented her doubts and her reasons for them to Lady Davenant, but she was not convinced. It was one of the few points on which she could justly be reproached with adhering to her fancy instead of listening to reason. The more Carlos was attacked, the more she adhered to him. In fact, it was not so much because he was a favourite, as because he was a protégé; he was completely dependent upon her protection: she had brought him to England, had saved him from his mother, a profligate camp-follower, had freed him from the most miserable condition possible, and had raised him to easy, happy, confidential life. To the generous the having conferred an obligation is in itself a tie hard to sever. All noble-minded people believe in fidelity, and never doubt of gratitude; they throw their own souls into those they oblige, and think and feel for them, as they, in their situation, would think and feel. Lady Davenant considered it an injustice to doubt the attachment of this boy, and a cruelty she deemed it to suspect him causelessly of being the most base of human creatures – he, a young defenceless orphan. Helen had more than once offended, by attempting to stop Lady Davenant from speaking imprudently before Carlos; she was afraid, even at this moment, to irritate her by giving utterance to her doubts; she determined, therefore, to keep them to herself till she had some positive grounds for her suspicions. She resolved to watch the boy very carefully. Presently, having finished her letters, Lady Davenant rang for him. Helen's eyes were upon Carlos the moment he entered, and her thoughts did not escape observation.

'You are wrong, Helen,' said Lady Davenant, as she lighted the taper to seal her letters.

'If I am not right,' said Helen, keeping her eyes upon the boy's changing countenance, 'I am too suspicious – but observe, am I not right, at this instant, in thinking that his countenance is *bad*?'

Lady Davenant could not but see that countenance change in an extraordinary manner, in spite of his efforts to keep it steady.

'You cause that of which you complain,' said she, going on sealing her letters deliberately. 'In courts of public justice, and in private equity,' the word *equity* she pronounced with an austere emphasis, 'how often is the change of countenance misinterpreted. The sensibility of innocence, that cannot bear to be suspected, is often mistaken for the confusion worse confounded of guilt.'

Helen observed that, as Lady Davenant spoke, and spoke in his favour, the boy's countenance cleared up; that vacillating expression of fear, and consciousness of having something within him unwhipt of justice, completely disappeared, and his whole air was now bold and open – towards Helen, almost an air of defiance.

'What do you think is the cause of this change in his countenance – you observe it, do you not?' asked Helen.

'Yes, and the cause is as plain as the change. He sees that I do not suspect him, though you do; and seeing, Helen, that he has at least one friend in the world, who will do him justice, the orphan boy takes courage.'

'I wish I could be as good as you are, my dearest Lady Davenant,' said Helen; 'but I cannot help still feeling, and saying, – I doubt. Now observe him, while I speak; I will turn my eyes away, that my terrible looks may not confound him. You say he knows that you do not suspect him, and that I do. How does he know it?'

'How!' said Lady Davenant. 'By the universal language of the eyes.'

'Not only by that universal language, I think,' said Helen; 'but I suspect he understands every word we say.'

Helen, without ever looking up from a bunch of seals which she was rubbing bright, slowly and very distinctly added,

'I think that he can speak, read, and write English.'

A change in the countenance of Carlos appeared, notwithstanding all his efforts to hold his features in the same position; instead of placid composure there was now grim rigidity.

'Give me the great seal with the coat of arms on it,' said Lady Davenant, dropping the wax on the letter, and watching the boy's eye as she spoke, without herself looking towards the seal she had described. He never stirred, and Helen began to fear she was unjust and suspicious. But again her doubts, at least of his disposition, occurred: as she was passing through Lady Davenant's dressing-room with her, when they were going down to dinner, the page following them, Helen caught his figure in a mirror, and saw that he was making a horrible grimace at her behind her back, his dark countenance expressing extreme hatred and revenge. Helen touched Lady Davenant's arm, but, before her eye could be directed to the glass, Carlos, perceiving that he was observed, pretended to be suddenly seized with the cramp in his foot, which obliged him to make these frightful contortions. Helen was shocked by his artfulness, but it succeeded with Lady Davenant: it was in vain to say more about it to her, so Helen let it pass. When she mentioned it afterwards to Lady Cecilia, she said – 'I am sorry, for your sake, Helen, that this happened; depend upon it, that revengeful little Portuguese gnome will work you mischief some time or other.' Helen did not think of herself – indeed she could not imagine any means by which he could possibly work her woe; but the face was so horrible, that it came again and again before her eyes, and she was more and more determined to watch Carlos constantly.

This was one of the public days at Clarendon Park, on which there was a good deal of company; many of the neighbouring gentry were to be at dinner. When Lady Davenant appeared, no inquiries concerning her health were made by her daughter or by the General – no allusion to her having been unwell. She seemed quite recovered, and Helen observed that she particularly exerted herself, and that her manner was more gracious than usual to commonplace people – more present to everything that was passing. She retired however early, and took Helen with her. The depression of her spirits, or rather the weight upon her mind, appeared again as soon as they were alone together. She took her writing-desk and looked over some letters which she said ought to be burned. She could not sleep in peace, she said – she ought not to sleep, till this was done. Several of these, as she looked over them, seemed to give her pain, and excited her indignation or contempt as she from time to time exclaimed – 'Meanness! – corruption! – ingratitude too! – all favours forgotten! To see – to feel this – is the common fate of all who have lived the life I have lived; of this I am not so inconsistent as to complain. But it is hard that my own character – the integrity of a whole life – should avail me nothing! And yet,' added she, after a moment's pause of reflection, 'to how few can my character be really known! Women cannot, like men, make their characters known by public actions. I have no right to complain; but if Lord Davenant's honour is to be – ' She paused; her thoughts seeming too painful for utterance. She completed the arrangement of the papers, and, as she pressed down the lid of her writing-box, and heard the closing sound of the lock, she said, – 'Now I may sleep in peace.' She put out the lamp, and went to her bedroom, carrying with her two or three books which she intended to read after she should be in bed; for, though she talked of sleeping, it was plain she thought she should not. Helen prevailed upon her to let her remain with her, and read to her.

She opened first a volume of Shakespeare, in which was Lady Davenant's mark. 'Yes,' said she, 'read that speech of Wolsey's; read that whole scene, the finest picture of ambition ever drawn.'

And, after she had heard the scene, she observed that there is no proof more certain of the truth of poetic description, than its recurring to us at the time we strongly feel. 'Those who tell us,' continued she, 'that it is unnatural to recollect poetry or eloquence at times of powerful emotion are much mistaken; they have not strong feelings or strong imaginations. I can affirm from my own experience that it is perfectly natural.' Lady Davenant rapidly mentioned some instances of this sort which she recollected, but seeing the anxiety of Helen's look, she added, 'You are afraid that I am feverish; you wish me to rest; then, go on reading to me.'

Helen read on, till Lady Davenant declared she would not let her sit up any longer. 'Only, before you go, my dear child, look here at what I have been looking at while you have been reading.' She made Helen place herself so as to see exactly in the same direction and light in which she was looking, and she pointed out to her, in the lining of the bed, a place where, from the falling of the folds and the crinkles in the material, a figure with the head, head-dress, and perfect profile of an old woman with a turned-up chin, appeared. At first Helen could not see it; but at last she caught it, and was struck with it. 'The same sort of curious effect of chance resemblance and coincidence which painters, Leonardo da Vinci in particular, have observed in the moss and stains on old stones,' observed Lady Davenant. 'But it struck me tonight, Helen, perhaps because I am a little feverish – it struck me in a new point of view – moral, not picturesque. If such be the effects of chance, or of coincidences, how cautious we should be in deciding from appearances, or pronouncing from circumstantial evidence upon the guilt of evil design in any human creature.'

'You mean this to apply to me about Carlos?' said Helen.

'I do. But not only of him and you was I thinking, but of myself and those who judge of me falsely from coincidences, attributing to me designs which I never had, and actions of which I am incapable.' She suddenly raised herself in her bed, and was going to say more, but the pendule striking at that instant two o'clock, she stopped abruptly, kissed Helen, and sent her away.

Helen gathered together and carried away with her all the books, that Lady Davenant might not be tempted to look at them more. As she had several piled on one arm, and had a taper in her hand, she was somewhat encumbered, and, though she managed to open the bedroom door, and to shut it again without letting any of the books fall, and crossed the little anteroom between the bed-chamber and dressing-room safely, yet, as she was opening the dressing-room door, and taking too much or too little care of some part of her pyramid of books, down came the whole pile with a noise which in the stillness of the night sounded tremendous. She was afraid it would disturb Lady Davenant, and was going back to tell her what it was, when she was startled by hearing, as she thought, the moving of a chair or table in the dressing-room: she stopped short to listen – all was silent; she thought she had mistaken the direction in which the noise came.

She softly opened the dressing-room door, and looked in – all was silent – no chair, or stool, or table overturned, everything was in its place exactly as they had left it, but there was a strong smell of a half-extinguished lamp: she thought it had been put out when they had left the room, she now supposed it had not been sufficiently lowered, she turned the screw, and took care now to see it completely extinguished; then went back for the books, and as people sometimes will, when most tired and most late, be most orderly, she would not go to bed without putting every volume in its place in the book-case. After reaching to put one book upon the highest shelf, as she was getting down she laid her hand on the top of Lady Davenant's writing-box, and, as she leaned on it, was surprised to hear the click of its lock closing. The sound was so peculiar she could not be mistaken; besides, she thought she had felt the lid give way under her pressure. There was no key left in the lock – she perfectly recollected the very sound of that click when Lady Davenant shut the lid down before leaving the room this night. She stood looking at the lock, and considering how this could be, and as she remained perfectly still, she heard, or thought she heard, someone breathing near her. Holding in her own breath, she listened and cautiously

looked round without stirring from the place where she stood –
one of the window curtains moved, so at least she thought – yes,
certainly there was some living thing behind it. It might be Lady
Davenant's great dog; but looking again at the bottom of the
curtain she saw a human foot. The page, Carlos! was her instant
suspicion, and his vengeful face came before her, and a vision of
a stiletto, or she did not well know what. She trembled all over;
yet she had presence of mind enough to recollect that she should
not seem to take notice. And, while she moved about the books
on the table, she gave another look, and saw that the foot was not
withdrawn. She knew she was safe still, it had not been perceived
that she had seen it; now what was she to do? 'Go up to that
curtain and draw it back and face the boy' – but she did not dare;
yet he was only a boy – But it might be a man and not the page.
Better go and call somebody – tell Lady Davenant. She MUST go
through the ante-chamber, and pass close to that curtain to open
the door. All this was the thought of one moment, and she went
on holding up the light to the book-shelves as if in quest of some
book, and kept coasting along to gain the door; she was afraid
when she was to pass the window-curtain, either of touching it,
or of stumbling over that foot. But she got past without touching
or stumbling, opened the door, whisked through – that was done
too quickly, but she could not help it, – she shut, bolted the door,
and ran across the ante-chamber to Lady Davenant's bed-room.
She entered softly, aware of the danger to her of sudden alarm.
But Lady Davenant was not asleep, was not alarmed, but was *effec-
tive* in a moment. First she asked: – 'Did you lock the door after
you?' 'Yes, bolted it.' 'That is well.' Neither of them said, 'Who do
you think it is?' But each knew what the other thought. They
returned through the ante-chamber to the dressing-room. But
when they opened the door, all was quiet – no one behind the
curtain, no one in the room – they searched under the sofas,
everywhere; there was no closet or hiding-place in which any
one could be concealed. The window fastenings were unstirred.
But the door into the gallery was unlocked, and the simple thing
appeared – that Helen, in her confusion, had thought only of

fastening the door into the ante-chamber, which also opened on the gallery, but had totally forgotten to lock that from the dressing-room into the gallery, by which whoever had been in the room had escaped without any difficulty. Lady Davenant rather inclined to believe that no one had been there, and that it was all Helen's imagination. But Helen persisted that she had seen what she had seen, and heard what she had heard. They went into the gallery – all silence, no creature visible, and the doors at the ends of the gallery locked outside.

After a fruitless search they retired, Lady Davenant to her own room, and Helen to hers, full of shame and regret that she had not had the courage to open the curtain at the right moment. Nothing could stir her belief, however, in the evidence of her senses; the boy must have been there, and must be still concealed somewhere in the gallery, or in some of the rooms opening into it. Some of these were unoccupied, but they were all locked up, as Lady Davenant had told her when she had proposed searching them; one or two they tried and found fastened. She stood at her own door, after having put down the candle on her table, still giving a lingering look-out, when, through the darkness in the gallery at the further end, she saw a ray of light on the floor, which seemed to come from under the door of a room unoccupied – Mr Mapletofft's room; he had gone to town with Lord Davenant. Helen went on tiptoe very softly along the gallery, almost to this door, when it suddenly opened, and the page stood before her, the lamp in his hand shining full on his face and on hers. Both started – then both were motionless for one second – but he, recovering instantly, shot back again into the room, flung to the door, and locked it.

'Seen him!' cried Lady Davenant, when Helen flew to her room and told her; 'seen him! do you say?' and then ringing her bell, she bade Helen run and knock at the General's door, while she went herself to Mr Mapletoift's room, commanding Carlos to open the door immediately. But he would not open it, nor make any answer; the servants came, and the General ordered one to go round to the windows of the room lest the boy should escape that way. It was too late, he had escaped; when the door was forced, one of the windows was found open; Carlos was not in the room; he must have swung himself down from the height by means of a tree which was near the window. The lamp was still burning, and papers half burnt smouldering on the table. There were sufficient remains to tell what they had been. Lady Davenant saw, in the handwriting of Carlos, copies of letters taken from her desk. One half-unburnt cover of the packet he had been making up, showed by its direction to whom it was to have been sent, and there were a few lines in the boy's own writing inside addressed to his employer, which revealed the whole. His employer was, as Lady Davenant had suspected – the diplomatist!

A duplicate Bramah key was found under the table, and she recollected that she had some months ago missed this duplicate key of her desk, and supposed she had dropped it from her watch-ring while out walking; she recollected, farther, that Carlos had with great zeal assisted her in the search for it all through the shrubbery walks. The proofs of this boy's artifice and long-premeditated treachery, accumulating upon Lady Davenant, shocked her so much that she could not think of anything else. 'Is it possible? is it in human nature?' she exclaimed. 'Such falsehood, such art, such ingratitude!' As she fixed her eyes upon the writing, scarcely yet dry, she repeated, 'It *is* his writing – I see it, yet can scarcely believe it! I, who taught him to write myself – guided that little hand to make the first letters that he ever formed! And this is in human nature! I could not have conceived it – it is dreadful to be so convinced, it lowers one's confidence in one's fellow-creatures. That is the worst of all!' She sighed deeply, and then, turning to Helen, said, 'But let us think no more of it tonight, we can do no more, they are in pursuit of him; I hope I may never, never, see him more.'

CHAPTER 29

SOME PEOPLE VALUE their friends most for active service, some for passive kindness. Some are won by tender expressions, some convinced by solid proofs of regard; others of a yet nobler kind, and of this sort was Lady Davenant, are apt to be best pleased, most touched, by proofs that their own character has been thoroughly understood, and that they have justly appreciated the good qualities of their friend. More than by all the kindness and sympathy Helen had ever before shown her was she now pleased and vouched by the respect for her feelings in this affair of the page; Helen never having at the moment of his detection or afterwards, by word or look, indulged in the self-triumph of 'You see how right I was!' which implies 'You see how wrong you were!' On the contrary, she gave what comfort she honestly could by showing that she knew from what humane motives and generous feelings Lady Davenant had persisted in supporting this boy to the last.

As to the little wretch himself, he appeared no more. Search was made for him in every direction, but he was not to be found, and Helen thought it was well that Lady Davenant should be spared the pain of seeing or hearing more about him.

The whole mystery was now solved, the difficulty for Lady Davenant in a fair way to be ended. She had felt an instinctive aversion to the fawning tone of the diplomatist, whom she had suspected of caballing against Lord Davenant secretly, and it was now proved that he had been base beyond what she could have conceived possible; had been in confederacy with this boy, whom he had corrupted, purchasing from him copies of private letters, and bribing him to betray his benefactress. The copy of that letter from an illustrious personage had been thus obtained. The proofs now brought home to the guilty person deprived him at once of all future means of injuring Lord Davenant. Completely in their power, he would be ready to ensure silence at any price, and, instead of caballing further, this low intriguer would now be compelled to return from whence he came, too happy to be permitted to retreat from his situation, and quit England without being brought to public disgrace. No notice of the report that had been in private circulation against Lady Davenant having yet appeared in the public prints, it was possible to prevent the mischief that even the mention of her name in such an affair must have occasioned. It was necessary, however, that letters should be written immediately to the different persons whom the private reports had reached; and Helen and her daughter trembled for her health in consequence of this extreme hurry and fatigue, but she repeated her favourite maxim – 'Better to wear out than to rust out' – and she accomplished all that was to be done. Lord Davenant wrote in triumph that all was settled, all difficulties removed, and they were to set out for Russia immediately.

And now Lady Davenant breathed freely. Relieved from the intolerable thought that the base finger of suspicion could point at her or at Lord Davenant, her spirits rose, her whole appearance renovated, and all the fears that Helen and her daughter had felt, lest she should not be able to sustain the hardships of a long voyage and the rigour of a northern climate, were now completely dispelled.

The day of departure was fixed – Lady Davenant remained, however, as long as she possibly could with her daughter; and she was anxious, too, to see Granville Beauclerc before she left Clarendon Park.

The number of the days of quarantine were gone over every morning at breakfast by Lady Cecilia and the General; they looked in the papers carefully for the arrivals at the hotel which Beauclerc usually frequented. This morning, in reading the list aloud, the General came to the name of Sir Thomas D'Aubigny, brother to the Colonel. The paragraph stated that Colonel D'Aubigny had left some manuscripts to his brother, which would soon be published, and then followed some puff in the usual style, which the General did not think it necessary to read. But one of the officers, who knew some of the D'Aubignys, went on talking of the Colonel, and relating various anecdotes to prove that his souvenirs would be amusing. Helen, who was conscious that she always blushed when Colonel D'Aubigny's name was mentioned, and that the General had observed it, was glad that he never looked up from what he was reading, and when she had courage to turn towards her she admired Cecilia's perfect self-possession. Beauclerc's name was not among the arrivals, and it was settled consequently that they should not see him this day.

Some time after they had left the breakfast-room, Helen found Lady Davenant in her own apartment, sitting, as it was very unusual with her, perfectly unemployed – her head leaning on her hand, and an expression of pain in her countenance. 'Are you not well, my dear Lady Davenant?' Helen asked.

'My mind is not well,' she replied, 'and that always affects my body, and I suppose my looks.' After a moment's silence she fixed her eyes on Helen, and said, 'You tell me that Colonel D'Aubigny never was a lover – never was an admirer of yours?'

'Never!' said Helen, low, but very decidedly. Lady Davenant sighed, but did not speak.

After a longer continuance of silence than had almost ever occurred when they two were alone together, Lady Davenant looked up, and said, 'I hope in God that I am mistaken. I pray that I may never live to see it.'

'To see what?' cried Helen.

'To see that one little black spot, invisible to you, Helen, the speck of evil in that heart – my daughter's heart – spread and taint, and destroy all that is good. It must be cut out – at any pain it must be cut away; if any part be unsound, the corruption will spread.'

'Corruption in Cecilia!' exclaimed. 'Oh! I know her – I know her from dear childhood! there is nothing corrupt in her, no, not a thought!'

'My dear Helen, you see her as she has been – as she is. I see her as she may become – very – frightfully different. Helen! if truth fail, if the principle of truth fail in her character, all will fail! All that charming nature, all that fair semblance, all that fair reality, all this bright summer's dream of happiness, even love – the supreme felicity of her warm heart – even love will fail her. Cecilia will lose her husband's affections!'

Helen uttered a faint cry.

'Worse!' continued Lady Davenant. 'Worse! she will lose her own esteem, she will sink, but I shall be gone,' cried she, and pressing her hand upon her heart, she faintly repeated, 'Gone!' And then abruptly added, 'Call Cecilia! I must see Cecilia, I must speak to her. But first I will tell you, from a few words that dropped this morning from General Clarendon, I suspect – I fear that Cecilia has deceived him!'

'Impossible! – about what – about whom?'

'That Colonel D'Aubigny,' said Lady Davenant.

'I know all about it, and it was all nothing but nonsense. Did you look at her when the General read that paragraph this morning – did you see that innocent countenance?'

'I saw it, Helen, and thought as you did, but I have been so deceived – so lately in countenance!'

'Not by hers – never.'

'Not by yours, Helen, never. And yet, why should I say so? This very morning, yours, had I not known you, yours would have misled me.'

'Oh, my foolish absurd habit of blushing, how I wish I could prevent it!' said Helen; 'I know it will make me betray somebody some time or other.'

'Betray! What have you to betray?' cried Lady Davenant, leaning forward with an eagerness of eye and voice that startled Helen from all power of immediate reply. After an instant's pause, however, she answered firmly, 'Nothing, Lady Davenant, and that there is nothing wrong to be known about Cecilia, I as firmly believe as that I stand here at this moment. Can you suspect anything really wrong?'

'Suspect! – wrong!' cried Lady Davenant, starting up, with a look in her eye which made Helen recoil. 'Helen, what can you conceive that I suspect wrong? – Cecilia? – Captain D'Aubigny? What did you mean? Wrong did you say? – of Cecilia? Could you mean – could you conceive Helen, that I, having such a suspicion, could be here – living with her – or – living anywhere – ' And she sank down on the sofa again, seized with sudden spasm – in a convulsion of agonising pain. But she held Helen's hand fast grasped, detaining her – preventing her from pulling the bell; and by degrees the pain passed off, the livid hue cleared away, the colour of life once more returned, but more tardily than before, and Helen was excessively alarmed.

'Poor child! my poor, dear child, I feel – I hear your heart beating. You are a coward, Helen, but a sweet creature; and I love you – and I love my daughter. What were we saying?'

'Oh, say no more! say no more now, for Heaven's sake,' said Helen, kneeling beside her; and, yielding to that imploring look, Lady Davenant, with a fond smile, parted the hair on her forehead, kissed her, and remained perfectly quiet and silent for some time.

'I am quite well again now,' said she, 'and quite composed. If Cecilia has told her husband the whole truth, she will continue to be, as she is, a happy wife; but if she have deceived him in the estimation of a single word – she is undone. With him, of all men, never will confidence, once broken, unite again. Now General Clarendon told me this morning – would I had known it before the marriage! – that he had made one point with my daughter, and only one, on the faith of which he married: the point was, that she should tell him if she had ever loved any other man. And she told him – I fear from some words which he said afterwards – I am sure he is in the belief – the certainty, that his wife never loved any man breathing but himself.'

'Nor did she,' said Helen. 'I can answer for it she has told him the truth – and she has nothing to fear, nor have you.'

'You give me new life!' cried Lady Davenant, her face becoming suddenly radiant with hope; 'but how can you answer for this, Helen? You had no part in any deceit, I am sure, but there was something about a miniature of you, which I found in Colonel D'Aubigny's hands one day. That was done, I thought, at the time, to deceive me, to make me believe that you were his object. Deceit there was.'

'On his part,' said Helen, 'much and always; but on Cecilia's there was only, from her over-awe of you, some little concealment; but the whole was broken off and repented of, whatever little there was, long since. And as to loving him, she never did; she told me so then, and often and often she has told me so since.'

'Convince me of that,' said Lady Davenant; 'convince me that she thought what she said. I believe, indeed, that till she met General Clarendon she never felt any enthusiastic attachment, but I thought she liked that man – it was all coquetry, flirting nonsense perhaps. Be it so – I am willing to believe it. Convince me but that she is true – there is the only point of consequence. The man is dead and gone, the whole in oblivion, and all that is of importance is her truth; convince me but of that, and I am a happy mother.'

Helen brought recollections, and proofs from conversations at the time and letters since, confirming at least Cecilia's own belief that she had never loved the man, that it was all vanity on her part and deception on his: Lady Davenant listened, willing to be convinced.

'And now,' said she, 'let us put this matter out of our minds entirely – I want to talk to you of yourself.'

She took Helen out with her in her pony-phaeton, and spoke of Granville Beauclerc, and of his and Helen's prospects of happiness.

Lady Cecilia, who was riding with her husband in some fields adjoining the park, caught a glimpse of the phaeton as it went along the avenue, and, while the General was giving some orders to the wood-ranger about a new plantation, she, telling him that she would be back in two minutes, cantered off to overtake her mother, and, making a short-cut across the fields, she leaped a wide ha-ha which came in her way. She was an excellent horse-woman, and Fairy carried her lightly over; and when she heard the General's voice in dismay and indignation at what she had done, she turned and laughed, and cantered on till she overtook the phaeton. The breeze had blown her hair most becomingly, and raised her colour, and her eyes were joyously bright, and her light figure, always well on horseback, now looked so grace-ful as she bent to speak to her mother, that her husband could not find it in his heart to scold her, and he who came to chide remained to admire. Her mother, looking up at her, could not help exclaiming,

'Well, certainly, you are an excessively pretty creature!'

'Bearers of good news always look well, I believe,' said she, smiling; 'so there is now some goodness in my face.'

'That there certainly is,' said her mother, fondly.

'But you certainly don't know what it is – you cannot know till I tell you, my dearest Helen – my dear mother, I mean. Gran-ville Beauclerc will be here to-day – I am sure of it. So pray do not go far from home – do not go out of the grounds: this was what I was in such a hurry to say to you.'

'But how do you know, Cecilia?'

'Just because I can read,' replied she, 'because I can read a newspaper through, which none of you newspaper-readers by profession could do this morning. After you all of you laid them down, I took them up, and found in that evening paper which your stupid aide-de-damp had been poring and boring over a fresh list of arrivals, and Mr Granville Beauclerc among them at full length. Now he would not stay a moment longer in town than was absolutely necessary, you know, or else he ought to be excommunicated. But it is not in his nature to delay; he will be here directly – I should not be surprised –

'You are right, Cecilia,' interrupted the General, 'I see a caleche on that road. It is he.'

The caleche turned into the park, and in a few minutes they met. Carriages, horses, and servants, were sent off to the house, while the whole party walked, and talked, and looked. Lady Cecilia was in delightful spirits, and so affectionately, so delicately joyful – so kind, that if Helen and Beauclerc had ever blamed, or had reason to blame her, it must now be for ever forgotten. As, in their walk, they came near that seat by the water's side where the lovers had parted, Cecilia whispered something to her mother, and instantly it was 'done as desired.' Beauclerc and Helen were left to their own explanations, and the rest of the party pursued their walk home. Of what passed in this explanatory scene no note has been transmitted to the biographer, and we must be satisfied with the result.

CHAPTER 30

'ALL IS RIGHT!' cried Lady Cecilia. 'O my dear mother, I am the happiest creature in the world, if you were not going away; could you not stay – a little, a very little longer – just till – '

'No, no, my dear, do not urge me to stay,' said Lady Davenant; 'I cannot – your father expects me to-morrow.'

All her preparations were made – in short, it must be so, and Lady Davenant begged her daughter would not spend the short remaining time they were to have together in entreaties, distressing and irritating to the feelings of those who ask and of those who must refuse. 'Let us enjoy in peace,' said she, 'all that is to be enjoyed this day before I go.'

When Helen entered the drawing-room before dinner, knowing that she was very late, she found assembled Lady Davenant, Beauclerc, and the officers, but Cecilia was not there, nor did the punctual General make his appearance; the dinner-hour was past, a servant had twice looked in to announce it, and, seeing neither my lady nor the General, had in surprise retired. Silence prevailed – what could be the matter? So unusual for the General to be late. The General came in, hurried – very uncommon in him, and, after saying a few words in a low voice to Lady Davenant, who immediately went upstairs, he begged pardon, was very sorry he had kept dinner waiting, but Lady Cecilia had been taken ill – had fainted – she was better – he hoped it was nothing that would signify – she was lying down – he begged they would go to dinner. And to dinner they went, and when Lady Davenant returned she put Helen's mind at rest by saying it was only a little faintishness from over-fatigue. She had prescribed rest, and Cecilia had herself desired to be left quite alone. After dinner Lady Davenant went up again to see her, found her not so well – feverish; she would not let Helen go to her – they would talk if they were together, and she thought it necessary to keep Cecilia very quiet. If she would but submit to this, she would be well again probably in the morning. At tea-time, and in the course of the evening twice, Cecilia sent to beg to speak to Helen; but Lady Davenant and the General joined in requesting her not to go. The General went himself to Lady Cecilia to enforce obedience, and he reported that she had submitted with a good grace.

Helen was happily engaged by Beauclerc's conversation during the rest of the evening. It was late before they retired, and when she went upstairs, Felicie said that her lady was asleep, and had been asleep for the last two hours, and she was sure that after such good rest her ladyship would be perfectly well in the morning. Without further anxiety about her friend, therefore, Helen went to her own room. It was a fine moonlight night, and she threw open the shutters, and stood for a moment looking out upon the moonlight, which she loved; and even after she had retired to bed it was long before she could sleep. The only painful thought in her mind was of Lady Davenant's approaching departure; without her, all happiness would be incomplete; but still, hope and love had much that was delightful to whisper, and as she at last sank to sleep, Beauclerc's voice seemed still speaking to her in soft sounds. Yet the dream which followed was uneasy; she thought that they were standing together in the library, at the open door of the conservatory, by moonlight, and he asked her to walk out, and when she did not comply, all changed, and she saw him walking with another – with Lady Castlefort; but then the figure changed to one younger – more beautiful – it must be, as the beating of Helen's heart in the dream told her – it must be Lady Blanche. Without seeing Helen, however, they seemed to come on, smiling and talking low to each other along the matted alley of the conservatory, almost to the very door where she was still, as she thought, standing with her hand upon the lock, and then they stopped, and Beauclerc pulled from an orange-tree a blossom which seemed the very same which Helen had given to him that evening; he offered it to Lady Blanche, and something he whispered; but at this moment the handle of the lock seemed to slip, and Helen awoke with a start; and when she was awake, the noise of her dream seemed to continue; she heard the real sound of a lock turning – her door slowly opened, and a white figure appeared. Helen started up in her bed, and awaking thoroughly, saw that it was only Cecilia in her dressing-gown.

'Cecilia! What's the matter, my dear? are you worse?'

Lady Cecilia put her finger on her lips, closed the door behind her, and said, 'Hush! hush! or you'll waken Felicie; she is sleeping in the dressing-room tonight. Mamma ordered it, in case I should want her.'

'And how are you now? What can I do for you?'

'My dear Helen, you can do something for me indeed. But don't get up. Lie down and listen to me. I want to speak to you.'

'Sit down, then, my dear Cecilia, sit down here beside me.'

'No, no, I need not sit down. I am very well, standing. Only let me say what I have to say. I am quite well.'

'Quite well! indeed you are not. I feel you all trembling. You must sit down, indeed, my dear,' said Helen, pressing her.

She sat down. 'Now listen to me – do not waste time, for I can't stay. Oh! if the General should awake and find me gone!'

'What is the matter, my dear Cecilia? Only tell me what I can do for you.'

'That is the thing; but I am afraid, now it is come to the point.' Lady Cecilia breathed quick and short. 'I am almost afraid to ask you to do this for me.'

'Afraid! my dear Cecilia, to ask me to do anything in this world for you! How can you be afraid? Tell me only what it is at once.'

'I am very foolish – I am very weak. I know you love me – would do anything for me, Helen. And this is the simplest thing in the world, but the greatest favour – the greatest service. It is only just to receive a packet, which the General will give you in the morning. He will ask if it is for you. And you will just accept of it. I don't ask you to say it is yours, or to say a word about it — only receive it for me.'

'Yes, I will, to be sure. But why should he give it to me, and not to yourself?'

'Oh, he thinks, and you must let him think, it is for you, that's all. Will you promise me?' But Helen made no answer. 'Oh, promise me, promise me, speak, for I can't stay. I will explain it all to you in the morning.' She rose to go.

'Stay, stay! Cecilia,' cried Helen, stopping her; 'stay! — you must, indeed, explain it all to me now — you must indeed!'

Lady Cecilia hesitated — said she had not time. 'You said, Helen, that you would take the packet, and you know you must; but I will explain it all as fast as I can. You know I fainted, but you do not know why. I will tell you exactly how it all happened: — you recollect my coming into the library after I was dressed, before you went upstairs, and giving you a sprig of orange flowers?'

'Oh yes, I was dreaming of it just now when you came in,' said Helen. 'Well, what of that?'

'Nothing, only you must have been surprised to hear so soon afterwards that I had fainted.'

'Yes,' Helen said, she had been very much surprised and alarmed; and again Lady Cecilia paused.

'Well, I went directly from you to Clarendon, to give him a rose, which you may remember I had in my hand for him. I found him in the study, talking to corporal somebody. He just smiled as I came in, took the rose, and said, "I shall be ready this moment": and looking to a table on which were heaps of letters and parcels which Granville had brought to town, he added, "I do not know whether there is anything there for you, Cecilia." I went to look, and he went on talking to his corporal. He was standing with his back to the table.'

Helen felt that Lady Cecilia had told all these minute details as if there was some fact to which she feared to come. Cecilia went on very quickly. 'I did not find anything for myself but in tossing over the papers I saw a packet directed to General Clarendon. I thought it was a feigned hand – and yet that I knew it – that I had seen it somewhere lately. There was one little flourish that I recollected; it was like the writing of that wretched Carlos.'

'Carlos!' cried Helen: 'well!'

'The more I looked at it,' continued Lady Cecilia, 'the more like I thought it; and I was going to say so to the General, only I waited till he had done his business: but as I was examining it through the outer cover, of very thin foreign paper, I could distinguish the writing of some of the inside, and it was like your hand or like mine. You know between our hands there is such a great resemblance, there is no telling one from another.'

Helen did not think so, but she remained silent.

'At least,' said Cecilia, answering her look of doubt, 'at least the General says so; he never knows our hands asunder. Well! I perceived that there was something hard inside – more than papers; and as I felt it, there came from it an uncommon perfume – a particular perfume, like what I used to have once, at the time – that time that I can never bear to think of, you know –'

'I know,' said Helen, and in a low voice she added, 'you mean about Colonel D'Aubigny.'

'The perfume, and altogether I do not know what, quite overcame me. I had just sense enough to throw the packet from me: I made an effort, and reached the window, and I was trying to open the sash, I remember; but what happened immediately after that, I cannot tell you. When I came to myself, I was in my husband's arms; he was carrying me upstairs – and so much alarmed about me he was! Oh, Helen, I do so love him! He laid me on the bed, and he spoke so kindly, reproaching me for not taking more care of myself – but so fondly! Somehow I could not bear it just then, and I closed my eyes as his met mine. He, I knew, could suspect nothing – but still! He stayed beside me, holding my hand: then dinner was ready; he had been twice summoned. It was a relief to me when he left me. Next, I believe, my mother came up, and felt my pulse, and scolded me for over-fatiguing myself, and for that leap; and I pleaded guilty, and it was all very well. I saw she had not an idea there was anything else. Mamma really is not suspicious, with all her penetration – she is not suspicious.'

'And why did you not tell her all the little you had to tell, dear Cecilia? If you had, long ago, when I begged of you to do so – if you had told your mother all about – '

'Told her!' interrupted Cecilia; 'told my mother! – oh no, Helen – '

Helen sighed, and feebly said, 'Go on.'

'Well! when you were at dinner, it came into my poor head that the General would open that parcel before I could see you again, and before I could ask your advice and settle with you – before I could know what was to be done. I was so anxious, I sent for you twice.'

'But Lady Davenant and the General forbade me to go to you.'

'Yes,' – Lady Cecilia said she understood that, and she had seen the danger of showing too much impatience to speak to Helen; she thought it might excite suspicion of her having something particular to say, she had therefore refrained from asking again. She was not asleep when Helen came to bed, though Felicie thought she was; she was much too anxious to sleep till she had seen her husband again; she was awake when he came into his room; she saw him come in with some letters and packets in his hand; by his look she knew all was still safe – he had not opened *that* particular packet – he held it among a parcel of military returns in his hand as he came to the side of the bed on tiptoe to see if she was asleep – to ask how she did; 'He touched my pulse,' said Lady Cecilia, – 'and I am sure he might well say it was terribly quick.

'Every instant I thought he would open that packet. He threw it, however, and all the rest, down on the table, to be read in the morning, as usual, as soon as he awoke. After feeling my pulse again, the last thing, and satisfying himself that it was better – 'Quieter now,' said he, he fell fast asleep, and slept so soundly, and I – '

Helen looked at her with astonishment, and was silent.

'Oh, speak to me!' said Lady Cecilia; 'what do you say, Helen?'

'I say that I cannot imagine why you are so much alarmed about this packet.'

'Because I am a fool, I believe, said Lady Cecilia, trying to laugh. 'I am so afraid of his opening it.'

'But why?' said Helen, 'what do you think there is in it?'

'I have told you, surely! Letters – foolish letters of mine to that D'Aubigny. Oh how I repent I ever wrote a line to him! And he told me, he absolutely swore, he had destroyed every note and letter I ever wrote to him. He was the most false of human beings!'

'He was a very bad man – I always thought so,' said Helen; 'but, Cecilia, I never knew that he had any letters of yours.'

'Oh yes, you did, my dear, at the time; do you not recollect I showed you a letter, and it was you who made me break off the correspondence?'

'I remember your showing me several letters of his,' said Helen, 'but not of yours – only one or two notes – asking for that picture back again which he had stolen from your portfolio.'

'Yes, and about the verses; surely you recollect my showing you another letter of mine, Helen!'

'Yes, but these were all of no consequence; there must be more, or you could not be so much afraid, Cecilia, of the General's seeing these, surely.' At this moment Lady Davenant's prophecy, all she had said about her daughter, flashed across Helen's mind, and with increasing eagerness she went on: – 'What is there in those letters that can alarm you so much?'

'I declare I do not know,' said Cecilia, 'that is the plain truth; I cannot recollect – I cannot be certain what there is in them.'

'But it is not so long ago, Cecilia – only two years?'

'That is true, but so many great events have happened since, and such new feelings, all that early nonsense was swept out of my mind. I never really loved that wretch – '

A gleam of joy came across Helen's face.

'Never, never,' repeated Lady Cecilia.

'Oh, I am happy still,' cried Helen. 'I told your mother I was sure of this.'

'Good heavens! Does she know about this packet?'

'No, no! – how could she? But what frightens you, my dear Cecilia? you say there is nothing wrong in the letters?'

'Nothing – nothing.'

'Then make no wrong out of nothing,' cried Helen. 'If you break confidence with your husband, that confidence will never, never unite again – your mother says so.'

'My mother!' cried Cecilia: 'good heavens! – so she does suspect? – tell me, Helen, tell me what she suspects.'

'That you did not at first – before you were married – tell the General the whole truth about Colonel D'Aubigny.'

Cecilia was silent.

'But it is not yet too late,' said Helen, earnestly; 'you can set it all right now – this is the moment, my dearest Cecilia. Do, do,' cried Helen, 'do tell him all – bid him look at the letters.'

'Look at them! Impossible! Impossible!' said Lady Cecilia. 'Bid me die rather.'

She turned quite away.

'Listen to me, Cecilia;' she held her fast. 'You must do it, Cecilia.'

'Helen, I cannot.'

'You can, indeed you can,' said Helen; 'only have courage now, and you will be happier all your life afterwards.'

'Do not ask it – do not ask it – it is all in vain, you are wasting time.'

'No, no – not wasting time; and in short, Cecilia, you must do what I ask of you, for it is right; and I will not do what you ask of me, for it is wrong.'

'You will not! You will not!' cried Lady Cecilia, breathless. 'After all! You will not receive the packet for me! you will not let the General believe the letters to be yours! Then I am undone! You will not do it! Then do not talk to me – do not talk to me – you do not know General Clarendon. If his jealousy were once roused, you have no idea what it would be.'

'If the man were alive,' said Helen, 'but since he is dead – '

'But Clarendon would never forgive me for having loved another – '

'You said you did not love him.'

'Nor did I ever *really* love that man; but still Clarendon, from even seeing those letters, might think I did. The very fact of having written such letters would be destruction to me with Clarendon. You do not know Clarendon. How can I convince you it is impossible for me to tell him? At the time he first proposed for me – oh! how I loved him, and feared to lose him. One day my mother, when I was not by, said something – I do not know what, about a first love, let fall something about that hateful D'Aubigny, and the General came to me in such a state! Oh, Helen, in such a state! I thought it was all at an end. He told me he never would marry any woman on earth who had ever loved another. I told him I never had, and that was true, you know; but then I went a little beyond perhaps. I said I had never THOUGHT of anybody else, for he made such a point of that. In short, I was a coward – a fool; I little foresaw – I laughed it off, and told him that what mamma had said was all a mistake, all nonsense; that Colonel D'Aubigny was a sort of universal flirt – and that was very true, I am sure; that he had admired us both, both you and me, but you last, you most, Helen, I said.'

'Oh, Cecilia, how could you say so, when you knew he never cared for me in the least?'

'Forgive me, my dear, for there was no other way; and what harm did it do you, or what harm can it ever do you? It only makes it the easier for you to help me – to save me now. And Granville,' continued Lady Cecilia, thinking that was the obstacle in Helen's mind, 'and Granville need never know it.'

Helen's countenance suddenly changed. 'Granville! I never thought of that!' and now that she did think of it she reproached herself with the selfishness of that fear. Till this moment, she knew her motives had been all singly for Cecilia's happiness; now the fear she felt of this some way hurting her with Beauclerc made her less resolute. Lady Cecilia saw her giving way and hurried on –

'Oh, my dear Helen! I know I have been very wrong, but you would not quite give me up, would you? Oh! for my mother's sake! Consider how it would be with my mother, so ill as you saw her! I am sure if anything broke out now, in my mother's state of health it would be fatal.'

Helen became excessively agitated.

'Oh, Helen! would you make me the death of that mother? Oh, Helen, save her! and do what you will with me afterwards. It will be only for a few hours – only a few hours!' repeated Lady Cecilia, seeing that these words made a great impression upon Helen, – 'Save me, Helen! save my mother.'

She sank upon her knees, clasping her hands in an agony of supplication. Helen bent down her head and was silent – she could no longer refuse. 'Then I must,' said she.

'Oh, thank you! bless you!' cried Lady Cecilia in an ecstasy – ' you will take the letters?'

'Yes,' Helen feebly said; 'yes, since it must be so.'

Cecilia embraced her, thanked her, blessed her, and hastily left the room, but in an instant afterward she returned, and said, 'One thing I forget, and I must tell you. Think of my forgetting it! The letters are not signed with my real name, they are signed Emma – Henry and Emma! – O, folly, folly! My dear, dear friend! save me but now, and I never will be guilty of the least deception again during my whole life; believe me, believe me! When once my mother is safely gone I will tell Clarendon all. Look at me, dear Helen, look at me and believe me.'

And Helen looked at her, and Helen believed her.

CHAPTER 31

HELEN SLEPT NO MORE this night. When alone in the stillness of the long hours, she went over and over again all that had passed, what Cecilia had said, what she had at first thought and afterwards felt, all the persuasions by which she had been wrought upon, and, on the contrary, all the reasons by which she ought to be decided; backward and forward her mind vibrated, and its painful vacillation could not be stilled.

'What am I going to do? To tell a falsehood! That cannot be right; but in the circumstances – yet this is Cecilia's own way of palliating the fault that her mother so fears in her – that her mother trusted to me to guard her against; and now, already, even before Lady Davenant has left us, I am going to assist Cecilia in deceiving her husband, and on that very dangerous point – Colonel D'Aubigny.' Lady Davenant's foreboding having already been so far accomplished struck Helen fearfully, and her warning voice in the dead silence of that night sounded, and her look was upon her, so strongly, that she for an instant hid her head to get rid of her image. 'But what *can* I do? her own life is at stake! No less a motive could move me, but this ought – must – shall decide me. Yet, if Lady Davenant were to know it! – and I, in the last hours I have to pass with her – the last I ever may have with her, shall I deceive her? But it is not deceit, only prudence – necessary prudence; what a physician would order, what even humanity requires. I am satisfied it is quite right, quite, and I will go to sleep that I may be strong, and calm, and do it all well in the morning. After all, I have been too cowardly; frightening myself about nothing; too scrupulous – for what is it I have promised? only to receive the letters as if they were mine. Not to *say* that they are mine; he will not ask me, Cecilia thinks he will not ask me. But how can she tell? if he should, what *can* I do? I must then answer that they are mine. Indeed it is the same thing, for I should lead him to believe it as much by my receiving them in silence; it will be telling or acting an absolute falsehood, and can that ever be right?' Back it came to the same point, and in vain her cheek settled on the pillow and she thought she could sleep. Then with closed eyes she considered how the General would look, and speak, or not speak. 'What will he think of me when he sees the picture – the letters? For he must open the packet. But he will not read them, no, he is too honourable. I do not know what is in them. There can be nothing, however, but nonsense, Cecilia says; yet even so, love-letters he must know they are, and a clandestine correspond-ence. I heard him once express such contempt for any clandestine affair. He, who is so nice, so strict, about women's conduct, how I shall sink in his esteem! Well, be it so, that concerns only myself; and it is for his own sake, too, to save his happiness; and Cecilia, my dear Cecilia, oh I can bear it, and it will be a pride to me to bear it, for I am grateful; my gratitude shall not be only in words; now, when I am put to the trial, I can do something for my friends. Yes, and I will, let the consequences be what they may.' Yet Beauclerc! that thought was at the bottom of her heart; the fear, the almost certainty, that some way or other – every way in which she could think of it, it would lead to difficulty with Beauclerc. But this fear was mere selfishness, she thought, and to counteract it came all her generous, all her grateful, all her long-cherished, romantic love of sacrifice – a belief that she was capable of self-devotion for the friends she loved; and upon the strength of this idea she fixed at last. Quieted, she soothed herself to repose, and, worn out with reasoning or flying to reason in vain, she at last, in spite of the morning light dawning upon her through the unclosed shutters, in a soft sort of enthusiastic vision fading away, fell asleep.

She slept long; when she awoke it was with that indescrib-able feeling that something painful had happened – that something dreadful was to be this day. She recollected, first, that Lady Davenant was to go. Then came all that had passed with Cecilia. It was late, she saw that her maid had been in the room, but had refrained from awakening her; she rose, and dressed as fast as she could. She was to go to Lady Davenant when her bell rang twice. How to appear before one who knew her countenance so well, without showing that anything had happened, was her first difficulty. She looked in her glass to see whether there was any alteration in her face; none that she could see, but she was no judge. 'How foolish to think so much about it all!' She dressed, and between times inquired from her maid if she had heard of any change in Lady Davenant's intentions of going. Had any counter-orders about the carriage been given? None; it was ordered to be at the door by twelve o'clock. 'That was well,' said Helen to herself. It would all soon be over. Lady Davenant would be safe, then she could bear all the rest; next she hoped, that any perturbation or extraordinary emotion in herself would not be observed in the hurry of departure, or would be thought natural at parting with Lady Davenant. 'So then, I come at every turn to some little deceit,' thought she, 'and I must, I must!' and she sighed.

'It is a sad thing for you, ma'am, Lady Davenant's going away,' said her maid.

Helen sighed again. 'Very sad indeed.' Suddenly a thought darted into her mind, that the whole danger might be avoided. A hope came that the General might not open the packet before Lady Davenant's departure, in which case Cecilia could not expect that she should abide by her promise, as it was only conditional. It had been made really on her mother's account; Cecilia had said that if once her mother was safe out of the house, she could then, and she would the very next day, tell the whole to her husband. Helen sprang from under the hands of her maid as she was putting up her hair behind, and ran to Cecilia's dressing-room, but she was not there. It was now her usual time for coming, and Helen left open the door between them, that she might go to her before Felicie should be rung for. She waited impatiently, but no Cecilia came. The time, to her impatience, seemed dreadfully long. But her maid observed, that as her lady-ship had not been well yesterday, it was no wonder she was later this morning than usual.

'Very true, but there is somebody coming along the gallery now, see if that is Lady Cecilia.'

'No, ma'am, Mademoiselle Felicie.'

Mademoiselle Felicie said ditto to Helen's own maid, and, moreover, supposed her lady might not have slept well. Just then, one little peremptory knock at the door was heard.

'*Bon Dieu! C'est Monsieur le Général!*' exclaimed Felicie.

It was so – Felicie went to the door and returned with the General's compliments to Miss Stanley, and he begged to see her as soon as it might suit her convenience in the library, before she went into the breakfast-room, and after she should have seen Lady Cecilia, who wished to see her immediately.

Helen found Lady Cecilia in bed, looking as if she had been much agitated, two spots of carnation colour high up in her cheeks, a well-known sign in her of great emotion. 'Helen!' she cried, starting up the moment Helen came in, 'he has opened the packet, and you see me alive. But I do believe I should have died, when it came to the point, but for you – dearest Helen, I should have been, and still but for you I must be, undone – and my mother – oh! if he had gone to her!'

'What has happened, tell me clearly, my dear Cecilia, and quickly, for I must go to General Clarendon; he has desired to see me as soon as I can after seeing you.'

'I know, I know,' said Cecilia, 'but he will allow time, and you had better be some time with me, for he thinks I have all to explain to you this morning – and so I have, a great deal to say to you; sit down – quietly – oh if you knew how I have been agitated. I am hardly able yet to tell anything rightly.' She threw herself back on the pillows, and drew a long breath, as if to relieve the oppression of mind and body. 'Now I think I can tell it.'

'Then do, my dear Cecilia – all – pray do! and exactly – O Cecilia, tell me all.'

'Every word, every look, to the utmost, as far as I can recollect, as if you had been present. Give me your hand, Helen, how cool you are – delightful! but how you tremble!'

'Never mind,' said Helen; 'but how burning hot your hand is!'

'No matter. If ever I am well or happy again in this world, Helen, I shall owe it to you. After I left you I found the General fast asleep, I do not believe he had ever awoke – I lay awake for hours, till past five o'clock in the morning, I was wide awake – feverish. But can you conceive it? just then, when I was most anxious to be awake, when I knew there was but one hour – not so much, till he would awake and read that packet, I felt an irresistible sleepiness come over me; I turned and turned, and tried to keep my eyes open, and pulled and pinched my fingers. But all would not do, and I fell asleep, dreaming that I was awake, and how long I slept I cannot tell you, so deep, so dead asleep I must have been; but the instant I did awake, I started up and drew back the curtain, and I saw – O Helen! there was Clarendon dressed – standing with his arms folded – a letter open hanging from his hand. His eyes were fixed upon me, waiting, watching for my first look: he saw me glance at the letter in his hand, and then at the packet on the table near the bed. For an instant neither of us spoke: I could not, nor exclaim even; but surprised, terrified, he must have seen I was. As I leaned forward, holding by the curtains, he pulled one of them suddenly back, threw open the shutters, and the full glare was upon my face. I shut my eyes – I could not help it – and shrank; but, gathering strength from absolute terror of his silence, I spoke: I asked, "For Heaven's sake! Clarendon, what is the matter? Why do you look so?"

'Oh, that look of his! still fixed on me – the same, as I once saw before we were married – once, and but once, when he came from my mother to me about this man, Well, I put my hands before my eyes; he stepped forward, drew them down, and placed the open letter before me, and then asked me, in a terrible sort of suppressed voice, "Cecilia, whose writing is this?"

'The writing was before my eyes, but I literally could not see it – it was all a sort of maze. He saw I could not read it, and calmly bade me "take time – examine – is it a forgery?"

'A forgery! – that had never crossed my mind, and for an instant I was tempted to say it was; but quickly I saw that would not do: there was the miniature, and that could not be a forgery. "No," I answered, "I do not think it is a forgery."

' "What then?" said he, so hastily that I could hardly hear; and before I could think what to answer, he said, "I must see Lady Davenant." He stepped towards the bell; I threw myself upon his arm – "Good Heavens! do not, Clarendon, if you are not out of your senses." "I am not out of my senses, Cecilia, but I am perfectly calm; answer me, one word only – is this your writing?" O my dear Helen! then it was that you saved me.'

'I!'

'Yes, forgive me, Helen, I answered, "There is a handwriting so like, that you never can tell it from mine. Ask me no more, Clarendon," I said.

'I saw a flash of light, as it were, come across his face – it was hope – but still it was not certainty. I saw this: oh! how quick one sees. He pointed to the first words of the letter, held his finger under them, and his hand trembled – think of his hand trembling! "Read," he said, and I read. How I brought myself to pronounce the words, I cannot imagine. I read what, as I hope for mercy, I had no recollection of ever having written – "My dear, too dear Henry."

"Colonel D'Aubigny?" said the General. I answered, "Yes." He looked astonished at my self-possession – and so was I. For another instant his finger rested, pressing down there under the words, and his eyes on my face, as if he would have read into my soul. "Ask me no more," I repeated, scarcely able to speak; and something I said, I believe, about honour and not betraying you. He turned to the signature, and, putting his hand down upon it, asked, "What name is signed to this letter?" I answered, I have seen – I know – I believe it is "Emma."

' "You knew then of this correspondence?" was his next question. I confessed I did. He said that was wrong, "but quite a

different affair" from having been engaged in it myself, or some such
word. His countenance cleared; that pale look of the forehead, the
fixed purpose of the eye, changed; Oh! I could see – I understood
it all with half a glance – saw the natural colour coming back,
and tenderness for me returning – yet some doubt lingering still.
He stood, and I heard some half-finished sentences. He said that
you must have been very young at that time; I said, "Yes, very
young" – "And the man was a most artful man," he observed; I
said, "Yes, very artful." That was true, I am sure. Clarendon then
recollected that you showed some emotion one day when Colonel
D'Aubigny was first mentioned – at that time, you know, when
we heard of his death. I said nothing. The General went on: "I
could scarcely have believed all this of Helen Stanley," he said. He
questioned no farther: – and oh! Helen, what do you think I did
next? but it was the only thing left me to put an end to doubts,
which, to *me*, must have been fatal – forgive me, Helen!'

'Tell me what you did,' said Helen.

'Cannot you guess?'

'You told him positively that I wrote the letters?'

'No, not so bad, I never said that downright falsehood – no, I
could not; but I did almost as bad.'

'Pray tell me at once, my dear Cecilia.'

'Then, in the first place, I stretched out my hand for the whole
packet of letters which lay on the table untouched.'

'Well?'

'Well, he put them into my hands and said, "There is no direction on these but to myself, I have not looked at any of them
except this, which in ignorance I first opened; I have not read
one word of any of the others."

'Well,' said Helen, 'and what did you do?'

'I said I was not going to read any of the letters, that I was
only looking for – now Helen, you know – I told you there was
something hard in the parcel, something more than papers, I was
sure what it must be – the miniature – the miniature of you,
which I painted, you know, that I might have it when you were
gone, and which *he* stole, and pretended before my mother to be

admiring as your likeness, but he kept it only because it was my painting. I opened the paper in which it was folded; Clarendon darted upon it – "It is Helen!" and then he said, "How like! how beautiful! how unworthy of that man!"

'But, oh, Helen, think of what an escape I had next. There was my name – my initials C.D. at the bottom of the picture, as the painter; and that horrible man, not content with his initials opposite to mine, had on the back written at full length, "For Henry D'Aubigny." Clarendon looked at it, and said between his teeth, "He is dead." "Thank God!" said I.

'Then he asked me how I came to paint this picture for that man; I answered – oh how happy then it was for me that I could tell the whole truth about that at least! – I answered that I did not do the picture for Colonel D'Aubigny; that it never was given to him; that he stole it from my portfolio, and that we both did what we could to get it back again from him, but could not. And that you even wanted me to tell my mother but of that I was afraid; and Clarendon said, "You were wrong there, my dear Cecilia."

'I was so touched when I heard him call me his dear Cecilia again, and in his own dear voice, that I burst into tears. This was a great relief to me, and I kept saying over and over again that I was wrong – very wrong indeed! and then he kneeled down beside me, and I so felt his tenderness, his confiding love for me – for me, unworthy as I am.' The tears streamed from Lady Cecilia's eyes as she spoke – 'Quite unworthy!'

'No, no, not quite unworthy,' said Helen; 'my poor dear Cecilia, what you must have felt!'

'Once,' continued Cecilia – 'once, Helen, as my head was lying on his shoulder, my face hid, I felt so much love, so much remorse, and knowing I had done nothing really bad, I was tempted to whisper all in his ear. I felt I should be so much happier for ever – ever – if I could!'

'Oh that you had! my dear Cecilia, I would give anything upon earth for *your* sake, that you had.'

'Helen, I could not – I could not. It was too late, I should have been undone if I had breathed but a word. When he even suspected the truth! that look – that voice – was so terrible. To see it – hear it again! I could not – oh, Helen, it would have been utter ruin – madness. I grant you, my dear Helen, it might have been done at first, before I was married; oh, would to Heaven it had! but it is useless thinking of that now. Helen, my whole earthly happiness is in your hands, this is all I have to say, may I – may I depend on you?'

'Yes, yes, depend upon me, my dearest Cecilia,' said Helen; 'now let me go.'

Lady Cecilia held her one instant longer, to say that she had asked Clarendon to leave it to her to return the letters, 'to save you the embarrassment, my dearest Helen; but he answered he must do this himself, and I did not dare to press the matter: but you need not be alarmed, he will be all gentleness to you, he said, "it is so different." Do not be afraid.'

'Afraid for myself?' said Helen; 'oh no – rest, dear Cecilia, and let me go.'

'Go then, go,' cried Cecilia; 'but for you what would have become of my mother! – of me! – you save us all.'

Believing this, Helen hastened to accomplish her purpose; resolved to go through with it, whatever it might cost; her scruples vanished, and she felt a sort of triumphant pleasure in the courage of sacrificing herself.

CHAPTER 32

GENERAL CLARENDON was sitting in the music-room, within the library, the door open, so that he could see Helen the moment she came in, and in that moment he threw down his book as he rose, and their eyes met: hers fell beneath his penetrating glance; he came forward immediately to meet her, with the utmost gentleness and kindness in his whole appearance and manner, took her hand, and, drawing her arm within his, said, in the most encouraging tone, 'Consider me as your brother, Helen; you know you have allowed me so to feel for you, and so, believe me, I do feel.'

This kindness quite overcame her, and she burst into tears. He hurried her across the library, into the inner room, seated her, and when he had closed the door, stood beside her, and began, as if he had been to blame, to apologise for himself.

'You must have been surprised at my having opened letters which did not belong to me, but there was no direction, no indication, that could stop me. They were simply in a cover directed to me. The purpose of whoever sent them must have been to make me read them; the ultimate purpose was, I doubt not, to ruin Lady Cecilia Clarendon in my opinion.'

'Or me,' said Helen.

'No, Miss Stanley, no; that at all events cannot be,' said the General. 'Supposing the letters to be acknowledged by you, still it would be quite a different affair. But in the first place look at them, they may be forgeries. You will tell me if they are forgeries?'

And he placed the packet in her hands. Scarcely looking at the writing, she answered, 'No, forgeries I am sure they are not.' The General looked again at the direction of the cover, and observed, 'This is a feigned hand. Whose can it be?'

Helen was on the brink of saying that Cecilia had told her it was like the writing of Carlos. Now this cover had not, to the General's knowledge, been seen by Cecilia, and that one answer might have betrayed all that she was to conceal, for he would instantly have asked how and when did Cecilia see it, and the cause of her fainting would have been then understood by him. Such hazards, in every, even the first, least, step in false-hood; such hazard in this first moment! But she escaped this peril, and Helen answered: 'It is something like the writing of the page, Carlos, but I do not think all that direction is his. There seem to be two different hands. I do not know, indeed, how it is.'

'Some time or other it will come out,' said the General. 'I will keep this cover, it will lead to the direction of that boy, or of whoever it was that employed him.'

To give her further time the General went on looking at the miniature, which he held in his hand. 'This is a beautiful like-ness,' said he, 'and not ill painted – by Cecilia, was it not?'

Helen looked at it, and answered, 'Yes, by Cecilia.'

'I am glad it is safe,' said the General, 'restored – Cecilia told me the history. I know that it was stolen, not given by you.'

'Given!' said Helen. 'Oh no! stolen.'

'Base!' said the General.

'He was base,' answered Helen.

General Clarendon held in his hand, along with the picture, one letter separated from the rest, open; he looked at it as if embarrassed, while Helen spoke the last words, and he repeated, 'Base! yes, he certainly was, or he would have destroyed these letters.'

Again Helen was on the point of saying that Colonel D'Aubigny had told Cecilia he had done so, but fortunately her agitation, in default of presence of mind, kept her silent.

'This is the first letter I opened,' said the General, 'before I was aware that they were not what I should read. I saw only the first words, I thought then that I had a right to read them. When these letters met my eyes, I conceived them to have been written by my wife. I had a right to satisfy myself respecting the nature of the correspondence; that done, I looked no farther. I bore my suspense – I waited till she awoke.'

'So she told me, Cecilia has told me all; but even if she had not, in any circumstances who could doubt your honour, General Clarendon?'

'Then trust to it, Miss Stanley, for the past, for the future, trust to it! You gratify me more than I can express – you do me justice. I wished to return these letters to you with my own hand,' continued he, 'to satisfy myself, in the first place, that there was no mistake. Of that your present candour, indeed, the first look of that ingenuous countenance, was sufficient.'

Helen felt that she blushed all over.

'Pardon me for distressing you, my dear Helen. It was a matter in which a man MUST be selfish, *must* in point of honour, *must* in point of feeling. I owe to your candour not merely relief from what I could not endure and live, but relief from suspicion, – suspicion of the truth of one dearer to me than life.'

Helen sat as if she had been transfixed.

'I owe to you,' continued he, 'the happiness of my whole future life.'

'Then I am happy,' cried Helen, 'happy in this, at all events, whatever may become of me.'

She had not yet raised her eyes towards the General; she felt as if her first look must betray Cecilia; but now she tried to fix her eyes upon him as he looked anxiously at her, and she said, 'Thank you, thank you, General Clarendon! Oh, thank you for all the kindness you have shown me; but I am the more grieved, it makes me more sorry to sink quite in your esteem.'

'To sink! You do not: your candour, your truth, raises you – '

'Oh! do not say that – '

'I do,' repeated the General, 'and you may believe me. I am incapable of deceiving you – this is no matter of compliment. Between friend and friend I should count a word, a look of falsehood, treason.'

Helen's tears stopped, and, without knowing what she did, she began hastily to gather up the packet of letters which she had let fall; the General assisted her in putting them into her bag, and she closed the strings, thanked him, and was rising, when he went on – 'I beg your indulgence while I say a few words of myself.'

She sat down again immediately. 'Oh! as many as you please.'

'I believe I may say I am not of a jealous temper.'

'I am sure you are not,' said Helen.

'I thank you,' said the General. 'May I ask on what your opinion is founded?'

'On what has now passed, and on all that I have heard from Lady Davenant.'

He bowed. 'You may have heard then, from Lady Davenant, of some unfortunate circumstances in my own and in a friend's family which happened a short time before my marriage?'

Helen said she had.

'And of the impression these circumstances made on my mind, my consequent resolve never to marry a woman who had ever had any previous attachment?'

Helen was breathless at hearing all this repeated.

'Were you informed of these particulars?' said the General.

'Yes,' Helen said faintly.

'I am not asking, Miss Stanley, whether you approved of my resolution; simply whether you heard of it?'

'Yes – certainly.'

'That's well. It was on an understanding between Cecilia and myself on this point that I married. Did you know this?'

'Yes,' said Helen.

'Some words,' continued the General, 'once fell from Lady Davenant concerning this Colonel D'Aubigny which alarmed me. Cecilia satisfied me that her mother was mistaken. Cecilia solemnly assured me that she had never loved him.' The General paused.

Helen, conceiving that he waited for and required her opinion, replied, 'So I always thought – so I often told Lady Davenant.' But at this moment recollecting the words at the beginning of that letter, 'My dear, too dear Henry,' Helen's voice faltered.

The General saw her confusion, but attributed it to her own consciousness. 'Had Lady Davenant not been mistaken,' resumed he, 'that is to say had there ever been – as might have happened not unnaturally – had there ever been an attachment; in short, had Cecilia ever loved him, and told me so, I am convinced that such truth and candour would have satisfied me, would have increased – as I now feel – increased my esteem. I am at this moment convinced that, in spite of my declared resolution, I should in perfect confidence have married.'

'Oh that Cecilia had but told him,' thought Helen.

'I should not, my dear Miss Stanley,' continued the General, 'have thus taken up your time talking of myself, had I not an important purpose in view. I was desirous to do away in your mind the idea of my great strictness – not on my own account, but on yours, I wished to dispel this notion. Now you will no longer, I trust, apprehend that my esteem for you is diminished. I assure you I can make allowances.'

She was shocked at the idea of allowances, yet thanked him for his indulgence, and she could hardly refrain from again bursting into tears.

'Still by your agitation I see you are afraid of me,' said he, smiling.

'No indeed; not afraid of you, but shocked at what you must think of me.'

'I am not surprised, but sorry to see that the alarm I gave my poor Cecilia has passed from her mind into yours. To her I must have appeared harsh: I *was* severe; but when I thought I had been deceived, duped, can you wonder?'

Helen turned her eyes away.

'My dear Miss Stanley, why will you not distinguish? the cases are essentially different. Nine out of ten of the young ladies who marry in these countries do not marry the first object of their fancy, and whenever there is, as there will be, I am sure, in your case, perfect candour, I do not apprehend the slightest danger to the happiness of either party. On the contrary, I should foretell an increase of esteem and love. Beauclerc has often – '

Beauclerc's voice was at this instant heard in the hall.

'Compose yourself, my dear Miss Stanley – this way,' said the General, opening a door into the conservatory, for he heard Beauclerc's step now in the library. The General followed Helen as she left the room, and touching the bag that contained the letters, said,

'Remember, whatever may be your hurry, lock this up first.'

'Thank you,' answered she; 'I will, I will!' and she hastened on, and in a moment she was safe across the hall and upstairs, without meeting any one, and in her own room, and the bag locked up in her cabinet. Lady Davenant's bell rang as she went to her apartment; she looked in at Cecilia, who started up in her bed.

'All is over,' said Helen, 'all is well. I have the letters locked up; I cannot stay.'

Helen disengaged herself almost forcibly from Cecilia's embrace, and she was in Lady Davenant's room in another minute. She bade her good morning as composedly as she could, she thought quite as usual. But that was impossible: so much the better, for it would not have been natural this last morning of Lady Davenant's stay, when nothing was as usual externally or internally. All was preparation for departure – her maids packing – Lady Davenant making some last arrangements – in the midst of which she stopped to notice Helen – pressed her in her arms, and after looking once in her face, said, 'My poor child! it must be so.'

Elliott interrupted, asking some question, purposely to draw off her attention; and while she turned about to give some orders to another servant, Elliott said to Miss Stanley, 'My lady was not well last night; she must be kept from all that can agitate her, as much as possible.'

Helen at that instant rejoiced that she had done what she had. She agreed with Elliott, she said, that all emotion which could be avoided should; and upon this principle busied herself, and was glad to employ herself in whatever she could to assist the preparations, avoiding all conversation with Lady Davenant.

'You are right, my love – quite right,' said Lady Davenant. 'The best way is always to employ oneself to the last. Yes, put up those drawings carefully, in this portfolio, Elliott; take silver paper, Helen.'

They were Helen's own drawings, so all went on, and all was safe – even when Cecilia was spoken of; while the silver paper went over the drawings, Helen answered that she had seen her. 'She was not well, but still not seriously ill, though – '

'Yes,' said Lady Davenant; 'only the General is too anxious about her – very naturally. He sent me word just now,' continued she, 'that he has forbidden her to get up before breakfast. I will go and see her now; dear Cecilia! I hope she will do well – every way – I feel sure of it, Helen – sure as you do yourself, my dear – But what is the matter?'

'Nothing!' said Helen. That was not quite true; but she could not help it – 'Nothing!' repeated she. 'Only I am anxious, my dear Lady Davenant,' continued poor Helen, blushing, unaccustomed to evasions – 'only I am very anxious you should go soon to Cecilia; I know she is awake now, and you will be hurried after breakfast.'

Elliott looked reproachfully at Miss Stanley, for she thought it much better for her lady to be engaged in more indifferent matters till after breakfast, when she would have but a few minutes to spend with her daughter; so Helen, correcting herself, added – 'But perhaps I am wrong, so do not let me interrupt you in whatever you are doing.'

'My dear child,' said Lady Davenant; 'you do not know what you are saying or doing yourself this morning.'

But no suspicion was excited in her mind, as she accounted for Helen's perturbation by the sorrow of their approaching separation, and by the hurry of her spirits at Beauclerc's arrival the day before.

And then came the meeting with the General at breakfast, which Helen dreaded; but so composed, so impenetrable, was he that she could hardly believe that anything could have occurred that morning to agitate him.

Lady Davenant, after being with her daughter, came to take leave of Helen, and said gravely, 'Helen! remember what I said of Cecilia's truth, my trust is in you. Remember, if I never see you again, by all the love and esteem I bear you, and all which you feel for me, remember this my last request – prayer – adjuration to you, support, save Cecilia!'

At that moment the General came in to announce that the carriage was ready: promptly he led her away, handed her in, and the order to 'drive on' was given. Lady Davenant's last look, her last anxious look, was upon Helen and Beauclerc as they stood beside each other on the steps, and she was gone.

Helen was so excessively agitated that Beauclerc did not attempt to detain her from hurrying to her own room, where she sat down, and endeavoured to compose herself. She repeated Lady Davenant's last words, 'Support, save Cecilia,' and, unlocking the cabinet in which she had deposited the fatal letters, she seized the bag that contained them, and went immediately to Cecilia. She was in her dressing-room, and the General sitting beside her on the sofa, upon which she was resting. He was sitting directly opposite to Helen as she entered; she started at the sight of him: his eyes instantly fell upon the bag, and she felt her face suddenly flush. He took out his watch, said he had an appointment, and was gone before Helen raised her eyes.

'My dearest friend, come to me, come close to me,' cried Cecilia, and throwing her arms round Helen, she said, 'Oh, I am the happiest creature now!'

'Are you?' said Helen.

'Yes, that I am, and I thank you for it; how much I thank you, Helen, it is impossible to express, and better I love you than anything upon earth but Clarendon himself, my best friend, my generous Helen. Oh, Clarendon has been so kind, so very kind! so sorry for having alarmed me! He is a noble, charming creature. I love him a thousand times better than I ever did, am happier than I ever was! and all this I owe to you, dearest Helen. But I cannot get your eyes from that bag, – what have you there?'

'The letters,' said Helen.

'The letters!' exclaimed Cecilia, springing up, 'give them to me,' seizing and opening the bag. 'Oh that dreadful perfume! Helen, open the window, and bolt the door, my dear – both doors.'

While Helen was doing so, Cecilia struck one little quick blow on a taper-lighter; it flared, and when Helen turned, one of the letters was in flames, and Cecilia continued feeding the flame with them as fast as ever it could devour.

'Burn! burn! there, there!' cried she, 'I would not look at any one of them again for the world; I know no more what is in them than if I had never written them, except those horrid, horrid words Clarendon saw and showed me. I cannot bear to think of it. There now,' continued she, as they burned, 'no one can ever know anything more about the matter: how glad I am to see them burning! – burnt! safe! The smell will go off in a minute or two. It is going, – yes, gone! is not it? Now we may breathe freely. But you look as if you did not know whether you were glad or sorry, Helen.'

'I believe it was right; the General advised me to lock them up,' said Helen, 'but then – '

'Did he? how thoughtful of him! But better to burn them at once; I am sure it was not my fault that they were not long ago destroyed. I was assured by that abominable man – but no matter, we will never think of him again. It is done now – no, not completely yet,' said she, looking close at the half-white, half-black burnt paper, in which words, and whole lines, still appeared in shrunken but yet quite legible characters. 'One cannot be too careful,' and she trampled on the burnt paper, and scattered the cinders. Helen was anxious to speak, she had something important to say, but hesitated; she saw that Cecilia's thoughts were so far from what she wanted to speak of that she could not instantly say it; she could not bear to overturn all Cecilia's present happiness, and yet said to herself, I must – I must – or what may happen hereafter? Then forcing herself to speak, she began, 'Your mother is safe now, Cecilia.'

'Oh yes, and thank you, thank you for that – '

'Then now, Cecilia – your promise.'

'My promise!' Lady Cecilia's eyes opened in unfeigned astonishment. 'What promise? Oh, I recollect, I promised – did I?'

'My dear Cecilia, surely you cannot have forgotten.'

'How was it?'

'You know the reason I consented was to prevent the danger of any shock to Lady Davenant.'

'Well, I know, but what did I promise?'

The words had in reality passed Lady Cecilia's lips at the time without her at all considering them as a promise, only as a means of persuasion to bring Helen to her point.

'What did I promise?' repeated she.

'You said, "As soon as my mother is safe, as soon as she is gone, I will tell my husband all," – Cecilia, you cannot forget what you promised.'

'Oh no, now I remember it perfectly, but I did not mean so soon. I never imagined you would claim it so soon: but some time I certainly will tell him all.'

'Do not put it off, dearest Cecilia. It must be done – let it be done to-day.'

'To-day!' Lady Cecilia almost screamed.

'I will tell you why,' said Helen.

'To-day!' repeated Lady Cecilia.

'If we let the present *now* pass,' continued Helen, 'we shall lose both the power and the opportunity, believe me.'

'I have not the power, Helen, and I do not know what you mean by the opportunity,' said Cecilia.

'We have a reason now to give General Clarendon – a true good reason, for what we have done.'

'Reason!' cried Lady Cecilia, 'what can you mean?'

'That it was to prevent danger to your mother, and now she is safe; and if you tell him directly, he will see this was really so.'

'That is true; but I cannot – wait till to-morrow, at least.'

'Every day will make it more difficult. The deception will be greater, and less pardonable. If we delay, it will become deliberate falsehood, a sort of conspiracy between us,' said Helen.

'Conspiracy! Oh, Helen, do not use such a shocking word, when it is really nothing at all.'

'Then why not tell it?' urged Helen.

'Because, though it is nothing at all in reality, Clarendon would think it dreadful – though I have done nothing really wrong.'

'So I say – so I know,' cried Helen; 'therefore – '

'Therefore let me take my own time,' said Cecilia. 'How can you urge me so, hurrying me so terribly, and when I am but just recovered from one misery, and when you had made me so happy, and when I was thanking you with all my heart?'

Helen was much moved, but answered as steadily as she could – 'It seems cruel, but indeed I am not cruel.'

'When you had raised me up,' continued Cecilia, 'to dash me down again, and leave me worse than ever!'

'Not worse – no, surely not worse, when your mother is safe.'

'Yes, safe, thank you – but oh, Helen, have you no feeling for your own Cecilia?'

'The greatest,' answered Helen; and her tears said the rest.

'You, Helen! I never could have thought you would have urged me so!'

'O Cecilia! If you knew the pain it was to me to make you unhappy again, – but I assure you it is for your own sake. Dearest Cecilia, let me tell you all that General Clarendon said about it, and then you will know my reasons.' She repeated as quickly as she could all that had passed between her and the General; and when she came to this declaration that, if Cecilia had told him plainly the fact before, he would have married with perfect confidence, and, as he believed, with increased esteem and love, Cecilia started up from the sofa on which she had thrown herself, and exclaimed,

'Oh that I had but known this at the time, and I *would* have told him.'

'It is still time,' said Helen.

'Time now? – impossible. His look this morning. Oh, that look!'

'But what is one look, my dear Cecilia, compared with a whole life of confidence and happiness?'

'A life of happiness! never, never for me; in that way at least, never.'

'In that way and no other, Cecilia, believe me. I am certain you never could endure to go on concealing this, living with him you love so, yet deceiving him.'

'Deceiving! do not call it deceiving, it is only suppressing a fact that would give him pain; and when he can have no suspicion, why give him that pain? I am afraid of nothing now but this timidity of yours – this going back. Just before you came in. Clarendon was saying how much he admired your truth and candour, how much he is obliged to you for saving him from endless misery; he said so to me, that was what made me so completely happy. I saw that it was all right for you as well as me, that you had not sunk, that you had risen, in his esteem.'

'But I must sink, Cecilia, in his esteem, and now it hangs upon a single point – upon my doing what I cannot do.' Then she repeated what the General had said about that perfect openness which he was sure there would be in this case between her and Beauclerc. 'You see what the General expects that I should do.'

'Yes,' said Cecilia; and then indeed she looked much disturbed. 'I am very sorry that this notion of your telling Beauclerc came into Clarendon's head – very, very sorry, for he will not forget it. And yet, after all,' continued she, 'he will never ask you point blank, "Have you told Beauclerc?" – and still more impossible that he should ask Beauclerc about it.'

'Cecilia!' said Helen, 'if it were only for myself I would say no more; there is nothing I would not endure – that I would not sacrifice – even my utmost happiness.' She stopped, and blushed deeply.

'Oh, my dearest Helen! do you think I could let you ever hazard that? If I thought there was the least chance of injuring you with Granville! – I would do anything – I would throw myself at Clarendon's feet this instant.'

'This instant – I wish he was here,' cried Helen.

'Good Heavens! do you?' cried Lady Cecilia, looking at the door with terror – she thought she heard his step.

'Yes, if you would but tell him. Oh let me call him!'

'Oh no, no! Spare me – spare me, I cannot speak now. I could not utter the words; I should not know what words to use. Tell him if you will, I cannot.'

'May I tell him?' Helen said eagerly.

'No, no – that would be worse; if anybody tells him it must be myself.'

'Then you will now – when he comes in?'

'He is coming!' cried Cecilia.

General Clarendon came to the door – it was bolted.

'In a few minutes,' said Helen. Lady Cecilia did not speak, but listened, as in agony, to his receding footsteps.

'In a few minutes, Helen, did you say? – then there is nothing for me, but to die – I wish I could die – I wish I was dead.'

Helen felt she was cruel, she began to doubt her own motives; she thought she had been selfish in urging Cecilia too strongly; and, going to her kindly, she said, 'Take your own time, my dear Cecilia: only tell him – tell him soon.'

'I will, I will indeed, when I can – but now I am quite exhausted.'

'You are indeed,' said Helen; 'how cruel I have been! – how pale you are!'

Lady Cecilia lay down on the sofa, and Helen covered her with a soft India shawl, trembling so much herself that she could hardly stand.

'Thank you, thank you, dear, kind Helen; tell him I am going to sleep, and I am sure I hope I shall.'

Helen closed the shutters – she had now done all she could; she feared she had done too much; and as she left the room, she said to herself, 'Oh, Lady Davenant! if you could see – if you knew – what it cost me!'

VOLUME THREE

THE OVERWROUGHT STATE of Helen's feeling was relieved by a walk with Beauclerc, not in the dressed part of the park, but in what was generally undiscovered country: a dingle, a bosky dell, which he had found out in his rambles, and which, though so little distant from the busy hum of men, had a wonderful air of romantic seclusion and stillness – the stillness of evening. The sun had not set; its rich, red light yet lingered on the still remaining autumn tints upon the trees. The birds hopped fearlessly from bough to bough, as if this sweet spot were all their own. The cattle were quietly grazing below, or slowly winding their way to the watering-place. By degrees the sounds of evening faded away upon the ear; a faint chirrup here and there from the few birds not yet gone to roost, and now only the humming of the flies over the water, were to be heard.

It was perfect repose, and Beauclerc and Helen sat down on the bank to enjoy it together. The sympathy of the woman he loved, especially in his enjoyment of the beauties of nature, was to Beauclerc an absolute necessity of life. Nor would he have been contented with that show taste for the picturesque, which is, as he knew, merely one of a modern young lady's many accomplishments. Helen's taste was natural, and he was glad to feel it so true, and for him here alone expressed with such peculiar heightened feeling, as if she had in all nature now a new sense of delight. He had brought her here, in hopes that she would be struck with this spot, not only because it was beautiful in itself, and his discovery, but because it was like another bushy dell and bosky bourne, of which he had been from childhood fond, in another place, of which he hoped she would soon be mistress. 'Soon! very soon, Helen!' he repeated, in a tone which could not be heard by her with indifference. He said that some of his friends in London told him that the report of their intended union had been spread everywhere – (by Lady Katrine Hawksby, probably, as Cecilia, when Lady Castlefort departed, had confided to her, to settle her mind about Beauclerc, that he was coming over as Miss Stanley's acknowledged lover). And since the report had been so spread, the sooner the marriage took place the better; at least, it was a plea which Beauclerc failed not to urge, and Helen's delicacy failed not to feel.

She sighed – she smiled. The day was named – and the moment she consented to be his, nothing could be thought of but him. Yet, even while he poured out all his soul – while he enjoyed the satisfaction there is in perfect unreservedness of confidence, Helen felt a pang mix with her pleasure. She felt there was one thing *she* could *not* tell him: he who had told her everything – all his faults and follies. 'Oh! why,' thought she, 'why cannot I tell him everything? I, who have no secrets of my own – why should I be forced to keep the secrets of another?' In confusion, scarcely finished, these ideas, came across her mind, and she sighed deeply. Beauclerc asked why, and she could not tell him! She was silent; and he did not reiterate the indiscreet question. He was sure she thought of Lady Davenant; and he now spoke of the regret he felt that she could not be present at their marriage, and Lord Davenant too! Beauclerc said he had hoped that Lord Davenant, who loved Helen as if she were his own daughter, would have been the person to act as her father at the ceremony. But the General, his friend and hers, would now, Beauclerc said, give her to him; and would, he was sure, take pleasure in thus publicly marking his approbation of his ward's choice.

They rose, and going on down the path to the river's side, they reached a little cove where he had moored his boat, and they returned home by water – the moon just visible, the air so still; all so placid, so delightful, and Beauclerc so happy that she could not but be happy; yes – quite happy too. They reached the shore just as the lamps were lighting in the house. As they went in, they met the General, who said, 'In good time'; and he smiled on Helen as she passed.

'It is all settled,' whispered Beauclerc to him; 'and you are to give her away.'

'With pleasure,' said the General.

As Helen went upstairs, she said to herself, 'I understand the General's smile; he thinks I have followed his advice; he thinks I have told all – and I – I can only be silent.'

There was a great dinner party, but the General, not thinking Cecilia quite equal to it, had engaged Mrs Holdernesse, a relation of his, to do the honours of the day.

Lady Cecilia came into the drawing-room in the evening; but, after paying her compliments to the company, she followed the General's advice, and retired to the music-room: Helen went with her, and Beauclerc followed. Lady Cecilia sat down to play at *écarté* with him, and Helen tuned her harp. The General came in for a few minutes, he said, to escape from two young ladies who had talked him half dead about craniology. He stood leaning on the mantelpiece, and looking over the game. Lady Cecilia wanted counters, and she begged Beauclerc to look for some which she believed he would find in the drawer of a table that was behind him. Beauclerc opened the drawer, but no sooner had he done so, than, in admiration of something he discovered there, he exclaimed, 'Beautiful! beautiful! and how like!' it was the miniature of Helen, and besides the miniature, farther back in the drawer, Lady Cecilia saw – how quick is the eye of guilty fear! – could it be? – yes – one of the fatal letters – *the* letter! Nothing but the picture had yet been seen by the General or by Beauclerc: Lady Cecilia stretched behind her husband, whose eyes were upon the miniature, and closed the drawer. It was all she could do, it was impossible for her to reach the drawer.

Beauclerc, holding the picture up to the light, repeated, 'Beautiful! who did it? whom is it for? General, look! do you know it?'

'Yes, to be sure,' replied the General; 'Miss Stanley.'

'You have seen it before?'

'Yes,' said the General coldly.

'It is very like. Who did it?'

'I did it,' cried Lady Cecilia, who now recovered her voice.

'You, my dear Lady Cecilia! Whom for? for me? is it for me?'

'For you? It may be, hereafter, perhaps.'

'Oh thank you, my dear Lady Cecilia!' cried Beauclerc.

'If you behave well, perhaps,' added she.

The General heard in his wife's tremulous tone, and saw in her half confusion, half attempt at playfulness, only an amiable anxiety to save her friend, and to give her time to recover from her dismay. He at once perceived that Helen had not followed the course he had suggested; that she had not told Beauclerc, and did not intend that he should be told, the whole truth. The General looked extremely grave; Beauclerc gave a glance round the room. 'Here is some mystery,' said he, now first seeing Helen's disconcerted countenance. Then he turned on the General a look of eager enquiry. 'Some mystery, certainly,' said he, 'with which I am not to be made acquainted?'

'If there be any mystery,' said the General, 'with which you are not to be made acquainted, I am neither the adviser nor abettor. Neither in jest nor in earnest am I ever an adviser of mystery.'

While her husband thus spoke, Lady Cecilia made another attempt to possess herself of the letter. This time she rose decidedly, and, putting aside the little *écarté* table which was in her way, pressed forward to the drawing, saying something about 'counters.' Her Cashmere caught on Helen's harp, and, in her eager spring forward, it would have been overset, but that the General felt, turned, and caught it.

'What are you about, my dear Cecilia? – what do you want?'

'Nothing, nothing, thank you, my dear; nothing now.' Then she did not dare to open the drawer, or to let him open it, and anxiously drew away his attention by pointing to a footstool which she seemed to want.

'Could not you ask for it, my dear, without disturbing yourself? What are men made for?'

Beauclerc, after a sort of absent effort to join in quest of the footstool, had returned eagerly to the picture, and looking at it more closely, he saw the letters C.D. written in small characters in one corner; and, just as his eye turned to the other corner, Lady Cecilia, recollecting what initials were there, started up and snatched it from his hand. 'Oh, Granville!' cried she, 'you must not look at this picture any more till I have done something to it.' Beauclerc was trying to catch another look at it, when Cecilia cried out, 'Take it, Helen! take it!' and she held it up on high, but as she held it, though she turned the face from him, she forgot, quite forgot, that Colonel D'Aubigny had written his name on the back of the picture; and there it was in distinct characters such as could be plainly read at that height, 'For Henry D'Aubigny.' Beauclerc saw, and gave one glance at Helen. He made no further attempt to reach the picture. Lady Cecilia, not aware of what he had seen, repeated, 'Helen! Helen! why don't you take it? – now! now!'

Helen could not stir. The General took the picture from his wife's hand, gave it to Miss Stanley, without looking at her, and said to Lady Cecilia, 'Pray keep yourself quiet, Cecilia. You have done enough, too much, to-day; sit down,' said he, rolling her arm-chair close, and seating her. 'Keep yourself quiet, I beg.' 'I beg,' in the tone of 'I insist.'

She sat down, but catching a view of Beauclerc was alarmed by his aspect – and Helen! her head was bent down behind the harp. Lady Cecilia did not know yet distinctly what had happened. The General pressed her to lean back on the cushions which he was piling up behind her. Beauclerc made a step towards Helen, but checking himself, he turned to the *écarté* table. 'Those counters, after all, that we were looking for – 'As he spoke he pulled open the drawer. The General with his back to him was standing before Cecilia; she could not see what Beauclerc was doing, but she heard the drawer open, and cried out, 'Not there, Beauclerc; no counters there – you need not look there.' But before she spoke, he had given a sudden pull to the drawer, which brought it quite out, and all the contents fell upon the floor, and there was the fatal letter, open, and the words, '*My dear, too dear Henry*,' instantly met his eyes; he looked no farther, but in that single glance the writing seemed to him to be Lady Cecilia's, and quick his eye turned upon her. She kept perfectly quiet, and appeared to him perfectly composed. His eye then darted in search of Helen; she had sunk upon a seat behind the harp. Through the harp-strings he caught a glimpse of her face, all pale – crimsoned it grew as he advanced: she rose instantly, took up the letter, and, without speaking or looking at any one, tore it to pieces, Beauclerc in motionless astonishment. Lady Cecilia breathed again. The General's countenance expressed 'I interfere no farther.' He left the room; and Beauclerc, without another look at Helen, followed him.

For some moments after Lady Cecilia and Helen were left alone, there was a dead silence. Lady Cecilia sat with her eyes fixed upon the door through which her husband and Beauclerc had passed. She thought that Beauclerc might return; but when she found that he did not, she went to Helen, who had covered her face with her hands.

'My dearest friend,' said Lady Cecilia, 'thank you! thank you! – you did the best that was possible!'

'O Cecilia!' exclaimed Helen, 'to what have you exposed me?'

'How did it all happen?' continued Cecilia. 'Why was not that letter burnt with the rest? How came it there? Can you tell me?'

'I do not know,' said Helen, 'I cannot recollect.' But after some effort, she remembered that in the morning, while the General had been talking to her, she had in her confusion, when she took the packet, laid the picture and that letter beside her on the arm of the chair. She had, in her hurry of putting the other letters into her bag, forgotten this and the picture, and she supposed that they had fallen between the chair and the wall, and that they had been found and put into the table-drawer by one of the servants.

Helen was hastening out of the room, Cecilia detained her. 'Do not go, my dear, for that would look as if you were guilty, and you know you are innocent. At the first sound of your harp Beauclerc will return – only command yourself for an hour or two.'

'Yes, it will only be for an hour or two,' said Helen, brightening with hope. 'You will tell the General tonight. Do you think Granville will come back? Where is the harp-key? – I dropped it – here it is.' She began to tune the harp. Crack went one string – then another.

'That is lucky,' said Lady Cecilia, 'it will give you something to do, my love, if the people come in.'

The aide-de-camp entered. 'I thought I heard harp-strings going,' said he.

'Several! – yes,' said Lady Cecilia, standing full in his way.

'Inauspicious sounds for us! bad omens for my embassy. Mrs Holdernesse sent me.'

'I know,' said Lady Cecilia, 'and you will have the goodness to tell her that Miss Stanley's harp is unstrung.'

'Can I be of any use, Miss Stanley?' said he, moving towards the harp.

'No, no,' cried Lady Cecilia, 'you are in my service, attend to me.'

'Dear me, Lady Cecilia! I did not hear what you said.'

'That is what I complain of – hear me now.'

'I am all attention, I am sure. What are your commands?'

She gave him as many as his head could hold. A long message to Mrs Holdernesse, and to Miss Holdernesse and Miss Anna about their music-books, which had been left in the carriage, and were to be sent for, and duets to be played, and glees, for the major and Lady Anne Ruthven.

'Good Heavens! I cannot remember any more,' cried the aide-de-camp.

'Then go off, and say and do all that before you come back again,' said Lady Cecilia.

'What amazing presence of mind you have!' said Helen. 'How can you say so much, and think of everything?'

The aide-de-camp performed all her behests to admiration, and was rewarded by promotion to the high office of turner-over-general of the leaves of the music-books, an office requiring, as her ladyship remarked to Miss Holdernesse, prompt

eye and ear, and all his distinguished gallantry. By such compliments she fixed him to the pianoforte, while his curiosity and
all his feelings, being subordinate to his vanity, were prevented
from straying to Miss Stanley and her harp-stringing, a work still
doing – still to do.

All the arrangements succeeded as Lady Cecilia's arrangements usually did. Helen heard the eternal buzz of conversation
and the clang of instruments, and then the harmony of music, all
as in a dream, or as at the theatre, when the thoughts are absent
or the feelings preoccupied; and in this dreamy state she performed the operation of putting in the harp-strings quite well:
and when she was at last called upon by Cecilia, who gave her
due notice and time, she sat and played automatically, without
soul or spirit – but so do so many others. It passed 'charmingly,'
till a door softly opened behind her, and she saw the shadow
on the wall, and some one stood, and passed from behind her.
There was an end of her playing; however, from her just dread
of making a scene, she commanded herself so powerfully, that,
except her timidity, nothing was observed by the company, and
that timidity was pitied by the good-natured Mrs Holdernesse,
who said to her daughter, 'Anne, we must not press Miss Stanley
any more; she, who is always so obliging, is tired now.' She then
made way for Helen to pass, who, thanking her with such a
look as might be given for a life saved, quitted the harp, and
the crowd, closing behind her, happily thought of her no more.
She retreated to the darkest part of the room, and sat down. She
did not dare to look towards what she most wished to see. Her
eyes were fixed upon the face of the young lady singing, and yet
she saw not one feature of that face, while she knew, without
looking, or seeming to look, exactly where Beauclerc stood. He
had stationed himself in a doorway into the drawing-room; there,
leaning back against the wall, he stood, and never stirred. Helen
was so anxious to get one clear view of the expression of his
countenance, that at last she ventured to move a little, and from
behind the broad back of a great man she looked: Beauclerc's
eyes met hers. How different from their expression when they

were sitting on the bank together but a few short hours before! He left the doorway instantly, and placed himself where Helen could see him no more.

Of all the rest of what passed this evening she knew nothing; she felt only a sort of astonishment at everybody's gaiety, and a sense of the time being intolerably long. She thought that all these people never would go away – that their carriages never would be announced. But before it came to that time, General Clarendon insisted upon Lady Cecilia's retiring. 'I must,' said he, 'play the tyrant, Cecilia; you have done too much to-day – Mrs Holdernesse shall hold your place.'

He carried Cecilia off, and Helen thought, or fancied, that he looked about for her. Glad to escape, she followed close behind. The General did not offer his arm or appear to notice her. When she came to the door leading to the staircase, there was Beauclerc, standing with folded arms, as in the music-room; he just bowed his head, and wished Lady Cecilia a good-night, and waited, without a word, for Helen to pass, or not to pass, as she thought fit. She saw by his look that he expected explanation; but till she knew what Cecilia meant to do, how could she explain? To say nothing – to bear to be suspected – was all she could do, without betraying her friend. That word *betray* – that thought ruled her. She passed him: 'Good-night' she could not then say. He bowed as she passed, and she heard no 'Good-night' – no sound. And there was the General in the hall to be passed also, before she could reach the staircase up which Cecilia was going. When he saw Helen, with a look of surprise – as it seemed to her, of disapproving surprise – he said, 'Are you gone, Miss Stanley?' The look, the tone, struck cold to her heart. He continued – 'Though I drove Cecilia away, I did not mean to drive you away too. It is early.'

'Is it? I thought it was very late.'

'No – and if you *can*, I hope you will return.' There was a meaning in his eye, which she well understood.

'Thank you,' said she; 'if I can certainly – '

'I hope you can and will.'

'Oh! thank you; but I must first – ' see Cecilia, she was going to say, but, afraid of implicating her, she changed the sentence to – 'I must first consider – '

'Consider! what the devil!' thought he, and his countenance was instantly angrily suited to the thought. Helen hesitated. 'Do not let me detain – distress you farther, Miss Stanley, unavailingly; and since I shall not have the pleasure of seeing you again this evening,' concluded he, in a constrained voice, 'I have the honour to wish you a good-night.' He returned to the music-room.

CHAPTER 34

HELEN INSTANTLY WENT to Cecilia's room; Felicie was with her. Helen expected Lady Cecilia would dismiss her instantly; but mademoiselle was chattering. Helen had sometimes thought Cecilia let her talk too much, but tonight it was insufferable. Helen was too impatient, too anxious, to bear it. 'Cecilia, my dear, I want to speak to you alone, as soon as you can, in my own room.'

'As soon as possible,' Cecilia answered in a voice not natural. And she came, but not as soon as possible – shut the door behind her, showing that she had not dismissed Felicie, and, with hair dishevelled, as if hastening back to her room, said, 'I am in a hurry; the General ordered me to make haste, and not to be an hour undressing.'

'I will not keep you a moment,' said Helen. 'I am in as great a hurry as you can be. Beauclerc is waiting for me.'

'Waiting for you at this time of night! Oh, my dear, he cannot be standing there with his arms folded all this time.'

Helen repeated what the General had said, and ended with 'I am determined to return.'

'No, no,' Lady Cecilia said. The General could not advise her going back at this time of night. And with rapidity and confusion, she poured out a multitude of dissuasive arguments, some contradicting the others. 'At this time of night! The world is not gone, and Beauclerc is in the midst of them by this time, you may be sure. You don't think he is standing alone there all this time. You could not speak to him before all the world – don't attempt it. You would only expose yourself. You would make a scene at last – undo all, and come to disgrace, and ruin me and yourself. I know you would. Helen. And if you were to send for him – into the library –alone! the servants would know it – and the company gone! And after all, for you, my dear, to make the first advance to reconciliation! If he is angry – I don't think that would be quite – dignified; quite like you, Helen.'

'The General thinks it right, and I am sure he not would advise anything improper – undignified. It does not signify, Cecilia, I am determined – I will go.' Trembling, she grew absolutely desperate from fear. 'I am afraid you have forgotten your promise, Cecilia; you said that if I could bear it for one hour, it would be over. Did you not promise me that if any difficulty came between me and – ' She stopped short. She had felt indignant; but when she looked at Cecilia, and saw her tears, she could not go on.

'O Helen!' cried Cecilia, 'I do not ask you to pity me. You cannot know what I suffer – you are innocent – and I have done so wrong! You cannot pity me.'

'I do, I do,' cried Helen, 'from the bottom of my heart. Only trust me, dear Cecilia; let me go down – '

Lady Cecilia sprang between her and the door. 'Hear me! hear me, Helen! Do not go tonight, and, cost what it will – cost me what it may, since it has come to this between you, I will confess all this night – I will tell all to the General, and clear you with him and with Granville. What more can you ask? – what more can I do, Helen? And will you go?'

'No, no, my dear Cecilia. Since you promise me this, I will not go now.'

'Be satisfied then, and rest – for me there is no rest'; so saying Cecilia slowly left the room.

Helen could not sleep: this was the second wretched night she had passed in that most miserable of all uncertainty – whether she was right or wrong.

In the morning, to Helen's astonishment, Cecilia's first words were about a dream – 'Oh, my dear Helen, I have had such a dream! I do not usually mind dreams in the least, but I must own to you that this has made an impression! My dear, I can hardly tell it; I can scarcely bear to think of it. I thought that Clarendon and I were sitting together, and my hand was on his shoulder; and I had worked myself up – I was just going to speak. He was winding up his watch, and I leaned forward to see his face better. He looked up – and it was not him: it was Colonel D'Aubigny come to life. The door opened, Clarendon appeared – his eyes were upon me; but I do not know what came afterwards; all was confusion and fighting. And then I was with that nurse my mother recommended, and an infant in her arms. I was going to take the child, when Clarendon snatched it, and threw it into the flames. Oh! I awoke with a scream!'

'How glad you must have been,' said Helen, 'to awake and find it was only a dream!'

'But when I screamed,' continued Cecilia, 'Clarendon started up, and asked if I was in pain. "Not of body," I said; – and then – oh, Helen! then I thought I would begin. "Not of body," I said, "but of mind"; then I added, "I was thinking of Helen and Beauclerc." Clarendon said, "So was I; but there is no use in thinking of it; we can do no good." "Then," I said, "suppose, Clarendon – only suppose that Helen, without saying anything, were to let this matter pass off with Beauclerc?" Clarendon answered, "It would not pass off with Beauclerc.""But," said I, "I do not mean without any explanation at all. Only suppose that Helen did not enter into any particulars, do not you think, Clarendon, that things would go on well enough." "No," he said decidedly, "no." "Do you mean," said I, "that things would not go on at all?" "I do not say, not at all," he answered; "but *well* they would not go on." '

'I am sure the General is right,' said Helen.

'Then,' continued Lady Cecilia, 'then I put the question differently. I wanted to feel my way, to try whether I could possibly venture upon my own confession. "Consider it this way, Clarendon," I said. "Take it for granted that Helen did somehow arrange that Beauclerc were to be satisfied without any formal explanation." "Formal!" said he, – "I will not say formal," said I; "but without a *full* explanation: in short, suppose that from mere timidity, Helen could not, did not, exactly tell him the whole before marriage – put it off till afterwards – then told him all candidly; do you think, Clarendon, that if you were in Beauclerc's place (I quite stammered when I came to this) – do you think you could pardon, or forgive, or esteem, or love," I intended to end with, but he interrupted me with – "I do not know," very shortly; and added, "I hope this is not what Miss Stanley intends to do?"

'Oh! what did you answer?' cried Helen.

'I said I did not know. My dear Helen, it was the only thing I could say. What would Clarendon have thought, after all my *supposes*, if I had said anything else? he must have seen the truth.'

'And that he is not to see,' said Helen: 'and how false he must think me!'

'No, no; for I told him,' continued Lady Cecilia, 'that I was sure you wished always to tell the whole truth about everything, but that there might be circumstances where you really could not; and where – I, knowing all the circumstances, could not advise it. He said, "Cecilia, I desire you will not advise or interfere any farther in this matter. Promise me, Cecilia!" He spoke sternly, and I promised as fast as I could. "Do nothing, say nothing, more about it," he repeated; and now, after that, could I go on, Helen?'

'No, indeed; I do not think you could. My dear Cecilia, I really think you could not,' said Helen, much moved.

'And do you forgive me, my. dear, good – ' But seeing Helen change colour, Lady Cecilia, following her eye, and looking out of the window, started up, exclaiming, 'There is Beauclerc; I see him in my mother's walk. I will go to him this minute; yes, I will trust him – I will tell him all instantly.'

Helen caught hold of her, and stopped her. Surprised, Cecilia said, 'Do not stop me. I may never have the courage again if stopped now. Do not stop me, Helen.'

'I must, Cecilia. General Clarendon desired you not to interfere in this matter.'

'But this is not interfering, only interposing to prevent mischief.'

'But, Cecilia,' continued Helen eagerly, 'another reason has just struck me.'

'I wish reasons would not strike you. Let me go. Oh, Helen; it is for you.'

'And it is for you I speak, Cecilia,' said Helen, as fast as she could. 'If you told Beauclerc, you never could afterwards tell the General; it would be a new difficulty. You know the General could never endure your having confessed this to any man but himself – trusted Beauclerc rather than your husband.'

Cecilia stopped, and stood silent.

'My dear Cecilia,' continued Helen, 'you must leave me to my own judgment now'; and, breaking from Cecilia, she left the room. She hurried out to meet Beauclerc. He stopped on seeing her, and then came forward with an air of evident deliberation.

'Do you wish to speak to me, Miss Stanley?'

'Miss Stanley!' cried Helen; 'is it come to this, and without hearing me?'

'Without hearing you, Helen? Was not I ready last night to hear you? Without hearing you! Have not you kept me in torture, the worst of tortures – suspense? Why did not you speak to me last night?'

'I could not.'

'Why, why?'

'I cannot tell you,' said she.

'Then I can tell you, Helen.'

'You can!'

'And will. Helen, you could not speak to me till you had con- sulted – arranged – settled what was to be said – what not to be said – what told – what left untold.'

Between each half-sentence he darted looks at her, defying hers to contradict – and she could not contradict by word or look. 'You could not speak,' continued he passionately, 'till you had well determined what was to be told, what left untold, to me! To me, Helen, your confiding – devoted – accepted lover! for I protest before Heaven, had I knelt at the altar with you, Helen Stanley, not more yours, not more mine could I have deemed

you – not more secure of your love and truth – your truth, for
what is love without it? – not more secure of perfect felicity
could I have been on earth than I was when we two sat together
but yesterday evening on that bank. Your words – your looks –
and still your looks – But what signify tears? – Tears, women's
tears! – Oh! what is woman? – and what is man that believes in
her? – weaker still!'

'Hear me! – hear me!'

'Hear you? No, Helen, do not now ask me to hear you. Do
not force me to hear you. Do not debase, do not sully, that perfect
image of truth. Do not sink yourself, Helen, from that height
at which it was my entranced felicity to see you. Leave me one
blessed, one sacred illusion. No,' cried he, with increasing vehe-
mence, 'say nothing of all you have prepared – not one arranged
word conned over in your midnight and your morning consulta-
tions,' pointing back to the window of her dressing-room, where
he had seen her and Lady Cecilia.

'You saw,' Helen began –

'Yes. Am I blind, think you? I wish I were. Oh that I could be
again the believing, fond, happy dupe I was but yesterday evening!'

'Dupe!' repeated Helen. 'But pour out all – all, dear Granville.
Think – say – what you will – reproach – abuse me as you please
– It is a relief – take it – for I have none to give.'

'None!' cried he, his tone suddenly changing, 'no relief to
give! What! have you nothing to say? No explanation? Why speak
to me then at all?'

'To tell you so at once – to end your suspense – to tell you that
I cannot explain. The midnight consultation and the morning,
were not to prepare for you excuse or apology, but to decide
whether I could tell you the whole; and since that cannot be, I
determined not to enter into any explanation. I am glad that you
do not wish to hear any.'

'Answer me one question,' said he: – 'that picture – did you
give it to Colonel D'Aubigny?'

'No. That is a question I can answer. No – he stole it from
Cecilia's portfolio. Ask me no more.'

'One question more – '

'No, not one more – I cannot tell you anything more.'

She was silent for a moment, he withdrew his eyes, and she went on.

'Granville! I must now put your love and esteem for me to the test. If that love be what I believe it to be, if your confidence in me is what I think it ought to be, I am now going to try it. There is a mystery which I cannot explain. I tell you this, and yet I expect you to believe that I am innocent of anything wrong but the concealment. There are circumstances which I cannot tell you.'

'But why?' interrupted Beauclerc. 'Ought there to be any circumstances which cannot be told to the man to whom you have plighted your faith? Away with this "cannot – this mystery"! Did I not tell you every folly of my life – every fault? And what is this? – in itself, nothing! – concealment everything – Oh, Helen – '

She was going to say, 'If it concerned only myself,' – but that would at once betray Cecilia, and she went on, – 'If it were in my opinion right to tell it to you, I would. On this point, Granville, leave me to judge and act for myself. This is the test to which I put your love – put mine to any test you will; but if your confidence in me is not sufficient to endure this trial, we can never be happy together.' She spoke very low: but Beauclerc listened with such intensity that he could not only distinguish every syllable she said, but could distinctly hear the beating of her heart, which throbbed violently, in spite of all her efforts to be calm. 'Can you trust me?' concluded she.

'I can,' cried he. 'I can! – I do! By Heaven I do! I think you an angel, and legions of devils could not convince me of the contrary. I trust your word – I trust that heavenly countenance – I trust entirely – ' He offered, and she took his offered hand. 'I trust entirely. Not one question more shall I ask – not a suspicion shall I have: you put me to the test, you shall find me stand it.'

'Can you?' said she; 'you know how much I ask. I acknowledge a mystery, and yet I ask you to believe that I am not wrong.'

'I know,' said he; 'you shall see.' And, both in happiness once more, they returned to the house.

'I love her a thousand times better than ever,' thought Beauclerc, 'for the independence of mind she shows in thus braving my opinion, daring to set all upon the cast – something noble in this! I am to form my own judgment of her, and I will, independently of what any other human being may say or think. The General, with his strict, narrow, conventional notions, has not an idea of the kind of woman I like, or of what Helen really is. He sees in Helen only the discreet proper-behaved young lady, adapted, so nicely adapted, to her place in society, to nitch and notch in, and to be of no sort of value out of it. Give me a being able to stand alone, to think and feel, decide and act for herself. Were Helen only what the General thinks her, she would not be for me; while she is what I think her, I love – I adore!' And when he saw his guardian, Beauclerc declared that, though Helen had entered into no explanations, he was perfectly satisfied.

The General answered, 'I am glad you *are* satisfied.'

Beauclerc perceived that the General was not; and in spite of all that he had just been saying to himself, this provoked and disgusted him. His theory of his own mind, if not quite false, was still a little at variance with his practice. His guardian's opinion swayed him powerfully, whenever he believed that it was not designed to influence him; when the opinion was repressed, he could not rest without drawing it out. 'Then, you think, General,' said he, 'that some explanation ought to have been made?'

'No matter what I think, Granville, the affair is yours. If you are satisfied, that is all that is necessary.'

Then even, because left on their own point of suspension to vibrate freely, the diamond-scales of Beauclerc's mind began to move, from some nice, unseen cause of variation. 'But,' said he, 'General Clarendon, no one can judge without knowing facts.'

'So I apprehend,' said the General.

'I may be of too easy faith,' replied Beauclerc. [No reply.] 'This is a point of honour.' [No denial.] 'My dear General, if there be anything which weighs with you, and which you know and I do not, I think, as my friend and guardian, you ought to tell it to me.'

'Pardon me,' said the General, turning away from Beauclerc as he spoke, and striking first one heel of his boot against the scraper at the hall-door, then the other – ' pardon me, Granville, I cannot admit you to be a better judge than I am myself of what I ought to do or not to do.'

The tone was dry and proud, but Beauclerc's provoked imagination conceived it to be also mysterious; the scales of his mind vibrated again, but he had said he would trust – trust entirely, and he would: yet he could not succeed in banishing all doubt, till an idea started into his head – 'That writing was Lady Cecilia's! I thought so at the first moment, and I let it go again. It is hers, and Helen is keeping her secret: – but how could Lady Cecilia be so ungenerous – so treacherous?' However, he had declared he would ask no questions; he was a man of honour, and he would ask none – none even of himself – a resolution which he found it surprisingly easy to keep when the doubt concerned only Lady Cecilia. Whenever the thought crossed his mind, he said to himself, 'I will ask nothing – suspect nobody; but if it is Lady Cecilia's affair, it is all the more generous in Helen.' And so, secure in this explanation, though he never allowed to himself that he admitted it, his trust in Helen was easy and complete, and his passion for her increased every hour.

But Lady Cecilia was disturbed even by the perfect confidence and happiness of Beauclerc's manner towards Helen. She could not but fear that he had guessed the truth; and it seemed as if everything which happened tended to confirm him in his suspicions; for, whenever the mind is strongly interested on any subject, something alluding to it seems wonderfully, yet accidentally, to occur in everything that we read, or hear in common conversation; and so it now happened: things were continually said by persons wholly unconcerned, which seemed to bear upon her secret. Lady Cecilia frequently felt this with pangs of confusion, shame, and remorse; and, though Beauclerc did not watch, or play the spy upon her countenance, he could not help sometimes observing the flitting colour – the guilty changes of countenance – the assumed composure: that mind, once so artless,

began to be degraded – her spirits sank; she felt that she 'had lost
the sunshine of a soul without a mystery.'

The day fixed for the marriage approached; Lady Cecilia had
undertaken the superintendence of the *trousseau*, and Felicie was
in anxious expectation of its arrival. Helen had written to the
Collingwoods to announce the intended event, asking for the
good bishop's sanction, as her guardian, and regretting that he
could not perform the ceremony. She had received from Lady
Davenant a few lines, written just before she sailed, warm with
all the enthusiasm of her ardent heart, and full of expectation
that Helen's lot would be one of the happiest this world could
afford. All seemed indeed to smile upon her prospects, and the
only clouds which dimmed the sunshine were Cecilia's insincerity, and her feeling that the General thought her acting unhand-
somely and unwisely towards his ward; but she consoled herself
with the thought that he could not judge of what he did not
know, that she did not deserve his displeasure, that Granville
was satisfied, and if he was, why should not General Clarendon
be so too? Much more serious, however, was the pain she felt
on Cecilia's account. She reproached herself with betraying the
trust Lady Davenant had reposed in her. That dreadful prophecy
seemed now accomplishing: Cecilia's natural generosity, that for
which Helen had ever most loved and admired her, the brightest,
fairest parts of her character, seemed failing now; what could be
more selfish than Cecilia's present conduct towards herself, more
treacherous to her noble-minded, her confiding husband? The
openness, the perfect unreserve, between the two friends, was
no longer what it had been. Helen, however, felt the constraint
between them the less as she was almost constantly with Beauclerc, and in her young happiness she hoped all would be right.
Cecilia would tell the General, and they would be as intimate, as
affectionate, as they had ever been.

One morning General Clarendon, stopping Cecilia as she was
coming down to breakfast, announced that he was obliged to set
off instantly for London, on business which could not be delayed,
and that she must settle with Miss Stanley whether they would

accompany him or remain at Clarendon Park. He did not know, he said, how long he might be detained.

Cecilia was astonished, and excessively curious; she tried her utmost address to discover what was the nature of his business, in vain. All that remained was to do as he required without more words. He left the room, and Cecilia decided at once that they had better accompany him. She dreaded some delay; she thought that, if the General went alone to town, he might be detained Heaven knows how long; and though the marriage must be postponed at all events, yet if they went with the General, the ceremony might be performed in town as well as at Clarendon Park; and she with some difficulty convinced Helen of this. Beauclerc feared nothing but delay. They were to go. Lady Cecilia announced their decision to the General, who immediately set off, and the others in a few hours followed him.

CHAPTER 35

'In my youth, and through the prime of manhood, I never entered London without feelings of hope and pleasure. It was to me the great theatre of intellectual activity, the field for every species of enterprise and exertion, the metropolis of the world, of business, thought, and action. There, I was sure to find friends and companions, to hear the voice of encouragement and praise. There, society of the most refined sort offered daily its banquets to the mind, and new objects of interest and ambition were constantly exciting attention either in politics, literature, or science.'

THESE FEELINGS, SO WELL described by a man of genius, have probably been felt more or less by most young men who have within them any consciousness of talent, or any of that enthusiasm, that eager desire to have or to give sympathy, which, especially in youth, characterises noble natures. But after even one or two seasons in a great metropolis these feelings often change long before they are altered by age. Granville Beauclerc had already persuaded himself that he now detested, as much as he had at first been delighted with, a London life. From his metaphysical habits of mind, and from the sensibility of his temper, he had been too soon disgusted by that sort of general politeness, which, as he said, takes up the time and place of real friendship; and as for the intellectual pleasures, they were, he said, too superficial for him; and his notions of independence, too, were at this time quite incompatible with the conventional life of a great capital. His present wish was to live all the year round in the country, with the woman he loved, and in the society of a few chosen friends. Helen quite agreed with him in his taste for the country; she had scarcely ever known any other life, and yet had always been happy; and whatever youthful curiosity had been awakened in her mind as to the pleasures of London had been now absorbed by stronger and more tender feelings. Her fate in life, she felt, was fixed, and wherever the man she loved wished to reside, that, she felt, must be her choice. With these feelings they arrived at General Clarendon's delightful house in town.

Helen's apartment, and Cecilia's, were on different floors, and had no communication with each other. It was of little consequence, as their stay in town was to be but short, yet Helen could not help observing that Cecilia did not express any regret at it, as formerly she would have done; it seemed a symptom of declining affection, of which even the slightest indication was marked and keenly felt by Helen, the more so because she had anticipated that such must be the consequence of all that had passed between them, and there was now no remedy.

Among the first morning visitors admitted were Lady Castlefort and Lady Katrine Hawksby. They did not, as it struck Cecilia, seem surprised to see that Miss Stanley was Miss Stanley still, though the day for the marriage had been announced in all the papers as fixed; but they did seem now full of curiosity to know how it had come to pass, and there was rather too apparent a hope that something was going wrong. Their first inquisitive look was met by Lady Cecilia's careless glance in reply, which said better than words could express, 'Nothing the matter, do not flatter yourself.' Then her expertness at general answers which give no information completely baffled the two curious impertinents. They could only learn that the day for the marriage was not fixed, that it could not be definitively named till some business should be settled by the General. Law business they supposed, of course. Lady Cecilia 'knew nothing about it. Lawyers are such provoking wretches, with their fast bind fast find. Such an unconscionable length of time as they do take for their parchment doings, heeding nought of that little impatient flapper Cupid.'

Certain that Lady Cecilia was only playing with their curiosity, yet unable to circumvent her, Lady Katrine changed the conversation, and Lady Castlefort preferred a prayer, which was, she said, the chief object of her visit, that Lady Cecilia and Miss Stanley would come to her on Monday; she was to have a few friends – a very small party, and independently of the pleasure she should have in seeing them, it would be advantageous, perhaps to Miss Stanley, as Lady Castlefort, in her softest voice, added, 'For from the marriage being postponed even for a few days, people might talk, and Mr Beauclerc and Miss Stanley appearing together would prevent anybody's thinking there was any little – Nothing so proper now as for a young lady to appear with her *futur*; so I shall expect you, my dear Cecilia, and Miss Stanley,' – and so saying, she departed. Helen's objections were all overruled, and when the engagement was made known to Beauclerc, he shrugged and shrank, and submitted; observing, 'that all men, and all women, must, from the moment they come within the precincts of London life, give up their time and their will to an imaginary necessity of going when we do not like it, where we do not wish, to see those whom we have no desire to see, and who do not care if they were never to see us again, except for the sake of their own reputation of playing well their own parts in the grand farce of mock civility.' Helen was sorry to have joined in making an engagement for him which he seemed so much to dislike. But Lady Cecilia, laughing, maintained that half his reluctance was affectation, and the other half a lover-like spirit of monopoly, in which he should not be indulged, and instead of pretending to be indifferent to what the world might think, he ought to be proud to show Helen as a proof of his taste.

In dressing Helen this night, Felicie, excited by her lady's exhortations, displayed her utmost skill. Mademoiselle Felicie had a certain *petite métaphysique de toilette*, of which she was justly vain. She could talk, and as much to the purpose as most people, of *le genre classique*, and *le genre romantique*, of the different styles of dress

that suit different styles of face; and while 'she worked and wondered at the work she made,' she threw out from time to time her
ideas on the subject to form the taste of Helen's little maid, Rose,
who, in mute attention, held the light and assiduously presented
pins. 'Not your pin so fast one after de other, Miss Rose – Tenez!
tenez!' cried mademoiselle. 'You fink in England always too much
of your pin in your dress, too little of our taste – too little of our
elegance, too much of your what you call *tidiness*, or God knows
what! But never you mind dat so much, Miss Rose; and you not
prim up your little mouth, but listen to me. Never you put in
one pin before you ask yourself, Miss Rose, what for I do it? In
every toilette that has taste there is above all – tenez – a character
– a sentiment to be support; suppose your lady is to be superbe,
or she will rather be elegante, or charmante, or intéressante, or
distinguée – well, dat is all ver' well, and you dress to that idée,
one or oder – but none of your wat you call *odd*. No, no, never,
Miss Rose – dat is not style noble; 'twill only become de petit
minois of your English originale. I wash my hand of dat always.'
The toilette superbe mademoiselle held to be the easiest of all
those which she had named with favour, it may, be accomplished
by any common hands; but *head* is requisite to reach the toilette
distinguée. The toilette superbe requires only cost – a toilette distinguée demands care. There was a happiness as well as care in
Felicie's genius for dress, which, ever keeping the height of fashion
in view, never lost sight of nature, adapting, selecting, combining
to form a perfect whole, in which art itself concealed appeared
only, as she expressed it, in the sublime of simplicity. In the midst
of all her talking, however, she went on with the essential business,
and as she finished, pronounced, '*Précepte commence, exemple achève.*'[1]

When they arrived at Lady Castlefort's, Lady Cecilia was surprised to find a line of carriages, and noise, and crowds of footmen.
How was this? She had understood that it was to be one of those
really small parties, those select reunions of some few of the high
and mighty families who chance to be in town before Christmas.

[1] what precept starts, example completes

'But how is this?' Lady Cecilia repeated to herself as she entered the hall, amazed to find it blazing with light, a crowd on the stairs, and in the anteroom a crowd, as she soon felt, of an unusual sort. It was not the soft crush of aristocracy, they found hard unaccustomed citizen elbows, – strange round-shouldered, square-backed men and women, so over-dressed, so bejewelled, so coarse – shocking to see, impossible to avoid; not one figure, one face, Lady Cecilia had ever seen before; till at last, from the midst of the throng emerged a fair form – a being as it seemed of other mould, certainly of different caste. It was one of Cecilia's former intimates – Lady Emily Greville, whom she had not seen since her return from abroad. Joyfully they met, and stopped and talked; she was hastening away, Lady Emily said, 'after having been an hour on duty; Lady Castlefort had made it a point with her to stay after dinner, she had dined there, and had stayed, and now guard was relieved.'

'But who are all these people? What is all this, my dear Lady Emily?' asked Cecilia.

'Do not you know? Louisa has trapped you into coming then, to-night, without telling you how it is?'

'Not a word did she tell me, I expected to meet only our own world.'

'A very different world you perceive this! A sort of farce this is to the "Double Distress," a comedy; – in short, one of Lord Castlefort's brothers is going to stand for the City, and citizens and citoyennes must be propitiated. When an election is in the case all other things give place; and, besides, he has just married the daughter of some amazing merchant, worth I don't know how many plums; so *le petit Bossu*, who is proud of his brother, for he is reckoned the genius of the family, made it a point with Louisa to do this. She put up her eyebrows, and stood out as long as she could, but Lord Castlefort had his way, for he holds the purse you know, – and so she was forced to make a party for these Goths and Vandals, and of course she thought it best to do it directly, out of season, you know, when nobody will see it – and she consulted me whether it should be large or small; I advised a large party, by all means, as crowded as possible.'

'Yes, yes, I understand,' said Cecilia; 'to hide the shame in the multitude; vastly well, very fair all this, except the trapping us into it, who have nothing to do with it.'

'Nothing to do with it! pardon me,' cried Lady Emily. 'It could not have been done without us. Entrapping us! – do not you understand that we are the baits to the traps? Bringing those animals here, wild beasts or tame, only to meet one another, would have been "doing business nohow." We are what they are "come for to see," or to have it to say that they have seen the Exclusives, Exquisites, or Transcendentals, or whatever else they call us.'

'Lady Emily Greville's carriage!' was now called in the ante-room.

'I must go, but first make me known to your friend Miss Stanley, you see I know her by instinct'; but 'Lady Emily Greville's carriage!' now resounded reiteratedly, and gentlemen with cloaks stood waiting, and as she put hers on, Lady Emily stooped forward and whispered,

'I do not believe one word of what they say of her,' and she was off, and Lady Cecilia stood for an instant looking after her, and considering what she could mean by those last words. Concluding, however, that she had not heard aright, or had missed some intervening name, and that these words, in short, could not possibly apply to Helen, Lady Cecilia turned to her, they resumed their way onward, and at length they reached the grand reception-room.

In the middle of that brilliantly-lighted saloon, immediately under the centre chandelier, was ample verge and space enough reserved for the *élite* of the world; circle it was not, nor square, nor form regularly defined, yet the bounds were guarded. There was no way of getting to the farther end of the saloon, or to the apartments open in the distance beyond it, except by passing through this enclosed space, in which fair entrance was practicable, and one ample exit full in view on the opposite side. Several gentlemen of fashionable bearing held the outposts of this privileged place, at back of sofa, or side of fauteuil, stationary, or wandering near. Some chosen few were within; two caryatides gentlemen leaned one on each side of the fireplace, and in the centre of the rug stood a remarkably handsome man, of fine figure, perfectly dressed, his whole air exquisitely scornful, excruciatingly miserable, and loftily abstract. 'Twas wonderful, 'twas strange, 'twas passing strange! how one lost to all sublunary concerns, so far above the follies of inferior mortals, as he looked, came here – so extremely well dressed too! How happened it? so nauseating the whole, as he seemed, so wishing that the business of the world were done! With half-closed dreamy eyelids he looked silent down upon two ladies who sat opposite to him, rallying, abusing, and admiring him to his vanity's content. They gave him his choice of three names, *l'Ennuyé*, *le Frondeur*, or *le Blasé*. [1] L'Ennuyé? he shook his head; too common; he would have none of it. Le Frondeur? no; too much trouble; he shrugged his abhorrence. Le Blasé, he allowed, might be too true. But would they hazard a substantive verb? He would give them four-and-twenty hours to consider, and he would take twenty-four himself to decide. They should have his definitive to-morrow, and he was sliding away, but Lady Castlefort, as he passed her, cried, 'Going, Lord Beltravers, going are you?' in an accent of surprise and disappointment; and she whispered, 'I am hard at work here, and acting receiver-general to these City worthies; and you do not pity me – cruel!' and she looked up with languishing eyes, that so begged for sympathy. He threw upon her one look of commiseration, reproachful. 'Pity you, yes! But why will you do these things? and why did you bring me here to do this horrid sort of work?' and he vanished.

Lady Cecilia Clarendon and Miss Stanley now appeared in the *offing*, and now reached the straits; Lady Castlefort rose with vivacity extraordinary, and went forward several steps. 'Dear Cecilia! Miss Stanley, so good! Mr Beauclerc, so happy! the General could not? so sorry!' Then with hand pressed on hers, 'Miss Stanley, so kind of you to come. Lady Grace, give me leave – Miss Stanley – Lady Grace Bland,' and in a whisper, 'Lord Beltravers's aunt.'

[1] Bored, Troublesome or Blasé

Lady Grace, with a haughty drawback motion, and a supercili-
ous arching of her brows, was 'happy to have the honour.' Honour
nasally prolonged, and some guttural sounds followed, but further
words, if words they were, which she syllabled between snuffling
and mumbling, were utterly unintelligible; and Helen, without
being 'very happy,' or happy at all, only returned bend for bend.

Lady Cecilia then presented her to a group of sister graces
standing near the sofas of mammas and chaperons – not each a different grace, but similar each, indeed upon the very same identical
pattern air of young-lady fashion – well bred, and apparently well
nurtured. No sooner was Miss Stanley made known to them by
Lady Cecilia, than, smiling just enough, not a muscle too much,
they moved; the ranks opened softly, but sufficiently, and Helen
was in the group; amongst them, but not *of* them – and of this she
became immediately sensible, though without knowing how or
why. One of these daughters had had expectations last season from
having been frequently Mr Beauclerc's partner, and the mother
was now fanning herself opposite to him. But Helen knew nought
of this: to her all was apparently soft, smooth, and smiling.

While, whenever any of the unprivileged multitude, the City
monsters, passed near this highborn, high-bred group, they looked
as though the rights of pride were infringed, and, smiling scorn,
they dropped from half-closed lips such syllables of withering contempt as they thought these vulgar victims merited; careless if they
heard or not, rather rejoicing to see the sufferers wince beneath
the wounds which they inflicted in their pride and pomp of sway.
'Pride!' thought Helen, 'was it pride?' If pride it was, how unlike
what she had been taught to consider the proper pride of aristocracy; how unlike that noble sort which she had seen, admired, and
loved! Helen fancied what Lady Davenant would have thought,
how ignoble; how mean, how vulgar, would she have considered
these sneers and scoffs from the nobly to the lowly born. How
unworthy of their rank and station in society! They who ought to
be the first in courtesy, because the first in place.

As these thoughts passed rapidly in Helen's mind, she involuntarily looked towards Beauclerc; but she was so encompassed by her

present companions that she could not discover him. Had she been able to see his countenance, she would have read in it at once how exactly he was at that instant feeling with her. More indignant than herself, for his high chivalrous devotion to the fair could ill endure the readiness with which the gentlemen, attendants at ottoman or sofa, lent their aid to mock and to embarrass every passing party of the City tribe, mothers and their hapless daughter-train.

At this instant Lady Bearcroft, who, if she had not good breeding, certainly had good-nature, came up to Beauclerc, and whispered earnestly, and with an expression of strong interest in her countenance, 'As you love her, do not heed one word you hear anybody say this night, for it's all on purpose to vex you; and I am certain as you are it's all false – all envy. And there she goes, Envy herself in the black jaundice,' continued she, looking at Lady Katrine Hawksby, who passed at that instant.

'Good Heavens!' cried Beauclerc, 'what can – '

'No, no,' interrupted Lady Bearcroft, 'no, no, do not ask – better not; best you should know no more – only keep your temper whatever happens. Go you up the hill, like the man in the tale, and let the black stones bawl themselves hoarse – dumb. Go you on, and seize your pretty singing thinking bird – the sooner the better. So fare you well.'

And she disappeared in the crowd. Beauclerc, to whom she was perfectly unknown (though she had made him out), totally at a loss to imagine what interest she could take in Helen or in him, or what she could possibly mean, rather inclined to suppose she was a mad woman, and he forget everything else as he saw Helen with Lady Cecilia emerging from the bevy of young ladies and approaching him. They stopped to speak to some acquaintance, and he tried to look at Helen as if he were an indifferent spectator, and to fancy what he should think of her if he saw her now for the first time. He thought that he should be struck not only with her beauty, but with her graceful air – her ingenuous countenance, so expressive of the freshness of natural sensibility. She was exquisitely well dressed too, and that, as Felicie observed, goes for much, even with your most sensible men.

Altogether he was charmed, whether considering her as with the eyes of an unbiased stranger or with his own. And all he heard confirmed, and, although he would not have allowed it, strengthened his feelings. He heard it said that, though there were some as handsome women in the room, there were none so interesting; and some of the young men added, 'As lovely as Lady Blanche, but with more expression.' A citizen, with whom Beauclerc could have shaken hands on the spot, said, 'There's one of the highbreds, now, that's well-bred too.' In the height of the rapture of his feelings he overtook Lady Cecilia, who, telling him that they were going on to another room, delivered Helen to his care, and herself taking the arm of some ready gentleman, they proceeded as fast as they could through the crowd to the other end of the room.

This was the first time Helen had ever seen Lady Cecilia in public, where certainly she appeared to great advantage. Not thinking about herself, but ever willing to be pleased; so bright, so gay, she was sunshine which seemed to spread its beams wherever she turned. And she had something to say to everybody, or to answer quick to whatever they said or looked, happy always in the *à propos* of the moment. Little there might be, perhaps, in what she said, but there was all that was wanted, just what did for the occasion.

In others there often appeared a distress for something to say, or a dread dulness of countenance opposite to you. From others, a too fast hazarded broadside of questions and answers – glads and sorrys in chain-shots that did no execution, because there was no good aim – congratulations and condolences playing at cross purposes. These were mistakes, misfortunes, which could never occur in Lady Cecilia's natural grace and acquired tact of manner. Helen was amused, as she followed her, in watching the readiness with which she knew how to exchange the necessary counters in the commerce of society; she was amused, till her attention was distracted by hearing, as she and Beauclerc passed, the whispered words – '*I promessi sposi*[1] – look – *La belle fiancée.*'[2] These words were repeated as they went on, and Lady Cecilia heard some one say, 'I thought it was broken off; that was all slander, then?' She recollected Lady Emily's words, and, terrified lest Helen should hear more of – she knew not what, she began to talk to her as fast as she could, while they were stopped in the doorway by a crowd. She succeeded for the moment with Helen; she had not heard the last speech, and she could not, as long as Lady Cecilia spoke, hear more; but Beauclerc again distinguished the words '*Belle fiancée*'; and as he turned to discover the speaker, a fat matron near him asked, 'Who is it?' and the daughter answered, 'It is that handsome girl, with the white rose in her hair.' 'Hush!' said the brother, on whose arm she leaned; 'Handsome is that handsome does.'

Handsome does! thought Beauclerc: and the mysterious warning of his unknown friend recurred to him. He was astonished, alarmed, furious; but the whispering party had passed on, and just then Lady Cecilia descrying Mr Churchill in the distance, she made towards him. He discerned them from afar, and was happily prepared both with a ready bit of wit and with a proper greeting. His meeting with Lady Cecilia was, of course, just the same as ever. He took it up where he left off at Clarendon Park; no difference, no hiatus. His bow to Beauclerc and Helen, to Helen and Beauclerc, joined in one little sweep of a congratulatory motion, was incomparable; it said everything that a bow could say, and more. It implied such a happy freedom from envy or jealousy; such a polite acquiescence in the decrees of fate; such a philosophic indifference; such a cool sarcastic superiority to the event; and he began to Lady Cecilia with one of his prepared impromptus: 'At the instant your ladyship came up, I am afraid I started, actually in a trance, I do believe. Methought I was – where do you think? In the temple of Jaggernaut.'

'Why?' said Lady Cecilia, smiling.

'Methought,' continued Horace, 'that I was in the temple of Jaggernaut – that one strange day in the year, when all castes meet, when all distinction of castes and ranks is forgotten – the abomination of mixing them all together permitted, for their sins no doubt – high caste and low, from the abandoned Pariah to the Brahmin prince, from their Billingsgate and Farringdon Without, suppose, up to their St James's Street and Grosvenor Square, mingle, mingle, ye

¹the betrothed   ²beautiful fiancée

who mingle may, white spirits and gray, black spirits and blue. Now pray, look around: is not this Jaggernaut night with Lady Castlefort?'

'And you,' said Lady Cecilia; 'are not you the great Jaggernaut himself, driving over all in your triumphant chariot of sarcasm, and crushing all the victims in your way?'

This took place with Horace; it put in him spirits, in train, and he fired away at Lady Castlefort, whom he had been flattering only five minutes before.

'I so admire that acting of sacrifice in your *belle cousine* tonight! Pasta herself could not do it better. There is a look of "Oh, ye just gods! what a victim am I!" and with those upturned eyes so charming! Well, and seriously it is a sad sacrifice. Fathers have flinty hearts by parental prescription; but husbands – *petit Bossus* especially – should have mercy for their own sakes; they should not strain their marital power too far.'

'But,' said Lady Cecilia, 'it is curious that one born and bred such an ultra exclusive as Louisa Castlefort should be obliged after her marriage immediately to open her doors and turn ultra liberale, or an universal suffragist – all in consequence of these *mésalliances*. [2] 'True, true,' said Churchill, with a solemn, pathetic shake of the head. 'Gentlemen and noblemen should consider before they make these low matches to save their studs, or their souls, or their entailed estates. Whatever be the necessity, there can be no apology for outraging all propriety. Necessity has no law, but it should have some decency. Think of bringing upon a foolish elder brother – But we won't be personal.'

'No, don't, pray, Horace,' said Lady Cecilia, moving on.

'But think, only think, my dear Lady Cecilia; think what it must be to be "*How-d'ye-doed*," and to be "dear sistered" by such bodies as these in public.'

'Sad! sad!' said Lady Cecilia.

'The old French nobility,' continued Churchill, 'used to call these low money-matches *mettre du fumier sur nos terres*.'[1] 'Dirty work at best,' said Lady Cecilia.

[1] to put dung on our fields

'But still,' said Horace, 'it might be done with decency if not with majesty.'

'But in the midst of all this,' said Lady Cecilia, 'I want some ice very much for myself, and for Helen more.'

'I have a notion we shall find some here,' replied he, 'if you will come on this way – in this *sanctum sanctorum* [1] of Lady Katrine's.'

He led them on to a little inner apartment, where, as he said, Lady Katrine Hawksby and her set do always scandal take, and sometimes tea. 'Tea and *ponch*,' [2] continued he, 'you know, in London now is quite *à la Française*, and it is astonishing to me, who am but a man, what strong punch ladies can take.'

'Only when it is iced,' said Lady Cecilia, smiling.

'Be it so,' said he, – 'very refreshing ice, and more refreshing scandal, and here we have both in perfection. Scandal hot and hot, and ice cold and cold.'

By this time they had reached the entrance to what he called Lady Katrine's *sanctum sanctorum*, where she had gathered round the iced punch and tea-table a select party, whom she had drawn together with the promise of the other half of a half-published report, – a report in which '*I promessi sposi*' and '*La belle fiancée*' were implicated!

'Stop here one moment,' cried Churchill, 'one moment longer. Let us see before we are seen. Look in, look in, pray, at this group. Lady Katrine herself on the sofa, finger up – holding forth; and the deaf old woman stretching forward to hear, while the other, with the untasted punch, sits suspended in curiosity. "What can it be?" she says, or seems to say. Now, now, see the pretty one's hands and eyes uplifted, and the ugly one, with that look of horror, is exclaiming, "You don't say so, my dear Lady Katrine!" Admirable creatures! Cant and scandal personified! I wish Wilkie were here – worth any money to him.'

'And he should call it "The scandal party," ' said Lady Cecilia. 'He told me he never could venture upon a subject unless he could give it a good name.'

[1] holy of holies   [2] punch

At this moment Lady Katrine, having finished her story, rose, and awakening from the abstraction of malice, she looked up and saw Helen and Lady Cecilia, and, as she came forward, Churchill whispered between them, 'Now – now we are going comfortably to enjoy, no doubt, Madame de Sévigné's pleasure *de mal dire du prochain,*[1] at the right hour too.'

Churchill left them there. Lady Katrine welcoming her victims – her unsuspicious victims – he slid off to the friends round the tea-table to learn from 'Cant' what 'Scandal' had been telling. Beauclerc was gone to inquire for the carriage. The instant Helen appeared, all eyes were fixed upon her, and '*Belle fiancée*' was murmured round, and Cecilia heard – 'He's much to be pitied.'

At this moment Lord Castlefort went up to Helen; she had always been a favourite of his; he was grateful to her for her constant kindness to him, and, peevish though the little man might be, he had a good heart, and he showed it now by instantly taking Helen out of the midst of the starers, and begging her opinion upon a favourite picture of his, a Madonna. Was it a Raffaelle, or was it not? He, and Mr Churchill, he said, were at issue about it. In short, no matter what he said, it engrossed Helen's attention, so that she could not hear anything that passed, and could not be seen by the starers; and he detained her in conversation till Beauclerc came to say – 'The carriage is ready, Lady Cecilia is impatient.' Lord Castlefort opened a door that led at once to the staircase, so that they had not to recross all the rooms, but got out immediately. The smallest service merits thanks, and Helen thanked Lord Castlefort by a look which he appreciated.

Even in the few words which Beauclerc had said as he announced the carriage, she had perceived that he was agitated, and, as he attended her in silence down the stairs, his look was grave and preoccupied; she saw he was displeased, and she thought he was displeased with her. When he had put them into the carriage, he wished them good-night.

'Are not you coming with us?' cried Lady Cecilia.

[1] to speak ill of one's neighbours

'No, he thanked her, he had rather walk, and,' he added – 'I shall not see you at breakfast – I am engaged.'

'Home!' said Lady Cecilia, drawing up the glass with a jerk.

Helen looked out anxiously. Beauclerc had turned away, but she caught one more glance of his face as the lamp flared upon it – she saw, and she was sure that – 'Something is very much the matter – I am certain of it.'

'Nonsense, my dear Helen,' said Lady Cecilia; 'the matter is that he is tired to death, as I am sure I am.'

'There's more than that,' said Helen, 'he is angry,' – and she sighed.

'Now, Helen, do not torment yourself about nothing,' said Cecilia, who, not being sure whether Beauclerc had heard anything, had not looked at his countenance or remarked his tone; her mind was occupied with what had passed while Helen was looking at the Madonna. Lady Cecilia had tried to make out the meaning of these extraordinary starings and whisperings – Lady Katrine would not tell her anything distinctly, but said, 'Strange reports – so sorry it had got into the papers, those vile libellous papers; of course she did not believe – of Miss Stanley. After all, nothing very bad – a little awkward only – might be hushed up. Better not talk of it tonight; but I will try, Cecilia, in the morning, to find those paragraphs for you.' Lady Cecilia determined to go as early as possible in the morning, and make out the whole; and, had she plainly told this to Helen, it would have been better for all parties: but she continued to talk of the people they had seen, to hide her thoughts from Helen, who all the time felt as in a feverish dream, watching the lights of the carriage flit by like fiery eyes, while she thought only of the strange words she had heard and why they should have made Beauclerc angry with her.

At last they were home. As they went in, Lady Cecilia inquired if the General had come in. Yes, he had been at home for some time, and was in bed. This was a relief. Helen was glad not to see any one, or to be obliged to say anything more that night. Lady Cecilia bade her 'be a good child, and go to sleep.' How much Helen slept may be left to the judgment of those who have any imagination.

CHAPTER 36

'*MILADI A UNE MIGRANIE AFFREUSE*[1] this morning,' said Felicie, addressing herself on the stairs to Rose. '*Mille amitiés de sa part*[2] to your young lady, Miss Rose, and *miladi* recommend to her to follow a good example, and to take her breakfast in her bed, and then to take one good sleep till you shall hear *midi sonné*.'

Miss Stanley, however, was up and dressed at the time when this message was brought to her, and a few minutes afterwards a footman came to the door, to give notice that the General was in the breakfast-room, waiting to know whether Miss Stanley was coming down or not. The idea of a *tête-à-tête* breakfast with him was not now quite so agreeable as it would have been to her formerly, but she went down. The General was standing with his back to the fire, newspapers hanging from his hand, his look ominously grave. After 'Good-mornings' had been exchanged with awful solemnity, Helen ventured to hope that there was no bad public news.

'No public news whatever,' said the General.

Next, she was sorry to hear that Cecilia had 'such a bad head-ache.'

'Tired last night,' said the General.

'It was, indeed, a tiresome, disagreeable party,' said Helen, hoping this would lead to how so? or why? but the General drily answered, 'Not the London season,' and went on eating his breakfast in silence.

---

[1] Miladi has a terrible migraine   [2] she sends her best regards

Such a constraint and awe came upon her, that she felt it would be taking too great a liberty, in his present mood, to put sugar and cream into his tea, as she was wont in happier times. She set sugar-bowl and cream before him, and whether he understood, or noticed not her feelings, she could not guess. He sugared, and creamed, and drank, and thought, and spoke not. Helen put out of his way a supernumerary cup, to which he had already given a push, and she said, 'Mr Beauclerc does not breakfast with us.'

'So I suppose,' said the General, 'as he is not here.'

'He said he was engaged to breakfast.'

'With some of his friends, I suppose,' said the General.

There the dialogue came to a full stop, and breakfast, uncomfortably on her part, and with a preoccupied air on his, went on in absolute silence. At length the General signified to the servant who was in waiting, by a nod, and a look towards the door, that his further attendance was dispensed with. At another time Helen would have felt such a dismissal as a relief, for she disliked, and recollected that her uncle particularly disliked, the fashion of having servants waiting at a family breakfast, which he justly deemed unsuited to our good old English domestic habits; but somehow it happened that at this moment she was rather sorry when the servant left the room. He returned however in a moment, with something which he fancied to be yet wanting, the General, after glancing at whatever he had brought, said, 'That will do, Cockburn; we want nothing more.'

Cockburn placed a screen between him and the fire; the General put it aside, and, looking at him, said sternly – 'Cockburn, no intelligence must ever go from my house to any newspapers.'

Cockburn bowed – 'None shall, sir, if I can prevent it; none ever did from me, General.'

'None must ever go from any one in my family – look to it.'

Cockburn bowed again respectfully, but with a look of reservation of right of remonstrance, answered by a look from his master, of 'No more must be said.' Yet Cockburn was a favourite; he had lived in the family from the time he was a boy. He moved hastily towards the door, and having turned the handle, rested upon it and said, 'General, I cannot answer for others.'

'Then, Cockburn, I must find somebody who can.'

Cockburn disappeared, but after closing the door the veteran opened it again, stood, and said stoutly, though seemingly with some impediment in his throat – 'General Clarendon, do me the justice to give me full powers.'

'Whatever you require: say, such are your orders from me, and that you have full power to dismiss whoever disobeys.' Cockburn bowed, and withdrew satisfied.

Another silence, when the General, hastily finishing his break-fast, took up the newspaper, and said, 'I wished to have spared you the pain of seeing these, Miss Stanley, but it must be done now. There have appeared in certain papers paragraphs alluding to Beauclerc and to you; these scandalous papers I never allow to enter my house, but I was informed that there were such paragraphs, and I was obliged to examine into them. I am sorry to find that they have some of them been copied into my paper to-day.'

He laid the newspaper before her. The first words which struck her eye were the dreaded whispers of last night; the para-graph was as follows:

'In a few days will be published the Memoirs of the late Colonel D'—, comprising anecdotes, and original love-letters; which will explain the mysterious allusions lately made in certain papers to "*La belle fiancée*," and "*I promessi sposi*." '

'What!' exclaimed Helen; 'the letters! published!'

The General had turned from her as she read, and had gone to his writing-desk, which was at the farthest end of the room; he unlocked it, and took from it a small volume, and turning over the leaves as he slowly approached Helen, he folded down some pages, laid the volume on the table before her, and then said, 'Before you look into these scandalous memoirs, Miss Stanley, let me assure you that nothing but the necessity of being empowered by you to say what is truth and what is falsehood could deter-mine me to give you this shock.'

She was scarcely able to put forward her hand; yet took the book, opened it, looked at it, saw letters which she knew could not be Cecilia's, but turning another leaf, she pushed it from her with horror. It was the letter – beginning with 'My dear – too dear Henry.'

'In print!' cried she; 'in print! published!'

'Not published yet, that I hope to be able to prevent,' said the General.

Whether she heard, whether she could hear him, he was not certain, her head was bent down, her hands clasping her forehead. He waited some minutes, then sitting down beside her, with a voice of gentleness and of commiseration, yet of steady determination, he went on: – 'I *must* speak, and you *must* hear me, Helen, for your own sake, and for Beauclerc's sake.'

'Speak,' cried she, 'I hear.'

'Hear then the words of a friend, who will be true to you through life – through life and death, if you will be but true to yourself, Helen Stanley – a friend who loves you as he loves Beauclerc; but he must do more, he must esteem you as he esteems Beauclerc, incapable of anything that is false.'

Helen listened with her breath suspended, not a word in reply.

'Then I ask – '

She put her hand upon his arm, as if to stop him; she had a foreboding that he was going to ask something that she could not, without betraying Cecilia, answer.

'If you are not yet sufficiently collected, I will wait; take your own time – my question is simple – I ask you to tell me whether all these letters are yours or not?'

'No,' cried Helen, 'these letters are not mine.'

'Not all,' said the General: 'this first one I know to be yours, because I saw it in your handwriting; but I am certain all cannot be yours: now will you show me which are and which are not.'

'I will take them to my own room and consider and examine.'

'Why not look at them here, Miss Stanley?'

She wanted to see Cecilia, she knew she could never answer the question without consulting her, but that she could not say;

still she had no other resource, so, conquering her trembling, she rose and said, 'I would rather go to – '

'Not to Cecilia,' said he; 'to that I object: what can Cecilia do for you? what can she advise, but what I advise, that the plain truth should be told?'

'If I could! Oh if I could!' cried Helen.

'What can you mean? Pardon me, Miss Stanley, but surely you can tell the plain fact; you can recollect what you have written – at least you can know what you have not written. You have not yet even looked beyond a few of the letters – pray be composed – be yourself. This business it was that brought me to town. I was warned by that young lady, that poetess of Mr Churchill's, whom you made your friend by some kindness at Clarendon Park – I was warned that there was a book to come out, these Memoirs of Colonel D'Aubigny, which would contain letters said to be yours, a publication that would be highly injurious to you. I need not enter into details of the measures I consequently took; but I ascertained that Sir Thomas D'Aubigny, the elder brother of the colonel, knows nothing more of the matter than that he gave a manuscript of his brother's, which he had never read, to be published: the rest is a miserable intrigue between booksellers and literary manufacturers, I know not whom; I have not been able to get to the bottom of it; sufficient for my present purpose I know, and must tell you. You have enemies who evidently desire to destroy your reputation, of course to break your marriage. For this purpose the slanderous press has been set at work, the gossiping part of the public has had its vile curiosity excited, the publication of this book is expected in a few days: this is the only copy yet completed, I believe, and this I could not get from the bookseller till this morning; I am now going to have every other copy destroyed directly.'

'Oh my dear, dear friend, how can I thank you?' Her tears gushed forth.

'Thank me not by words, Helen, but by actions; no tears, summon your soul – be yourself.'

'Oh if I could but retrieve one false step!' – she suddenly checked herself.

He stood aghast for an instant, then recovering himself as he looked upon her and marked the nature of her emotion, he said, 'There can be no false step that you could ever have taken that cannot be retrieved. There can have been nothing that is irretrievable, except falsehood.'

'Falsehood! No,' cried she, 'I will not say what is false – therefore I will not say anything.'

'Then since you cannot speak,' continued the General, 'will you trust me with the letters themselves? Have you brought them to town with you?'

'The original letters?'

'Yes, those in the packet which I gave to you at Clarendon Park.'

'They are burned.'

'All? – one, this first letter, I saw you tear; did you burn all the rest?'

'They are burned,' repeated she, colouring all over. She could not say, 'I burned them.'

He thought it a poor evasion. 'They are burned,' continued he, 'that is, you burned them: unfortunate. I must then recur to my first appeal. Take this pencil, and mark, I pray you, the passages that are yours. I may be called on to prove the forgery of these passages: if you do not show me, and truly, which are yours, and which are not, how can I answer for you, Helen?'

'One hour,' said Helen, – 'only leave me for one hour, and it shall be done.'

'Why this cowardly delay?'

'I ask only one hour – only leave me for one hour.'

'I obey, Miss Stanley, since it must be so. I am gone.'

He went, and Helen felt how sunk she was in his opinion, – sunk for ever, she feared! but she could not think distinctly, her mind was stunned; she felt that she must wait for somebody, but did not at first recollect clearly that it was for Cecilia. She leaned back on the sofa, and sank into a sort of dreamy state. How long she remained thus unconscious she knew not; but she was roused at last by the sound, as she fancied, of a carriage stopping at the door: she started up, but it was gone, or it had not been. She perceived that the breakfast things had been removed, and, turning her eyes upon the clock, she was surprised to see how late it was. She snatched up the pages which she hated to touch, and ran upstairs to Cecilia's room, – door bolted; – she gave a hasty tap – no answer; another louder, no answer. She ran into the dressing-room for Felicie, who came with a face of mystery, and the smile triumphant of one who knows what is not to be known. But the smile vanished on seeing Miss Stanley's face.

'*Bon Dieu!* Miss Stanley – how pale! *mais qu'est ce que c'est? Mon Dieu, qu'est ce que c'est donc?*' [1]

'Is Lady Cecilia's door bolted withinside?' said Helen.

'No, only lock by me,' said Mademoiselle Felicie. 'Miladi charge me not to tell you she was not dere. And I had de presentiment you might go up to look for her in her room. Her head is got better quite. She is all up and dress; she is gone out in the carriage, and will soon be back no doubt. I know not to where she go, but in my opinion to my Lady Katrine. If you please, you not mention I say dat, as miladi charge me not to speak of dis to you. *Apparemment quelque petit mystère.*' [2]

Poor Helen felt as if her last hope was gone, and now in a contrary extreme from the dreamy torpor in which she had been before, she was seized with a nervous impatience for the arrival of Cecilia, though whether to hope or fear from it, she did not distinctly know. She went to the drawing-room, and listened and listened, and watched and watched, and looked at the clock, and felt a still-increasing dread that the General might return before Lady Cecilia, and that she should not have accomplished her promise. She became more and more impatient. As it grew later, the rolling of carriages increased, and their noise grew louder, and continually as they came near she expected that one would stop at the door. She expected and expected, and feared, and grew sick with fear long deferred. At last one carriage did stop, and then came a thundering knock – louder, she thought, than

[1] but what is it? My God, what is it?   [2] Apparently some little mystery

usual; but before she could decide whether it was Cecilia or not, the room-door opened, and the servant had scarcely time to say that two ladies who did not give their names had insisted upon being let up – when the two ladies entered. One in the extreme of foreign fashion, but an Englishwoman, of assured and not pre-possessing appearance; the other, half hid behind her companion, and all timidity, struck Helen as the most beautiful creature she had ever beheld.

'A thousand pardons for forcing your doors,' said the foremost lady; 'but I bear my apology in my hand: a precious little box of Roman cameos from a friend of Lady Cecilia Clarendon's, which I was desired to deliver myself.'

Helen was, of course, sorry that Lady Cecilia was not at home.

'I presume I have the honour of speaking to Miss Stanley,' continued the assured lady, and she gave her card, 'Comtesse de St Cymon.' Then half turning to the beauty, who now became visible – 'Allow me to *mention* – Lady Blanche Forrester.'

At that name Helen did not start, but she felt as if she had received an electric shock. How she went through the necessary forms of civility she knew not; but even in the agony of passion the little habits of life hold their sway. The customary motions were made, and words pronounced; yet when Helen looked at that beautiful Lady Blanche, and saw how beautiful! there came a spasm at her heart.

The comtesse, in answer to her look towards a chair, did not 'choose to sit down – could not stay – would not intrude on Miss Stanley.' So they stood, Helen supporting herself as best she could, and preserving, apparently, perfect composure, seeming to listen to what further Madame de St Cymon was saying; but only the sounds reached her ear, and a general notion that she spoke of the box in her hand. She gave Helen some message to Lady Cecilia, explanatory of her waiting or not waiting upon her ladyship, to all which Helen answered with proper signs of civility: and while the comtesse was going on, she longed to look again at Lady Blanche, but dared not. She saw a half-curtsey and a receding motion; and she knew they were going, and she curtsied mechanically. She felt inexpressible relief when Madame de St Cymon turned her back and moved towards the door. Then Helen looked again at Lady Blanche, and saw again her surpassing beauty and perfect tranquillity. The tranquillity gave her courage, it passed instantaneously into herself, through her whole existence. The comtesse stopped in her way out to look at a china table. 'Ha! beautiful! Sèvres – enamel – by Jaquetot, is it not?'

Helen was able to go forward, and answer to all the questions asked. Not one word from the Lady Blanche; but she wished to hear the sound of her voice. She tried – she spoke to her; but to whatever Helen said, no answer came, but the sweetest of smiles. The comtesse, with easy assurance and impertinent ill-breeding, looked at all that lay in her way, and took up and opened the miniature pictures that were on the table. 'Lady Cecilia Clarendon – charming! – Blanche, you never saw her yet. Quite charming, is it not?'

Not a word from Lady Blanche, but a smile, a Guido smile. Another miniature taken up by the curious comtesse. 'Ah! very like indeed! not flattered though. Do you know it, Blanche – eh?'

It was Beauclerc. Lady Blanche then murmured some few words indistinctly, in a very sweet voice, but showed no indication of feeling, except, as Helen gave one glance, she thought she saw a slight colour, like the inside of a shell, delicately beautiful; but it might be only the reflection from the crimson silk curtain near which she stood: it was gone, and the picture put down; and in a lively tone from the comtesse, '*Au revoir*,' and exit, a graceful bend from the silent beauty, and the vision vanished.

Helen stood for some moments fixed to the spot where they left her. She questioned her inmost thoughts. 'Why was I struck so much, so strangely, with that beauty – so painfully? It cannot be envy; I never was envious of any one, though so many I have seen so much handsomer than myself. Jealousy? surely not; for there is no reason for it – no possibility of danger. Yet now, alas! when he has so much cause to doubt me? perhaps he might change. He seemed so displeased last night, and he has never been here all the morning!' She recollected the look and accent of

Madame de St Cymon, as she said the words '*au revoir*.' Helen did
not like the words, or the look. She did not like anything about
Madame de St Cymon: 'Something so assured, so impertinent!
And all that unintelligible message about those cameos! – a mere
excuse for making this unreasonable pushing visit – just pushing
for the acquaintance. The General will never permit it, though –
that is one comfort. But why do I say comfort?' Back went the
circle of her thoughts to the same point. 'What can I do? – the
General will return, he will find I have not obeyed him. But what
can be done till Cecilia returns? If she were but here, I could
mark – we could settle. O Cecilia! where are you? But,' thought
she, 'I had better look at the whole. I will have courage to read
these horrible letters.' To prevent all hazard of further interrup-
tion, she now went into an inner room, bolted the doors, and sat
down to her dreaded task. And there we leave her.

CHAPTER 37

THAT FORTUNE IS NOT NICE in her morality, that she frequently favours those who do not adhere to truth more than those who do, we have early had occasion to observe. But whether Fortune may not be in this, as in all the rest, treacherous and capricious; whether she may not by her first smiles and favours lure her victims on to their cost, to their utter undoing at last, remains to be seen.

It is time to inquire what has become of Lady Cecilia Clarendon. Before we follow her on her very early morning visit to her cousin's, we must take leave to pause one moment to remark, not in the way of moralising by any means, but simply as a matter of history, that the first little fib in which Lady Cecilia, as a customary license of speech, indulged herself the moment she awoke this morning, though it seemed to answer its purpose exactly at the time, occasioned her ladyship a great deal of superfluous toil and trouble during the course of the day. In reply to the first question her husband had asked, or in evasion of that question, she had answered, 'My dear love, don't ask me any questions, for I have such a horrid headache that I really can hardly speak.'

Now a headache, such as she had at that moment, certainly never silenced any woman. Slighter could not be – scarce enough to swear by. There seemed no great temptation to prevarication either, for the General's question was not of a formidable nature, not what the lawyers call a leading question, rather one that led to nothing. It was only, 'Had you a pleasant party at Lady Castlefort's last night, my dear Cecilia?' But with that prescience with which some nicely foresee how the truth, seemingly most innocent, may do harm, her ladyship foreboded that, if she answered straight forward – 'no' – that might lead to – why? how? or wherefore? – and this might bring out the history of the strange rude manner in which '*la belle fiancée*' had been received. That need not necessarily have followed, but, even if it had, it would have done her no harm – rather would have served at once her purpose in the best manner possible, as time will show. Her husband, unsuspicious man, asked no more questions, and only gave her the very advice she wished him to give, that she should not get up to breakfast – that she should rest as long as she could. Further, as if to forward her schemes, even without knowing them, he left the house early, and her headache conveniently going off, she was dressed with all despatch – carriage at the door as soon as husband out of sight, and away she went, as we have seen, without Helen's hearing, seeing, or suspecting her so well contrived and executed project.

She was now in good spirits. The infection of fear, which she had caught perhaps from the too sensitive Helen last night, she had thrown off this morning. It was a sunny day, and the bright sunshine dispelled, as ever with her, any black notions of the night, all melancholy ideas whatsoever. She had all the constitutional hopefulness of good animal spirits. But though no fears remained, curiosity was as strong as ever. She was exceedingly eager to know what had been the cause of all these strange appearances. She guessed it must be some pitiful jealousy of Lady Katrine's – some poor spite against Helen. Anything that should really give Beauclerc uneasiness, she now sincerely believed to be out of the question. Nonsense – only Helen and Beauclerc's love of tormenting themselves – quite nonsense! And nonsense! three times ejaculated, quite settled the matter, and assured her in the belief that there could be nothing serious to be apprehended. In five minutes she should be at the bottom of all things, and in half an hour return triumphant to Helen, and make her laugh at her cowardly self. The carriage rolled on, Lady Cecilia's spirits rising as she moved rapidly onwards, so that by the time she arrived at Lady Castlefort's she was not only in good but in high spirits. To her askings,

'Not at home' never echoed. Even at hours undue, such as at the present, she, privileged, penetrated. Accordingly, unquestioned, unquestioning, the alert step was let down, opened wide was the hall-door, and lightly tripped she up the steps; but the first look into the hall told her that company was in the house already – yes – a breakfast – all were in the breakfast-room, except Lady Castlefort, not yet come down – above, the footman believed, in her boudoir. To the boudoir Cecilia went, but Lady Castlefort was not there, and Cecilia was surprised to hear the sound of music in the drawing-room, Lady Castlefort's voice singing. While she waited in the next room for the song to be finished, Cecilia turned over the books on the table, richly gilt and beautifully bound, except one in a brown paper parcel, which seemed unsuited to the table, yet excited more attention than all the others, because it was directed '*Private – for Lady Katherine Hawksby – to be returned before two o'clock.*' What could it be? thought Lady Cecilia. But her attention was now attracted by the song which Lady Castlefort seemed to be practising; the words were distinctly pronounced, uncommonly distinctly, so as to be plainly heard –

> Had we never loved so kindly,
> Had we never loved so blindly,
> Never met, or never parted,
> We had ne'er been broken-hearted.

As Cecilia listened, she cast her eyes upon a card which lay on the table – 'Lord Beltravers,' and a new light flashed upon her, a light favourable to her present purpose; for since the object was altered with Lady Castlefort, since it was not Beauclerc any longer, there would be no further ill-will towards Helen. Lady Castlefort was not of the violent vindictive sort, with her there was no long-lasting *dépit amoureux*.[1] She was not that fury, a woman scorned, but that blessed spirit, a woman believing herself always admired. 'Soft, silly, sooth – not one of the hard, wicked, is Louisa,' thought Cecilia. And as Lady Castlefort, slowly opening

---

[1] resentment of spurned love

the door, entered, timid, as if she knew some particular person was in the room, Cecilia could not help suspecting that Louisa had intended her song for other ears than those of her dear cousin, and that the superb negligence of her dress was not unstudied; but that well-prepared, well-according sentimental air, changed instantly on seeing – not the person expected, and with a start she exclaimed, 'Cecilia Clarendon!'

'Lousia Castleford' cried Lady Cecilia, answering that involuntary start of confusion with a well-acted start of admiration. 'Louisa Castlefort, *si belle, si belle*, so beautifully dressed!'

'Beautifully dressed – nothing extraordinary!' said Lady Castlefort, advancing with a half-embarrassed, half-*nonchalant* air, – 'One must make something of a *toilette de matin*, you know, when one has people to breakfast.'

'So elegent, so negligent!' continued Lady Cecilia.

'There is the point,' said Lady Castlefort. 'I cannot bear anything that is studied in costume, for dress is really a matter of so little consequence! I never bestow a thought upon it. Angelique rules my toilette as she pleases.'

'Angelique has the taste of an angel fresh from Paris,' cried Lady Cecilia.

'And now tell me, Cecilia,' pursued Lady Castlefort, quite in good humour, 'tell me, my dear, to what do I owe this pleasure? what makes you so *matinale*? It must be something very extraordinary.'

'Not at all, only a little matter of curiosity.'

Then, from Lady Castlefort, who had hitherto, as if in absence of mind, stood, there was a slight 'Won't you sit?' motion.

'No, no, I can't sit, can't stay,' said Lady Cecilia.

A look, quickly visible and quickly suppressed, showed Lady Castlefort's sense of relief; then came immediately greater pressing to sit down, 'Pray do not be in such a hurry.'

'But I am keeping you; have you breakfasted?'

'Taken coffee in my own room,' said Lady Castlefort.

'But you have people to breakfast; must not you go down?'

'No, no, I shall not go down, for this is Katrine's affair, as I will explain to you.'

Lady Cecilia was quite content, without any explanation; and sitting down, she drew her chair close to Lady Castlefort, and said, 'Now, my dear, my little matter of curiosity.'

Lady Cecilia ought to have been aware that when once her dear cousin Louisa's little heart opened, and she became confidential, very, it was always of her own domestic grievances she began to talk, and that, once, the sluice opened, out poured from the deep reservoir the long-collected minute drops of months and years.

'You have no idea what a life I lead with Katrine – now she is grown blue.'

'Is she?' said Lady Cecilia, quite indifferent.

'Deep blue! shocking: and this is a blue breakfast, and all the people at it are blue bores, and a blue bore is, as Horace Churchill says, one of the most mischievous creatures breathing; and he tells me the only way of hindering them from doing mischief is by *ringing* them; but first you must get rings. Now, in this case, for Katrine not a ring to be had for love or money. So there is no hope for me.'

'No hope for me,' thought Lady Cecilia, throwing herself back in her chair, submissive, but not resigned.

'If it had but pleased Heaven,' continued Lady Castlefort, 'in its mercy, to have sent Katrine a husband of any kind, what a blessing it would have been! If she could but have been married to anybody – now anybody – '

'Anybody is infinitely obliged to you,' said Cecilia, 'but since that is out of the question, let us say no more about it – no use.'

'No use! that is the very thing of which I complain; the very thing which must ever – ever make me miserable.'

'Well, well, my dear,' cried Lady Cecilia, no longer capable of patience; 'do not be miserable any more just now; never mind Katrine just now.'

'Never mind her! Easy for you to say, Cecilia, who do not live with Katrine Hawksby, and do not know what it is to have such a plague of a sister, watching one – watching every turn, every look one gives – worse than a jealous husband. Can I say more?'

'No,' cried Cecilia; 'therefore say no more about it. I understand it all perfectly; and I pity you from the bottom of my heart; so now, my dear Louisa – '

'I tell you, my dear Cecilia,' pursued Lady Castlefort, continuing her own thoughts, 'I tell you, Katrine is envious of me. Envy has been her fault from a child. Envy of poor me! Envy, in the first place, of whatever good looks it pleased Providence to give me.' A glance at the glass. 'And now Katrine envies me for being Lady Castlefort. Heaven knows! now, Cecilia, and you know, she need not envy me so when she looks at Lord Castlefort; that is what she sometimes says herself, which you know is very wrong of her to say to me – unnecessary too, when she knows I had no more hand in my marriage – '

'Than heart!' Cecilia could not forbear saying.

'Than heart!' readily responded Lady Castlefort; 'never was a truer word said. Never was there a more complete sacrifice than my mother made of me; you know, Cecilia, a poor, young, innocent, helpless sacrifice, if ever there was one upon earth.'

'To a coronet,' said Lady Cecilia.

'Absolutely dragged to the altar,' continued Lady Castlefort.

'In Mechlin lace, that was some comfort,' said Cecilia, laughing, and she laughed on in hope of cutting short this sad chapter of sacrifices. But Lady Castlefort did not understand raillery upon this too tender point. 'I don't know what you mean by Mechlin lace,' cried she pettishly. 'Is this your friendship for me, Cecilia?'

Cecilia, justly in fear of losing the reward of all her large lay-out of flattery, fell to protesting the tenderest sympathy. 'But only, now it was all over, why make her heart bleed about what could not be helped?'

'Cannot be helped! Oh! there is the very thing I must ever, ever mourn.'

The embroidered cambric handkerchief was taken out of the bag; no tears, indeed, came, but there were sobs, and Cecilia, not knowing how far it might go, apprehending that her ladyship meditated hysterics, seized a smelling-bottle, threw out the stopper, and presented it close under the nostrils. The good

English smelling salts of which Felicie always acknowledged the unrivalled potency, did their business effectually. Back went the head, with an exclamation of 'That's enough! Oh, oh! too much! too much, Cecilia!'

'Are you better, my dear?' inquired Cecilia; 'but indeed you must not give way to low spirits; indeed, you must not: so now to change the conversation, Louisa – '

'Not so fast, Lady Cecilia; not yet'; and now Louisa went on with a medical maundering. 'As to low spirits, my dear Cecilia, I must say I agree with Sir Sib Pennyfeather, who tells me it is not mere common low spirits, but really all mind, too much mind; mind preying upon my nerves. Oh! I knew it myself. At first he thought it was rather constitutional; poor dear Sir Sib! he is very clever, Sir Sib; and I convinced him he was wrong; and so we agreed that it was all upon my mind – all; all – '

At that instant a green parrot, who had been half asleep in the corner, awoke on Lady Castlefort's pronouncing, in an elevated tone, 'All, all!' and conceiving himself in some way called upon, answered, 'Poll! Poll! bit o' sugar Poll!' No small difficulty had Lady Cecilia at that moment in keeping her risible muscles in order; but she did, for Helen's sake, and she was rewarded, for after Lady Castlefort had, all unconscious of ridicule, fed Poll from her amber *bonbonnière*, and sighed out once more, 'Mind! too much mind!' she turned to Cecilia, and said, 'But, my dear, you wanted something; you had something to ask me.'

At once, and as fast as she could speak, Lady Cecilia poured out her business about Helen Stanley. She told of the ill-bred manner in which Helen had been received last night; inquired why the words *promessi sposi* and *belle fiancée* were so oddly repeated, as if they had been watchwords, and asked what was meant by all those strange whisperings in the *sanctum sanctorum*.

'Katrine's set,' observed Lady Castlefort coolly. 'Just like them; just like her!'

'I should not care about it in the least,' said Lady Cecilia, 'if it were only Katrine's ill-nature, or their ill-breeding. Ill-breeding always recoils on the ill-bred, and does nobody else any harm.

But I should be glad to be quite clear that there is nothing more at the bottom.'

Lady Castlefort made no reply, but took up a bunch of seals, and looked at them one after another. Lady Cecilia, more afraid now than she had yet been that there was something at the bottom, still bravely went on, 'What is it? If you know, tell me at once.'

'Nay, ask Katrine,' said Lady Castlefort.

'No, I ask you, I would rather ask you, for you are good-natured, Louisa – so tell me.'

'But I daresay it is only slander,' said the good-natured Louisa.

'Slander!' repeated Lady Cecilia, 'slander did you say?'

'Yes; what is there to surprise you so much in that word? did you never hear of such a thing? I am sure I hear too much of it; Katrine lives and breathes and fattens upon it; as Churchill says, she eats slander, drinks slander, sleeps upon slander.'

'But tell me, what of Helen? that is all I want to hear,' cried Lady Cecilia: 'Slander! of Helen Stanley! what is it that Katrine says about poor Helen? what spite, what vengeance, can she have against her? – tell me, tell me.'

'If you would ask one question at a time, I might be able to answer you,' said Lady Castlefort. 'Do not hurry me so; you fidget my nerves. First as to the spite, you know yourself that Katrine, from the beginning, never could endure Helen Stanley; for my part, I always rather liked her than otherwise, and shall defend her to the last.'

'Defend her!'

'But Katrine was always jealous of her, and lately worse than ever, for getting into her place, as she says, with you; that made her hate her all the more.'

'Let her hate on, that will never make me love Helen the less.'

'So I told her; and besides, Miss Stanley is going to be married.'

'To be sure; – well?'

'And Katrine naturally hates everybody that is going to be married. If you were to see the state she is in always reading the announcements of marriages in High Life! Churchill, I do believe, had Miss Stanley's intended match put into every paper continually, on purpose for the pleasure of plaguing Katrine; and if you could have seen her long face, when she saw it announced in the Court Gazette – good authority, you know – really it was pitiable.'

'I don't care, I don't care about that – Oh pray go on to the facts about Helen.'

'Well, but the fact is as I tell you; you wanted to know what sufficient cause for vengeance, and am I not telling you? If you would not get into such a state of excitement! – as Sir Sib says, excitements should be avoided. La! my dear,' continued Lady Castlefort, looking up at her with unfeigned astonishment, 'what agitation! why, if it were a matter that concerned yourself – '

'It concerns my friend, and that is the same thing.'

'So one says; but – you look really, such a colour.'

'No matter what colour I look,' cried Cecilia; 'go on.'

'Do you never read the papers?' said Lady Castlefort.

'Sometimes,' said Lady Cecilia; 'but I have not looked at a paper these three days; was there anything in particular? tell me.'

'My dear! tell you! as if I could remember by heart all the scandalous paragraphs I read.' She looked round the room, and not seeing the papers, said, 'I do not know what has become of those papers; but you can find them when you go home.'

She mentioned the names of two papers, noted for being personal, scandalous, and scurrilous.

'Are those the papers you mean?' cried Lady Cecilia; 'the General never lets them into the house.'

'That is a pity – that's hard upon you, for then you never are, as you see, *au courant du jour*, and all your friends might be abused to death without your knowing it, if some kind person did not tell you.'

'Do tell me, then, the substance; I don't want the words.'

'But the words are all. Somehow it is nothing without the words.'

In her now excited state of communicativeness, Lady Castlefort rose and looked all about the room for the papers, saying, 'They were here, they were there, all yesterday; Katrine had them showing them to Lady Masham in the morning, and to all her blue set afterwards – Lord knows what she has done with them. So tiresome looking for things! how I hate it.'

She rang the bell and inquired from the footman if he knew what had become of the papers. Of course he did not know, could not imagine — servants never know, nor can imagine, what has become of newspapers — but he would inquire. While he went to inquire, Lady Castlefort sank down again into her *bergère*, and again fell into admiration of Cecilia's state of impatience.

'How curious you are! Now I am never really curious about anything that does not come home to myself; I have so little interest about other people.'

This was said in all the simplicity of selfishness, not from candour, but from mere absence of shame, and utter ignorance of what others think, what others feel, which always characterises, and often betrays, the selfish, even where the head is best capable of supplying the deficiencies of the heart. But Louisa Castlefort had no head to hide her want of heart; while Cecilia, who had both head and heart, looked down upon her cousin with surprise, pity, and contempt, quick succeeding each other, in a sort of parenthesis of feeling, as she moved her eyes for a moment from the door on which they had been fixed, and to which they recurred, while she stood waiting for the appearance of those newspapers. The footman entered with them. 'In Mr Landrum's room they were, my lady.'

Lady Cecilia did not hear a word that was said, nor did she see that the servant laid a note on the table. It was well that Louisa had that note to read, and to answer, while Cecilia looked at the paragraphs in these papers; else her start must have been seen, her exclamation must have been heard: it must have been marked that the whole character of her emotion changed from generous sympathy with her friend to agony of fear for herself. The instant she cast her eyes on that much-read paper, she saw the name of Colonel D'Aubigny; all the rest swam before her eyes. Lady Castlefort, without looking up from her writing, asked — What day of the month? Cecilia could not answer, but, recalled to herself by the sound of the voice, she now tried to read — she scarcely read the words, but some way took the sense into her mind at a glance.

CHAPTER 38

THE FIRST OF THESE paragraphs caught the eye by its title in capital letters.

'LA BELLE FIANCÉE.

'Though quite unknown in the London world, this young lady cannot fail to excite some curiosity among our fashionables as the successful rival of one whom the greatest painter of the age has pronounced to be *the fairest of the fair* – the Lady B. F—. This new *Helen* is, we understand, of a respectable family, niece to a late dean, distinguished for piety much and *virtù* more. It was reported that the niece was a great heiress, but after the proposal had been made, it was discovered that *Virtù* had made away with every shilling of her fortune. This made no difference in the eyes of her inamorato, who is as rich as he is generous, and who saw with the eyes of a youth "Of Age to-morrow." His guardian, a wary general, demurred – but *nursery tactics* prevailed. The young lady, though she had never been out, bore the victory from him of many campaigns. The day for the marriage was fixed as announced by us. – But we are concerned to state that a *postponement* of this marriage for mysterious reasons has taken place. Delicacy forbids us to say more at present.'

Delicacy, however, did not prevent their saying in the next paper, in a paragraph headed, 'MYSTERY SOLVED,' 'We understand that in the course of a few days will appear the "Memoirs of the late Colonel D—y; or, Reminiscences of a Roué, well known in the Fashionable World." This little volume bids fair to engross the attention of the higher circles, as it contains, besides innumerable curious, personal, and secret anecdotes, the original love-letters of a certain *belle fiancée*, now residing with a noble family in Grosvenor Square.'

Lady Cecilia saw at once the whole dreadful danger – her own letters to Colonel D'Aubigny they must be! How could they have got them? They would be seen by her husband – published to the whole world – if the General found out they were hers, he would cast her off forever. If they were believed to be Helen's – Helen was undone, sacrificed to her folly, her cowardice. 'Oh! if I had but told Clarendon, he would have stopped this dreadful, dreadful publication.' And what false-hoods it might contain, she did not even dare to think. All was remorse, terror, confusion – fixed to the spot like one stupe-fied, she stood. Lady Castlefort did not see it – she had been completely engrossed with what she had been writing, she was now looking for her most sentimental seal, and not till she had pressed that seal down and examined the impression, did she look up or notice Cecilia – Then struck indeed with a sense of something unusual – 'My dear,' said she, 'you have no idea how odd you look – so strange, Cecilia – quite *ébahie*!' [1] Giving two pulls to the bell as she spoke, and her eyes on the door, impatient for the servant, she added, – 'After all, Cecilia – Helen Stanley is no relation even – only a friend. Take this note' – to the footman who answered the bell; and the moment he left the room, continuing, in the same tone, to Lady Cecilia, she said – 'You will have to give her up at last – that's all; so you had better make your mind up to it.'

When Lady Cecilia tried to speak, she felt her tongue cleave to the roof of her mouth; and when she did articulate, it was in a sort of hoarse sound, 'Is the book published?' She held the paper before Lady Castlefort's eyes and pointed to the name she could not utter.

'D'Aubigny's book – is it published, do you mean?' said Lady Castlefort. 'Absolutely published, I cannot say, but it is all in print, I know. I do not understand about publishing. There's something about presentation copies: I know Katrine was wild to have one before anybody else, so she is to have the first copy, I know, and, I

---

[1] amazed

believe, is to have it this very morning for the people at breakfast: it is to be the dainty morsel of the business.'

'What has Katrine to do with it? – Oh, tell me, quick!'

'Dear me, Cecilia, what a fuss you are in! – you make me quite nervous to look at you. You had better go down to the breakfast-room, and you will hear all about it from the fountain-head.'

'Has Katrine the book or not?' cried Lady Cecilia.

'Bless me! I will inquire, my dear, if you will not look so dreadful.' She rang and coolly asked – 'Did that man, that book-seller, Stone, send any parcel or book this morning, do you know, for Lady Katrine?'

'Yes, my lady; Landrum had a parcel for Lady Katrine – it is on the table, I believe.'

'Very well.' The man left the room.

Lady Cecilia darted on the brown paper parcel she had seen directed to Lady Katrine, and seized it before the amazed Louisa could prevent her. 'Stop, stop!' cried she, springing forward, 'stop, Cecilia; Katrine will never forgive me!'

But Lady Cecilia, seizing a penknife, cut the first knot. 'O Cecilia, I am undone if Katrine comes in! Make haste, make haste! I can only let you have a peep or two. We must do it up again as well as ever,' continued Lady Castlefort, while Lady Cecilia, fast as possible, went on cut, cut, cutting the packthread to bits, and she tore off the brown paper cover, then one of silver paper, that pro-tected the silk binding.

Lady Castlefort took up the outer cover and read, 'To be returned before two o'clock.' 'What can that mean? Then it is only lent; not her own. Katrine will not understand this – will be outrageously disappointed. I'm sure I don't care. But here is a note from Stone, however, which may explain it.' She opened and read – 'Stone's respects – existing circumstances make it neces-sary her ladyship's copy should be returned. Will be called for at two o'clock.

'Cecilia, Cecilia, make haste! But Katrine does not know yet – Still she may come up.' Lady Castlefort rang and inquired, – '

'Have they done breakfast?'

'Breakfast is over, my lady,' said the servant who answered the bell, 'but Landrum thinks the gentlemen and ladies will not be up immediately, on account of one of the ladies being *performing* a poem.'

'Very well, very good,' added her ladyship, as the man left the room. 'Then, Cecilia, you will have time enough, for when once they begin *performing*, as Sylvester calls it, there is no end of it.'

'O Heavens!' cried Cecilia, as she turned over the pages, 'O Heavens! what is here? Such absolute falsehood! Shocking, shocking!' she exclaimed, as she looked on, terrified at what she saw: 'absolutely false − a forgery.'

'Whereabouts are you?' said Lady Castlefort, approaching to read along with her.

'Oh, do not read it,' cried Cecilia, and she hastily closed the book.

'What signifies shutting the book, my dear,' said Louisa, 'as if you could shut people's eyes? I know what it is; I have read it.'

'Read it!'

'Read it! I really can read, though it seems to astonish you.'

'But it is not published?'

'One can read in manuscript.'

'And did you see the manuscript.'

'I had a glimpse. Yes − I know more than Katrine thinks I know.'

'Oh tell me, Louisa; tell me all,' cried Cecilia.

'I will, but you must never tell that I told it to you.'

'Speak, speak,' cried Cecilia.

'It is a long story,' said Lady Castlefort.

'Make it short them. Oh tell me quick, Louisa!'

'There is a literary *dessous des cartes*,' [1] said Lady Castlefort, a little vain of knowing a literary *dessous des cartes*; 'Churchill being at the head of everything of that sort, you know, the bookseller brought him the manuscript which Sir Thomas D'Aubigny had offered him, and wanted to know whether it would do or not.

[1] showing one's hand

Mr Churchill's answer was that it would never do without more pepper and salt, meaning gossip and scandal, and all that. But you are reading on, Cecilia, not listening to me.'

'I am listening, indeed.'

'Then never tell how I came to know everything. Katrine's maid has a lover; who is, as she phrases it, one of the gentlemen connected with the press. Now, my Angelique, who cannot endure Katrine's maid, tells me that this man is only a *wonder-maker*, a half-crown paragraph writer. So, through Angelique, and indeed from another person – ' she stopped; and then went on – 'through Angelique it all came up to me.'

'All what?' cried Cecilia; 'go on, go on to the facts.'

'I will, if you will not hurry me so. The letters were not in Miss Stanley's handwriting.'

'No! I am sure of that,' said Cecilia.'

'Copies were all that they pretended to be; so they may be forgeries after all, you see.'

'But how did Katrine or Mr Churchill come by the copies?'

'I have a notion, but of this I am not quite sure – I have a notion, from something I was told by – in short I suspect that Carlos, Lady Davenant's page, somehow got at them, and gave them, or had them given, to the man who was to publish the book. Lady Katrine and Churchill laid their heads together; here, in this very *sanctum sanctorum*. They thought I knew nothing, but I knew everything. I did not believe Horace had anything to do with it, except saying that the love-letters would be just the thing for the public if they were bad enough. I remember, too, that it was he who added the second-title, "Reminiscences of a Roué." and said something about alliteration's artful aid. And now,' concluded Lady Castlefort, 'it is coming to the grand catastrophe, as Katrine calls it. She has already told the story, and to-day she was to give all her set what she calls ocular demonstration. Cecilia, now, quick, finish; they will be here this instant. Give me the book; let me do it up this minute.'

'No, no; let me put it up,' cried Lady Cecilia, keeping possession of the book and the brown paper. 'I am a famous hand at doing up a parcel, as famous as any Bond Street shopman: your hands are not made for such work.'

Anybody but Lady Castlefort would have discerned that Lady Cecilia had some further design, and she was herself afraid it would be perceived; but taking courage from seeing what a fool she had to deal with, Lady Cecilia went on more boldly: 'Louisa, I must have more packthread; this is all cut to bits.'

'I will ring and ask for some.'

'No, no; do not ring for the footman; he might observe that we had opened the parcel. Cannot you get a string without ringing? Look in that basket.'

'None there, I know,' said Lady Castlefort, without stirring.

'In your own room, then; Angelique has some.'

'How do you know?'

'I know! never mind how. Go, and she will give you pack-thread. I must have it before Katrine comes up. So go, Louisa, go.'

'Go,' in the imperative mood, operated, and she went; she did not know why.

That instant Lady Cecilia drew the book out of the half-folded paper, and quick, quick, tore out page after page – every page of those letters that concerned herself or Helen, and into the fire thrust them, and as they blazed held them down bravely – had the boldness to wait till all was black: all the while she trembled, but stood it, and they were burnt, and the book in its brown paper cover was left on the table, and she down stairs, before Lady Castlefort's dressing-room door opened, and she crossed the hall without meeting a soul except the man in waiting there. The breakfast-room was at the back of the house looking into the gardens, and her carriage at the front door had never been seen by Lady Katrine or any of her blue set. She cleared out of the house into her carriage – and off – 'To the Park,' said she. She was off, but just in time. The whole tribe came out of the break-fast-room before she had turned the corner of the street. She threw herself back in the carriage and took breath, congratulating herself upon this hairbreadth 'scape. For this hour, this minute, she had escaped! – she was reprieved!

And now what was next to be done? This was but a momentary reprieve. Another copy would be had – no, not till tomorrow though. The sound of the words that had been read from the bookseller's note by Lady Castlefort, though scarcely noticed at the time, recurred to her now; and there was hope something might to-day be done to prevent the publication. It might still be kept for ever from her husband's and from Beauclerc's knowledge. One stratagem had succeeded – others might.

She took a drive round the Park to compose the excessive flurry of her spirits. Letting down all the glasses, she had the fresh air blowing upon her, and ere she was half round, she was able to think of what yet remained to do. Money! oh! any money she could command she would give to prevent this publication. She was not known to the bookseller – no matter. Money is money from whatever hand. She would trust the matter to no one but herself, and she would go immediately – not a moment to be lost. 'To Stone's, the bookseller's.'

Arrived. 'Do not give my name; only say, a lady wants to speak to Mr Stone.'

The people at Mr Stone's did not know the livery, or the carriage, but such a carriage and such a lady commanded the deference of the shopman. 'Please to walk in, madam,' and by the time she had walked in, the man changed madam into your ladyship – 'Mr Stone will be with your ladyship in a moment – only in the warehouse. If your ladyship will please to walk up into the back drawing-room – there's a fire.' The maid followed to blow it; and while the bellows wheezed and the fire did not burn, Lady Cecilia looked out of the window in eager expectation of seeing Mr Stone returning from the warehouse with all due celerity. No Mr Stone, however, appeared; but there was a good fire in the middle of the courtyard, as she observed to the maid who was plying the wheezing bellows; and who answered that they had had a great fire there this morning past 'burning of papers.' And at that moment a man came out with his arms full of a huge pile – sheets of a book, Lady Cecilia saw – it was thrown on the fire. Then came out and stood before the fire –

could she be mistaken? – impossible – it was like a dream – the General!

Cecilia's first thought was to run away before she should be seen; but the next moment that thought was abandoned, for the time to execute it was now past. The messenger sent across the yard had announced that a lady in the back drawing-room wanted Mr Stone. Eyes had looked up – the General had seen and recognised her, and all she could now do was to recognise him in return, which she did as eagerly and gracefully as possible. The General came up to her directly, not a little astonished that she, whom he fancied at home in her bed, incapacitated by a headache that had prevented her from speaking to him, should be here, so far out of her usual haunts, and, as it seemed, out of her element – 'What can bring you here, my dear Cecilia?'

'The same purpose which, if I rightly spell, brought you here, my dear General,' and her eyes intelligently glanced at the burning papers in the yard.

'Do you know then, Cecilia, what those papers are? How did you know?'

Lady Cecilia told her history, keeping as strictly to facts as the nature of the case admitted. Her headache, of course, she had found much better for the sleep she had taken. She had set off, she told him, as soon as she was able, for Lady Castlefort's to inquire into the meaning of the strange whispers of the preceding night. Then she told of the scandalous paragraphs she had seen; how she had looked over the book; and how successfully she had torn out and destroyed the whole chapter; and then how, hoping to be able to prevent the publication, she had driven directly to Mr Stone's.

Her husband, with confiding, admiring eyes, looked at her and listened to her, and thought all she said so natural, so kind, that he could not but love her the more for her zeal of friendship, though he blamed her for interfering, in defiance of his caution. 'Had you consulted me, or listened to me, my dear Cecilia, this morning, I could have saved you all this trouble; I should have told you that I would settle with Stone, and stop the publication, as I have done.'

'But that copy which had been sent to Lady Katrine, surely I did some good there by burning those pages; for if once it had got among her set, it would have spread like wildfire, you know, Clarendon.'

He acknowledged this, and said, smiling – 'Be satisfied with yourself, my love; I acknowledge that you made there a capital *coup de main*.'

Just then in came Mr Stone with an account in his hand, which the General stepped forward to receive, and, after one glance at the amount, he took up a pen, wrote, and signed his name to a cheque on his banker. Mr Stone received it, bowed obsequiously, and assured the General that every copy of the offensive chapter had been withdrawn and burnt – 'that copy excepted which you have yourself, General, and that which was sent to Lady Katrine Hawksby, which we expect *in* every minute, and it shall be sent to Grosvenor Square immediately. I will bring it myself, to prevent all danger.'

The General, who knew there was no danger there, smiled at Cecilia, and told the bookseller that he need take no further trouble about Lady Katrine's copy; the man bowed, and looking again at the amount of the cheque, retired well satisfied.

'You come home with me, my dear Clarendon, do not you?' said Lady Cecilia.

They drove off. On their way, the General said – 'It is always difficult to decide whether to contradict or to let such publications take their course: but in the present case, to stop the scandal instantly and completely was the only thing to be done. There are cases of honour, when women are concerned, where law is too slow: it must not be remedy, it must be prevention. If the finger of scorn dares to point, it must be – cut off.' After a pause of grave thought, he added – 'Upon the manner in which Helen now acts will depend her happiness – her character – her whole future life.'

Lady Cecilia summoned all her power to prevent her from betraying herself: the danger was great, for she could not command her fears so completely as to hide the look of alarm with which she listened to the General; but in his eyes her agitation appeared no more than was natural for her to feel about her friend.

'My love,' continued he, 'if Helen is worthy of your affection, she will show it now. Her only resource is in perfect truth: tell her so, Cecilia – impress it upon her mind. Would to Heaven I had been able to convince her of this at first! Speak to her strongly, Cecilia; as you love her, impress upon her that my esteem, Beauclerc's love, the happiness of her life, depend upon her truth!' As he repeated these words, the carriage stopped at their own door.

CHAPTER 39

WE LEFT HELEN in the back drawing-room, the door bolted, and beginning to read her dreaded task. The paragraphs in the newspapers, we have seen, were sufficiently painful, but when she came to the book itself – to the letters – she was in consternation, greater even that what she had felt in the General's presence under the immediate urgency of his eye and voice. Her conviction was that in each of these letters there were some passages, some expressions, which certainly were Cecilia's, but mixed with others, which as certainly were not hers. The internal evidence appeared to her irresistibly strong: and even in those passages which she knew to be Cecilia's writing, it too plainly appeared that, however playfully, however delicately expressed, there was more of real attachment for Colonel D'Aubigny than Cecilia had ever allowed Helen to believe; and she felt that Cecilia must shrink from General Clarendon's seeing these as her letters, after she had herself assured him that he was her first love. The falsehood was here so indubitable, so proved, that Helen herself trembled at the thought of Cecilia's acknowledging the plain facts to her husband. The time for it was past. Now that they were in print, published perhaps, how must he feel! If even candid confession were made to him, and made for best motives, it would to him appear only forced by necessity – forced, as he would say to himself, because her friend would not submit to be sacrificed.

Such were Helen's thoughts on reading the two or three first letters, but, as she went on, her alarm increased to horror. She saw things which she felt certain Cecilia could never have written;

yet truth and falsehood were so mixed up in every paragraph, circumstances which she herself had witnessed so misrepresented, that it was all to her inextricable confusion. The passages which were to be marked could not now depend upon her opinion, her belief; they must rest upon Cecilia's integrity – and how could she depend upon it? The impatience which she had felt for Lady Cecilia's return now faded away, and merged in the more painful thought that, when she did come, the suspense would not end – the doubts would never he satisfied.

She lay down upon the sofa and tried to rest, kept herself perfectly still, and resolved to think no more; and, as far as the power of the mind over itself can stay the ever-rising thoughts, she controlled hers, and waited with a sort of forced, desperate composure for the event. Suddenly she heard that knock, that ring, which she knew announced Lady Cecilia's return. But not Cecilia alone; she heard the General also coming upstairs, but Cecilia first, who did not stop for more than an instant at the drawing-room door: – she looked in, as Helen guessed, and seeing that no one was there, ran very quickly up the next flight of stairs. Next came the General: – on hearing his step, Helen's anxiety became so intense that she could not, at the moment he came near, catch the sound or distinguish which way he went. Strained beyond its power, the faculty of hearing seemed suddenly to fail – all was confusion, an indistinct buzz of sounds. The next moment, however, recovering, she plainly heard his step in the front drawing-room, and she knew that he twice walked up and down the whole length of the room, as if in deep thought. Each time as he approached the folding doors she was breathless. At last he stopped, his hand was on the lock – she recollected that the door was bolted, and as he turned the handle she, in a powerless voice, called to tell him, but not hearing her, he tried again, and as the door shook she again tried to speak, but could not. Still she heard, though she could not articulate. She heard him say, 'Miss Stanley, are you there? Can I see you?'

But the words – the voice seemed to come from afar – sounded dull and strange. She tried to rise from her seat – found a difficulty – made an effort – stood up – she summoned resolution – struggled – hurried across the room – drew back the bolt – threw open the door – and that was all she could do. In that effort strength and consciousness failed – she fell forward and fainted at the General's feet. He raised her up, and laid her on the sofa in the inner room. He rang for her maid, and went upstairs to prevent Cecilia's being alarmed. He took the matter coolly; he had seen many fainting young ladies, he did not like them – his own Cecilia excepted – in his mind always excepted from every unfavourable suspicion regarding the sex. Helen, on the contrary, was at present subject to them all, and, under the cloud of distrust, he saw in a bad light everything that occurred; the same appearances which, in his wife, he would have attributed to the sensibility of true feeling, he interpreted in Helen as the consciousness of falsehood, the proof of cowardly duplicity. He went back at once to his original prejudice against her, when, as he first thought, she had been forced upon him in preference to his own sister. He had been afterwards convinced that she had been perfectly free from all double dealing; yet now he slid back again, as people of his character often do, to their first opinion. 'I thought so at first, and I find, as I usually do, that my first thought was right.'

What had been but an adverse feeling was now considered as a prescient judgment. And he did not go upstairs the quicker for these thoughts, but calmly and coolly, when he reached Lady Cecilia's dressing-room, knocked at the door, and, with all the precautions necessary to prevent her from being alarmed, told her what had happened. 'You had better not go down, my dear Cecilia, I beg you will not. Miss Stanley has her own maid, all the assistance that can be wanted. My dear, it is not fit for you. I desire you will not go down.'

But Lady Cecilia would not listen, could not be detained; as she escaped from her husband, and ran down to Helen. Excessively alarmed she was, and well she might be, knowing herself to be the cause, and not certain in any way how it might end. She found Helen a little recovered, but still pale as white marble;

and when Lady Cecilia took her hand, it was still quite cold. She came to herself but very slowly. For some minutes she did not recover perfect consciousness or clear recollection. She saw figures of persons moving about her, she felt them as if too near, and wished them away; wanted air, but could not say what she wished. She would have moved, but her limbs would not obey her will. At last, when she had with effort half raised her head, it sank back again before she could distinguish all the persons in the room. The shock of cold water on her forehead revived her; then, coming clearly to powers of perception, she saw Cecilia bending over her. But still she could not speak, and yet she understood distinctly, saw the affectionate anxiety, too, in her little maid Rose's countenance; she felt that she loved Rose, and that she could not endure Felicie, who had now come in, and was making exclamations, and advising various remedies, all of which, when offered, Helen declined. It was not merely that Felicie's talking, and tone of voice, and superabundant action, were too much for her; but that Helen had at this moment a sort of intuitive perception of insincerity and of exaggeration. In that dreamy state, hovering between life and death, in which people are on coming out of a swoon, it seems as if there was need for a firm hold of reality; the senses and the understanding join in the struggle, and become most acute in their perception of what is natural or what is unnatural, true or false, in the expressions and feelings of the bystanders. Lady Cecilia understood her look, and dismissed Felicie, with all her smelling-bottles. Rose, though not ordered away, judiciously retired as soon as she saw that her services were of no further use, and that there was something upon her young lady's mind, for which hartshorn and sal volatile could be of no avail.

Cecilia would have kissed her forehead, but Helen made a slight withdrawing motion, and turned away her face: the next instant, however, she looked up, and taking Cecilia's hand, pressed it kindly, and said, 'You are more to be pitied than I am; sit down, sit down beside me, my poor Cecilia; how you tremble! and yet you do not know what is coming upon you.'

'Yes, yes, I do – I do,' cried Lady Cecilia, and she eagerly told Helen all that had passed, ending with the assurance that the publication had been completely stopped by her dear Clarendon; that the whole chapter containing the letters had been destroyed, that not a single copy had got abroad. 'The only one in existence is this,' said she, taking it up as she spoke, and she made a movement as if going to tear out the leaves, but Helen checked her hand, 'That must not be, the General desired – '

And almost breathless, yet distinctly, she repeated what the General had said, that he might be called upon to prove what parts were forged, and which true, and that she had promised to mark the passages. 'So now, Cecilia, here is a pencil, and mark what is and what is not yours.'

Lady Cecilia instantly took the pencil, and in great agitation obeyed. 'Oh, my dear Helen, some of these the General could not think yours. Very wicked these people have been! – so the General said; he was sure, he knew, all could not be yours.'

'Finish, my dear Cecilia,' interrupted Helen; 'finish what you have to do, and in this last trial, give me this one proof of your sincerity. Be careful in what you are now doing, mark truly – O Cecilia! every word you recollect – as your conscience tells you. Will you, Cecilia? this is all I ask, as I am to answer for it – will you?'

Most fervently she protested she would. She had no difficulty in recollecting, in distinguishing, her own; and at first she marked truly, and was glad to separate what was at worst only foolish girlish nonsense from things which had been interpolated to make out the romance: things which never could have come from her mind.

There is some comfort in having our own faults overshadowed, outdone, by the greater faults of others. And here it was flagrant wickedness in the editor, and only weakness and imprudence in the writer of the real letters. Lady Cecilia continually solaced her conscience by pointing out to Helen, as she went on, the folly, literally the folly, of the deception she had practised on her husband; and her exclamations against herself were so vehement that Helen would not add to her pain by a single reproach, since she had decided that the time was past for urging her confession to the General. She now only said, 'Look to the future, Cecilia, the past we cannot recall. This will be a lesson you can never forget.'

'Oh, never, never, can I forget it. You have saved me, Helen.'

Tears and protestations followed these words, and at the moment they were all sincere; and yet, can it be believed? even in this last trial, when it came to this last proof, Lady Cecilia was not perfectly true. She purposely avoided putting her mark of acknowledgment to any of those expressions which most clearly proved her love for Colonel D'Aubigny; for she still said to herself that the time might come, though at present it could not be, when she might make a confession to her husband, – in his joy at the birth of a son, she thought she might venture; she still looked forward to doing justice to her friend at some future period, and to make this easier – to make this possible – as she said to herself, she must now leave out certain expressions, which might, if acknowledged, remain for ever fixed in Clarendon's mind, and for which she could never be forgiven.

Helen, when she looked over the pages, observed among the unmarked passages some of those expressions which she had thought were Cecilia's, but she concluded she was mistaken: she could not believe that her friend could at such a moment deceive her, and she was even ashamed of having doubted her sincerity; and her words, look, and manner, now gave assurance of perfect unquestioning confidence.

This delicacy in Helen struck Lady Cecilia to the quick. Ever apt to be more touched by her refined feelings than by any strong appeal to her reason or her principles, she was now shocked by the contrast between her own paltering meanness and her friend's confiding generosity. As this thought crossed her mind, she stretched out her hand again for the book, took up the pencil, and was going to mark the truth; but, the impulse past, cowardice prevailed, and cowardice whispered, 'Helen is looking at me, Helen sees at this moment what I am doing, and, after having marked them as not mine, how can I now acknowledge them? – it is too late – it is impossible.'

'I have done as you desired,' continued she, 'Helen, to the best of my ability. I have marked all this, but what can it signify now, my dear, except – ?'

Helen interrupted her. 'Take the book to the General this moment, will you, and tell him that all the passages are marked as he desired; stay, I had better write.'

She wrote upon a slip of paper a message to the same effect, having well considered the words by which she might, without further step in deception, save her friend, and take upon herself the whole blame – the whole hazardous responsibility.

When Cecilia gave the marked book to General Clarendon, he said, as he took it, 'I am glad she has done this, though it is unnecessary now, as I was going to tell her if she had not fainted; unnecessary, because I have now in my possession the actual copies of the original letters; I found them here on my return. That good little poetess found them for me at the printer's – but she could not discover – I have not yet been able to trace where they came from, or by whom they were copied.'

'Oh, let me see them,' cried Lady Cecilia.

'Not yet, my love,' said he; 'you would know nothing more by seeing them; they are in a feigned hand evidently.'

'But,' interrupted Cecilia, 'you cannot want the book now, when you have the letters themselves'; and she attempted to draw it from his hand, for she instantly perceived the danger of the discrepancies between her marks and the letters being detected. She made a stronger effort to withdraw the book, but he held it fast.

'Leave it with me now, my dear; I want it; it will settle my opinion as to Helen's truth.'

Slowly, and absolutely sickened with apprehension, Lady Cecilia withdrew. When she returned to Helen, and found how pale she was and how exhausted she seemed, she entreated her to lie down again and try to rest.

'Yes, I believe I had better rest before I see Granville,' said Helen; 'where can he have been all day?'

'With some friends of his, I suppose,' said Cecilia, and she insisted on Helen's saying no more, and keeping herself perfectly quiet. She further suggested that she had better not appear at dinner.

'It will only be a family party, some of the General's relations. Miss Clarendon is to be here, and she is one, you know, trying to the spirits; and she is not likely to be in her most suave humour this evening, as she has been under a course of the toothache, and has been all day at the dentist's.'

Helen readily consented to remain in her own room, though she had not so great a dread of Miss Clarendon as Lady Cecilia seemed to feel. Lady Cecilia was indeed in the greatest terror lest Miss Clarendon should have heard some of these reports about Helen and Beauclerc, and would in her blunt way ask directly what they meant, and go on with some of her point-blank questions, which Cecilia feared might be found unanswerable. However, as Miss Clarendon had only just come to town from Wales, and come only about her teeth, she hoped that no reports could have reached her; and Cecilia trusted much to her own address and presence of mind in moments of danger, in turning the conversation the way it should go.

But things were now come to a point where none of the little skilful interruptions or lucky hits by which she had so frequently profited, could avail her further than to delay what must be. Passion and character pursue their course unalterably, unimpeded by small external circumstances; interrupted they may be in their progress, but as the stream opposed bears against the obstacle, sweeps it away, or foams and passes by.

Before Lady Cecilia's toilette was finished her husband was in her dressing-room; came in without knocking, – a circumstance so unusual with him, that Mademoiselle Felicie's eyes were opened to their utmost orbit, and, without waiting for word or look, she vanished, leaving the bracelet half clasped on her lady's arm.

'Cecilia!' said the General.

He spoke in so stern a tone that she trembled from head to foot; her last falsehood about the letters – all her falsehoods, all her concealments, were, she thought, discovered; unable to support herself, she sank into his arms. He seated her, and went on in a cool, inexorable tone, 'Cecilia, I am determined not to sanction by any token of my public approbation this marriage, which I no longer in my private conscience desire or approve; I will not be the person to give Miss Stanley to my ward.'

Lady Cecilia almost screamed: her selfish fears forgotten, she felt only terror for her friend. She exclaimed, 'Clarendon, will you break off the marriage? Oh! Helen, what will become of her? Clarendon, what can you mean?'

'I mean that I have compared the passages that Helen marked in the book wtih those copies of the letters which were given to the bookseller before the interpolations were made – the letters as Miss Stanley wrote them. The passages in the letters and the passages marked in the book do not agree.'

'Oh, but she might have forgotten, it might be accident,' cried Cecilia, overwhelmed with confusion.

'No, Cecilia,' pursued the General, in a tone which made her heart die within her – 'no, Cecilia, it is not accident, it is design. I perceive that every strong expression, every word, in short, which could show her attachment to that man, has been purposely marked as not her own, and the letters themselves prove that they were her own. The truth is not in her.'

In an agitation, which prevented all power of thought, Cecilia exclaimed, 'She mistook – she mistook; I could not, I am sure, recollect; she asked me if I remembered any.'

'She consulted you, then?'

'She asked my advice, – told me that – '

'I particularly requested her,' interrupted the General, 'not to ask your advice; I desired her not to speak to you on the subject – not to consult you. Deceit – double-dealing in everything she does, I find.'

'No, no, it is my fault; everything I say and do is wrong,' cried Lady Cecilia. 'I recollect now – it was just after her fainting, when I brought the book, and when she took it to mark she really was not able. It was not that she consulted me, but I forced my counsel upon her. I looked over the letters, and said what I thought – if anybody is wrong, it is I, Clarendon. Oh do not visit my sins upon Helen so cruelly! I assure you, if you do this, I never could forgive myself.'

The General looked at her in silence: she did not dare to meet his eyes, desperately anxious as she was to judge by his countenance what was passing within. He clasped for her that bracelet which her trembling hands were in vain attempting to close.

'Poor thing, how its heart beats!' said her husband, pressing her to him as he sat down beside her. Cecilia thought she might venture to speak. 'You know, my dear Clarendon, I never oppose – interfere with – any determination of yours when once it is fixed – '

'This is fixed,' interrupted the General.

'But after all you have done for her this very day, for which I am sure she – I am sure I thank you from my soul, would you now undo it all?'

'She is saved from public shame,' said the General, 'from private contempt I cannot save her: who can save those who have not truth? But my determination *is* fixed; it is useless to waste words on the subject. Esther is come; I must go to her. And now, Cecilia, I conjure you, when you see Beauclerc – I have not seen him all day – I do not know where he has been – I conjure you – I command you not to interfere between him and Helen.'

'But you would not have me give her up! I should be the basest of human beings.'

'I do not know what you mean, Cecilia; you have done for her all that an honourable friend could do.'

'I am not an honourable friend,' was Cecilia's bitter consciousness, as she pressed her hand upon her heart, which throbbed violently with contending fears.

'You have done all that an honourable friend could do; more must not be done,' continued the General. – 'And now recollect, Cecilia, that you are my wife as well as Miss Stanley's friend': and, as he said these words, he left the room.

—◆❧ CHAPTER 40 ❧◆—

THAT KNOWING FRENCH minister, Louvois, whose power is said to have been maintained by his surpassing skill in collecting and spreading secret and swift intelligence, had in his pay various classes of unsuspected agents, dancing-masters, fencing-masters, language-masters, milliners, hairdressers, and barbers – dentists he would have added, had he lived to our times; and not all Paris could have furnished him with a person better suited to his purpose than the most fashionable London dentist of the day, St Leger Swift. Never did Frenchman exceed him in volubility of utterance, or in gesture significant, supplying all that words might fear or fail to tell; never was he surpassed by prattling barber or privileged hunchback in ancient or modern story, Arabian or Persian; but he was not a malicious, only a coxcomb scandal-monger, triumphing in his *sçavoir dire*. St Leger Swift was known to everybody – knew everybody in London that was to be or was not to be known, every creature dead or alive that ever had been, or was about to be, celebrated, fashionable, or rich, or clever, or notorious, *roué* or murderer, about to be married, or about to be hanged – for that last class of persons enjoys in our days a strange kind of heroic celebrity, of which Voltaire might well have been jealous. St Leger was, of course, hand and glove with all the royal family; every illustrious personage – every most illustrious personage – had in turn sat in his chair; he had had all their heads, in their turns, in his hands, and he had capital anecdotes and sayings of each, with which he charmed away the sense of pain in loyal subjects. But with scandal for the fair was he especially provided.

Never did man or woman skim the surface tittle-tattle of society, or dive better, breathless, into family mysteries; none, with more careless air, could at the same time talk and listen – extract your news and give you his *on dit*, or tell the secret which you first reveal. There was in him and about him such an air of reckless, cordial coxcombry, it warmed the coldest, threw the most cautious off their guard, brought out family secrets as if he had been one of your family – your secret purpose as though he had been a secular father confessor; as safe everything told to St Leger Swift, he would swear to you, as if known only to yourself; he would swear, and you would believe, unless peculiarly constituted, as was the lady who, this morning, took her seat in his chair –

Miss Clarendon. She was accompanied by her aunt, Mrs Pennant.

'Ha! old lady and young lady, fresh from the country. Both, I see, persons of family – of condition,' said St Leger to himself. On that point his practised eye could not mistake, even at first glance; and accordingly it was really doing himself a pleasure, and these ladies, as he conceived it, a pleasure, a service, and an honour, to put them, immediately on their arrival in town, *au courant du jour*. Whether to pull or not to pull a tooth that had offended, was the professional question before him.

Miss Clarendon threw back her head, and opened her mouth.

'Fine teeth, fine! Nothing to complain of here surely,' said St Leger. 'As fine a show of ivory as ever I beheld. 'Pon my reputation, I know many a fine lady who would give – all but her eyes for such a set.'

'I must have this tooth out,' said Miss Clarendon, pointing to the offender.

'I see; certainly, ma'am, as you say.'

'I hope, sir, you don't think it necessary,' said her tender-hearted aunt: 'if it could be any way avoided – '

'By all means, madam, as you say. We must do nothing without consideration.'

'I have considered, my dear aunt,' said Miss Clarendon. 'I have not slept these three nights.'

'But you do not consider that you caught cold getting up one night for me; and it may be only an accidental cold, my dear Esther. I should be so sorry if you were to lose a tooth. Don't be in a hurry; once gone, you cannot get it back again.'

'Never was a truer, wiser word spoken, madam,' said St Leger, swiftly whisking himself round, and as if looking for some essential implement. 'May be a mere twinge, accidental cold, rheumatism, or may be – My dear madam' (to the aunt), 'I will trouble you; let me pass. I beg pardon – one word with you,' and with his back to the patient in the chair, while he rummaged among ivory-handled instruments on the table, he went on in a low voice to the aunt – 'Is she nervous? is she nervous, eh, eh, eh?'

Mrs Pennant looked, but did not hear, for she was a little deaf.

'Yes, yes, yes; I see how it is. A word to the wise,' replied he, with a nod of intelligence. 'Every lady's nervous nowadays, more or less. Where the deuce did I put this thing? Yes, yes – nerves; – all the same to me; know how to manage. Make it a principle – professional, to begin always by talking away nerves. You shall see, you shall see, my dearest madam; you shall soon see – you shall hear, you shall hear how I'll talk this young lady – your niece – out of her nerves fairly. Beg pardon, miss – , one instant. I am searching for – where have I put it?'

'I beg your pardon, sir; I am a little deaf,' said Mrs Pennant.

'Deaf – hey? Ha! a little deaf. So everybody is nowadays; even the most illustrious personages, more or less. Death and deafness common to all – *mors omnibus*. I have it. Now, my dear young lady, let us have another look and touch at these beautiful teeth. Your head will do very – vastly well, my dear ma'am – miss – um, um, um!' hoping the name would be supplied. But that Miss Clarendon did not tell.

So raising his voice to the aunt as he went on looking, or seeming to look, at the niece's tooth, he continued rapidly – 'From Wales you are, ma'am? a beautiful country, Wales, ma'am. Very near being born there myself, like, ha, ha, ha! that Prince of Wales – first Prince – Caernarvon Castle – you know the historical anecdote. Never saw finer teeth, upon my reputation. Are you

ladies, may I ask, for I've friends in both divisions – are you North
or South Wales, eh, eh?'

'South, sir. Llansillen.'

'Ay, South. The most picturesque certainly. Llansillen, Llansillen; know it; know everybody ten miles round. Respectable
people – all – very; most respectable people come up from Wales
continually. Some of our best blood from Wales, as a great personage observed lately to me, – Thick, thick! not thicker blood
than the Welsh. His late Majesty, *à propos*, was pleased to say to
me once – '

'But,' interrupted Miss Clarendon, 'what do you say to my
tooth?'

'Sound as a roach, my dear ma'am; I will insure it for a thousand pounds.'

'But that, the tooth you touch, is not the tooth I mean: pray
look at this, sir.'

'Excuse me, my dear madam, a little in my light,' said he to the
aunt. 'May I beg the favour of your name?'

'Pennant! ah! ah! ah!' with his hands in uplifted admiration –
'I thought so – Pennant. I said so to myself, for I know so many
Pennants – great family resemblance – Great naturalist of that
name – any relation? Oh yes – No – I thought so from the first.
Yes – and can assure you, to my private certain knowledge, that
man stood high on the pinnacle of favour with a certain royal
personage, – for, often sitting in this very chair –

'Keep your mouth open – a little longer – little wider, my
good Miss Pennant. Here's a little something for me to do,
nothing of any consequence – only touch and go – nothing to
be taken away, no, no, must not lose one of these fine teeth. That
most illustrious personage said one day to me, sitting in this very
chair – "Swift," said he, "St Leger Swift," familiarly, condescend-
ingly, colloquially – "St Leger Swift, my good fellow," said he –

'But positively, my dear miss – um, um, if you have not
patience – you must sit still – pardon me, professionally I must be
peremptory. Impossible I could hurt – can't conceive – did not
touch – only making a perquisition – inquisition – say what you

please, but you are nervous, ma'am; I am only taking a general survey.

'*À propos* – general survey – General – a friend of mine, General Clarendon, is just come to town. My ears must have played me false, but I thought my man said something like Clarendon when he showed you up.'

No answer from Miss Clarendon, who held her mouth open wide, as desired, resolved not to satisfy his curiosity, but to let him blunder on.

'Be that as it may, General Clarendon's come to town – fine teeth he has too – and a fine kettle of fish – not very elegant, but expressive still – he and his ward have made of that marriage announced. Fine young man, though, that Beauclerc – finest young man, almost, I ever saw!'

But here Mr St Leger Swift, starting suddenly, withdrawing his hand from Miss Clarendon's mouth, exclaimed, –

'My finger, ma'am! but never mind, never mind, all in the day's work. Casualty – contingencies – no consequence. But as I was saying, Mr Granville Beauclerc – '

Then poured out, on the encouragement of one look of curiosity from Mrs Pennant, all the *on dits* of Lady Katrine Hawksby, and all her chorus, and all the best authorities; and St Leger Swift was ready to pledge himself to the truth of every word. He positively knew that the marriage was off, and thought, as everybody did, that the young gentleman was well off too; for besides the young lady's great fortune turning out not a *sous* – and here he supplied the half-told tale by a drawn-up ugly face and shrugging gesture.

'Shocking! shocking! all came to an *éclat* – *esclandre*; [1] a scene quite, last night, I am told, at my friend Lady Castlefort's. Sad – sad – so young a lady! But to give you a general idea, love-letters to come out in the Memoirs of that fashionable Roué – friend of mine too – fine fellow as ever breathed – only a little – you understand; Colonel D'Aubigny – Poor D'Aubigny, heigho – only if the book comes out – Miss Stanley – '

---

[1] unpleasant notoriety

Mrs Pennant looked at her niece in benevolent anxiety; Miss Clarendon was firmly silent; but St Leger, catching from the expression of both ladies' countenances that they were interested in the contrary direction to what he had anticipated, turned to the right about, and observed, –

'This may be all scandal, one of the innumerable daily false reports that are always flying about town; scandal all, I have no doubt – Your head a little to the right, if you please – And the publication will be stopped, of course, and the young lady's friends – you are interested for her, I see; so am I – always am for the young and fair, that's my foible; and indeed, confidentially, I can inform you – If you could keep your head still, my dear madam.'

But Miss Clarendon could bear it no longer; starting from under his hand, she exclaimed, 'No more, thank you – no more at present, sir: we can call another day – no more': and added as she hastily left the room, 'Better bear the toothache,' and ran down-stairs. Mrs Pennant slipped into the dentist's hand, as he pulled the bell, a double fee; for though she did not quite think he deserved it much, yet she felt it necessary to make amends for her niece's way of running off, which might not be thought quite civil.

'Thank you, ma'am – thank ye, ma'am – not the least occa-sion – don't say a word about it – Young lady's nervous, said so from the first. Nerves! nerves! all – open the door there – Nerves all,' were the last words, at the top of the stairs, St Leger Swift was heard to say.

And the first words of kind Mrs Pennant, as soon as she was in the carriage and had drawn up the glass, were 'Do you know, Esther, my dear, I am quite sorry for this poor Miss Stanley. Though I don't know her, yet, as you described her to me, she was such a pretty, young, interesting creature! I am quite sorry.'

'I don't believe a word of it,' said Miss Clarendon.

'But even to have such things said must be so distressing to her and to her lover, your friend Mr Beauclerc – so very distressing!'

'I hope they are not such fools as to be distressed about such stuff. All this insufferable talking man's invention, I daresay.'

'Why do people tell such things?' said Mrs Pennant. 'But, my dear Esther, even supposing it to be all false, it is shocking to have such things spoken of. I pity the poor young lady and her lover. Do you not think, my dear, we shall be able to inquire into the truth of the matter from your brother this evening? He must know, he ought to know, about it: whether the report be true or false, he should hear of it. He can best judge what should be done, if anything should be done, my dear.'

Miss Clarendon quite agreed with all this; indeed she almost always agreed with this aunt of hers, who, perhaps from the peculiar gentleness of her manner, joined to a simplicity and sincerity of character, she could never doubt, had an ascendency over her, which no one, at first view, could have imagined.

They had many country commissions to execute this morning, which naturally took up a good deal of aunt Pennant's attention. But between each return from shop to carriage, in the intervals between one commission off her hands and another on her mind, she returned regularly to 'that poor Miss Stanley, and those love-letters!' and she sighed. Dear kind-hearted old lady! she had always a heart, as well as a hand, open as day to melting charity – charity in the most enlarged sense of the word: charity in judging as well as charity in giving. She was all indulgence for human nature, for youth and love especially.

'We must take care, my dear Esther,' said she, 'to be at General Clarendon's early, as you will like to have some little time with him to yourself before any one else arrives – shall you not, my dear?'

'Certainly,' replied Miss Clarendon; 'I shall learn the truth from my brother in five minutes, if Lady Cecilia does not come between.'

'Nay, my dear Esther, I cannot think so ill of Lady Cecilia; I cannot believe – '

'No, my dear aunt, I know you cannot think ill of anybody. Stay till you know Lady Cecilia Clarendon as I do. If there is anything wrong in this business, you will find that some falsehood of hers is at the bottom of it.'

'Oh, my dear, do not say so before you know; perhaps, as you thought at first, we shall find that it is all only a mistake of that giddy dentist's; for your brother's sake try to think as well as you can of his wife; she is a charming agreeable creature, I am sure.'

'You've only seen her once, my dear aunt,' said Miss Clarendon. 'For my brother's sake I would give up half her agreeableness for one ounce – for one scruple – of truth.'

'Well, well, take it with some grains of allowance, my dear niece; and, at any rate, do not suffer yourself to be so prejudiced as to conceive she can be in fault in this business.'

'We shall see to-day,' said Miss Clarendon; 'I will not be prejudiced; but I remember hearing at Florence that this Colonel D'Aubigny had been an admirer of Lady Cecilia's. I will get at the truth.'

With this determination, and in pursuance of the resolve to be early, they were at General Clarendon's full a quarter of an hour before the arrival of any other company; but Lady Cecilia entered so immediately after the General that Miss Clarendon had no time to speak with her brother alone. Determined, however, as she was, to get at the truth, without preface, or even smoothing her way to her object, she rushed into the middle of things at once. 'Have you heard any reports about Miss Stanley, brother?'

'Yes.'

'And you, Lady Cecilia?'

'Yes.'

'What have you heard?'

Lady Cecilia was silent, looked at the General, and left it to him to speak as much or as little as he pleased. She trusted to his laconic mode of answering, which, without departing from truth, defied curiosity. Her trust in him upon the present occasion was, however, a little disturbed by her knowledge of his being at this moment particularly displeased with Helen. But, had she known the depths as well as she knew the surface of his character, her confidence in his caution would have been increased, instead of being diminished, by this circumstance: Helen was lost in his esteem, but she was still under his protection; her secrets were not only sacred, but, as far as truth and honour could admit, he would still serve and save her. Impenetrable, therefore, was his look, and brief was his statement to his sister. A rascally bookseller had been about to publish a book, in which were some letters which paragraphs in certain papers had led the public to believe were Miss Stanley's; the publication had been stopped, the offensive chapter suppressed, and the whole impression destroyed.'

'But, brother,' pursued Miss Clarendon, 'were the letters Miss Stanley's, or not? You know I do not ask from idle curiosity, but from regard for Miss Stanley'; and she turned her inquiring eyes full upon Lady Cecilia.

'I believe, my dear Esther,' said Lady Cecilia, 'I believe we had better say no more; you had better inquire no further.'

'That must be a bad case which can bear no inquiry,' said Miss Clarendon; 'which cannot admit any further question, even from one most disposed to think well of the person concerned – a desperately bad case.'

'Bad! no, Esther. It would be cruel of you so to conclude: and falsely it would be – might be; indeed, Esther! my dear Esther! – '

Her husband's eyes were upon Lady Cecilia, and she did not dare to justify Helen decidedly; her imploring look and tone, and her confusion, touched the kind aunt, but did not stop the impenetrable niece.

'Falsely, do you say? Do you say, Lady Cecilia, that it would be to conclude falsely? Perhaps not falsely though, upon the data given to me. The data may be false.'

'Data! I do not know what you mean exactly, Esther,' said Lady Cecilia, in utter confusion.

'I mean exactly what I say,' pursued Miss Clarendon, 'that if I reason wrong, and come to a false conclusion, or what you call a cruel conclusion, it is not my fault, but the fault of those who do not plainly tell me the facts.'

She looked from Lady Cecilia to her brother, and from her brother to Lady Cecilia. On her brother no effect was produced: calm, unalterable, looked he; as though his face had been turned to stone. Lady Cecilia struggled in vain to be composed. 'I wish

I could tell you, Esther,' said she; 'but facts cannot always – all facts – even the most innocent – that is, even with the best intentions – cannot always be all told, even in the defence of one's best friend.'

'If this be the best defence you can make for your best friend, I am glad you will never have to defend me, and I am sorry for Helen Stanley.'

'Oh, my dear Esther!' said her aunt, with a remonstrating look; for, though she had not distinctly heard all that was said, she saw that things were going wrong, and that Esther was making them worse. 'Indeed, Esther, my dear, we had better let this matter rest.'

'Let this matter rest!' repeated Miss Clarendon; 'that is not what you would say, my dear aunt, if you were to hear any evil report of me. If any suspicion fell like a blast on my character, you would never say "let it rest." '

Fire lighted in her brother's eyes, and the stone face was all animated, and he looked sudden sympathy, and he cried, 'You are right, sister, in principle, but wrong in – fact.'

'Set me right where only I am wrong then,' cried she.

He turned to stone again, and her aunt, in a low voice, said, 'Not now.'

'Now or never,' said the sturdy champion; 'it is for Miss Stanley's character. You are interested for her, are not you, aunt?'

'Certainly, I am indeed; but we do not know all the circumstances – we cannot – '

'But we must. You do not know, brother, how public these reports are. Mr St Leger Swift, the dentist, has been chattering to us all morning about them. So, to go to the bottom of the business at once, will you, Lady Cecilia, answer me one straightforward question?'

Straightforward question! what is coming? thought Lady Cecilia: her face flushed, and taking up a hand-screen, she turned away, as if from the scorching fire; but it was not a scorching fire, as everybody, or at least as Miss Clarendon, could see. The face turned away from Miss Clarendon was full in view of aunt Pennant, who was on her other side; and she, seeing the distressed

state of the countenance, pitied, and gently laying her hand upon
Lady Cecilia's arm, said, in her low voice, 'This must be a very
painful subject to you, Lady Cecilia. I am sorry for you.'

'Thank you,' said Lady Cecilia, pressing her hand with quick
gratitude for her sympathy. 'It is indeed to me a painful subject,
for Helen has been my friend from childhood, and I have so
much reason for loving her!'

Many contending emotions struggled in Cecilia's countenance, and she could say no more; but what she had said, what
she had looked, had been quite enough to interest tenderly in
her favour that kind heart to which it was addressed; and Cecilia's
feeling was true at the instant; she forgot all but Helen; the screen
was laid down; tears stood in her eyes – those beautiful eyes! 'If
I could but tell you the whole – oh if I could! without destroying – '

Miss Clarendon at this moment placed herself close opposite
to Cecilia, and, speaking so low that neither her brother nor her
aunt could hear her, said, 'Without destroying yourself, or your
friend – which?'

Lady Cecilia could not speak.

'You need not – I am answered,' said Miss Clarendon; and
returning to her place, she remained silent for some minutes.

The General rang, and inquired if Mr Beauclerc had come in.
'No.'

The General made no observation, and then began some
indifferent conversation with Mrs Pennant, in which Lady Cecilia
forced herself to join; she dreaded even Miss Clarendon's silence
– that grim repose, – and well she might.

'D'Aubigny's Memoirs, I think was the title of the book, aunt,
that the dentist talked of? That is the book you burnt, is not it,
brother? – a chapter in that book?'

'Yes,' said the General.

And again Miss Clarendon was silent; for though she well
recollected what she had heard at Florence, and however strong
were her suspicions, she might well pause; for she loved her
brother before everything but truth and justice, – she loved her

brother too much to disturb his confidence. 'I have no proof,' thought she; 'I might destroy his happiness by another word, and I may be wrong.'

'But shall we not see Miss Stanley?' said Mrs Pennant.

Lady Cecilia was forced to explain that Helen was not very well, would not appear till after dinner – nothing very much the matter – a little faintish.

'Fainted,' said the General.

'Yes, quite worn out – she was at Lady Castlefort's last night – such a crowd!' She went on to describe its City horrors.

'But where is Mr Beauclerc all this time?' said Miss Clarendon: 'has he fainted too? or is he faintish?'

'Not likely,' said Lady Cecilia; 'faint heart never won fair lady. He is not of the faintish sort.'

At this moment a thundering knock at the door announced the rest of the company, and never was company more welcome. But Beauclerc did not appear. Before dinner was served, however, a note came from him to the General. Lady Cecilia stretched out her hand for it, and read,

> 'MY DEAR FRIENDS – I am obliged to dine out of town. I shall not return tonight, but you will see me at breakfast-time to-morrow. –
> Yours ever, GRANVILLE BEAUCLERC.'

Cockburn now entered with a beautiful bouquet of hot-house flowers, which, he said, Mr Beauclerc's man had brought with the note, and which were, he said, for Miss Stanley. Lady Cecilia's countenance grew radiant with joy, and she exclaimed, 'Give them to me, – I must have the pleasure of taking them to her myself.'

And she flew off with them. Aunt Pennant smiled on her as she passed, and, turning to her niece as Lady Cecilia left the room, said, 'What a bright creature! so warm, so affectionate!'

Miss Clarendon was indeed struck with the indisputably natural sincere satisfaction and affection in Cecilia's countenance; and, herself of such a different nature, could not comprehend the possibility of such contradiction in any character: she could not imagine the existence of such variable, transitory feelings – she could not believe any human being capable of sacrificing her friend to save herself, while she still so loved her victim, could still feel such generous sympathy with her. She determined at least to suspend her judgment; she granted Lady Cecilia a reprieve from her terrific questions and her as terrific looks. Cecilia recovered her presence of mind, and dinner went off delightfully, to her at least, with the sense of escape in recovered self-possession, and 'spirits light, to every joy in tune.'

From the good breeding of the company there was no danger that the topic she dreaded should be touched upon. Whatever reports might have gone forth, whatever any one present might have heard, nothing would assuredly be said of her friend Miss Stanley, to her, or before her, unless she or the General introduced the subject; and she was still more secure of his discretion than of her own. The conversation kept safe on London-dinner generalities and frivolities. Yet often things that were undesignedly said touched upon the *taboo'd* matter; and those who knew when, where, and how it touched, looked at or from one another, and almost equally dangerous was either way of looking. Such perfect neutrality of expression is not given to all men in these emergencies as to General Clarendon.

The dessert over, out of the dinner-room and in the drawing-room, the ladies alone together, things were not so pleasant to Lady Cecilia. Curiosity peeped out more and more in great concern about Miss Stanley's health; and when ladies trifled over their coffee, and saw through all things with their half-shut eyes, they asked, and Lady Cecilia answered, and parried, and explained, and her conscience winced, and her countenance braved, and Miss Clarendon listened with that dreadfully good memory, that positive point-blank recollection, which permits not the slightest variation of statement. Her doubts and her suspicions returned, but she was silent; and sternly silent she remained the rest of the evening.

CHAPTER 41

IF 'TRIFLES LIGHT AS AIR are to the jealous confirmations strong as proofs of Holy Writ,' and that they are no one since the time of Othello could ever doubt, it may be some consolation to observe, on the credit side of human nature, that, to those who are not cursed with a jealous infirmity, trifles light as air are often confirmations strong of the constancy of affection. Well did Lady Cecilia know this when she was so eager to be the bearer of the flowers which were sent by Beauclerc. She foresaw and enjoyed the instant effect, the quick smile and blush of delight with which that bouquet was received by Helen.

'Oh, thank you! How kind of him!' and 'all's well,' was her immediate conclusion. When she saw his note, she never even took notice that he did not particularly mention her. The flowers from him were enough; she knew his sincerity so well, trusted to it so completely, that she was quite sure, if he had been angry with her, he would not have sent these tokens of his love, – slight tokens, though they were all-sufficient for her. Her fears had taken but one direction, and in that direction they were all dispelled. He would be at breakfast to-morrow, when she should know where he had been, and what had detained him from her the whole of this day. She told Cecilia that she was now quite well, but that she would not attempt to go down stairs. And Cecilia left her happy, so far at least; and when she was alone with her flowers, she doubly enjoyed them, inhaling the fragrance of each which she knew he particularly liked, and thanking him in her heart for the careful choice, for she was certain that they were not accidentally put together. Some of them were associated with little circumstances known only to themselves, awakening recollections of bright, happy moments, and selected, she was sure, with reference to a recent conversation they had had on the language of flowers.

Whether Helen fancied half this, or whether it was all true, it had the effect of soothing and pleasing her anxious, agitated mind; and she was the more ready to indulge in that pleasant reverie from all she had previously suffered herself, and all that she feared Beauclerc had yet to endure. She knew too well how much these reports would affect him – and hear them he must. She considered what trials he had already borne, and might still have to bear, for her sake, whatever course she might now pursue. Though soon, very soon, the whole would be told to him, yet still, though she might stand clear in his eyes as to the main points, he must, and would, blame her weakness in first consenting to this deception – he who was above deceit. She had not absolutely *told*, but she had *admitted* a falsehood; she had *acted* a falsehood. This she could not extenuate. Her motive at first, to save Lady Davenant's life, was good; but then her weakness afterwards, in being persuaded time after time by Cecilia, could not well be excused. She was conscious that she had sunk step by step, dragged down that slippery path by Cecilia, instead of firmly making a stand, as she ought to have done, and upholding by her own integrity her friend's failing truth. With returning anguish of self-reproach she went over and over these thoughts; she considered the many unforeseen circumstances that had occurred. So much public shame, so much misery, had been brought upon herself and on all she loved by this one false step! And how much more might still await her, notwithstanding all that best of friends, the General, had done! She recollected how much he had done for her! – thinking of her too, as he must, with lowered esteem, and that was the most painful thought of all; – to Beauclerc she could and would soon clear her truth, but to the General – never, perhaps, completely!

Her head was leaning on her hand, as she was sitting deep in these thoughts, when she was startled by an unusual knock at her door. It was Cockburn with a packet, which General Clarendon had ordered him to deliver into Miss Stanley's own hands. The instant she saw the packet she knew that it contained *the book*; and on opening it she found manuscript letters inserted between the marked pages, and there was a note from General Clarendon. She trembled – she foreboded ill.

The note began by informing Miss Stanley how the enclosed manuscript letters came into General Clarendon's hands from a person whom Miss Stanley had obliged, and who had hoped in return to do her some service. The General next begged Miss Stanley to understand that these letters had been put into his possession since his conversation with her at breakfast time; his only design in urging her to mark her share in the printed letters had been to obtain her authority for serving her to the best of his ability; but he had since compared them: – and then came references, without comment, to the discrepancies between the marked passages, the uniform character of the omissions, followed only by a single note of admiration at each from the General's pen. And at last, in cold polite phrase, came his regret that he had not been able to obtain that confidence which he had trusted he had deserved, and his renunciation of all future interference in her affairs – *or concerns*, had been written, but a broad dash of the pen had erased the superfluous words; and then came the inevitable conclusion, on which Helen's eyes fixed, and remained immovable for some time – that determination which General Clarendon had announced to his wife in the first heat of indignation, but which, Lady Cecilia had hoped, could be evaded, changed, postponed – would not at least be so suddenly declared to Helen; therefore she had given her no hint, had in no way prepared her for the blow, – and with the full force of astonishment it came upon her – 'General Clarendon cannot have the pleasure he had proposed to himself, of giving Miss Stanley at the altar to his ward. He cannot by any public act of his attest his consent to that marriage, of which, in his private opinion, he no longer approves.'

'And he is right. O Cecilia!' was Helen's first thought, when she could think after this shock – not of her marriage, not of herself, not of Beauclerc, but of Cecilia's falsehood – Cecilia's selfish cowardice, she thought, and could not conceive it possible, – could not believe it, though it was there. Incredible – yet proved – there – there – before her eyes – brought home keen to her heart! after all! at such a time – after her most solemn promise, with so little temptation, so utterly false – with every possible motive that a good mind could have to be true – in this last trial – her friend's whole character at stake – ungenerous – base! 'O Cecilia! how different from what I thought you – or how changed! And I have helped to bring her to this! – I – I have been the cause. I will not stay in this house – I will leave her. To save her – to save myself – save my own truth and my own real character – let the rest go as it will – the world think what it may! Farther and farther, lower and lower, I have gone; I will not go lower – I will struggle up again at any risk, at any sacrifice. This is a sacrifice Lady Davenant would approve of: she said that if ever I should be convinced that General Clarendon did not wish me to be his guest – if he should ever cease to esteem me – I should go, that instant – and I will go.' But where? To whom could she fly, to whom turn? The Collingwoods were gone; all her uncle's friends passed rapidly through her recollection. Since she had been living with General and Lady Cecilia Clarendon, several had written to invite her; but Helen knew a little more of the world now than formerly, and she felt that there was not one, no, not one of these to whom she could now, at her utmost need, turn and say, 'I am in distress, receive me! my character is attacked, defend me! my truth is doubted, believe in me!' And, her heart beating with anxiety, she tried to think what was to be done. There was an old Mrs Medlicott, who had been a housekeeper of her uncle's, living at Seven Oaks – she would go there – she should be safe – she should be independent. She knew that she was then in town, and was to go to Seven Oaks the next day; she resolved to send Rose early in the morning to Mrs Medlicott's lodging, which was near Grosvenor Square, to desire her to call at General Clarendon's as she went out of town, at eight o'clock. She could then go with her to Seven Oaks; and, by setting out before Cecilia could be up, she should avoid seeing her again.

There are minds which totally sink, and others that wonderfully rise, under the urgency of strong motive and of perilous
circumstance. It is not always the mind apparently strongest or
most daring that stands the test. The firm of principle are those
most courageous in time of need. Helen had determined what
her course should be, and, once determined, she was calm. She
sat down and wrote to General Clarendon.

'Miss Stanley regrets that she cannot explain to General
Clarendon the circumstances which have so much displeased him. She assures him that no want of confidence
has been, on her part, the cause; but she cannot expect that,
without further explanation, he should give her credit for
sincerity. She feels that with his view of her conduct, and
in his situation, his determination is right – that it is what
she has deserved, – that it is just towards his ward and due
to his own character. She hopes, however, that he will not
think it necessary to announce to Mr Beauclerc his determination of withdrawing his approbation and consent to
his marriage, when she informs him that it will now never
be by her claimed or accepted. She trusts that General
Clarendon will permit her to take upon herself the breaking off this union. She encloses a letter to Mr Beauclerc,
which she begs may be given to him to-morrow. General
Clarendon will find she has dissolved their engagement
as decidedly as he could desire, and that her decision will
be irrevocable. And since General Clarendon has ceased
to esteem her, Miss Stanley cannot longer accept his protection, or encroach upon his hospitality. She trusts that
he will not consider it as any want of respect, that she
has resolved to retire from his family as soon as possible.
She is certain of having a safe and respectable home with
a former housekeeper of her uncle Dean Stanley's, who
will call for her at eight o'clock to-morrow, and take her
to Seven Oaks, where she resides. Miss Stanley has named
that early hour, that she may not meet Mr Beauclerc

before she goes; she wishes also to avoid the struggle and agony of parting with Lady Cecilia. She entreats General Clarendon will prevent Lady Cecilia from attempting to see her in the morning, and permit her to go unobserved out of the house at her appointed hour.

'So now farewell, my dear friend – yes, friend, this last time you must permit me to call you; for such I feel you have ever been, and ever would have been, to me, if my folly would have permitted. Believe me – notwithstanding the deception of which I acknowledge I have been guilty towards you, General Clarendon – I venture to say, *believe me*, I am not ungrateful. At this instant my heart swells with gratitude, while I pray that you may be happy – as you deserve to be. But you will read this with disdain, as mere idle words: so be it.

Farewell!   HELEN STANLEY.'

Next, she was to write to Beauclerc, himself. Her letter was as follows: –

'With my whole heart, dear Granville, I thank you for the generous confidence you have shown towards me, and for the invariable steadiness of your faith and love. For your sake I rejoice. One good has at least resulted from the trials you have gone through: you must now and hereafter feel sure of your own strength of mind. With me it has been different, for I have not a strong mind. I have been all weakness, and must now be miserable; but wicked I will not be – and wicked I should be if I took advantage of your confiding love. I must disappoint your affection, but your confidence I will not betray. When I put your love to that test which it has so nobly stood, I had hoped that a time would come when all doubts would be cleared up, and when I could reward your constancy by the devotion of my whole happy life – but that hope is past: I cannot prove my innocence – I will no longer allow you to take it upon my assertion. I cannot indeed, with truth, even assert that I have done no wrong; for though I am not false, I have gone on step by step in deception, and might go on, I know not how far, nor to what dreadful consequences, if I did not now stop – and I do stop. On my own head be the penalty of my fault – upon my own happiness – my own character. I will not involve yours – therefore we part. You have not yet heard all that has been said of me; but you soon will, and you will feel, as I do, that I am not fit to be your wife. Your wife should not be suspected; I have been – I am. All the happiness I can ever have in this world must be henceforth in the thought of having saved from misery, if not secured the happiness of, those I love. Leave me this hope – O Granville, do not tell me, do not make me believe, that you will never be happy without me! You will – indeed you will. I only pray Heaven that you may find love as true as mine, and strength to abide by the truth! Do not write to me – do not try to persuade me to change my determination: it is irrevocable. Further writing or meeting could be only useless anguish to us both. Give me the sole consolation I can now have, and which you alone can give – let me hear from Cecilia that you and your noble-minded guardian are, after I am gone, as good friends as you were before you knew me. I shall be gone from this house before you are here again; I cannot stay where I can do no good, and might do much evil by remaining even a few hours longer. As it is, comfort your generous heart on my account with the assurance that I am sustained by the consciousness that I am now, to the best of my power, doing right. Adieu, Granville! Be happy! you can – you have done no wrong. Be happy, and that will console

  Your affectionate   HELEN STANLEY.'

This, enclosed to General Clarendon, she sent by Cockburn, who delivered it to his master immediately.

Though she could perfectly depend upon her maid Rose's fidelity, Helen did not tell her that she was going away in the morning, to avoid bringing her into any difficulty if she were questioned by Lady Cecilia; and besides, no note of preparation would be heard or seen. She would take with her only sufficient for the day, and would leave Rose to pack up all that belonged to her, after her departure, and to follow her. Thanks to her own late discretion, she had no money difficulties – no debts but such as Rose could settle, and she had now only to write to Cecilia; but she had not yet recovered from the tumult of mind which the writing to the General and to Beauclerc had caused. She lay down upon the sofa, and closing her trembling eyelids, she tried to compose herself sufficiently to think at least of what she was going to say. As she passed the table in going to the sofa, she, without perceiving it, threw down some of the flowers; they caught her eye, and she said to herself, 'Lie there! lie there! Granville's last gifts! last gifts to me! All over now; lie there and wither! Joys that are past, wither! All happiness for me, gone! Lie there, and wither, and die! – and so shall I soon, I hope – if that only hope is not wrong.'

Someone knocked at the door; she started up, and said, 'I cannot see you, Cecilia!'

A voice not Cecilia's, a voice she did not recollect, answered, 'It is not Cecilia; let me see you. I come from General Clarendon.'

Helen opened the door, and saw – Miss Clarendon. Her voice had sounded so much lower and gentler than usual, that Helen had not guessed it to be hers. She was cloaked, as if prepared to go away; and in the outer room was another lady seated with her back towards them, and with her cloak on also.

'My aunt Pennant – who will wait for me. As she is a stranger, she would not intrude upon you, Miss Stanley; but will you allow me one minute?'

Helen, surprised, begged Miss Clarendon to come in, moved a chair towards her, and stood breathless with anxiety. Miss Clarendon sat down, and resuming her abruptness of tone, said, 'I feel that I have no right to expect that you should have confidence in me, and yet I do. I believe in your sincerity, even from the little I know of you, and I have a notion you believe in mine. Do you?'

'I do.'

'I wish it had pleased Heaven,' continued Miss Clarendon, 'that my brother had married a woman who could speak truth! But you need not be afraid; I will not touch on your secrets. On any matter you have in keeping, my honour as well as yours will command my silence – as will also my brother's happiness, which I have somewhat at heart; not that I think it can be preserved by the means you take. But this is not what I came to say. You mean to go away from this house to-morrow morning?'

'Yes,' said Helen.

'You are right. I would not stay where I did not esteem or where I had reason to believe that I was not esteemed. You are quite right to go, and to go directly, but not to your old house-keeper.'

'Why not?' said Helen.

'Because, though I daresay she is vastly respectable, – an excellent person in her own way, I am convinced, – yet my brother says she might not be thought just the sort of person to whom you should go now – not just the thing for you at present; though, at another time, it would be very well and condescending; but now, when you are attacked, you must look to appearances – in short, my brother will not allow you to go to this old lady's boarding-house, or cottage, or whatever it may be, at Seven Oaks; he must be able to say for you where you are gone. You must be with me; you must be at Llansillen. Llansillen is a place that can be named. You must be with me – with General Clarendon's sister. You must – you will, I am sure, my dear Miss Stanley. I never was so happy in having a house of my own as at this moment. You will not refuse to return with my aunt and me to Llansillen, and make our home yours? We will try and make it a happy home to you. Try; you see the sense of it: the world can say nothing when you are known to be with Miss Clarendon; and you will, I hope, feel the comfort of it, out of the stir and din of this London world. I know you like the country, and Llansillen is a beautiful place

– romantic too; a fine castle, an excellent library, beautiful conservatory; famous for our conservatories we are in South Wales; and no neighbours – singular blessing! And my aunt Pennant, you will love her so! Will you try? Come! say that you will.'

But Helen could not; she could only press the hand that Miss Clarendon held out to her. There is nothing more touching, more overcoming, than kindness at the moment the heart is sunk in despair. 'But did General Clarendon really wish you to ask me?' said Helen, when she could speak. 'Did he think so much and so carefully for me to the last? And with such a bad opinion as he must have of me!'

'But there you know he is wrong.'

'It is like himself,' continued Helen; 'consistent in protecting me to the last. Oh, to lose such a friend!'

'Not lost, only mislaid,' said Miss Clarendon. 'You will find him again some fair day or other; truth always comes to light. Meanwhile, all is settled. I must run and tell my aunt, and bless the fates and Lady Emily Greville, that Lady Cecilia did not come up in the middle of it. Luckily, she thinks I am gone, and knows nothing of my being with you; for my brother explained all this to me in his study, after we had left the saloon, and he desires me to say that his carriage shall be ready for you at your hour, at eight o'clock. We shall expect you; and now, farewell till to-morrow.'

She was gone, and her motto might well be, though in a different acceptation from that of our greatest modern politician – '*Tout faire sans paraître.*' [1]

But before Helen could go to rest, she must write to Lady Cecilia, and her thoughts were in such perplexity and her feelings in such conflict, that she knew not how to begin. At last she wrote only a few hasty lines of farewell, and referred for her determination, and for all explanations, to her letter to the General. It came to 'Farewell, dear Cecilia.'

Dear! yes, still dear she was to Helen – she must be as Lady Davenant's daughter – still dear for her own sake was Cecilia, the

---

[1] do everything without appearing to

companion of her childhood, who had shown her such generous affection early, such fondness always, who was so charming, with so many good qualities, so much to win love – loved she must be still. 'Farewell, Cecilia; may you be happy!'

But as Helen wrote these words, she thought it impossible, she could scarcely in the present circumstances wish it possible, that Cecilia was happy. How could she, unless her conscience had become quite callous?

She gave her note to Rose, with orders to deliver it herself to Lady Cecilia tonight, when she should demand admittance. And soon she came, the very instant Lady Emily Greville went away – before Helen was in bed she heard Cecilia at her door; she left her to parley with Rose – heard her voice in the first instance, eager, peremptory for admittance. Then a sudden silence. Helen comprehended that she had opened her note – and in another instant she heard her retreating step. On seeing the first words referring for explanation to Helen's letter to the General, panic-struck, Lady Cecilia hurried to her own room to read the rest privately.

Helen now tried to recollect whether everything had been said, written, done, that ought to be done; and at last went to bed and endeavoured to sleep for a few hours.

CHAPTER 42

HELEN WAS JUST DRESSED, and had given her last orders to her bewildered maid, when she heard a knock at the door, and Mademoiselle Felicie's voice. She could not at this instant endure to hear her heartless exclamatory speeches; she would not admit her. Mademoiselle gave Rose a note for her young lady – it was from Cecilia.

> 'DEAREST HELEN – The General will not allow me to take leave of you this morning, but I shall certainly go to you in the course of to-day. I cannot understand or make you understand anything till I see you. I *will* see you to-day. Your affectionate
>
> CECILIA.'

'I understand it too well!' thought Helen.

The carriage was announced, Helen was ready; she hurried into it, and she was gone! And thus she parted from the friend of her childhood – the friend she had but a few months before met with such joy, such true affection; and her own affection was true to the last.

As Helen drove from the door, she saw the General – yes, it was certainly the General riding off – at this unusual hour? Was it to avoid her? But she was in too great anguish to dwell upon that or any other circumstance; her only thought now was to subdue her emotion before she was seen by Miss Clarendon and Mrs Pennant. And by the time she arrived, she thought she had quite recovered herself, and was not aware that any traces of tears remained; but to Mrs Pennant's sympathising eyes they were visible, and after the first introductions and salutations were over, that kind lady, as she seated her at the breakfast-table, gently pressing her hand, said, 'Poor thing! no wonder – parting with old friends for new is a sad trial: but you know we shall become old friends in time: we will make what haste we can, my dear Miss Stanley, and Esther will help me to make you forget that you have not known us all your life.'

'There is very little to be known; no mysteries, that is one comfort,' said Miss Clarendon; 'so now to breakfast. You are very punctual, Miss Stanley; and that is a virtue which aunt Pennant likes, and can estimate to a fraction of a minute with that excellent watch of hers.'

There was some history belonging to that family-watch, which then came out; and then the conversation turned upon little family anecdotes and subjects which were naturally interesting to the aunt and niece, and not exciting to Helen, whose mind, they saw, needed quiet, and freedom from all observation.

From the first awkwardness of her situation, from the sense of intrusion, and the suddenness of change, she was thus as far as possible gradually and almost imperceptibly relieved. By their perfect good-breeding, as well as good-nature, from their making no effort to show her particular attention, she felt received at once into their family as one of themselves; and yet, though there was no effort, she perceived in the most minute circumstances the same sort of consideration which would be shown to an intimate friend. They not only did not expect, but did not wish, that she should make any exertion to appear to be what she could not be; they knew the loneliness of heart she must feel, the weight that must be upon her spirits. They left her, then, quite at liberty to be with them or alone, as she might like, and she was glad to be alone with her own thoughts; they soon fixed upon Beauclerc. She considered how he would feel, what he would think, when he should receive her letter: she pictured his looks while reading it; considered whether he would write immediately, or attempt, notwithstanding her prohibition, to see her. He would know from General Clarendon, that is, if the General thought proper to tell him, where she was, and that she would remain all this day in town. Though her determination was fixed, whether he wrote or came, to abide by her refusal, and for the unanswerable reasons which she had given, or which she had laid down to herself; yet she could not, and who, loving as she did, could help wishing that Beauclerc should desire to see her again? she hoped that he would make every effort to change her resolution, even though it might cost them both pain. Yet in some pain there is pleasure; or to be without it is a worse kind of suffering. Helen was conscious of the inconsistency in her mind, and sighed, and endeavoured to be reasonable. And, to do her justice, there was not the slightest wavering as to the main point. She thought that the General might, perhaps, have some relenting towards her. Hope would come into her mind, though she tried to keep it out; she had nothing to expect, she repeatedly said to herself, except that either Cecilia would send, or the General would call this morning, and Rose must come at all events.

The morning passed on, however, and no one came so soon as Helen had expected. She was sitting in a back room where no knocks at the door could be heard; but she would have been called, surely, if General Clarendon had come. He had come, but he had not asked for her; he had at first inquired only for his sister, but she was not at home, gone to the dentist's. The General then desired to see Mrs Pennant, and when she supposed that she had not heard rightly, and that Miss Stanley must be the person he wished to see, he had answered, 'By no means; I particularly wish not to see Miss Stanley. I beg to see Mrs Pennant alone.'

It fell to the lot of this gentle-hearted lady to communicate to Helen the dreadful intelligence he brought: a duel had taken place! When Helen had seen the General riding off, he was on his way to Chalk Farm. Just as the carriage was coming round for Miss Stanley, Mr Beauclerc's groom had requested in great haste to see the General; he said he was sure something was going wrong about his master; he had heard the words Chalk Farm. The General was off instantly, but before he reached the spot the duel had been fought. A duel between Beauclerc and Mr Churchill. Beauclerc was safe, but Mr Churchill was gravely wounded; the medical people present could not answer for his life. At the time the General saw him he was speechless, but when Beauclerc and his second, Lord Beltravers, had come up to him, he had extended his hand in token of forgiveness to one or the other, but to which he had addressed the only words he had uttered could not be ascertained; the words were, '*You* are not to blame! – escape! – fly!' Both had fled to the Continent. General Clarendon said that he had no time for explanations, he had not been able to get any intelligible account of the cause of the affair. Lord Beltravers had named Miss Stanley, but Beauclerc had stopped him, and had expressed the greatest anxiety that Miss Stanley's name should not be implicated, should not be mentioned. He took the whole blame upon himself – said he would write – there was no time for more.

Mrs Pennant listened with the dread of losing a single word: but, however brief his expressions, the General's manner of speaking, notwithstanding the intensity of his emotion, was so distinct that every word was audible, except the name of Lord Beltravers, which was not familiar to her. She asked again the name of Mr Beauclerc's second. 'Lord Beltravers,' the General repeated with a forcible accent, and, loosening his neckcloth with his finger, he added, 'Rascal! as I always told Beauclerc that he was, and so he will find him – too late.'

Except this exacerbation, the General was calmly reserved in speech, and Mrs Pennant felt that she could not ask him a single question beyond what he had communicated. When he rose to go, which he did the moment he had finished what he had to say, she had, however, courage enough to hope that they should soon hear again, when the General should learn something more of Mr Churchill.

Certainly he would let her know whatever he could learn of Mr Churchill's state.

Her eyes followed him to the door with anxious eagerness to penetrate farther into what his own opinion of the danger might be. His rigidity of composure made her fear that he had no hope, 'otherwise certainly he would have said something.'

He opened the door again, and returning, said, 'Depend upon it you shall hear how he is, my dear Mrs Pennant, before you leave town to-morrow.'

'We will not go to-morrow,' she replied. 'We will stay another day at least. Poor Miss Stanley will be so anxious – '

'I advise you not to stay in town another day, my dear madam. You can do no good by it. If Mr Churchill survive this day, he will linger long, I am assured. Take Helen – take Miss Stanley out of town, as soon as may be. Better go to-morrow, as you had determined.'

'But it will be so long, my dear General! – one moment – if we go, it will be so long before we can hear any further news of your ward.'

'I will write.'

'To Miss Stanley – Oh, thank you.'

'To my sister,' he looked back to say, and repeated distinctly, 'To my sister.'

'Very well – thank you, at all events.'

Mrs Pennant saw that, in General Clarendon's present disposition towards Miss Stanley, the less she said of him the better, and she confined herself strictly to what she had been commissioned to say, and all she could do was to prevent the added pain of suspense; it was told to Helen in the simplest shortest manner possible: – but the facts were dreadful. Beauclerc was safe! – safe! but under what circumstances? 'And it was for me, I am sure,' cried Helen, 'I am sure it was for me! I was the cause! I am the cause of that man's death – of Beauclerc's agony.'

For some time Helen had not power or thought for any other idea. The promise that they should hear as soon as they could learn anything more of Mr Churchill's state was all she could rely upon or recur to.

When her maid Rose arrived from General Clarendon's she said that when Lady Cecilia heard of the duel she had been taken very ill, but had since recovered sufficiently to drive out with the

General. Miss Clarendon assured Helen there was no danger. 'It is too deep a misfortune for Lady Cecilia. Her feelings have not depth enough for it, you will see. You need not be afraid for her, Helen'.

The circumstances which led to the duel were not clearly known till long afterwards, but may now be related. The moment Beauclerc had parted from Helen when he turned away at the carriage-door after the party at Lady Castlefort's he went in search of one, who, as he hoped, could explain the strange whispers he had heard. The person of whom he went in search was his friend, his friend as he deemed him, Lord Beltravers. Churchill had suggested that if anybody knew the bottom of the matter, except that origin of all evil, Lady Katrine herself, – it must be Lord Beltravers, with whom Lady Castlefort was, it was said, *fortement éprise*,[1] and as Horace observed, 'the secrets of scandal are common property between lovers, much modern love being cemented by hate.'

Without taking in the full force of this observation in its particular application to the hatred which Lord Beltravers might feel to Miss Stanley, as the successful rival of his sister Blanche, Beauclerc hastened to act upon his suggestion. His lordship was not at home; his people thought he had been at Lady Castlefort's; did not know where he might be if not there. At some gambling-house Beauclerc at last found him, and Lord Beltravers was sufficiently vexed in the first place at being there found, for he had pretended to his friend Granville that he no longer played. His embarrassment was increased by the questions which Beauclerc so suddenly put to him; but he had *nonchalante* impudence enough to brave it through, and he depended with good reason on Beauclerc's prepossession in his favour. He protested he knew nothing about it; and he returned Churchill's charge by throwing the whole blame upon him; said he knew he was in league with Lady Katrine; – mentioned that one morning, some time ago, he had dropped in unexpectedly early at Lady Castlefort's,

[1] smitten

and had been surprised to find the two sisters, contrary to their wont, together – their heads and Horace Churchill's over some manuscript, which was shuffled away as he entered. This was true, all but the shuffling away; and here it is necessary to form a clear opinion, clearer than Lord Beltravers will give, of the different shares of wrong; of wrong knowingly and unknowingly perpetrated by the several scandal-mongers concerned in this affair.

Lord Beltravers could be in no doubt as to his own share, for he it was who had furnished the editor of Colonel D'Aubigny's Memoirs with the famous letters. When Carlos, Lady Davenant's runaway page, escaped from Clarendon Park, having changed his name, he got into the service of Sir Thomas D'Aubigny, who was just at this time arranging his brother's papers. Now it had happened that Carlos had been concealed behind the screen in Lady Davenant's room the day of her first conversation with Helen about Colonel D'Aubigny, and he had understood enough of it to perceive that there was some mystery about the Colonel with either Helen or Lady Cecilia; and chancing one day, soon after he entered Sir Thomas's service, to find his escritoire open, he amused himself with looking over his papers, among which he discovered the packet of Lady Cecilia's letters. Carlos was not perfectly sure of the handwriting, he thought it was Lady Cecilia's; but when he found the miniature of Miss Stanley along with them, he concluded that the letters must be hers. And having special reasons for feeling vengeance against Helen, and certain at all events of doing mischief, he sent them to General Clarendon: not, however, forgetting his old trade, he copied them first. This was just at the time when Lord Beltravers returned from abroad after his sister's divorce. He by some accident found out who Carlos was, and whence he came, and full of his own views for his sister, he cross-examined him as to everything he knew about Miss Stanley; and partly by bribes, partly by threats of betraying him to Lady Davenant, he contrived to get from him the copied letters. Carlos soon after returned with his master to Portugal, and was never more heard of. Lord Beltravers took these purloined copies of the letters, thus surreptitiously obtained, to the editor into whose hands Sir Thomas D'Aubigny (who knew nothing of books or book-making) had put his brother's memoirs. This editor, as has been mentioned, had previously consulted Mr Churchill, and in consequence of his pepper-and-salt hint, Lord Beltravers himself made those interpolations which he hoped would ruin his sister's rival in the eyes of her lover.

Mr Churchill, however, except this hint, and except his vanity in furnishing a good title, and his coxcombry of literary patronage, and his general hope that Helen's name being implicated in such a publication would avenge her rejection of himself, had had nothing to do with the business. This Lord Beltravers well knew, and yet when he found that the slander made no impression upon Beauclerc, and that he was only intent upon discovering the slanderer, he, with dextrous treachery, contrived to turn the tables upon Churchill, and to direct all Beauclerc's suspicions towards him. He took his friend home with him, and showed him all the newspaper paragraphs – paragraphs which he himself had written! Yes, this man of romantic friendship, this *blasé*, this hero oppressed with his own sensibility, could condescend to write anonymous scandal, to league with newsmongers, and to bribe waiting-women to supply him with information, for Mademoiselle Felicie had, though Lady Katrine's maid, told all, and more than all she knew, of what passed at General Clarendon's; and on this foundation did he construct those paragraphs, which he hoped would blast the character of the woman to whom his dearest friend was engaged. And now he contrived to say all that could convince Beauclerc that Mr Churchill was the author of these very paragraphs. And, hot and rash, Beauclerc rushed on to that conclusion. He wrote a challenge to Churchill, and as soon as it was possible in the morning, he sent it by Lord Beltravers. Mr Churchill named Sir John Luttrell as his friend: Lord Beltravers would enter into no terms of accommodation; the challenge was accepted, Chalk Farm appointed as the place of meeting, and the time fixed for eight o'clock next morning. And thus, partly by his own warmth of temper, and partly by the falsehood of others, was Beauclerc urged on to the action he detested, to be the thing he hated. Duelling and duelists had, from the time he could think, been his abhorrence, and now he was to end his life, or to take the life of a fellow-creature perhaps, in a duel.

There was a dread interval. And it was during the remainder of this day and night that Beauclerc felt most strongly, compared with all other earthly ties, his attachment, his passionate love, for Helen. At every pause, at every close of other thoughts forced upon him, his mind recurred to Helen – what Helen would feel – what Helen would think – what she would suffer – and in the most and in the least important things his care was for her. He recalled the last look that he had seen at the carriage-door when they parted, recollected that it expressed anxiety, was conscious that he had turned away abruptly – that in the preoccupied state of his mind he had not spoken one word of kindness – and this might be the last impression of him left on her mind. He knew that her anxiety would increase, when all that day must pass without his return, and it was then he thought of sending her those flowers which would, he knew, reassure her better than any words he could venture to write.

Meanwhile his false friend coldly calculated what were the chances in his sister's favour; and when Churchill fell, and even in the hurry of their immediate departure, Lord Beltravers wrote to Madame de St Cymon, over whom the present state of her affairs gave him command, to order her to set out immediately, and to take Blanche with her to Paris, without asking the consent of that fool and prude, her aunt Lady Grace.

It was well for poor Helen, even in the dreadful uncertainty in which she left London, that she did not know *all* these circumstances. It may be doubted, indeed, whether we should be altogether happier in this life if that worst of evils, as it is often called, suspense, were absolutely annihilated, and if human creatures could clearly see their fate, or even know what is most likely to happen.

CHAPTER 43

ACCORDING TO the General's advice, Mrs Pennant did not delay her journey, and Helen left London the next day with her and Miss Clarendon. The last bulletin of Mr Churchill had been that he was still in great danger, and a few scarce legible lines Helen had received from Cecilia, saying that the General would not allow her to agitate herself by going to take leave of her, that she was glad that Helen was to be out of town till all blew over, and that she was so much distracted by this horrible event, she scarcely knew what she wrote.

As they drove out of town, Miss Clarendon, in hopes of turning Helen's thoughts, went on talking. 'Unless,' said she, 'we could, like Madam de Genlis, "promote the post-boys into agents of mystery and romance," we have but little chance, I am afraid, of any adventures on our journey to Llansillen, my dear Miss Stanley.'

She inveighed against the stupid safety, convenience, luxury, and expedition of travelling nowadays all over England, even in Wales, 'so that one might sleep the whole way from Hyde Park Corner to Llansillen gate,' said she, 'and have no unconscionably long nap either. No difficulties on the road, nothing to complain of at inns, no enjoying one's dear delight in being angry, no opportunity even of showing one's charming resignation. Dreadfully bad this for the nervous and bilious, for all the real use and benefit of travelling is done away; all too easy for my taste; one might as well be a doll, or a dolt, or a parcel in the coach.'

Helen would have been glad to have been considered merely as a parcel in the coach. During the whole journey, she took no notice of anything till they came within a few miles of Llansillen; then, endeavouring to sympathise with her companions, she looked out of the carriage window at the prospect which they admired. But, however charming, Llansillen had not for Helen the chief charm of early, fond, old associations with a happy home. To her it was to be, she doubted not, as happy as kindness could make it, but still it was new; and in that thought, that feeling, there was something inexpressibly melancholy; and the contrast, at this moment, between her sensations and those of her companions, made the pain the more poignant; they perceived this, and were silent. Helen was grateful for this consideration for her, but she could not bear to be a constraint upon them, therefore she now exerted herself, sat forward – admired and talked when she was scarcely able to speak. By the time they came to Llansillen gate, however, she could say no more; she was obliged to acknowledge that she was not well; and when the carriage at last stopped at the door, there was such a throbbing in her temples, and she was altogether so ill, that it was with the greatest difficulty she could, leaning on Miss Clarendon's arm, mount the high steps to the hall-door. She could scarcely stand when she reached the top, but, making an effort, she went on, crossed the slippery floor of that great hall, and came to the foot of the black oak staircase, of which the steps were so very low that she thought she could easily go up, but found it impossible, and she was carried directly up to Miss Clarendon's room, no other having been yet prepared. The rosy Welsh maids looked with pity on the pale stranger. They hurried to and fro, talking Welsh to one another very fast; and Helen felt as if she were in a foreign land, and in a dream. The end of the matter was, that she had a low fever which lasted long. It was more dispiriting than dangerous – more tedious than alarming. Her illness continued for many weeks, during which time she was attended most carefully by her two new friends – by Miss Clarendon with the utmost zeal and activity – by Mrs Pennant with the greatest solicitude and tenderness.

Her history for these weeks – indeed for some months afterwards – can be only the diary of an invalid and of a convalescent. Miss Clarendon meanwhile received from her brother, punctually, once a week, bulletins of Churchill's health; the surgical details, the fears of the formation of internal abscess, reports of continual exfoliations of bone, were judiciously suppressed, and the laconic General reported only 'Much the same – not progressing – cannot be pronounced out of danger.' These bulletins were duly repeated to Helen, whenever she was able to hear them; and at last she was considered well enough to read various letters, which had arrived for her during her illness; several were from Lady Cecilia, but little in them. The first was full only of expressions of regret, and self-reproach; in the last, she said, she *hoped soon to have a right to claim Helen back again*. This underlined passage Helen knew alluded to the promise she had once made, that at the birth of her child all should be told; but words of promise from Cecilia had lost all value – all power to excite even hope, as she said to herself as she read the words, and sighed.

One of her letters mentioned what she would have seen in the first newspaper she had opened, that Lady Blanche Forrester was gone with her sister, the Comtesse de St Cymon, to Paris, to join her brother Lord Beltravers. But Lady Cecilia observed that Helen need not be alarmed by this paragraph, which she was sure was inserted on purpose to plague her. Lady Cecilia seemed to take it for granted that her rejection of Beauclerc was only a lover's ruse, and went on with her usual hopes, now vague and more vague every letter – that things would end well some time, somehow or other.

Helen only sighed on reading these letters, and, quick as she glanced her eye over them, threw them from her on the bed; and Miss Clarendon said, 'Ah! you know her now, I see!'

Helen made no reply: she was careful not to make any comment which could betray how much, or what sort of reason she had to complain of Lady Cecilia; but Miss Clarendon, confident that she had guessed pretty nearly the truth, was satisfied with her own penetration, and then, after seeming to doubt for a few moments, she put another letter into Helen's hand, and with one of those looks of tender interest which sometimes softened her countenance, she left the room.

The letter was from Beauclerc; it appeared to have been written immediately after he had received Helen's letter, and was as follows: —

'Not write to you, my dearest Helen! Renounce my claim to your hand! submit to be rejected by you, my affianced bride! No, never — never! Doubt! suspicion! — suspicion of you! — you, angel as you are — you, who have devoted, sacrificed, yourself to others. No, Helen, my admiration, my love, my trust in you, are greater than they ever were. And do *I* dare to say these words to you? *I*, who am perhaps a murderer! I ought to imitate your generosity, I ought not to offer you a hand stained with blood: — I ought at least to leave you free till I know when I may return from banishment. I have written this at the first instant I have been able to command during my hurried journey, and as you know something of what led to this unhappy business, you shall in my next letter hear the whole; till then, adieu!'

'GRANVILLE BEAUCLERC.'

The next day, when she thought Helen sufficiently recovered from the agitation of reading Beauclerc's letter, aunt Pennant produced one letter more, which she had kept for the last, because she hoped it would give pleasure to her patient. Helen sat up in her bed eagerly, and stretched out her hand. The letter was directed by General Clarendon, but that was only the outer cover, they knew, for he had mentioned in his last despatch that the letter enclosed for Miss Stanley was from Lady Davenant. Helen tore off the cover, but the instant she saw the inner direction, she sank back, turned, and hid her face on the pillow.

It was directed — 'To Mrs Granville Beauclerc.'

Lady Davenant had unfortunately taken it for granted that nothing could have prevented the marriage.

Aunt Pennant blamed herself for not having foreseen and prevented this accident, which she saw distressed poor Helen so much. But Miss Clarendon wondered that she was so shocked, and supposed she would get over it in a few minutes, or else she must be very weak. There was nothing that tended to raise her spirits much in the letter itself, to make amends for the shock the direction had given. It contained but a few lines in Lady Davenant's own handwriting, and a postscript from Lord Davenant. She wrote only to announce their safe arrival at Petersburg, as she was obliged to send off her letter before she had received any despatches from England; and she concluded with, 'I am sure the first will bring me the joyful news of Beauclerc's happiness and yours, my dear child.'

Lord Davenant's postscript added that in truth Lady Davenant much needed such a cordial, for that her health had suffered even more than he had feared it would. He repented that he had allowed her to accompany him to such a rigorous climate.

Au that could be said to allay the apprehensions this postscript might excite, was of course said in the best way by aunt Pennant. But it was plain that Helen did not recover during the whole of this day from the shock she had felt 'from that foolish direction,' as Miss Clarendon said. She could not be prevailed upon to rise this day, though Miss Clarendon, after feeling her pulse, had declared that she was very well able to get up. 'It was very bad for her to remain in bed.' This was true, no doubt. And Miss Clarendon remarked to her aunt that she was surprised to find Miss Stanley so weak. Her aunt replied that it was not surprising that she should be rather weak at present, after such a long illness.

'Weakness of mind and body need not go together,' said Miss Clarendon.

'Need not, perhaps,' said her aunt, 'but they are apt to do so.'

'It is to be hoped the weakness of mind will go with the weakness of body, and soon,' said Miss Clarendon.

'We must do what we can to strengthen and fatten her, poor thing!' said Mrs Pennant.

'Fatten the body, rather easier than to strengthen the mind. Strength of mind cannot be thrown in, as you would throw in the bark, or the chicken broth.'

'Only have patience with her,' said Mrs Pennant, 'and you will find that she will have strength of mind enough when she gets quite well. Only have patience.'

During Helen's illness Miss Clarendon had been patient, but now that she was pronounced convalescent, she became eager to see her quite well. In time of need Miss Clarendon had been not only the most active and zealous, but a most gentle and – doubt it who may – soft-stepping, soft-voiced nurse; but now, when Doctor Tudor had assured them that all fever was gone, and agreed with her that the patient would soon be well, if she would only think so, Miss Clarendon deemed it high time to use something more than her milder influence, to become, if not a rugged, at least a stern nurse, and she brought out some of her rigid lore.

'I intend that you should get up in seasonable time to-day, Helen,' said she, as she entered her room.

'Do you?' said Helen in a languid voice.

'I do,' said Miss Clarendon; 'and I hope you do not intend to do as you did yesterday, to lie in bed all day.'

Helen turned, sighed, and Mrs Pennant said, 'Yesterday is over, Esther – no use in talking of yesterday.'

'Only to secure our doing better to-day, ma'am,' replied Miss Clarendon, with prompt ability.

Helen was all submission, and she got up, and that was well. Miss Clarendon went in quest of arrow-root judiciously; and aunt Pennant stayed and nourished her patient meanwhile with 'the fostering dew of praise'; and let her dress as slowly and move as languidly as she liked, though Miss Clarendon had admonished her 'not to *dawdle*.'

As soon as she was dressed, Helen went to the window and threw up the sash for the first time to enjoy the fresh air, and to see the prospect, which she was told was beautiful; and she saw that it was beautiful, and, though it was still winter, she felt that the air was balmy; and the sun shone bright, and the grass began to be green, for spring approached. But how different to her from the spring-time of former years! Nature the same, but all within herself how changed! And all which used to please, and to seem to her most cheerful, now came over her spirits with a sense of sadness; – she felt as if all the life of life was gone. Tears filled her eyes, large tears rolled slowly down as she stood fixed, seeming to gaze from that window at she knew not what. Aunt Pennant unperceived stood beside her, and let the tears flow unnoticed. 'They will do her good; they are a great relief sometimes.'

Miss Clarendon returned, and the tears were dried, but the glaze remained, and Miss Clarendon saw it, and gave a reproach-ful look at her aunt, as much as to say, 'Why did you let her cry?' And her aunt's look in reply was, 'I could not help it, my dear.'

'Eat your arrow-root,' was all that transpired to Helen. And she tried to eat it, but could not; and Miss Clarendon was not well pleased, for the arrow-root was good, and she had made it; she felt Miss Stanley's pulse, and said that 'it was as good a pulse as could be, only low and a little fluttered.'

'Do not flutter it any more, then, Esther, my dear,' said Mrs Pennant.

'What am I doing or saying, ma'am, that should flutter anybody that has common sense?'

'Some people don't like to have their pulse felt,' said aunt Pennant.

'Those people have not common sense,' replied the niece.

'I believe I have not common sense,' said Helen.

'Sense you have enough – resolution is what you want, Helen, I tell you.'

'I know,' said Helen, 'too true – '

'True, but not too true – nothing can be too true.'

'True,' said Helen, with languid submission.

Helen was not in a condition to chop logic, or ever much inclined to it; now less than ever, and least of all with Miss Clarendon, so able as she was. There is something very provoking sometimes in perfect submission, because it is unanswerable. But the languor, not the submission, afforded some cause for further remark and remonstrance.

'Helen, you are dreadfully languid to-day.'

'Sadly,' said Helen.

'If you could have eaten more arrow-root before it grew cold, you would have been better.'

'But if she could not, my dear Esther,' said aunt Pennant.

'*Could* not, ma'am! As if people could not eat if they pleased.'

'But if people have no appetite, my dear, I am afraid eating will not do much good.'

'I am afraid, my dear aunt, you will not do Miss Stanley much good,' said Miss Clarendon, shaking her head; 'you will only spoil her.'

'I am quite spoiled, I believe,' said Helen; 'you must unspoil me, Esther.'

'Not so very easy,' said Esther; 'but I shall try, for I am a sincere friend.'

'I am sure of it,' said Helen.

Then what more could be said? Nothing at that time – Helen's look was so sincerely grateful, and 'gentle as a lamb,' as aunt Pennant observed; and Esther was not a wolf quite – at heart not at all.

Miss Clarendon presently remarked that Miss Stanley really did not seem glad to be better – glad to get well. Helen acknowledged that, instead of being glad, she was rather sorry. 'If it had pleased Heaven, I should have been glad to die.'

'Nonsense about dying, and worse than nonsense,' cried Miss Clarendon, 'when you see that it did not please Heaven that you should die – '

'I am content to live,' said Helen.

'Content! to be sure you are,' said Miss Clarendon. 'Is this your thankfulness to Providence?'

'I am resigned – I am thankful – I will try to be more so – but I cannot be glad.'

General Clarendon's bulletins continued with little variation for some time; they were always to his sister – he never mentioned Beauclerc, but confined himself to the few lines or words necessary to give his promised regular accounts of Mr Churchill's state, the sum of which continued to be for a length of time: 'Much the same.' 'Not in immediate danger.' 'Cannot be pronounced out of danger.' Not very consolatory, Helen felt. 'But while there is life, there is hope,' as aunt Pennant observed.

'Yes, and fear,' said Helen; and her hopes and fears on this subject alternated with fatiguing reiteration, and with a total incapacity of forming any judgment.

Beauclerc's letter of explanation arrived, and other letters came from him from time to time, which, as they were only repetitions of hopes and fears as to Churchill's recovery, and of uncertainty as to what might be his own future fate, only increased Helen's misery; and as even their expressions of devoted attachment could not alter her own determination, while she felt how cruel her continued silence must appear, they only agitated without relieving her mind. Mrs Pennant sympathised with and soothed her, and knew how to soothe, and how to raise, and to sustain a mind in sorrow, suffering under disappointed affection, and sunk almost to despondency; for aunt Pennant, besides her softness of manner, and her quick intelligent sympathy, had power of consolation of a higher sort, beyond any which this world can give. She was very religious, of a cheerfully religious turn of mind – of that truly Christian spirit which hopeth all things. When she was a child somebody asked her if she was bred up in the fear of the Lord. She said no, but in the love of God. And so she was, in that love which casteth out fear. And now the mildness of her piety, and the whole tone and manner of her speaking and thinking, reminded Helen of that good dear uncle by whom she had been educated. She listened with affectionate reverence, and she truly and simply said, 'You do me good – I think you have done me a great deal of good – and you shall see it.' And see it she did afterwards, and Miss Clarendon thought it was her doing, and so her aunt let it pass, and was only glad the good was done.

The first day Helen went down to the drawing-room, she found there a man who looked, as she thought at first glance, like a tradesman – some person, she supposed, come on business, standing waiting for Miss Clarendon, or Mrs Pennant. She scarcely looked at him, but passed on to the sofa, beside which was a little table set for her, and on it a beautiful work-box, which she began to examine and admire.

'Not nigh so handsome as I could have wished it, then, for you, Miss Helen – I ask pardon, Miss Stanley.'

Helen looked up, surprised at hearing herself addressed by one whom she had thought a stranger; but yet she knew the voice, and a reminiscence came across her mind of having seen him somewhere before.

'Old David Price, ma'am. Maybe you forget him, you being a child at that time. But since you grew up, you have been the saving of me and many more – ' Stepping quite close to her, he whispered that he had been paid under her goodness's order by Mr James, along with *the other creditors* that had been *left*.

Helen by this time recollected who the poor Welshman was – an upholsterer and cabinet-maker, who had been years before employed at the Deanery. Never have been paid at the time, a very considerable debt had been accumulated, and having neither note nor bond, Mr Price said that he had despaired of ever obtaining the amount of his earnings. He had, however, since the Dean's death, been paid in full, and had been able to retire to his native village, which happened to be near Llansillen, and most grateful he was; and as soon as he perceived that he was recognised, his gratitude became better able to express itself. Not well, however, could it make its way out for some time; between crying and laughing, and between two languages, he was at first scarcely intelligible. Whenever much moved, David Price had recourse to his native Welsh, in which he was eloquent; and Mrs Pennant, on whom, knowing that she understood him, his eyes turned, was good enough to interpret for him. And when once fairly set agoing, there was danger that poor David's garrulous gratitude should flow for ever. But it was all honest; not a word of flattery; and his old face was in a glow and radiant with feeling, and the joy of telling Miss Helen all, how, and about it; particularly concerning the last day when Mr James paid him, and them, and all of them: that was a day Miss Stanley ought to have seen; pity she could not have witnessed it; it would have done her good to the latest hour of her life. Pity she should never see the faces of many, some poorer they might have been than himself; many richer, that would have been ruined for ever but for her. For his own part, he reckoned himself one of the happiest of them all, in being allowed to see her face to face. And he hoped, as soon as she was able to get out so far – but it was not so far – she would come to see how comfortable he was in his own house. It ended at last in his giving a shove to the work-box on the table, which, though nothing worth otherwise, he knew she could not mislike, on account it was made out of all the samples of wood the Dean, her uncle, had given to him in former times.

Notwithstanding the immoderate length of his speeches, and the impossibility he seemed to find of ending his visit, Helen was not much tired. And when she was able to walk so far, Mrs Pennant took her to see David Price, and in a most comfortable house she found him; and every one in that house, down to the youngest child, gathered round her by degrees, some more, some less shy, but all with gratitude beaming and smiling in their faces. It was delightful to Helen; for there is no human heart, so engrossed by sorrow, so overwhelmed by disappointment, so closed against hope of happiness, that will not open to the touch of gratitude.

CHAPTER 44

BUT THERE WAS STILL in Helen's mind one deceitful hope. She thought she had pulled it up by the roots many times, and the last time completely; but still a little fibre lurked; and still it grew again. It was the hope that Cecilia would keep that last promise, though at the moment Helen had flung from her the possibility; yet now she took it up again, and she thought it was possible that Cecilia might be true to her word. IF her child should be born alive, and IF it should be a boy! It became a heart-breaking suspense as the time approached, and every day the news might be expected. The post came but three times a week at Llansillen, and every post day Miss Clarendon repeated her prophecy to her aunt, 'You will see, ma'am, the child will be born in good time, and alive. You who have always been so much afraid for Lady Cecilia, will find she has not feeling enough to do her any harm.'

In due time a note came from the General. 'A boy! child and mother doing well. Give me joy.'

The joy to Miss Clarendon was much increased by the triumph in her own perfectly right opinion. Mrs Pennant's was pure affectionate joy for the father, and for Lady Cecilia, for whom, all sinner as she was in her niece's eyes, this good soul had compassion. Helen's anxiety to hear again and again every post was very natural the aunt thought; quite superfluous the niece deemed it: Lady Cecilia would do very well, no doubt, she prophesied again, and laughed at the tremor, the eagerness, with which Helen every day asked if there was any letter from Cecilia. At last one came, the first in her own handwriting, and it was to Helen herself, and it extinguished all hope. Helen could only articulate, 'O Cecilia!'

Her emotion, her disappointment, were visible, but unaccountable; she could give no reason for it to Miss Clarendon, whose wondering eye was upon her; nor even to sympathising aunt Pennant could she breathe a word without betraying Cecilia; she was silent, and there was all that day, and many succeeding days, a hopelessness of languor in her whole appearance. There was, as Miss Clarendon termed it, a 'backsliding in her recovery,' which grieved aunt Pennant, and Helen had to bear imputation of caprice and of indolence from Miss Clarendon; but even that eye immediately upon her, that eye more severe than ever, had not power to rouse her. Her soul was sunk within, nothing further to hope; there was a dead calm, and the stillness and loneliness of Llansillen made that calm almost awful. The life of great excitation which she had led previous to her illness rendered her more sensible of the change, of the total want of stimulus. The walks to Price's cottage had been repeated, but, though it was a very bright spot, the eye could not always be fixed upon it.

Bodily exertion being more easy to her now than mental, she took long walks, and came in boasting how far she had been, and looking quite exhausted. And Miss Clarendon wondered at her wandering out alone; then she tried to walk with Miss Clarendon, and she was more tired, though the walks were shorter – and that was observed, and was not agreeable either to the observer or to the observed. Helen endeavoured to make up for it; she followed Miss Clarendon about in all her various occupations, from flower-garden to conservatory, and from conservatory to pheasantry, and to all her pretty cottages, and her schools, and she saw and admired all the good that Esther did so judiciously, and with such extraordinary, such wonderful energy.

'Nothing wonderful in it,' Miss Clarendon said: and as she ungraciously rejected praise, however sincere, and required not sympathy, Helen was reduced to be a mere silent, stupid, useless stander-by, and she could not but feel this a little awkward. She tried to interest herself for the poor people in the neighbourhood, but their language was unintelligible to her, and hers to them, and it is hard work trying to make objects for oneself in quite a new place, and with a preoccupying sorrow in the mind all the time. It was not only hard work to Helen, but it seemed labour in vain – bringing soil by handfuls to a barren rock, where, after all, no plant will take root. Miss Clarendon thought that labour could never be in vain.

One morning, when it must be acknowledged that Helen had been sitting in the same position with her head leaning on her hand, Miss Clarendon in her abrupt voice asked, 'How much longer, Helen, do you intend to sit there, doing only what is the worst thing in the world for you – thinking?'

Helen started, and said she feared she had been sitting too long idle.

'If you wish to know how long, I can tell you,' said Miss Clarendon; 'just one hour and thirteen minutes.'

'By the stop watch,' said Helen, smiling.

'By my watch,' said grave Miss Clarendon; 'and in the meantime look at the quantity of work I have done.'

'And done so nicely!' said Helen, looking at it with admiration.

'Oh, do not think to bribe me with admiration; I would rather see you do something yourself than hear you praise my doings.'

'If I had anybody to work for. I have so few friends now in the world who would care for anything I could do! But I will try – you shall see, my dear Esther, by and by.'

'By and by! no, no – now. I cannot bear to see you any longer, in this half-alive, half-dead state.'

'I know,' said Helen, 'that all you say is for my good. I am sure your only object is for my happiness.'

'Your happiness is not in my power or in yours, but it is in your power to deserve to be happy, by doing what is right – by exerting yourself: – that is my object, for I see you are in danger of being lost in indolence. Now you have the truth and the whole truth.'

Many a truth would have come mended from Miss Clarendon's tongue if it had been uttered in a softer tone, and if she had paid a little more attention to times and seasons: but she held it the sacred duty of sincerity to tell a friend her faults as soon as seen, and without circumlocution.

The next day Helen set about a drawing. She made it an object to herself to try to copy a view of the dear Deanery in the same style as several beautiful drawings of Miss Clarendon's.

While she looked over her portfolio, several of her old sketches recalled remembrances which made her sigh frequently; Miss Clarendon heard her, and said – 'I wish you would cure yourself of that habit of sighing; it is very bad for you.'

'I know it,' said Helen.

'Despondency is not penitence,' continued Esther: 'reverie is not reparation.'

She felt as desirous as ever to make Helen happy at Llansillen, but she was provoked to find it impossible to do so. Of a strong body herself, capable of great resistance, powerful reaction under disappointment or grief, she could ill make allowance for feebler health and spirits – perhaps feebler character. For great misfortunes she had great sympathy, but she could not enter into the details of lesser sorrows, especially any of the sentimental kind, which she was apt to class altogether under the head – 'Sorrows of my Lord Plumcake!' an expression which had sovereignly taken her fancy, and which her aunt did not relish, or quite understand.

Mrs Pennant was, indeed, as complete a contrast to her niece in these points as nature and habit joined could produce. She was naturally of the most exquisitely sympathetic mimosa-sensibility, shrinking and expanding to the touch of others' joy or woe; and instead of having by long use worn this out, she had preserved it wonderfully fresh in advancing years. But, notwithstanding the contrast and seemingly incompatible difference between this aunt and niece, the foundations of their characters both being good, sound and, true, they lived on together well, and loved each other dearly. They had seldom differed so much on any point as in the present case, as to the treatment of their patient and their guest. Scarcely a day passed in which they did not come to some mutual remonstrance; and sometimes when she was by, which was not pleasant to her, as may be imagined. Yet perhaps even these little altercations and annoyances, though they tried Helen's temper or grieved her heart at the moment, were of use to her upon the whole, by drawing her out of herself. Besides, these daily vicissitudes – made by human temper, manner, and character – supplied in some sort the total want of events, and broke the monotony of these tedious months.

The General's bulletins, however, became at last more favourable: Mr Churchill was decidedly better; his physician hoped he might soon be pronounced out of danger. The General said nothing of Beauclerc, but that he was, he believed, still at Paris. And from this time forward no more letters came from Beauclerc to Helen; as his hopes of Churchill's recovery increased, he expected every day to be released from his banishment, and was resolved to write no more till he could say that he was free. But Helen, though she did not allow it to herself, felt this deeply: she thought that her determined silence had at last convinced him that all pursuit of her was vain; and that he submitted to her rejection: she told herself it was what should be, and yet she felt it bitterly. Lady Cecilia's letters did not mention him, indeed they scarcely told anything; they had become short and constrained: the General, she said, advised her to go out more, and her letters often concluded in haste, with 'Carriage at the door,' and all the usual excuses of a London life.

One day when Helen was sitting intently drawing, Miss Clarendon said 'Helen!' so suddenly that she started and looked round; Miss Clarendon was seated on a low stool at her aunt's feet, with one arm thrown over her great dog's neck; he had laid his head on her lap, and resting on him, she looked up with a steadiness, a fixity of repose, which brought to Helen's mind Raphael's beautiful figure of Fortitude leaning on her lion; she thought she had never before seen Miss Clarendon look so handsome, so graceful, so interesting; she took care not to say so, however.

'Helen!' continued Miss Clarendon, 'do you remember the time when I was at Clarendon Park and quitted it so abruptly?

My reasons were good, whatever my manner was; the opinion of the world I am not apt to fear for myself, or even for my brother, but to the whispers of conscience I do listen. Helen! I was conscious that certain feelings in my mind were too strong, – in me, you would scarcely believe it – too tender. I had no reason to think that Granville Beauclerc liked me; it was therefore utterly unfit that I should think of him: I felt this, I left Clarendon Park, and from that moment I have refused myself the pleasure of his society, I have altogether ceased to think of him. This is the only way to conquer a hopeless attachment. But you, Helen, though you have commanded him never to attempt to see you again, have not been able to command your own mind. Since Mr Churchill is so much better, you expect that he will soon be pronounced out of danger – you expect that Mr Beauclerc will come over – come here, and be at your feet!'

'I expect nothing,' said Helen in a faltering voice, and then added resolutely, 'I cannot foresee what Mr Beauclerc may do; but of this be assured, Miss Clarendon, that until I stand as I once stood, and as I deserve to stand, in the opinion of your brother; unless, above all, I can bring *proofs* to Granville's confiding heart that I have ever been unimpeachable of conduct and of mind, and in all but one circumstance true – true as yourself, Esther – never, never, though your brother and all the world consented, never till I myself felt that I was *proved* to be as worthy to be his wife as I think I am, would I consent to marry him – no, not though my heart were to break.'

'I believe it,' said Mrs Pennant; 'and I wish – oh, how I wish – '

'That Lady Cecilia were hanged, as she deserves,' said Miss Clarendon; 'so do I, I am sure; but that is nothing to the present purpose.'

'No, indeed,' said Helen.

'Helen!' continued Esther, 'remember that Lady Blanche Forrester is at Paris.'

Helen shrank.

'Lady Cecilia tells you there is no danger; I say there is.'

'Why should you say so, my dear Esther?' said her aunt.

'Has not this friend of yours always deceived, misled you, Helen?'

'She can have no motive for deceiving me in this,' said Helen: 'I believe her.'

'Believe her then!' cried Miss Clarendon; 'believe her, and do not believe me, and take the consequences: I have done.'

Helen sighed, but though she might feel the want of the charm of Lady Cecilia's suavity of manner, of her agreeable, and her agreeing temper, yet she felt the safe solidity of principle in her present friend, and admired, esteemed, and loved, without fear of change, her unblenching truth. Pretty ornaments of gold cannot be worked out of the native ore; to fashion the rude mass some alloy must be used, and when the slight filigree of captivating manner comes to be tested against the sterling worth of unalloyed sincerity, weighed in the just balance of adversity, we are glad to seize the solid gold, and leave the ornaments to those that they deceive.

The fear about Lady Blanche Forrester was, however, soon set at rest, and this time Lady Cecilia was right. A letter from her to Helen announced that Lady Blanche was married! — actually married, and not to Granville Beauclerc, but to some other English gentleman at Paris, no matter whom. Lord Beltravers and Madame de St Cymon, disappointed, had returned to London; Lady Cecilia had seen Lord Beltravers, and heard the news from him. There could be no doubt of the truth of the intelligence, and scarcely did Helen herself rejoice in it with more sincerity than did Miss Clarendon, and Helen loved her for her candour as well as for her sympathy.

Time passed; week after week rolled away. At last General Clarendon announced to his sister, but without one word to Helen, that Mr Churchill was pronounced out of danger. The news had been sent to his ward, the General said, and he expected Granville would return from his banishment immediately.

Quite taken up in the first tumult of her feelings at this intelligence, Helen scarcely observed that she had no letter from Cecilia. But even aunt Pennant was obliged to confess, in reply to her niece's observation, that this was 'certainly very odd; but we shall soon hear some explanation, I hope.'

Miss Clarendon shook her head; she said that she had always thought how matters would end; she judged from her brother's letters that he began to find out that he was not the happiest of men. Yet nothing to that effect was ever said by him; one phrase only excepted, in his letter to her on her last birthday, which began with, 'In our happy days, my dear Esther.'

Miss Clarendon said nothing to Helen on this subject; she refrained altogether from mentioning Lady Cecilia.

Two, three post-days passed without bringing any letter to Helen. The fourth, very early in the morning long before the usual time for the arrival of the post, Rose came into her room with a letter in her hand, saying, 'From General Clarendon, ma'am. His own man, Mr Cockburn, has just this minute arrived, ma'am – from London.'

With a trembling hand Helen tore the letter open: not one word from General Clarendon! It was only a cover, containing two notes; one from Lord Davenant to the General, the other from Lady Davenant to Helen.

Lord Davenant said that Lady Davenant's health had declined so alarmingly after their arrival at Petersburg that he had insisted upon her return to England, and that, as soon as the object of his mission was accomplished, he should immediately follow her. A vessel, he said, containing letters from England had been lost, so that they were in total ignorance of what had occurred at home; and indeed it appeared from the direction of Lady Davenant's note to Helen, written on her landing in England, that she had left Russia without knowing that the marriage had been broken off, or that Helen had quitted General Clarendon's. She wrote – 'Let me see you and Granville once more before I die. Be in London, at my own house, to meet me. I shall be there as soon as I can be moved.'

The initials only of her name were signed. Elliott added a postscript, saying that her lady had suffered much from an unusually long passage, and that she was not sure what day they could be in town.

There was nothing from Lady Cecilia. Cockburn said that her ladyship had not been at home when he set out; that his master had ordered him to travel all night, to get to Llansillen as fast as possible, and to make no delay in delivering the letter to Miss Stanley.

To set out instantly, to be in town at her house to meet Lady Davenant, was, of course, Helen's immediate determination. General Clarendon had sent his travelling carriage for her; and under the circumstances, her friends could have no wish but to speed her departure. Miss Clarendon expressed surprise at there being no letter from Lady Cecilia, and would see and question Cockburn herself; but nothing more was to be learned than what he had already told, that the packet from Lady Davenant had come by express to his master after Lady Cecilia had driven out, as it had been her custom of late, almost every day, to Kensington, to see her child. Nothing could be more natural, Mrs Pennant thought, and she only wondered at Esther's unconvinced look of suspicion. 'Nothing, surely, can be more natural, my dear Esther.' To which Esther replied, 'Very likely, ma'am.'

Helen was too much hurried and too much engrossed by the one idea of Lady Davenant to think of what they had said. At parting she had scarcely time even to thank her two friends for all their kindness, but they understood her feelings, and, as Miss Clarendon said, words on that point were unnecessary. Aunt Pennant embraced her again and again, and then let her going, saying, 'I must not detain you, my dear.'

'But I must,' said Miss Clarendon, 'for one moment. There is one point on which my parting words are necessary. Helen! keep clear of Lady Cecilia's affairs, whatever they may be. Hear none of her secrets.'

Helen wished she had never heard any; did not believe there were any more to hear; but she promised herself and Miss Clarendon that she would observe this excellent counsel.

And now she was in the carriage, and on her road to town. And now she had leisure to breathe, and to think, and to feel. Her thoughts and feelings, however, could be only repetitions of fears and hopes about Lady Davenant, and uncertainty and dread of what would happen when she should require explanation of all that had occurred in her absence. And how would Lady Cecilia be able to meet her mother's penetration? – ill or well, Lady Davenant was so clear-sighted. 'And how shall I,' thought Helen, 'without plunging deeper in deceit, avoid revealing the truth? Shall I assist Cecilia to deceive her mother in her last moments; or shall I break my promise, betray Cecilia's secret, and at last be the death of her mother by the shock?' It is astonishing how often the mind can go over the same thoughts and feelings without coming to any conclusion, any ease from racking suspense. In the meantime, on rolled the carriage, and Cockburn, according to his master's directions, got her over the ground with all conceivable speed.

CHAPTER 45

WHEN THEY WERE WITHIN the last stage of London the carriage suddenly stopped, and Helen, who was sitting far back, deep in her endless reverie, started forward – Cockburn was at the door.

'My lady, coming to meet you, Miss Stanley.'

It was Cecilia herself. But Cecilia so changed in her whole appearance that Helen would scarcely have known her. She was so much struck that she hardly knew what was said: but the carriage-doors were opened, and Lady Cecilia was beside her, and Cockburn shut the door without permitting one moment's delay, and on they drove.

Lady Cecilia was excessively agitated. Helen had not power to utter a word, and was glad that Cecilia went on speaking very fast; though she spoke without appearing to know well what she was saying: of Helen's goodness in coming so quickly, of her fears that she would never have been in time – 'but she was in time, – her mother had not yet arrived. Clarendon had gone to meet her on the road, she believed – she was not quite certain.'

That seemed very extraordinary to Helen. 'Not quite certain?' said she.

'No, I am not,' replied Cecilia, and she coloured; her very pale cheek flushed; but she explained not at all, she left that subject, and spoke of the friends Helen had left at Llansillen – then suddenly of her mother's return – her hopes – her fears – and then, without going on to the natural idea of seeing her mother, and of how soon they should see her, began to talk of Beauclerc – of

Mr Churchill's being quite out of danger – of the General's expectation of Beauclerc's immediate return. 'And then, my dearest Helen,' said she, 'all will be –

'Oh! I do not know how it will be!' cried she, her tone changing suddenly; and, from the breathless hurry in which she had been running on, sinking at once to a low broken tone and speaking very slowly. 'I cannot tell what will become of any of us. We can never be happy again – any one of us. And it is all my doing – and I cannot die. O Helen, when I tell you – '

She stopped, and Miss Clarendon's warning, counsel, all her own past experience, were full in Helen's mind; and after a moment's silence, she stopped Cecilia just as she seemed to have gathered power to speak, and begged that she would not tell her anything that was to be kept secret. She could not, would not, hear any secrets; she turned her head aside, and let down the glass, and looked out, as if determined not to be compelled to receive this confidence.

'Have you, then, lost all interest, all affection, for me, Helen? I deserve it! But you need not fear me now, Helen: I have done with deception, would to Heaven I had never begun with it!'

It was the tone and look of truth – she steadily fixed her eyes upon Helen – and instead of the bright beams that used to play in those eyes, there was now a dark deep-seated sorrow, almost despair. Helen was touched to the heart: it was indeed impossible for her – it would have been impossible for any one who had any feeling – to have looked upon Lady Cecilia Clarendon at that moment, and to have recollected what she had so lately been, without pity. The friend of her childhood looked upon her with all the poignant anguish of compassion –

'O my dear Cecilia! how changed!'

Helen was not sensible that she uttered the words 'how changed!'

'Changed! yes, I believe I am,' said Lady Cecilia, in a calm voice, 'very much changed in appearance, but much more in reality; my mind is more altered than my person. O Helen! if you could see into my mind at this moment, and know how completely it is changed – but it is all in vain now! You have suffered, and suffered for me! but your sufferings could not equal mine. You lost love and happiness, but still conscious of deserving both: I had both at my command, and I could enjoy neither under the consciousness, the torture, of remorse.'

Helen threw her arms round her, and exclaimed, 'Do not think of me! – all will be well – since you have resolved on the truth, all will yet be well.'

Cecilia sighed deeply and went on. 'I am sure, Helen, you were surprised that my child was born alive; at least I was. I believe its mother had not feeling enough to endanger its exist- ence. Well, Clarendon has that comfort at all events, and, as a boy, it will never put him in mind of his mother. Well, Helen, I had hopes of myself to the last minute; I really and truly hoped, as I told you, that I should have had courage to tell him all when I put the child into his arms. But his joy! – I could not dash his joy – I could not! – and then I thought I never could. I knew you would give me up; I gave up all hope of myself. I was very unhappy, and Clarendon thought I was very ill; and I acknowledge that I was anxious about you, and let all the blame fall on you, innocent, generous creature! I heard my husband perpetually upbraiding you when he saw me ill – all, he said, the consequences of your falsehood – and all the time I knew it was my own.

'My dear Helen, it is impossible to tell you all the daily, hourly necessities for dissimulation which occurred. Every day, you know, we were to send to inquire for Mr Churchill; and every day when Clarendon brought me the bulletin, he pitied me, and blamed you; and the double-dealing in my countenance he never suspected – always interpreted favourably. Oh, such con- fidence as he had in me – and how it has been wasted, abused! Then letters from Beauclerc – how I bore to hear them read I cannot conceive: and at each time that I escaped, I rejoiced and reproached myself – and reproached myself and rejoiced. I suc- ceeded in every effort at deception, and was cursed by my own success. Encouraged to proceed, I soon went on without shame and without fear. The General heard me defending you against the various reports which my venomous cousin had circulated, and he only admired what he called "my amiable zeal." His love for me increased, but it gave me no pleasure: for, Helen, now I am going to tell you an extraordinary turn which my mind took, for which I cannot account – I can hardly believe it – it seems out of human nature – my love for him decreased! – not only because I felt that he would hate me if he discovered my deceit, but because he was lowered in my estimation! I had always had, as everybody has, even my mother, the highest opinion of his judgment. To that judgment I had always looked up; it had raised me in my own opinion; it was a motive to me to be equal to what he thought me: but now that motive was gone, I no longer looked up to him; his credulous affection had blinded his judgment – he was my dupe! I could not reverence – I could not love one who was my dupe. But I cannot tell you how shocked I was at myself when I felt my love for him decrease every time I saw him.

'I thought myself a monster; I had grown used to everything but that – that I could not endure; it was a darkness of the mind – a coldness; it was as if the sun had gone out of the universe; it was more – it was worse – it was as if I was alone in the world. Home was a desert to me. I went out every evening; sometimes, but rarely, Clarendon accompanied me: he had become more retired; his spirits had declined with mine; and though he was glad I should go out and amuse myself, yet he was always exact as to the hours of my return. I was often late – later than I ought to have been, and I made a multitude of paltry excuses; this it was, I believe, which first shook his faith in my truth; but I was soon detected in a more decided failure.

'You know I never had the least taste for play of any kind: you may remember I used to be scolded for never minding what I was about at *écarté*; in short, I never had the least love for it – it wearied me; but now that my spirits were gone it was a sort of intoxication in which I cannot say I indulged – for it was no indulgence – but to which I had recourse. Louisa Castlefort, you know, was always fond of play – got into her first difficulties by that means – she led me on. I lost a good deal of money to her, and did not care about it as long as I could pay; but presently it came to a time when I could not pay without applying to the General: I applied to him, but under false pretence – to pay this bill or that, or to buy something, which I never bought: this occurred so often, and to such an extent that he suspected – he discovered how it went; he told me so. He spoke in that low, suppressed, that terrible voice which I had heard once before; I said, I know not what, in deprecation of his anger. "I am not angry, Cecilia," said he. I caught his hand and would have detained him; he withdrew that hand, and, looking at me, exclaimed, "Beautiful creature! half those charms would I give for *truth!*" He left the room, and there was contempt in his look.

'All my love – all my reverence – returned for him in an instant; but what could I say? He never recurred to the subject; and now, when I saw the struggle in his mind, my passion for him returned in all its force.

'People who flattered me often, you know, said I was fascinating, and I determined to use my powers of fascination to regain my husband's heart; how little I knew that heart! I dressed to please him – oh! I never dressed myself with such care in my most coquettish days; – I gave a splendid ball; I dressed to please him – he used to be delighted with my dancing: he had said, no matter what, but I wanted to make him say it – feel it – again; he neither said nor felt it. I saw him standing looking at me, and at the close of the dance I heard from him one sigh. I was more in love with him than when first we were married, and he saw it, but that did not restore me to his confidence – his esteem; nothing could have done that but – what I had not. One step in dissimulation led to another.

'After Lord Beltravers returned from Paris on Lady Blanche's marriage, I used to meet him continually at Louisa Castlefort's. As for play, that was over with me for ever, but I went to Louisa's continually, because it was the gayest house I could go to; I used to meet Lord Beltravers there, and he pretended to pay me a vast deal of attention, to which I was utterly indifferent, but his object was to push his sister into society again by my means. He took advantage of that unfortunate note which I had received from Madame de St Cymon when she was at Old Forest; he wanted me to admit her among my acquaintance; he urged it in every possible way, and was excessively vexed that it would not do: not that he cared for her; he often spoke of her in a way that shocked me, but it hurt his pride that she should be excluded from the society to which her rank entitled her. I had met her at Louisa's once or twice; but when I find that for her brother's sake she was always to be invited, I resolved to go there no more, and I made a merit of this with Clarendon. He was pleased; he said, 'That is well, that is right, my dear Cecilia.' And he went out more with me. One night at the opera, the Comtesse de St Cymon was in the box opposite to us, no lady with her, only some gentlemen. She watched me; I did all I could to avoid her eye, but at an unlucky moment she caught mine, bent forward, and had the assurance to bow. The General snatched the open-glass from my hand, made sure who it was, and then said to me,

' "How does that woman dare to claim your notice, Lady Cecilia? I am afraid there must have been some encouragement on your part."

' "None," said I, "nor ever shall be; you see I take no notice."

' "But you must have taken notice, or this could never be."

' "No indeed!" persisted I.

'Helen! I really forgot at the moment that first unfortunate note. An instant afterwards I recollected it, and the visit about the cameos, but that was not my fault. I had, to be sure, dropped a card in return at her door, and I ought to have mentioned that, but I really did not recollect it till the words had passed my lips, and then it was too late, and I did not like to go back and spoil my case by an exception. The General did not look quite satisfied; he did not receive my assertions as implicitly as formerly. He left the box afterwards to speak to some one, and while he was gone in came Lord Beltravers. After some preliminary nothings, he went directly to the point; and said in an assured manner, "I believe you do not know my sister at this distance. She has been endeavouring to catch your eye."

' "The Comtesse de St Cymon does me too much honour," said I, with a slight inclination of the head, and elevation of the eyebrow, which spoke sufficiently plainly.

'Unabashed, and with a most provoking, almost sneering look he replied, "Madame de St Cymon had wished to say a few words to your ladyship on your own account; am I to understand this cannot be?"

' "On my own account?" said I, "I do not in the least understand your lordship." "I am not sure," said he, "that I perfectly comprehend it. But I know that you sometimes drive to Kensington, and sometimes take a turn in the gardens there. My sister lives at Kensington, and could not she, without infringing etiquette, meet you in your walk, and have the honour of a few words with you? Something she wants to say to you," and here he lowered his voice, "about a locket, and Colonel D'Aubigny."

'Excessively frightened, and hearing some one at the door, I answered, "I do not know, I believe I shall drive to Kensington to-morrow." He bowed delighted, and relieved me from his presence that instant. The moment afterwards General Clarendon came in. He asked me, "Was not that Lord Beltravers whom I met?"

' "Yes," said I; "he came to reproach me for not noticing his sister, and I answered him in such a manner as to make him clear that there was no hope."

' "You did right," said he, "if you did so." My mind was in such confusion that I could not quite command my countenance, and I put up my fan as if the lights hurt me.

' "Cecilia," said he, "take care what you are about. Remember, it is not my request only, but my command to my wife" (he laid solemn stress on the words) "that she should have no communication with this woman."

' "My dear Clarendon, I have not the least wish."

' "I do not ask what your wishes may be: I require only your obedience."

'Never have I heard such austere words from him. I turned to the stage, and I was glad to seize the first minute I could to get away. But what was to be done? If I did not go to Kensington, there was this locket, and I knew not what, standing out against me. I knew that this wretched woman had had Colonel D'Aubigny in her train abroad, and supposed that he must –treacherous profligate as he was – have given the locket to her, and now I was so afraid of its coming to Clarendon's eyes or ears! – and yet why should I have feared his knowing about it? Colonel D'Aubigny stole it, just as he stole the picture. I had got it for you, do you recollect?'

'Perfectly,' said Helen, 'and your mother missed it.'

'Yes,' continued Lady Cecilia. 'Oh that I had had the sense to do nothing about it! But I was so afraid of its somehow bringing everything to light: my cowardice – my conscience – my consciousness of that first fatal falsehood before my marriage has haunted me at the most critical moments: it has risen against me, and stood like an evil spirit threatening me from the right path.

'I went to Kensington, trusting to my own good fortune, which had so often stood me in stead; but Madame de St Cymon was too cunning for me, and so interested, so mean, she actually bargained for giving up the locket. She hinted that she knew Colonel D'Aubigny had never been your lover, and ended by saying that she had not the locket with her; and though I made her understand that the General would never allow me to receive her at my own house, yet she "hoped I could manage an introduction for her to some of my friends, and that she would bring the locket on Monday, if I would in the meantime try, at least with Lady Emily Greville and Mrs Holdernesse."

'I felt her meanness, and yet I was almost as mean myself, for I agreed to do what I could. Monday came, Clarendon saw me as I was going out, and, as he handed me into the carriage, he asked me where I was going. To Kensington I said, and added – O Helen, I am ashamed to tell you, I added, – I am going to see my child. And there I found Madame de St Cymon, and I had to tell her of my failure with Lady Emily and Mrs Holdernesse. I softened their refusal as much as I could, but I might have spared myself the trouble, for she only retorted by something about English prudery. At this moment a shower of rain came on, and she insisted upon my taking her home; "Come in," said she, when the carriage stopped at her door; "if you will come in, I will give it to you now, and you need not have the trouble of calling again." I had the folly to yield, though I saw that it was a trick to decoy me into her house, and to make it pass for a visit. It all flashed upon me, and yet I could not resist, for I thought I must obtain the locket at all hazards. I resolved to get it from her before I left the house, and then I thought all would be finished.

'She looked triumphant as she followed me into her saloon, and gave a malicious smile, which seemed to say, "You see you are visiting me after all." After some nonsensical conversation, meant to detain me, I pressed for the locket, and she produced it: it was indeed the very one that had been made for you. But just at that instant, while she still held it in her hand, the door suddenly opened, and Clarendon stood opposite to me!

'I heard Madame de St Cymon's voice, but of what she said I have no idea. I heard nothing but the single word "rain," and with scarcely strength to articulate, I attempted to follow up that excuse. Clarendon's look of contempt! But he commanded himself, advanced calmly to me, and said, "I came to Kensington with these letters; they have just arrived by express. Lady Davenant is in England – she is ill." He gave me the packet, and left the room, and I heard the sound of his horse's feet for the next instant as he rode off. I broke from Madame de St Cymon, forgetting the locket and everything. I asked my servants which way the General had gone. "To town." I perceived that he must have been going to look for me at the nurse's, and had seen the carriage at Madame de St Cymon's door. I hasted after him, and then I recollected that I had left the locket on the table at Madame de St Cymon's, that locket for which I had hazarded – lost – everything! The moment I reached home, I ran to Clarendon's room; he was not there, and oh, Helen, I have not seen him since!

'From some orders which he left about horses, I suppose he went to meet my mother. I dared not follow him. She had desired me to wait for her arrival at her own house. All yesterday, all last night, Helen, what I have suffered! I could not bear it any longer, and then I thought of coming to meet you. I thought I must see you before my mother arrived – my mother! but Clarendon will not have met her till to-day. O Helen! you feel all that I fear – all that I foresee.'

Lady Cecilia sank back, and Helen, overwhelmed with all she had heard, could for some time only pity her in silence; and at last could only suggest that the General would not have time for any private communication with Lady Davenant, as her woman would be in the carriage with her, and the General was on horse-back.

It was late in the day before they reached town. As they came near Grosvenor Square, Cockburn inquired whether they were to drive home, or to Lady Davenant's.

'To my mother's, certainly, and as fast as you can.'

Lady Davenant had not arrived, but there were packages in the hail, her courier, and her servants, who said that General Clarendon was with her, but not in the carriage; he had sent them on. No message for Lady Cecilia, but that Lady Davenant would be in town this night.

Tonight – some hours still of suspense! As long as there were arrangements to be made, anything to do or to think of but that meeting of which they dared not think, it was endurable, but too soon all was settled; nothing to be done, but to wait and watch, to hear the carriages roll past, and listen, and start, and look at each other, and sink back disappointed. Lady Cecilia walked from the sofa to the window, and looked out, and back again – continually, continually, till at last Helen begged her to sit down. She sat down before an old pianoforte of her mother's, on which her eyes fixed; it was one on which she had often played with Helen when they were children. 'Happy, innocent days,' said she; 'never shall we be so happy again, Helen! But I cannot think of it'; she rose hastily, and threw herself on the sofa.

A servant, who had been watching at the hall-door, came in – 'The carriage, my lady! Lady Davenant is coming.'

Lady Cecilia started up; they ran downstairs; the carriage stopped, and in the imperfect light they saw the figure of Lady

Davenant, scarcely altered, leaning upon General Clarendon's arm. The first sound of her voice was feebler, softer, than formerly – quite tender, when she said, as she embraced them both by turns, 'My dear children!'

'You have accomplished your journey, Lady Davenant, better than you expected,' said the General.

Something struck her in the tone of his voice. She turned quickly, saw her daughter lay her hand upon his arm, and saw that arm withdrawn!

They all entered the saloon – it was a blaze of light; Lady Davenant, shading her eyes with her hand, looked round at the countenances, which she had not yet seen. Lady Cecilia shrank back. The penetrating eyes turned from her, glanced at Helen, and fixed upon the General.

'What is all this?' cried she.

Helen threw her arms round Lady Davenant. 'Let us think of you first, and only – be calm.'

Lady Davenant broke from her, and pressing forwards exclaimed, 'I must see my daughter – if I have still a daughter! Cecilia!'

The General moved. Lady Cecilia, who had sunk upon a chair behind him, attempted to rise. Lady Davenant stood opposite to her; the light was now full upon her face and figure; and her mother saw how it was changed! and looking back at Helen, she said in a low, awful tone, 'I see it; the black spot has spread!'

Scarcely had Lady Davenant pronounced these words, when she was seized with violent spasms. The General had but just time to save her from falling; he could not leave her. All was terror! Even her own woman, so long used to these attacks, said it was the worst she had ever seen, and for some time evidently feared it would terminate fatally. At last slowly she came to herself, but perfectly in possession of her intellects, she sat up, looked round, saw the agony in her daughter's countenance, and holding out her hand to her, said, 'Cecilia, if there is anything that I ought to know, it should be said now.'

Cecilia caught her mother's hand, and threw herself upon her knees. 'Helen, Helen, stay!' cried she; 'do not go, Clarendon!'

He stood leaning against the chimneypiece, motionless, while Cecilia, in a faltering voice, began; her voice gaining strength, she went on, and poured out all – even from the very beginning, that first suppression of the truth, that first cowardice, then all that followed from that one falsehood – all – even to the last degradation, when in the power, in the presence, of that bad woman, her husband found and left her. She shuddered as she came to the thought of that last look of his, and not daring, not having once dared while she spoke, to turn towards him, her eyes fixed upon her mother's; but as she finished speaking, her head sank, she laid her face on the sofa beside her; she felt her mother's arm thrown over her and she sobbed convulsively.

There was silence.

'I have still a daughter!' were the first words that broke the silence. 'Not such as I might have had, but that is my own fault.'

'O mother!'

'I have still a daughter!' repeated Lady Davenant. 'There is,' continued she, turning to General Clarendon, 'there is a redeeming power in truth. She may yet be more worthy to be your wife than she has ever yet been!'

'Never!' exclaimed the General. His countenance was rigid as iron; then suddenly it relaxed, and going up to Helen, he said,

'I have done you injustice, Miss Stanley. I have been misled. I have done you injustice, and by Heaven! I will do you public justice, cost me what it will. Beauclerc will be in England in a few days; at the altar I will give you to him publicly; in the face of all the world will I mark my approbation of his choice; publicly will I repair the wrong I have done you. I will see his happiness and yours before I leave England for ever!'

Lady Cecilia started up: 'Clarendon!' was all she could say.

'Yes, Lady Cecilia Clarendon,' said he, all the stem fixedness of his face returning at once – 'Yes, Lady Cecilia Clarendon, we separate, now and for ever.'

Then turning from her, he addressed Lady Davenant. 'I shall be ordered on some foreign service. Your daughter, Lady Davenant, will remain with you, while I am still in England, unless you wish otherwise – '

'Leave my daughter with me, my dear General, till my death,' said Lady Davenant. She spoke calmly, but the General, after a respectful – an affectionate pressure of the hand she held out to him, said, 'That may be far distant, I trust in God, and we shall at all events meet again the day of Helen's marriage.'

'And if that day is to be a happy day to me,' cried Helen, 'to me or to your own beloved ward, General Clarendon, it must be happy to Cecilia!'

'As happy as she has left it in my power to make her. When I am gone, my fortune – '

'Name it not as happiness for my daughter,' interrupted Lady Davenant, 'or you do her injustice, General Clarendon.'

'I name it but to do her justice,' said he. 'It is all that she has left it in my power to give'; and then his long-suppressed passion suddenly bursting forth, he turned to Cecilia. 'All I can give to one so false – false from the first moment to the last – false to me – to me! who so devotedly, fondly, blindly loved her!' He rushed out of the room.

Then Lady Davenant, taking her daughter in her arms, said, 'My child, return to me!'

She sank back exhausted. Mrs Elliott was summoned, she wished them all out of the room, and said so; but Lady Davenant would have her daughter stay beside her, and with Cecilia's hand in hers she fell into a profound slumber.

CHAPTER 46

ON AWAKENING IN THE MORNING, after some long-expected event has happened, we feel in doubt whether it has really occurred, or whether it is all a dream. Then comes the awful sense of waking truth, and the fear that what has been done, or said, is irremediable, and then the astonishment that it really is done.

'It is over!' Helen repeated to herself; repeated aloud, before she could well bring herself from that state of half-belief, before she could recover her stunned faculties.

Characters which she thought she perfectly understood had each appeared, in these new circumstances, different from what she had expected. From Cecilia she had scarcely hoped, even at the last moment, for such perfect truth in her confession. From Lady Davenant not so much indulgence, not all that tenderness for her daughter. From the General, less violence of expression, more feeling for Cecilia; he had not allowed the merit of her candour, her courage, at the last. It was a perfectly voluntary confession, all that concerned Colonel D'Aubigny and the letters could never have been known to the General by any other means. Disappointed love, confidence duped, and his pride of honour, had made him forget himself in anger, even to cruelty. Helen thought he would feel this hereafter, fancied he must feel it even now, but that, though he might relent, he would not recede; though he might regret that he had made the determination, he would certainly abide by it; that which he had resolved to do would certainly be done, – the separation between him and Cecilia would take place. And though all was clear and bright in Helen's own prospects, the General's esteem restored, his approbation to be publicly marked, Beauclerc to be convinced of her perfect innocence! Beauclerc, freed from all fear and danger, returning all love and joy; yet she could not be happy – it was all mixed with bitterness, anguish for Cecilia.

She had so often so forcibly urged her to this confession! and now it was made, did Helen regret that it was made? No, independently of her own cleared character, she was satisfied, even for Cecilia's sake, for it was right, whatever were the consequences; it was right, and in the confusion and discordance of her thoughts and feelings, this was the only fixed point. To this conclusion she had come, but had not been able further to settle her mind, when she was told that Lady Davenant was now awake, and wished to see her.

Lady Davenant, renovated by sleep, appeared to Helen, even when she saw her by daylight, scarcely altered in her looks. There was the same life, and energy, and elasticity, and strength, Helen hoped, not only of mind, but of body, and quick as that hope rose, as she stood beside her bed, and looked upon her, Lady Davenant marked it, and said, 'You are mistaken, my dear Helen, I shall not last long; I am now to consider how I am to make the most of the little life that remains. How to repair as far as may be, as far as can be, in my last days, the errors of my youth! You know, Helen, what I mean, and it is now no time to waste words, therefore I shall not begin by wasting upon you, Helen, any reproaches. Foolish, generous, weak creature that you are, and as the best of human beings will ever be – I must be content with you as you are; and so,' continued she, in a playful tone, 'we must love one another, perhaps all the better, for not being too perfect. And indeed, my poor child, you have been well punished already, and the worst of criminals need not be punished twice. Of the propensity to sacrifice your own happiness for others you will never be cured, but you will, I trust, in future, when I am gone never to return, be true to yourself. Now as to my daughter – '

Lady Davenant then went over with Helen every circumstance in Cecilia's confession, and showed how, in the midst of the shock she had felt at the disclosure of so much falsehood, hope for her daughter's future truth had risen in her mind even from the courage, and fullness, and exactness of her confession. 'And it is not,' continued she, 'a sudden reformation; I have no belief in sudden reformations. I think I see that this change in Cecilia's mind has been some time working out by her own experience of the misery, the folly, the degradation of deceit.'

Helen earnestly confirmed this from her own observations, and from the expressions which had burst forth in the fullness of Cecilia's heart and strength of her conviction, when she told her all that had passed in her mind.

'That is well!' pursued Lady Davenant; 'but principles cannot be depended upon till confirmed by habit; and Cecilia's nature is so variable – impressions on her are easily, even deeply made, but all in sand; they may shift with the next tide – may be blown away by the next wind.'

'Oh no,' exclaimed Helen, 'there is no danger of that. I see the impression deepening, every hour, from your kindness and – ' Helen hesitated, 'and besides – '

'*Besides*,' said Lady Davenant, 'usually comes as the *arrière-ban* [1] of weak reasons; you mean to say that the sight of my sufferings must strengthen, must confirm, all her principles – her taste for truth. Yes,' continued she, in her most firm tone; 'Cecilia's being with me during my remaining days will be painful but salutary to her. She sees, as you do, that all the falsehood meant to save me has been in vain; that at last the shock has only hastened my end: it must be so, Helen. Look at it steadily, in the best point of view – the evil you cannot avert; take the good and be thankful for it.'

And Cecilia – how did she feel? Wretched she was, but still in her wretchedness there was within her a relieved conscience and the sustaining power of truth; and she had now the support of her mother's affection, and the consolation of feeling that she had at last done Helen justice! To her really generous, affection-ate disposition, there was in the return of her feelings to their

---

[1] rearguard

natural course an indescribable sense of relief. Broken, crushed, as were all her own hopes, her sympathy, even in the depths of her misery, now went pure, free from any windings of deceit, direct to Helen's happy prospects, in which she shared with all the eagerness of her warm heart.

Beauclerc arrived, found the General at home expecting him, and in his guardian's countenance and voice he saw and heard only what was natural to the man. The General was prepared, and Beauclerc was himself in too great impatience to hear the facts, to attend much to the manner in which things were told.

'Lady Davenant has returned ill; her daughter is with her, and Helen – '

'And Helen – '

'And you may be happy, Beauclerc, if there be truth in woman,' said the General. 'Go to her – you will find I can do justice. Go, and return when you can tell me that your wedding-day is fixed. And, Beauclerc,' he called after him, 'let it be as soon as possible.'

'The only unnecessary advice my dear guardian has ever given me,' Beauclerc, laughing, replied.

The General's prepared composure had not calculated upon this laugh, this slight jest; his features gave way. Beauclerc, struck with a sudden change in the General's countenance, released his hand from the congratulatory shake in which its power failed. The General turned away as if to shun inquiry, and Beauclerc, however astonished, respected his feelings, and said no more. He hastened to Lady Davenant with all a lover's speed – with all a lover's joy he saw the first expression in Helen's eyes; and with all a friend's sorrow for Lady Davenant and for the General, heard all that was to be told of Lady Cecilia's affairs: her mother undertook the explanation, Cecilia herself did not appear.

In the first rush of Beauclerc's joy in Helen's cleared fame, he was ready to forgive all the deceit; yes, to forgive all; but it was such forgiveness as contempt can easily grant, which can hardly be received by any soul not lost to honour. This Lady Davenant felt, and felt so keenly, that Helen trembled for her: she remained silent, pressing her hand upon her heart, which told her sense of approaching danger. It was averted by the calmness, the truth, the justice with which Helen spoke to Beauclerc of Cecilia. As she went on, Lady Davenant's colour returned and Beauclerc's ready sympathy went with her as far as she pleased, till she came to one point, from which he instantly started back. Helen proposed, if Beauclerc would consent, to put off their marriage till the General should be reconciled to Cecilia.

'Attempt it not, Helen,' cried Lady Davenant; 'delay not for any consideration. Your marriage must be as soon as possible, for my sake, for Cecilia's — mark me! — for Cecilia's sake, as soon as possible let it be; it is but justice that her conscience should be so far relieved, let her no longer obstruct your union. Let me have the satisfaction of seeing it accomplished; name the day, Helen, I may not have many to live.'

The day, the earliest possible, was named by Helen; and the moment it was settled, Lady Davenant hurried Beauclerc away, saying — 'Return to General Clarendon — spare him suspense — it is all we can do for him.'

The General's wishes in this, and in all that followed, were to be obeyed. He desired that the marriage should be public, that all should be bidden of rank, fashion, and note — all their family connections. Lady Katrine Hawksby he especially named. To do justice to Helen seemed the only pleasurable object now remaining to him. In speaking to Beauclerc, he never once named Lady Cecilia; it seemed a tacit compact between him and Beauclerc that her name should not be pronounced. They talked of Lady Davenant; the General said he did not think her in such danger as she seemed to consider herself to be: his opinion was, he declared, confirmed by his own observation; by the strength of mind and of body which she had shown since her arrival in England. Beauclerc could only hope that he was right; and the General went on to speak of the service upon which he was to be employed; said that all *arrangements*, laying an emphasis upon the word, would be transacted by his man of business. He spoke of what would happen after he quitted England, and left his ward a legacy of some favourite horse which he used to ride at

Clarendon Park, and seemed to take it for granted that Beauclerc and Helen would be sometimes there when he was gone. Then, having cleared his throat several times, the General desired that Lady Cecilia's portrait, which he designated only as 'the picture over the chimneypiece in my room,' should be sent after him. And taking leave of Beauclerc, he set off for Clarendon Park, where he was to remain till the day before the wedding; – the day following he had fixed for his departure from England.

When Beauclerc was repeating this conversation to Helen, Lady Davenant came into the room just as he was telling these last particulars. She remarked the smile, the hope that was excited, but shook her head, and said, 'Raise no false hopes in my daughter's mind, I conjure you'; and she turned the conversation to other subjects. Beauclerc had been to see Mr Churchill, and of that visit Lady Davenant wished to hear.

As to health, Beauclerc said that Mr Churchill had recovered almost perfectly; 'but there remains, and I fear will always remain, a little lameness, not disabling, but disfiguring – an awkward-ness in moving, which, to a man of his personal pretensions, is trying to the temper; but after noticing the impediment as he advanced to meet me, he shook my hand cordially, and smiling, said, "You see I am a marked man; I always wished to be so, you know, so pray do not repent, my good friend." He saw I was too much moved for jesting, then he took it more seriously, but still kindly, assuring me that I had done him real service; it is always of service, he said, to be necessitated to take time for quiet reflection, of which he had had sufficient in his hours of solitary confine-ment – this little adversity had left him leisure to be good.

'And then,' continued Beauclerc, 'Churchill adverting to our foolish quarrel, to clear that off my mind, threw the whole weight of the blame at once comfortably upon the absent – on Beltravers. Churchill said we had indeed been a couple of bravely blind fools; he ought, as he observed, to have recollected in time, that

'Anger is like
A full hot horse, who being allowed his way,
Self-mettle tires him.

'So that was good, and Horace, in perfect good humour with me and himself, and all the world, played on with the past and the future, glad he had no more of his bones to exfoliate; glad, after so many months of failure in "the first intention," to find himself in a whole skin, and me safe returned from transportation – spoke of Helen seriously; said that his conduct to her was the only thing that weighed upon his mind, but he hoped that his sincere penitence, and his months of suffering, would be considered as sufficient atonement for his having brought her name before the public; and he finished by inviting himself to our wedding, if it were only for the pleasure of seeing what sort of face Lady Katrine Hawksby will have upon the occasion. It was told of a celebrated statesman, jealous of his colleagues, Horace says, that every commonly good speech cost him a twinge of the gout; and every uncommonly good one sent him to bed with a regular fit. Now Horace protests that every commonly decent marriage of her acquaintance costs Lady Katrine at least a sad headache; but Miss Stanley's marriage, likely as it is to be so happy after all, as he politely said, foredooms poor Lady Katrine to a month's heart-ache at the least, and a face full ell long.'

Whether in his penitence he had forsworn slander or not, it was plain that Churchill had not lost either his taste, talent, or power of sarcasm, and of this Beauclerc could have given, and in time gave, further illustrations; but it was in a case which came home to him rather too nearly, and on which his reports did not flow quite so fluently – touching Lord Beltravers, it was too tender a subject. Beauclerc was ashamed of himself for having been so deceived when, after all his guardian had done to save his fortune, after all that noble sacrifice had been made, he found that it was to no good end, but for the worst purpose possible. Lord Beltravers, as it was now clear, never had the slightest intention of living in that house of his ancestors on which Beauclerc had lavished his thousands, ay, and tens of thousands; but while he was repairing, and embellishing, and furnishing Old Forest, fit for an English aristocrat of the first water, the Lord Beltravers at the gaming-table pledged it, and lost it, and sold it; and it went to the hammer. This came out in the first fury of Lord Beltravers upon his sister's marriage at Paris: and then and there Beauclerc first came to the perception that his good friend had predestined him and his fortune for the Lady Blanche, whom, all the time, he considered as a fool and a puppet, and for whom he had not the slightest affection: it was all for his own interested purposes.

Beauclerc suddenly opened his eyes wide, and saw it all at once; how it happened that they had never seen it before, notwithstanding all that the General on one side, and Lady Davenant on the other, had done to force them open, was incomprehensible; but, as Lady Davenant observed, 'A sort of cataract comes over the best eyes for a time, and the patient will not suffer himself to be couched; and if you struggle to perform the operation that is to do him good against his will, it is odds but you blind him for life.'

Helen could not, however, understand how Granville could have been so completely deceived, except that it had been impossible for him to imagine the exquisite meanness of that man's mind.

'There,' cried Beauclerc, 'you see my fault was having too little, instead of too much imagination.'

Lady Davenant smiled, and said, 'It has been admirably observed, that "it is among men as among certain tribes of animals, it is sometimes only necessary that one of the herd should step forward and lead the way, to make all the others follow with alacrity and submission"; Lord Mahon and I solve the whole difficulty thus: I suppose that Lord Beltravers, just following Beauclerc's lead, succeeded in persuading him that he was a man of genius and a noble fellow, by allowing all Beauclerc's own paradoxes, adopting all his ultra-original opinions, and, in short, sending him back the image of his own mind, till Granville had been caught by it, and had fairly fallen in love with it – a mental metaphysical Narcissus.

'After all,' continued Lady Davenant, smiling, 'of all the follies of youth, the dangerous folly of trying to do good – that for which you stand convicted – may be the most easily pardoned, the most safely left to time and experience to cure. You know,

Granville, that ever since the time of Alexander the Great's great tutor, the characteristic faults of youth and age have been the "*too much*" and the "*too little*." In youth, the too much confidence in others and in themselves, the too much of enthusiasm – too much of benevolence; – in age, alas! too little. And with this youth, who has the *too much* in everything – what shall we do with him, Helen? Take him, for better for worse, you must; and I must love him as I have done from his childhood, a little while longer – to the end of my life.'

'A little longer, to the end of her life!' said Beauclerc to himself, as leaning on the back of Helen's chair he looked at Lady Davenant. 'I cannot believe that she whom I see before me is passing away, to be with us but a little longer; so full of life as she appears; such energy divine! No, no, she will live, live long!'

And as his eyes looked that hope, Helen caught it, and yet she doubted, and sighed, but still she had hope. Cecilia had none; she was sitting behind her mother; she looked up at Helen, and shook her head; she had seen more of her mother's danger, she had been with her in nights of fearful struggle. She had been with her just after she had written to Lord Davenant what she must have felt to be a farewell letter – a letter, too, which contained the whole history of Cecilia's deception and Helen's difficulties, subjects so agitating that the writing of them had left her mother in such a state of exhaustion that Cecilia could think only with terror for her, yet she exerted all her power over herself to hide her anguish, not only for her mother's but for Helen's sake.

The preparations for the wedding went on, pressed forward by Lady Davenant as urgently as the General could desire. The bridesmaids were to be Lady Emily Greville's younger sister, Lady Susan, and, at Helen's particular request, Miss Clarendon. Full of joy, wonder, and sympathy, in wedding haste Miss Clarendon and Mrs Pennant arrived, both delighted that it was all happily settled for Helen: which most, it was scarcely possible to say; but which most curious as to the means by which it had been settled, it was very possible to see. When Miss Clarendon had secured a private moment with Helen, she began,

'Now tell me – tell me everything about yourself.'

Helen could only repeat what the General had already written to his sister – that he was now convinced that the reports concerning Miss Stanley were false, his esteem restored, his public approbation to be given, Beauclerc satisfied, and her rejection honourably retracted.

'I will ask you no more, Helen, by word or look,' said Esther; 'I understand it all, my brother and Lady Cecilia are separated for life. And now let us go to aunt Pennant: she will not annoy you by her curiosity, but how she will be able to manage her sympathy amongst you with these crossing demands I know not; Lady Cecilia's wretchedness will almost spoil my aunt's joy for you – it cannot be pure joy.'

Pure joy! how far from it Helen's sigh told; and Miss Clarendon had scarcely patience enough with Lady Cecilia to look at her again; had scarcely seconded, at least with good grace, a suggestion of Mrs Pennant's that they should prevail on Lady Cecilia to take a turn in the Park with them, she looked so much in want of fresh air.

'We can go now, my dear Esther, you know, before it is time for that picture sale, at which you are to be before two o'clock.' Lady Davenant desired Cecilia to go. 'Helen will be with me, do, my dear Cecilia, go.'

She went, and before the awkwardness of Miss Clarendon's silence ceased, and before Mrs Pennant had settled which glass or which blind was best up or down, Lady Cecilia burst into tears, thanked aunt Pennant for her sympathy, and now, above the fear of Miss Clarendon – above all fear but that of doing further wrong by concealment, she at once told the whole truth, that they might, as well as the General, do full justice to Helen, and that they might never, never blame Clarendon for the separation which was to be.

That he should have mentioned nothing of her conduct even to his sister was not surprising. 'I know his generous nature,' said Cecilia.

'But I never knew yours till this moment, Cecilia,' cried Miss Clarendon, embracing her; 'my sister, now, – separation or not.'

'But there need be no separation,' said kind aunt Pennant.

Cecilia sighed, and Miss Clarendon repeated, 'You will find in me a sister at all events.'

She now saw Cecilia as she really was – faults and virtues. Perhaps indeed in this moment of revulsion of feeling, in the surprise of gratified confidence, she overvalued Lady Cecilia's virtues, and was inclined to do her more than justice, in her eagerness to make generous reparation for unjust suspicion.

CHAPTER 47

AFTER SETTING DOWN Lady Cecilia at her mother's, the aunt and niece proceeded to the picture sale which Miss Clarendon was eager to attend, as she was in search of a pendant to a famous Berghem she possessed; and while she was considering the picture, she had the advantage of hearing a story, which seemed, indeed, to be told for the amusement of the whole room, by a party of fashionables who were standing near her: – a wonderful story of a locket, which was going about; it was variously told, but all agreed in one point – that a young married lady of high rank had never dared to appear in the world since her husband had seen this locket in her hands – it had brought out something – something which had occurred before marriage – and here mysterious nods were exchanged.

Another version stated that the story had not yet been filly explained to the husband, that he had found the locket on the table in a room that he had suddenly entered, where he discovered her kneeling to the person in question, – 'the person in question' being sometimes a woman and sometimes a man.

Then leaned forward, stretching her scraggy neck, one who had good reason to believe that the husband would soon speak out – the public would soon hear of a separation: and everybody must be satisfied that there could not be a separation without good grounds.

Miss Clarendon inquired from a gentleman near them, who the lady was with the outstretched scraggy neck – Lady Katrine Hawksby.

Miss Clarendon knew her only by reputation. She did not know Miss Clarendon either by reputation or by sight; and she went on to say she would 'venture any wager that the separation would take place within a month. In short, there could be no doubt that before marriage,' – and she ended with a look which gave a death-blow to the reputation.

Exceedingly shocked, Miss Clarendon, not only from a sense of justice to Lady Cecilia, but from feeling for her brother's honour, longed to reply in defence; but she constrained herself for once, and having been assured by Lady Cecilia that all had been confessed to her mother, she thought that Lady Davenant must be the best person to decide what should be done. She went to her house immediately, sent in word that she begged to see Lady Davenant for two or three minutes alone, was admitted; Cecilia immediately vacated the chair beside her mother's bed, and left the room. Miss Clarendon felt some difficulty in beginning, but she forced herself to repeat all she had heard. Then Lady Davenant started up in her bed, and the colour of life spread over her face –

'Thank you, thank you, Miss Clarendon! a second time I have to thank you for an inestimable service. It is well for Cecilia that she made the whole truth known to us both – made you her friend; now we *can* act for her. I will have that locket from Madame de St Cymon before the sun goes down.'

Now Lady Davenant had Madame de St Cymon completely in her power, from her acquaintance with a disgraceful transaction which had come to her knowledge at Florence. The locket was surrendered, returned with humble assurances that Madame de St Cymon now perfectly understood the thing in its true light, and was quite convinced that it had been stolen, not given. Lady Davenant glanced over her note with scorn and was going to throw it from her into the fire, but did not. When Miss Clarendon called upon her again that evening as she had appointed, she showed it to her, and desired that she would, when her brother arrived next day, tell him what she had heard, what Lady Davenant had done, and how the locket was now in her possession.

Some people who pretend to know, maintain that the passion of love is of such an all-engrossing nature that it swallows up every other feeling; but we, who judge more justly of our kind, hold differently, and rather believe that love in generous natures imparts a strengthening power, a magnetic touch, to every good feeling. Helen was incapable of being perfectly happy while her friend was miserable; and even Beauclerc, in spite of all the suffering she had caused, could not help pitying Lady Cecilia, and he heartily wished the General could be reconciled to her; yet it was a matter in which he could not properly interfere; he did not attempt it.

Lady Davenant determined to give a breakfast to all the bridal party after the marriage. In her state of health, Helen and Cecilia remonstrated, but Lady Davenant had resolved upon it, and at last they agreed that it would be better than parting at the church-door – better that she should at her own house take leave of Helen and Beauclerc, who would set out immediately after the breakfast for Thorndale.

And now equipages were finished, and wedding paraphernalia sent home – the second time that wedding-dresses had been furnished for Miss Stanley; – and never once were these looked at by the bride-elect, nor even by Cecilia, but to see that all was as it should be – that seen, she sighed, and passed on.

Felicie's ecstasies were no more to be heard; we forgot to mention that she had, before Helen's return from Llansillen, departed, dismissed in disgrace; and happy was it for Lady Cecilia and Helen to be relieved from her jabbering, and not exposed to her spying and reporting. Nevertheless, the gloom that hung over the world above could not but be observed by the world below; it was, however, naturally accounted for by Lady Davenant's state of health, and by the anxiety which Lady Cecilia must feel for the General, who, as it had been officially announced by Mr Cockburn, was to set out on foreign service the day after the marriage.

Lady Cecilia, notwithstanding the bright hopefulness of her temper, and her habits of sanguine belief that all would end well in which she and her good fortune had any concern, seemed now, in this respect, to have changed her nature; and ever since her husband's denunciations, had continued quite resigned to misery, and submissive to the fate which she thought she had deserved. She was much employed in attendance upon her mother, and thankful that she was so permitted to be. She never mentioned her husband's name, and if she alluded to him, or to what had been decreed by him, it was with an emotion that scarcely dared to touch the point. She spoke most of her child, and seemed to look to the care of him as her only consolation. The boy had been brought from Kensington for Lady Davenant to see, and was now at her house. Cecilia once said she thought he was very like his father, and hoped that he would at least take leave of his boy at the last. To that last hour – that hour when she was to see her husband once more, when they were to meet but to part, to meet first at the wedding ceremony, and at a breakfast in a public company, – altogether painful as it must be, yet she looked forward to it with a sort of longing ardent impatience. 'True, it will be dreadful, yet still – still I shall see him again, see him once again, and he cannot part with his once so dear Cecilia without some word, some look, different from his last.'

The evening before the day on which the wedding was to be, Lady Cecilia was in Lady Davenant's room, sitting beside the bed while her mother slept. Suddenly she was startled from her still and ever the same recurring train of melancholy thoughts by a sound which had often made her heart beat with joy – her husband's knock; she ran to the window, opened it, and was out on the balcony in an instant. His horse was at the door, he had alighted, and was going up the steps; the leaned over the rails of the balcony, and as she leaned, a flower she wore broke off – it fell at the General's feet: he looked up, and their eyes met. There he stood, waiting on those steps, some minutes, for an answer to his inquiry how Lady Davenant was; and when the answer was brought out by Elliott, whom, as it seemed, he had desired to see, he remounted his horse, and rode away without ever again looking up to the balcony.

Lady Davenant had awakened, and when Cecilia returned on hearing her voice, her mother, as the light from the half-open shutters shone upon her face, saw that she was in tears; she kneeled down by the side of the bed, and wept bitterly; she made her mother understand how it had been.

'Not that I had hoped more, but still – still to feel it so! Oh, mother, I am bitterly punished!'

Then Lady Davenant, seizing those clasped hands, and raising herself in her bed, fixed her eyes earnestly upon Cecilia, and asked – '

'Would you, Cecilia – tell me, would you if it were now, this moment, in your power – would you retract your confession?'

'Retract! impossible!'

'Do you repent – regret having made it, Cecilia?'

'Repent – regret having made it! No, mother, no!' replied Cecilia firmly. 'I only regret that it was not sooner made. Retract! impossible I could wish to retract the only right thing I have done, the only thing that redeems me in my inmost soul from uttermost contempt. No! rather would I be as I am, and lose that noble heart, than hold it as I did, unworthily. There is, mother, as you said, as I feel, a sustaining, a redeeming power in truth.'

Her mother threw her arms round her.

'Come to me, my heart, my child, close – close to my heart. Heaven bless you! You have my blessing – my thanks, Cecilia. Yes, my thanks, – for now I know – I feel, my dear daughter, that my neglect of you in childhood has been repaired. You make me forgive myself, you make me happy, you have my thanks – my blessing – my warmest blessing!'

A smile of delight was on her pale face, and tears ran down as Cecilia answered – 'Oh, mother, mother! blind that I have been. Why did not I sooner know this tenderness of your heart?'

'And why, my child, did I not sooner know you? The fault was mine, the suffering has been yours, – not yours alone, though.'

'Suffer no more for me, mother, for now, after this, come what may, I can bear it. I can be happy, even if – ' There she paused, and then eagerly looking into her mother's eyes she asked –

'What do you say, mother, about him? do you think I may hope?'

'I dare not bid you hope,' replied her mother.

'Do you bid me despair?'

'No, despair in this world is only for those who have lost their own esteem, who have no confidence in themselves, for those who cannot repent, reform, and trust. My child, you must not despair. Now leave me to myself,' continued she; 'open a little more of the shutter, and put that book within my reach.'

As soon as Miss Clarendon heard that her brother had arrived in town, she hastened to him, and as Lady Davenant had desired, told him of all the reports that were in circulation, and of all that Lady Cecilia had spontaneously confided to her. Esther watched his countenance as she spoke, and observed that he listened with eager attention to the proofs of exactness in Cecilia; but he said nothing, and whatever his feelings were, his determination, she could not doubt, was still unshaken; even she did not dare to press his confidence.

Miss Clarendon reported to Lady Davenant that she had obeyed her command, and she described as nearly as she could all that she thought her brother's countenance expressed. Lady Davenant seemed satisfied, and this night she slept, as she told Cecilia in the morning, better than she had done since she returned to England. And this was the day of trial –

The hour came, and Lady Davenant was in the church with her daughter. This marriage was to be, as described in olden times, 'celebrated with all the lustre and pomp imaginable'; and so it was, for Helen's sake, Helen, the pale bride –

'Beautiful!' the whispers ran as she appeared, 'but too pale.' Leaning on General Clarendon's arm she was led up the aisle to the altar. He felt the tremor of her arm on his, but she looked composed and almost firm. She saw no one individual of the assembled numbers, not even Cecilia or Lady Davenant. She knelt at the altar beside him to whom she was to give her faith, and General Clarendon, in the face of all the world, proudly gave her to his ward, and she, without fear, low and distinctly pronounced the sacred vow. And as Helen rose from her knees, the sun shone out, and a ray of light was on her face, and it was lovely. Every heart said so – every heart but Lady Katrine Hawksby's – And why do we think of her at such a moment? and why does Lady Davenant think of her at such a moment? Yet she did; she looked to see if she were present, and she bade her to the breakfast.

And now all the salutations were given and received, and all the murmur of congratulations rising, the living tide poured out of the church; and then the noise of carriages, and all drove off to Lady Davenant's; and Lady Davenant had gone through it all so far, well. And Lady Cecilia knew that it had been; and her eyes had been upon her husband, and her heart had been full of another day when she had knelt beside him at the altar. And did he, too, think of that day? She could not tell, his countenance discovered no emotion, his eyes never once turned to the place where she stood. And she was now to see him for one hour, but one hour longer, and at a public breakfast! but still she was to see him.

And now they are all at breakfast. The attention of some was upon the bride and bridegroom; of others, on Lady Cecilia and on the General; of others, on Lady Davenant; and of many, on themselves. Lady Davenant had Beauclerc on one side, General Clarendon on the other, and her daughter opposite to him. Lady Katrine was there, with her '*tristeful* visage,' as Churchill justly called it, and more *tristeful* it presently became.

When breakfast was over, seizing her moment when conversation flagged, and when there was a pause, implying 'What is to be said or done next?' Lady Davenant rose from her seat with an air of preparation, and somewhat of solemnity. All eyes were instantly upon her. She drew out a locket, which she held up to public view; then, turning to Lady Kathrine Hawksby, she said – 'This bauble has been much talked of, I understand, by your ladyship, but I question whether you have ever yet seen it, or know the truth concerning it. This locket was *stolen* by a worthless man, given by him to a worthless woman, from whom

I have obtained it; and now I give it to the person for whom it was originally destined.'

She advanced towards Helen, and put it round her neck. This done, her colour flitted – her hand was suddenly to her heart; yet she commanded – absolutely commanded, the paroxysm of pain. The General was at her side; her daughter, Helen, and Beauclerc, were close to her instantly. She was just able to walk: she slowly left the room – and was no more seen by the world!

She suffered herself to be carried up the steps into her own apartment by the General, who laid her on the sofa in her dressing-room. She looked round on them, and saw that all were there whom she loved; but there was an alteration in her appearance which struck them all, and most the General, who had least expected it. She held out her hand to him, and fixing her eyes upon him with deathfiil expression, calmly smiled, and said – 'You would not believe this could be; but now you see it must be, and soon. We have no time to lose,' continued she, and moving very cautiously and feebly, she half-raised herself – 'Yes,' said she, 'a moment is granted to me, thank Heaven!' She rose with sudden power and threw herself on her knees at the General's feet: it was done before he could stop her.

'For God's sake!' cried he, 'Lady Davenant! – I conjure you – '

She would not be raised. 'No,' said she, 'here I die if I appeal to you in vain – to your justice, General Clarendon, to which, as far as I know, none ever appealed in vain – and shall I be the first? – a mother for her child – a dying mother for your wife – for my dear Cecilia, once dear to you.'

His face was instantly covered with his hands.

'Not to your love,' continued she – 'if that be gone – to your justice I appeal, and MUST be heard, if you are what I think you: if you are not, why go – go, instantly – go, and leave your wife, innocent as she is, to be deemed guilty – Part from her, at the moment when the only fault she committed has been repaired – Throw her from you when, by the sacrifice of all that was dear to her, she has proved her truth – Yes, you know that she has spoken the whole, the perfect truth – '

'I know it,' exclaimed he.

'Give her up to the whole world of slanderers! – destroy her character! If now her husband separate from her, her good name is lost for ever! If now her husband protect her not – '

Her husband turned, and clasped her in his arms. Lady Davenant rose and blessed him – blessed them both: they knelt beside her, and she joined their hands.

'Now,' said she, 'I give my daughter to a husband worthy of her, and she more worthy of that noble heart than when first his. Her only fault was mine – my early neglect: it is repaired – I die in peace! You make my last moments the happiest! Helen, my dearest Helen, now, and not till now, happy – perfectly happy in Love and Truth!'